A QUARTETTE OF COMEDIES

A Quartette of Comedies

BY

H. G. Wells

LONDON: ERNEST BENN LIMITED
BOUVERIE HOUSE, FLEET STREET
M.CM.XXVIII

First published 1928

MADE AND PRINTED IN GREAT BRITAIN BY
BILLING AND SONS, LTD., GUILDFORD AND ESHER

CONTENTS

KIPPS

THE STORY OF A SIMPLE SOUL

THE HISTORY OF MR. POLLY

BEALBY

LOVE AND MR. LEWISHAM

CONTENTS

I*

KIPPS

THE STORY OF A SIMPLE SOUL

"Those individuals who have led secluded or isolated lives, or have hitherto moved in other spheres than those wherein well-bred people move, will gather all the information necessary from these pages to render them thoroughly conversant with the manners and amenities of society."—*Manners and Rules of Good Society,* by a Member of the Aristocracy.

BOOK I
THE MAKING OF KIPPS

CHAPTER THE FIRST

The Little Shop at New Romney

§ 1

UNTIL he was nearly arrived at manhood it did
not become clear to Kipps how it was that he had come
into the care of an aunt and uncle instead of having a
father and mother like other little boys. He had vague
memories of a somewhere else—a dim room, a window
looking down on white buildings, and of a someone else
who talked to forgotten people and who was his mother.
He could not recall her features very distinctly, but he
remembered with extreme definition a white dress she
wore, with a pattern of little sprigs of flowers and little
bows upon it, and a girdle of straight-ribbed white
ribbon about the waist. Linked with this, he knew not
how, were clouded, half-obliterated recollections of
scenes in which there was weeping, weeping in which
he was inscrutably moved to join. Some terrible tall
man with a loud voice played a part in these scenes,

15

and either before or after them there were impressions of looking for interminable periods out of the windows of railway trains in the company of these two people. . . .

He knew, though he could not remember that he had ever been told, that a certain faded, wistful face that looked at him from a plush and gilt-framed daguerreotype above the mantel of the "sitting-room," was the face of his mother. But that knowledge did not touch his dim memories with any elucidation. In the photograph she was a girlish figure, leaning against a photographer's stile, and with all the self-conscious shrinking natural to that position. She had curly hair and a face far younger and prettier than any other mother in his experience. She swung a Dolly Varden hat by the string, and looked with obedient respectful eyes at the photographer-gentleman who had commanded the pose. She was very slight and pretty. But the phantom mother who haunted his memory so elusively was not like that, though he could not remember how she differed. Perhaps she was older, or a little less shrinking, or, it may be, only dressed in a different way. . . .

It is clear she handed him over to his aunt and uncle at New Romney with explicit directions and a certain endowment. One gathers she had something of that fine sense of social distinctions that subsequently played so large a part in Kipps' career. He was not to go to a "common" school, she provided, but to a certain seminary in Hastings that was not only a "middle-class academy," with mortar-boards and every evidence of a higher social tone, but also remarkably cheap. She seems to have been animated by the desire to do her best for Kipps, even at a certain sacrifice of herself, as though Kipps were in some way a superior sort of person. She sent pocket-money to him from time to time for a year or more after Hastings had begun for him, but her face he never saw in the days of his lucid memory.

His aunt and uncle were already high on the hill of life when first he came to them. They had married for comfort in the evening or at any rate in the late afternoon of their days. They were at first no more than vague figures in the background of proximate realities, such realities as familiar chairs and tables, quiet to ride and drive, the newel of the staircase, kitchen furniture, pieces of firewood, the boiler tap, old newspapers, the cat, the High Street, the back yard and the flat fields that are always so near in that little town. He knew all the stones in the yard individually, the creeper in the corner, the dustbin and the mossy wall, better than many men know the faces of their wives. There was a corner under the ironing-board which, by means of a shawl, could be made, under propitious gods, a very decent cubby-house, a corner that served him for several years as the indisputable hub of the world; and the stringy places in the carpet, the knots upon the dresser, and the several corners of the rag hearthrug his uncle had made, became essential parts of his mental foundations. The shop he did not know so thoroughly; it was a forbidden region to him, yet somehow he managed to know it very well.

His aunt and uncle were the immediate gods of this world, and, like the gods of the world of old, occasionally descended right into it, with arbitrary injunctions and disproportionate punishments. And, unhappily, one rose to their Olympian level at meals. Then one had to say one's "grace," hold one's spoon and fork in mad, unnatural ways called "properly," and refrain from eating even nice sweet things "too fast." If he "gobbled" there was trouble, and at the slightest *abandon* with knife, fork, and spoon, his aunt rapped his knuckles, albeit his uncle always finished up his gravy with his knife. Sometimes, moreover, his uncle would come pipe in hand out of a sedentary remoteness in the most disconcerting way when a little boy was doing the most natural and attractive things, with

" Drat and drabbit that young rascal! What's he
a-doing of now?" And his aunt would appear at door
or window to interrupt interesting conversation with
children who were upon unknown grounds considered
" low " and undesirable, and call him in.   The
pleasantest little noises, however softly you did them,
drumming on tea-trays, trumpeting your fists, whistling
on keys, ringing chimes with a couple of pails, or playing tunes on the window-panes, brought down the gods
in anger. Yet what noise is fainter than your finger on
the window—gently done? Sometimes, however, these
gods gave him broken toys out of the shop, and then
one loved them better—for the shop they kept was,
among other things, a toy-shop. The other things
included books to read and books to give away, and
local photographs; it had some pretensions also to be a
china-shop, and the fascia spoke of glass; it was also a
stationer's shop with a touch of haberdashery about it,
and in the windows and odd corners were mats and
terra-cotta dishes, and milking-stools for painting; and
there was a hint of picture-frames, and fire-screens, and
fishing-tackle, and air-guns, and bathing-suits, and tents
—various things, indeed, but all cruelly attractive to a
small boy's fingers. Once his aunt gave him a trumpet
if he would *promise* faithfully not to blow it, and afterwards took it away again. And his aunt made him say
his catechism, and something she certainly called the
" Colic for the Day," every Sunday in the year.

As the two grew old as he grew up, and as his impression of them modified insensibly from year to year,
it seemed to him at last that they had always been as
they were when in his adolescent days his impression of
things grew fixed; his aunt he thought of as always lean,
rather worried looking, and prone to a certain obliquity
of cap, and his uncle massive, many-chinned, and careless about his buttons. They neither visited nor
received visitors. They were always very suspicious
about their neighbours and other people generally; they

feared the "low" and they hated and despised the "stuck-up," and so they "kept themselves *to* themselves," according to the English ideal. Consequently little Kipps had no playmates, except through the sin of disobedience. By inherent nature he had a sociable disposition. When he was in the High Street he made a point of saying "Hello!" to passing cyclists, and he would put his tongue out at the Quodling children whenever their nursemaid was not looking. And he began a friendship with Sid Pornick, the son of the haberdasher next door, that, with wide intermissions, was destined to last his lifetime through.

Pornick the haberdasher, I may say at once, was, according to old Kipps, a "blaring jackass"; he was a teetotaller, a "nyar, nyar, 'im-singing Methodis'," and altogether distasteful and detrimental, he and his together, to true Kipps ideals, so far as little Kipps could gather them. This Pornick certainly possessed an enormous voice, and he annoyed old Kipps greatly by calling, "You—Arn" and "Siddee," up and down his house. He annoyed old Kipps by private choral services on Sunday, all his family "nyar, nyar-ing"; and by mushroom culture, by behaving as though the pilaster between the two shops was common property; by making a noise of hammering in the afternoon when old Kipps wanted to be quiet after his midday meal, by going up and down uncarpeted stairs in his boots, by having a black beard, by attempting to be friendly, and by—all that sort of thing. In fact, he annoyed old Kipps. He annoyed him especially with his shop-door mat. Old Kipps never beat his mat, preferring to let sleeping dust lie; and, seeking a motive for a foolish proceeding, he held that Pornick waited until there was a suitable wind in order that the dust disengaged in that operation might defile his neighbour's shop. These issues would frequently develop into loud and vehement quarrels, and on one occasion came so near to violence as to be subsequently described by Pornick (who read his newspaper) as a "Disgraceful Frackass." On that occasion he certainly went into his own shop with extreme celerity.

But it was through one of these quarrels that the friendship of little Kipps and Sid Pornick came about. The two small boys found themselves one day looking through the gate at the doctor's goats together; they exchanged a few contradictions about which goat could fight which, and then young Kipps was moved to remark that Sid's father was a "blaring jackass." Sid said he wasn't, and Kipps repeated that he was, and quoted his authority. Then Sid, flying off at a tangent rather alarmingly, said he could fight young Kipps with one hand, an assertion young Kipps with a secret want of confidence denied. There were some vain repetitions, and the incident might have ended there, but happily a sporting butcher-boy chanced on the controversy at this stage, and insisted upon seeing fair play.

The two small boys under his pressing encouragement did at last button up their jackets, square and fight an edifying drawn battle, until it seemed good to the butcher-boy to go on with Mrs. Holyer's mutton. Then, according to his directions and under his experienced stage management, they shook hands and made it up. Subsequently, a little tear-stained perhaps, but flushed with the butcher-boy's approval ("tough little kids"), and with cold stones down their necks as he advised, they sat side by side on the doctor's gate, projecting very much behind, stanching an honourable bloodshed and expressing respect for one another. Each had a bloody nose and a black eye——three days later they matched to a shade——neither had given in, and, though this was tacit, neither wanted any more.

It was an excellent beginning. After this first encounter the attributes of their parents and their own relative value in battle never rose between them, and if anything was wanted to complete the warmth of their regard it was found in a joint dislike of the eldest

Quodling. The eldest Quodling lisped, had a silly sort
of straw hat and a large pink face (all covered over with
self-satisfaction), and he went to the National School
with a green baize bag—a contemptible thing to do.
They called him names and threw stones at him, and
when he replied by threatenings ("Look 'ere, young
Art Kipth, you better *thtoppit!*") they were moved to
attack and put him to flight.

And after that they broke the head of Ann Pornick's
doll, so that she went home weeping loudly—a wicked
and endearing proceeding. Sid was whacked, but, as
he explained, he wore a newspaper tactically adjusted
during the transaction, and really it didn't hurt him at
all. . . . And Mrs. Pornick put her head out of the
shop door suddenly, and threatened Kipps as he passed.

§ 2

"Cavendish Academy," the school that had won the
limited choice of Kipps' vanished mother, was established in a battered private house in the part of Hastings
remotest from the sea; it was called an Academy for
Young Gentlemen, and many of the young gentlemen
had parents in "India" and other unverifiable places.
Others were the sons of credulous widows anxious, as
Kipps' mother had been, to get something a little
"superior" to a board school education as cheaply as
possible, and others again were sent to demonstrate the
dignity of their parents and guardians. And of course
there were boys from France.

Its "principal" was a lean long creature of indifferent digestion and temper, who proclaimed himself
on a gilt-lettered board in his front areas George Garden
Woodrow, F.S.Sc., letters indicating that he had paid
certain guineas for a bogus diploma. A bleak white-
washed outhouse constituted his schoolroom, and the
scholastic quality of its carved and worn desks and forms
was enhanced by a slippery blackboard and two large

yellow out-of-date maps, one of Africa and the other of Wiltshire, that he had picked up cheap at a sale. There were other maps and globes in his study, where he interviewed inquiring parents, but these his pupils never saw. And in a glass cupboard in the passage was several shillings' worth of test tubes and chemicals, a tripod, a glass retort, and a damaged Bunsen burner, manifesting that the "Scientific laboratory" mentioned in the prospectus was no idle boast.

This prospectus, which was in dignified but incorrect English, laid particular stress on the sound preparation for a commercial career given in the Academy, but the army, navy, and civil service were glanced at in an ambiguous sentence. There was something vague in the prospectus about "examinational successes"—though Woodrow, of course, disapproved of "cram"—and a declaration that the curriculum included "art," "modern foreign languages" and "a sound technical and scientific training." Then came insistence upon the "moral well-being" of the pupils, and an emphatic boast of the excellence of the religious instruction, "so often neglected nowadays even in schools of wide repute." "That's bound to fetch 'em," Mr. Woodrow had remarked when he drew up the prospectus. And in conjunction with the mortar-boards it certainly did. Attention was directed to the "motherly" care of Mrs. Woodrow—in reality a small partially effaced woman with a plaintive face and a mind above cookery; and the prospectus concluded with a phrase intentionally vague, "Fare unrestricted, and our own milk and produce."

The memories Kipps carried from that school into after life were set in an atmosphere of stuffiness and mental muddle; and included countless pictures of sitting on creaking forms bored and idle, of blot licking and the taste of ink, of torn books with covers that set one's teeth on edge, of the slimy surface of the laboured slates, of furtive marble-playing, whispered story-telling, and of pinches, blows, and a thousand such petty annoyances being perpetually " passed on " according to the custom of the place, of standing up in class and being hit suddenly and unreasonably for imaginary misbehaviour, of Mr. Woodrow's raving days, when a scarcely sane injustice prevailed, of the cold vacuity of the hour of preparation before the bread-and-butter breakfast, and of horrible headaches and queer, unprecedented, internal feelings resulting from Mrs. Woodrow's motherly rather than intelligent cookery. There were dreary walks, when the boys marched two by two, all dressed in the mortar-board caps that so impressed the widowed mothers; there were dismal half-holidays when the weather was wet and the spirit of evil temper and evil imagination had the pent boys to work its will on; there were unfair, dishonourable fights and miserable defeats and victories, there was bullying and being bullied. A coward boy Kipps particularly afflicted, until at last he was goaded to revolt by incessant persecution, and smote Kipps to tolerance with whirling fists. There were memories of sleeping three in a bed, of the dense leathery smell of the schoolroom when one returned thither after ten minutes' play, of a playground of mud and incidental sharp flints. And there was much furtive foul language.

"Our Sundays are our happiest days," was one of Woodrow's formulæ with the inquiring parent, but Kipps was not called in evidence. They were to him terrible gaps of inanity—no work, no play, a drear expanse of time with the mystery of church twice and plum duff once in the middle. The afternoon was given up to furtive relaxations, among which figured " Torture Chamber " games with the less agreeable weaker boys. It was from the difference between this day and common days that Kipps derived his first definite conceptions of the nature of God and heaven. His instinct was to evade any closer acquaintance as long as he could.

The solid work varied according to the prevailing

mood of Mr. Woodrow. Sometimes that was a despondent lethargy, copy-books were distributed or sums were " set," or the great mystery of book-keeping was declared in being, and beneath these superficial activities lengthy conversations and interminable guessing games with marbles went on while Mr. Woodrow sat inanimate at his desk heedless of school affairs, staring in front of him at unseen things. At times his face was utterly inane, at times it had an expression of stagnant amazement, as if he saw before his eyes with pitiless clearness the dishonour and mischief of his being. . . .

At other times the F.S.Sc. roused himself to action, and would stand up a wavering class and teach it, goading it with bitter mockery and blows through a chapter of Ahn's " First French Course," or " France and the French," or a Dialogue about a traveller's washing, or the parts of an opera-house. His own knowledge of French had been obtained years ago in another English private school, and he had refreshed it by occasional weeks of loafing and mean adventure in Dieppe. He would sometimes in their lessons hit upon some reminiscence of these brighter days, and then he would laugh inexplicably and repeat French phrases of an unfamiliar type.

Among the commoner exercises he prescribed the learning of long passages of poetry from a " Poetry Book," which he would delegate an elder boy to " hear," and there was reading aloud from the Holy Bible, verse by verse—it was none of your " godless " schools!—so that you counted the verses up to your turn and then gave yourself to conversation—and sometimes one read from a cheap History of this land. They did, as Kipps reported, " loads of catechism." Also there was much learning of geographical names and lists, and sometimes Woodrow in an outbreak of energy would see these names were actually found on a map. And once, just once, there was a chemistry lesson—a lesson of indescribable excitement—glass things of the strangest shape, a smell like bad eggs, something bubbling in something, a smash and stench, and Mr. Woodrow saying quite distinctly—they thrashed it out in the dormitory afterwards—" Damn !" followed by the whole school being kept in, with extraordinary severities, for an hour. . . .

But interspersed with the memories of this grey routine were certain patches of brilliant colour—the holidays, his holidays, which in spite of the feud between their seniors, he spent as much as possible with Sid Pornick, the son of the irascible black-bearded haberdasher next door. They seemed to be memories of a different world. There were glorious days of " mucking about " along the beach, the siege of unresisting Martello towers, the incessant interest of the mystery and motion of windmills, the windy excursions with boarded feet over the yielding shingle to Dungeness lighthouse—Sid Pornick and he far adrift from reality, smugglers and armed men from the moment they left Great Stone behind them—wanderings in the hedgeless reedy marsh, long excursions reaching even to Hythe, where the machine-guns of the Empire are for ever whirling and tapping, and to Rye and Winchelsea, perched like dream-cities on their little hills. The sky in these memories was the blazing hemisphere of the marsh heavens in summer, or its wintry tumult of sky and sea; and there were wrecks, real wrecks, in it (near Dymchurch pitched high and blackened and rotting were the ribs of a fishing-smack flung aside like an empty basket when the sea had devoured its crew); and there was bathing all naked in the sea, bathing to one's armpits and even trying to swim in the warm sea-water (spite of his aunt's prohibition), and (with her indulgence) the rare eating of dinner from a paper parcel, miles away from home. Toke and cold ground-rice puddin' with plums it used to be—there is no better food at all. And for the background, in the place of

Woodrow's mean and fretting rule, were his aunt's spare but frequently quite amiable figure——for though she insisted on his repeating the English Church Catechism every Sunday, she had an easy way over dinners that one wanted to take abroad——and his uncle, corpulent and irascible, but sedentary and easily escaped. And freedom!

The holidays were indeed very different from school. They were free, they were spacious, and though he never knew it in these words——they had an element of beauty. In his memory of his boyhood they shone like strips of stained-glass window in a dreary waste of scholastic wall, they grew brighter and brighter as they grew remoter. There came a time at last and moods when he could look back to them with a feeling akin to tears.

The last of these windows was the brightest, and instead of the kaleidoscopic effects of its predecessors its glory was a single figure. For in the last of his holidays, before the Moloch of Retail Trade got hold of him, Kipps made his first tentative essays at the mysterious shrine of Love. Very tentative they were, for he had become a boy of subdued passions, and potential rather than actual affectionateness.

And the object of these first stirrings of the great desire was no other than Ann Pornick, the head of whose doll he and Sid had broken long ago, and rejoiced over long ago, in the days when he had yet to learn the meaning of a heart.

§ 3

Negotiations were already on foot to make Kipps into a draper before he discovered the lights that lurked in Ann Pornick's eyes. School was over, absolutely over, and it was chiefly present to him that he was never to go to school again. It was high summer. The " breaking up " of school had been hilarious; and the excellent maxim, "Last Day's Pay Day," had been observed by him with a scrupulous attention to his honour. He had punched the heads of all his enemies, wrung wrists and kicked shins; he had distributed all his unfinished copy-books, all his school books, his collection of marbles and his mortar-board cap among such as loved him; and he had secretly written in obscure pages of their books, "remember Art Kipps." He had also split the anæmic Woodrow's cane, carved his own name deeply in several places about the premises, and broken the scullery window. He had told everybody so often that he was to learn to be a sea captain that he had come almost to believe the thing himself. And now he was home, and school was at an end for him evermore.

He was up before six on the day after his return, and out in the hot sunlight of the yard. He set himself to whistle a peculiarly penetrating arrangement of three notes, supposed by the boys of the Hastings Academy and himself and Sid Pornick, for no earthly reason whatever, to be the original Huron war-cry. As he did this he feigned not to be doing it, because of the hatred between his uncle and the Pornicks, but to be examining with respect and admiration a new wing of the dustbin recently erected by his uncle—a pretence that would not have deceived a nestling tomtit.

Presently there came a familiar echo from the Pornick hunting-ground. Then Kipps began to sing, "Ar pars eight tra-la, in the lane be'ind the church." To which an unseen person answered, "Ar pars eight it is, in the lane be'ind the church." The "tra-la" was considered to render this sentence incomprehensible to the un-initiated. In order to conceal their operations still more securely, both parties to this duet then gave vent to a vocalisation of the Huron war-cry again, and after a lingering repetition of the last and shrillest note, dispersed severally, as became boys in the enjoyment of holidays, to light the house fires for the day.

Half-past eight found Kipps sitting on the sunlit

gate at the top of the long lane that runs towards the sea, clashing his boots in a slow rhythm, and whistling with great violence all that he knew of an excruciatingly pathetic air. There appeared along by the churchyard wall a girl in a short frock, brown-haired, quick-coloured, and with dark blue eyes. She had grown so that she was a little taller than Kipps, and her colour had improved. He scarcely remembered her, so changed was she since last holidays—if indeed he had seen her last holidays, a thing he could not clearly remember.

Some vague emotion arose at the sight of her. He stopped whistling and regarded her, oddly tongue-tied.

"He can't come," said Ann, advancing boldly. "Not yet."

"What—not Sid?"

"No. Father's made him dust all his boxes again."

"What for?"

"I dunno. Father's in a stew 'smorning."

"Oh!"

Pause. Kipps looked at her, and then was unable to look at her again. She regarded him with interest. "You left school?" she remarked after a pause.

"Yes."

"So's Sid."

The conversation languished. Ann put her hands on the top of the gate, and began a stationary hopping, a sort of ineffectual gymnastic experiment.

"Can you run?" she said presently.

"Run you any day," said Kipps.

"Gimme a start?"

"Where for?" said Kipps.

Ann considered, and indicated a tree. She walked towards it, and turned. "Gimme to here?" she called.

Kipps, standing now and touching the gate, smiled to express conscious superiority. "Further!" he said.

"Here?"

"Bit more!" said Kipps, and then, repenting of his

magnanimity, said " Orf !" suddenly, and so recovered his lost concession.

They arrived abreast at the tree, flushed and out of breath.

" Tie !" said Ann, throwing her hair back from her face with her hand.

" I won," panted Kipps.

They disputed firmly but quite politely.

" Run it again, then," said Kipps. " *I* don't mind."

They returned towards the gate.

" You don't run bad," says Kipps temperately, expressing sincere admiration. " I'm pretty good, you know."

Ann sent her hair back by an expert toss of the head. " You give me a start," she allowed.

They became aware of Sid approaching them.

" You better look out, young Ann," said Sid, with that irreverent want of sympathy usual in brothers. " You been out nearly 'arf-'our. Nothing ain't been done upstairs. Father said he didn't know where you was, but when he did he'd warm y'r young ear."

Ann prepared to go.

" How about that race ?" asked Kipps.

" Lor' !" cried Sid, quite shocked. " You ain't been racing *her !*"

Ann swung herself round the end of the gate with her eyes on Kipps, and then turned away suddenly and ran off down the lane.

Kipps' eyes tried to go after her, and came back to Sid's.

" I give her a lot of start," said Kipps apologetically. " It wasn't a proper race." And so the subject was dismissed. But Kipps was *distrait* for some seconds, perhaps, and the mischief had begun in him.

§ 4

They proceeded to the question of how two accomplished Hurons might most satisfactorily spend the morning. Manifestly their line lay straight along the lane to the sea.

"There's a new wreck," said Sid, "and my—don't it stink just!"

"Stink?"

"Fair make you sick. It's rotten wheat."

They fell to talking of wrecks, and so came to ironclads and wars and suchlike manly matters.

Half-way to the wreck Kipps made a casual irrelevant remark. "Your sister ain't a bad sort," he said offhandedly.

"I clout her a lot," said Sidney modestly, and after a pause the talk reverted to more suitable topics.

The new wreck was full of rotting grain, and smelt abominably, even as Sid had said. This was excellent. They had it all to themselves. They took possession of it in force, at Sid's suggestion, and had speedily to defend it against enormous numbers of imaginary "natives," who were at last driven off by loud shouts of *bang, bang,* and vigorous thrusting and shoving of sticks. Then, also at Sid's direction, they sailed with it into the midst of a combined French, German, and Russian fleet, demolishing the combination unassisted, and having descended to the beach, clambered up the side and cut out their own vessel in brilliant style, they underwent a magnificent shipwreck (with vocalised thunder) and floated "waterlogged"—so Sid insisted—upon an exhausted sea.

These things drove Ann out of mind for a time. But at last, as they drifted without food or water upon a stagnant ocean, haggard-eyed, chins between their hands, looking in vain for a sail, she came to mind again abruptly.

"It's rather nice 'aving sisters," remarked one perishing mariner.

Sid turned round and regarded him thoughtfully. "Not it!" he said.

"No?"

"Not a bit of it."

He grinned confidentially. "Know too much," he said, and afterwards "get out of things."

He resumed his gloomy scrutiny of the hopeless horizon. Presently he fell to spitting jerkily between his teeth, as he had read was the way with such ripe manhood as chews its quid.

"Sisters," he said, "is rot. That's what sisters are. Girls if you like, but sisters—*no!*"

"But ain't sisters girls?"

"*N-eaow!*" said Sid, with unspeakable scorn.

And Kipps answered, "Of course. I didn't mean—— I wasn't thinking of that."

"You got a girl?" asked Sid, spitting very cleverly again.

Kipps admitted his deficiency. He felt compunction.

"You don't know who *my* girl is, Art Kipps—I bet."

"Who *is,* then?" asked Kipps, still chiefly occupied by his own poverty.

"Ah!"

Kipps let a moment elapse before he did his duty. "Tell us!"

Sid eyed him and hesitated. "Secret?" he said.

"Secret."

"Dying solemn?"

"Dying solemn!" Kipps' self-concentration passed into curiosity.

Sid administered a terrible oath. Even after that precaution he adhered lovingly to his facts. "It begins with a Nem," he said, doling them out parsimoniously. "MAUD," he spelled, with a stern eye on Kipps, "CHARTERIS."

2

Now Maud Charteris was a young person of eighteen
and the daughter of the vicar of St. Bavon's,—besides
which she had a bicycle,—so that as her name unfolded
the face of Kipps lengthened with respect. " Get out ! "
he gasped incredulously.   " She ain't your girl, Sid
Pornick."

" She is ! " answered Sid stoutly.

" What—truth ? "

" *Truth.* "

Kipps scrutinised his face.   " Reely ? "

Sid touched wood, whistled, and repeated a binding
doggerel with great solemnity.

Kipps still struggled with the amazing new light on
the world about him.   " D'you mean—she knows ? "

Sid flushed deeply, and his aspect became stern and
gloomy.   He resumed his wistful scrutiny of the sunlit
sea.   " I'd die for that girl, Art Kipps," he said
presently, and Kipps did not press a question he felt to
be ill timed.   " I'd do anything she asked me to do,"
said Sid—" just anything.   If she was to ask me to
chuck myself into the sea."   He met Kipps' eye.   " I
would," he said.

They were pensive for a space, and then Sid began
to discourse in fragments of Love, a theme upon which
Kipps had already in a furtive way meditated a little,
but which, apart from badinage, he had never yet heard
talked about in the light of day.   Of course many and
various aspects of life had come to light in the muffled
exchange of knowledge that went on under the shadow
of Woodrow, but this of Sentimental Love was not
among them.   Sid, who was a boy with an imagination,
having once broached this topic, opened his heart, or at
any rate a new wing of his heart, to Kipps, and found
no fault with Kipps for a lack of return.   He produced
a thumbed novelette that had played a part in his
sentimental awakening; he proffered it to Kipps, and
confessed there was a character in it, a baronet, singularly like himself.   This baronet was a person of

volcanic passions which he concealed beneath a
demeanour of "icy cynicism." The utmost expression
he permitted himself was to grind his teeth; and now
his attention was called to it, Kipps remarked that Sid
also had a habit of grinding his teeth—and indeed had
had all the morning. They read for a time, and
presently Sid talked again. The conception of love Sid
made evident was compact of devotion and much
spirited fighting and a touch of mystery; but through
all that cloud of talk there floated before Kipps a face
that was flushed and hair that was tossed aside.

So they budded, sitting on the blackening old wreck
in which men had lived and died, looking out to sea,
talking of that other sea upon which they must presently
embark. . . .

They ceased to talk, and Sid read; but Kipps falling
behind with the reading and not wishing to admit
that he read slowlier than Sid, whose education was
of the inferior Elementary School brand, lapsed into
meditation.

"I *would* like to 'ave a girl," said Kipps. "I mean
just to talk to and all that. . . ."

A floating sack distracted them at last from this
obscure topic. They abandoned the wreck and followed
the new interest a mile along the beach, bombarding it
with stones until it came to land. They had inclined
to a view that it would contain romantic mysteries, but
it was simply an ill-preserved kitten—too much even for
them. And at last they were drawn dinnerward and
went home hungry and pensive side by side.

§ 5

But Kipps' imagination had been warmed by that
talk of love, and in the afternoon, when he saw Ann
Pornick in the High Street and said "Hello!" it was
a different "hello" from that of their previous intercourse. And when they had passed they both looked

back and caught each other doing so. Yes, he *did* want
a girl badly. . . .

Afterwards he was diverted by a traction engine
going through the town, and his aunt had got some
sprats for supper. When he was in bed, however,
sentiment came upon him again in a torrent quite
abruptly and abundantly, and he put his head under
the pillow and whispered very softly, "I love Ann
Pornick," as a sort of supplementary devotion.

In his subsequent dreams he ran races with Ann, and
they lived in a wreck together, and always her face was
flushed and her hair about her face. They just lived
in a wreck and ran races, and were very, very fond of
one another. And their favourite food was rock-
chocolate, dates, such as one buys off barrows, and
sprats—fried sprats. . . .

In the morning he could hear Ann singing in the
scullery next door. He listened to her for some time,
and it was clear to him that he must put things before
her.

Towards dusk that evening they chanced on one
another at the gate by the church; but though there
was much in his mind, it stopped there with a resolute
shyness until he and Ann were out of breath catching
cockchafers, and were sitting on that gate of theirs
again. Ann sat up upon the gate, dark against vast
masses of flaming crimson and darkling purple, and her
eyes looked at Kipps from a shadowed face. There
came a stillness between them and quite abruptly he
was moved to tell his love.

"Ann," he said, "I *do* like you. I wish you was my
girl. . . . I say, Ann : will you *be* my girl?"

Ann made no pretence of astonishment. She weighed
the proposal for a moment with her eyes on Kipps.
"If you like, Artie," she said lightly, "*I* don't mind
if I am."

"All right," said Kipps, breathless with excitement,
"then you are."

"All right," said Ann.

Something seemed to fall between them, and they no longer looked openly at one another. "Lor'!" cried Ann suddenly, "see that one!" and jumped down and darted after a cockchafer that had boomed within a yard of her face. And with that they were girl and boy again. . . .

They avoided their new relationship painfully.

They did not recur to it for several days, though they met twice. Both felt that there remained something before this great experience was complete, but there was an infinite diffidence about the next step. Kipps talked in fragments of all sorts of matters, telling particularly of the great things that were being done to make a man and a draper of him, how he had two new pairs of trousers and a black coat and four new shirts. And all the while his imagination was urging him to that unknown next step, and when he was alone and in the dark he became even an enterprising wooer. It became evident to him that it would be nice to take Ann by the hand; even the decorous novelettes Sid affected egged him on to that greater nearness of intimacy.

Then a great idea came to him, in a paragraph called "Lovers' Tokens" that he read in a torn fragment of *Tit-Bits*. It fell in to the measure of his courage—a divided sixpence! He secured his aunt's best scissors, fished a sixpence out of his jejune tin money-box, and jabbed his finger in a varied series of attempts to get it in halves. When they met again the sixpence was still undivided. He had not intended to mention the matter to her at that stage, but it came up spontaneously. He endeavoured to explain the theory of broken sixpences and his unexpected failure to break one.

"But what do you break it for?" said Ann. "It's no good if it's broke."

"It's a Token," said Kipps.

"Like . . .?"

"Oh, you keep half and I keep half, and when we're sep'rated you look at your half and I look at mine—see! Then we think of each other."

"Oh!" said Ann, and appeared to assimilate this information.

"Only *I* can't get it in 'arf nohow," said Kipps.

They discussed this difficulty for some time without illumination. Then Ann had a happy thought. "Tell you what," she said, starting away from him abruptly and laying a hand on his arm, "you let *me* 'ave it, Artie. I know where father keeps his file."

Kipps handed her the sixpence, and they came upon a pause.

"I'll easy do it," said Ann.

In considering the sixpence side by side, his head had come near her cheek. Quite abruptly he was moved to take his next step into the unknown mysteries of love.

"Ann," he said, and gulped at his temerity, "I *do* love you. Straight. I'd do anything for you, Ann. Reely—I would."

He paused for breath. She answered nothing, but she was no doubt enjoying herself. He came yet closer to her—his shoulder touched hers. "Ann, I wish you'd——"

He stopped.

"What?" said Ann.

"Ann—lemme kiss you."

Things seemed to hang for a space; his tone, the drop of his courage, made the thing incredible as he spoke. Kipps was not of that bold order of wooers who impose conditions.

Ann perceived that she was not prepared for kissing after all. Kissing, she said, was silly, and when Kipps would have displayed a belated enterprise, she flung away from him. He essayed argument. He stood afar off, as it were—the better part of a yard—and said she *might* let him kiss her, and then that he didn't see what good it was for her to be his girl if he couldn't kiss her.

She repeated that kissing was silly. A certain estrangement took them homeward. They arrived in the dusky High Street not exactly together, and not exactly apart, but straggling. They had not kissed, but all the guilt of kissing was between them. When Kipps saw the portly contours of his uncle standing dimly in the shop doorway his footsteps faltered, and the space between our young couple increased. Above, the window over Pornick's shop was open, and Mrs. Pornick was visible, taking the air. Kipps assumed an expression of extreme innocence. He found himself face to face with his uncle's advanced outposts of waistcoat buttons.

" Where ye bin, my boy ?"

" Bin for a walk, uncle."

" Not along of that brat of Pornick's ?"

" Along of who ?"

" That gell "—indicating Ann with his pipe.

" Oh, no, uncle !"—very faintly.

" Run in, my boy."

Old Kipps stood aside, with an oblique glance upward, and his nephew brushed clumsily by him and vanished out of sight of the street, into the vague obscurity of the little shop. The door closed behind old Kipps with a nervous jangle of its bell, and he set himself to light the single oil lamp that illuminated his shop at nights. It was an operation requiring care and watching, or else it flared and " smelt." Often it smelt after all. Kipps for some reason found the dusky living-room with his aunt in it too populous for his feelings, and went upstairs.

" That brat of Pornick's !" It seemed to him that a horrible catastrophe had occurred. He felt he had identified himself inextricably with his uncle, and cut himself off from her for ever by saying " Oh, no !" At supper he was so visibly depressed that his aunt asked him if he wasn't feeling well. Under this imminent threat of medicine he assumed an unnatural cheerfulness.

He lay awake for nearly half an hour that night, groaning because things had all gone wrong—because Ann wouldn't let him kiss her, and because his uncle had called her a brat. It seemed to Kipps almost as though he himself had called her a brat. . . .

There came an interval during which Ann was altogether inaccessible. One, two, three days passed, and he did not see her. Sid he met several times; they went fishing, and twice they bathed; but though Sid lent and received back two further love stories, they talked no more of love. They kept themselves in accord, however, agreeing that the most flagrantly sentimental story was "proper." Kipps was always wanting to speak of Ann, and never daring to do so. He saw her on Sunday evening going off to chapel. She was more beautiful than ever in her Sunday clothes, but she pretended not to see him because her mother was with her. But he thought she pretended not to see him because she had given him up for ever. Brat!—who could be expected ever to forgive that? He abandoned himself to despair, he ceased even to haunt the places where she might be found.

§ 6

With paralysing unexpectedness came the end.

Mr. Shalford, the draper at Folkestone to whom he was to be bound apprentice, had expressed a wish to "shape the lad a bit" before the autumn sale. Kipps became aware that his box was being packed, and gathered the full truth of things on the evening before his departure. He became feverishly eager to see Ann just once more. He made silly and needless excuses to go out into the yard, he walked three times across the street without any excuse at all, to look up at the Pornick windows. Still she was hidden. He grew desperate. It was within half an hour of his departure that he came on Sid.

"Hello!" he said. "I'm orf!"

"Business?"

"Yes."

Pause.

"I say, Sid. You going 'ome?"

"Straight now."

"D'you mind? Ask Ann about that."

"About what?"

"She'll know."

And Sid said he would. But even that, it seemed, failed to evoke Ann.

At last the Folkestone bus rumbled up, and he ascended. His aunt stood in the doorway to see him off. His uncle assisted with the box and portmanteau. Only furtively could he glance up at the Pornick windows, and still it seemed Ann hardened her heart against him. "Get up!" said the driver, and the hoofs began to clatter. No—she would not come out even to see him off. The bus was in motion, and old Kipps was going back into his shop. Kipps stared in front of him, assuring himself that he did not care.

He heard a door slam, and instantly craned out his neck to look back. He knew that slam so well. Behold! out of the haberdasher's door a small untidy figure in homely pink print had shot resolutely into the road, and was sprinting in pursuit. In a dozen seconds she was abreast of the bus. At the sight of her Kipps' heart began to beat very quickly, but he made no immediate motion of recognition.

"Artie!" she cried breathlessly, "Artie! Artie! You know! I got *that!*"

The bus was already quickening its pace, and leaving her behind again, when Kipps realized what "that" meant. He became animated, he gasped, and gathered his courage together, and mumbled an incoherent request to the driver to "stop jest a jiff for sunthin'."

2*

The driver grunted, as the disparity of their years demanded, and then the bus had pulled up and Ann was below.

She leapt up upon the wheel. Kipps looked down into Ann's face, and it was foreshortened and resolute. He met her eyes just for one second as their hands touched. He was not a reader of eyes. Something passed quickly from hand to hand, something that the driver, alert at the corner of his eye, was not allowed to see. Kipps hadn't a word to say, and all she said was, "I done it, 'smorning." It was like a blank space in which something pregnant should have been written and wasn't. Then she dropped down, and the bus moved forward.

After the lapse of about ten seconds it occurred to him to stand and wave his new bowler hat at her over the corner of the bus top, and to shout hoarsely, "Goo'-bye, Ann! Don't forget me—while I'm away!"

She stood in the road looking after him, and presently she waved her hand.

He remained standing unstably, his bright, flushed face looking back at her, and his hair fluffing in the wind, and he waved his hat until at last the bend of the road hid her from his eyes. Then he turned about and sat down, and presently he began to put the half sixpence he held clenched in his hand into his trouser pocket. He looked sideways at the driver, to judge how much he had seen.

Then he fell a-thinking. He resolved that, come what might, when he came back to New Romney at Christmas, he would by hook or by crook kiss Ann.

Then everything would be perfect and right, and he would be perfectly happy.

CHAPTER THE SECOND

The Emporium

§ 1

WHEN Kipps left New Romney, with a small yellow tin box, a still smaller portmanteau, a new umbrella, and a keepsake half-sixpence, to become a draper, he was a youngster of fourteen, thin, with whimsical drakes' tails at the poll of his head, smallish features, and eyes that were sometimes very light and sometimes very dark, gifts those of his birth; and by the nature of his training he was indistinct in his speech, confused in his mind, and retreating in his manners. Inexorable fate had appointed him to serve his country in commerce, and the same national bias towards private enterprise and leaving bad alone, which had left his general education to Mr. Woodrow, now indentured him firmly into the hands of Mr. Shalford, of the Folkestone Drapery Bazaar. Apprenticeship is still the recognised English way to the distributing branch of

the social service. If Mr. Kipps had been so unfortunate as to have been born a German he might have
been educated in an elaborate and costly special school
(" over-educated—crammed up "—old Kipps) to fit him
for his end—such being their pedagogic way. He
might . . . But why make unpatriotic reflections in a
novel? There was nothing pedagogic about Mr.
Shalford.

He was an irascible, energetic little man, with hairy
hands, for the most part under his coat tails, a long
shiny bald head, a pointed aquiline nose a little askew,
and a neatly trimmed beard. He walked lightly and
with a confident jerk, and he was given to humming.
He had added to exceptional business " push," bankruptcy under the old dispensation, and judicious matrimony. His establishment was now one of the most
considerable in Folkestone, and he insisted on every
inch of frontage by alternate stripes of green and yellow
down the houses over the shops. His shops were
numbered 3, 5, and 7 on the street, and on his bill-
heads 3 to 7. He encountered the abashed and awe-
stricken Kipps with the praises of his System and
himself. He spread himself out behind his desk with
a grip on the lapel of his coat and made Kipps a sort of
speech. "We expect y'r to work, y'r know, and we
expect y'r to study our interests," explained Mr. Shalford in the regal and commercial plural. "Our System
here is the best system y'r could have. I made it, and I
ought to know. I began at the very bottom of the
ladder when I was fourteen, and there isn't a step in it
I don't know. Not a step. Mr. Booch in the desk will
give y'r the card of rules and fines. Jest wait a
minute." He pretended to be busy with some dusty
memoranda under a paper-weight, while Kipps stood in
a sort of paralysis of awe regarding his new master's oval
baldness. "Two thous'n three forty-seven pounds,"
whispered Mr. Shalford audibly, feigning forgetfulness
of Kipps. Clearly a place of great transactions!

Mr. Shalford rose, and handing Kipps a blotting-pad and an inkpot to carry—mere symbols of servitude, for he made no use of them—emerged into a counting-house where three clerks had been feverishly busy ever since his door handle had turned. "Booch," said Mr. Shalford, "'ave y'r a copy of the rules?" and a down-trodden, shabby little old man with a ruler in one hand and a quill pen in his mouth, silently held out a small book with green and yellow covers, mainly devoted, as Kipps presently discovered, to a voracious system of fines. He became acutely aware that his hands were full, and that everybody was staring at him. He hesitated a moment before putting the inkpot down to free a hand.

"Mustn't fumble like *that*," said Mr. Shalford as Kipps pocketed the rules. "Won't do here. Come along, come along," and he cocked his coat tails high, as a lady might hold up her dress, and led the way into the shop.

A vast interminable place it seemed to Kipps, with unending shining counters and innumerable faultlessly dressed young men and presently Houri-like young women staring at him. Here there was a long vista of gloves dangling from overhead rods, there ribbons and baby-linen. A short young lady in black mittens was making out the account of a customer, and was clearly confused in her addition by Shalford's eagle eye.

A thickset young man with a bald head and a round, very wise face, who was profoundly absorbed in adjusting all the empty chairs down the counter to absolutely equal distances, awoke out of his preoccupation and answered respectfully to a few Napoleonic and quite unnecessary remarks from his employer. Kipps was told that this young man's name was Mr. Buggins, and that he was to do whatever Mr. Buggins told him to do.

They came round a corner into a new smell, which was destined to be the smell of Kipps' life for many years, the vague, distinctive smell of Manchester goods.

A fat man with a large nose jumped—actually jumped
—at their appearance, and began to fold a pattern of
damask in front of him exactly like an automaton that
is suddenly set going.

"Carshot, see to this boy to-morrow," said the
master. "See he don't fumble. Smart'n 'im up."

"Yussir," said Carshot fatly, glanced at Kipps, and
resumed his pattern-folding with extreme zeal.

"Whatever Mr. Carshot says y'r to do, ye *do*," said
Mr. Shalford, trotting onward; and Carshot blew out
his face with an appearance of relief.

They crossed a large room full of the strangest things
Kipps had ever seen. Ladylike figures, surmounted by
black wooden knobs in the place of the refined heads
one might have reasonably expected, stood about with a
lifelike air of conscious fashion.

"Costume room," said Shalford.

Two voices engaged in some sort of argument—"I
can assure you, Miss Mergle, you are entirely mistaken
—entirely, in supposing I should do anything so un-
womanly"—sank abruptly, and they discovered two
young ladies, taller and fairer than any of the other
young ladies, and with black trains to their dresses, who
were engaged in writing at a little table. Whatever
they told him to do, Kipps gathered he was to do. He
was also, he understood, to do whatever Carshot and
Booch told him to do. And there were also Buggins
and Mr. Shalford. And not to forget or fumble!

They descended into a cellar called "The Warehouse," and Kipps had an optical illusion of errand
boys fighting. Some aerial voice said, "Teddy!" and
the illusion passed. He looked again, and saw quite
clearly that they were packing parcels and always would
be, and that the last thing in the world that they would
or could possibly do was to fight. Yet he gathered from
the remarks Mr. Shalford addressed to their busy backs
that they had been fighting—no doubt at some past
period of their lives.

Emerging in the shop again among a litter of toys and what are called "fancy articles," Shalford withdrew a hand from beneath his coat tails to indicate an overhead change-carrier. He entered into elaborate calculations to show how many minutes in one year were saved thereby, and lost himself among the figures. "Seven tums-eight seven nine—was it? Or seven eight nine? Now, *now!* Why, when I was a boy your age I c'd do a sum like that as soon as hear it. We'll soon get y'r into better shape than that. Make you Fishent. Well, y'r must take my word, it comes to pounds and pounds saved in the year—pounds and pounds. System! System everywhere. Fishency." He went on murmuring "Fishency" and "System" at intervals for some time.

They passed into a yard, and Mr. Shalford waved his hand to his three delivery vans all striped green and yellow—"uniform—green, yell'r—System." All over the premises were pinned absurd little cards. "This door locked after 7.30.—By order, Edwin Shalford," and the like.

Mr. Shalford always wrote "By order," though it conveyed no earthly meaning to him. He was one of those people who collect technicalities upon them as the Reduvius bug collects dirt. He was the sort of man who is not only ignorant, but absolutely incapable of English. When he wanted to say he had a sixpenny-ha'penny longcloth to sell, he put it thus to startled customers: "Can do you one, six half if y' like." He always omitted pronouns and articles and so forth; it seemed to him the very essence of the efficiently businesslike. His only preposition was "as" or the compound "as per." He abbreviated every word he could; he would have considered himself the laughing-stock of Wood Street if he had chanced to spell socks in any way but "sox." But on the other hand, if he saved words here, he wasted them there: he never acknowledged an order that was not an esteemed favour,

nor sent a pattern without begging to submit it. He
never stipulated for so many months' credit, but bought
in November " as Jan." It was not only words he
abbreviated in his London communications. In paying
his wholesalers his " System" admitted of a constant
error in the discount of a penny or twopence, and it
" facilitated business," he alleged, to ignore odd pence
in the cheques he wrote. His ledger clerk was so struck
with the beauty of this part of the System that he
started a private one on his own account with the stamp
box, that never came to Shalford's knowledge.

This admirable British merchant would glow with a
particular pride of intellect when writing his London
orders.

" Ah! do y'r think *you*'ll ever be able to write
London orders?" he would say with honest pride to
Kipps, waiting impatiently long after closing time to
take these triumphs of commercial efficiency to post, and
so end the interminable day.

Kipps shook his head, anxious for Mr. Shalford to
get on.

" Now, here, f' example, I've written—see?—' 1
piece 1 in. cott. blk, elas. 1/or.' What do I mean by
that *or,* eh?—d'ye know?"

Kipps promptly hadn't the faintest idea.

" And then, ' 2 ea. silk net as per patts. herewith' :
ea., eh?"

" Dunno, sir."

It was not Mr. Shalford's way to explain things.
" Dear, dear! Pity you couldn't got some c'mercial
education at your school. 'Stid of all this lit'ry stuff.
Well, my boy, if y' don't 'ussel a bit y'll never write
London orders, *that*'s pretty plain. Jest stick stamps
on all those letters, and mind y'r stick 'em right way
up, and try and profit a little more by the opportunities
your aunt and uncle have provided ye. Can't say
what'll happen t'ye if ye don't."

And Kipps, tired, hungry, and belated, set about stamping with vigour and despatch.

"Lick the *envelope*," said Mr. Shalford, "lick the *envelope*," as though he grudged the youngster the postage-stamp gum. "It's the little things mount up," he would say; and, indeed, that was his philosophy of life—to bustle and save, always to bustle and save. His political creed linked Reform, which meant nothing, with Efficiency which meant a sweated service, and Economy which meant a sweated expenditure, and his conception of a satisfactory municipal life was to "keep down the rates." Even his religion was to save his soul, and to preach a similar cheeseparing to the world.

§ 2

The indentures that bound Kipps to Mr. Shalford were antique and complex : they insisted on the latter gentleman's parental privileges; they forbade Kipps to dice and game; they made him over body and soul to Mr. Shalford for seven long years, the crucial years of his life. In return there were vague stipulations about teaching the whole art and mystery of the trade to him; but as there was no penalty attached to negligence, Mr. Shalford, being a sound, practical business man, considered this a mere rhetorical flourish, and set himself assiduously to get as much out of Kipps and to put as little into him as he could in the seven years of their intercourse.

What he put into Kipps was chiefly bread and margarine, infusions of chicory and tea-dust, colonial meat by contract at threepence a pound, potatoes by the sack, and watered beer. If, however, Kipps chose to buy any supplementary material for growth, Mr. Shalford had the generosity to place his kitchen resources at his disposal free—if the fire chanced to be going. He was also allowed to share a bedroom with eight other young Englishmen, and to sleep in a bed which, except in very severe weather, could be made with the help of his overcoat and private underlinen, not to mention newspapers, quite sufficiently warm for any reasonable soul. In addition Kipps was taught the list of fines; and how to tie up parcels; to know where goods were kept in Mr. Shalford's systematised shop; to hold his hands extended upon the counter and to repeat such phrases as "What can I have the pleasure. . . .?" "No trouble, I 'ssure you," and the like; to block, fold, and measure materials of all sorts; to lift his hat from his head when he passed Mr. Shalford abroad, and to practise a servile obedience to a large number of people. But he was not, of course, taught the "cost" mark of the goods he sold, nor anything of the method of buying such goods. Nor was his attention directed to the unfamiliar social habits and fashions to which his trade ministered. The use of half the goods he saw sold and was presently to assist in selling he did not understand; materials for hangings, cretonnes, chintzes and the like, serviettes and all the bright, hard white wear of a well-ordered house, pleasant dress materials, linings, stiffenings—they were to him from first to last no more than things heavy and difficult to handle in bulk, that one folded up, unfolded, cut in lengths and saw dwindle and pass away out into that mysterious happy world in which the customer dwells. Kipps hurried from piling linen table-cloths, that were collectively as heavy as lead, to eat off oilcloth in a gas-lit dining-room underground; and beneath his overcoat, spare undershirt, and three newspapers he dreamt of combing endless blankets. So he had at least the chance of learning the beginnings of philosophy.

In return for these benefits he worked so that he commonly went to bed exhausted and footsore. His round began at half-past six in the morning, when he would descend unwashed and shirtless, in old clothes and a scarf, and dust boxes and yawn, and take down wrappers and clean the windows until eight. Then in half an hour he would complete his toilet and take an austere breakfast of bread and margarine and what only an Imperial Englishman would admit to be coffee, after which refreshment he ascended to the shop for the labours of the day. Commonly these began with a mighty running to and fro with planks and boxes and goods for Carshot, the window-dresser, who, whether he worked well or ill, nagged persistently by reason of a chronic indigestion, until the window was done. Sometimes the costume window had to be dressed, and then Kipps staggered down the whole length of the shop from the costume room with one after another of those ladylike shapes grasped firmly but shamefully, each about her single ankle of wood. Such days as there was no window-dressing, there was a mighty carrying and lifting of blocks and bales of goods into piles and stacks. After this there were terrible exercises, at first almost despairfully difficult : certain sorts of goods that came in folded had to be rolled upon rollers, and for the most part refused absolutely to be rolled, at any rate by Kipps; and certain other sorts of goods that came from the wholesalers rolled had to be measured and folded, which folding makes young apprentices wish they were dead. All of it, too, quite avoidable trouble, you know, that is not avoided because of the cheapness of the genteeler sorts of labour and the dearness of forethought in the world. And then consignments of new goods had to be marked off and packed into proper parcels; and Carshot packed like conjuring tricks, and Kipps packed like a boy with tastes in some other direction—not ascertained. And always Carshot nagged.

He had a curious formula of appeal to his visceral œconomy, had Carshot, that the refinement of the times and the earnest entreaties of my friends induce me to render by an anæmic paraphrase.

"My heart and lungs! I never see such a boy," so I present Carshot's refrain; and even when he was within a foot or so of the customer's face the disciplined ear of Kipps would still at times develop a featureless, intercalary murmur into—well, "my heart and lungs!"

There came blessed intervals when Kipps was sent abroad "matching." This consisted chiefly in supplying unexpected defects in buttons, ribbon, lining, and so forth in the dressmaking department. He was given a written paper of orders with patterns pinned thereto, and discharged into the sunshine and interest of the street. Then, until he thought it wise to return and stand the racket of his delay, he was a free man, clear of all reproach.

He made remarkable discoveries in topography, as for example that the most convenient way from the establishment of Mr. Adolphus Davis to the establishment of Messrs. Plummer, Roddis & Tyrrel, two of his principal places of call, is not as is generally supposed down the Sandgate Road, but up the Sandgate Road, round by West Terrace, and along the Leas to the lift, watch the lift up and down *twice,* but not longer, because that wouldn't do, back along the Leas, watch the Harbour for a short time, and then round by the churchyard, and so (hurrying) into Church Street and Rendezvous Street. But on some exceptionally fine days the route lay through Radnor Park to the pond where the little boys sail ships and there are interesting swans.

He would return to find the shop settling down to the business of serving customers. And now he had to stand by to furnish any help that was necessary to the seniors who served, to carry parcels and bills about the shop, to clear away "stuff" after each engagement, to hold up curtains until his arms ached, and what was more difficult than all, to do nothing, and not stare disconcertingly at customers when there was nothing for him to do. He plumbed an abyss of boredom, or stood a mere carcass, with his mind far away, fighting the enemies of the Empire, or steering a dream ship perilously into unknown seas. To be recalled sharply to our higher civilisation by some bustling senior's " Nar then, Kipps. *Look* alive! Ketch 'old. (My heart and lungs!)"

At half-past seven o'clock—except on late nights—a feverish activity of "straightening up" began, and when the last shutter was up outside, Kipps with the speed of an arrow leaving a bow would start hanging wrappers over the fixtures and over the piles of wares upon the counters, preparatory to a vigorous scattering of wet sawdust and the sweeping out of the shop.

Sometimes people would stay long after the shop was closed—"They don't mind a bit at Shalford's," these ladies used to say—it is always ladies do this sort of thing—and while they loitered it was forbidden to touch a wrapper, or take any measures to conclude the day until the doors closed behind them.

Mr. Kipps would watch these later customers from the shadow of a stack of goods, and death and disfigurement was the least he wished for them. Rarely much later than nine, a supper of bread and cheese and watered beer awaited him upstairs, and, that consumed, the rest of the day was entirely at his disposal for reading, recreation, and the improvement of his mind. . . .

The front door was locked at half-past ten, and the gas in the dormitory extinguished at eleven.

§ 3

On Sundays he was obliged to go to church once, and commonly he went twice, for there was nothing else to do. He sat in the free seats at the back; he was too shy to sing, and not always clever enough to keep his place in the prayer-book, and he rarely listened to the sermon. But he had developed a sort of idea that going to church had a tendency to alleviate life. His aunt wanted to have him confirmed, but he evaded this ceremony for some years.

In the intervals between services he walked about Folkestone with an air of looking for something. Folkestone was not so interesting on Sundays as on week-days, because the shops were shut; but on the other hand there was a confusing brilliance along the front of the Leas in the afternoon. Sometimes the apprentice next above him would condescend to go with him; but when the apprentice next but one above him condescended to go with the apprentice next above him, then Kipps, being habited as yet in ready-made clothes without tails, and unsuitable therefore to appear in such company, went alone.

Sometimes he would strike out into the country—still as if looking for something he missed—but the rope of meal-times haled him home again; and sometimes he would invest the major portion of the weekly allowance of a shilling that old Booch handed out to him, in a sacred concert on the pier. He would sometimes walk up and down the Leas between twenty and thirty times after supper, desiring much the courage to speak to some other person in the multitude similarly employed. Almost invariably he ended his Sunday footsore.

He never read a book; there were none for him to read, and besides, in spite of Mr. Woodrow's guidance through a cheap and cheaply annotated edition of the *Tempest* (English Literature), he had no taste that way; he never read any newspapers, except occasionally *Tit-Bits* or a ha'penny "comic." His chief intellectual stimulus was an occasional argey-bargey that sprang up between Carshot and Buggins at dinner. Kipps listened as if to unparalleled wisdom and wit, and treasured all the gems of repartee in his heart against the time when he, too, should be a Buggins and have the chance and courage for speech.

At times there came breaks in this routine—sale

times, darkened by extra toil and work past midnight, but brightened by a sprat supper and some shillings in the way of "premiums." And every year—not now and then, but every year—Mr. Shalford, with parenthetic admiration of his own generosity and glancing comparisons with the austerer days when *he* was apprenticed, conceded Kipps no less than ten days' holiday— ten whole days every year! Many a poor soul at Portland might well envy the fortunate Kipps. Insatiable heart of man! but how those days were grudged and counted as they snatched themselves away from him one after another!

Once a year came stock-taking, and at intervals gusts of "marking off" goods newly arrived. Then the splendours of Mr. Shalford's being shone with oppressive brilliancy. "System!" he would say, "system. Come! 'ussel!" and issue sharp, confusing, contradictory orders very quickly. Carshot trotted about, confused, perspiring, his big nose up in the air, his little eye on Mr. Shalford, his forehead crinkled, his lips always going to the formula "Oh, my heart and lungs!" The smart junior and the second apprentice vied with one another in obsequious alacrity. The smart junior aspired to Carshot's position, and that made him almost violently subservient to Shalford. They all snapped at Kipps. Kipps held the blotting-pad and the safety inkpot and a box of tickets, and ran and fetched things. If he put the ink down before he went to fetch things Mr. Shalford usually knocked it over, and if he took it away Mr. Shalford wanted it before he returned. "You make my tooth ache, Kipps," Mr. Shalford would say. "You gimme n'ralgia. You got no more System in you than a bad potato." And at the times when Kipps carried off the inkpot Mr. Shalford would become purple in the face and jab round with his dry pen at imaginary inkpots and swear, and Carshot would stand and vociferate, and the smart junior would run to the corner of the department and vociferate, and the second

apprentice would pursue Kipps, vociferating, "Look
Alive, Kipps! Look Alive! Ink, Man! Ink!"

A vague self-disgust, that shaped itself as an intense
hate of Shalford and all his fellow-creatures, filled the
soul of Kipps during these periods of storm and stress.
He felt that the whole business was unjust and idiotic,
but the why and the wherefore was too much for his
unfortunate brain. His mind was a welter. One desire,
the desire to dodge some at least of a pelting storm of
disagreeable comment, guided him through a fumbling
performance of his duties. His disgust was infinite! It
was not decreased by the inflamed ankles and sore feet
that form a normal incident in the business of making
an English draper; and the senior apprentice, Minton,
a gaunt, sullen-faced youngster with close-cropped, wiry
black hair, a loose ugly mouth, and a moustache like a
smudge of ink, directed his attention to deeper aspects
of the question and sealed his misery.

"When you get too old to work they chuck you
away," said Minton. "Lor'! you find old drapers
everywhere—tramps, beggars, dock labourers, bus con-
ductors—Quod. Anywhere but in a crib."

"Don't they get shops of their own?"

"Lord! 'Ow are they to get shops of their own?
They 'aven't any capital! How's a draper's shopman
to save up five hundred pounds even? I tell you it
can't be done. You got to stick to cribs until it's over.
I tell you we're in a blessed drainpipe, and we've got to
crawl along it till we die."

The idea that fermented perpetually in the mind of
Minton was to "hit the little beggar slap in the eye"—
the little beggar being Mr. Shalford—"and see how his
blessed System met that."

The threat filled Kipps with splendid anticipations
whenever Shalford went marking off in Minton's department. He would look at Minton and look at Shalford,
and decide where he would best like Shalford hit. . . .
But for reasons known to himself Shalford never pished

and tushed with Minton as he did at the harmless Carshot, and this interesting experiment upon the System was never attempted.

§ 4

There were times when Kipps would lie awake, all others in the dormitory asleep and snoring, and think dismally of the outlook Minton pictured. Dimly he perceived the thing that had happened to him—how the great stupid machine of retail trade had caught his life into its wheels, a vast irresistible force which he had neither strength of will nor knowledge to escape. This was to be his life until his days should end. No adventures, no glory, no change, no freedom. Neither —though the force of that came home to him later— might he dream of effectual love and marriage. And there was a terrible something called the "swap," or "the key of the street," and "crib hunting," of which the talk was scanty but sufficient. Night after night he would resolve to enlist, to run away to sea, to set fire to the warehouse, or drown himself; and morning after morning he rose up and hurried downstairs in fear of a sixpenny fine. He would compare his dismal round of servile drudgery with those windy, sunlit days of Littlestone, those windows of happiness shining ever brighter as they receded. The little figure of Ann seemed in all those windows now.

She, too, had happened on evil things. When Kipps went home for the first Christmas after he was bound, that great suspended resolve of his to kiss her flared up to hot determination, and he hurried out and whistled in the yard. There was a still silence, and then Old Kipps appeared behind him.

"It's no good your whistling there, my boy," said Old Kipps in a loud clear tone, designed to be audible over the wall. "They've cleared out all you 'ad any truck with. *She's* gone as help to Ashford, my boy.

Help! Slavey is what we used to call 'em, but times are changed. Wonder they didn't say lady-'elp while they was about it. It 'ud be like 'em."

And Sid? Sid had gone, too. "Arrand boy or somethink," said Old Kipps. "To one of these here brasted cicycle shops."

"*Has* 'e!" said Kipps, with a feeling that he had been gripped about the chest, and he turned quickly and went indoors.

Old Kipps, still supposing him present, went on to further observations of an anti-Pornick hue. . . .

When Kipps got upstairs safe in his own bedroom, he sat down on the bed and stared at nothing. They were caught—they were all caught. All life took on the hue of one perpetual, dismal Monday morning. The Hurons were scattered, the wrecks and the beach had passed away from him, the sun of those warm evenings at Littlestone had set for evermore. . . .

The only pleasure left for the brief remainder of his holiday after that was to think he was not in the shop. Even that was transient. Two more days—one more day—half a day. When he went back there were one or two very dismal nights indeed. He went so far as to write home some vague intimation of his feelings about business and his prospects, quoting Minton. But Mrs. Kipps answered him, "Did he want the Pornicks to say he wasn't good enough to be a draper?" This dreadful possibility was of course conclusive in the matter. "No," he resolved they should not say he failed at that.

He derived much help from a "manly" sermon delivered in an enormous voice by a large, fat, sun-red clergyman, just home from a colonial bishopric he had resigned on the plea of ill-health, exhorting him that whatever his hand found to do, he was to do with all his might; and the revision of his Catechism preparatory to his confirmation reminded him that it behoved him

" to do his duty in that state of life unto which it shall please God to call him. . . ."

After a time the sorrows of Kipps grew less acute, and save for a miracle the brief tragedy of his life was over. He subdued himself to his position even as his Church required of him, seeing moreover no way out of it.

The earliest mitigation of his lot was that his soles and ankles became indurated to the perpetual standing. The next was an unexpected weekly whiff of freedom that came every Thursday. Mr. Shalford, after a brave stand for what he called " Innyvishal lib'ty " and the " Idea of my System," a stand which he explained he made chiefly on patriotic grounds, was at last, under pressure of certain of his customers, compelled to fall in line with the rest of the local Early Closing Association, and Mr. Kipps could emerge in daylight and go where he listed for long, long hours. Moreover Minton, the pessimist, reached the end of his appointed time and left——to enlist in a cavalry regiment and go about this planet leading an insubordinate but interesting life, that ended at last in an intimate, vivid and really you know by no means painful or tragic night grapple in the Terah Valley. In a little while Kipps cleaned windows no longer; he was serving customers (of the less important sort) and taking goods out on approval; and presently he was third apprentice, and his moustache was visible, and there were three apprentices whom he might legally snub and cuff. But one was (most dishonestly) too big to cuff in spite of his greener years.

§ 5

There came still other distractions, the natural distractions of adolescence, to take his mind off the inevitable. His costume, for example, began to interest him more; he began to realise himself as a visible object,

to find an interest in the costume-room mirrors and the
eyes of the girl apprentices.

In this he was helped by counsel and example.
Pierce, his immediate senior, was by way of being what
was called a Masher, and preached his cult. During
slack times grave discussions about collars, ties, the cut
of trouser legs, and the proper shape of a boot-toe,
were held in the Manchester department. In due
course Kipps went to a tailor, and his short jacket was
replaced by a morning coat with tails. Stirred by this,
he purchased at his own expense three stand-up collars
to replace his former turn-down ones. They were
nearly three inches high, higher than those Pierce wore,
and they made his neck quite sore and left a red mark
under his ears. . . . So equipped, he found himself fit
company even for this fashionable apprentice, who had
now succeeded Minton in his seniority.

Most potent help of all in the business of forgetting
his cosmic disaster was this, that so soon as he was in
tail coats the young ladies of the establishment began to
discover that he was no longer a "horrid little boy."
Hitherto they had tossed heads at him and kept him in
his place. Now they discovered that he was a "nice
boy," which is next door at least to being a "feller,"
and in some ways even preferable. It is painful to
record that his fidelity to Ann failed at their first onset.
I am fully sensible how entirely better this story would
be from a sentimental point of view if he had remained
true to that early love. Only then it would have been
a different story altogether. And at least Kipps was
thus far true, that with none of these later loves was
there any of that particular quality that linked Ann's
flushed face and warmth and the inner things of life so
inseparably together. Though they were not without
emotions of various sorts.

It was one of the young ladies in the costume-room
who first showed by her manner that he was a visible
object and capable of exciting interest. She talked to

him, she encouraged him to talk to her, she lent him a book she possessed and darned a sock for him, and said she would be his elder sister. She allowed him to escort her to church with a great air of having induced him to go. Then she investigated his eternal welfare, overcame a certain affectation of virile indifference to religion, and extorted a promise that he would undergo "confirmation." This excited the other young lady in the costumes, her natural rival, and she set herself with great charm and subtlety to the capture of the ripening heart of Kipps. She took a more worldly line. She went for a walk with him to the pier on Sunday afternoon, and explained to him how a gentleman must always walk "outside" a lady on a pavement, and how all gentlemen wore, or at least carried, gloves, and generally the broad beginnings of the British social ideal. Afterwards the ladies exchanged "words," upon Sabbatical grounds. In this way was the *toga virilis* bestowed on Kipps, and he became recognised as a suitable object for that Platonic Eros whose blunted darts devastate even the very highest-class establishments. In this way, too, did that pervading ambition of the British young man to be, if not a "gentleman," at least mistakably like one, take root in his heart.

He took to these new interests with quite natural and personal zest. He became initiated into the mysteries of "flirting," and—at a slightly later stage, and with some leading hints from Pierce, who was of a communicative disposition in these matters—of the milder forms of "spooning." Very soon he was engaged. Before two years were out he had been engaged six times, and was beginning to be rather a desperate fellow, so far as he could make out. Desperate, but quite gentlemanly, be it understood, and without let or hindrance to the fact that he was, in four brief lessons, "prepared" by a distant-mannered and gloomy young curate, and "confirmed" a member of the Established Church.

The engagements in drapery establishments do not necessarily involve a subsequent marriage. They are essentially more refined, less coarsely practical, and altogether less binding than the engagements of the vulgar rich. These young ladies do not like not to be engaged—it is so unnatural; and Mr. Kipps was as easy to get engaged to as one could wish. There are, from the young lady's point of view, many conveniences in being engaged. You get an escort for church and walks and so forth. It is not quite the thing to walk abroad with a "feller," much more to "spoon" with him, when he is neither one's *fiancé* nor an adopted brother; it is considered either a little fast, or else as savouring of the "walking-out" habits of the servant girls. Now such is the sweetness of human charity, that the shop young lady in England has just the same horror of doing anything that savours of the servant girl as the lady journalist, let us say, has to anything savouring of the shop girl, or the really quite nice young lady has of anything savouring of any sort of girl who has gone down into the economic battlefield to earn herself a living. . . . But the very deepest of these affairs was still among the shallow places of love; at best it was paddling where it is decreed that men must sink or swim. Of the deep and dangerous places, and of the huge buoyant lift of its waves, he tasted nothing. Affairs of clothes and vanities they were, jealousies about a thing said, flatteries and mutual boastings, climaxes in the answering grasp of hands, the temerarious use of Christian names, culminations in a walk, or a near confidence, or a little pressure more or less. Close-sitting on a seat after twilight, with some little fondling, was indeed the boldest of a lover's adventures, the utmost limit of his enterprises in the service of that stark Great Lady, who is daughter of Uranus and the sea. The "young ladies" who reigned in his heart came and went like people in an omnibus : there was the vehicle, so to speak, upon the road, and they entered and left it without any cataclysm of emotion. For all that, this development of the sex interest was continuously very interesting to Kipps, and kept him going as much as anything through all these servile years.

§ 6

For a tailpiece to this chapter one may vignette one of those little affairs.

It is a bright Sunday afternoon; the scene is a secluded little seat half-way down the front of the Leas, and Kipps is four years older than when he parted from Ann. There is a quite perceptible down upon his upper lip, and his costume is just as tremendous a "mash" as lies within his means. His collar is so high that it scars his inaggressive jawbone, and his hat has a curly brim, his tie shows taste, his trousers are modestly brilliant, and his boots have light cloth uppers and button at the side. He jabs at the gravel before him with a cheap cane, and glances sideways at Flo Bates, the young lady from the cash desk. She is wearing a brilliant blouse and a gaily trimmed hat. There is an air of fashion about her that might disappear under the analysis of a woman of the world, but which is quite sufficient to make Kipps very proud to be distinguished as her particular "feller," and to be allowed at temperate intervals to use her Christian name.

The conversation is light and gay in the modern style, and Flo keeps on smiling, good temper being her special charm.

"Ye see, you don' mean what *I* mean," he is saying.

"Well, what do *you* mean?"

"Not what you mean!"

"Well, tell me."

"*Ah!* That's another story."

Pause. They look meaningly at one another.

"You *are* a one for being roundabout," says the lady.

"Well, you're not so plain, you know."

" Not plain?"

" No."

" You don't mean to say I'm roundabout?"

" No. I mean to say . . . though———"

Pause.

" Well?"

" You're not a bit plain—you're " (his voice jumps up to a squeak) " pretty. See?"

" Oh, get *out!*" her voice lifts also—with pleasure.

She strikes at him with her glove, then glances suddenly at a ring upon her finger. Her smile disappears momentarily. Another pause. Eyes meet and the smile returns.

" I wish I knew———" says Kipps.

" Knew———?"

" Where you got that ring."

She lifts the hand with the ring until her eyes just show (very prettily) over it. " You'd just *like* to know," she says slowly, and smiles still more brightly with the sense of successful effect.

" I dessay I could guess."

" I dessay you couldn't."

" Couldn't I?"

" No!"

" Guess it in three."

" Not the name."

" Ah!"

" *Ah!*"

" Well, anyhow lemme look at it."

He looks at it. Pause. Giggles, slight struggle, and a slap on Kipps' coat-sleeve. A passer-by appears down the path, and she hastily withdraws her hand.

She glances at the face of the approaching man. They maintain a bashful silence until he has passed.

CHAPTER THE THIRD

The Wood-Carving Class

§ 1

THOUGH these services to Venus Epipontia, the seaside Venus, and these studies in the art of dress, did much to distract his thoughts and mitigate his earlier miseries, it would be mere optimism to present Kipps as altogether happy. A vague dissatisfaction with life drifted about him and every now and again enveloped him like a sea fog. During these periods it was greyly evident that there was something, something vital in life, lacking. For no earthly reason that Kipps could discover, he was haunted by a suspicion that life was going wrong or had already gone wrong in some irrevocable way. The ripening self-consciousness of adolescence developed this into a clearly felt insufficiency. It was all very well to carry gloves, open doors, never say "Miss" to a girl, and walk "outside," but were there not other things, conceivably even deeper things, before the complete thing was attained? For example, certain matters of knowledge. He perceived great bogs of ignorance about him, fumbling traps, where other people, it was alleged, *real* gentlemen and ladies for example, and the clergy, had knowledge and assurance, bogs which it was sometimes difficult to elude. A girl arrived in the millinery department who could, she said, *speak* French and German. She snubbed certain advances, and a realisation of inferiority blistered Kipps. But he tried to pass the thing off as a joke by saying, " Parlez-vous Francey," whenever he met her, and inducing the junior apprentice to say the same.

He even made some dim half-secret experiments towards remedying the deficiencies he suspected. He spent five shillings on five serial numbers of a Home Educator, and bought (and even thought of reading) a Shakespeare and a Bacon's " Advancement of Learning " and the poems of Herrick from a chap who was hard up. He battled with Shakespeare all one Sunday afternoon, and found the " English Literature " with which Mr. Woodrow had equipped him had vanished down some crack in his mind. He had no doubt it was very splendid stuff, but he couldn't quite make out what it was all about. There was an occult meaning, he knew, in literature, and he had forgotten it. Moreover he discovered one day, while taunting the junior apprentice with ignorance, that his " rivers of England " had also slipped his memory, and he laboriously restored that fabric of rote learning : " Ty Wear Tees 'Umber. . . ."

I suppose some such phase of discontent is a normal thing in every adolescence. The ripening mind seeks something upon which its will may crystallise, upon which its discursive emotions, growing more abundant with each year of life, may concentrate. For many, though not for all, it takes a religious direction, but in those particular years the mental atmosphere of Folkestone was exceptionally free from any revivalistic disturbance that might have reached Kipps' mental being. Sometimes they fall in love. I have known this un-

easiness end in different cases in a vow to read one book
(not a novel) every week, to read the Bible through in a
year, to pass in the Honours division of the London
Matriculation examination, to become an accomplished
chemist, and never more to tell a lie. It led Kipps
finally into Technical Education as we understand it in
the south of England.

It was in the last year of his apprenticeship that he
had pursued his researches after that missing qualifica-
tion into the Folkestone Young Men's Association,
where Mr. Chester Coote prevailed. Mr. Chester
Coote was a young man of semi-independent means who
inherited a share in a house agency, read Mrs. Humphry
Ward, and took an interest in social work. He was a
whitish-faced young man with a prominent nose, pale
blue eyes, and a quivering quality in his voice. He was
very active upon committees; he was very prominent
and useful on all social occasions, in evidence upon
platforms and upon all those semi-public occasions when
the Great descend. He lived with an only sister. To
Kipps and his kind in the Young Men's Association he
read a stimulating paper on "Self-Help." He said it
was the noblest of all our distinctive English characteristics, and he was very much down upon the "over
educated" Germans. At the close a young German
hairdresser made a few commendatory remarks which
developed somehow into an oration on Hanoverian
politics. As he became excited he became guttural and
obscure; the meeting sniggered cheerfully at such
ridiculous English, and Kipps was so much amused that
he forgot a private project to ask this Chester Coote
how he might set about a little self-help on his own
account in such narrow margins of time as the System
of Mr. Shalford spared him. But afterwards in the
night-time it came to him again.

It was a few months later, and after his apprenticeship was over and Mr. Shalford had with depreciatory
observations taken him on as an improver at twenty

pounds a year, that this question was revived by a casual article on Technical Education in a morning paper that a commercial traveller had left behind him. It played the rôle of the word in season. Something in the nature of conversion, a faint sort of concentration of purpose, really occurred in him then. The article was written with penetrating vehemence, and it stimulated him to the pitch of inquiring about the local Science and Art Classes; and after he had told everybody in the shop about it and taken the advice of all who supported his desperate resolution, he joined. At first he attended the class in Freehand, that being the subject taught on early closing night; and he had already made some progress in that extraordinary routine of reproducing freehand "copies" which for two generations had passed with English people for instruction in art, when the dates of the classes were changed. Thereby just as the March winds were blowing he was precipitated into the wood-carving class, and his mind diverted first to this useful and broadening pursuit, and then to its teacher.

§ 2

The class in wood-carving was an extremely select class, conducted at that time by a young lady named Walshingham; and as this young lady was destined by fortune to teach Kipps a great deal more than wood-carving, it will be well if the reader gets the picture of her correctly in mind. She was only a year or so older than he was; she had a pale, intellectual face, dark grey eyes, and black hair, which she wore over her forehead in an original and striking way that she had adopted from a picture by Rossetti in the South Kensington Museum. She was slender, so that without ungainliness she had an effect of being tall, and her hands were shapely and white when they came into contrast with hands much exercised in rolling and blocking. She dressed in those loose and pleasant forms and those soft and tempered shades that arose in England in the socialistic-æsthetic epoch and remain to this day among us as the badge of those who read Turgenev's novels, scorn current fiction, and think on higher planes. I think she was as beautiful as most beautiful people, and to Kipps she was altogether beautiful. She had, Kipps learnt, matriculated at London University, an astounding feat to his imagination; and the masterly way in which she demonstrated how to prod and worry honest pieces of wood into useless and unedifying patterns in relief extorted his utmost admiration.

At first, when Kipps had learnt he was to be taught by a "girl," he was inclined to resent it, the more so as Buggins had recently been very strong on the gross injustice of feminine employment.

"We have to keep wives," said Buggins (though as a matter of fact he did not keep even one), "and how are we to do it with a lot of girls coming in to take the work out of our mouths?"

Afterwards Kipps, in conjunction with Pierce, looked at it from another point of view, and thought it would be rather a "lark." Finally when he saw her, and saw her teaching and coming nearer to him with an impressive deliberation, he was breathless with awe and the quality of her dark, slender femininity.

The class consisted of two girls and a maiden lady of riper years, friends of Miss Walshingham's, and anxious rather to support her in an interesting experiment than to become really expert wood-carvers; an oldish young man with spectacles and a black beard, who never spoke to anyone, and who was evidently too short-sighted to see his work as a whole; a small boy who was understood to have a "gift" for wood-carving; and a lodging-house keeper who "took classes" every winter, she told Mr. Kipps, as though they were a tonic, and "found they did her good." And occasionally Mr. Chester Coote—refined and gentlemanly— would come into the class, with or without papers,

ostensibly on committee business, but in reality to talk
to the less attractive one of the two girl students; and
sometimes a brother of Miss Walshingham, a slender,
dark young man with a pale face and fluctuating
resemblances to the young Napoleon, would arrive
just at the end of the class-time to take his sister
home.

All these personages impressed Kipps with a sense of
inferiority that in the case of Miss Walshingham became
positively abysmal. The ideas and knowledge they
appeared to have, their personal capacity and freedom,
opened a new world to his imagination. These people
came and went, with a sense of absolute assurance,
against an overwhelming background of plaster casts,
diagrams and tables, benches and a blackboard—a background that seemed to him to be saturated with recon-
dite knowledge and the occult and jealously guarded
tips and secrets that constitute Art and the Higher Life.
They went home, he imagined, to homes where the
piano was played with distinction and freedom, and
books littered the tables, and foreign languages were
habitually used. They had complicated meals, no
doubt—with serviettes. They "knew etiquette," and
how to avoid all the errors for which Kipps bought
penny manuals, "What to Avoid," "Common Errors
in Speaking," and the like. He knew nothing about it
all—nothing whatever; he was a creature of the outer
darkness blinking in a blinding unrevealing light.

He heard them speak easily and freely to one another
of examinations, of books and paintings, of "last year's
Academy"—a little contemptuously; and once, just at
the end of the class-time, Mr. Chester Coote and young
Walshingham and the two girls argued about something
or other called, he fancied, "Vagner" or "Vargner"—
they seemed to say it both ways—and which presently
shaped itself more definitely as the name of a man who
made up music. (Carshot and Buggins weren't in it
with them.) Young Walshingham, it appeared, said

something or other that was an "epigram," and they all
applauded him. Kipps, I say, felt himself a creature of
outer darkness, an inexcusable intruder in an altitudinous
world. When the epigram happened, he first of all
smiled, to pretend he understood, and instantly suppressed the smile to show he did not listen. Then he
became extremely hot and uncomfortable, though nobody had noticed either phase.

It was clear his only chance of concealing his bottom-
less baseness was to hold his tongue, and meanwhile he
chipped with earnest care, and abased his soul before the
very shadow of Miss Walshingham. She used to come
and direct and advise him, with, he felt, an effort to
conceal the scorn she had for him; and indeed it is true
that at first she thought of him chiefly as the clumsy
young man with the red ears.

And as soon as he emerged from the first effect of
pure and awestricken humility—he was greatly helped
to emerge from that condition to a perception of
human equality by the need the lodging-house keeper
was under to talk while she worked, and as she didn't
like Miss Walshingham and her friends very much, and
the young man with spectacles was deaf, she naturally
talked to Kipps—he perceived that he was in a state
of adoration for Miss Walshingham that it seemed
almost a blasphemous familiarity to speak of as being
in love.

This state, you must understand, had nothing to do
with "flirting" or "spooning" and that superficial
passion that flashes from eye to eye upon the Leas and
pier—absolutely nothing. That he knew from the first.
Her rather pallid, intelligent young face, beneath those
sombre clouds of hair, put her in a class apart; towards
her the thought of "attentions" paled and vanished.
To approach such a being, to perform sacrifices and to
perish obviously for her, seemed the limit he might
aspire to, he or any man. For if his love was abasement,
at any rate it had this much of manliness, that it

covered all his sex. It had not yet come to Kipps to acknowledge any man as his better in his heart of hearts. When one does that the game is played and one grows old indeed.

The rest of his sentimental interests vanished altogether in this great illumination. He meditated about her when he was blocking cretonne; her image was before his eyes at tea-time and blotted out the more immediate faces, and made him silent and preoccupied and so careless in his bearing that the junior apprentice, sitting beside him, mocked at and parodied his enormous bites of bread and butter unreproved. He became conspicuously less popular on the "fancy" side, the "costumes" was chilly with him and the "millinery" cutting. But he did not care. An intermittent correspondence with Flo Bates, that had gone on since she left Mr. Shalford's desk for a position at Tonbridge "nearer home," and which had roused Kipps in its earlier stages to unparalleled heights of epistolatory effort, died out altogether by reason of his neglect. He heard with scarcely a pang that, as a consequence perhaps of his neglect, Flo was "carrying on with a chap who managed a farm."

Every Thursday he jabbed and gouged at his wood, jabbing and gouging intersecting circles and diamond traceries and that laboured inane which our mad world calls ornament, and he watched Miss Walshingham furtively whenever she turned away. The circles in consequence were jabbed crooked; and his panels, losing their symmetry, became comparatively pleasing to the untrained eye—and once he jabbed his finger. He would cheerfully have jabbed all his fingers if he could have found some means of using the opening to express himself of the vague emotions that possessed him. But he shirked conversation just as earnestly as he desired it; he feared that profound general ignorance of his might appear.

§ 3

There came a time when she could not open one of the classroom windows. The man with the black beard pored over his chipping heedlessly. . . .

It did not take Kipps a moment to grasp his opportunity. He dropped his gouge and stepped forward. "Lem *me*," he said. . . .

He could not open the window either!

"Oh, please don't trouble," she said.

"'Sno trouble," he gasped.

Still the sash stuck. He felt his manhood was at stake. He gathered himself together for a tremendous effort, and the pane broke with a snap, and he thrust his hand into the void beyond.

"*There!*" said Miss Walshingham, and the glass fell ringing into the courtyard below.

Then Kipps made to bring his hand back, and felt the keen touch of the edge of the broken glass at his wrist. He turned dolefully. "I'm tremendously sorry," he said in answer to the accusation in Miss Walshingham's eyes. "I didn't think it would break like that,"—as if he had expected it to break in some quite different and entirely more satisfactory manner. The boy with the gift of wood-carving having stared at Kipps' face for a moment, became involved in a Laocoön struggle with a giggle.

"You've cut your wrist," said one of the girl friends, standing up and pointing. She was a pleasant-faced, greatly freckled girl, with a helpful disposition, and she said "You've cut your wrist," as brightly as if she had been a trained nurse.

Kipps looked down, and saw a swift line of scarlet rush down his hand. He perceived the other man student regarding this with magnified eyes. "You *have* cut your wrist," said Miss Walshingham, and Kipps regarded his damage with greater interest.

"He's cut his wrist," said the maiden lady to the

3*

lodging-house keeper, and seemed in doubt what a
lady should do. " It's——" she hesitated at the word
" bleeding," and nodded to the lodging-house keeper
instead.

" Dreadfully," said the maiden lady, and tried to
look and tried not to look at the same time.

" Of *course* he's cut his wrist," said the lodging-house
keeper, momentarily quite annoyed at Kipps; and the
other young lady, who thought Kipps rather common,
went on quietly with her wood-cutting with an air of
its being the proper thing to do—though nobody else
seemed to know it.

" You must tie it up," said Miss Walshingham.

" We must tie it up," said the freckled girl.

" I 'adn't the slightest idea that window was going
to break like that," said Kipps, with candour. " Nort
the slightest."

He glanced again at the blood on his wrist, and it
seemed to him that it was on the very point of dropping
on the floor of that cultured classroom. So he very
neatly licked it off, feeling at the same time for his
handkerchief. " Oh, *don't!*" said Miss Walshingham as
he did so, and the girl with the freckles made a movement of horror. The giggle got the better of the boy
with the gift, and celebrated its triumph by unseemly
noises; in spite of which it seemed to Kipps at the
moment that the act that had made Miss Walshingham
say " Oh, *don't!*" was rather a desperate and manly
treatment of what was after all a creditable injury.

" It ought to be tied up," said the lodging-house
keeper, holding her chisel upright in her hand. " It's
a bad cut to bleed like that."

" We must tie it up," said the freckled girl, and
hesitated in front of Kipps. " Have you got a handkerchief?" she said.

" I dunno 'ow I managed *not* to bring one," said
Kipps. " I—Not 'aving a cold I suppose some'ow I
didn't think——"

He checked a further flow of blood.

The girl with the freckles caught Miss Walshingham's eye, and held it for a moment. Both glanced at Kipps' injury. The boy with the gift, who had reappeared with a chastened expression from some noisy pursuit beneath his desk, made the neglected motions of one who proffers shyly. Miss Walshingham under the spell of the freckled girl's eye produced a handkerchief. The voice of the maiden lady could be heard in the background. "I've been through all the technical education ambulance classes twice, and I know you go *so* if it's a vein, and *so* if it's an artery—at least you go *so* for one and *so* for the other, whichever it may be; but . . ."

"If you will give me your hand," said the freckled girl, and proceeded with Miss Walshingham's assistance to bandage Kipps in a most businesslike way. Yes, they actually bandaged Kipps. They pulled up his cuffs— happily they were not a very frayed pair—and held his wrist, and wrapped the soft handkerchief round it, and tightened the knot together. And Miss Walshingham's face, the face of that almost divine Over-human, came close to the face of Kipps.

"We're not hurting you, are we?" she said.

"Not a bit," said Kipps, as he would have said if they had been sawing his arm off.

"We're not experts, you know," said the freckled girl.

"I'm sure it's a dreadful cut," said Miss Walshingham.

"It ain't much reely," said Kipps; "and you're taking a lot of trouble. I'm sorry I broke that window. I can't think what I could have been doing."

"It isn't so much the cut at the time, it's the poisoning afterwards," came the voice of the maiden lady.

"Of course I'm quite willing to pay for the window," panted Kipps opulently.

"We must make it just as tight as possible, to stop the bleeding," said the freckled girl.

"I don't think it's much reely," said Kipps. "I'm awful sorry I broke that window, though."

"Put your finger on the knot, dear," said the freckled girl.

"Eh?" said Kipps; "I mean——"

Both the young ladies became very intent on the knot, and Mr. Kipps was very red and very intent upon the two young ladies.

"Mortified, and had to be sawn off," said the maiden lady.

"Sawn off?" said the lodging-house keeper.

"Sawn *right* off," said the maiden lady, and jabbed at her mangled design.

"*There*," said the freckled girl, "I think that ought to do. You're sure it's not too tight?"

"Not a bit," said Kipps.

He met Miss Walshingham's eye, and smiled to show how little he cared for wounds and pain. "It's only a little cut," he added.

The maiden lady appeared as an addition to their group. "You should have washed the wound, dear," she said. "I was just telling Miss Collis." She peered through her glasses at the bandage. "That doesn't look *quite* right," she remarked critically. "You should have taken the ambulance classes. But I suppose it will have to do. Are you hurting?"

"Not a bit," said Kipps, and he smiled at them all with the air of a brave soldier in hospital.

"I'm sure it *must* hurt," said Miss Walshingham.

"Anyhow, you're a very good patient," said the girl with the freckles.

Mr. Kipps became quite pink. "I'm only sorry I broke the window—that's all," he said. "But who would have thought it was going to break like that?"

Pause.

"I'm afraid you won't be able to go on carving to-night," said Miss Walshingham.

"I'll try," said Kipps. "It reely doesn't hurt—not anything to matter."

Presently Miss Walshingham came to him as he carved heroically with his hand bandaged in her handkerchief. There was a touch of a novel interest in her eyes. "I'm afraid you're not getting on very fast," she said.

The freckled girl looked up and regarded Miss Walshingham.

"I'm doing a little, anyhow," said Kipps. "I don't want to waste any time. A feller like me hasn't much time to spare."

It struck the girls that there was a quality of modest disavowal about that "feller like me." It gave them a light into this obscure person, and Miss Walshingham ventured to commend his work as "promising" and to ask whether he meant to follow it up. Kipps didn't "altogether know"—"things depended on so much," but if he was in Folkestone next winter he certainly should. It did not occur to Miss Walshingham at the time to ask why his progress in art depended upon his presence in Folkestone. There were some more questions and answers—they continued to talk to him for a little time, even when Mr. Chester Coote had come into the room—and when at last the conversation had died out it dawned upon Kipps just how much his cut wrist had done for him. . . .

He went to sleep that night revising that conversation for the twentieth time, treasuring this and expanding that, and inserting things he might have said to Miss Walshingham, things he might still say about himself—in relation more or less explicit to her. He wasn't quite sure if he wouldn't like his arm to mortify a bit, which would make him interesting, or to heal up absolutely, which would show the exceptional purity of his blood.

§ 4

The affair of the broken window happened late in
April, and the class came to an end in May. In that
interval there were several small incidents and great
developments of emotion. I have done Kipps no justice
if I have made it seem that his face was unsightly. It
was, as the freckled girl pointed out to Helen Walshingham, an "interesting" face, and that aspect of him
which presented chiefly erratic hair and glowing ears
ceased to prevail.

They talked him over, and the freckled girl discovered there was something "wistful" in his manner.
They detected a "natural delicacy," and the freckled
girl set herself to draw him out from that time forth.
The freckled girl was nineteen, and very wise and
motherly and benevolent, and really she greatly preferred drawing out Kipps to wood-carving. It was quite
evident to her that Kipps was in love with Helen
Walshingham, and it struck her as a queer and romantic
and pathetic and extremely interesting phenomenon.
And as at that time she regarded Helen as "simply
lovely," it seemed only right and proper that she should
assist Kipps in his modest efforts to place himself in a
state of absolute *abandon* upon her altar.

Under her sympathetic management the position of
Kipps was presently defined quite clearly. He was
unhappy in his position—misunderstood. He told her
he "didn't seem to get on like" with customers, and
she translated this for him as "too sensitive." The
discontent with his fate in life, the dreadful feeling
that education was slipping by him, troubles that time
and usage were glazing over a little, revived to their old
acuteness but not to their old hopelessness. As a basis
for sympathy indeed they were even a source of
pleasure.

And one day at dinner it happened that Carshot and

Buggins fell talking of "these here writers," and how Dickens had been a labeller of blacking and Thackeray "an artist who couldn't sell a drawing," and how Samuel Johnson had walked to London without any boots, having thrown away his only pair "out of pride." "It's luck," said Buggins, "to a very large extent. They just happen to hit on something that catches on, and there you are!"

"Nice easy life they have of it, too," said Miss Mergle. "Write just an hour or so, and done for the day! Almost like gentlefolks."

"There's more work in it than you'd think," said Carshot, stooping to a mouthful.

"I wouldn't mind changing, for all that," said Buggins. "I'd like to see one of these here authors marking off with Jimmy."

"I think they copy from each other a good deal," said Miss Mergle.

"Even then (chup, chup, chup)," said Carshot, "there's writing it out in their own hands."

They proceeded to enlarge upon the literary life, on its ease and dignity, on the social recognition accorded to those who led it, and on the ample gratifications their vanity achieved. "Pictures everywhere—never get a new suit without being photographed—almost like Royalty," said Miss Mergle.

And all this talk impressed the imagination of Kipps very greatly. Here was a class that seemed to bridge the gulf. On the one hand essentially Low, but by factitious circumstances capable of entering upon those levels of social superiority to which all true Englishmen aspire, those levels from which one may tip a butler, scorn a tailor, and even commune with those who lead "men" into battle. "Almost like gentlefolks"—that was it! He brooded over these things in the afternoon, until they blossomed into day-dreams. Suppose, for example, he had chanced to write a book, a well-known book, under an assumed name, and yet kept on being a draper all the time. . . . Impossible, of course, but *suppose*—it made quite a long dream.

And at the next wood-carving class he let it be drawn from him that his real choice in life was to be a Nawther—"only one doesn't get a chance."

After that there were times when Kipps had that pleasant sense that comes of attracting interest. He was a mute, inglorious Dickens, or at any rate something of that sort, and they were all taking him at that. The discovery of this indefinable "something in" him, the development of which was now painfully restricted and impossible, did much to bridge the gulf between himself and Miss Walshingham. He was unfortunate, he was futile, but he was not "common." Even now with help . . . ? The two girls, and the freckled girl in particular, tried to "stir him up" to some effort to do his imputed potentialities justice. They were still young enough to believe that to nice and niceish members of the male sex—more especially when under the stimulus of feminine encouragement—nothing is finally impossible.

The freckled girl was, I say, the stage manager of this affair, but Miss Walshingham was the presiding divinity. A touch of proprietorship came into her eyes at times when she looked at him. He was hers—unconditionally—and she knew it.

To her directly Kipps scarcely ever made a speech. The enterprising things that he was continually devising to say to her, he usually did not say, or he said them in a suitably modified form to the girl with the freckles. And one day the girl with the freckles smote him to the heart. She said to him, with the faintest indication of her head across the classroom to where her friend reached a cast from the shelf, "I do think Helen Walshingham is sometimes the most lovely person in the world. Look at her now!"

Kipps gasped for a moment. The moment

lengthened, and she regarded him as an intelligent young surgeon might regard an operation without anæsthetics.

"You're right," he said, and then looked at her with an entire abandonment of visage.

She coloured under his glare of silent avowal, and he blushed brightly.

"I think so too," he said hoarsely, cleared his throat, and after a meditative moment proceeded sacramentally with his wood-carving.

"You *are* wonderful," said the freckled girl to Miss Walshingham, apropos of nothing, as they went on their way home together. "He simply adores you."

"But, my dear, what have I done?" said Helen.

"That's just it," said the freckled girl. "What *have* you done?"

And then with a terrible swiftness came the last class of the course, to terminate this relationship altogether. Kipps was careless of dates, and the thing came upon him with an effect of abrupt surprise. Just as his petals were expanding so hopefully, "Finis," and the thing was at an end. But Kipps did not fully appreciate that the end was indeed and really and truly the end, until he was back in the Emporium after the end was over.

The end began practically in the middle of the last class, when the freckled girl broached the topic of terminations. She developed the question of just how he was going on after the session. She hoped he would stick to certain resolutions of self-improvement he had breathed. She said quite honestly that he owed it to himself to develop his possibilities. He expressed firm resolve, but dwelt on difficulties. He had no books. She instructed him how to get books from the public library. He was to get a form of application for a ticket signed by a ratepayer; and he said "of course," when she said Mr. Shalford would do that, though all the time he knew perfectly well it would "never do" to ask Mr. Shalford for anything of the sort. She explained that she was going to North Wales for the summer, information he received without immediate regret. At intervals he expressed his intention of going on with wood-carving when the summer was over, and once he added " If——"

She considered herself extremely delicate not to press for the completion of that " if——"

After that talk there was an interval of languid wood-carving and watching Miss Walshingham.

Then presently there came a bustle of packing, a great ceremony of hand-shaking all round by Miss Collis and the maiden lady of ripe years, and then Kipps found himself outside the classroom, on the landing with his two friends. It seemed to him he had only just learnt that this was the last class of all. There came a little pause, and the freckled girl suddenly went back into the classroom, and left Kipps and Miss Walshingham alone together for the first time. Kipps was instantly breathless. She looked at his face with a glance of mingled sympathy and curiosity, and held out her white hand.

" Well, good-bye, Mr. Kipps," she said.

He took her hand and held it. " I'd do anything," said Kipps, and had not the temerity to add, " for you." He stopped awkwardly. He shook her hand and said, " Good-bye."

There was a little pause.

" I hope you will have a pleasant holiday," she said.

" I shall come back to the class next year, anyhow," said Kipps valiantly, and turned abruptly to the stairs.

" I hope you will," said Miss Walshingham.

He turned back towards her. " Reely ?" he said.

" I hope everybody will come back."

" I will—anyhow," said Kipps. " You may count on that," and he tried to make his tones significant.

They looked at one another through a little pause.

" Good-bye," she said.

Kipps lifted his hat. She turned towards the class-room.

"Well?" said the freckled girl, coming back towards her.

"Nothing," said Helen. "At least—presently." And she became very energetic about some scattered tools on a desk.

The freckled girl went out and stood for a moment at the head of the stairs. When she came back she looked very hard at her friend. The incident struck her as important—wonderfully important. It was unassimilable, of course, and absurd, but there it was, the thing that is so cardinal to a girl, the emotion, the subservience, the crowning triumph of her sex. She could not help feeling that Helen took it, on the whole, a little too hardly.

CHAPTER THE FOURTH

Chitterlow

§ 1

THE hour of the class on the following Thursday found Kipps in a state of nearly incredible despondency. He was sitting with his eyes on the reading-room clock, his chin resting on his fists and his elbows on the accumulated comic papers that were comic alas! in vain! He paid no heed to the little man in spectacles glaring opposite to him, famishing for *Fun*. In this place it was he had sat night after night, each night more precious than the last, waiting until it should be time to go to Her! And then—bliss! And now the hour had come and there was no class! There would be no class now until next October; it might be that for him there would never be a class again.

It might be there would never be a class again, for Shalford, taking exception at a certain absent-mindedness that led to mistakes and more particularly to the ticketing of several articles in Kipps' Manchester window upside down, had been "on to" him for the past few days in an exceedingly onerous manner. . . .

He sighed profoundly, pushed the comic papers back —they were instantly rent away from him by the little man in spectacles—and tried the old engravings of Folkestone in the past, that hung about the room. But these, too, failed to minister to his bruised heart. For a time he wandered about the corridors and watched the library indicator for a while. Wonderful thing that! But it did not hold him for long. People came and laughed near him and that jarred on him dreadfully. He went out of the building and a beastly cheerful barrel organ mocked him in the street. He was moved to a desperate resolve to go down to the beach. There it might be he would be alone. The sea might be rough—and attuned to him. It would certainly be dark.

"If I 'ad a penny I'm blest if I wouldn't go and chuck myself off the end of the pier. . . . *She'd* never miss me. . . ." He followed a deepening vein of thought.

"Penny though! It's tuppence," he said after a space.

He went down Dover Street in a state of profound melancholia—at the pace and mood as it were of his own funeral procession—and he crossed at the corner of Tontine Street heedless of all mundane things. And there it was that Fortune came upon him, in disguise and with a loud shout, the shout of a person endowed with an unusually rich, full voice, followed immediately by a violent blow in the back.

His hat was over his eyes and an enormous weight rested on his shoulders and something kicked him in the back of his calf.

Then he was on all fours in some mud that Fortune, in conjunction with the Folkestone corporation and in the pursuit of equally mysterious ends, had heaped together even lavishly for his reception.

He remained in that position for some seconds awaiting further developments, and believing almost anything
broken before his heart. Gathering at last that this
temporary violence of things in general was over, and
being perhaps assisted by a clutching hand, he arose,
and found himself confronting a figure holding a bicycle
and thrusting forward a dark face in anxious scrutiny.

"You aren't hurt, Matey?" gasped the figure.

"Was that *you* 'it me?" said Kipps.

"It's these handles, you know," said the figure with
an air of being a fellow-sufferer. "They're too *low*.
And when I go to turn, if I don't remember, Bif!—
and I'm *in* to something."

"Well—you give me a oner in the back—anyhow,"
said Kipps, taking stock of his damages.

"I was coming down hill, you know," explained
the bicyclist. "These little Folkestone hills are a Fair
Treat. It isn't as though I'd been on the level. I came
rather a whop."

"You did *that*," said Kipps.

"I was back-pedalling for all I was worth anyhow,"
said the bicyclist. "Not that I *am* worth much back-
pedalling."

He glanced round and made a sudden movement
almost as if to mount his machine. Then he turned as
rapidly to Kipps again, who was now stooping down,
pursuing the tale of his injuries.

"Here's the back of my trouser leg all torn down,"
said Kipps, "and I believe I'm bleeding. You reely
ought to be more careful——"

The stranger investigated the damage with a rapid
movement. "Holy Smoke, so you are!" He laid a
friendly hand on Kipps' arm. "I say—look here!
Come up to my diggings and sew it up. I'm—— Of
course I'm to blame, and I say——" his voice sank to
a confidential friendliness. "Here's a slop. Don't let
on I ran you down. Haven't a lamp, you know.
Might be a bit awkward, for *me*."

Kipps looked up towards the advancing policeman. The appeal to his generosity was not misplaced. He immediately took sides with his assailant. He stood up as the representative of the law drew nearer. He assumed an air which he considered highly suggestive of an accident not having happened.

"All right," he said, "go on!"

"Right you are," said the cyclist promptly, and led the way; and then, apparently with some idea of deception, called over his shoulder, "I'm tremendously glad to have met you, old chap.

"It really isn't a hundred yards," he said after they had passed the policeman, "it's just round the corner."

"Of course," said Kipps, limping slightly. "I don't want to get a chap into trouble. Accidents *will* happen. Still——"

"Oh! *rather!* I believe you. Accidents *will* happen. Especially when you get *me* on a bicycle." He laughed. "You aren't the first I've run down, not by any manner of means! I don't think you can be hurt much either. It isn't as though I was scorching. You didn't see me coming. I was back-pedalling like anything. Only naturally it seems to you I must have been coming fast. And I did all I could to ease off the bump as I hit you. It was just the treadle I think came against your calf. But it was All Right of you about that policeman, you know. That was a Fair Bit of All Right. Under the Circs, if you'd told him I was riding it might have been forty bob! Forty bob! I'd have had to tell 'em Time is Money. Just now for Mr. H. C.

"I shouldn't have blamed you either, you know. Most men after a bump like that might have been spiteful. The least I can do is to stand you a needle and thread. And a clothes brush. It isn't everyone who'd have taken it like you.

"Scorching! Why if I'd been scorching you'd have ——coming as we did——you'd have been knocked silly.

"But I tell you, the way you caught on about that slop was something worth seeing. When I asked you, I didn't half expect it. Bif! Right off. Cool as a cucumber. Had your line at once. I tell you that there isn't many men would have acted as you have done, I *will* say that. You acted like a gentleman over that slop."

Kipps' first sense of injury disappeared. He limped along a pace or so behind, making depreciatory noises in response to these flattering remarks and taking stock of the very appreciative person who uttered them.

As they passed the lamps he was visible as a figure with a slight anterior plumpness, progressing buoyantly on knickerbockered legs with quite enormous calves, legs that, contrasting with Kipps' own narrow practice, were even exuberantly turned out at the knees and toes. A cycling cap was worn very much on one side, and from beneath it protruded carelessly straight wisps of dark red hair, and ever and again an ample nose came into momentary view round the corner. The muscular cheeks of this person and a certain generosity of chin he possessed were blue shaven, and he had no moustache. His carriage was spacious and confident, his gestures up and down the narrow deserted back street they traversed were irresistibly suggestive of ownership; a suggestion of broadly gesticulating shadows were born squatting on his feet and grew and took possession of the road and reunited at last with the shadows of the infinite, as lamp after lamp was passed. Kipps saw by the flickering light of one of them that they were in Little Fenchurch Street, and then they came round a corner sharply into a dark court and stopped at the door of a particularly ramshackle-looking little house, held up between two larger ones—like a drunken man between policemen.

The cyclist propped his machine carefully against the window, produced a key and blew down it sharply. "The lock's a bit tricky," he said, and devoted himself for some moments to the task of opening the door. Some mechanical catastrophe ensued and the door was open.

"You'd better wait here a bit while I get the lamp," he remarked to Kipps; "very likely it isn't filled," and vanished into the blackness of the passage. "Thank God for matches!" he said, and Kipps had an impression of a passage in the transitory pink flare and the bicyclist disappearing into a further room. Kipps was so much interested by these things that for the time he forgot his injuries altogether.

An interval and Kipps was dazzled by a pink-shaded kerosene lamp. "You go in," said the red-haired man, "and I'll bring in the bike," and for a moment Kipps was alone in the lamp-lit room. He took in rather vaguely the shabby ensemble of the little apartment, the round table covered with a torn, red, glass-stained cover on which the lamp stood, a mottled looking-glass over the fireplace reflecting this, a disused gas bracket, an extinct fire, a number of aged postcards and memoranda stuck round the glass, a dusty paper-rack on the mantel crowded with a number of cabinet photographs, a side table littered with papers and cigarette ash and a siphon of soda water. Then the cyclist reappeared and Kipps saw his blue-shaved, rather animated face and bright-reddish, brown eyes for the first time. He was a man perhaps ten years older than Kipps, but his beardless face made them in a way contemporary.

"You behaved all right about that policeman—anyhow," he repeated as he came forward.

"I don't see 'ow else I could 'ave done," said Kipps quite modestly. The cyclist scanned his guest for the first time and decided upon hospitable details.

"We'd better let that mud dry a bit before we brush it. Whisky there is, good old Methusaleh, Canadian Rye, and there's some brandy that's all right. Which'll you have?"

"*I* dunno," said Kipps, taken by surprise, and then

seeing no other course but acceptance, "well—whisky, then."

"Right you are, old boy, and if you'll take my advice you'll take it neat. I may not be a particular judge of this sort of thing, but I do know old Methusaleh pretty well. Old Methusaleh—three stars. That's me! Good old Harry Chitterlow and good old Methusaleh. Leave 'em together. Bif! He's gone!"

He laughed loudly, looked about him, hesitated and retired, leaving Kipps in possession of the room and free to make a more precise examination of its contents.

§ 2

He particularly remarked the photographs that adorned the apartment. They were chiefly photographs of ladies, in one case in tights, which Kipps thought a "bit 'ot," but one represented the bicyclist in the costume of some remote epoch. It did not take Kipps long to infer that the others were probably actresses and that his host was an actor, and the presence of the half of a large coloured playbill seemed to confirm this. A note set up in an Oxford frame that was a little too large for it, he presently demeaned himself to read. "Dear Mr. Chitterlow," it ran its brief course, "if after all you will send the play you spoke of I will endeavour to read it," followed by a stylish but absolutely illegible signature, and across this was written in pencil, "What price Harry now?" And in the shadow by the window was a rough and rather able sketch of the bicyclist in chalk on brown paper, calling particular attention to the curvature of the forward lines of his hull and calves and the jaunty carriage of his nose, and labelled unmistakably "Chitterlow." Kipps thought it "rather a take-off." The papers on the table by the siphon were in manuscript, Kipps observed; manuscript of a particularly convulsive and blottesque sort and running obliquely across the page.

Presently he heard the metallic clamour as if of a series of irreparable breakages with which the lock of the front door discharged its function, and then Chitterlow reappeared, a little out of breath as if from running, and with a starry labelled bottle in his large freckled hand.

"Sit down, old chap," he said, "sit down. I had to go out for it after all. Wasn't a solitary bottle left. However, it's all right now we're here. No, don't sit on that chair, there's sheets of my play on that. That's the one—with the broken arm. I think this glass is clean, but anyhow wash it out with a squizz of siphon and shy it in the fireplace. Here! I'll do it! Lend it here!"

As he spoke Mr. Chitterlow produced a corkscrew from a table drawer, attacked and overcame good old Methusaleh's cork in a style a bar-tender might envy, washed out two tumblers in his simple, effectual manner, and poured a couple of inches of the ancient fluid into each. Kipps took his tumbler, said "Thenks" in an off-hand way, and after a momentary hesitation whether he should say "here's to you!" or not, put it to his lips without that ceremony. For a space fire in his throat occupied his attention to the exclusion of other matters, and then he discovered Mr. Chitterlow with an intensely bulldog pipe alight, seated on the opposite side of the empty fireplace and pouring himself out a second dose of whisky.

"After all," said Mr. Chitterlow, with his eye on the bottle and a little smile wandering to hide amidst his larger features, "this accident might have been worse. I wanted someone to talk to a bit, and I didn't want to go to a pub, leastways not a Folkestone pub, because as a matter of fact I'd promised Mrs. Chitterlow, who's away, not to, for various reasons, though of course if I'd wanted to I'm just that sort I should have all the same, and here we are! It's curious how one runs up against people out bicycling!"

"Isn't it!" said Kipps, feeling that the time had
come for him to say something.

"Here we are, sitting and talking like old friends,
and half an hour ago we didn't know we existed. Leastways we didn't know each other existed. I might have
passed you in the street perhaps and you might have
passed me, and how was I to tell that put to the test
you would have behaved as decently as you have
behaved? Only it happened otherwise, that's all.
You're not smoking!" he said. "Have a cigarette?"

Kipps made a confused reply that took the form of
not minding if he did, and in his confusion drank
another sip of old Methusaleh. He was able to follow
the subsequent course of that sip for quite a long way.
It was as though the old gentleman was brandishing a
burning torch through his vitals, lighting him here and
lighting him there until at last his whole being was in
a glow. Chitterlow produced a tobacco pouch and
cigarette papers; and with an interesting parenthesis
that was a little difficult to follow about some lady
named Kitty something or other who had taught him
the art when he was as yet only what you might call a
nice boy, made Kipps a cigarette, and with a consideration that won Kipps' gratitude suggested that after all
he might find a little soda water an improvement with
the whisky. "Some people like it that way," said
Chitterlow, and then with voluminous emphasis, "*I*
don't."

Emboldened by the weakened state of his enemy
Kipps promptly swallowed the rest of him and had his
glass at once hospitably replenished. He began to feel
he was of a firmer consistency than he commonly
believed, and turned his mind to what Chitterlow was
saying with the resolve to play a larger part in the
conversation than he had hitherto done. Also he
smoked through his nose quite successfully, an art he
had only very recently acquired.

Meanwhile Chitterlow explained that he was a playwright, and the tongue of Kipps was unloosened to respond that he knew a chap, or rather one of their fellows knew a chap, or at least to be perfectly correct this fellow's brother did, who had written a play. In response to Chitterlow's inquiries he could not recall the title of the play, nor where it had appeared nor the name of the manager who produced it, though he thought the title was something about " Love's Ransom " or something like that.

" He made five 'undred pounds by it, though," said Kipps. " I know that."

" That's nothing," said Chitterlow, with an air of experience that was extremely convincing. " Nothing. May seem a big sum to *you,* but *I* can assure you it's just what one gets any day. There's any amount of money, an-ny amount, in a good play."

" I dessay," said Kipps, drinking.

" Any amount of money !"

Chitterlow began a series of illustrative instances. He was clearly a person of quite unequalled gift for monologue. It was as though some conversational dam had burst upon Kipps, and in a little while he was drifting along upon a copious rapid of talk about all sorts of theatrical things by one who knew all about them, and quite incapable of anticipating whither that rapid meant to carry him. Presently somehow they had got to anecdotes about well-known theatrical managers, little Teddy Bletherskite, artful old Chumps, and the magnificent Behemoth, " petted to death, you know, fair sickened, by all these society women." Chitterlow described various personal encounters with these personages, always with modest self-depreciation, and gave Kipps a very amusing imitation of old Chumps in a state of intoxication. Then he took two more stiff doses of old Methusaleh in rapid succession.

Kipps reduced the hither end of his cigarette to a pulp as he sat " dessaying " and " quite believing " Chitterlow in the sagest manner, and admiring the easy

way in which he was getting on with this very novel
and entertaining personage. He had another cigarette
made for him, and then Chitterlow, assuming by in-
sensible degrees more and more of the manner of a rich
and successful playwright being interviewed by a young
admirer, set himself to answer questions which sometimes Kipps asked and sometimes Chitterlow, about the
particulars and methods of his career. He undertook
this self-imposed task with great earnestness and vigour,
treating the matter indeed with such fulness that at
times it seemed lost altogether under the thicket of
parentheses, footnotes, and episodes that branched and
budded from its stem. But it always emerged again,
usually by way of illustration, to its own digressions.
Practically it was a mass of material for the biography of
a man who had been everywhere and done everything
(including the Honourable Thomas Norgate, which was
a Record), and in particular had acted with great distinction and profit (he dated various anecdotes, "when
I was getting thirty, or forty, or fifty dollars a week")
throughout America and the entire civilised world.

And as he talked on and on in that full, rich, satisfying voice he had, and as old Methusaleh, indisputably a most drunken old reprobate of a whisky, busied
himself throughout Kipps, lighting lamp after lamp
until the entire framework of the little draper was
illuminated and glowing like some public building on a
festival, behold Chitterlow and Kipps with him and
the room in which they sat were transfigured!
Chitterlow became in very truth that ripe, full man of
infinite experience and humour and genius, fellow of
Shakespeare and Ibsen and Maeterlinck (three names
he placed together quite modestly far above his own)
and no longer ambiguously dressed in a sort of yachting
costume with cycling knickerbockers, but elegantly if
unconventionally attired, and the room ceased to be a
small and shabby room in a Folkestone slum, and grew
larger and more richly furnished, and the fly-blown

photographs were curious old pictures, and the rubbish
on the walls the most rare and costly bric-à-brac, and
the indisputable paraffin lamp a soft and splendid light.
A certain youthful heat that to many minds might have
weakened old Methusaleh's starry claim to a ripe
antiquity, vanished in that glamour, two burnt holes
and a claimant darn in the tablecloth, moreover, became
no more than the pleasing contradictions natural in the
house of genius, and as for Kipps!——Kipps was a bright
young man of promise, distinguished by recent quick,
courageous proceedings not too definitely insisted upon,
and he had been rewarded by admission to a sanctum
and confidences for which the common prosperous, for
which " society women " even, were notoriously sighing
in vain. " Don't *want* them, my boy; they'd simply
play old Harry with the work, you know! Chaps
outside, bank clerks and university fellows, think the
life's all *that* sort of thing. Don't you believe 'em.
Don't you believe 'em."

And then——!

" Boom . . . Boom . . . Boom . . . Boom . . ." right
in the middle of a most entertaining digression on flats
who join touring companies under the impression that
they are actors, Kipps much amused at their flatness as
exposed by Chitterlow.

" Lor'!" said Kipps like one who awakens, " that's
not eleven!"

" Must be," said Chitterlow. " It was nearly ten
when I got that whisky. It's early yet——"

" All the same I must be going," said Kipps, and
stood up. " Even now—maybe. Fact is—I 'ad *no*
idea. The 'ouse door shuts at 'arf past ten, you know.
I ought to 'ave thought before."

" Well, if you *must* go——! I tell you what. I'll
come too. . . . Why! There's your leg, old man!
Clean forgot it! You can't go through the streets like
that. I'll sew up the tear. And meanwhile have
another whisky."

"I ought to be getting on *now*," protested Kipps feebly, and then Chitterlow was showing him how to kneel on a chair in order that the rent trouser leg should be attainable, and old Methusaleh on his third round was busy repairing the temporary eclipse of Kipps' arterial glow. Then suddenly Chitterlow was seized with laughter, and had to leave off sewing to tell Kipps that the scene wouldn't make a bad bit of business in a farcical comedy, and then he began to sketch out the farcical comedy, and that led him to a digression about another farcical comedy of which he had written a ripping opening scene which wouldn't take ten minutes to read. It had something in it that had never been done on the stage before, and was yet perfectly legitimate, namely, a man with a live beetle down the back of his neck trying to seem at his ease in a roomful of people. . . .

"*They* won't lock you out," he said, in a singularly reassuring tone, and began to read and act what he explained to be (not because he had written it, but simply because he knew it was so on account of his exceptional experience of the stage), and what Kipps also quite clearly saw to be, one of the best opening scenes that had ever been written.

When it was over Kipps, who rarely swore, was inspired to say the scene was "damned fine" about six times over, whereupon as if by way of recognition, Chitterlow took a simply enormous portion of the inspiring antediluvian, declaring at the same time that he had rarely met a "finer" intelligence than Kipps' (stronger there might be, *that* he couldn't say with certainty as yet, seeing how little after all they had seen of each other, but a finer *never*); that it was a shame such a gallant and discriminating intelligence should be nightly either locked up or locked out at ten—well, ten thirty then—and that he had half a mind to recommend old somebody or other (apparently the editor of a London daily paper) to put on Kipps forthwith as a dramatic critic in the place of the current incapable.

"I don't think I've ever made up anything for print," said Kipps; "—ever. I'd have a thundering good try, though, if ever I got a chance. I would that! I've written window tickets often enough. Made 'em up and everything. But that's different."

"You'd come to it all the fresher for not having done it before. And the way you picked up every point in that scene, my boy, was a Fair Treat! I tell you, you'd knock William Archer into fits. Not so literary, of course, you'd be, but I don't believe in literary critics any more than in literary playwrights. Plays *aren't* literature—that's just the point they miss. Plays are plays. No! That won't hamper you anyhow. You're wasted down here, I tell you. Just as I was, before I took to acting. I'm hanged if I wouldn't like your opinion on these first two acts of that tragedy I'm on to. I haven't told you about that. It wouldn't take me more than an hour to read. . . ."

§ 3

Then so far as he could subsequently remember, Kipps had "another," and then it would seem that suddenly, regardless of the tragedy, he insisted that he "reely *must* be getting on," and from that point his memory became irregular. Certain things remained quite clear, and as it is a matter of common knowledge that intoxicated people forget what happens to them, it follows that he was not intoxicated. Chitterlow came with him partly to see him home and partly for a freshener before turning in. Kipps recalled afterwards very distinctly how in Little Fenchurch Street he discovered that he could not walk straight, and also that Chitterlow's needle and thread in his still unmended trouser leg was making an annoying little noise on the pavement behind him. He tried to pick up the needle

4

suddenly by surprise and somehow tripped and fell, and then Chitterlow, laughing uproariously, helped him up. "It wasn't a bicycle this time, old boy," said Chitterlow, and that appeared to them both at the time as being a quite extraordinarily good joke indeed. They punched each other about on the strength of it.

For a time Kipps certainly pretended to be quite desperately drunk and unable to walk, and Chitterlow entered into the pretence and supported him. After that Kipps remembered being struck with the extremely laughable absurdity of going down hill to Tontine Street in order to go up hill again to the Emporium, and trying to get that idea into Chitterlow's head and being unable to do so on account of his own merriment or Chitterlow's evident intoxication, and his next memory after that was of the exterior of the Emporium, shut and darkened and, as it were, frowning at him with all its stripes of yellow and green. The chilly way in which " Shalford " glittered in the moonlight printed itself with particular vividness on his mind. It appeared to Kipps that that establishment was closed to him for evermore. Those gilded letters, in spite of appearances, spelt FINIS for him and exile from Folkestone. He would never do wood-carving, never see Miss Walshingham again. Not that he had ever hoped to see her again. But this was the knife, this was final. He had stayed out, he had got drunk, there had been that row about the Manchester window dressing only three days ago. . . . In the retrospect he was quite sure that he was perfectly sober then and at bottom extremely unhappy, but he kept a brave face on the matter nevertheless, and declared stoutly he didn't care if he *was* locked out.

Whereupon Chitterlow slapped him on the back very hard and told him that was a " Bit of All Right," and assured him that when he himself had been a clerk in Sheffield before he took to acting he had been locked out sometimes for six nights running.

"What's the result?" said Chitterlow. "I could go back to that place now, and they'd be glad to have me. . . . Glad to have me," he repeated, and then added, "that is to say, if they remember me—which isn't very likely."

Kipps asked a little weakly, "What am I to do?"

"Keep out," said Chitterlow. "You can't knock 'em up now—that would give you Right away. You'd better try and sneak in in the morning with the Cat. That'll do you. You'll probably get in all right in the morning if nobody gives you away."

Then for a time—perhaps as the result of that slap on the back—Kipps felt decidedly queer, and acting on Chitterlow's advice went for a bit of a freshener along the Leas. After a time he threw off the temporary queerness, and found Chitterlow patting him on the shoulder and telling him that he'd be all right now in a minute and all the better for it—which he was. And the wind having dropped and the night being now a really very beautiful moonlit night indeed, and all before Kipps to spend as he liked and with only a very little tendency to spin round now and again to mar its splendour, they set out to walk the whole length of the Leas to the Sandgate lift and back, and as they walked Chitterlow spoke first of moonlight transfiguring the sea and then of moonlight transfiguring faces, and so at last he came to the topic of Love, and upon that he dwelt a great while, and with a wealth of experience and illustrative anecdote that seemed re- markably pungent and material to Kipps. He forgot his lost Miss Walshingham and his outraged employer again. He became as it were a desperado by reflection.

Chitterlow had had adventures, a quite astonishing variety of adventures in this direction; he was a man with a past, a really opulent past, and he certainly seemed to like to look back and see himself amidst its opulence.

He made no consecutive history, but he gave Kipps vivid, momentary pictures of relations and entangle-

ments.   One moment he was in flight—only too
worthily in flight—before the husband of a Malay
woman in Cape Town.   At the next he was having
passionate complications with the daughter of a clergyman in York.   Then he passed to a remarkable grouping
at Seaford.

"They say you can't love two women at once," said
Chitterlow.   "But I tell you——"   He gesticulated
and raised his ample voice.   "It's *Rot! Rot!*"

"I know that," said Kipps.

"Why, when I was in the smalls with Bessie
Hopper's company there were three."   He laughed and
decided to add, "Not counting Bessie, that is."

He set out to reveal Life as it is lived in touring
companies, a quite amazing jungle of interwoven
"affairs" it appeared to be, a mere amorous winepress
for the crushing of hearts.

"People say this sort of thing's a nuisance and inter-
feres with Work.   I tell you it isn't.   The Work
couldn't go on without it.   They *must* do it.   They
haven't the Temperament if they don't.   If they hadn't
the Temperament they wouldn't want to act, if they
have—Bif!"

"You're right," said Kipps.   "I see that."

Chitterlow proceeded to a close criticism of certain
historical indiscretions of Mr. Clement Scott respecting
the morals of the stage.   Speaking in confidence and
not as one who addresses the public, he admitted regretfully the general truth of these comments.   He proceeded to examine various typical instances that had
almost forced themselves upon him personally, and with
especial regard to the contrast between his own conduct
towards women and that of the Honourable Thomas
Norgate, with whom it appeared he had once been on
terms of great intimacy. . . .

Kipps listened with emotion to these extraordinary
recollections.   They were wonderful to him, they were
incredibly credible.   This tumultuous, passionate,

irregular course was the way life ran—except in high-class establishments! Such things happened in novels, in plays—only he had been fool enough not to understand they happened. His share in the conversation was now indeed no more than faint writing in the margin; Chitterlow was talking quite continuously. He expanded his magnificent voice into huge guffaws, he drew it together into a confidential intensity, it became drawlingly reminiscent, he was frank, frank with the effect of a revelation, reticent also with the effect of a revelation, a stupendously gesticulating, moonlit black figure, wallowing in itself, preaching Adventure and the Flesh to Kipps. Yet withal shot with something of sentiment, with a sort of sentimental refinement, very coarsely and egotistically done. The Times he had had!—even before he was as old as Kipps he had had innumerable Times.

Well, he said with a sudden transition, he had sown his wild oats; one had to somewhen; and now—he fancied he had mentioned it earlier in the evening—he was happily married. She was, he indicated, a "born lady." Her father was a prominent lawyer, a solicitor in Kentish Town, "done a lot of public-house business"; her mother was second cousin to the wife of Abel Jones, the fashionable portrait painter—"almost Society people in a way." That didn't count with Chitterlow. He was no snob. What *did* count was that she possessed what he ventured to assert, without much fear of contradiction, was the very finest completely untrained contralto voice in all the world. ("But to hear it properly," said Chitterlow, "you want a Big Hall.") He became rather vague and jerked his head about to indicate when and how he had entered matrimony. She was, it seemed, "away with her people." It was clear that Chitterlow did not get on with these people very well. It would seem they failed to appreciate his playwriting, regarding it as an unremunerative pursuit, whereas as he and Kipps knew, wealth beyond the dreams of avarice would presently accrue. Only patience and persistence were needful.

He went off at a tangent to hospitality. Kipps must come down home with him. They couldn't wander about all night, with a bottle of the right sort pining at home for them. "You can sleep on the sofa. You won't be worried by broken springs anyhow, for I took 'em all out myself two or three weeks ago. I don't see what they ever put 'em in for. It's a point I know about. I took particular notice of it when I was with Bessie Hopper. Three months we were, and all over England, North Wales, and the Isle of Man, and I never struck a sofa in diggings anywhere that hadn't a broken spring. Not once—all the time."

He added almost absently: "It happens like that at times."

They descended the slant road towards Harbour Street and went on past the Pavilion Hotel.

§ 4

They came into the presence of old Methusaleh again; and that worthy under Chitterlow's direction at once resumed the illumination of Kipps' interior with the conscientious thoroughness that distinguished him. Chitterlow took a tall portion to himself with an air of asbestos, lit the bulldog pipe again, and lapsed for a space into meditation, from which Kipps roused him by remarking that he expected "a nacter 'as a lot of ups and downs like, now and then."

At which Chitterlow seemed to bestir himself. "Ra-ther," he said. "And sometimes it's his own fault and sometimes it isn't. Usually it is. If it isn't one thing it's another. If it isn't the manager's wife it's bar-bragging. I tell you things happen at times. I'm a fatalist. The fact is, Character has you. You can't get away from it. You may think you do, but you don't."

He reflected for a moment. "It's that what makes tragedy. Psychology really. It's the Greek irony— Ibsen and—all that. Up to date."

He emitted this exhaustive summary of high-toned modern criticism as if he was repeating a lesson while thinking of something else, but it seemed to rouse him as it passed his lips, by including the name of Ibsen.

He became interested in telling Kipps, who was indeed open to any information whatever about this quite novel name, exactly where he thought Ibsen fell short, points where it happened that Ibsen was defective just where it chanced that he, Chitterlow, was strong. Of course he had no desire to place himself in any way on an equality with Ibsen; still the fact remained that his own experience in England and America and the colonies was altogether more extensive than Ibsen could have had. Ibsen had probably never seen "one decent bar scrap" in his life. That, of course, was not Ibsen's fault or his own merit, but there the thing was. Genius, he knew, was supposed to be able to do anything or to do without anything; still he was now inclined to doubt that. He had a play in hand that might perhaps not please William Archer—whose opinion, after all, he did not value as he valued Kipps' opinion—but which, he thought, was at any rate as well constructed as anything Ibsen ever did.

So with infinite deviousness Chitterlow came at last to his play. He decided he would not read it to Kipps, but tell him about it. This was the simpler, because much of it was still unwritten. He began to explain his plot. It was a complicated plot, and all about a nobleman who had seen everything and done everything and knew practically all that Chitterlow knew about women; that is to say, "all about women" and such-like matters. It warmed and excited Chitterlow. Presently he stood up to act a situation—which could not be explained It was an extremely vivid situation.

Kipps applauded the situation vehemently. "Tha's dam' fine," said the new dramatic critic, quite familiar with his part now, striking the table with his fist and almost upsetting his third portion (in the second series) of old Methusaleh. "Tha's *dam*' fine, Chit'low!"

"You see it?" said Chitterlow, with the last vestiges of that incidental gloom disappearing. "Good old boy! I thought you'd see it. But it's just the sort of thing the literary critic can't see. However, it's only a beginning——"

He replenished Kipps and proceeded with his exposition.

In a little while it was no longer necessary to give that over-advertised Ibsen the purely conventional precedence he had hitherto had. Kipps and Chitterlow were friends, and they could speak frankly and openly of things not usually admitted. "Any'ow," said Kipps a little irrelevantly, and speaking over the brim of the replenishment, "what you read jus' now was dam' fine. Nothing can't alter that."

He perceived a sort of faint, buzzing vibration about things that was very nice and pleasant, and with a little care he had no difficulty whatever in putting his glass back on the table. Then he perceived Chitterlow was going on with the scenario, and then that old Methusaleh had almost entirely left his bottle. He was glad there was so little more Methusaleh to drink, because that would prevent his getting drunk. He knew that he was not drunk now, but he knew that he had had enough. He was one of those who always know when they have had enough. He tried to interrupt Chitterlow to tell him this, but he could not get a suitable opening. He doubted whether Chitterlow might not be one of those people who did not know when they had had enough. He discovered that he disapproved of Chitterlow. Highly. It seemed to him that Chitterlow went on and on like a river. For a time he was explicably and quite unjustly cross with

Chitterlow and wanted to say to him, "you got the gift of the gab," but he only got so far as to say "the gift," and then Chitterlow thanked him and said he was better than Archer any day. So he eyed Chitterlow with a baleful eye until it dawned upon him that a most extraordinary thing was taking place. Chitterlow kept mentioning someone named Kipps. This presently began to perplex Kipps very greatly. Dimly but decidedly he perceived this was wrong.

"Look 'ere," he said suddenly, "*what* Kipps?"

"This chap Kipps I'm telling you about."

"What chap Kipps you're telling which about?"

"I told you."

Kipps struggled with a difficulty in silence for a space. Then he reiterated firmly, "*What* chap Kipps?"

"This chap in my play—man who kisses the girl."

"Never kissed a girl," said Kipps; "leastways——" and subsided for a space. He could not remember whether he had kissed Ann or not—he knew he had meant to. Then suddenly in a tone of great sadness and addressing the hearth, he said, "*My* name's Kipps."

"Eh?" said Chitterlow.

"Kipps," said Kipps, smiling a little cynically.

"What about him?"

"He's me." He tapped his breastbone with his middle finger to indicate his essential self.

He leant forward very gravely towards Chitterlow. "Look 'ere, Chit'low," he said, "you haven't no business putting my name into play. You mustn't do things like that. You'd lose me my crib, right away." And they had a little argument—so far as Kipps could remember. Chitterlow entered upon a general explanation of how he got his names. These, he had for the most part got out of a newspaper that was still, he believed, "lying about." He even made to look for it, and while he was doing so Kipps went on with the argument, addressing himself more particularly to the photograph of the girl in tights. He said that at first

4*

her costume had not commended her to him, but now he perceived she had an extremely sensible face. He told her she would like Buggins if she met him; he could see she was just that sort. She would admit, all sensible people would admit, that using names in plays was wrong. You could, for example, have the law of him.

He became confidential. He explained that he was already in sufficient trouble for stopping out all night, without having his name put in plays. He was certain to be in the deuce of a row, the deuce of a row. Why had he done it? Why hadn't he gone at ten? Because one thing leads to another. One thing, he generalised, always does lead to another. . . .

He was trying to tell her that he was utterly unworthy of Miss Walshingham, when Chitterlow gave up the search and suddenly accused him of being drunk and talking " Rot——"

CHAPTER THE FIFTH

"Swapped"

§ 1

HE awoke on the thoroughly comfortable sofa that
had had all its springs removed, and although he had
certainly not been intoxicated, he awoke with what
Chitterlow pronounced to be, quite indisputably, a
Head and a Mouth. He had slept in his clothes and
he felt stiff and uncomfortable all over, but the head
and mouth insisted that he must not bother over little
things like that. In the head was one large, angular
idea that it was physically painful to have there. If he
moved his head the angular idea shifted about in the
most agonising way. This idea was that he had lost his
situation and was utterly ruined and that it really
mattered very little. Shalford was certain to hear of
his escapade, and that, coupled with that row about
the Manchester window——!

He raised himself into a sitting position under
Chitterlow's urgent encouragement.

He submitted apathetically to his host's attentions.

Chitterlow, who admitted being a "bit off it" himself and in need of an egg-cupful of brandy, just an egg-cupful neat, dealt with that Head and Mouth as a mother might deal with the fall of an only child. He compared it with other Heads and Mouths that he had met, and in particular to certain experienced by the Honourable Thomas Norgate. "Right up to the last," said Chitterlow, "he couldn't stand his liquor. It happens like that at times." And after Chitterlow had pumped on the young beginner's head and given him some anchovy paste piping hot on buttered toast, which he preferred to all the other remedies he had encountered, Kipps resumed his crumpled collar, brushed his clothes, tacked up his trouser-leg, and prepared to face Mr. Shalford and the reckoning for this wild, unprecedented night—the first "night out" that ever he had taken.

Acting on Chitterlow's advice to have a bit of a freshener before returning to the Emporium, Kipps walked some way along the Leas and back, and then went down to a shop near the Harbour to get a cup of coffee. He found that extremely reinvigorating, and he went on up the High Street to face the inevitable terrors of the office, a faint touch of pride in his depravity tempering his extreme self-abasement. After all, it was not an unmanly headache; he had been out all night, and he had been drinking and his physical disorder was there to witness the fact. If it wasn't for the thought of Shalford he would have been even a proud man to discover himself at last in such a condition. But the thought of Shalford was very dreadful. He met two of the apprentices snatching a walk before shop began. At the sight of them he pulled his spirits together, put his hat back from his pallid brow, thrust his hands into his trouser pockets and adopted an altogether more dissipated carriage; he met their innocent faces with a wan smile. Just for a moment he was glad that the rent in his trousers was, after all, visible and that some at least of the mud on his clothes had refused to move at Chitterlow's brushing. What wouldn't they think he had been up to? He passed them without speaking. He could imagine how they regarded his back. Then he recollected Mr. Shalford. . . .

The deuce of a row certainly and perhaps——! He tried to think of plausible versions of the affair. He could explain he had been run down by rather a wild sort of fellow who was riding a bicycle, almost stunned for the moment (even now he felt the effects of the concussion in his head), and had been given whisky to restore him, and "the fact is, sir"——with an upward inflection of the voice, an upward inflection of the eyebrows and an air of its being the last thing one would have expected whisky to do, the manifestation indeed of a practically unique physiological weakness—— "it got into my *'ed!*"

Put like that it didn't look so bad.

He got to the Emporium a little before eight, and the housekeeper with whom he was something of a favourite ("There's no harm in Mr. Kipps," she used to say) seemed to like him if anything better for having broken the rules, and gave him a piece of dry toast and a good hot cup of tea.

"I suppose the G. V.——" began Kipps.

"He knows," said the housekeeper.

He went down to shop a little before time, and presently Booch summoned him to the presence.

He emerged from the private office after an interval of ten minutes.

The junior clerk scrutinised his visage. Buggins put the frank question.

Kipps answered with one word.

"Swapped!" said Kipps.

§ 2

Kipps leant against the fixtures with his hands in his pockets and talked to the two apprentices under him.

"I don't care if I *am* swapped," said Kipps. "I been sick of Teddy and his System some time. I was a good mind to chuck it when my time was up. Wish I 'ad now."

Afterwards Pierce came round and Kipps repeated this.

"What's it for?" said Pierce. "That row about the window tickets?"

"No fear!" said Kipps and sought to convey a perspective of splendid depravity. "I wasn't in las' night," he said and made even Pierce, "man about town" Pierce, open his eyes.

"Why! where did you get to?" asked Pierce.

He conveyed that he had been "fair round the town." "With a Nactor chap I know.

"One can't *always* be living like a curit," he said.

"No fear," said Pierce, trying to play up to him.

But Kipps had the top place in that conversation.

"My lor'!" said Kipps, when Pierce had gone, "but wasn't my mouth and 'ed bad this morning before I 'ad a pick-me-up!"

"What jer 'ave?"

"Anchovy on 'ot buttered toast. It's the very best pick-me-up there is. You trust me, Rodgers. I never take no other and I don't advise you to. See?"

And when pressed for further particulars, he said again he had been "fair all *round* the town, with a Nactor chap" he knew. They asked curiously all he had done and he said, "Well, what do *you* think?" And when they pressed for still further details he said there were things little boys ought not to know, and laughed darkly and found them some huckaback to roll.

And in this manner for a space did Kipps fend off the contemplation of the "key of the street" that Shalford had presented him.

§ 3

This sort of thing was all very well when junior apprentices were about, but when Kipps was alone with himself it served him not at all. He was uncomfortable inside and his skin was uncomfortable, the Head and Mouth, palliated perhaps but certainly not cured, were still with him. He felt, to tell the truth, nasty and dirty and extremely disgusted with himself. To work was dreadful and to stand still and think still more dreadful. His patched knee reproached him. These were the second best of his three pairs of trousers, and they had cost him thirteen and sixpence. Practically ruined they were. His dusting pair was unfit for shop and he would have to degrade his best. When he was under inspection he affected the slouch of a desperado; but directly he found himself alone, this passed insensibly into the droop.

The financial aspect of things grew large before him. His whole capital in the world was the sum of five pounds in the Post Office Savings Bank and four and sixpence cash. Besides this there would be two months' "screw." His little tin box upstairs was no longer big enough for his belongings; he would have to buy another, let alone that it was not calculated to make a good impression in a new "crib." Then there would be paper and stamps needed in some abundance for answering advertisements, and railway fares when he went "crib hunting." He would have to write letters, and he had never written letters. There was spelling, for example, to consider. Probably if nothing turned up before his month was up he would have to go home to his Uncle and Aunt.

How would they take it? . . .

For the present at any rate he resolved not to write to them.

Such disagreeable things as this it was that lurked below the fair surface of Kipps' assertion, "I've been wanting a change. If 'e 'adn't swapped me, I should very likely 'ave swapped *'im*."

In the perplexed privacies of his own mind he could not understand how everything had happened. He had been the Victim of Fate, or at least of one as inexorable—Chitterlow. He tried to recall the successive steps that had culminated so disastrously. They were difficult to recall. . . .

Buggins that night abounded in counsel and reminiscence.

"Curious thing," said Buggins, "but every time I've had the swap I've never believed I should get another Crib—never. But I have," said Buggins. "Always. So don't lose heart, whatever you do. . . .

"Whatever you do," said Buggins, "keep hold of your collars and cuffs—shirts if you can, but collars anyhow. Spout them last. And anyhow, it's summer! —you won't want your coat. . . . You got a good umbrella. . . .

"You'll no more get a shop from New Romney than—anything. Go straight up to London, get the cheapest room you can find—and hang out. Don't eat too much. Many a chap's put his prospects in his stomach. Get a cup o' coffee and a slice—egg if you like—but remember you got to turn up at the Warehouse tidy. The best places *now,* I believe, are the old cabmen's eating houses. Keep your watch and chain as long as you can. . . . .

"There's lots of shops going," said Buggins. "Lots!"

And added reflectively, "But not this time of year perhaps."

He began to recall his own researches. "'Stonishing lot of chaps you see," he said. "All sorts. Look like Dukes some of 'em. High hat. Patent boots. Frock coat. All there. All right for a West End crib. Others—Lord! It's a caution, Kipps. Boots been inked in some reading rooms—*I* used to write in a Reading

Room in Fleet Street, regular penny club—hat been wetted, collar frayed, tail coat buttoned up, black chest-plaster tie—spread out. Shirt, you know, gone—" Buggins pointed upward with a pious expression.

"No shirt, I expect?"

"Ate it," said Buggins.

Kipps meditated. "I wonder where old Minton is," he said at last. "I often wondered about 'im."

§ 4

It was the morning following Kipps' notice of dismissal that Miss Walshingham came into the shop. She came in with a dark slender lady, rather faded, rather tightly dressed, whom Kipps was to know some day as her mother. He discovered them in the main shop at the counter of the ribbon department. He had come to the opposite glove counter with some goods enclosed in a parcel that he had unpacked in his own department. The two ladies were both bent over a box of black ribbon.

He had a moment of tumultuous hesitations. The etiquette of the situation was incomprehensible. He put down his goods very quietly and stood hands on counter, staring at these two ladies. Then, as Miss Walshingham sat back, the instinct of flight seized him. . . .

He returned to his Manchester shop wildly agitated. Directly he was out of sight of her he wanted to see her. He fretted up and down the counter, and addressed some snappish remarks to the apprentice in the window. He fumbled for a moment with a parcel, untied it needlessly, began to tie it up again and then bolted back into the main shop. He could hear his own heart beating.

The two ladies were standing in the manner of those who have completed their purchases and are waiting for their change. Mrs. Walshingham regarded some

remnants with impersonal interest; Helen's eyes
searched the shop. They distinctly lit up when they
discovered Kipps.

He dropped his hands to the counter by habit and
stood for a moment regarding her awkwardly. What
would she do? Would she cut him? She came across
the shop to him.

"How are *you*, Mr. Kipps?" she said in her clear
distinct tones, and she held out her hand.

"Very well, thank you," said Kipps; "how are
you?"

She said she had been buying some ribbon.

He became aware of Mrs. Walshingham very much
surprised. This checked something allusive about the
class, and he said instead that he supposed she was glad
to be having her holidays now. She said she was, it
gave her more time for reading and that sort of thing.
He supposed that she would be going abroad, and she
thought that perhaps they *would* go to Knocke or
Bruges for a time.

Then came a pause and Kipps' soul surged within
him. He wanted to tell her he was leaving and would
never see her again. He could find neither words nor
voice to say it. The swift seconds passed. The girl in
the ribbons was handing Mrs. Walshingham her change.
"Well," said Miss Walshingham, "good-bye," and gave
him her hand again.

Kipps bowed over her hand. His manners, his
counter manners, were the easiest she had ever seen
upon him. She turned to her mother. It was no good
now, no good. Her mother! You couldn't say a
thing like that before her mother! All was lost but
politeness. Kipps rushed for the door. He stood at
the door bowing with infinite gravity, and she smiled
and nodded as she went out. She saw nothing of the
struggle within him, nothing but a gratifying emotion.
She smiled like a satisfied goddess as the incense
ascends.

Mrs. Walshingham bowed stiffly and a little awkwardly.

He remained holding the door open for some seconds after they had passed out, then rushed suddenly to the back of the "costume" window to watch them go down the street. His hands tightened on the window rack as he stared. Her mother appeared to be asking discreet questions. Helen's bearing suggested the off-hand replies of a person who found the world a satisfactory place to live in. "Really, Mumsie, you cannot expect me to cut my own students dead," she was in fact saying. . . .

They vanished round Henderson's corner.

Gone! And he would never see her again——never! It was as though someone had struck his heart with a whip. Never! Never! Never! And she didn't know! He turned back from the window, and the department with its two apprentices was impossible. The whole glaring world was insupportable.

He hesitated, and made a rush head down for the cellar that was his Manchester warehouse. Rodgers asked him a question that he pretended not to hear.

The Manchester warehouse was a cellar apart from the general basement of the building and dimly lit by a small gas flare. He did not turn that up, but rushed for the darkest corner, where on the lowest shelf the sale window tickets were stored. He drew out the box of these with trembling hands and upset them on the floor, and so having made himself a justifiable excuse for being on the ground with his head well in the dark, he could let his poor bursting little heart have its way with him for a space.

And there he remained until the cry of "Kipps! Forward!" summoned him once more to face the world.

CHAPTER THE SIXTH

The Unexpected

§ 1

NOW in the slack of that same day, after the mid-day dinner and before the coming of the afternoon customers, this disastrous Chitterlow descended upon Kipps with the most amazing coincidence in the world. He did not call formally, entering and demanding Kipps, but privately, in a confidential and mysterious manner.

Kipps was first aware of him as a dark object bobbing about excitedly outside the hosiery window. He was stooping and craning and peering in the endeavour to see into the interior between and over the socks and stockings. Then he transferred his attention to the door, and after a hovering scrutiny, tried the baby-linen display. His movements and gestures suggested a suppressed excitement.

Seen by daylight, Chitterlow was not nearly such a magnificent figure as he had been by the subdued nocturnal lightings and beneath the glamour of his own interpretation. The lines were the same indeed, but the texture was different. There was quality about the yachting cap, an indefinable finality of dustiness, a shiny finish on all the salient surfaces of the reefer coat. The red hair and the profile, though still forcible and fine, were less in the quality of Michael Angelo and more in that of the merely picturesque. But it was a bright brown eye still that sought amidst the interstices of the baby-linen.

Kipps was by no means anxious to interview Chitterlow again. If he had felt sure that Chitterlow would not enter the shop he would have hid in the warehouse until the danger was past, but he had no idea of Chitterlow's limitations. He decided to keep up the shop in the shadows until Chitterlow reached the side window of the Manchester department, and then to go outside as if to inspect the condition of the window and explain to him that things were unfavourable to immediate intercourse. He might tell him he had already lost his situation. . . .

"'Ullo, Chit'low," he said, emerging.

"Very man I want to see," said Chitterlow, shaking with vigour. "Very man I want to see." He laid a hand on Kipps' arm. "How *old* are you, Kipps?"

"One and twenty," said Kipps. "Why?"

"Talk about coincidences! And your name now? Wait a minute." He held out a finger. "*Is* it Arthur?"

"Yes," said Kipps.

"You're the man," said Chitterlow.

"What man?"

"It's about the thickest coincidence I ever struck," said Chitterlow, plunging his extensive hand into his breast coat pocket. "Half a jiff and I'll tell you your mother's Christian name." He laughed and struggled with his coat for a space, produced a washing book and two pencils, which he deposited in his side pocket; then, in one capacious handful, a bent but by no means finally disabled cigar, the rubber proboscis of a bicycle pump, some twine and a lady's purse, and finally a small pocket book, and from this, after dropping and recovering several visiting cards, he extracted a carelessly torn piece of newspaper. "Euphemia," he read and brought his face close to Kipps'. "Eh?" He laughed noisily. "It's about as fair a Bit of All Right as anyone *could* have—outside a coincidence play. Don't say her name wasn't Euphemia, Kipps, and spoil the whole blessed show."

"Whose name—Euphemia?" asked Kipps.

"Your mother's."

"Lemme see what it says on the paper."

Chitterlow handed him the fragment and turned away. "You may say what you like," he said, addressing a vast, deep laugh to the street generally.

Kipps attempted to read. "WADDY or KIPPS. If Arthur Waddy or Arthur Kipps, the son of Margaret Euphemia Kipps, who——"

Chitterlow's finger swept over the print. "I went down the column and every blessed name that seemed to fit my play I took. I don't believe in made-up names. As I told you. I'm all with Zola in that. Documents whenever you can. I like 'em hot and real. See? Who was Waddy?"

"Never heard his name."

"Not Waddy?"

"No!"

Kipps tried to read again and abandoned the attempt. "What does it mean?" he said. "I don't understand."

"It means," said Chitterlow, with a momentary note of lucid exposition, "so far as I can make out that you're going to strike it Rich. Never mind about the Waddy—that's a detail. What does it usually mean? You'll hear of something to your advantage—very well. I took that newspaper up to get my names by the merest chance. Directly I saw it again and read that— I knew it was you. I believe in coincidences. People say they don't happen. *I* say they do. Everything's a coincidence. Seen properly. Here you are. Here's one! Incredible? Not a bit of it! See? It's you! Kipps! Waddy be damned! It's a Mascot. There's luck in my play. Bif! You're there. *I'm* there. Fair *in* it! Snap!" And he discharged his fingers like a pistol. "Never you mind about the 'Waddy.'"

"Eh?" said Kipps, with a nervous eye on Chitterlow's fingers.

"You're all right," said Chitterlow; "you may bet the seat of your only breeches on that! Don't you worry about the Waddy—that's as clear as day. You're about as right side up as a billiard ball—whatever you do. Don't stand there gaping, man! Read the paper if you don't believe me. Read it!"

He shook it under Kipps' nose.

Kipps became aware of the second apprentice watching them from the shop. His air of perplexity gave place to a more confident bearing.

—"'who was born at East Grinstead.' I certainly was born there. I've 'eard my Aunt say——"

"I knew it," said Chitterlow, taking hold of one edge of the paper and bringing his face close alongside Kipps'.

"'——on September the first, eighteen hundred and seventy-eight——'"

"*That's* all right," said Chitterlow. "It's all, all right, and all you have to do is to write to Watson and Bean and get it——"

"Get what?"

"Whatever it is."

Kipps sought his moustache. "You'd write?" he asked.

"Ra-ther."

"But what d'you think it is?"

"That's the fun of it!" said Chitterlow, taking three steps in some as yet uninvented dance. "That's where the joke comes in. It may be anything—it may be a million. If so! Where does little Harry come in? Eh?"

Kipps was trembling slightly. "But——" he said, and thought. "If you was me——" he began. "About that Waddy——?"

He glanced up and saw the second apprentice disappear with amazing swiftness from behind the goods in the window.

"*What?*" asked Chitterlow, but he never had an answer.

"Lor'! There's the guv'nor!" said Kipps and made a prompt dive for the door.

He dashed in only to discover that Shalford, with the junior apprentice in attendance, had come to mark off remnants of Kipps' cotton dresses and was demanding him. "Hullo, Kipps," he said, "outside——?"

"Seein' if the window was straight, Sir," said Kipps.

"Umph!" said Shalford.

For a space Kipps was too busily employed to think at all of Chitterlow or the crumpled bit of paper in his trouser pocket. He was, however, painfully aware of a suddenly disconnected excitement at large in the street. There came one awful moment when Chitterlow's nose loomed interrogatively over the ground glass of the department door, and his bright little red-brown eye sought for the reason of Kipps' disappearance, and then it became evident that he saw the high light of Shalford's baldness and grasped the situation and went away. And then Kipps (with that advertisement in his pocket) was able to come back to the business in hand.

He became aware that Shalford had asked a question. "Yessir, nosir, rightsir. I'm sorting up zephyrs tomorrow, Sir," said Kipps.

Presently he had a moment to himself again, and, taking up a safe position behind a newly unpacked pile of summer lace curtains, he straightened out the piece of paper and re-perused it. It was a little perplexing. That "Arthur Waddy or Arthur Kipps"—did that

imply two persons or one? He would ask Pierce or
Buggins. Only——

It had always been impressed upon him that there
was something demanding secrecy about his mother.

"Don't you answer no questions about your mother,"
his aunt had been wont to say. "Tell them you don't
know, whatever it is they ask you."

"Now this——?"

Kipps' face became portentously careful and he tugged
at his moustache, such as it was, hard.

He had always represented his father as being a
"gentleman farmer." "It didn't pay," he used to say
with a picture in his own mind of a penny magazine
aristocrat prematurely worn out by worry. "I'm a
Norfan, both sides," he would explain, with the air of
one who had seen trouble. He said he lived with his
uncle and aunt, but he did not say that they kept a
toy shop, and to tell anyone that his uncle had been a
butler—*a servant*—would have seemed the maddest of
indiscretions. Almost all the assistants in the Emporium
were equally reticent and vague, so great was their
horror of "Lowness" of any sort. To ask about this
"Waddy or Kipps" would upset all these little fictions.
He was not, as a matter of fact, perfectly clear about
his real status in the world (he was not, as a matter of
fact, perfectly clear about anything), but he knew that
there was a quality about his status that was—detrimental.

Under the circumstances——?

It occurred to him that it would save a lot of trouble
to destroy the advertisement there and then.

In which case he would have to explain to Chitterlow!

"Eng!" said Mr. Kipps.

"Kipps," cried Carshot, who was shopwalking;
"Kipps, Forward!"

He thrust back the crumpled paper into his pocket
and sallied forth to the customer.

"I want," said the customer, looking vaguely about

her through glasses, " a little bit of something to cover a little stool I have. Anything would do—a remnant or anything——"

The matter of the advertisement remained in abeyance for half an hour, and at the end the little stool was still a candidate for covering and Kipps had a thoroughly representative collection of the textile fabrics in his department to clear away. He was so angry about the little stool that the crumpled advertisement lay for a space in his pocket absolutely forgotten.

§ 2

Kipps sat on his tin box under the gas bracket that evening, and looked up the name Euphemia and learnt what it meant in the " Enquire Within About Everything " that constituted Buggins' reference library. He hoped Buggins, according to his habit, would ask him what he was looking for, but Buggins was busy turning out his week's washing. " Two collars," said Buggins, " half pair socks, two dickeys. Shirt? . . . M'm. There ought to be another collar somewhere."

" Euphemia," said Kipps at last, unable altogether to keep to himself this suspicion of a high origin that floated so delightfully about him, " Eu—phemia; it isn't a name *common* people would give to a girl, is it?"

" It isn't the name any decent people would give to a girl," said Buggins, " —common or not."

" Lor'!" said Kipps. " Why?"

" It's giving girls names like that," said Buggins, " that nine times out of ten makes 'em go wrong. It unsettles 'em. If ever I was to have a girl, if ever I was to have a dozen girls, I'd call 'em all Jane. Every one of 'em. You couldn't have a better name than that. Euphemia indeed! What next? . . . Good Lord! . . . That isn't one of my collars there, is it, under your bed? . . ."

Kipps got him the collar.

"I don't see no great 'arm in Euphemia," he said as he did so.

After that he became reckless. "I'm a good mind to write that letter," he said, and then, finding Buggins preoccupied wrapping his washing up in the "half sox," added to himself, "a thundering good mind."

So he got his penny bottle of ink, borrowed the pen from Buggins and, with no very serious difficulty in spelling or composition, did as he had resolved.

He came back into the bedroom about an hour afterwards, a little out of breath and pale. "Where you been?" said Buggins, who was now reading the *Daily World Manager,* which came to him in rotation from Carshot.

"Out to post some letters," said Kipps, hanging up his hat.

"Crib hunting?"

"Mostly," said Kipps.

"Rather," he added with a nervous laugh; "what else?"

Buggins went on reading. Kipps sat on his bed and regarded the back of the *Daily World Manager* thoughtfully.

"Buggins," he said at last.

Buggins lowered his paper and looked.

"I say, Buggins, what do these here advertisements mean that say so-and-so will hear of something greatly to his advantage."

"Missin' people," said Buggins, making to resume reading.

"How d'yer mean?" asked Kipps. "Money left and that sort of thing?"

Buggins shook his head. "Debts," he said, "more often than not."

"But that ain't to his advantage."

"They put that to get 'old of 'em," said Buggins. "Often it's wives."

" What you mean ?"

" Deserted wives try and get their husbands back that way."

" I suppose it *is* legacies sometimes, eh ? Perhaps if someone was left a hundred pounds by someone——"

" Hardly ever," said Buggins.

" Well, 'ow——?" began Kipps and hesitated.

Buggins resumed reading. He was very much excited by a leader on Indian affairs. " By Jove!" he said, " it won't do to give these here Blacks votes."

" No fear," said Kipps.

" They're different altogether," said Buggins. " They 'aven't the sound sense of Englishmen, and they 'aven't the character. There's a sort of tricky dishonesty about 'em—false witness and all that—of which an English-man has no idea. Outside their courts of law—it's a pos'tive fact, Kipps—there's witnesses waitin' to be 'ired. Reg'lar trade. Touch their 'ats as you go in. Englishmen 'ave no idea, I tell you—not ord'nary Englishmen. It's in their blood. They're too timid to be honest. Too slavish. They aren't used to being free like we are, and if you gave 'em freedom they wouldn't make a proper use of it. Now *we*— Oh, *Damn!*"

For the gas had suddenly gone out, and Buggins had the whole column of Society Club Chat still to read.

Buggins could talk of nothing after that but Shalford's meanness in turning off the gas, and after being extremely satirical about their employer, undressed in the dark, hit his bare toe against a box and subsided after unseemly ejaculations into silent ill-temper.

Though Kipps tried to get to sleep before the affair of the letter he had just posted resumed possession of his mind, he could not do so. He went over the whole thing again, exhaustively. Now that his first terror was abating he couldn't quite determine whether he was glad or sorry that he had posted that letter. If it *should* happen to be a hundred pounds !

It *must* be a hundred pounds!

If it was he could hold out for a year, for a couple of years even, before he got a Crib.

Even if it was fifty pounds——!

Buggins was already breathing regularly when Kipps spoke again. "Bug-gins," he said.

Buggins pretended to be asleep, and thickened his regular breathing (a little too hastily) to a snore.

"I say, Buggins," said Kipps after an interval.

"What's up now?" said Buggins unamiably.

"S'pose *you* saw an advertisement in a paper, with your name in it, see, asking you to come and see some-one, like, so as to hear of something very much to your——"

"Hide," said Buggins shortly.

"But——"

"I'd hide."

"Er?"

"Goo'-night, o' man," said Buggins, with convincing earnestness. Kipps lay still for a long time, then blew profoundly, turned over and stared at the other side of the dark.

He had been a fool to post that letter!

Lord! *Hadn't* he been a fool!

§ 3

It was just five days and a half after the light had been turned out while Buggins was reading, that a young man with a white face, and eyes bright and wide-open, emerged from a side road upon the Leas front. He was dressed in his best clothes, and, although the weather was fine, he carried his umbrella, just as if he had been to church. He hesitated and turned to the right. He scanned each house narrowly as he passed it, and presently came to an abrupt stop. "Hughenden," said the gateposts in firm, black letters, and the fanlight in gold repeated "Hughenden." It

was a stucco house fit to take your breath away, and
its balcony was painted a beautiful sea-green, enlivened
with gilding. He stood looking up at it.

"Gollys!" he said at last in an awestricken whisper.

It had rich-looking crimson curtains to all the lower
windows and brass-railed blinds above. There was a
splendid tropical plant in a large artistic pot in the
drawing-room window. There was a splendid bronzed
knocker (ring also) and two bells—one marked
"servants." "Gollys! *Servants,* eh?"

He walked past it, with his eyes regarding it, and
then turned and came back. He passed through a
further indecision, and finally drifted away to the sea
front and sat down on a seat a little way along the
Leas and put his arm over the back and regarded
"Hughenden." He whistled an air very softly to himself, put his head first on one side and then on the
other. Then for a space he scowled fixedly at it.

A very stout old gentleman, with a very red face
and very protuberant eyes, sat down beside Kipps, removed a Panama hat of the most abandoned desperado
cut, and mopped his brow and blew. Then he began
mopping the inside of his hat. Kipps watched him
for a space, wondering how much he might have a
year, and where he bought his hat. Then "Hughenden" reasserted itself.

An impulse overwhelmed him. "I say," he said,
leaning forward, to the old gentleman.

The old gentleman started and stared.

"*Whad* do you say?" he asked fiercely.

"You wouldn't think," said Kipps, indicating with
his forefinger, "that that 'ouse there belongs to
me."

The old gentleman twisted his neck round to look
at "Hughenden." Then he came back to Kipps,
looked at his mean little garments with apoplectic
intensity and blew at him by way of reply.

"It does," said Kipps, a little less confidently.

"Don't be a Fool," said the old gentleman, and put his hat on and wiped out the corners of his eyes. "It's hot enough," panted the old gentleman indignantly, "without Fools." Kipps looked from the old gentleman to the house and back to the old gentleman. The old gentleman looked at Kipps and snorted and looked out to sea, and again, snorting very contemptuously, at Kipps.

"Mean to say it doesn't belong to me?" said Kipps.

The old gentleman just glanced over his shoulder at the house in dispute and then fell to pretending Kipps didn't exist. "It's been lef' me this very morning," said Kipps. "It ain't the only one that's been lef' me, neither."

"Aw!" said the old gentleman, like one who is sorely tried. He seemed to expect the passers-by presently to remove Kipps.

"It 'as," said Kipps. He made no further remark to the old gentleman for a space, but looked with a little less certitude at the house. . . .

"I got——" he said and stopped.

"It's no good telling you if you don't believe," he said.

The old gentleman, after a struggle with himself, decided not to have a fit. "Try that game on with me," he panted. "Give you in charge."

"What game?"

"Wasn't born yesterday," said the old gentleman, and blew. "Besides," he added, "*look* at you! I know you," and the old gentleman coughed shortly and nodded to the horizon and coughed again.

Kipps looked dubiously from the house to the old gentleman and back to the house. Their conversation, he gathered, was over. Presently he got up and went slowly across the grass to its stucco portal again. He stood, and his mouth shaped the precious word, "Hughenden." It was all *right!* He looked over his shoulder as if in appeal to the old gentleman, then turned and went his way. The old gentleman was so evidently past all reason!

He hung for a moment some distance along the parade, as though some invisible string was pulling him back. When he could no longer see the house from the pavement he went out into the road. Then with an effort he snapped the string.

He went on down a quiet side street, unbuttoned his coat furtively, took out three bank notes in an envelope, looked at them and replaced them. Then he fished out five new sovereigns from his trouser pocket and examined them. To such a confidence had his exact resemblance to his dead mother's portrait carried Messrs. Watson and Bean.

It was right enough.

It really was *all* right.

He replaced the coins with grave precaution and went his way with a sudden briskness. It was all right—he had it now—he was a rich man at large. He went up a street and round a corner and along another street, and started towards the Pavilion and changed his mind and came round back, resolved to go straight to the Emporium and tell them all.

He was aware of someone crossing the road far off ahead of him, someone curiously relevant to his present extraordinary state of mind. It was Chitterlow. Of course it was Chitterlow who had told him first of the whole thing! The playwright was marching buoyantly along a cross street. His nose was in the air, the yachting cap was on the back of his head and the large freckled hand grasped two novels from the library, a morning newspaper, a new hat done up in paper and a lady's net bag full of onions and tomatoes. . . .

He passed out of sight behind the wine merchant's at the corner, as Kipps decided to hurry forward and tell him of the amazing change in the Order of the Universe that had just occurred.

Kipps uttered a feeble shout, arrested as it began, and waved his umbrella. Then he set off at a smart pace in pursuit. He came round the corner and Chitterlow had gone; he hurried to the next and there was no Chitterlow; he turned back unavailingly and his eyes sought some other possible corner. His hand fluttered to his mouth and he stood for a space at the pavement edge, staring about him. No good!

But the sight of Chitterlow was a wholesome thing, it connected events together, joined him on again to the past at a new point, and that was what he so badly needed. . . .

It was all right—all right.

He became suddenly very anxious to tell everybody at the Emporium, absolutely everybody, all about it. That was what wanted doing. He felt that telling was the thing to make this business real. He gripped his umbrella about the middle and walked very eagerly.

He entered the Emporium through the Manchester department. He flung open the door (over whose ground glass he had so recently, in infinite apprehension, watched the nose of Chitterlow) and discovered the second apprentice and Pierce in conversation. Pierce was prodding his hollow tooth with a pin and talking in fragments about the distinctive characteristics of Good Style.

Kipps came up in front of the counter.

"I say," he said; "what d'yer think?"

"What?" said Pierce over the pin.

"Guess."

"You've slipped out because Teddy's in London."

"Something more."

"What?"

"Been left a fortune."

"Garn!"

"I 'ave."

"Get out!"

5

"Straight. I been lef' twelve 'undred pounds—twelve 'undred pounds a year!"

He moved towards the little door out of the department into the house, moving, as heralds say, *regardant passant*. Pierce stood with mouth wide open and pin poised in air. "No!" he said at last.

"It's right," said Kipps, "and I'm going."

And he fell over the doormat into the house.

§ 4

It happened that Mr. Shalford was in London buying summer sale goods—and no doubt also interviewing aspirants to succeed Kipps.

So that there was positively nothing to hinder a wild rush of rumour from end to end of the Emporium. All the masculine members began their report with the same formula. "Heard about Kipps?"

The new girl in the cash desk had had it from Pierce, and had dashed out into the fancy shop to be the first with the news on the fancy side. Kipps had been left a thousand pounds a year, twelve thousand pounds a year. Kipps had been left twelve hundred thousand pounds. The figures were uncertain, but the essential facts they had correct. Kipps had gone upstairs. Kipps was packing his box. He said he wouldn't stop another day in the old Emporium, not for a thousand pounds! It was said that he was singing ribaldry about old Shalford.

He had come down! He was in the counting house. There was a general movement thither. Poor old Buggins had a customer and couldn't make out what the deuce it was all about! Completely out of it was Buggins.

There was a sound of running to and fro and voices saying this, that and the other thing about Kipps. Ring-a-dinger, ring-a-dinger went the dinner bell all unheeded. The whole of the Emporium was suddenly bright-eyed, excited, hungry to tell somebody, to find at any cost somebody who didn't know and be first to tell them, "Kipps has been left thirty—forty—fifty thousand pounds!"

"*What?*" cried the senior porter, "Him?" and ran up to the counting house as eagerly as though Kipps had broken his neck.

"One of our chaps just been left sixty thousand pounds," said the first apprentice, returning after a great absence to his customer.

"Unexpectedly?" said the customer.

"Quite," said the first apprentice. . . .

"I'm sure if Anyone deserves it, it's Mr. Kipps," said Miss Mergle, and her train rustled as she hurried to the counting house.

There stood Kipps amidst a pelting shower of congratulations. His face was flushed and his hair disordered. He still clutched his hat and best umbrella in his left hand. His right hand was anyone's to shake rather than his own. (Ring-a-dinger, ring-a-dinger ding, ding, ding, dang you! went the neglected dinner bell.)

"Good old Kipps," said Pierce, shaking. "Good old Kipps."

Booch rubbed one anæmic hand upon the other. "You're sure it's all right, Mr. Kipps," he said in the background.

"I'm sure we all congratulate him," said Miss Mergle.

"Great Scott!" said the new young lady in the glove department. "Twelve hundred a year! Great Scott! You aren't thinking of marrying anyone are you, Mr. Kipps?"

"Three pounds, five and ninepence a day," said Mr. Booch, working in his head almost miraculously. . . .

Everyone, it seemed, was saying how glad they were it was Kipps, except the junior apprentice, upon whom —he being the only son of a widow and used to having

the best of everything as a right—an intolerable envy,
a sense of unbearable wrong, had cast its gloomy shade.
All the rest were quite honestly and simply glad—
gladder perhaps at that time than Kipps because they
were not so overpowered. . . .

Kipps went downstairs to dinner, emitting fragmentary, disconnected statements. "Never expected
anything of the sort. . . . When this here old Bean
told me, you could have knocked me down with a
feather. . . . He says, 'You b'en lef' money.' Even
then I didn't expect it'd be mor'n a hundred pounds
perhaps. Something like that."

With the sitting down to dinner and the handing of
plates the excitement assumed a more orderly quality.
The housekeeper emitted congratulations as she carved
and the maidservant became dangerous to clothes with
the plates—she held them anyhow; one expected to see
one upside down even—she found Kipps so fascinating
to look at. Everyone was the brisker and hungrier for
the news (except the junior apprentice) and the housekeeper carved with unusual liberality. It was High Old
Times there under the gaslight, High Old Times.
"I'm sure if Anyone deserves it," said Miss Mergle—
"pass the salt, please—it's Mr. Kipps."

The babble died away a little as Carshot began barking across the table at Kipps. "You'll be a bit of a
Swell, Kipps," he said. "You won't hardly know
yourself."

"Quite the gentleman," said Miss Mergle.

"Many real gentlemen's families," said the housekeeper, "have to do with less."

"See you on the Leas," said Carshot. "My gu—!"
He met the housekeeper's eye. She had spoken about
that expression before. "My eye!" he said tamely,
lest words should mar the day.

"You'll go to London, I reckon," said Pierce.
"You'll be a man about town. We shall see you

mashing 'em, with violets in your button'ole, down the Burlington Arcade."

"One of these West End Flats. That'd be *my* style," said Pierce. "And a first-class club."

"Aren't these clubs a bit 'ard to get into?" asked Kipps, open-eyed, over a mouthful of potato.

"No fear. Not for Money," said Pierce. And the girl in the laces, who had acquired a cynical view of Modern Society from the fearless exposures of Miss Marie Corelli, said "Money goes everywhere nowadays, Mr. Kipps."

But Carshot showed the true British strain.

"If I was Kipps," he said, pausing momentarily for a knifeful of gravy, "I should go to the Rockies and shoot bears."

"I'd certainly 'ave a run over to Boulogne," said Pierce, "and look about a bit. I'm going to do that next Easter myself, anyhow—see if I don't."

"Go to Oireland, Mr. Kipps," came the soft insistence of Biddy Murphy, who managed the big workroom, flushed and shining in the Irish way as she spoke. "Go to Oireland. Ut's the loveliest country in the world. Outside Car-rs. Fishin', shootin', huntin'. An' pretty gals! Eh! You should see the Lakes of Killarney, Mr. Kipps!" And she expressed ecstasy by a facial pantomime and smacked her lips.

And presently they crowned the event.

It was Pierce who said, "Kipps, you ought to stand Sham!"

And it was Carshot who found the more poetical word, "Champagne."

"Rather!" said Kipps hilariously, and the rest was a question of detail and willing emissaries. "Here it comes!" they said as the apprentice came down the staircase. "How about the shop?" said someone. "Oh, *hang* the shop!" said Carshot and made gruntulous demands for a corkscrew with a thing to cut the

wire. Pierce, the dog! had a wire cutter in his pocket
knife. How Shalford would have stared at the gold-
tipped bottles if he had chanced to take an early train!
Bang with the corks, and bang! Gluck, gluck, gluck,
and sizzle!

When Kipps found them all standing about him
under the gas flare, saying almost solemnly "Kipps!"
with tumblers upheld—"Have it in tumblers," Carshot
had said; "have it in tumblers. It isn't a wine like
you have in glasses. Not like port and sherry. It
cheers you up, but you don't get drunk. It isn't hardly
stronger than lemonade. They drink it at dinner, some
of 'em, every day."

"What! At three and six a bottle!" said the housekeeper incredulously.

"*They* don't stick at *that*," said Carshot; "not the
champagne sort."

The housekeeper pursed her lips and shook her
head. . . .

When Kipps, I say, found them all standing up to
toast him in that manner, there came such a feeling in
his throat and face that for the life of him he scarcely
knew for a moment whether he was not going to cry.
"Kipps!" they all said, with kindly eyes. It was
very good of them, and hard there wasn't a stroke of
luck for them all!

But the sight of upturned chins and glasses pulled
him together again. . . .

They did him honour. Unenviously and freely they
did him honour.

For example, Carshot being subsequently engaged in
serving cretonne and desiring to push a number of
rejected blocks up the counter in order to have space
for measuring, swept them by a powerful and ill-
calculated movement of the arm, with a noise like
thunder, partly on to the floor and partly on to the
foot of the still gloomily preoccupied junior apprentice.
And Buggins, whose place it was to shopwalk while

Carshot served, shopwalked with quite unparalleled dignity, dangling a new season's sunshade with a crooked handle on one finger. He arrested each customer who came down the shop with a grave and penetrating look. " Showing very 'tractive line new sheason's shun-shade," he would remark, and, after a suitable pause, " 'Markable thing, one our 'sistant leg'sy twelve 'undred a year. V'ry 'tractive. Nothing more to-day, mum? No!" And he would then go and hold the door open for them with perfect decorum and with the sunshade dangling elegantly from his left hand. . . .

And the second apprentice, serving a customer with cheap ticking, and being asked suddenly if it was strong, answered remarkably,

" Oo! *no,* mum! Strong! Why, it ain't 'ardly stronger than lemonade. . . ."

The head porter, moreover, was filled with a virtuous resolve to break the record as a lightning packer and make up for lost time. Mr. Swaffenham of the Sandgate Riviera, for example, who was going out to dinner that night at seven, received at half-past six, instead of the urgently needed dress shirt he expected, a corset specially adapted to the needs of persons inclined to embonpoint. A parcel of summer underclothing selected by the elder Miss Waldershawe, was somehow distributed in the form of gratis additions throughout a number of parcels of a less intimate nature, and a box of millinery on approval to Lady Pamshort (at Wampachs) was enriched by the addition of the junior porter's cap. . . .

These little things, slight in themselves, witness perhaps none the less eloquently to the unselfish exhilaration felt throughout the Emporium at the extraordinary and unexpected enrichment of Mr. Kipps.

§ 5

The bus that plies between New Romney and Folkestone is painted a British red and inscribed on either side with the word "Tip-top" in gold amidst voluptuous scrolls. It is a slow and portly bus. Below it swings a sort of hold, hung by chains between the wheels, and in the summer time the top has garden seats. The front over the two dauntless unhurrying horses rises in tiers like a theatre; there is first a seat for the driver and his company, and above that a seat and above that, unless my memory plays me false, a seat. There are days when this bus goes and days when it doesn't go—you have to find out. And so you get to New Romney.

This bus it was, this ruddy, venerable and immortal bus, that came down the Folkestone hill with unflinching deliberation, and trundled through Sandgate and Hythe, and out into the windy spaces of the Marsh, with Kipps and all his fortunes on its brow. You figure him there. He sat on the highest seat diametrically above the driver and his head was spinning and spinning with champagne and this stupendous Tomfoolery of Luck; and his heart was swelling, swelling indeed at times as though it would burst him, and his face towards the sunlight was transfigured. He said never a word, but ever and again as he thought of this or that, he laughed. He seemed full of chuckles for a time, detached and independent chuckles, chuckles that rose and burst in him like bubbles in a wine. . . . He held a banjo sceptre-fashion and restless on his knee. He had always wanted a banjo, and now he had got one at Malchior's while he was waiting for the bus.

There sat beside him a young servant who was sucking peppermint and a little boy with a sniff, whose flitting eyes showed him curious to know why ever and again Kipps laughed, and beside the driver were two young men in gaiters talking about "tegs." And there sat Kipps, all unsuspected, twelve hundred a year, as it were, disguised as a common young man. And the young man in gaiters to the left of the driver eyed Kipps and his banjo, and especially his banjo, ever and again as if he found it and him, with his rapt face, an insoluble enigma. And many a King has ridden into a conquered city with a lesser sense of splendour than Kipps.

Their shadows grew long behind them and their faces were transfigured in gold as they rumbled on towards the splendid West. The sun set before they had passed Dymchurch, and as they came lumbering into New Romney past the windmill the dusk had come.

The driver handed down the banjo and the portmanteau, and Kipps having paid him—"That's aw right," he said to the change, as a gentleman should—turned about and ran the portmanteau smartly into old Kipps, whom the sound of the stopping of the bus had brought to the door of the shop in an aggressive mood and with his mouth full of supper.

"'Ullo, Uncle, didn't see you," said Kipps.

"Blunderin' ninny," said old Kipps. "What's brought *you* here? Ain't early closing, is it? Not Toosday?"

"Got some news for you, Uncle," said Kipps, dropping the portmanteau.

"Ain't lost your situation, 'ave you? What's that you got there? I'm blowed if it ain't a banjo. Goo'-lord! Spendin' your money on banjos! Don't put down your portmanty there—anyhow. Right in the way of everybody. I'm blowed if ever I saw such a boy as you've got lately. Here! Molly! And, look here! What you got a portmanty for? Why! Goo'-lord! You ain't *really* lost your place, 'ave you?"

"Somethin's happened," said Kipps, slightly dashed. "It's all right, Uncle. I'll tell you in a minute."

Old Kipps took the banjo as his nephew picked up the portmanteau again.

5*

The living-room door opened quickly, showing a table equipped with elaborate simplicity for supper, and Mrs. Kipps appeared.

"If it ain't young Artie," she said. "Why! Whatever's brought *you* 'ome?"

"'Ullo, Aunt," said Artie. "I'm coming in. I got somethin' to tell you. I've 'ad a bit of Luck."

He wouldn't tell them all at once. He staggered with the portmanteau round the corner of the counter, set a bundle of children's tin pails into clattering oscillation, and entered the little room. He deposited his luggage in the corner beside the tall clock, and turned to his Aunt and Uncle again. His Aunt regarded him doubtfully, the yellow light from the little lamp on the table escaped above the shade and lit her forehead and the tip of her nose. It would be all right in a minute. He wouldn't tell them all at once. Old Kipps stood in the shop door with the banjo in his hand, breathing noisily. "The fact is, Aunt, I've 'ad a bit of Luck."

"You ain't been backin' gordless 'orses, Artie?" she asked.

"No fear."

"It's a draw he's been in," said old Kipps, still panting from the impact of the portmanteau; "it's a dratted draw. Jest look here, Molly! He's won this 'ere trashy banjer and thrown up his situation on the strength of it—that's what he's done. Goin' about singing. Dash and plunge! Jest the very fault poor Pheamy always 'ad. Blunder right in and no one mustn't stop 'er!"

"You ain't thrown up your place, Artie, 'ave you?" said Mrs. Kipps.

Kipps perceived his opportunity. "I 'ave," he said; "I've throwed it up."

"What for?" said old Kipps.

"So's to learn the banjo!"

"Goo' *Lord!*" said old Kipps, in horror to find himself verified.

"I'm going about playing!" said Kipps with a giggle. "Goin' to black my face, Aunt, and sing on the beach. I'm going to 'ave a most tremenjous lark and earn any amount of money—you see. Twenty-six fousand pounds I'm going to earn just as easy as nothing!"

"Kipps," said Mrs. Kipps, "he's been drinking!"

They regarded their nephew across the supper table with long faces. Kipps exploded with laughter and broke out again when his Aunt shook her head very sadly at him. Then suddenly he fell grave. He felt he could keep it up no longer. "It's all right, Aunt. Reely. I ain't mad and I ain't been drinking. I been lef' money. I been lef' twenty-six fousand pounds."

Pause.

"And you thrown up your place?" said old Kipps.

"Yes," said Kipps. "Rather!"

"And bort this banjer, put on your best noo trousers and come right on 'ere?"

"Well," said Mrs. Kipps, "*I* never did."

"These ain't my noo trousers, Aunt," said Kipps regretfully. "My noo trousers wasn't done."

"I shouldn't ha' thought that *even you* could ha' been such a fool as that," said old Kipps.

Pause.

"It's *all* right," said Kipps, a little disconcerted by their distrustful solemnity. "It's all right—reely! Twenny-six fousan' pounds. And a 'ouse——"

Old Kipps pursed his lips and shook his head.

"A 'ouse on the Leas. I could have gone there. Only I didn't. I didn't care to. I didn't know what to say. I wanted to come and tell you."

"How d'yer know the 'ouse——?"

"They told me."

"Well," said old Kipps, and nodded his head portentously towards his nephew, with the corners of his mouth pulled down in a portentous, discouraging way. "Well, you *are* a young Gaby."

"I didn't *think* it of you, Artie!" said Mrs. Kipps.

"Wadjer mean?" asked Kipps faintly, looking from one to the other with a withered face.

Old Kipps closed the shop door. "They been 'avin' a lark with you," said old Kipps in a mournful undertone. "That's what I mean, my boy. They jest been seein' what a Gaby like you 'ud do."

"I dessay that young Quodling was in it," said Mrs. Kipps. "'E's jest that sort."

(For Quodling of the green baize bag had grown up to be a fearful dog, the terror of New Romney.)

"It's somebody after your place very likely," said old Kipps.

Kipps looked from one sceptical, reproving face to the other, and round him at the familiar, shabby little room, with his familiar cheap portmanteau on the mended chair, and that banjo amidst the supper things like some irrevocable deed. Could he be rich indeed? Could it be that these things had really happened? Or had some insane fancy whirled him hither?

Still—perhaps a hundred pounds——

"But," he said, "it's all right, reely, Uncle. You don't think——? I 'ad a letter."

"Got up," said old Kipps.

"But I answered it and went to a norfis."

Old Kipps felt staggered for a moment, but he shook his head and chins sagely from side to side. As the memory of Bean and Shalford revived, the confidence of Kipps came back to him.

"I saw a nold gent, Uncle—perfect gentleman. And 'e told me all about it. Mos' respectable 'e was. Said 'is name was Watson and Bean—leastways 'e was Bean. Said it was lef' me—" Kipps suddenly dived into his breast pocket. "By my Grandfather——"

The old people started.

Old Kipps uttered an exclamation and wheeled round

towards the mantelshelf above which the daguerreotype of his lost younger sister smiled its fading smile
upon the world.

"Waddy 'is name was," said Kipps, with his hand
still deep in his pocket. "It was '*is* son was my
father——"

"Waddy!" said old Kipps.

"Waddy!" said Mrs. Kipps.

"She'd never say," said old Kipps.

There was a long silence.

Kipps fumbled with a letter, a crumpled advertisement and three bank notes. He hesitated between these
items.

"Why! That young chap what was arsting questions——" said old Kipps, and regarded his wife with an
eye of amazement.

"Must 'ave been," said Mrs. Kipps.

"Must 'ave been," said old Kipps.

"James," said Mrs. Kipps, in an awestricken voice,
"after all—perhaps—it's true!"

"'*Ow* much did you say?" asked old Kipps. "'Ow
much did you say 'e'd lef' you, me b'y?"

It was thrilling, though not quite in the way Kipps
had expected. He answered almost meekly across the
meagre supper things, with his documentary evidence in
his hand :

"Twelve 'undred pounds. 'Proximately, he said.
Twelve 'undred pounds a year. 'E made 'is will, jest
before 'e died—not more'n a month ago. When 'e
was dying, 'e seemed to change like, Mr. Bean said.
'E'd never forgiven 'is son, never—not till then. 'Is
son 'ad died in Australia, years and years ago, and *then*
'e 'adn't forgiven 'im. You know—'is son what was my
father. But jest when 'e was ill and dying 'e seemed
to get worried like and longing for someone of 'is own.
And 'e told Mr. Bean it was 'im that had prevented
them marrying. So 'e thought. That's 'ow it all come
about. . . ."

§ 6

At last Kipps' flaring candle went up the narrow uncarpeted staircase to the little attic that had been his shelter and refuge during all the days of his childhood and youth. His head was whirling. He had been advised, he had been warned, he had been flattered and congratulated, he had been given whisky and hot water and lemon and sugar, and his health had been drunk in the same. He had also eaten two Welsh rarebits—an unusual supper. His Uncle was chiefly for his going into Parliament, his Aunt was consumed with a great anxiety. "I'm afraid he'll go and marry beneath 'im."

"Y'ought to 'ave a bit o' shootin' somewheer," said old Kipps.

"It's your *duty* to marry into a county family, Artie. Remember that."

"There's lots of young noblemen'll be glad to 'ang on to you," said old Kipps. "You mark my words. And borry your money. And then, good day to ye."

"I got to be precious Careful," said Kipps. "Mr. Bean said that."

"And you got to be precious careful of this old Bean," said old Kipps. "We may be out of the world in Noo Romney, but I've 'eard a bit about s'licitors, for all that. You keep your eye on old Bean, me b'y.

"'Ow do we know what 'e's up to, with your money, even now?" said old Kipps, pursuing this uncomfortable topic.

"'E *looked* very respectable," said Kipps. . . .

Kipps undressed with great deliberation, and with vast gaps of pensive margin. Twenty-six thousand pounds!

His Aunt's solicitude had brought back certain matters into the foreground that his "Twelve 'Undred a year!" had for a time driven away altogether. His thoughts went back to the wood-carving class. Twelve Hundred a Year. He sat on the edge of the bed in profound meditation and his boots fell "whop" and "whop" upon the floor, with a long interval between each "whop." Twenty-six thousand pounds. "By Gum!" He dropped the remainder of his costume about him on the floor, got into bed, pulled the patchwork quilt over him and put his head on the pillow that had been first to hear of Ann Pornick's accession to his heart. But he did not think of Ann Pornick now.

It was about everything in the world except Ann Pornick that he seemed to be trying to think of—simultaneously. All the vivid happenings of the day came and went in his overtaxed brain; "that old Bean" explaining and explaining, the fat man who wouldn't believe, an overpowering smell of peppermint, the banjo, Miss Mergle saying he deserved it, Chitterlow's vanishing round a corner, the wisdom and advice and warnings of his Aunt and Uncle. She was afraid he would marry beneath him, *was* she? She didn't know. . . .

His brain made an excursion into the wood-carving class and presented Kipps with the picture of himself amazing that class by a modest yet clearly audible remark, "I been left twenty-six thousand pounds." Then he told them all quietly but firmly that he had always loved Miss Walshingham, always, and so he had brought all his twenty-six thousand pounds with him to give to her there and then. He wanted nothing in return. . . . Yes, he wanted nothing in return. He would give it to her all in an envelope and go. Of course he would keep the banjo—and a little present for his Aunt and Uncle—and a new suit perhaps—and one or two other things she would not miss. He went off at a tangent. He might buy a motor car, he might buy one of these here things that will play you a piano—that would make old Buggins sit up! He could pretend he had learnt to play—he might buy a bicycle and a cyclist suit. . . .

A terrific multitude of plans of what he might do, and in particular what he might buy, came crowding into his brain, and he did not so much fall asleep as pass into a disorder of dreams in which he was driving a four-horse Tip-Top coach down Sandgate Hill ("I shall have to be precious careful"), wearing innumerable suits of clothes, and through some terrible accident wearing them all wrong. Consequently he was being laughed at. The coach vanished in the interest of the costume. He was wearing golfing suits and a silk hat. This passed into a nightmare that he was promenading on the Leas in a Highland costume, with a kilt that kept shrinking, and Shalford was following him with three policemen. "He's my assistant," Shalford kept repeating; "he's escaped. He's an escaped Improver. Keep by him and in a minute you'll have to run him in. I know 'em. We say they wash, but they won't. . . ." He could feel the kilt creeping up his legs. He would have tugged at it to pull it down only his arms were paralysed. He had an impression of giddy crisis. He uttered a shriek of despair. "*Now!*" said Shalford. He woke in horror, his quilt had slipped off the bed.

He imagined he had just been called, that he had somehow overslept himself and missed going down for dusting. Then he perceived it was still night and light by reason of the moonshine, and that he was no longer in the Emporium. He wondered where he could be. He had a curious fancy that the world had been swept and rolled up like a carpet and that he was nowhere. It occurred to him that perhaps he was mad. "Buggins!" he said. There was no answer, not even the defensive snore. No room, no Buggins, nothing!

Then he remembered better. He sat on the edge of his bed for some time. Could anyone have seen his face they would have seen it white and drawn with staring eyes. Then he groaned weakly. "Twenty-six thousand pounds!" he whispered.

Just then it presented itself in an almost horribly overwhelming mass.

He remade his bed and returned to it. He was still dreadfully wakeful. It was suddenly clear to him that he need never trouble to get up punctually at seven again. That fact shone out upon him like a star through clouds. He was free to lie in bed as long as he liked, get up when he liked, go where he liked, have eggs every morning for breakfast or rashers or bloater paste or . . . Also he was going to astonish Miss Walshingham. . . .

Astonish her and astonish her. . . .

    *   *   *   *   *

He was awakened by a thrush singing in the fresh dawn. The whole room was flooded with warm golden sunshine. "I say!" said the thrush. "I say! I say! Twelve 'undred a year! Twelve 'Undred a Year. Twelve 'UNDRED a Year! I say! I say! I say!"

He sat up in bed and rubbed the sleep from his eyes with his knuckles. Then he jumped out of bed and began dressing very eagerly. He did not want to lose any time in beginning the new life.

END OF BOOK I

BOOK II
MR. COOTE THE CHAPERON

CHAPTER THE FIRST

The New Conditions

§ 1

THERE comes a gentlemanly figure into these events and for a space takes a leading part therein, a Good Influence, a refined and amiable figure, Mr. Chester Coote. You must figure him as about to enter our story, walking with a curious rectitude of bearing through the evening dusk towards the Public Library, erect, large-headed—he had a great big head that suggested a powerful mind well under control—with a large official-looking envelope in his white and knuckly hand. In the other he carries a gold-handled cane. He wears a silken grey jacket suit, buttoned up, and anon he coughs behind the official envelope. He has a prominent nose, slaty grey eyes and a certain heaviness about the mouth. His mouth hangs breathing open, with a slight protrusion of the lower jaw. His straw hat is pulled down a little in front, and he looks each person he passes in the eye, and directly his look is answered looks away.

Thus Mr. Chester Coote, as he was on the evening when he came upon Kipps. He was a local house agent and a most active and gentlemanly person, a conscious gentleman, equally aware of society and the serious side of life. From amateur theatricals of a nice refined sort to science classes, few things were able to get along without him. He supplied a fine full bass, a little flat and quavery perhaps, but very abundant, to the St. Stylites' choir. . . .

He passes on towards the Public Library, lifts the envelope in salutation to a passing curate, smiles and enters. . . .

It was in the Public Library that he came upon Kipps.

By that time Kipps had been rich a week or more, and the change in his circumstances was visible upon his person. He was wearing a new suit of drab flannels, a Panama hat and a red tie for the first time, and he carried a silver-mounted stick with a tortoiseshell handle. He felt extraordinarily different, perhaps more different than he really was, from the meek Improver of a week ago. He felt as he felt dukes must feel, yet at bottom he was still modest. He was leaning on his stick and regarding the indicator with a respect that never palled. He faced round to meet Mr. Coote's overflowing smile.

"What are you doang hea?" said Mr. Chester Coote.

Kipps was momentarily abashed. "Oh," he said slowly, and then, "Mooching round a bit."

That Coote should address him with this easy familiarity was a fresh reminder of his enhanced social position. "Jes' mooching round," he said. "I been back in Folkestone free days now. At my 'ouse, you know."

"Ah!" said Mr. Coote. "I haven't yet had an opportunity of congratulating you on your good fortune."

Kipps held out his hand. "It was the cleanest surprise that ever was," he said. "When Mr. Bean told me of it—you could have knocked me down with a feather."

"It must mean a tremendous change for you."

"Oo. Rather. Change? Why, I'm like the chap in the song they sing, I don't 'ardly know where I are. *You* know."

"An extraordinary change," said Mr. Coote. "I can quite believe it. Are you stopping in Folkestone?"

"For a bit. I got a 'ouse, you know. What my gran'father 'ad. I'm stopping there. His housekeeper was kep' on. Fancy—being in the same town and everything!"

"Precisely," said Mr. Coote. "That's it!" and coughed like a sheep behind four straight fingers.

"Mr. Bean got me to come back to see to things. Else I was out in New Romney, where my Uncle and Aunt live. But it's a Lark coming back. In a way. . . ."

The conversation hung for a moment.

"Are you getting a book?" asked Coote.

"Well, I 'aven't got a ticket yet. But I shall get one all right, and have a go in at reading. I've often wanted to. Rather. I was just 'aving a look at this Indicator. First-class idea. Tells you all you want to know."

"It's simple," said Coote, and coughed again, keeping his eyes fixed on Kipps. For a moment they hung, evidently disinclined to part. Then Kipps jumped at an idea he had cherished for a day or more—not particularly in relation to Coote, but in relation to anyone.

"You doing anything?" he asked.

"Just called with a paypah about the classes."

"Because— Would you care to come up and look at my 'ouse and 'ave a smoke and a chat? Eh?" He made indicative back jerks of the head, and was smitten with a horrible doubt whether possibly this invitation might not be some hideous breach of etiquette. Was it, for example, the correct hour? "I'd be awfully glad if you would," he added.

Mr. Coote begged for a moment while he handed the

official-looking envelope to the librarian and then declared himself quite at Kipps' service. They muddled a moment over precedence at each door they went through, and so emerged to the street.

"It feels awful rum to me at first, all this," said Kipps. "'Aving a 'ouse of my own and all that. It's strange, you know. 'Aving all day. Reely I don't 'ardly know what to do with my time.

"D'ju smoke?" he said suddenly, proffering a magnificent gold decorated pigskin cigarette case, which he produced from nothing almost as though it was some sort of trick. Coote hesitated and declined, and then, with great liberality, "Don't let me hinder you. . . ."

They walked a little way in silence, Kipps being chiefly concerned to affect ease in his new clothes and keeping a wary eye on Coote. "It's rather a big windfall," said Coote presently. "It yields you an income——?"

"Twelve 'undred a year," said Kipps. "Bit over— if anything."

"Do you think of living in Folkestone?"

"Don't know 'ardly yet. I *may*. Then again, I may not. I got a furnished 'ouse, but I may let it."

"Your plans are undecided?"

"That's jest it," said Kipps.

"Very beautiful sunset it was to-night," said Coote, and Kipps said, "Wasn't it?" and they began to talk of the merits of sunsets. Did Kipps paint? Not since he was a boy. He didn't believe he could now. Coote said his sister was a painter and Kipps received this intimation with respect. Coote sometimes wished he could find time to paint himself—but one couldn't do everything and Kipps said that was "jest it."

They came out presently upon the end of the Leas and looked down to where the squat dark masses of the harbour and harbour station, gemmed with pin-point lights, crouched against the twilit grey of the sea. "If one could do *that*," said Coote, and Kipps was inspired to throw his head back, cock it on one side, regard the harbour with one eye shut and say that it would take some doing. Then Coote said something about "Abend," which Kipps judged to be in a foreign language and got over by lighting another cigarette from his by no means completed first one. "You're right, *puff*, *puff*."

He felt that so far he had held up his end of the conversation in a very creditable manner, but that extreme discretion was advisable.

They turned away and Coote remarked that the sea was good for crossing, and asked Kipps if he had been over the water very much. Kipps said he hadn't been— "much," but he thought very likely he'd have a run over to Boulogne soon, and Coote proceeded to talk of the charms of foreign travel, mentioning quite a number of unheard-of places by name. He had been to them! Kipps remained on the defensive, but behind his defences his heart sank. It was all very well to pretend, but presently it was bound to come out. *He* didn't know anything of all this. . . .

So they drew near the house. At his own gate Kipps became extremely nervous. It was a fine, impressive door. He knocked neither a single knock nor a double, but about one and a half—an apologetic half. They were admitted by an irreproachable housemaid with a steady eye, before which Kipps cringed dreadfully. He hung up his hat and fell about over hall chairs and things. "There's a fire in the study, Mary?" he had the audacity to ask, though evidently he knew, and led the way upstairs panting. He tried to shut the door and discovered the housemaid behind him coming to light his lamp. This enfeebled him further. He said nothing until the door closed behind her. Meanwhile to show his *sang froid* he hummed and flitted towards the window, and here and there.

Coote went to the big hearthrug and turned and surveyed his host. His hand went to the back of his head and patted his occiput—a gesture frequent with him.

"'Ere we are," said Kipps, hands in his pockets and glancing round him.

It was a gaunt Victorian room with a heavy, dirty cornice, and the ceiling enriched by the radiant plaster ornament of an obliterated gas chandelier. It held two large glass-fronted bookcases, one of which was sur-mounted by a stuffed terrier encased in glass. There was a mirror over the mantel, and hangings and cur-tains of magnificent crimson patternings. On the mantel were a huge black clock of classical design, vases in the Burslem Etruscan style, spills and toothpicks in large receptacles of carved rock, large lava ash trays and an exceptionally big box of matches. The fender was very great and brassy. In a favourable position, under the window, was a spacious rosewood writing desk, and all the chairs and other furniture were of rosewood and well stuffed.

"This," said Kipps, in something near an under-tone, "was the o' gentleman's study—my grandfather that was. 'E used to sit at that desk and write."

"Books?"

"No. Letters to *The Times,* and things like that. 'E's got 'em all cut out—stuck in a book. . . . Least-ways, he *'ad.* It's in that bookcase. . . . Won't you sit down?"

Coote did, blowing very slightly, and Kipps secured his vacated position on the extensive black skin rug. He spread out his legs, compass-fashion and tried to appear at his ease. The rug, the fender, the mantel and mirror conspired with great success to make him look a trivial and intrusive little creature amidst their common-place hauteur, and his own shadow on the opposite wall seemed to think everything a great lark and mocked and made tremendous fun of him. . . .

§ 2

For a space Kipps played a defensive game and Coote drew the lines of the conversation. They kept away from the theme of Kipps' change of fortune, and Coote made remarks upon local and social affairs. "You must take an interest in these things now," was as much as he said in the way of personalities. But it speedily became evident that he was a person of wide and commanding social relationships. He spoke of "society" being mixed in the neighbourhood and of the difficulty of getting people to work together, and "do" things; they were cliquish. Incidentally he alluded quite familiarly to men with military titles, and once even to someone with a title, a Lady Punnet. Not snobbishly, you understand, nor deliberately, but quite in passing. He had, it appeared, talked to Lady Punnet about private theatricals! In connection with the Hospitals. She had been unreasonable and he had put her right, gently of course, but firmly. "If you stand up to these people," said Coote, "they like you all the better." It was also very evident he was at his ease with the clergy; "My friend Mr. Densemore—a curate, you know, and rather curious, the Reverend *and* Honourable." Coote grew visibly in Kipps' eyes as he said these things; he became not only the exponent of "Vagner or Vargner," the man whose sister had painted a picture to be exhibited at the Royal Academy, the type of the hidden thing called culture, but a delegate, as it were, or at least an intermediary from that great world "up there," where there were men servants, where there were titles, where people dressed for dinner, drank wine at meals, wine costing very often as much as three and sixpence the bottle, and followed through a maze of etiquette the most stupendous practices. . . .

Coote sat back in the armchair smoking luxuriously and expanding pleasantly, with the delightful sense of Savoir Faire; Kipps sat forward, his elbows on his chair arm, alert, and his head a little on one side. You figure him as looking little and cheap and feeling smaller and cheaper amidst his new surroundings. But it was a most stimulating and interesting conversation. And soon it became less general and more serious and intimate. Coote spoke of people who had got on and of people who hadn't, of people who seemed to be *in* everything and people who seemed to be *out* of everything, and then he came round to Kipps.

"You'll have a good time," he said abruptly, with a smile that would have interested a dentist.

"I dunno," said Kipps.

"There's mistakes, of course."

"That's jest it."

Coote lit a new cigarette. "One can't help being interested in what you will do," he remarked. "Of course—for a young man of spirit, come suddenly into wealth—there's temptations."

"I got to go careful," said Kipps. "O' Bean told me that at the very first."

Coote went on to speak of pitfalls, of Betting, of Bad Companions. "I know," said Kipps, "I know." "There's Doubt again," said Coote. "I know a young fellow—a solicitor—handsome, gifted. And yet, you know—utterly sceptical. Practically altogether a Sceptic."

"Lor'!" said Kipps, "not a Natheist?"

"I fear so," said Coote. "Really, you know, an awfully fine young fellow—Gifted! But full of this dreadful Modern Spirit—Cynical! All this Overman stuff. Nietzsche and all that. . . . I wish I could do something for him."

"Ah!" said Kipps and knocked the ash off his cigarette. "I knew a chap—one of our apprentices he was—once. Always scoffing. . . . He lef'!"

He paused. "Never wrote for his refs," he said, in a deep tone proper to a moral tragedy, and then, after a pause—"Enlisted!"

"Ah!" said Coote.

"And often," he said, after a pause, "it's just the most spirited chaps, just the chaps one likes best, who Go Wrong."

"It's temptation," Kipps remarked.

He glanced at Coote, leant forward, knocked the ash from his cigarette into the mighty fender. "That's jest it," he said; "you get tempted. Before you know where you are."

"Modern life," said Coote, "is so—complex. It isn't everyone is Strong. Half the young fellows who go wrong, aren't really bad."

"That's jest it," said Kipps.

"One gets a tone from one's surroundings——"

"That's exactly it," said Kipps.

He meditated. "*I* picked up with a chap," he said. "A Nacter. Leastways he writes plays. Clever feller. But——"

He implied extensive moral obloquy by a movement of his head. "Of course it's seeing life," he added.

Coote pretended to understand the full implications of Kipps' remark. "Is it *worth* it?" he asked.

"That's jest it," said Kipps.

He decided to give some more. "One gets talking," he said. "Then it's ''ave a drink!' Old Methusaleh three stars—and where *are* you? *I* been drunk," he said in a tone of profound humility, and added, "lots of times."

"Tt. Tt.," said Coote.

"Dozens of times," said Kipps, smiling sadly, and added, "Lately."

His imagination became active and seductive. "One thing leads to another. Cards, p'r'aps. Girls——"

"I know," said Coote; "I know."

Kipps regarded the fire and flushed slightly. He borrowed a sentence that Chitterlow had recently used. "One can't tell tales out of school," he said.

"I can imagine it," said Coote.

Kipps looked with a confidential expression into Coote's face. "It was bad enough when money was limited," he remarked. "But now——" He spoke with raised eyebrows, "I got to steady down."

"You *must,*" said Coote, protruding his lips into a sort of whistling concern for a moment.

"I must," said Kipps, nodding his head slowly with raised eyebrows. He looked at his cigarette end and threw it into the fender. He was beginning to think he was holding his own in this conversation rather well, after all.

Kipps was never a good liar. He was the first to break silence. "I don't mean to say I been reely bad or reely bad drunk. A 'eadache perhaps—three or four times, say. But there it is!"

"I have never tasted alcohol in my life," said Coote with an immense frankness, "never!"

"No?"

"Never. I don't feel I should be likely to get drunk at all—it isn't that. And I don't go so far as to say even that in small quantities—at meals—it does one harm. But if I take it, someone else who doesn't know where to stop—you see?"

"That's jest it," said Kipps, with admiring eyes.

"I smoke," admitted Coote. "One doesn't want to be a Pharisee."

It struck Kipps what a tremendously Good chap this Coote was, not only tremendously clever and educated and a gentleman and one knowing Lady Punnet, but Good. He seemed to be giving all his time and thought to doing good things to other people. A great desire to confide in him arose. At first Kipps hesitated whether he should confide an equal desire for Benevolent activities or for further Depravity—either was in his mind. He rather affected the pose of the Good Intentioned Dog. Then suddenly his impulses took quite a different turn, fell indeed into what was a far more serious rut in his mind. It seemed to him

Coote might be able to do for him something he very much wanted done.

"Companionship accounts for so much," said Coote.

"That's jest it," said Kipps. "Of course, you know, in my new position—— That's just the difficulty."

He plunged boldly at his most secret trouble. He knew that he wanted refinement—culture. It was all very well—but he knew. But how was one to get it? He knew no one, knew no people—— He rested on the broken sentence. The shop chaps were all very well, very good chaps and all that, but not what one wanted. "I feel be'ind," said Kipps. "I feel out of it. And consequently I feel it's no good. And then if temptation comes along——"

"Exactly," said Coote.

Kipps spoke of his respect for Miss Walshingham and her freckled friend. He contrived not to look too self-conscious. "You know, I'd like to talk to people like that, but I can't. A chap's afraid of giving himself away."

"Of course," said Coote, "of course."

"I went to a middle-class school, you know. You mustn't fancy I'm one of these here board-school chaps, but you know it reely wasn't a first-class affair. Least-ways he didn't take pains with us. If you didn't want to learn you needn't—I don't believe it was *much* better than one of these here national schools. We wore mortar-boards, o' course. But what's *that?*

"I'm a regular fish out of water with this money. When I got it—it's a week ago—reely I thought I'd got everything I wanted. But I dunno what to *do.*"

His voice went up into a squeak. "Practically," he said, "it's no good shuttin' my eyes to things—I'm a gentleman."

Coote indicated a serious assent.

"And there's the responsibilities of a gentleman," he remarked.

"That's jest it," said Kipps.

"There's calling on people," said Kipps. "If you want to go on knowing Someone you knew before like. People that's refined." He laughed nervously. "I'm a regular fish out of water," he said, with expectant eyes on Coote.

But Coote only nodded for him to go on.

"This actor chap," he meditated, "is a good sort of chap. But 'e isn't what *I* call a gentleman. I got to 'old myself in with 'im. 'E'd make me go it wild in no time. 'E's pretty near the on'y chap I know. Except the shop chaps. They've come round to 'ave supper once already and a bit of a sing-song afterwards. I sang. I got a banjo, you now, and I vamp a bit. Vamping—you know. Haven't got far in the book— ''Ow to Vamp'—but still I'm getting on. Jolly of course, in a way, but what does it lead to? . . . Besides that, there's my Aunt and Uncle. *They're* very good old people—very—jest a bit interfering p'r'aps and thinking one isn't grown up, but Right enough. Only— It isn't what I *want*. I feel I've got be'ind with everything. I want to make it up again. I want to get with educated people who know 'ow to do things —in the regular, proper way."

His beautiful modesty awakened nothing but benevolence in the mind of Chester Coote.

"If I had someone like you," said Kipps, "that I knew regular like——"

From that point their course ran swift and easy. "If I *could* be of any use to you," said Coote. . . .

"But you're so busy and all that."

"Not *too* busy. You know, your case is a very interesting one. It was partly that made me speak to you and draw you out. Here you are with all this money and no experience, a spirited young chap——"

"That's jest it," said Kipps.

"I thought I'd see what you were made of, and I

must confess I've rarely talked to anyone that I've found quite so interesting as you have been——"

"I seem able to say things to you like, somehow," said Kipps.

"I'm glad. I'm tremendously glad."

"I want a Friend. That's it—straight."

"My dear chap, if I——"

"Yes, but——"

"*I* want a Friend, too."

"Reely?"

"Yes. You know, my dear Kipps—if I may call you that——"

"Go on," said Kipps.

"I'm rather a lonely dog myself. *This* to-night— I've not had anyone I've spoken to so freely of my Work for months."

"No?"

"Yes. And, my dear chap, if I can do anything to guide or help you——"

Coote displayed all his teeth in a kindly tremulous smile and his eyes were shiny. "Shake 'ands," said Kipps, deeply moved, and he and Coote rose and clasped with mutual emotion.

"It's reely too good of you," said Kipps.

"Whatever I can do I will," said Coote.

And so their compact was made. From that moment they were Friends, intimate, confidential, high-thinking, sotto voce friends. All the rest of their talk (and it inclined to be interminable) was an expansion of that. For that night Kipps wallowed in self-abandonment and Coote behaved as one who had received a great trust. That sinister passion for pedagogy to which the Good Intentioned are so fatally liable, that passion of infinite presumption that permits one weak human being to arrogate the direction of another weak human being's affairs, had Coote in its grip. He was to be a sort of lay confessor and director of Kipps, he was to

6

help Kipps in a thousand ways, he was in fact to chaperon Kipps into the higher and better sort of English life. He was to tell him his faults, advise him about the right thing to do——

"It's all these things I don't know," said Kipps. "I don't know, for instance, what's the right sort of dress to wear—I don't even know if I'm dressed right now——"

"All these things"—Coote stuck out his lips and nodded rapidly to show he understood—"Trust me for that," he said, "trust me."

As the evening wore on Coote's manner changed, became more and more the manner of a proprietor. He began to take up his rôle, to survey Kipps with a new, with a critical affection. It was evident the thing fell in with his ideas. "It will be awfully interesting," he said. "You know, Kipps, you're really good stuff." (Every sentence now he said "Kipps" or "my dear Kipps" with a curiously authoritative intonation.)

"I know," said Kipps, "only there's such a lot of things I don't seem to be up to some'ow. That's where the trouble comes in."

They talked and talked, and now Kipps was talking freely. They rambled over all sorts of things. Among others Kipps' character was dealt with at length. Kipps gave valuable lights on it. "When I'm reely excited," he said, "I don't seem to care *what* I do. I'm like that." And again, "I don't like to do anything under'and. I *must* speak out. . . ."

He picked a piece of cotton from his knee, the fire grimaced behind his back, and his shadow on the wall and ceiling was disrepectfully convulsed.

§ 3

Kipps went to bed at last with an impression of important things settled, and he lay awake for quite a long time. He felt he was lucky. He had known—in fact Buggins and Carshot and Pierce had made it very clear indeed—that his status in life had changed and that stupendous adaptations had to be achieved, but the problem of achievement had driven them into the realm of the incredible. Here in the simplest, easiest way was the adapter. The thing had become possible. Not of course easy, but possible.

There was much to learn, sheer intellectual toil, methods of address, bowing, an enormous complexity of laws. One broken, you are an outcast. How, for example, would one encounter Lady Punnet? It was quite possible some day he might really have to do that. Coote might introduce him. "Lord!" he said aloud to the darkness between grinning and dismay. He figured himself going into the Emporium to buy a tie, for example, and there in the face of Buggins, Carshot, Pierce and the rest of them, meeting "my friend, Lady Punnet!" It might not end with Lady Punnet! His imagination plunged and bolted with him, galloped, took wings and soared to romantic, to poetical altitudes. . . .

Suppose some day one met Royalty. By accident, say! He soared to that! After all—twelve hundred a year is a lift, a tremendous lift. How did one address Royalty? "Your Majesty's Goodness," it would be, no doubt—something like that—and on the knees. He became impersonal. Over a thousand a year made him an Esquire, didn't it? He thought that was it. In which case, wouldn't he have to be presented at court? Velvet breeches like you wear cycling, and a sword! What a curious place a court must be! Kneeling and bowing, and what was it Miss Mergle used to talk about? Of course!—ladies with long trains walking

about backward. Everybody walked about backward at
court, he knew, when not actually on their knees.
Perhaps, though, some people regular stood up to the
King! Talked to him, just as one might talk to
Buggins, say. Cheek, of course! Dukes, it might be,
did that—by permission? Millionaires? . . .

From such thoughts this free citizen of our Crowned
Republic passed insensibly into dreams, turgid dreams
of that vast ascent which constitutes the true-born
Briton's social scheme, which terminates with retrogres-
sive progression and a bending back.

§ 4

The next morning he came down to breakfast looking grave—a man with much before him in the
world. . . .

Kipps made a very special thing of his breakfast.
Daily once hopeless dreams came true then. It had
been customary in the Emporium to supplement Shalford's generous, indeed unlimited, supply of bread and
butter-substitute by private purchases, and this had given
Kipps very broad, artistic conceptions of what the meal
might be. Now there would be a cutlet or so or a
mutton chop—this splendour Buggins had reported from
the great London clubs—haddock, kipper, whiting or
fish-balls, eggs, boiled or scrambled, or eggs and bacon,
kidney also frequently and sometimes liver. Amidst
a garland of such themes, sausages, black and white
puddings, bubble and squeak, fried cabbage and scallops
came and went. Always as camp followers came potted
meat in all varieties, cold bacon, German sausage, brawn,
marmalade and two sorts of jam, and when he had
finished these he would sit among his plates and smoke
a cigarette and look at all these dishes crowded round
him with beatific approval. It was his principal meal.
He was sitting with his cigarette regarding his apartment
with the complacency begotten of a generous plan of

feeding successfully realised, when newspapers and post arrived.

There were several things by the post, tradesmen's circulars and cards and two pathetic begging letters—his luck had got into the papers—and there was a letter from a literary man and a book to enforce his request for ten shillings—to put down Socialism. The book made it very clear that prompt action on the part of property owners was becoming urgent, if property was to last out the year. Kipps dipped in it and was seriously perturbed. And there was a letter from old Kipps saying it was difficult to leave the shop and come over and see him again just yet, but that he had been to a sale at Lydd the previous day and bought a few good old books and things it would be difficult to find the equal of in Folkestone. "They don't know the value of these things out here," wrote old Kipps, "but you may depend upon it they are valuable," and a brief financial statement followed. "There is an engraving someone might come along and offer you a lot of money for one of these days. Depend upon it, these old things are about the best investments you could make. . . ."

Old Kipps had long been addicted to sales, and his nephew's good fortune had converted what had once been but a looking and a craving—he had rarely even bid for anything in the old days except the garden tools or the kitchen gallipots or things like that, things one gets for sixpence and finds a use for—into a very active pleasure. Sage and penetrating inspection, a certain mystery of bearing, tactical bids and Purchase!—Purchase!—the old man had had a good time.

While Kipps was rereading the begging letters and wishing he had the sound, clear common sense of Buggins to help him a little, the Parcels Post brought along the box from his uncle. It was a large insecure-looking case held together by a few still loyal nails, and by what the British War Office would have recognised at once as an Army Corps of string, rags and odds and ends tied together. Kipps unpacked it with a table knife, assisted at a critical point by the poker, and found a number of books and other objects of an antique type.

There were three bound volumes of early issues of *Chambers' Journal,* a copy of Punch's Pocket Book for 1875, Sturm's Reflections, an early version of Gill's Geography (slightly torn), an illustrated work on Spinal Curvature, an early edition of Kirke's Human Physiology, " The Scottish Chiefs " and a little volume on the Language of Flowers. There was a fine steel engraving, oak-framed and with some rusty spots, done in the Colossal style and representing the Handwriting on the Wall. There were also a copper kettle, a pair of candle snuffers, a brass shoehorn, a tea caddy to lock, two decanters (one stoppered) and what was probably a portion of an eighteenth-century child's rattle.

Kipps examined these objects one by one and wished he knew more about them. Turning over the pages of the Physiology again he came upon a striking plate in which a youth of agreeable profile displayed his interior in an unstinted manner to the startled eye. It was a new view of humanity altogether for Kipps, and it arrested his mind.

" Chubes," he whispered. " Chubes."

This anatomised figure made him forget for a space that he was " practically a gentleman " altogether, and he was still surveying its extraordinary complications when another reminder of a world quite outside those spheres of ordered gentility into which his dreams had carried him overnight, arrived (following the servant) in the person of Chitterlow.

§ 5

" ''Ul-*lo* !'' said Kipps, rising.

" Not busy ?'' said Chitterlow, enveloping Kipps' hand for a moment in one of his own and tossing the yachting cap upon the monumental carved-oak sideboard.

" Only a bit of reading,'' said Kipps.

" Reading, eh ?'' Chitterlow cocked the red eye at the books and other properties for a moment and then, " I've been expecting you round again one night.''

" I been coming round,'' said Kipps. " On'y there's a chap 'ere— I was coming round last night on'y I met 'im.''

He walked to the hearthrug. Chitterlow drifted round the room for a time, glancing at things as he talked. " I've altered that play tremendously since I saw you,'' he said. " Pulled it all to pieces.''

" What play's that, Chit'low ?''

" The one we were talking about. You know. You said something—I don't know if you meant it—about buying half of it. Not the tragedy. I wouldn't sell my own twin brother a share in that. That's my investment. That's my Serious Work. No! I mean that new farce I've been on to. Thing with the business about a beetle.''

" Oo yes,'' said Kipps. " *I* remember.''

" I thought you would. Said you'd take a fourth share for a hundred pounds. *You* know.''

" I seem to remember something———''

" Well, it's all different. Every bit of it. I'll tell you. You remember what you said about a butterfly? You got confused, you know—Old Meth. Kept calling the beetle a butterfly and that set me off. I've made it quite different. Quite different. Instead of Popplewaddle—thundering good farce name that, you know—for all that it came from a Visitors' List— instead of Popplewaddle getting a beetle down his neck and rushing about, I've made him a collector—

collects butterflies, and this one you know's a rare one. Comes in at window, centre." Chitterlow began to illustrate with appropriate gestures. "Pop rushes about after it. Forgets he mustn't let on he's in the house. After that— Tells 'em. Rare butterfly worth lots of money. Some are, you know. Everyone's on to it after that. Butterfly can't get out of room every time it comes out to have a try, rush and scurry. Well, I've worked on that. Only——"

He came very close to Kipps. He held up one hand horizontally and tapped it in a striking and confidential manner with the fingers of the other. "Something else," he said. "That's given me a Real Ibsenish Touch —like the Wild Duck. You know that woman—I've made her lighter—and she sees it. When they're chasing the butterfly the third time, she's on! She looks. 'That's me!' she says. Bif! Pestered Butterfly. *She's* the Pestered Butterfly. It's legitimate. Much more legitimate than the Wild Duck—where there isn't a duck!

"Knock 'em! The very title ought to knock 'em. I've been working like a horse at it. . . . You'll have a gold mine in that quarter share, Kipps. . . . *I* don't mind. It's suited me to sell it, and suited you to buy. Bif!"

Chitterlow interrupted his discourse to ask, "You haven't any brandy in the house, have you? Not to drink, you know. But I want just an eggcupful to pull me steady. My liver's a bit queer. . . . It doesn't matter, if you haven't. Not a bit. I'm like that. Yes, whisky'll do. Better!"

Kipps hesitated for a moment, then turned and fumbled in the cupboard of his sideboard. Presently he disinterred a bottle of whisky and placed it on the table. Then he put out first one bottle of soda water and after the hesitation of a moment another. Chitterlow picked up the bottle and read the label. "Good old Methusaleh," he said. Kipps handed him the corkscrew and then his hand fluttered up to his mouth. "I'll have to ring now," he said, "to get glasses." He hesitated for a moment before doing so, leaning doubtfully as it were towards the bell.

When the housemaid appeared he was standing on the hearthrug with his legs wide apart, with the bearing of a desperate fellow. And after that they had both had whiskies—"You know a decent whisky," Chitterlow remarked and took another "just to drink"—Kipps produced cigarettes and the conversation flowed again.

Chitterlow paced the room. He was, he explained, taking a day off; that was why he had come round to see Kipps. Whenever he thought of any extensive change in a play he was writing he always took a day off. In the end it saved time to do so. It prevented his starting rashly upon work that might have to be rewritten. There was no good in doing work when you might have to do it over again, none whatever.

Presently they were descending the steps by the Parade *en route* for the Warren, with Chitterlow doing the talking and going with a dancing drop from step to step. . . .

They had a great walk, not a long one, but a great one. They went up by the Sanatorium, and over the East Cliff and into that queer little wilderness of slippery and tumbling clay and rock under the chalk cliffs, a wilderness of thorn and bramble, wild rose and wayfaring tree, that adds so greatly to Folkestone's charm. They traversed its intricacies and clambered up to the crest of the cliffs at last by a precipitous path that Chitterlow endowed in some mysterious way with suggestions of Alpine adventure. Every now and then he would glance aside at sea and cliffs with a fresh boyishness of imagination that brought back New Romney and the stranded wrecks to Kipps' memory; but mostly he talked of his great obsession of plays and playwriting, and that empty absurdity that is so serious to his kind, his Art. That was a thing that needed a monstrous lot

6*

of explaining. Along they went, sometimes abreast
sometimes in single file, up the little paths and down
the little paths, and in among the bushes and out along
the edge above the beach, and Kipps went along trying
ever and again to get an insignificant word in edgeways,
and the gestures of Chitterlow flew wide and far and
his great voice rose and fell, and he said this and he
said that and he biffed and banged into the circumambient Inane.

It was assumed that they were embarked upon no
more trivial enterprise than the Reform of the British
Stage, and Kipps found himself classed with many
opulent and even royal and noble amateurs—the
Honourable Thomas Norgate came in here—who had
interested themselves in the practical realisation of high
ideals about the Drama. Only he had a finer understanding of these things, and instead of being preyed
upon by the common professional—" and they *are* a
lot," said Chitterlow; " I haven't toured for nothing "
—he would have Chitterlow. Kipps gathered few
details. It was clear he had bought the quarter of a
farcical comedy—practically a gold mine—and it would
appear it would be a good thing to buy the half. A
suggestion, or the suggestion of a suggestion, floated out
that he should buy the whole play and produce it
forthwith. It seemed he was to produce the play upon
a royalty system of a new sort, whatever a royalty
system of any sort might be. Then there was some
doubt, after all, whether that farcical comedy was in
itself sufficient to revolutionise the present lamentable
state of the British Drama. Better perhaps for such a
purpose was that tragedy—as yet unfinished—which was
to display all that Chitterlow knew about women, and
which was to centre about a Russian nobleman embody-
ing the fundamental Chitterlow personality. Then it
became clearer that Kipps was to produce several plays.
Kipps was to produce a great number of plays. Kipps
was to found a National Theatre.

It is probable that Kipps would have expressed some sort of disavowal, if he had known how to express it. Occasionally his face assumed an expression of whistling meditation, but that was as far as he got towards protest.

In the clutch of Chitterlow and the Incalculable, Kipps came round to the house in Fenchurch Street, and was there made to participate in the midday meal. He came to the house, forgetting certain confidences, and was reminded of the existence of a Mrs. Chitterlow (with the finest completely untrained contralto voice in England) by her appearance. She had an air of being older than Chitterlow, although probably she wasn't, and her hair was a reddish brown, streaked with gold. She was dressed in one of those complaisant garments that are dressing gowns or tea gowns or bathing wraps or rather original evening robes according to the exigencies of the moment—from the first Kipps was aware that she possessed a warm and rounded neck, and her well-moulded arms came and vanished from the sleeves—and she had large, expressive brown eyes that he discovered ever and again fixed in an enigmatical manner upon his own.

A simple but sufficient meal had been distributed with careless spontaneity over the little round table in the room with the photographs and looking-glass; and when a plate had by Chitterlow's direction been taken from under the marmalade in the cupboard and the kitchen fork and a knife that was not loose in its handle had been found for Kipps, they began and made a tumultuous repast. Chitterlow ate with quiet enormity, but it did not interfere with the flow of his talk. He introduced Kipps to his wife very briefly; she had evidently heard of Kipps before, and he made it vaguely evident that the production of the comedy was the thing chiefly settled. His reach extended over the table, and he troubled nobody. When Mrs. Chitterlow, who for a little while seemed socially self-conscious, reproved him for taking a potato with a jab of his fork, he answered, "Well, you shouldn't have married a man of Genius," and from a subsequent remark it was perfectly clear that Chitterlow's standing in this respect was made no secret of in his household.

They drank old Methusaleh and siphon soda, and there was no clearing away; they just sat among the plates and things, and Mrs. Chitterlow took her husband's tobacco pouch and made a cigarette and smoked and blew smoke and looked at Kipps with her large brown eyes. Kipps had seen cigarettes smoked by ladies before, "for fun," but this was real smoking. It frightened him rather. He felt he must not encourage this lady—at any rate in Chitterlow's presence.

They became very cheerful after the repast, and as there was now no waste to deplore, such as one experiences in the windy open air, Chitterlow gave his voice full vent. He fell to praising Kipps very highly and loudly. He said he had known Kipps was the right sort, he had seen it from the first, almost before he got up out of the mud on that memorable night. "You can," he said, "sometimes. That was why—" He stopped, but he seemed on the verge of explaining that it was his certainty of Kipps being the right sort had led him to confer this great Fortune upon him. He left that impression. He threw out a number of long sentences and material for sentences of a highly philosophical and incoherent character about Coincidences. It became evident he considered dramatic criticism in a perilously low condition. . . .

About four Kipps found himself stranded, as it were, by a receding Chitterlow on a seat upon the Leas.

He was chiefly aware that Chitterlow was an overwhelming personality. He puffed his cheeks and blew.

No doubt this was seeing life, but had he particularly wanted to see life that day? In a way Chitterlow had interrupted him. The day he had designed for himself was altogether different from this. He had been going to read through a precious little volume called "Don't" that Coote had sent round for him, a book of invaluable hints, a summary of British deportment that had only the one defect of being at points a little out of date.

That reminded him he had intended to perform a difficult exercise called an Afternoon Call upon the Cootes, as a preliminary to doing it in deadly earnest upon the Walshinghams. It was no good to-day, anyhow, now.

He came back to Chitterlow. He would have to explain to Chitterlow he was taking too much for granted, he would have to do that. It was so difficult to do in Chitterlow's presence though; in his absence it was easy enough. This half share, and taking a theatre and all of it, was going too far.

The quarter share was right enough, he supposed, but even that—! A hundred pounds! What wealth is there left in the world after one has paid out a hundred pounds from it?

He had to recall that in a sense Chitterlow had indeed brought him his fortune before he could face even that.

You must not think too hardly of him. To Kipps, you see, there was as yet no such thing as proportion in these matters. A hundred pounds went to his horizon. A hundred pounds seemed to him just exactly as big as any other large sum of money.

CHAPTER THE
SECOND

The Walshinghams

§ 1

THE Cootes lived in a little house in Bouverie Square with a tangle of Virginia creeper up the veranda.

Kipps had been troubled in his mind about knocking double or single—it is these things show what a man is made of—but happily there was a bell.

A queer little maid with a big cap admitted Kipps and took him through a bead curtain and a door into a little drawing-room, with a black and gold piano, a glazed bookcase, a Moorish cosy corner and a draped looking-glass over-mantel bright with Regent Street ornaments and photographs of various intellectual lights. A number of cards of invitation to meetings and the match list of a Band of Hope cricket club were stuck into the looking-glass frame with Coote's name as a Vice-President. There was a bust of Beethoven over the bookcase and the walls were thick with conscientiously executed but carelessly selected "views" in oil and water-colours and gilt frames. At the end of the room facing the light was a portrait that struck Kipps

172

at first as being Coote in spectacles and feminine costume, and that he afterwards decided must be Coote's mother. Then the original appeared, and he discovered that it was Coote's elder and only sister, who kept house for him. She wore her hair in a knob behind, and the sight of the knob suggested to Kipps an explanation for a frequent gesture of Coote's, a patting exploratory movement to the back of his head. And then it occurred to him that this was quite an absurd idea altogether.

She said, " Mr. Kipps, I believe," and Kipps laughed pleasantly and said, " That's it!" and then she told him that " Chester " had gone down to the art school to see about sending off some drawings or other, and that he would be back soon. Then she asked Kipps if he painted, and showed him the pictures on the wall. Kipps asked her where each one was " of," and when she showed him some of the Leas slopes he said he never would have recognised them. He said it was funny how things looked in a picture very often. " But they're awfully *good*," he said. " Did you do them?" He would look at them with his neck arched like a swan's, his head back and on one side, and then suddenly peer closely into them. " They *are* good. I wish I could paint." " That's what Chester says," she answered. " I tell him he has better things to do." Kipps seemed to get on very well with her.

Then Coote came in, and they left her and went upstairs together and had a good talk about reading and the Rules of Life. Or rather Coote talked, and the praises of thought and reading were in his mouth. . . .

You must figure Coote's study, a little bedroom put to studious uses, and over the mantel an array of things he had been led to believe indicative of culture and refinement : an autotype of Rossetti's " Annunciation," an autotype of Watts' " Minotaur," a Swiss carved pipe with many joints and a photograph of Amiens Cathedral (these two the spoils of travel), a phrenological bust, and some broken fossils from the Warren. A rotating bookshelf carried the Encyclopædia Britannica (tenth edition), and on the top of it were lying a large official-looking, age-grubby envelope bearing the mystic words, "On His Majesty's Service," a number or so of the *Bookman,* and a box of cigarettes. A table under the window bore a little microscope, some dust in a saucer, some grimy glass slips and broken cover glasses; for Coote had "gone in for" biology a bit. The longer side of the room was given over to bookshelves, neatly edged with pinked American cloth and with an array of books—no worse an array of books than you find in any public library; an almost haphazard accumulation of obsolete classics, contemporary successes, the Hundred Best Books (including Samuel Warren's "Ten Thousand a Year"), old school books, directories, *The Times* Atlas, Ruskin in bulk, Tennyson complete in one volume, Longfellow, Charles Kingsley, Smiles and Mrs. Humphry Ward, a guide book or so, several medical pamphlets, odd magazine numbers, and much indescribable rubbish—in fact a compendium of the contemporary British mind. And in front of this array stood Kipps, ill-taught and untrained, respectful, awestricken and, for the moment at any rate, willing to learn, while Coote, the exemplary Coote, talked to him of reading and the virtue in books.

"Nothing enlarges the mind," said Coote, "like Travel and Books. . . . And they're both so easy nowadays, and so cheap!"

"I've often wanted to 'ave a good go in at reading," Kipps replied.

"You'd hardly believe," Coote said, "how much you can get out of books. Provided you avoid trashy reading, that is. You ought to make a rule, Kipps, and read one Serious Book a week. Of course, we can Learn even from Novels, Nace Novels that is, but it isn't the same thing as serious reading. I made a rule, One Serious Book and One Novel—no more. There are some of the serious books I've been reading lately——on that table; 'Sartor Resartus'——Mrs. Twaddletome's 'Pond Life,' the 'Scottish Chiefs,' 'Life and Letters of Dean Farrer.' . . ."

§ 2

There came at last the sound of a gong, and Kipps descended to tea in that state of nervous apprehension at the difficulties of eating and drinking that his Aunt's knuckle rappings had implanted in him for ever. Over Coote's shoulder he became aware of a fourth person in the Moorish cosy corner, and he turned, leaving incomplete something incoherent he was saying to Miss Coote about his modest respect and desire for literature, to discover this fourth person was Miss Helen Walshingham, hatless and looking very much at home.

She rose at once with an extended hand to meet his hesitation.

"You're stopping in Folkestone, Mr. Kipps?"

"'Ere on a bit of business," said Kipps. "I thought you was away in Bruges."

"That's later," said Miss Walshingham. "We're stopping until my brother's holiday begins, and we're trying to let our house. Where are you staying in Folkestone?"

"I got a 'ouse of mine——on the Leas."

"I've heard all about your good fortune——this afternoon."

"Isn't it a Go!" said Kipps. "I 'aven't nearly got to believe it's reely 'appened yet. When that Mr. Bean told me of it you could 'ave knocked me down with a feather. . . . It's a tremenjous change for me."

He discovered Miss Coote was asking him whether he took milk and sugar. "*I* don't mind," said Kipps. "Jest as you like."

Coote became active handing tea and bread-and-butter. It was thinly cut, and the bread was rather new, and the half of the slice that Kipps took fell upon the floor. He had been holding it by the edge, for he was not used to this migratory method of taking tea without plates or table. This little incident ruled him out of the conversation for a time, and when he came to attend to it again they were talking about something or other prodigious—a performer of some sort—that was coming, called, it seemed, " Padrooski." So Kipps, who had dropped quietly into a chair, ate his bread-and-butter, said " No, thenk you " to any more, and by this discreet restraint got more freedom with his cup and saucer.

Apart from the confusion natural to tea, he was in a state of tremulous excitement on account of the presence of Miss Walshingham. He glanced from Miss Coote to her brother and then at Helen. He regarded her over the top of his cup as he drank. Here she was, solid and real. It was wonderful. He remarked, as he had done at times before, the easy flow of the dark hair back from her brow over her ears, the shapeliness of the white hands that came out from her simple white cuffs, the delicate pencilling of her brow.

Presently she turned her face to him almost suddenly, and smiled with the easiest assurance of friendship.

" You will go, I suppose," she said, and added, " to the Recital."

" If I'm in Folkestone I shall," said Kipps, clearing away a little hoarseness. " I don't *know* much about music, but what I do know I like."

" I'm sure you'll like Paderewski," she said.

" If you do," he said, " I dessay I shall."

He found Coote very kindly taking his cup.

" Do you think of living in Folkestone?" asked Miss Coote, in a tone of proprietorship, from the hearthrug.

" No," said Kipps, " that's jest it—I hardly know." He also said that he wanted to look round a bit before doing anything. " There's so much to consider," said Coote, smoothing the back of his head.

" I may go back to New Romney for a bit," said

Kipps. " I got an Uncle and Aunt there. I reely don't know."

Helen regarded him thoughtfully for a moment.

" You must come and see us," she said, " before we go to Bruges."

" Oo, rather!" said Kipps. " If I may."

" Yes, do," she said, and suddenly stood up before Kipps could formulate an inquiry when he should call.

" You're sure you can spare that drawing board?" she said to Miss Coote, and the conversation passed out of range.

And when he had said " Good-bye " to Miss Walshingham and she had repeated her invitation to call, he went upstairs again with Coote to look out certain initiatory books they had had under discussion. And then Kipps, blowing very resolutely, went back to his own place, bearing in his arm (1) " Sesame and Lilies," (2) " Sir George Tressady," (3) an anonymous book on " Vitality " that Coote particularly esteemed. And having got to his own sitting-room, he opened " Sesame and Lilies " and read it with ruthless determination for some time.

§ 3

Presently he leant back and gave himself up to the business of trying to imagine just exactly what Miss Walshingham could have thought of him when she saw him. Doubts about the precise effect of the grey flannel suit began to trouble him. He turned to the mirror over the mantel, and then got on to a chair to study the hang of the trousers. It looked all right. Luckily, she had not seen the Panama hat. He knew that he had the brim turned up wrong, but he could not find out which way the brim was right. However, that she had not seen. He might perhaps ask at the shop where he bought it.

He meditated for awhile on his reflected face— doubtful whether he liked it or not—and then got down again and flitted across to the sideboard where there lay two little books, one in a cheap, magnificent cover of red and gold, and the other in green canvas. The former was called, as its cover witnessed, " Manners and Rules of Good Society, by a Member of the Aristocracy," and after the cover had indulged in a band of gilded decoration, light-hearted but natural under the circumstances, it added " TWENTY-FIRST EDITION." The second was that admirable classic, " The Art of Conversing." Kipps returned with these to his seat, placed the two before him, opened the latter with a sigh and flattened it under his hand.

Then with knitted brows he began to read onward from a mark, his lips moving.

" Having thus acquired possession of an idea, the little ship should not be abruptly launched into deep waters, but should be first permitted to glide gently and smoothly into the shallows, that is to say, the conversation should not be commenced by broadly and roundly stating a fact, or didactically expressing an opinion, as the subject would be thus virtually or summarily disposed of, or perhaps be met with a ' Really ' or ' Indeed,' or some equally brief monosyllabic reply. If an opposite opinion were held by the person to whom the remark were addressed, he might not, if a stranger, care to express it in the form of a direct contradiction, or actual dissent. To glide imperceptibly into conversation is the object to be attained."

At this point Mr. Kipps rubbed his fingers through his hair with an expression of some perplexity and went back to the beginning.

§ 4

When Kipps made his call on the Walshinghams, it all happened so differently from the " Manners and Rules " prescription (" Paying Calls ") that he was quite lost from the very outset. Instead of the footman or maidservant proper in these cases, Miss Walshingham opened the door to him herself. "I'm so glad you've come," she said, with one of her rare smiles.

She stood aside for him to enter the rather narrow passage.

"I thought I'd call," he said, retaining his hat and stick.

She closed the door and led the way to a little drawing-room, which impressed Kipps as being smaller and less emphatically coloured than that of the Cootes, and in which at first only a copper bowl of white poppies upon the brown tablecloth caught his particular attention.

"You won't think it unconventional to come in, Mr. Kipps, will you?" she remarked. "Mother is out."

"I don't mind," he said, smiling amiably, "if you don't."

She walked round the table and stood regarding him across it, with that same look between speculative curiosity and appreciation that he remembered from the last of the art class meetings.

"I wondered whether you would call or whether you wouldn't before you left Folkestone."

"I'm not leaving Folkestone for a bit, and any'ow, I should have called on you."

"Mother will be sorry she was out. I've told her about you, and she wants, I know, to meet you."

"I saw 'er—if that was 'er—in the shop," said Kipps.

"Yes—you did, didn't you! . . . She has gone out to make some duty calls, and I didn't go. I had something to write. I write a little, you know."

"Reely!" said Kipps.

"It's nothing much," she said, "and it comes to nothing." She glanced at a little desk near the window, on which there lay some paper. "One must do something." She broke off abruptly. "Have you seen our outlook?" she asked, and walked to the window, and Kipps came and stood beside her. "We look on the Square. It might be worse, you know. That outporter's truck there is horrid—and the railings, but it's better than staring one's social replica in the face, isn't it? It's pleasant in early spring—bright green laid on with a dry brush—and it's pleasant in autumn."

"I like it," said Kipps. "That laylock there is pretty, isn't it?"

"Children come and pick it at times," she remarked.

"I dessay they do," said Kipps.

He rested on his hat and stick and looked appreciatively out of the window, and she glanced at him for one swift moment. A suggestion that might have come from "The Art of Conversing" came into his head. "Have you a garden?" he said.

She shrugged her shoulders. "Only a little one," she said, and then, "perhaps you would like to see it."

"I like gardenin'," said Kipps, with memories of a pennyworth of nasturtiums he had once trained over his uncle's dustbin.

She led the way with a certain relief.

They emerged through a four-seasons coloured glass door to a little iron veranda that led by iron steps to a minute walled garden. There was just room for a patch of turf and a flower-bed; one sturdy variegated Euonymus grew in the corner. But the early June flowers, the big narcissus, snow-upon-the-mountains, and a fine show of yellow wallflowers shone gay.

"That's our garden," said Helen. "It's not a very big one, is it?"

"I like it," said Kipps.

"It's small," she said, "but this is the day of small things."

Kipps didn't follow that.

"If you were writing when I came," he remarked, "I'm interrupting you."

She turned round with her back to the railing and rested, leaning on her hands. "I had finished," she said. "I couldn't get on."

"Were you making up something?" asked Kipps.

There was a little interval before she smiled. "I try—quite vainly—to write stories," she said. "One must do something. I don't know whether I shall ever do any good—at that—anyhow. It seems so hopeless. And, of course, one must study the popular taste. But now my brother has gone to London, I get a lot of leisure."

"I seen your brother, 'aven't I?"

"He came to the class once or twice. Very probably you have. He's gone to London to pass his examinations and become a solicitor. And then, I suppose, he'll have a chance. Not much, perhaps, even then. But he's luckier than I am."

"You got your classes and things."

"They ought to satisfy me. But they don't. I suppose I'm ambitious. We both are. And we hadn't much of a springboard." She glanced over his shoulder at the cramped little garden with an air of reference in her gesture.

"I should think you could do anything if you wanted to," said Kipps.

"As a matter of fact I can't do anything I want to."

"You done a good deal."

"What?"

"Well, didn't you pass one of these here University things?"

"Oh! I matriculated!"

"I should think I was no end of a swell if *I* did, I know that."

"Mr. Kipps, do you know how many people matriculate into London University every year?"

"How many then?"

"Between two and three thousand."

"Well, just think how many don't!"

Her smile came again, and broke into a laugh. "Oh, *they* don't count," she said, and then realising that might penetrate Kipps if he was left with it, she hurried on to, "The fact is, I'm a discontented person, Mr. Kipps. Folkestone, you know, is a Sea Front, and it values people by sheer vulgar prosperity. We're not prosperous and we live in a back street. We have to live here because this is our house. It's a mercy we haven't to 'let.' One feels one hasn't opportunities. If one had, I suppose one wouldn't use them. Still——"

Kipps felt he was being taken tremendously into her confidence. "That's jest it," he said, very sagely.

He leant forward on his stick and said, very earnestly, "I believe you could do anything you wanted to, if you tried."

She threw out her hands in disavowal.

"I know," said he, very sagely, and nodding his head. "I watched you once or twice when you were teaching that wood-carving class."

For some reason this made her laugh—a rather pleasant laugh, and that made Kipps feel a very witty and successful person. "It's very evident," she said, "that you're one of those rare people who believe in me, Mr. Kipps," to which he answered, "Oo, I *do!*" and then suddenly they became aware of Mrs. Walshingham coming along the passage. In another moment she appeared through the four-seasons door, bonneted and ladylike and a little faded, exactly as Kipps had seen her in the shop. Kipps felt a certain apprehension at her appearance, in spite of the reassurances he had had from Coote.

"Mr. Kipps has called on us," said Helen, and Mrs. Walshingham said it was very kind of him, and added that new people didn't call on them very much nowadays. There was nothing of the scandalised surprise Kipps had seen in the shop; she had heard, perhaps, he was a gentleman now. In the shop he had thought her

rather jaded and haughty, but he had scarcely taken her
hand, which responded to his touch with a friendly
pressure, before he knew how mistaken he had been.
She then told her daughter that someone called Mrs.
Wace had been out, and turned to Kipps again to ask
him if he had had tea. Kipps said he had not, and
Helen moved towards some mysterious interior. " But
I say," said Kipps; " don't you on my account——!"

Helen vanished, and he found himself alone with
Mrs. Walshingham. Which, of course, made him
breathless and Boreas-looking for a moment.

"You were one of Helen's pupils in the wood-carving
class?" asked Mrs. Walshingham, regarding him with
the quiet watchfulness proper to her position.

" Yes," said Kipps, " that's 'ow I 'ad the pleasure
——"

" She took a great interest in her wood-carving class.
She is so energetic, you know, and it gives her an
Outlet."

" I thought she taught something splendid!"

" Everyone says she did very well. Helen, I think,
would do anything well that she undertook to do.
She's so very clever. And she throws herself into
things so."

She untied her bonnet strings with a pleasant in-
formality.

" She has told me all about her class. She used to
be full of it. And about your cut hand."

" Lor'!" said Kipps; " fancy telling that!"

" Oh, yes! And how brave you were."

(Though, indeed, Helen's chief detail had been his
remarkable expedient for checking bloodshed.)

Kipps became bright pink. " She said you didn't
seem to feel it a bit."

Kipps felt he would have to spend weeks over " The
Art of Conversing."

While he still hung fire Helen returned with the
apparatus for afternoon tea upon a tray.

"Do you mind pulling out the table?" asked Mrs.
Walshingham.

That, again, was very homelike. Kipps put down his
hat and stick in the corner and, amidst an iron thunder,
pulled out a little rusty, green-painted table, and then
in the easiest manner followed Helen in to get chairs.

So soon as he had got rid of his teacup—he refused
all food, of course, and they were merciful—he became
wonderfully at his ease. Presently he was talking. He
talked quite modestly and simply about his changed
condition and his difficulties and plans. He spread
what indeed had an air of being all his simple little soul
before their eyes. In a while his clipped, defective
accent had become less perceptible to their ears, and
they began to realise, as the girl with the freckles had
long since realised, that there were passable aspects of
Kipps. He confided, he submitted; and for both of
them he had the reallest, the most seductively flattering
undertone of awe and reverence.

He remained about two hours, having forgotten how
terribly incorrect it is to stay at such a length. They
did not mind at all.

CHAPTER THE THIRD

Engaged

§ 1

WITHIN two months, within a matter of three and fifty days, Kipps had clambered to the battlements of Heart's Desire.

It all became possible by the Walshinghams—it would seem at Coote's instigation—deciding, after all, not to spend the holidays at Bruges. Instead, they remained in Folkestone, and this happy chance gave Kipps just all those opportunities of which he stood in need.

His crowning day was at Lympne, and long before the summer warmth began to break, while indeed August still flamed on high. They had organised— no one seemed to know who suggested it first—a water party on the still reaches of the old military canal at Hythe, the canal that was to have stopped Napoleon if the sea failed us, and they were to picnic by the brick bridge, and afterwards to clamber to Lympne

185

Castle. The host of the gathering, it was understood very clearly, was Kipps.

They went, a merry party. The canal was weedy with only a few inches of water at the shallows, and so they went in three Canadian canoes. Kipps had learned to paddle—it had been his first athletic accomplishment, and his second—with the last three or four of ten private lessons still to come—was to be cycling. But Kipps did not paddle at all badly; muscles hardened by lifting pieces of cretonne could cut a respectable figure by the side of Coote's exertions, and the girl with the freckles, the girl who understood him, came in his canoe. They raced the Walshinghams, brother and sister; and Coote, in a liquefying state and blowing mightily, but still persistent and always quite polite and considerate, toiled behind with Mrs. Walshingham. She could not be expected to paddle (though, of course, she " offered ") and she reclined upon specially adjusted cushions under a black and white sunshade and watched Kipps and her daughter, and feared at intervals that Coote was getting hot.

They were all more or less in holiday costume, the eyes of the girls looked out under the shade of wide-brimmed hats; even the freckled girl was unexpectedly pretty, and Helen, swinging sunlit to her paddle, gave Kipps, almost for the first time, the suggestion of a graceful body. Kipps was arrayed in the completest boating costume, and when his fashionable Panama was discarded and his hair blown into disorder he became, in his white flannels, as sightly as most young men. His complexion was a notable asset.

Things favoured him, the day favoured him, everyone favoured him. Young Walshingham, the girl with the freckles, Coote and Mrs. Walshingham, were playing up to him in the most benevolent way, and between the landing place and Lympne, Fortune, to crown their efforts, had placed a small convenient field entirely at the disposal of an adolescent bull. Not a big, real, resolute bull, but, on the other hand, no calf; a young bull, at the same stage of emotional development as Kipps, "standing where brook and river meet." Detachedly our party drifted towards him.

When they landed, young Walshingham, with the simple directness of a brother, abandoned his sister to Kipps and secured the freckled girl, leaving Coote to carry Mrs. Walshingham's light wool wrap. He started at once, in order to put an effectual distance between himself and his companions, on the one hand, and a certain pervasive chaperonage that went with Coote, on the other. Young Walshingham, I think I have said, was dark, with a Napoleonic profile, and it was natural for him, therefore, to be a bold thinker and an epigrammatic speaker, and he had long ago discovered great possibilities of appreciation in the freckled girl. He was in a very happy frame that day because he had just been entrusted with the management of Kipps' affairs (old Bean inexplicably dismissed), and that was not a bad beginning for a solicitor of only a few months' standing, and, moreover, he had been reading Nietzsche, and he thought that in all probability he was the Non-Moral Overman referred to by that writer. He wore fairly large-sized hats. He wanted to expand the theme of the Non-Moral Overman in the ear of the freckled girl, to say it over, so to speak, and in order to seclude his exposition they went aside from the direct path and trespassed through a coppice, avoiding the youthful bull. They escaped to these higher themes but narrowly, for Coote and Mrs. Walshingham, subtle chaperons both, and each indisposed for excellent reasons to encumber Kipps and Helen, were hot upon their heels. These two kept the direct route to the stile of the bull's field, and the sight of the animal at once awakened Coote's innate aversion to brutality in any shape or form. He said the stiles were too high, and that they could do better by going round by the hedge, and Mrs. Walshingham, nothing loath, agreed.

This left the way clear for Kipps and Helen, and

they encountered the bull. Helen did not observe the
bull, Kipps did; but that afternoon at any rate, he
was equal to facing a lion. And the bull really came at
them. It was not an affair of the bull-ring exactly, no
desperate rushes and gorings; but he came; he regarded
them with a large, wicked, bluish eye, opened a mouth
below his moistly glistening nose and booed, at any
rate, if he did not exactly bellow; and he shook his
head wickedly and showed that tossing was in his mind.
Helen was frightened, without any loss of dignity, and
Kipps went extremely white. But he was perfectly
calm, and he seemed to her to have lost the last vestiges
of his accent and his social shakiness. He told her to
walk quietly to the stile, and made an oblique advance
towards the bull.

"You be orf!" he said. . . .

When Helen was well over the stile Kipps withdrew in good order. He got over the stile under cover
of a feint, and the thing was done—a small thing, no
doubt, but just enough to remove from Helen's mind
an incorrect deduction that a man who was so terribly
afraid of a teacup as Kipps must necessarily be abjectly
afraid of everything else in the world. In her moment
of reaction she went perhaps too far in the opposite
direction. Hitherto Kipps had always had a certain
flimsiness of effect for her. Now suddenly he was discovered solid. He was discovered possible in many new
ways. Here, after all, was the sort of back a woman
can get behind! . . .

As they went past the turf-crowned mass of Portus
Lemanus up the steep slopes towards the castle on the
crest, the thing was almost manifest in her eyes.

§ 2

Everyone who stays in Folkestone goes sooner or
later to Lympne. The castle became a farmhouse long
ago, and the farmhouse, itself now ripe and venerable,

wears the walls of the castle as a little man wears a big man's coat. The kindliest of farm ladies entertains a perpetual stream of visitors, and shows her vast mangle and her big kitchen, and takes you out upon the sunniest little terrace garden in all the world, and you look down the sheep-dotted slopes to where, beside the canal and under the trees, the crumpled memories of Rome sleep for ever. For hither to this lonely spot the galleys once came, the legions, the emperors, masters of the world. The castle is but a thing of yesterday, King Stephen's time or thereabouts, in that retrospect. One climbs the Keep, up a tortuous spiral of stone, worn now to the pitch of perforation, and there one is lifted to the centre of far more than a hemisphere of view. Away below one's feet, almost at the bottom of the hill, the Marsh begins, and spreads and spreads in a mighty crescent that sweeps about the sea, the Marsh dotted with the church towers of forgotten medieval towns and breaking at last into the low blue hills of Winchelsea and Hastings; east hangs France, between the sea and the sky, and round the north, bounding the wide perspective of farms and houses and woods, the Downs, with their hangers and chalk-pits, sustain the passing shadows of the sailing clouds.

And here it was, high out of the world of every day, and in the presence of spacious beauty, that Kipps and Helen found themselves agreeably alone. All six, it had seemed, had been coming for the Keep, but Mrs. Walshingham had hesitated at the horrid little stairs, and then suddenly felt faint, and so she and the freckled girl had remained below, walking up and down in the shadow of the house, and Coote had remembered they were all out of cigarettes, and had taken off young Walshingham into the village. There had been shouting to explain between ground and parapet, and then Helen and Kipps turned again to the view, and commended it and fell silent.

Helen sat fearlessly in an embrasure, and Kipps stood beside her.

"I've always been fond of scenery," Kipps repeated, after an interval.

Then he went off at a tangent. "D'you reely think that was right what Coote was saying?"

She looked interrogation.

"About my name."

"Being really C-U-Y-P-S? I have my doubts. I thought at first—— What makes Mr. Coote add an S to Cuyp?"

"I dunno," said Kipps, foiled. "I was jest thinking——"

She shot one wary glance at him and then turned her eyes to the sea.

Kipps was out for a space. He had intended to lead from this question to the general question of surnames and change of names; it had seemed a light and witty way of saying something he had in mind, and suddenly he perceived that this was an unutterably vulgar and silly project. The hitch about that "S" had saved him. He regarded her profile for a moment, framed in weather-beaten stone, and backed by the blue elements.

He dropped the question of his name out of existence and spoke again of the view. "When I see scenery—and things that—that are beautiful, it makes me feel——"

She looked at him suddenly, and saw him fumbling for his words.

"Silly like," he said.

She took him in with her glance, the old look of proprietorship it was, touched with a certain warmth. She spoke in a voice as unambiguous as her eyes. "You needn't," she said. "You know, Mr. Kipps, you hold yourself too cheap."

Her eyes and words smote him with amazement. He stared at her like a man who awakens. She looked down.

"You mean——" he said; and then, "don't you hold me cheap?"

She glanced up again and shook her head.

"But—for instance—you don't think of me—as an equal like."

"Why not?"

"Oo! But reely——"

His heart beat very fast.

"If I thought," he said; and then, "you know so much."

"That's nothing," she said.

Then for a long time, as it seemed to them, both kept silence, a silence that said and accomplished many things.

"I know what I am," he said at length. . . . "If I thought it was possible . . . if I thought *you* . . . I believe I could do anything——"

He stopped, and she sat downcast and strikingly still.

"Miss Walshingham," he said, "is it possible that you . . . could care for me enough to—to 'elp me? Miss Walshingham, do you care for me at all?"

It seemed she was never going to answer. She looked up at him. "I think," she said, "you are the most generous—look at what you have done for my brother! —the most generous and the most modest of men. And this afternoon—I thought you were the bravest."

She turned her head, glanced down, waved her hand to someone on the terrace below, and stood up.

"Mother is signalling," she said. "We must go down."

Kipps became polite and deferential by habit, but his mind was a tumult that had nothing to do with that.

He moved before her towards the little door that opened on the winding stairs—"always precede a lady down or up stairs"—and then on the second step he turned resolutely. "But," he said, looking up out of the shadow, flannel-clad and singularly like a man.

She looked down on him, with her hand upon the stone lintel.

7

He held out his hand as if to help her. "Can you tell me?" he said. "You must know——"

"What?"

"If you care for me?"

She did not answer for a long time. It was as if everything in the world was drawn to the breaking point, and in a minute must certainly break.

"Yes," she said, at last, "I know."

Abruptly, by some impalpable sign, he knew what the answer would be, and he remained still.

She bent down over him and softened to her wonderful smile.

"Promise me," she insisted.

He promised with his still face.

"If *I* do not hold you cheap, you will never hold yourself cheap——"

"If you do not hold me cheap! You mean——?"

She bent down quite close beside him. "I hold you," she said, and then whispered, " *dear*."

"Me?"

She laughed aloud.

He was astonished beyond measure. He stipulated, lest there might be some misconception, "You will marry me?"

She was laughing, inundated by the sense of bountiful power, of possession and success. He looked quite a nice little man to have. "Yes," she laughed. "What else could I mean?" and, "Yes."

He felt as a praying hermit might have felt, snatched from the midst of his quiet devotions, his modest sackcloth and ashes, and hurled neck and crop over the glittering gates of Paradise, smack among the iridescent wings, the bright-eyed Cherubim. He felt like some lowly and righteous man dynamited into Bliss. . . .

His hand tightened upon the rope that steadies one upon the stairs of stone. He was for kissing her hand and did not.

He said not a word more. He turned about, and

with something very like a scared expression on his face led the way into the obscurity of their descent.

§ 3

Everyone seemed to understand. Nothing was said, nothing was explained, the merest touch of the eyes sufficed. As they clustered in the castle gateway Coote, Kipps remembered afterward, laid hold of his arm as if by chance and pressed it. It was quite evident he knew. His eyes, his nose, shone with benevolent congratulations, shone, too, with the sense of a good thing conducted to its climax. Mrs. Walshingham, who had seemed a little fatigued by the hill, recovered, and was even obviously stirred by affection for her daughter. There was, in passing, a motherly caress. She asked Kipps to give her his arm in walking down the steep. Kipps in a sort of dream obeyed. He found himself trying to attend to her, and soon he was attending.

She and Kipps talked like sober, responsible people and went slowly, while the others drifted down the hill together, a loose little group of four. He wondered momentarily what they would talk about, and then sank into his conversation with Mrs. Walshingham. He conversed, as it were, out of his superficial personality, and his inner self lay stunned in unsuspected depths within. It had an air of being an interesting and friendly talk, almost their first long talk together. Hitherto he had had a sort of fear of Mrs. Walshingham, as of a person possibly satirical; but she proved a soul of sense and sentiment, and Kipps, for all of his abstraction, got on with her unexpectedly well. They talked a little upon scenery and the inevitable melancholy attaching to old ruins and the thought of vanished generations.

" Perhaps they jousted here," said Mrs. Walshingham.

" They was up to all sorts of things," said Kipps, and then the two came round to Helen. She spoke of her daughter's literary ambitions. "She will do some-thing, I feel sure. You know, Mr. Kipps, it's a great responsibility to a mother to feel her daughter is—exceptionally clever."

"I dessay it is," said Kipps. "There's no mistake about that."

She spoke, too, of her son—almost like Helen's twin—alike, yet different. She made Kipps feel quite fatherly. "They are so quick, so artistic," she said, "so full of ideas. Almost they frighten me. One feels they need opportunities—as other people need air."

She spoke of Helen's writing. "Even when she was quite a little dot she wrote verse."

(Kipps, sensation.)

"Her father had just the same tastes—" Mrs. Walshingham turned a little beam of half-pathetic reminiscence on the past. "He was more artist than business man. That was the trouble. . . . He was misled by his partner, and when the crash came every-one blamed him. . . . Well, it doesn't do to dwell on horrid things—especially to-day. There are bright days, Mr. Kipps, and dark days. And mine have not always been bright."

Kipps presented a face of Coote-like sympathy.

She diverged to talk of flowers, and Kipps' mind was filled with the picture of Helen bending down towards him in the Keep. . . .

They spread the tea under the trees before the little inn, and at a certain moment Kipps became aware that everyone in the party was simultaneously and furtively glancing at him. There might have been a certain tension had it not been first of all for Coote and his tact, and afterwards for a number of wasps. Coote was resolved to make this memorable day pass off well, and displayed an almost boisterous sense of fun. Then young Walshingham began talking of the Roman remains below Lympne, intending to lead up to the Overman.

" These old Roman chaps," he said, and then the wasps arrived. They killed three in the jam alone.

Kipps killed wasps as it were in a dream, and handed things to the wrong people, and maintained a thin surface of ordinary intelligence with the utmost difficulty. At times he became aware, aware with an extraordinary vividness, of Helen. Helen was carefully not looking at him and behaving with amazing coolness and ease. But just for that one time there was the faintest suggestion of pink beneath the ivory of her cheeks. . . .

Tacitly the others conceded to Kipps the right to paddle back with Helen; he helped her into the canoe and took his paddle, and, paddling slowly, dropped behind the others. And now his inner self stirred again. He said nothing to her. How could he ever say anything to her again? She spoke to him at rare intervals about reflections and the flowers and the trees and he nodded in reply. But his mind moved very slowly forward now from the point at which it had fallen stunned in the Lympne Keep, moving forward to the beginnings of realisation. As yet he did not say even in the recesses of his heart that she was his. But he perceived that the goddess had come from her altar, amazingly, and had taken him by the hand!

The sky was a vast splendour, and then close to them were the dark, protecting trees and the shining, smooth, still water. He was an erect black outline to her; he plied his paddle with no unskilful gesture, the water broke to snaky silver and glittered far behind his strokes. Indeed, he did not seem so bad to her. Youth calls to youth the wide world through, and her soul rose in triumph over his subjection. And behind him was money and opportunity, freedom and London, a great background of seductively indistinct hopes. To him her face was a warm dimness. In truth he could not see her eyes, but it seemed to his love-witched brain he did, and that they shone out at him like dusky stars.

All the world that evening was no more than a

shadowy frame of darkling sky and water and dipping boughs about Helen. He seemed to see through things with an extraordinary clearness; she was revealed to him, certainly, as the cause and essence of it all.

He was indeed at his Heart's Desire. It was one of those times when there seems to be no future, when Time has stopped and we are at the end. Kipps, that evening, could not have imagined a to-morrow; all that his imagination had pointed towards was attained. His mind stood still, and took the moments as they came.

§ 4

About nine that night Coote came round to Kipps' new apartment in the Upper Sandgate Road—the house on the Leas had been let furnished—and Kipps made an effort toward realisation. He was discovered sitting at the open window and without a lamp, quite still. Coote was deeply moved, and he pressed Kipps' palm and laid a knobbly white hand on his shoulder and displayed the sort of tenderness becoming in a crisis. Kipps too was moved that night, and treated Coote like a very dear brother.

" She's splendid," said Coote, coming to it abruptly.

" Isn't she?" said Kipps.

" I couldn't help noticing her face," said Coote. . . . " You know, my dear Kipps, this is better than a legacy."

" I don't deserve it," said Kipps.

" You can't say that."

" I don't. I can't 'ardly believe it. I can't believe it at all. No!"

There followed an expressive stillness.

" It's wonderful," said Kipps. " It takes me like that."

Coote made a faint blowing noise, and so again they came for a time on silence.

" And it began—before your money?"

"When I was in 'er class," said Kipps solemnly.

Coote, speaking out of a darkness which he was illuminating strangely with efforts to strike a match, said that it was beautiful. He could not have *wished* Kipps a better fortune. . . .

He lit a cigarette, and Kipps was moved to do the same, with a sacramental expression. Presently speech flowed more freely.

Coote began to praise Helen and her mother and brother. He talked of when "it" might be, he presented the thing as concrete and credible. "It's a county family, you know," he said. "She is connected, you know, with the Beaupres family—you know Lord Beaupres."

"No!" said Kipps, "reely!"

"Distantly, of course," said Coote. "Still——"

He smiled a smile that glimmered in the twilight.

"It's too much," said Kipps, overcome. "It's so all like that."

Coote exhaled. For a time Kipps listened to Helen's praises and matured a point of view.

"I say, Coote," he said. "What ought I to do now?"

"What do you mean?" said Coote.

"I mean about calling on 'er and all that."

He reflected. "Naturally, I want to do it all right."

"Of course," said Coote.

"It would be awful to go and do something—now—all wrong."

Coote's cigarette glowed as he meditated. "You must call, of course," he decided. "You'll have to speak to Mrs. Walshingham."

"'Ow?" said Kipps.

"Tell her you mean to marry her daughter."

"I dessay she knows," said Kipps, with defensive penetration.

Coote's head was visible, shaking itself judicially.

"Then there's the ring," said Kipps. "What 'ave I to do about that?"

"What ring do you mean?"

"'Ngagement Ring. There isn't anything at all about that in 'Manners and Rules of Good Society'— not a word."

"Of course you must get something—tasteful. Yes."

"What sort of a ring?"

"Something nace. They'll show you in the shop."

"Of course. I s'pose I got to take it to 'er, eh? Put it on 'er finger."

"Oh, no! Send it. Much better."

"Ah!" said Kipps, for the first time with a note of relief.

"Then, 'ow about this call—on Mrs. Walshingham, I mean? 'Ow ought one to go?"

"Rather a ceremonial occasion," reflected Coote.

"Wadyer mean? Frock coat?"

"I *think* so," said Coote, with discrimination.

"Light trousers and all that?"

"Yes."

"Rose?"

"I think it might run to a buttonhole."

The curtain that hung over the future became less opaque to the eyes of Kipps. To-morrow, and then other days, became perceptible at least as existing. Frock coat, silk hat and a rose! With a certain solemnity he contemplated himself in the process of slow transformation into an English gentleman. Arthur Cuyps, frock-coated on occasions of ceremony, the familiar acquaintance of Lady Punnet, the recognised wooer of a distant connection of the Earl of Beaupres.

Something like awe at the magnitude of his own fortune came upon him. He felt the world was open-ing out like a magic flower in a transformation scene at the touch of this wand of gold. And Helen, nestling beautiful in the red heart of the flower. Only ten weeks ago he had been no more than the shabbiest of improvers and shamefully dismissed for dissipation, the mere soil-buried seed, as it were, of these glories. He resolved the engagement ring should be of expressively excessive quality and appearance, in fact the very best they had.

"Ought I to send 'er flowers?" he speculated.

"Not necessarily," said Coote. "Though, of course, it's an attention. . . ."

Kipps meditated on flowers.

"When you see her," said Coote, "you'll have to ask her to name the day."

Kipps started. "That won't be just yet a bit, will it?"

"Don't know any reason for delay."

"Oo, but—a year, say."

"Rather a long taime," said Coote.

"Is it?" said Kipps, turning his head sharply. "But——"

There was quite a long pause.

"I say!" he said at last, and in an altered voice, "you'll 'ave to 'elp me about the wedding."

"Only too happy," said Coote.

"Of course," said Kipps, "I didn't think——" He changed his line of thought. "Coote," he asked, "wot's a 'tate-eh-tate'?"

"A 'tate-ah-tay'!" said Coote improvingly, "is a conversation alone together."

"Lor'!" said Kipps, "but I thought— It says *strictly* we oughtn't to enjoy a tater-tay, not sit together, walk together, ride together or meet during any part of the day. That don't leave much time for meeting, does it?"

"The book says that?" asked Coote.

"I jest learnt it by 'eart before you came. I thought that was a bit rum, but I s'pose it's all right."

"You won't find Mrs. Walshingham so strict as all that," said Coote. "I think that's a bit extreme. They'd only do that now in very strict old aristocratic

7*

families. Besides, the Walshinghams are so modern—
advanced, you might say. I expect you'll get plenty of
chances of talking together."

"There's a tremendous lot to think about," said
Kipps, blowing a profound sigh. "D'you mean—
p'r'aps we might be married in a few months or so."

"You'll *have* to be," said Coote. "Why not? . . ."

Midnight found Kipps alone, looking a little tired
and turning over the leaves of the red-covered textbook
with a studious expression. He paused for a moment
at page 233, his eye caught by the words:

"FOR AN UNCLE OR AUNT BY MARRIAGE
the period is six weeks black, with jet trimmings."

"No," said Kipps, after a vigorous mental effort.
"That's not it." The pages rustled again. He
stopped and flattened out the little book decisively at
the beginning of the chapter on "Weddings."

He became pensive. He stared at the lamp wick.
"I suppose I ought to go over and tell them," he said
at last.

§ 5

Kipps called on Mrs. Walshingham, attired in the
proper costume for Ceremonial Occasions in the Day.
He carried a silk hat, and he wore a deep-skirted frock
coat, his boots were patent leather and his trousers dark
grey. He had generous white cuffs with gold links, and
his grey gloves, one thumb of which had burst when he
put them on, he held loosely in his hand. He carried a
small umbrella rolled to an exquisite tightness. A sense
of singular correctness pervaded his being and warred
with the enormity of the occasion for possession of his
soul. Anon he touched his silk cravat. The world
smelt of his rosebud.

He seated himself on a newly re-covered chintz armchair and stuck out the elbow of the arm that held
his hat.

"I know," said Mrs. Walshingham, "I know everything," and helped him out most amazingly. She deepened the impression he had already received of her sense and refinement. She displayed an amount of tenderness that touched him.

"This is a great thing," she said, "to a mother," and her hand rested for a moment on his impeccable coat sleeve.

"A daughter, Arthur," she explained, "is so much more than a son."

Marriage, she said, was a lottery, and without love and toleration there was much unhappiness. Her life had not always been bright—there had been dark days and bright days. She smiled rather sweetly. "This is a bright one," she said.

She said very kind and flattering things to Kipps, and she thanked him for his goodness to her son. ("That wasn't anything," said Kipps.) And then she expanded upon the theme of her two children. "Both so accomplished," she said, "so clever. I call them my Twin Jewels."

She was repeating a remark she had made at Lympne, that she always said her children needed opportunities as other people needed air, when she was abruptly arrested by the entry of Helen. They hung on a pause, Helen perhaps surprised by Kipps' weekday magnificence. Then she advanced with outstretched hand.

Both the young people were shy. "I jest called round," began Kipps, and became uncertain how to end.

"Won't you have some tea?" asked Helen.

She walked to the window, looked at the familiar outporter's barrow, turned, surveyed Kipps for a moment ambiguously, said, "I will get some tea," and so departed again.

Mrs. Walshingham and Kipps looked at one another and the lady smiled indulgently. "You two young people mustn't be shy of each other," said Mrs. Walshingham, which damaged Kipps considerably.

She was explaining how sensitive Helen always had been, even about quite little things, when the servant appeared with the tea things; and then Helen followed, and taking up a secure position behind the bamboo tea table, broke the ice with officious teacup clattering. Then she introduced the topic of a forthcoming open-air performance of "As You Like It," and steered past the worst of the awkwardness. They discussed stage illusion. "I mus' say," said Kipps, "I don't quite like a play in a theayter. It seems sort of unreal, some'ow."

"But most plays are written for the stage," said Helen, looking at the sugar.

"I know," admitted Kipps.

They got through tea. "Well," said Kipps, and rose.

"You mustn't go yet," said Mrs. Walshingham, rising and taking his hand. "I'm sure you two must have heaps to say to each other," and so she escaped towards the door.

§ 6

Among other projects that seemed almost equally correct to Kipps at that exalted moment was one of embracing Helen with ardour so soon as the door closed behind her mother, and one of headlong flight through the open window. Then he remembered he ought to hold the door open for Mrs. Walshingham, and turned from that duty to find Helen still standing, beautifully inaccessible, behind the tea things. He closed the door and advanced towards her with his arms akimbo and his hands upon his coat skirts. Then, feeling angular, he moved his right hand to his moustache. Anyhow, he was dressed all right. Somewhere at the back of his mind, dim and mingled with doubt and surprise, appeared the perception that he felt now quite differently towards her, that something between them

had been blown from Lympne Keep to the four winds
of heaven. . . .

She regarded him with an eye of critical proprietorship.

"Mother has been making up to you," she said,
smiling slightly.

She added, "It was nice of you to come round to
see her."

They stood through a brief pause, as though each
had expected something different in the other and
was perplexed at its not being there. Kipps found he
was at the corner of the brown-covered table, and he
picked up a little flexible book that lay upon it to
occupy his mind.

"I bought you a ring to-day," he said, bending the
book and speaking for the sake of saying something, and
then he was moved to genuine speech. "You know,"
he said, "I can't 'ardly believe it."

Her face relaxed slightly again. "No?" she said,
and may have breathed. "Nor I."

"No," he went on. "It's as though everything 'ad
changed. More even than when I got my money.
'Ere we are going to marry. It's like being someone
else. What I feel is——"

He turned a flushed and earnest face to her. He
seemed to come alive to her with one natural gesture.
"I don't *know* things. I'm not good enough. I'm not
refined. The more you see of me the more you'll find
me out."

"But I'm going to help you."

"You'll 'ave to 'elp me a fearful lot."

She walked to the window, glanced out of it, made
up her mind, turned and came towards him, with her
hands clasped behind her back.

"All these things that trouble you are very little
things. If you don't mind—if you will let me tell you
things——"

"I wish you would."

"Then I will."

"They're little things to you, but they aren't to me."

"It all depends, if you don't mind being told."

"By you?"

"I don't expect you to be told by strangers."

"Oo!" said Kipps, expressing much.

"You know, there are just a few little things. For instance, you know, you are careless with your pronunciation. . . . You don't mind my telling you?"

"I like it," said Kipps.

"There are aitches."

"I know," said Kipps, and then, endorsingly, "I been told. Fact is, I know a chap, a Nacter, *he's* told me. He's told me, and he's going to give me a lesson or so."

"I'm glad of that. It only requires a little care."

"Of course, on the stage they got to look out. They take regular lessons."

"Of course," said Helen, a little absently.

"I dessay I shall soon get into it," said Kipps.

"And then there's dress," said Helen, taking up her thread again.

Kipps became pink, but he remained respectfully attentive.

"You don't mind?" she said.

"Oo, no."

"You mustn't be too—too dressy. It's possible to be over-conventional, over-elaborate. It makes you look like a shop—like a common, well-off person. There's a sort of easiness that is better. A real gentleman looks right, without looking as though he had tried to be right."

"Jest as though 'e'd put on what came first?" said the pupil, in a faded voice.

"Not exactly that, but a sort of ease."

Kipps nodded his head intelligently. In his heart

he was kicking his silk hat about the room in an ecstasy of disappointment.

"And you must accustom yourself to be more at your ease when you are with people," said Helen. "You've only got to forget yourself a little and not be anxious——"

"I'll try," said Kipps, looking rather hard at the teapot. "I'll do my best to try."

"I know you will," she said, and laid a hand for an instant upon his shoulder and withdrew it.

He did not perceive her caress. "One has to learn," he said. His attention was distracted by the strenuous efforts that were going on in the back of his head to translate, "I say, didn't you ought to name the day?" into easy as well as elegant English, a struggle that was still undecided when the time came for them to part. . . .

He sat for a long time at the open window of his sitting-room with an intent face, recapitulating that interview. His eyes rested at last almost reproachfully on the silk hat beside him. "'Ow *is* one to know?" he asked. His attention was caught by a rubbed place in the nap, and, still thoughtful, he rolled up his handkerchief skilfully into a soft ball and began to smooth this down.

His expression changed slowly.

"'Ow the Juice is one to know?" he said, putting down the hat with some emphasis.

He rose up, went across the room to the sideboard, and, standing there, opened and began to read in "Manners and Rules."

CHAPTER THE FOURTH

The Bicycle Manufacturer

§ 1

SO Kipps embarked upon his engagement, steeled himself to the high enterprise of marrying above his breeding. The next morning found him dressing with a certain quiet severity of movement, and it seemed to his landlady's housemaid that he was unusually dignified at breakfast. He meditated profoundly over his kipper and his kidney and bacon. He was going to New Romney to tell the old people what had happened and where he stood. And the love of Helen had also given him courage to do what Buggins had once suggested to him as a thing he would do were he in Kipps' place, and that was to hire a motor car for the afternoon. He had an early cold lunch, and then, with an air of quiet resolution, assumed a cap and coat he had purchased to this end, and thus equipped strolled round, blowing slightly, to the motor shop. The transaction was un-

206

expectedly easy, and within the hour Kipps, spectacled and wrapped about, was tootling through Dymchurch.

They came to a stop smartly and neatly outside the little toy shop. "Make that thing 'oot a bit, will you?" said Kipps. "Yes, that's it." "Whup," said the motor car. "Whurrup!"

Both his Aunt and Uncle came out on the pavement. "Why, it's Artie," cried his Aunt, and Kipps had a moment of triumph.

He descended to hand claspings, removed wraps and spectacles, and the motor driver retired to take "an hour off." Old Kipps surveyed the machinery and disconcerted Kipps for a moment by asking him in a knowing tone what they asked him for a thing like that. The two men stood inspecting the machine and impressing the neighbours for a time, and then they strolled through the shop into the little parlour for a drink.

"They ain't settled," old Kipps had said at the neighbours. "They ain't got no further than experiments. There's a bit of take-in about each. You take my advice and wait, me boy, even if it's a year or two, before you buy one for your own use."

(Though Kipps had said nothing of doing anything of the sort.)

"'Ow d'you like that whisky I sent?" asked Kipps, dodging the old familiar bunch of children's pails.

Old Kipps became tactful. "It's a very good whisky, my boy," said old Kipps. "I 'aven't the slightest doubt it's a very good whisky and cost you a tidy price. But—dashed if it soots me! They put this here Foozle Ile in it, my boy, and it ketches me jest 'ere." He indicated his centre of figure. "Gives me the heartburn," he said, and shook his head rather sadly.

"It's a very good whisky," said Kipps. "It's what the actor-manager chaps drink in London, I 'appen to know."

"I dessay they do, my boy," said old Kipps, "but then they've 'ad their livers burnt out, and I 'aven't.

They ain't dellicat like me. My stummik always 'as
been extry dellicat. Sometimes it's almost been as
though nothing would lay on it. But that's in passing.
I liked those segars. You can send me some more of
them segars. . . ."

You cannot lead a conversation straight from the
gastric consequences of Foozle Ile to Love, and so
Kipps, after a friendly inspection of a rare old engraving after Morland (perfect except for a hole kicked
through the centre) that his Uncle had recently purchased by private haggle, came to the topic of the old
people's removal.

At the outset of Kipps' great fortune there had been
much talk of some permanent provision for them. It
had been conceded they were to be provided for comfortably, and the phrase "retire from business" had
been very much in the air. Kipps had pictured an
ideal cottage, with a creeper always in exuberant flower
about the door, where the sun shone for ever and the
wind never blew and a perpetual welcome hovered in
the doorway. It was an agreeable dream, but when it
came to the point of deciding upon this particular
cottage or that, and on this particular house or that,
Kipps was surprised by an unexpected clinging to the
little home, which he had always understood to be the
worst of all possible houses.

"We don't want to move in a 'urry," said Mrs.
Kipps.

"When we want to move, we want to move for life.
I've had enough moving about in my time," said old
Kipps.

"We can do here a bit more, now we done here so
long," said Mrs. Kipps.

"You lemme look about a bit *fust*," said old Kipps.

And in looking about old Kipps found perhaps a
finer joy than any mere possession could have given.
He would shut his shop more or less effectually against
the intrusion of customers, and toddle abroad seeking

new matter for his dream; no house was too small and none too large for his knowing inquiries. Occupied houses took his fancy more than vacant ones, and he would remark, "You won't be a-livin' 'ere for ever, even if you think you will," when irate householders protested against the unsolicited examination of their more intimate premises. . . .

Remarkable difficulties arose of a totally unexpected sort.

"If we 'ave a larger 'ouse," said Mrs. Kipps with sudden bitterness, "we shall want a servant, and I don't want no gells in the place larfin' at me, sniggerin' and larfin' and prancin' and trapesin', lardy da!"

"If we 'ave a smaller 'ouse," said Mrs. Kipps, "there won't be room to swing a cat."

Room to swing a cat, it seemed, was absolutely essential. It was an infrequent but indispensable operation.

"When we *do* move," said old Kipps, "if we could get a bit of shootin'——

"I don't want to sell off all this here stock for nothin'," said old Kipps. "It's took years to 'cumulate. I put a ticket in the winder sayin' 'sellin' orf,' but it 'asn't brought nothing like a roosh. One of these 'ere dratted visitors pretendin' to want an air gun, was all we 'ad in yesterday. Jest an excuse for spyin' round and then go away and larf at you. No-thanky to everything, it didn't matter what. . . . That's 'ow *I* look at it, Artie."

They pursued meandering fancies about the topic of their future settlement for a space; and Kipps became more and more hopeless of any proper conversational opening that would lead to his great announcement, and more and more uncertain how such an opening should be taken. Once indeed old Kipps, anxious to get away from this dangerous subject of removals, began : "And what are you a-doin' of in Folkestone? I shall have to come over and see you one of these days," but before Kipps could get in upon that, his Uncle had passed into a general exposition of the proper treatment of landladies and their humbugging, cheating ways, and so the opportunity vanished. It seemed to Kipps the only thing to do was to go out into the town for a stroll, compose an effectual opening at leisure, and then come back and discharge it at them in its consecutive completeness. And even out-of-doors and alone, he found his mind distracted by irrelevant thoughts.

§ 2

His steps led him out of the High Street towards the church, and he leant for a time over the gate that had once been the winning post of his race with Ann Pornick, and presently found himself in a sitting position on the top rail. He had to get things smooth again, he knew; his mind was like a mirror of water after a breeze. The image of Helen and his great future was broken and mingled into fragmentary reflections of remoter things, of the good name of Old Methusaleh Three Stars, of long dormant memories the High Street saw fit, by some trick of light and atmosphere, to arouse that afternoon. . . .

Abruptly a fine, full voice from under his elbow shouted, "What-o, Art!" and, behold, Sid Pornick was back in his world, leaning over the gate beside him, and holding out a friendly hand.

He was oddly changed and yet oddly like the Sid that Kipps had known. He had the old broad face and mouth, abundantly freckled, the same short nose, and the same blunt chin, the same odd suggestion of his sister Ann without a touch of her beauty; but he had quite a new voice, loud and a little hard, and his upper lip carried a stiff and very fair moustache.

Kipps shook hands. "I was jest thinking of *you*, Sid," he said, "jest this very moment, and wondering if ever I should see you again, ever. And 'ere you are!"

"One likes a look round at times," said Sid. "How are *you*, old chap?"

"All right," said Kipps. "I just been lef'——"

"You aren't changed much," interrupted Sid.

"Ent I?" said Kipps, foiled.

"I knew your back directly I came round the corner. Spite of that 'at you got on. Hang it, I said, that's Art Kipps or the devil. And so it was."

Kipps made a movement of his neck as if he would look at his back and judge. Then he looked Sid in the face. "You got a moustache, Sid," he said.

"I s'pose you're having your holidays?" said Sid.

"Well, partly. But I just been lef'——"

"*I'm* taking a bit of a holiday," Sid went on. "But the fact is, I have to give *myself* holidays nowadays. I've set up for myself."

"Not down here?"

"No fear! I'm not a turnip. I've started in Hammersmith, manufacturing." Sid spoke offhand as though there was no such thing as pride.

"Not drapery?"

"No fear! Engineer. Manufacture bicycles." He clapped his hand to his breast pocket and produced a number of pink handbills. He handed one to Kipps and prevented him reading it by explanations and explanatory dabs of a pointing finger. "That's our make, my make to be exact, The Red Flag, see?—I got a transfer with my name—Pantocrat tyres, eight pounds— yes, *there*—Clinchers ten, Dunlop's eleven, Ladies' one pound more—that's the lady's. Best machine at a democratic price in London. No guineas and no discounts—honest trade. I build 'em—to order. I've built," he reflected, looking away seaward—"seventeen. Counting orders in 'and. . . ."

"Come down to look at the old place a bit," said Sid. "Mother likes it at times."

"Thought you'd all gone away——"

"What! after my father's death? No! My

mother's come back, and she's living at Muggett's
cottages. The sea air suits 'er. She likes the old place
better than Hammersmith . . . and I can afford it.
Got an old crony or so here. . . . Gossip . . . have
tea. . . . S'pose *you* ain't married, Kipps?"

Kipps shook his head. " I——" he began.

" *I* am," said Sid. " Married these two years and got
a nipper. Proper little chap."

Kipps got his word in at last. " I got engaged day
before yesterday," he said.

" Ah!" said Sid airily. " That's all right. Who's
the fortunate lady?"

Kipps tried to speak in an offhand way. He stuck
his hands in his pockets as he spoke. " She's a solicitor's
daughter," he said, " in Folkestone. Rather'r nice set.
County family. Related to the Earl of Beaupres——"

" Steady on!" cried Sid.

" You see, I've 'ad a bit of luck, Sid. Been lef'
money."

Sid's eye travelled instinctively to mark Kipps'
garments. " How much?" he asked.

" 'Bout twelve 'undred a year," said Kipps, more
offhandedly than ever.

" Lord!" said Sid, with a note of positive dismay, and
stepped back a pace or two.

" My granfaver it was," said Kipps, trying hard to be
calm and simple. " 'Ardly knew I 'ad a granfaver. And
then—bang! When o' Bean, the solicitor, told me of
it, you could 'ave knocked me down——"

" '*Ow* much?" demanded Sid, with a sharp note in
his voice.

" Twelve 'undred pound a year—'proximately, that
is. . . ."

Sid's attempt at genial unenvious congratulation did
not last a minute. He shook hands with an unreal
heartiness and said he was jolly glad. " It's a bloomin'
stroke of Luck," he said.

" It's a bloomin' stroke of Luck," he repeated; "that's

what it is," with the smile fading from his face. "Of course, better you 'ave it than me, o' chap. So I don't envy you, anyhow. *I* couldn't keep it, if I did 'ave it."

"'Ow's that?" said Kipps, a little hipped by Sid's patent chagrin.

"I'm a Socialist, you see," said Sid. "I don't 'old with Wealth. What *is* Wealth? Labour robbed out of the poor. At most it's only yours in Trust. Leastways, that 'ow *I* should take it."

He reflected. "The Present distribution of Wealth," he said and stopped.

Then he let himself go, with unmasked bitterness. "It's no sense at all. It's jest damn foolishness. Who's going to work and care in a muddle like this? Here first you do—something anyhow—of the world's work, and it pays you hardly anything, and then it invites you to do nothing, nothing whatever, and pays you twelve hundred pounds a year. Who's going to respect laws and customs when they come to damn silliness like that?"

He repeated, "Twelve hundred pounds a year!"

At the sight of Kipps' face he relented slightly.

"It's not you I'm thinking of, o' man; it's the system. Better you than most people. Still——"

He laid both hands on the gate and repeated to himself, "Twelve 'undred a year. . . . Gee-whiz, Kipps! You'll be a swell!"

"I shan't," said Kipps with imperfect conviction. "No fear."

"You can't 'ave money like that and not swell out. You'll soon be too big to speak to——'ow do they put it?—a mere mechanic like me."

"No fear, Siddee," said Kipps with conviction. "I ain't that sort."

"Ah!" said Sid, with a sort of unwilling scepticism, "money 'll be too much for you. Besides——you're caught by a swell already."

"'Ow d'yer mean?"

"That girl you're going to marry. Masterman says——"

"Oo's Masterman?"

"Rare good chap I know—takes my first floor front room. Masterman says it's always the wife pitches the key. Always. There's no social differences—till women come in."

"Ah!" said Kipps profoundly. "You don't know."

Sid shook his head. "Fancy!" he reflected, "Art Kipps! . . . Twelve 'Undred a Year!"

Kipps tried to bridge that opening gulf. "Remember the Hurons, Sid?"

"Rather," said Sid.

"Remember that wreck?"

"I can smell it now—sort of sour smell."

Kipps was silent for a moment with reminiscent eyes on Sid's still troubled face.

"I say, Sid, 'ow's Ann?"

"*She's* all right," said Sid.

"Where is she now?"

"In a place . . . Ashford."

"Oh!"

Sid's face had become a shade sulkier than before.

"The fact is," he said, "we don't get on very well together. *I* don't hold with service. We're common people, I suppose, but I don't like it. I don't see why a sister of mine should wait at other people's tables. No. Not even if they got Twelve 'Undred a Year."

Kipps tried to change the point of application. "Remember 'ow you came out once when we were racing here? . . . She didn't run bad for a girl."

And his own words raised an image brighter than he could have supposed, so bright it seemed to breathe before him, and did not fade altogether even when he was back in Folkestone an hour or so later.

But Sid was not to be deflected from that other rankling theme by any reminiscences of Ann.

"I wonder what you will do with all that money,"

he speculated. " I wonder if you will do any good at all. I wonder what you *could* do. You should hear Masterman. He'd tell you things. Suppose it came to me, what should I do? It's no good giving it back to the state as things are. Start an Owenite profit-sharing factory perhaps. Or a new Socialist paper. We want a new Socialist paper."

He tried to drown his personal chagrin in elaborate exemplary suggestions. . . .

§ 3

" I must be gettin' on to my motor," said Kipps at last, having to a large extent heard him out.

" What! Got a motor?"

" No!" said Kipps apologetically. " Only 'ired for the day."

" 'Ow much?"

" Five pounds."

" Keep five families for a week! Good Lord!" That seemed to crown Sid's disgust.

Yet drawn by a sort of fascination he came with Kipps and assisted at the mounting of the car. He was pleased to note it was not the most modern of cars, but that was the only grain of comfort. Kipps mounted at once, after one violent agitation of the little shop-door to set the bell a-jingle and warn his Uncle and Aunt. Sid assisted with the great fur-lined overcoat and examined the spectacles.

" Good-bye, o' chap!" said Kipps.

" Good-bye, o' chap!" said Sid.

The old people came out to say good-bye.

Old Kipps was radiant with triumph. " 'Pon my Sammy, Artie! I'm a goo' mind to come with you," he shouted, and then, " I got something you might take with you!"

He dodged back into the shop and returned with the perforated engraving after Morland.

"You stick to this, my boy," he said. "You get it repaired by someone who knows. It's the most vallyble thing I got you so far, you take my word."

"Warrup!" said the motor, and tuff, tuff, tuff, and backed and snorted while old Kipps danced about on the pavement as if foreseeing complex catastrophes, and told the driver, "That's all right."

He waved his stout stick to his receding nephew. Then he turned to Sid. "Now if you could make something like that, young Pornick, you *might* blow a bit!"

"I'll make a doocid sight better than that before I done," said Sid, hands deep in his pockets.

"Not *you*," said old Kipps.

The car set up a prolonged sobbing moan and vanished around the corner. Sid stood motionless for a space, unheeding some further remark from old Kipps. The young mechanic had just discovered that to have manufactured seventeen bicycles, including orders in hand, is not so big a thing as he had supposed, and such discoveries try one's manhood. . . .

"Oh well!" said Sid at last, and turned his face towards his mother's cottage.

She had got a hot teacake for him, and she was a little hurt that he was dark and preoccupied as he consumed it. He had always been such a boy for teacake, and then when one went out specially and got him one——!

He did not tell her—he did not tell anyone—he had seen young Kipps. He did not want to talk about Kipps for a bit to anyone at all.

CHAPTER THE FIFTH

The Pupil Lover

§ 1

WHEN Kipps came to reflect upon his afternoon's work he had his first inkling of certain comprehensive incompatibilities lying about the course of true love in his particular case. He had felt without understanding the incongruity between the announcement he had failed to make and the circle of ideas of his Aunt and Uncle. It was this rather than the want of a specific intention that had silenced him, the perception that when he travelled from Folkestone to New Romney he travelled from an atmosphere where his engagement to Helen was sane and excellent to an atmosphere where it was only to be regarded with incredulous suspicion. Coupled and associated with this jar was his sense of the altered behaviour of Sid Pornick, the evident shock to that ancient alliance caused by the fact of his enrichment, the touch of hostility in his "You'll soon be swelled too big to speak to a poor mechanic like me."

217

Kipps was unprepared for the unpleasant truth that the path of social advancement is and must be strewn with broken friendships. This first protrusion of that fact caused a painful confusion in his mind. It was speedily to protrude in a far more serious fashion in relation to the " hands " from the Emporium, and Chitterlow.

From the day at Lympne Castle his relations with Helen had entered upon a new footing. He had prayed for Helen as good souls pray for Heaven, with as little understanding of what it was he prayed for. And now that period of standing humbly in the shadows before the shrine was over, and the goddess, her veil of mystery flung aside, had come down to him and taken hold of him, a good, strong, firm hold and walked by his side. . . . She liked him. What was singular was that very soon she had kissed him thrice, whimsically upon the brow, and he had never kissed her at all. He could not analyse his feelings, only he knew the world was wonderfully changed about them; but the truth was that though he still worshipped and feared her, though his pride in his engagement was ridiculously vast, he loved her now no more. That subtle something woven of the most delicate strands of self-love and tenderness and desire had vanished imperceptibly; and was gone now for ever. But that she did not suspect in him, nor as a matter of fact did he.

She took him in hand in perfect good faith. She told him things about his accent, she told him things about his bearing, about his costume and his way of looking at things. She thrust the blade of her intelligence into the tenderest corners of Kipps' secret vanity, she slashed his most intimate pride to bleeding tatters. He sought very diligently to anticipate some at least of these informing thrusts by making great use of Coote. But the unanticipated made a brave number. . . .

She found his simple willingness a very lovable thing.

Indeed she liked him more and more. There was a touch of motherliness in her feelings towards him.

But his upbringing and his associations had been, she diagnosed, "awful." At New Romney she glanced but little; that was remote. But in her inventory—she went over him as one might go over a newly taken house, with impartial thoroughness—she discovered more proximate influences, surprising intimations of nocturnal "sing-songs"—she pictured it as almost shocking that Kipps should sing to the banjo—much low-grade wisdom treasured from a person called Buggins—"Who *is* Buggins?" said Helen—vague figures of indisputable vulgarity, Pierce and Carshot, and more particularly a very terrible social phenomenon, Chitterlow.

Chitterlow blazed upon them with unheralded oppressive brilliance the first time they were abroad together.

They were going along the front of the Leas to see a school play in Sandgate—at the last moment Mrs. Walshingham had been unable to come with them—when Chitterlow loomed up into the new world. He was wearing the suit of striped flannel and the straw hat that had followed Kipps' payment in advance for his course of elocution, his hands were deep in his side pockets and animated the corners of his jacket, and his attentive gaze at the passing loungers, the faint smile under his boldly drawn nose, showed him engaged in studying character—no doubt for some forthcoming play.

"What HO!" said he, at the sight of Kipps, and swept off his straw hat with so ample a clutch of his great, flat hand that it suggested to Helen's startled mind a conjurer about to palm a half-penny.

"'Ello, Chit'low," said Kipps a little awkwardly, and not saluting.

Chitterlow hesitated. "Half a mo', my boy," he said, and arrested Kipps by extending a large hand over his chest. "Excuse me, my dear," he said, bowing like his Russian count by way of apology to Helen, and with a smile that would have killed at a hundred yards. He effected a semi-confidential grouping of himself and Kipps, while Helen stood in white amazement.

"About that play," he said.

"'Ow about it?" asked Kipps, acutely aware of Helen.

"It's all right," said Chitterlow. "There's a strong smell of syndicate in the air, I may tell you—Strong."

"That's aw right," said Kipps.

"You needn't tell everybody," said Chitterlow with a transitory, confidential hand to his mouth, which pointed the application of the "everybody" beyond any possibility of error. "But I think it's coming off. However— I mustn't detain you now. So long. You'll come round, eh?"

"Right you are," said Kipps.

"To-night?"

"At eight."

And then, and more in the manner of a Russian prince than any common count, Chitterlow bowed and withdrew. Just for a moment he allowed a conquering eye to challenge Helen's, and noted her for a girl of quality. . . .

There was a silence between our lovers for a space.

"That," said Kipps with an allusive movement of the head, "was Chit'low."

"Is he—a friend of yours?"

"In a way. . . . You see—I met 'im. Leastways 'e met me. Run into me with a bicycle, 'e did, and so we got talking together."

He tried to appear at his ease. The young lady scrutinised his profile.

"What is he?"

"'E's a Nacter chap," said Kipps. "Leastways 'e writes plays."

"And sells them?"

"Partly."

"To whom?"

"Different people. Shares he sells. . . . It's all right, reely—I meant to tell you about him before."

Helen looked over her shoulder to catch a view of

Chitterlow's retreating aspect. It did not compel her complete confidence.

She turned to her lover and said in a tone of quiet authority, "You must tell me all about Chitterlow. Now."

The explanation began. . . .

The School Play came almost as a relief to Kipps. In the flusterment of going in he could almost forget for a time his Laocoön struggle to explain, and in the intervals he did his best to keep forgetting. But Helen, with a gentle insistence, resumed the explanation of Chitterlow as they returned towards Folkestone.

Chitterlow was confoundedly difficult to explain. You could hardly imagine!

There was an almost motherly anxiety in Helen's manner, blended with the resolution of a schoolmistress to get to the bottom of the affair. Kipps' ears were soon quite brightly red.

"Have you seen one of his plays?"

"'E's tole me about one."

"But on the stage."

"No. He 'asn't 'ad any on the stage yet. That's all coming. . . ."

"Promise me," she said in conclusion, "you won't do anything without consulting me."

And of course Kipps promised. "Oo—no!"

They went on their way in silence.

"One can't know everybody," said Helen in general.

"Of course," said Kipps; "in a sort of way it was him that helped me to my money." And he indicated in a confused manner the story of the advertisement. "I don't like to drop 'im all at once," he added.

Helen was silent for a space, and when she spoke she went off at a tangent. "We shall live in London —soon," she remarked. "It's only while we are here."

It was the first intimation she gave him of their post-nuptial prospects.

"We shall have a nice little flat somewhere, not too

far west, and there we shall build up a circle of our own."

All that declining summer Kipps was the pupil lover. He made an extraordinary open secret of his desire for self-improvement; indeed Helen had to hint once or twice that his modest frankness was excessive; and all this new circle of friends did, each after his or her manner, everything that was possible to supplement Helen's efforts and help him to ease and skill in the more cultivated circles to which he had come. Coote was still the chief teacher, the tutor—there are so many little difficulties a man may take to another man that he would not care to propound to the woman he loves—but they were all, so to speak, upon the staff. Even the freckled girl said to him once in a pleasant way, "You mustn't say 'contre temps,' you must say 'contraytom,'" when he borrowed that expression from "Manners and Rules," and she tried at his own suggestion to give him clear ideas upon the subject of "as" and "has." A certain confusion between these words was becoming evident, the first fruits of a lesson from Chitterlow on the aspirate. Hitherto he had discarded that dangerous letter almost altogether, but now he would pull up at words beginning with "h" and draw a sawing breath—rather like a startled kitten—and then aspirate with vigour.

Said Kipps one day, "As 'e?—I should say, ah—Has 'e? Ye know I got a lot of difficulty over them two words, which is which?"

"Well, 'as' is a conjunction and 'has' is a verb."

"I know," said Kipps, "but when is 'has' a conjunction and when is 'as' a verb?"

"Well," said the freckled girl, preparing to be very lucid, "it's has when it means one has, meaning having, but if it isn't it's as. As for instance one says 'e—I mean he—He has. But one says 'as he has.'"

"I see," said Kipps. "So I ought to say ' as 'e '?"

"No, if you are asking a question you say *has* 'e—I mean he—'as he?" She blushed quite brightly, but still clung to her air of lucidity.

"I see," said Kipps. He was about to say something further, but he desisted. "I got it much clearer now. *Has* 'e? *Has* 'e as. Yes."

"If you remember about having."

"Oo I will," said Kipps.

Miss Coote specialised in Kipps' artistic development. She had early formed an opinion that he had considerable artistic sensibility, his remarks on her work had struck her as decidedly intelligent, and whenever he called round to see them she would show him some work of art, now an illustrated book, now perhaps a colour print of a Botticelli, now the Hundred Best Paintings, now "Academy Pictures," now a German art handbook and now some magazine of furniture and design. "I know you like these things," she used to say, and Kipps said, "Oo I *do*." He soon acquired a little armoury of appreciative sayings. When presently the Walshinghams took him up to the Arts and Crafts, his deportment was intelligent in the extreme. For a time he kept a wary silence and suddenly pitched upon a colour print. "That's rather nace," he said to Mrs. Walshingham. "That lill' thing. There." He always said things like that by preference to the mother rather than the daughter unless he was perfectly sure.

He quite took to Mrs. Walshingham. He was impressed by her conspicuous tact and refinement; it seemed to him that the ladylike could go no further. She was always dressed with a delicate fussiness that was never disarranged, and even a sort of faded quality about her hair and face and bearing and emotions contributed to her effect. Kipps was not a big man, and commonly he did not feel a big man, but with Mrs. Walshingham he always felt enormous and distended,

8

as though he was a navvy who had taken some disagreeable poison which puffed him up inside his skin
as a preliminary to bursting. He felt, too, as though
he had been rolled in clay and his hair dressed with
gum. And he felt that his voice was strident and his
accent like somebody swinging a crowded pig's pail in
a free and careless manner. All this increased and
enforced his respect for her. Her hand, which flitted
often and again to his hand and arm, was singularly
well shaped and cool. "Arthur," she called him from
the very beginning.

She did not so much positively teach and tell him
as tactfully guide and infect him. Her conversation
was not so much didactic as exemplary. She would
say, "I *do* like people to do" so and so. She would
tell him anecdotes of nice things done, of gentlemanly
feats of graceful consideration; she would record her
neat observations of people in trains and omnibuses;
how, for example, a man had passed her change to the
conductor, "quite a common man he looked," but he
had lifted his hat. She stamped Kipps so deeply with
the hat-raising habit that he would uncover if he found
himself in the same railway ticket office with a lady,
and so stand ceremoniously until the difficulties of
change drove him to an apologetic provisional oblique
resumption of his headgear. . . . And robbing these
things of any air of personal application, she threw
about them an abundant talk about her two children—
she called them her Twin Jewels quite frequently—
about their gifts, their temperaments, their ambition,
their need of opportunity. They needed opportunity,
she would say, as other people needed air. . . .

In his conversations with her Kipps always assumed,
and she seemed to assume, that she was to join that
home in London Helen foreshadowed, but he was surprised one day to gather that this was not to be the
case. "It wouldn't do," said Helen, with decision.
"We want to make a circle of our own."

"But won't she be a bit lonely down here?" asked Kipps.

"There are the Waces, and Mrs. Prebble, and Mrs. Bindon Botting and—lots of people she knows." And Helen dismissed this possibility. . . .

Young Walshingham's share in the educational syndicate was smaller. But he shone out when they went to London on that Arts and Crafts expedition. Then this rising man of affairs showed Kipps how to buy the more theatrical weeklies for consumption in the train, how to buy and what to buy in the way of cigarettes with gold tips and shilling cigars, and how to order hock for lunch and sparkling Moselle for dinner, how to calculate the fare of a hansom cab—penny a minute while he goes—how to look intelligently at an hotel tape, and how to sit still in a train like a thoughtful man instead of talking like a fool and giving yourself away. And he, too, would glance at the good time coming when they were to be in London for good and all.

That prospect expanded and developed particulars. It presently took up a large part of Helen's conversation. Her conversations with Kipps were never of a grossly sentimental sort, there was a shyness of speech in that matter with both of them; but these new adumbrations were at least as interesting and not so directly disagreeable as the clear-cut intimations of personal defect that for a time had so greatly chastened Kipps' delight in her presence. The future presented itself with an almost perfect frankness as a joint campaign of Mrs. Walshingham's Twin Jewels upon the Great World, with Kipps in the capacity of baggage and supply. They would still be dreadfully poor, of course—this amazed Kipps, but he said nothing—until "Brudderkins" began to succeed, but if they were clever and lucky they might do a great deal.

When Helen spoke of London a brooding look, as of one who contemplates a distant country, came into

her eyes. Already it seemed they had the nucleus of
a set. Brudderkins was a member of the Theatrical
Judges, an excellent and influential little club of
journalists and literary people, and he knew Shimer
and Stargate and Whiffle, of the "Red Dragon," and
besides these were the Revels. They knew the Revels
quite well. Sidney Revel, before his rapid rise to
prominence as a writer of epigrammatic essays that were
quite above the ordinary public, had been an assistant
master at one of the best Folkestone schools, Brudderkins
had brought him home to tea several times, and it was
he had first suggested Helen should try to write. "It's
perfectly easy," Sidney had said. He had been writing
occasional things for the evening papers and for the
weekly reviews even at that time. Then he had gone
up to London and had almost unavoidably become a
dramatic critic. Those brilliant essays had followed,
and then "Red Hearts a-Beating," the romance that
had made him. It was a tale of spirited adventure,
full of youth and beauty and naïve passion and generous
devotion, bold, as the *Bookman* said, and frank in places,
never in the slightest degree morbid. He had met and
married an American widow with quite a lot of money,
and they had made a very distinct place for themselves,
Kipps learnt, in the literary and artistic society of
London. Helen seemed to dwell on the Revels a great
deal; it was her exemplary story; and when she spoke
of Sidney—she often called him Sidney—she would
become thoughtful. She spoke most of him naturally
because she had still to meet Mrs. Revel. . . .
Certainly they would be in the world in no time, even
if the distant connection with the Beaupres family came
to nothing.

Kipps gathered that with his marriage and the movement to London they were to undergo that subtle
change of name Coote had first adumbrated. They
were to become "Cuyps," Mr. and Mrs. Cuyps. Or,
was it Cuyp?

"It'll be rum at first," said Kipps.

"I dessay I shall soon get into it," he said. . . .

So in their several ways they all contributed to enlarge and refine and exercise the intelligence of Kipps. And behind all these other influences, and, as it were, presiding over and correcting these influences, was Kipps' nearest friend, Coote, a sort of master of the ceremonies. You figure his face, blowing slightly with solicitude, his slate-coloured, projecting but not unkindly eye intent upon our hero. The thing, he thought, was going off admirably. He studied Kipps' character immensely. He would discuss him with his sister, with Mrs. Walshingham, with the freckled girl, with anyone who would stand it. "He is an interesting character," he would say, "likeable—a sort of gentleman by instinct. He takes to all these things. He improves every day. He'll soon get Sang Froid. We took him up just in time. He wants now—well— Next year, perhaps, if there is a good Extension Literature course, he might go in for it. He wants to go in for something like that."

"He's going in for his bicycle now," said Mrs. Walshingham.

"That's all right for summer," said Coote, "but he wants to go in for some serious intellectual interest, something to take him out of himself a little more. Savoir Faire and self-forgetfulness is more than half the secret of Sang Froid."

§ 3

The world as Coote presented it was in part an endorsement, in part an amplification and in part a rectification of the world of Kipps, the world that derived from the old couple in New Romney and had been developed in the Emporium; the world, in fact, of common British life. There was the same subtle sense of social gradation that had moved Mrs. Kipps to prohibit intercourse with labourers' children, and the same dread of anything "common" that had kept the personal quality of Mr. Shalford's establishment so high. But now a certain disagreeable doubt about Kipps' own position was removed and he stood with Coote inside the sphere of gentlemen assured. Within the sphere of gentlemen there are distinctions of rank indeed, but none of class; there are the Big People and the modest, refined, gentlemanly little people like Coote, who may even dabble in the professions and counterless trades; there are lords and magnificences, and there are gentlefolk who have to manage; but they can all call on one another, they preserve a general equality of deportment throughout, they constitute that great state within the state, Society.

"But reely," said the Pupil, "not what you call being in Society?"

"Yes," said Coote. "Of course, down here one doesn't see much of it, but there's local society. It has the same rules."

"Calling and all that?"

"Precisely," said Coote.

Kipps thought, whistled a bar, and suddenly broached a question of conscience. "I often wonder," he said, "whether I oughtn't to dress for dinner—when I'm alone 'ere."

Coote protruded his lips and reflected. "Not full dress," he adjudicated; "that would be a little excessive. But you should *change*, you know. Put on a mess jacket and that sort of thing—easy dress. That is what *I* should do, certainly, if I wasn't in harness—and poor."

He coughed modestly and patted his hair behind.

And after that the washing bill of Kipps quadrupled, and he was to be seen at times by the bandstand with his light summer overcoat unbuttoned to give a glimpse of his nice white tie. He and Coote would be smoking the gold-tipped cigarettes young Walshingham had

prescribed as *chic,* and appreciating the music highly.
"That's—puff—a very nice bit," Kipps would say, or
better, "That's nace." And at the first grunts of the
loyal anthem up they stood with religiously uplifted
hats. Whatever else you might call them, you could
never call them disloyal.

The boundary of Society was admittedly very close
to Coote and Kipps, and a leading solicitude of the
true gentleman was to detect clearly those "beneath"
him and to behave towards them in a proper spirit.
"It's jest there it's so 'ard for me," said Kipps. He
had to cultivate a certain "distance," to acquire altogether the art of checking the presumption of bounders
and old friends. It was difficult, Coote admitted.

"I got mixed up with this lot 'ere," said Kipps.
"That's what's so harkward—I mean awkward."

"You could give them a hint," said Coote.

"'Ow?"

"Oh!—the occasion will suggest something."

The occasion came one early-closing night when
Kipps was sitting in a canopy chair near the bandstand
with his summer overcoat fully open and a new Gibus
pulled slightly forward over his brow, waiting for
Coote. They were to hear the band for an hour and
then go down to assist Miss Coote and the freckled girl
in trying over some Beethoven duets, if they remembered them, that is, sufficiently well. And as Kipps
lounged back in his chair and occupied his mind with
his favourite amusement on such evenings, which consisted chiefly in supposing that everyone about him was
wondering who he was, came a rude rap at the canvas
back and the voice of Pierce.

"It's nice to be a gentleman," said Pierce, and
swung a penny chair into position while Buggins
appeared smiling agreeably on the other side and leant
upon his stick. *He was smoking a common briar
pipe!*

Two real ladies, very fashionably dressed and sitting

close at hand, glanced quickly at Pierce and then away again, and it was evident *their* wonder was at an end.

"*He's* all right," said Buggins, removing his pipe and surveying Kipps.

"'Ello, Buggins!" said Kipps, not too cordially. "'Ow goes it?"

"All right. Holidays next week. If you don't look out, Kipps, I shall be on the Continong before you. Eh?"

"You going t'Boologne?"

"Ra-ther. Parley vous Francey. You bet."

"*I* shall 'ave a bit of a run over there one of these days," said Kipps.

There came a pause. Pierce applied the top of his stick to his mouth for a space and regarded Kipps. Then he glanced at the people about them.

"I say, Kipps," he said in a distinct, loud voice, "see 'er Ladyship lately?"

Kipps perceived the audience was to be impressed, but he responded half-heartedly. "No, I 'aven't," he said.

"She was along of Sir William the other night," said Pierce, still loud and clear, "and she asked to be remembered to you."

It seemed to Kipps that one of the two ladies smiled faintly and said something to the other, and then certainly they glanced at Pierce. Kipps flushed scarlet. "*Did* she?" he answered.

Buggins laughed good-humouredly over his pipe.

"Sir William suffers a lot from his gout," Pierce continued unabashed.

(Buggins much amused, with his pipe between his teeth.)

Kipps became aware of Coote at hand.

Coote nodded rather distantly to Pierce. "Hope I haven't kept you waiting, Kipps," he said.

"I kep' a chair for you," said Kipps and removed a guardian foot.

" But you've got your friends," said Coote.

" Oh! *we* don't mind," said Pierce cordially, " the more the merrier," and, " why don't you get a chair, Buggins?" Buggins shook his head in a sort of aside to Pierce and Coote coughed behind his hand.

" Been kep' late at business?" asked Pierce.

Coote turned quite pale and pretended not to hear. His eyes sought in space for a time, and with a convulsive movement he recognised a distant acquaintance and raised his hat.

Pierce had also become a little pale. He addressed himself to Kipps in an undertone.

" Mr. Coote, isn't he?" he asked.

Coote addressed himself to Kipps directly and exclusively. His manner had the calm of extreme tension.

" I'm rather late," he said. " I think we ought almost to be going on *now*."

Kipps stood up. " That's all right," he said.

" Which way are you going?" said Pierce, standing also, and brushing some crumbs of cigarette ash from his sleeve.

For a moment Coote was breathless. " Thank you," he said, and gasped. Then he delivered the necessary blow; " I don't think we're in need of your society, you know," and turned away.

Kipps found himself falling over chairs and things in the wake of Coote, and then they were clear of the crowd.

For a space Coote said nothing; then he remarked abruptly and quite angrily for him, " I think that was *awful* Cheek!"

Kipps made no reply. . . .

The whole thing was an interesting little object lesson in distance, and it stuck in the front of Kipps' mind for a long time. He had particularly vivid the face of Pierce, with an expression between astonishment and anger. He felt as though he had struck Pierce in the face under circumstances that gave Pierce no power

8*

to reply. He did not attend very much to the duets, and even forgot at the end of one of them to say how perfectly lovely it was.

§ 4

But you must not imagine that the national ideal of a gentleman, as Coote developed it, was all a matter of deportment and selectness, a mere isolation from debasing associations. There is a Serious Side, a deeper aspect of the true True Gentleman. But it is not vocal. The True Gentleman does not wear his heart on his sleeve. For example, he is deeply religious, as Coote was, as Mrs. Walshingham was; but outside the walls of a church it never appears, except perhaps now and then in a pause, in a profound look, in a sudden avoidance. In quite a little while Kipps also had learnt the pause, the profound look, the sudden avoidance, that final refinement of spirituality, impressionistic piety.

And the True Gentleman is patriotic also. When one saw Coote lifting his hat to the National Anthem, then perhaps one got a glimpse of what patriotic emotions, what worship, the polish of a gentleman may hide. Or singing out his deep notes against the Hosts of Midian, in the St. Stylites' choir; then indeed you plumbed his spiritual side.

> " *Christian, dost thou heed them,*
>   *On the holy ground,*
>   *How the hosts of Mid-i-ăn,*
>   *Prowl and prowl around!*
>   *Christian, up and smaĭ-it them. . . .*"

But these were but gleams. For the rest, Religion, Nationality, Passion, Money, Politics, much more so those cardinal issues, Birth and Death, the True Gentleman skirted about and became facially rigid towards, and ceased to speak and panted and blew.

"One doesn't talk of that sort of thing," Coote would say with a gesture of the knuckly hand.

"O' course," Kipps would reply, with an equal significance.

Profundities. Deep, as it were, blowing to deep.

One does not talk, but on the other hand one is punctilious to do. Actions speak. Kipps—in spite of the fact that the Walshinghams were more than a little lax—Kipps, who had formerly flitted Sunday after Sunday from one Folkestone church to another, had now a sitting of his own, duly paid for at St. Stylites. There he was to be seen, always at the surpliced evening service, and sometimes of a morning, dressed with a sober precision, and with an eye on Coote in the chancel. No difficulties now about finding the place in his book. He became a communicant again—he had lapsed soon after his confirmation when the young lady in the costume-room, who was his adopted sister, left the Emporium—and he would sometimes go round to the Vestry for Coote after the service. One evening he was introduced to the Hon. and Rev. Densemore. He was much too confused to say anything, and the noble cleric had nothing to say, but indisputably they were introduced. . . .

No! you must not imagine that the national ideal of a gentleman is without its "serious side," without even its stern and uncompromising side. The imagination no doubt refuses to see Coote displaying extraordinary refinements of courage upon the stricken field, but in the walks of peace there is sometimes sore need of sternness. Charitable as one may be, one must admit there are people who *do* things, impossible things; people who place themselves "out of it" in countless ways; people, moreover, who are by a sort of pre-destination out of it from the beginning, and against these Society has invented a terrible protection for its Cootery, the Cut. The cut is no joke for anyone. It is excommunication. You may be cut by individual,

you may be cut by a set, or you may be—and this is so
tragic that beautiful romances have been written about
it—"Cut by the County." One figures Coote dis-
charging this last duty and cutting somebody—Coote,
erect and pale, never speaking, going past with eyes of
pitiless slate, lower jaw protruding a little, face pursed
up and cold and stiff. . . .

It never dawned upon Kipps that he would one day
have to face this terrible front, to be to Coote not only
as one dead, but as one gone more than a stage or so in
decay, cut and passed, banned and outcast for ever. It
never dawned upon either of them.

Yet so it was to be!

One cannot hide any longer that all this fine progress
of Kipps is doomed to end in collapse. So far indeed
you have seen him ascend. You have seen him becoming more refined and careful day by day, more carefully
dressed, less clumsy in the uses of social life. You have
seen the gulf widening between himself and his former
low associates. I have brought you at last to the vision
of him, faultlessly dressed and posed, in an atmosphere
of candlelight and chanting, in his own sitting in one
of the most fashionable churches in Folkestone. . . . I
have refrained from the lightest touch upon the tragic
note that must now creep into my tale. Yet the net of
his low connections has been about his feet, and moreover there was something interwoven in his being. . . .

CHAPTER THE SIXTH

Discords

§ 1

ONE day Kipps set out upon his newly mastered bicycle to New Romney to break the news of his engagement to his Uncle and Aunt—positively. He was now a finished cyclist, but as yet an unseasoned one; the southwest wind, even in its summer guise, as one meets it on the Marsh, is the equivalent of a reasonable hill, and ever and again he got off and refreshed himself by a spell of walking. He was walking just outside New Romney preparatory to his triumphal entry (one hand off) when abruptly he came upon Ann Pornick.

It chanced he was thinking about her at the time. He had been thinking curious things; whether, after all, the atmosphere of New Romney and the Marsh had not some difference, some faint impalpable quality that was missing in the great and fashionable world of Folkestone behind there on the hill. Here there was a homeliness, a familiarity. He had noted as he passed that old Mr. Cliffordown's gate had been mended with

235

a fresh piece of string. In Folkestone he didn't take notice and he didn't care if they built three hundred houses. Come to think of it, that was odd. It was fine and grand to have twelve hundred a year; it was fine to go about on trams and omnibuses and think not a person aboard was as rich as oneself; it was fine to buy and order this and that and never have any work to do and to be engaged to a girl distantly related to the Earl of Beaupres, but yet there had been a zest in the old time out here, a rare zest in the holidays, in sunlight, on the sea beach and in the High Street, that failed from these new things. He thought of those bright windows of holiday that had seemed so glorious to him in the retrospect from his apprentice days. It was strange that now, amidst his present splendours, they were glorious still!

All those things were over now—perhaps that was it! Something had happened to the world and the old light had been turned out. He himself was changed, and Sid was changed, terribly changed, and Ann no doubt was changed.

He thought of her with the hair blown about her flushed cheeks as they stood together after their race. . . .

Certainly she must be changed, and all the magic she had been fraught with to the very hem of her short petticoats gone no doubt for ever. And as he thought that, or before and while he thought it, for he came to all these things in his own vague and stumbling way, he looked up, and there was Ann!

She was seven years older and greatly altered; yet for the moment it seemed to him that she had not changed at all. "Ann!" he said, and she, with a lifting note, "It's Art Kipps!"

Then he became aware of changes—improvements. She was as pretty as she had promised to be, her blue eyes as dark as his memory of them, and with a quick, high colour, but now Kipps by several inches was the taller again. She was dressed in a simple grey dress that showed her very clearly as a straight and healthy

little woman, and her hat was Sundayfied with pink
flowers. She looked soft and warm and welcoming.
Her face was alight to Kipps with her artless gladness
at their encounter.

" It's Art Kipps!" she said.

" Rather," said Kipps.

" You got your holidays?"

It flashed upon Kipps that Sid had not told her of
his great fortune. Much regretful meditation upon
Sid's behaviour had convinced him that he himself was
to blame for exasperating boastfulness in that affair, and
this time he took care not to err in that direction. So
he erred in the other.

" I'm taking a bit of a 'oliday," he said.

" So'm I," said Ann.

" You been for a walk?" asked Kipps.

Ann showed him a bunch of wayside flowers.

" It's a long time since I seen you, Ann. Why, 'ow
long must it be? Seven—eight years nearly."

" It don't do to count," said Ann.

" It don't look like it," said Kipps, with the slightest
emphasis.

" You got a moustache," said Ann, smelling her
flowers and looking at him over them, not without
admiration.

Kipps blushed. . .

Presently they came to the bifurcation of the roads.

" I'm going down this way to mother's cottage," said
Ann.

" I'll come a bit your way if I may."

In New Romney social distinctions that are primary
realities in Folkestone are absolutely non-existent, and
it seemed quite permissible for him to walk with Ann,
for all that she was no more than a servant. They
talked with remarkable ease to one another, they slipped
into a vein of intimate reminiscence in the easiest
manner. In a little while Kipps was amazed to find
Ann and himself at this :

"You r'member that half sixpence? What we cut togevver?"

"Yes."

"I got it still."

She hesitated. "Funny, wasn't it?" she said, and then, "You got yours, Artie?"

"Rather," said Kipps. "What do *you* think?" and wondered in his heart of hearts why he had never looked at that sixpence for so long.

Ann smiled at him frankly.

"I didn't expect you'd keep it," she said. "I thought often—it was silly to keep mine.

"Besides," she reflected, "it didn't mean anything really."

She glanced at him as she spoke and met his eye.

"Oh, didn't it!" said Kipps, a little late with his response, and realising his infidelity to Helen even as he spoke.

"It didn't mean much anyhow," said Ann. "You still in the drapery?"

"I'm living at Folkestone," began Kipps and decided that that sufficed. "Didn't Sid tell you he met me?"

"No! Here?"

"Yes. The other day. 'Bout a week or more ago."

"That was before I came."

"Ah! that was it," said Kipps.

"'E's got on," said Ann. "Got 'is own shop now, Artie."

"'E tole me."

They found themselves outside Muggett's Cottages. "You going in?" said Kipps.

"I s'pose so," said Ann.

They both hung upon the pause. Ann took a plunge.

"D'you often come to New Romney?" she said.

"I ride over a bit at times," said Kipps.

Another pause. Ann held out her hand.

"I'm glad I seen you," she said.

Extraordinary impulses arose in neglected parts of Kipps' being. "Ann," he said and stopped.

"Yes," said she, and was bright to him.

They looked at one another.

All and more than all of those first emotions of his adolescence had come back to him. Her presence banished a multitude of countervailing considerations. It was Ann more than ever. She stood breathing close to him, with her soft-looking lips a little apart and gladness in her eyes.

"I'm awful glad to see you again," he said; "it brings back old times."

"Doesn't it?"

Another pause. He would have liked to have had a long talk to her, to have gone for a walk with her or something, to have drawn nearer to her in any conceivable way, and, above all, to have had some more of the appreciation that shone in her eyes, but a vestige of Folkestone still clinging to him told him it "wouldn't do." "Well," he said, "I must be getting on," and turned away reluctantly, with a will under compulsion. . . .

When he looked back from the corner she was still at the gate. She was perhaps a little disconcerted by his retreat. He felt that. He hesitated for a moment, half turned, stood and suddenly did great things with his hat. That hat! The wonderful hat of our civilisation! . . .

In another minute he was engaged in a similarly absent-minded conversation with his Uncle about the usual topics.

His Uncle was very anxious to buy him a few upright clocks as an investment for subsequent sale. And there were also some very nice globes, one terrestrial and the other celestial, in a shop at Lydd that would look well in a drawing-room and inevitably increase in value. . . . Kipps either did or did not agree to this purchase; he was unable to recollect.

The south-west wind perhaps helped him back; at any rate he found himself through Dymchurch without having noticed the place. There came an odd effect as he drew near Hythe. The hills on the left and the trees on the right seemed to draw together and close in upon him until his way was straight and narrow. He could not turn round on that treacherous, half-tamed machine, but he knew that behind him, he knew so well, spread the wide vast flatness of the Marsh shining under the afternoon sky. In some way this was material to his thoughts. And as he rode through Hythe he came upon the idea that there was a considerable amount of incompatibility between the existence of one who was practically a gentleman and of Ann.

In the neighbourhood of Seabrook he began to think he had, in some subtle way, lowered himself by walking along by the side of Ann. . . . After all, she was only a servant.

Ann!

She called out all the least gentlemanly instincts of his nature. There had been a moment in their conversation when he had quite distinctly thought it would really be an extremely nice thing for someone to kiss her lips. . . . There was a warming quality about Ann—at least for Kipps. She impressed him as having during their vast interval of separation contrived to make herself in some distinctive way his.

Fancy keeping that half sixpence all this time!

It was the most flattering thing that had ever happened to Kipps.

§ 2

He found himself presently sitting over " The Art of Conversing," lost in the strangest musings. He got up, walked about, became stagnant at the window for a space, roused himself, and by way of something lighter tried " Sesame and Lilies." From that, too, his atten-

tion wandered. He sat back. Anon he smiled, anon
sighed. He arose, pulled his keys from his pocket,
looked at them, decided, and went upstairs. He
opened the little yellow box that had been the nucleus
of all his possessions in the world, and took out a small
" Escritoire," the very humblest sort of present, and
opened it—kneeling. And there, in the corner, was a
little packet of paper, sealed as a last defence against
any prying invader with red sealing wax. It had gone
untouched for years. He held this little packet between
finger and thumb for a moment, regarding it, and then
put down the escritoire and broke the seal. . . .

As he was getting into bed that night he remembered
something for the first time !

" Dash it !" he said. " Dashed if I told 'em *this*
time. . . . *Well!*

" I shall 'ave to go over to New Romney again !"

He got into bed and remained sitting pensively on
the pillow for a space.

" It's a rum world," he reflected after a vast
interval.

Then he recalled that she had noticed his moustache
and embarked upon a sea of egotistical musing.

He imagined himself telling Ann how rich he was.
What a surprise that would be for her !

Finally he sighed profoundly, blew out his candle
and snuggled down, and in a little while he was
asleep. . . .

But the next morning and at intervals afterwards he
found himself thinking of Ann—Ann the bright, the
desirable, the welcoming, and with an extraordinary
streakiness he wanted quite badly to go, and then as
badly not to go, over to New Romney again.

Sitting on the Leas in the afternoon, he had an idea.
" I ought to 'ave told 'er, I suppose, about my being
engaged.

" Ann !"

All sorts of dreams and impressions that had gone

clean out of his mental existence came back to him, changed and brought up to date to fit her altered presence. He thought of how he had gone back to New Romney for his Christmas holidays, determined to kiss her, and of the awful blankness of the discovery that she had gone away.

It seemed incredible now, and yet not wholly incredible, that he had cried real tears for her—how many years was it ago?

§ 3

Daily I should thank my Maker that He did not appoint me Censor of the world of men. I should temper a fierce injustice with a spasmodic indecision that would prolong rather than mitigate the bitterness of the Day. For human dignity, for all conscious human superiority I should lack the beginnings of charity, for bishops, prosperous schoolmasters, judges and all large respect-pampered souls. And more especially bishops, towards whom I bear an atavistic Viking grudge, dreaming not infrequently and with invariable zest of galleys and landings and well-known living ornaments of the episcopal bench sprinting inland on twinkling gaiters before my thirsty blade—all these people, I say, I should treat below their deserts; but, on the other hand, for such as Kipps— There the exasperating indecisions would come in. The Judgment would be arrested at Kipps. Everyone and everything would wait. The balance would sway and sway, and whenever it heeled towards an adverse decision, my finger would set it swaying again. Kings, warriors, statesmen, brilliant women, personalities, panting with indignation, headline humanity in general, would stand undamned, unheeded, or be damned in the most casual manner for their importunity, while my eye went about for anything possible that could be said on behalf of Kipps. . . . Albeit I fear nothing can save him from condemnation upon this present score, that within two days he was talking to Ann again.

One seeks excuses. Overnight there had been, in his presence, an encounter of Chitterlow and young Walshingham that had certainly warped his standards. They had called within a few minutes of each other, and the two, swayed by virile attentions to Old Methusaleh Three Stars, had talked against each other, over and at the hospitable presence of Kipps. Walshingham had seemed to win at the beginning, but finally Chitterlow had made a magnificent display of vociferation and swept him out of existence. At the beginning Chitterlow had opened upon the great profits of playwrights and young Walshingham had capped him at once with a cynical, but impressive, display of knowledge of the High Finance. If Chitterlow boasted his thousands, young Walshingham boasted his hundreds of thousands, and was for a space left in sole possession of the stage, juggling with the wealth of nations. He was going on by way of Financial Politics to the Overman, before Chitterlow recovered from his first check, and came back to victory. "Talking of Women," said Chitterlow, coming in abruptly upon some things not generally known, beyond Walshingham's more immediate circle, about a recently departed Empire-builder; "Talking of Women and the way they Get at a man——"

[Though as a matter of fact they had been talking of the Corruption of Society by Speculation.]

Upon this new topic Chitterlow was soon manifestly invincible. He knew so much, he had known so many. Young Walshingham did his best with epigrams and reservations, but even to Kipps it was evident that this was a book-learned depravity. One felt Walshingham had never known the inner realities of passion. But Chitterlow convinced and amazed. He had run away with girls, he had been run away with by girls, he had been in love with several at a time—"not counting

Bessie "—he had loved and lost, he had loved and refrained, and he had loved and failed. He threw remarkable lights upon the moral state of America—in which country he had toured with great success. He set his talk to the tune of one of Mr. Kipling's best-known songs. He told an incident of simple romantic passion, a delirious dream of love and beauty in a Saturday to Monday steamboat trip up the Hudson, and tagged his end with, " I learnt about women from 'er !" After that he adopted the refrain, and then lapsed into the praises of Kipling. " Little Kipling," said Chitterlow, with the familiarity of affection, " *he* knows," and broke into quotation :

> " ' *I've taken my fun where I've found it;*
> *I've rogued and I've ranged in my time;*
> *I've 'ad my picking of sweet' earts,*
> *An' four of the lot was Prime.*' "

(These things, I say, affect the moral standards of the best of us.)

" *I'd* have liked to have written that," said Chitterlow. " That's Life, that is ! But go and put it on the Stage, put even a bit of the Realities of Life on the Stage, and see what they'll do to you ! Only Kipling could venture on a job like that. That Poem KNOCKED me ! I don't say Kipling hasn't knocked me before and since, but that was a Fair Knock Out. And yet—you know—there's one thing in it . . . this :

> " ' *I've taken my fun where I've found it,*
> *And now I must pay for my fun,*
> *For the more you 'ave known o' the others,*
> *The less will you settle to one——*'

Well. In my case anyhow—I don't know how much that proves, seeing I'm exceptional in so many things and there's no good denying it—but so far as I'm concerned—I tell you two, but of course you needn't let it go any further—I've been perfectly faithful to Muriel ever since I married her—ever since. . . . Not once. Not even by accident have I ever said or done anything in the slightest—" His little brown eye became pensive after this flattering intimacy and the gorgeous draperies of his abundant voice fell into graver folds. "*I learnt about women from 'er,*" he said impressively.

"Yes," said Walshingham, getting into the hinder spaces of that splendid pause, "a man must know about women. And the only sound way of learning is the experimental method."

"If you want to know about the experimental method, my boy," said Chitterlow, resuming. . . .

So they talked. *Ex pede Herculem,* as Coote, that cultivated polyglot, would have put it. And in the small hours Kipps went to bed, with his brain whirling with words and whisky, and sat for an unconscionable time upon his bed edge, musing sadly upon the unmanly monogamy that had cast its shadow upon his career, musing with his thoughts pointing around more and more certainly to the possibility of at least duplicity with Ann.

§ 4

For a whole day he had refrained with some insistence from going off to New Romney again. . . .

I do not know if this may count in palliation of his misconduct. Men, real Strong-Souled, Healthy Men, should be, I suppose, impervious to conversational atmospheres, but I have never claimed for Kipps a place at these high levels. The fact remains that the next day he spent the afternoon with Ann and found no scruple in displaying himself a budding lover.

He had met her in the High Street, had stopped her, and almost on the spur of the moment had boldly proposed a walk, "for the sake of old times."

"*I* don't mind," said Ann.

Her consent almost frightened Kipps. His imagination had not carried him to that. "It would be a lark," said Kipps, and looked up the street and down. "Now?" he said.

"I don't mind a bit, Artie. I was just going for a walk along towards St. Mary's."

"Let's go that way be'ind the church," said Kipps; and presently they found themselves drifting seaward in a mood of pleasant commonplace. For a while they talked of Sid. It went clean out of Kipps' head even at that early stage that Ann was a "girl" according to the exposition of Chitterlow, and for a time he remembered only that she was Ann. But afterwards, with the reek of that talk in his head, he lapsed a little from that personal relation. They came out upon the beach and sat down in a tumbled pebbly place where a meagre grass and patches of sea poppy were growing, and Kipps reclined on his elbow and tossed pebbles in his hand, and Ann sat up, sunlit, regarding him. They talked in fragments. They exhausted Sid, they exhausted Ann, and Kipps was chary of his riches.

He declined to a faint love-making. "I got that 'arf sixpence still," he said.

"Reely?"

That changed the key. "I always kept mine, some'ow," said Ann, and there was a pause.

They spoke of how often they had thought of each other during those intervening years. Kipps may have been untruthful, but Ann perhaps was not. "I met people here and there," said Ann; "but I never met anyone quite like you, Artie."

"It's jolly our meeting again, anyhow," said Kipps. "Look at that ship out there. She's pretty close in. . . ."

He had a dull period, became indeed almost pensive, and then he was enterprising for a while. He tossed up his pebbles so that as if by accident they fell on Ann's hand. Then, very penitently, he stroked the place.

That would have led to all sorts of coquetries on the part of Flo Bates, for example, but it disconcerted and checked Kipps to find Ann made no objection, smiled pleasantly down on him, with eyes half shut because of the sun. She was taking things very much for granted.

He began to talk, and Chitterlow standards resuming possession of him he said he had never forgotten her.

" I never forgotten you either, Artie," she said. " Funny, isn't it?"

It impressed Kipps also as funny.

He became reminiscent, and suddenly a warm summer's evening came back to him. " Remember them cockchafers, Ann?" he said. But the reality of the evening he recalled was not the chase of cockchafers. The great reality that had suddenly arisen between them was that he had never kissed Ann in his life. He looked up and there were her lips.

He had wanted to very badly, and his memory leaped and annihilated an interval. That old resolution came back to him, and all sorts of new resolutions passed out of mind. And he had learnt something since those boyish days. This time he did not ask. He went on talking, his nerves began very faintly to quiver, and his mind grew bright.

Presently, having satisfied himself that there was no one to see, he sat up beside her and remarked upon the clearness of the air, and how close Dungeness seemed to them. Then they came upon a pause again.

" Ann," he whispered, and put an arm that quivered about her.

She was mute and unresisting, and, as he was to remember, solemn.

He turned her face towards him, and kissed her lips, and she kissed him back again—kisses frank and tender as a child's.

§ 5

It was curious that in the retrospect he did not find
nearly the satisfaction in this infidelity he had imagined
was there. It was no doubt desperately doggish, doggish to an almost Chitterlowesque degree, to recline
on the beach at Littlestone with a "girl," to make love
to her and to achieve the triumph of kissing her, when
he was engaged to another "girl" at Folkestone, but
somehow these two people were not "girls," they were
Ann and Helen. Particularly Helen declined to be
considered as a "girl." And there was something in
Ann's quietly friendly eyes, in her frank smile, in the
naïve pressure of her hand, there was something un-
defended and welcoming that imparted a flavour to the
business upon which he had not counted. He had
learnt about women from her. That refrain ran
through his mind and deflected his thoughts, but as
a matter of fact he had learnt about nothing but
himself.

He wanted very much to see Ann some more and
explain. He did not clearly know what it was he
wanted to explain.

He did not clearly know anything. It is the last
achievement of the intelligence to get all of one's life
into one coherent scheme, and Kipps was only in a
measure more aware of himself as a whole than is a
tree. His existence was an affair of dissolving and
recurring moods. When he thought of Helen or Ann
or any of his friends, he thought sometimes of this
aspect and sometimes of that—and often one aspect was
finally incongruous with another. He loved Helen, he
revered Helen. He was also beginning to hate her
with some intensity. When he thought of that expedition to Lympne, profound, vague, beautiful emotions
flooded his being; when he thought of paying calls with
her perforce, or of her latest comment on his bearing,
he found himself rebelliously composing fierce and

pungent insults, couched in the vernacular. But Ann, whom he had seen so much less of, was a simpler memory. She was pretty, she was almost softly feminine, and she was possible to his imagination just exactly where Helen was impossible. More than anything else, she carried the charm of respect for him, the slightest glance of her eyes was balm for his perpetually wounded self-conceit.

Chance suggestions set the tune of his thoughts, and his state of health and repletion gave the colour. Yet somehow he had this at least almost clear in his mind, that to have gone to see Ann a second time, to have implied that she had been in possession of his thoughts through all this interval, and, above all, to have kissed her, was shabby and wrong. Only unhappily this much of lucidity had come now just a few hours after it was needed.

§ 6

Four days after this it was that Kipps got up so late. He got up late, cut his chin while shaving, kicked a slipper into his sponge bath and said " Desh !"

Perhaps you know those intolerable mornings, dear Reader, when you seem to have neither the heart nor the strength to rise, and your nervous adjustments are all wrong and your fingers thumbs, and you hate the very birds for singing. You feel inadequate to any demand whatever. Often such awakenings follow a poor night's rest, and commonly they mean indiscriminate eating, or those subtle mental influences old Kipps ascribed to " Foozle Ile " in the system, or worry. And with Kipps—albeit Chitterlow had again been his guest overnight—assuredly worry had played a leading rôle. Troubles had been gathering upon him for days, there had been a sort of concentration of these hosts of Midian overnight, and in the grey small hours Kipps had held his review.

The predominating trouble marched under this banner :

MR. KIPPS

MRS. BINDON BOTTING

AT HOME

Thursday, September 16th

Anagrams, 4 to 6.30.   *R.S.V.P.*

a banner that was the facsimile of a card upon his looking glass in the room below. And in relation to this terribly significant document things had come to a pass with Helen that he could only describe in his own expressive idiom as " words."

It had long been a smouldering issue between them that Kipps was not availing himself with any energy or freedom of the opportunities he had of social exercises, much less was he seeking additional opportunities. He had, it was evident, a peculiar dread of that universal afternoon enjoyment, the Call, and Helen made it un-ambiguously evident that this dread was " silly " and had to be overcome. His first display of this unmanly weakness occurred at the Cootes' on the day before he kissed Ann. They were all there, chatting very pleasantly, when the little servant with the big cap announced the younger Miss Wace.

Whereupon Kipps manifested a lively horror and rose partially from his chair. " O Gum!" he protested. " Carn't I go upstairs?"

Then he sank back, for it was too late. Very prob-ably the younger Miss Wace had heard him as she came in.

Helen said nothing of that, though her manner may have shown her surprise, but afterwards she told Kipps he must get used to seeing people, and suggested that he should pay a series of calls with Mrs. Walshingham and herself. Kipps gave a reluctant assent at the time and afterwards displayed a talent for evasion that she had not suspected in him. At last she did succeed in securing him for a call upon Miss Punchafer of Radnor Park—a particularly easy call because Miss Punchafer, being so deaf, one could say practically what one liked —and then outside the gate he shirked again. "I can't go in," he said in a faded voice.

"You *must*," said Helen, beautiful as ever, but even more than a little hard and forbidding.

"I can't."

He produced his handkerchief hastily, thrust it to his face, and regarded her over it with rounded, hostile eyes.

"'Possible," he said, in a hoarse, strange voice out of the handkerchief. "Nozzez bleedin'."

But that was the end of his power of resistance, and when the rally for the Anagram Tea occurred she bore down his feeble protests altogether. She insisted. She said frankly, "I am going to give you a good talking to about this," and she did. . . .

From Coote he gathered something of the nature of Anagrams and Anagram parties. An anagram, Coote explained, was a word spelt the same way as another, only differently arranged, as, for instance, T. O. C. O. E. would be an anagram for his own name, Coote.

"T. O. C. O. E.," repeated Kipps very carefully.

"Or T. O. E. C. O.," said Coote.

"Or T. O. E. C. O.," said Kipps, assisting his poor head by nodding it at each letter.

"Toe Company like," he said in his efforts to comprehend.

When Kipps was clear what an anagram meant, Coote came to the second heading, the Tea. Kipps gathered there might be from thirty to sixty people present, and that each one would have an anagram; pinned on. "They give you a card to put your guesses on, rather like a dence programme, and then, you know, you go round and guess," said Coote. "It's rather good fun."

" Oo rather !" said Kipps, with stimulated gusto.

" It shakes everybody up together," said Coote.

Kipps smiled and nodded. . . .

In the small hours all his painful meditations were threaded by the vision of that Anagram Tea; it kept marching to and fro and in and out of all his other troubles, from thirty to sixty people, mostly ladies and callers, and a great number of the letters of the alphabet, and more particularly P. I. K. P. S. and T. O. E. C. O., and he was trying to make one word out of the whole interminable procession. . . .

This word, as he finally gave it with some emphasis to the silence of the night, was " *Demn !*"

Then, wreathed as it were in this lettered procession, was the figure of Helen as she had appeared at the moment of "words"; her face a little hard, a little irritated, a little disappointed. He imagined himself going around and guessing under her eye. . . .

He tried to think of other things, without lapsing upon a still deeper uneasiness that was decorated with yellow sea poppies; and the figures of Buggins, Pierce and Carshot, three murdered Friendships, rose reproachfully in the stillness and changed horrible apprehensions into unspeakable remorse. Last night had been their customary night for the banjo, and Kipps, with a certain tremulous uncertainty, had put old Methusaleh amidst a retinue of glasses on the table and opened a box of choice cigars. In vain. They were in no need, it seemed, of *his* society. But instead Chitterlow had come, anxious to know if it was all right about that syndicate plan. He had declined anything but a very weak whisky and soda, "just to drink," at least until business was settled, and had then opened the whole affair with an effect of great orderliness to Kipps. Soon he was taking another whisky by sheer inadvertency, and the complex fabric of his conversation was running more easily from the broad loom of his mind. Into that pattern had inter-woven a narrative of extensive alterations in the Pestered Butterfly—the neck and beetle business was to be restored—the story of a grave difference of opinion with Mrs. Chitterlow where and how to live after the play had succeeded, the reasons why the Hon. Thomas Norgate had never financed a syndicate, and much matter also about the syndicate now under discussion. But if the current of their conversation had been vortical and crowded, the outcome was perfectly clear. Kipps was to be the chief participator in the syndicate, and his contribution was to be two thousand pounds. Kipps groaned and rolled over, and found Helen, as it were, on the other side. " Promise me," she had said, " you won't do anything without consulting me."

Kipps at once rolled back to his former position, and for a space lay quite still. He felt like a very young rabbit in a trap.

Then suddenly, with extraordinary distinctness, his heart cried out for Ann; and he saw her as he had seen her at New Romney, sitting amidst the yellow sea poppies with the sunlight on her face. His heart called out for her in the darkness as one calls for rescue. He knew, as though he had known it always, that he loved Helen no more. He wanted Ann, he wanted to hold her and be held by her, to kiss her again and again, to turn his back for ever on all these other things. . . .

He rose late, but this terrible discovery was still there, undispelled by cockcrow or the day. He rose in a shattered condition, and he cut himself while shaving, but at last he got into his dining-room and could pull the bell for the hot constituents of his multifarious breakfast. And then he turned to his letters. There were two real letters in addition to the customary electric-belt advertisement, continental lottery circular and betting tout's card. One was in a slight-mourning envelope and addressed in an unfamiliar hand. This he opened first and discovered a note :

> Mrs. RAYMOND WACE
> requests the pleasure of
> Mr. KIPPS'
> Company at Dinner
> *on Tuesday, September 21st, at 8 o'clock*
>
> *R.S.V.P.*

With a hasty movement Kipps turned his mind to the second letter. It was an unusually long one from his Uncle, and ran as follows :

"My Dear Nephew :

"We are considerably startled by your letter though expecting something of the sort and disposed to hope for the best. If the young lady is a relation to the Earl of Beaupres well and good but take care you are not being imposed upon for there are many who will be glad enough to snap you up now your circumstances are altered. I waited on the old Earl once while in service and he was remarkably close with his tips and suffered from corns. A hasty old gent and hard to please—I daresay he has forgotten me altogether—and anyhow there is no need to rake up bygones. To-morrow is bus day and as you say the young lady is living near by we shall shut up shop for there is really nothing doing now what with all the visitors bringing everything with them down to their very children's pails and say how de do to her and give her a bit of a kiss and encouragement if we think her suitable—she will be pleased to see your old uncle. We wish we could have had a look at her first but still there is not much mischief done and hoping that all will turn out well yet I am

"Your affectionate Uncle
"Edward George Kipps.

"My heartburn still very bad. I shall bring over a few bits of rhubub I picked up, a sort you won't get in Folkestone and if possible a good bunch of flowers for the young lady."

"Comin' over to-day," said Kipps, standing help-lessly with the letter in his hand.

"'Ow the Juice——?

"I carn't.

"Kiss 'er!"   .

A terrible anticipation of that gathering framed itself in his mind—a hideous, impossible disaster.

"I carn't even face 'er——"

His voice went up to a note of despair, "And it's too late to telegrarf and stop 'em!"

§ 7

About twenty minutes after this, an outporter in Castle Hill Avenue was accosted by a young man with a pale, desperate face, an exquisitely rolled umbrella and a heavy Gladstone bag.

"Carry this to the station, will you?" said the young man. "I want to ketch the nex' train to London. . . . You'll 'ave to look sharp—I 'aven't very much time."

CHAPTER THE SEVENTH

London

LONDON was Kipps' third world. There were no
doubt other worlds, but Kipps knew only these three;
firstly, New Romney and the Emporium, constituting his
primary world, his world of origin, which also contained Ann; secondly, the world of culture and refinement, the world of which Coote was chaperon, and
into which Kipps was presently to marry, a world it
was fast becoming evident absolutely incompatible
with the first; and thirdly, a world still to a large
extent unexplored, London. London presented itself
as a place of great grey spaces and incredible multitudes
of people, centring about Charing Cross Station and
the Royal Grand Hotel, and containing at unexpected
arbitrary points shops of the most amazing sort, statuary,
squares, restaurants—where it was possible for clever
people like Walshingham to order a lunch item by
item, to the waiters' evident respect and sympathy—
exhibitions of incredible things—the Walshinghams had

taken him to the Arts and Crafts and to a picture gallery—and theatres. London, moreover, is rendered habitable by hansom cabs. Young Walshingham was a natural cab-taker, he was an all-round large-minded young man, and he had in the course of their two days' stay taken Kipps into no less than nine, so that Kipps was singularly not afraid of these vehicles. He knew that wherever you were, so soon as you were thoroughly lost you said " Hi!" to a cab, and then " Royal Grand Hotel." Day and night these trusty conveyances are returning the strayed Londoner back to his point of departure; and were it not for their activity, in a little while the whole population, so vast and incomprehensible is the intricate complexity of this great city, would be hopelessly lost for ever. At any rate, that is how the thing presented itself to Kipps, and I have heard much the same from American visitors.

His train was composed of corridor carriages, and he forgot his trouble for a time in the wonders of this modern substitute for railway compartments. He went from the non-smoking to the smoking carriage and smoked a cigarette, and strayed from his second-class carriage to a first and back. But presently Black Care got aboard the train and came and sat beside him. The exhilaration of escape had evaporated now, and he was presented with a terrible picture of his Aunt and Uncle arriving at his lodgings and finding him fled. He had left a hasty message that he was called away suddenly on business, " ver' important business," and they were to be sumptuously entertained. His immediate motive had been his passionate dread of an encounter between these excellent but unrefined old people and the Walshinghams, but now that end was secured, he could see how thwarted and exasperated they would be.

How to explain to them?

He ought never to have written to tell them!

He ought to have got married and told them afterwards.

He ought to have consulted Helen.

" Promise me," she had said.

" Oh, *desh!*" said Kipps, and got up and walked back into the smoking-car and began to consume cigarettes.

Suppose, after all, they found out the Walshinghams' address and went there!

At Charing Cross, however, were distractions again. He took a cab in an entirely Walshingham manner, and was pleased to note the enhanced respect of the cabman when he mentioned the Royal Grand. He followed Walshingham's routine on their previous visit with perfect success. They were very nice in the office, and gave him an excellent room at fourteen shillings the night.

He went up and spent a considerable time examining the furniture of his room, scrutinising himself in its various mirrors and sitting on the edge of the bed whistling. It was a vast and splendid apartment, and cheap at fourteen shillings. But finding the figure of Ann inclined to resume possession of his mind, he roused himself and descended by the staircase after a momentary hesitation before the lift. He had thought of lunch, but he drifted into the great drawing-room and read a guide to the Hotels of Europe for a space, until a doubt whether he was entitled to use this palatial apartment without extra charge arose in his mind. He would have liked something to eat very much now, but his inbred terror of the table was strong. He did at last get by a porter in uniform towards the dining-room, but at the sight of a number of waiters and tables, with remarkable complications of knives and glasses, terror seized him, and he backed out again with a mumbled remark to the waiter in the doorway about this not being the way.

He hovered in the hall and lounge until he thought the presiding porter regarded him with suspicion, and then went up to his room again by the staircase, got his hat and umbrella and struck boldly across the courtyard. He would go to a restaurant instead.

He had a moment of elation in the gateway. He felt all the Strand must notice him as he emerged through the great gate of the hotel. "One of these here rich swells," they would say. "Don't they go it just!" A cabman touched his hat. "No fear," said Kipps pleasantly.

Then he remembered he was hungry.

Yet he decided he was in no great hurry for lunch, in spite of an internal protest, and turned eastward along the Strand in a leisurely manner. He would find a place to suit him soon enough. He tried to remember the sort of dishes Walshingham had ordered. Before all things he didn't want to go into a place and look like a fool. Some of these places rook you dreadful, besides making fun of you. There was a place near Essex Street where there was a window brightly full of chops, tomatoes and lettuce. He stopped at this and reflected for a time, and then it occurred to him that you were expected to buy these things raw and cook them at home. Anyhow, there was sufficient doubt in the matter to stop him. He drifted on to a neat window with champagne bottles, a dish of asparagus and a framed menu of a two-shilling lunch. He was about to enter, when fortunately he perceived two waiters looking at him over the back screen of the window with a most ironical expression, and he sheered off at once. There was a wonderful smell of hot food half way down Fleet Street and a nice-looking tavern with several doors, but he could not decide which door. His nerve was going under the strain.

He hesitated at Farringdon Street and drifted up to St. Paul's and round the churchyard, full chiefly of dead bargains in the shop windows, to Cheapside. But now Kipps was getting demoralised, and each house of refreshment seemed to promise still more complicated obstacles to food. He didn't know how you went in and what was the correct thing to do with your hat; he didn't know what you said to the waiter or what you called the different things; he was convinced absolutely he would "fumble," as Shalford would have said, and look like a fool. Somebody might laugh at him! The hungrier he got the more unendurable was the thought that anyone should laugh at him. For a time he considered an extraordinary expedient to account for his ignorance. He would go in and pretend to be a foreigner. . . . Presently he had drifted into a part of London where there did not seem to be any refreshment places at all.

"Oh, *desh!*" said Kipps, in a sort of agony of indecisiveness. "The very nex' place I see, in I go."

The next place was a fried-fish shop in a little side street, where there were also sausages on a gas-lit grill.

He would have gone in, but suddenly a new scruple came to him, that he was too well dressed for the company he could see dimly through the steam sitting at the counter and eating with a sort of nonchalant speed.

§ 2

He was half minded to resort to a hansom and brave the terrors of the dining-room of the Royal Grand— they wouldn't know why he had gone out really— when the only person he knew in London appeared (as the only person one does know will do in London) and slapped him on the shoulder. Kipps was hovering at a window a few yards from the fish shop, pretending to examine some really strikingly cheap pink baby linen, and trying to settle finally about those sausages.

"Hullo, Kipps!" cried Sid; "spending the millions?"

Kipps turned, and was glad to perceive no lingering vestige of the chagrin that had been so painful at New Romney. Sid looked grave and important, and he wore a quite new silk hat that gave a commercial touch to a generally socialistic costume. For a moment the sight of Sid uplifted Kipps wonderfully. He saw him as a friend and helper, and only presently did it come clearly into his mind that this was the brother of Ann.

He made amiable noises.

"I've just been up this way," Sid explained, "buying a second-hand 'namelling stove. . . . I'm going to 'namel myself."

"Lor'!" said Kipps.

"Yes. Do me a lot of good. Let the customer choose his colour. See? What brings *you* up?"

Kipps had a momentary vision of his foiled Uncle and Aunt. "Jest a bit of a change," he said.

Sid came to a swift decision. "Come down to my little show. I got someone I'd like to see talking to you."

Even then Kipps did not think of Ann in this connection.

"Well," he said, trying to invent an excuse on the spur of the moment. "Fact is," he explained, "I was jest looking round to get a bit of lunch."

"Dinner we call it," said Sid. "But that's all right. You can't get anything to eat hereabout. If you're not too haughty to do a bit of slumming, there's some mutton spoiling for me now——"

The word "mutton" affected Kipps greatly.

"It won't take us 'arf an hour," said Sid, and Kipps was carried.

He discovered another means of London locomotion in the Underground Railway, and recovered his self-possession in that interest. "You don't mind going third?" asked Sid and Kipps said, "Nort a *bit* of it." They were silent in the train for a time, on account of strangers in the carriage, and then Sid began to explain who it was that he wanted Kipps to meet. "It's a chap named Masterman—do you no end of good.

"He occupies our first floor front room, you know. It isn't so much for gain I let as company. We don't *want* the whole 'ouse, that's one thing, and another is

I knew the man before. Met him at our Sociological, and after a bit he said he wasn't comfortable where he was. That's how it came about. He's a first-class chap —first class. Science! You should see his books!

"Properly he's a sort of journalist. He's written a lot of things, but he's been too ill lately to do very much. Poetry he's written, all sorts. He writes for the *Commonweal* sometimes, and sometimes he reviews books. He's got 'eaps of books—'eaps. Besides selling a lot.

"He knows a regular lot of people, and all sorts of things. He's been a dentist, and he's a qualified chemist, an' I seen him often reading German and French. Taught 'imself. He was here——"

Sid indicated South Kensington, which had come opportunely outside the carriage windows, with a nod of his head, "—three years. Studying science. But you'll see 'im. When he really gets to talking—he *pours* it out."

"Ah!" said Kipps, nodding sympathetically, with his two hands on his umbrella knob.

"He'll do big things some day," said Sid. "He's written a book on science already. 'Physiography,' it's called. 'Elementary Physiography'! Some day he'll write an Advanced—when he gets time."

He let this soak into Kipps.

"I can't introduce you to lords and swells," he went on, "but I *can* show you a Famous Man, that's going to be. I *can* do that. Leastways—unless——"

Sid hesitated.

"He's got a frightful cough," he said.

"He won't care to talk to me," weighed Kipps.

"That's all right; *he* won't mind. He's fond of talking. He'd talk to anyone," said Sid reassuringly, and added a perplexing bit of Londonised Latin. "He doesn't *pute* anything, *non alienum*. You know."

"*I* know," said Kipps intelligently, over his umbrella knob, though of course that was altogether untrue.

§ 3

Kipps found Sid's shop a practical-looking establishment, stocked with the most remarkable collection of bicycles and pieces of bicycle that he had ever beheld. "My hiring stock," said Sid, with a wave to this ironmongery, "and there's the best machine at a democratic price in London, The Red Flag, built by *me*. See?"

He indicated a graceful grey-brown framework in the window. "And there's my stock of accessories—store prices.

"Go in for motors a bit," added Sid.

"Mutton?" said Kipps, not hearing him distinctly.

"Motors, I *said*. . . . 'Owever, Mutton Department 'ere," and he opened a door that had a curtain-guarded window in its upper panel, to reveal a little room with red walls and green furniture, with a white-clothed table and the generous promise of a meal. "Fanny!" he shouted. . "Here's Art Kipps."

A bright-eyed young woman of five or six and twenty in a pink print appeared, a little flushed from cooking, and wiped a hand on an apron and shook hands and smiled, and said it would all be ready in a minute. She went on to say she had heard of Kipps and his luck, and meanwhile Sid vanished to draw the beer, and returned with two glasses for himself and Kipps.

"Drink that," said Sid, and Kipps felt all the better for it.

"I give Mr. Masterman '*is* upstairs a hour ago," said Mrs. Sid. "I didn't think 'e ought to wait."

A rapid succession of brisk movements on the part of everyone, and they were all four at dinner—the fourth person being Master Walt Whitman Pornick, a cheerful young gentleman of one and a half, who was given a spoon to hammer on the table with to keep him quiet, and who got "Kipps" right at the first effort and kept it all through the meal, combining it first with this previous acquisition, and then that. "Peacock Kipps"

9*

said Master Walt, at which there was great laughter, and also "More Mutton Kipps."

"He's a regular oner," said Mrs. Sid, "for catching up words. You can't say a word but what 'e's on to it."

There were no serviettes and less ceremony, and Kipps thought he had never enjoyed a meal so much. Everyone was a little excited by the meeting and chatting and disposed to laugh, and things went easily from the very beginning. If there was a pause Master Walt filled it in. Mrs. Sid, who tempered her enormous admiration for Sid's intellect and his socialism and his severe business methods by a motherly sense of her sex and seniority, spoke of them both as "you boys," and dilated—when she was not urging Kipps to have some more of this or that—on the disparity between herself and her husband.

"Shouldn't ha' thought there was a year between you," said Kipps; "you seem jest a match."

"I'm *his* match, anyhow," said Mrs. Sid, and no epigram of young Walshingham's was ever better received.

"Match," said young Walt, coming in on the tail of the joke and getting a round for himself.

Any sense of superior fortune had long vanished from Kipps' mind, and he found himself looking at host and hostess with enormous respect. Really old Sid was a wonderful chap, here in his own house at two and twenty, carving his own mutton and lording it over wife and child. No legacies needed by him! And Mrs. Sid, so kind and bright and hearty! And the child, old Sid's child! Old Sid had jumped round a bit. It needed the sense of his fortune at the back of his mind to keep Kipps from feeling abject. He resolved he'd buy young Walt something tremendous in toys at the first opportunity.

"Drop more beer, Art?"

"Right you are, old man."

"Cut Mr. Kipps a bit more bread, Sid."

"Can't I pass *you* a bit?"

Sid was all right, Sid was; there was no mistake about that.

It was growing up in his mind that Sid was the brother of Ann, but he said nothing about her for excellent reasons. After all, Sid's irritation at her name when they had met in New Romney seemed to show a certain separation. They didn't tell each other much. . . . He didn't know how things might be between Ann and Mrs. Sid either.

Still, for all that, Sid was Ann's brother.

The furniture of the room did not assert itself very much above the cheerful business of the table, but Kipps was impresesd with the idea that it was pretty. There was a dresser at the end with a number of gay plates and a mug or so, a Labour Day poster, by Walter Crane, on the wall, and through the glass and over the blind of the shop door one had a glimpse of the bright-coloured advertisement cards of bicycle dealers, and a shelf full of boxes labelled, The Paragon Bell, The Scarum Bell, and The Patent Omi! Horn. . . .

It seemed incredible that he had been in Folkestone that morning, that even now his Aunt and Uncle——!

Brrr. It didn't do to think of his Aunt and Uncle.

§ 4

When Sid repeated his invitation to come and see Masterman, Kipps, now flushed with beer and Irish stew, said he didn't mind if he did, and after a preliminary shout from Sid that was answered by a voice and a cough, the two went upstairs.

"Masterman's a rare one," said Sid over his arm and in an undertone. "You should hear him speak at a meeting. . . . If he's in form, that is."

He rapped and went into a large, untidy room.

"This is Kipps," he said. "You know. The chap I told you of. With twelve 'undred a year."

Masterman sat gnawing at an empty pipe, and as close to the fire as though it was alight and the season midwinter. Kipps concentrated upon him for a space, and only later took in something of the frowsy furniture, the little bed half behind, and evidently supposed to be wholly behind, a careless screen, the spittoon by the fender, the remains of a dinner on the chest of drawers and the scattered books and papers. Masterman's face showed him a man of forty or more, with curious hollows at the sides of his forehead and about his eyes. His eyes were very bright; there was a spot of red in each cheek, and the wiry black moustache under his short red nose had been trimmed with scissors into a sort of brush along his upper lip. His teeth were darkened ruins. His jacket collar was turned up about a knitted white neck wrap, and his sleeves betrayed no cuffs. He did not rise to greet Kipps, but held out a thin-wristed hand and pointed with the other to a bedroom armchair.

"Glad to see you," he said. "Sit down and make yourself at home. Will you smoke?"

Kipps said he would, and produced his store. He was about to take one, and then, with a civil afterthought, handed the packet first to Masterman and Sid. Masterman pretended surprise to find his pipe out before he took one. There was an interlude of matches. Sid pushed the end of the screen out of his way, sat down on the bed thus frankly admitted, and prepared, with a certain quiet satisfaction of manner, to witness Masterman's treatment of Kipps.

"And how does it feel to have twelve hundred a year?" asked Masterman, holding his cigarette to his nose tip in a curious manner.

"It's rum," confided Kipps, after a reflective interval. "It feels juiced rum."

"I've never felt it," said Masterman.

"It takes a bit of getting into," said Kipps. "I can tell you that."

Masterman smoked and regarded Kipps with curious eyes.

"I expect it does," he said presently.

"And has it made you perfectly happy?" he asked abruptly.

"I couldn't 'ardly say *that*," said Kipps.

Masterman smiled. "No," he said. "Has it made you much happier?"

"It did at first."

"Yes. But you got used to it. How long, for example, did the real delirious excitement last?"

"Oo, *that!* Perhaps a week," said Kipps.

Masterman nodded his head. "That's what discourages *me* from amassing wealth," he said to Sid. "You adjust yourself. It doesn't last. I've always had an inkling of that, and it's interesting to get it confirmed. I shall go on sponging for a bit longer on *you*, I think."

"You don't," said Sid. "No fear."

"Twenty-four thousand pounds," said Masterman, and blew a cloud of smoke. "Lord! Doesn't it worry you?"

"It is a bit worrying at times. . . . Things 'appen."

"Going to marry?"

"Yes."

"H'm. Lady, I guess, of a superior social position?"

"Rather," said Kipps. "Cousin to the Earl of Beaupres."

Masterman readjusted his long body with an air of having accumulated all the facts he needed. He snuggled his shoulder-blades down into the chair and raised his angular knees. "I doubt," he said, flicking cigarette ash into the atmosphere, "if any great gain or loss of money does—as things are at present—make more than the slightest difference in one's happiness. It ought to—if money was what it ought to be, the token given for service; one ought to get an increase in power and happiness for every pound one got. But the plain fact is the times are out of joint, and money——money, like everything else, is a deception and a disappointment."

He turned his face to Kipps and enforced his next words with the index finger of his lean, lank hand. " If I thought otherwise," he said, " I should exert myself to get some. But if one sees things clearly, one is so discouraged. So confoundedly discouraged. . . . When you first got your money, you thought that it meant you might buy just anything you fancied?"

" I was a bit that way," said Kipps.

" And you found that you couldn't. You found that for all sorts of things it was a question of where to buy and how to buy, and what you didn't know how to buy with your money, straight away this world planted something else upon you——"

" I got rather done over a banjo first day," said Kipps. " Leastways, my Uncle says so."

" Exactly," said Masterman.

Sid began to speak from the bed. " That's all very well, Masterman," he said, " but after all money *is* Power, you know. You can do all sorts of things——"

" I'm talking of happiness," said Masterman. " You can do all sorts of things with a loaded gun in the Hammersmith Broadway, but nothing—practically—that will make you or anyone else very happy. Nothing. Power's a different matter altogether. As for happiness, you want a world in order before money or property, or any of those things have any real value; and this world, I tell you, is hopelessly out of joint. Man is a social animal with a mind nowadays that goes round the globe, and a community cannot be happy in one part and unhappy in another. It's all or nothing, no patching any more for ever. It is the standing mistake of the world not to understand that. Consequently people think there is a class or order somewhere, just above them or just below them, or a country or place somewhere, that is really safe and happy. The fact is,

Society is one body, and it is either well or ill. That's
the law. This society we live in is ill. It's a fractious,
feverish invalid, gouty, greedy and ill-nourished. You
can't have a happy left leg with neuralgia, or a happy
throat with a broken leg. That's my position, and
that's the knowledge you'll come to. I'm so satisfied
of it that I sit here and wait for my end quite calmly,
sure that I can't better things by bothering—in my
time, and so far as I am concerned, that is. I'm not
even greedy any more—my egotism's at the bottom of
a pond, with a philosophical brick round its neck. The
world is ill, my time is short and my strength is small.
I'm as happy here as anywhere."

He coughed and was silent for a moment, then
brought the index finger round to Kipps again.
"You've had the opportunity of sampling two grades
of society, and you don't find the new people you're
among much better or any happier than the old?"

"No," said Kipps reflectively. "No. I 'aven't
seen it quite like that before, but— No. They're
not."

"And you might go all up the scale and down the
scale and find the same thing. Man's a gregarious
beast, a gregarious beast, and no money will buy you
out of your own time—any more than out of your
own skin. All the way up and all the way down the
scale there's the same discontent. No one is quite sure
where they stand, and everyone's fretting. The herd's
uneasy and feverish. All the old tradition goes or has
gone, and there's no one to make a new tradition.
Where are your nobles now? Where are your gentlemen? They vanished directly the peasant found out
he wasn't happy and ceased to be a peasant. There's
big men and little men mixed up together, that's all.
None of us know where we are. Your cads in a bank
holiday train and your cads on a two thousand pound
motor, except for a difference in scale, there's not a pin
to choose between them. Your smart society is as low

and vulgar and uncomfortable for a balanced soul as a gin palace, no more and no less; there's no place or level of honour or fine living left in the world; so what's the good of climbing?"

"'Ear, 'ear," said Sid.

"It's true," said Kipps.

"*I* don't climb," said Masterman, and accepted Kipps' silent offer of another cigarette.

"No," he said. "This world is out of joint. It's broken up, and I doubt if it will heal. I doubt very much if it'll heal. We're in the beginning of the Sickness of the World."

He rolled his cigarette in his lean fingers and repeated with satisfaction : "The Sickness of the World."

"It's we've got to make it better," said Sid, and looked at Kipps.

"Ah, Sid's an optimist," said Masterman.

"So are you, most times," said Sid.

Kipps lit another cigarette with an air of intelligent participation.

"Frankly," said Masterman, recrossing his legs and expelling a jet of smoke luxuriously, "frankly, I think this civilisation of ours is on the topple."

"There's Socialism," said Sid.

"There's no imagination to make use of it."

"We've got to *make* one," said Sid.

"In a couple of centuries perhaps," said Masterman. "But meanwhile we're going to have a pretty acute attack of universal confusion. Universal confusion. Like one of those crushes when men are killed and maimed for no reason at all, going into a meeting or crowding for a train. Commercial and Industrial Stresses. Political Exploitation. Tariff Wars. Revolutions. All the bloodshed that will come of some fools calling half the white world yellow. These things alter the attitude of everybody to everybody. Everybody's going to feel 'em. Every fool in the world panting and shoving. We're all going to be as happy and comfortable as a household during a removal. What else can we expect?"

Kipps was moved to speak, but not in answer to Masterman's inquiry. "I've never rightly got the 'eng of this Socialism," he said. "What's it going to do, like?"

They had been imagining that he had some elementary idea in the matter, but as soon as he had made it clear that he hadn't, Sid plunged at exposition, and in a little while Masterman, abandoning his pose of the detached man ready to die, joined in. At first he joined in only to correct Sid's version, but afterwards he took control. His manner changed. He sat up and rested his elbow on his knees, and his cheek flushed a little. He expanded his case against property and the property class with such vigour that Kipps was completely carried away, and never thought of asking for a clear vision of the thing that would fill the void this abolition might create. For a time he quite forgot his own private opulence. And it was as if something had been lit in Masterman. His languor passed. He enforced his words by gestures of his long, thin hands. And as he passed swiftly from point to point of his argument, it was evident he grew angry.

"To-day," he said, "the world is ruled by rich men; they may do almost anything they like with the world. And what are they doing? Laying it waste!"

"Hear, hear!" said Sid, very sternly.

Masterman stood up, gaunt and long, thrust his hands in his pockets and turned his back to the fireplace.

"Collectively, the rich to-day have neither heart nor imagination. No! They own machinery, they have knowledge and instruments and powers beyond all previous dreaming, and what are they doing with them? Think what they are doing with them, Kipps, and think what they might do. God gives them a power like the motor car, and all they can do with it is to go careering about the roads in goggled masks killing children and making machinery hateful to the soul of man! ("True," said Sid, "true.") God gives them means of communication, power unparalleled of every sort, time and absolute liberty. They waste it all in folly! Here under their feet (and Kipps' eyes followed the direction of a lean index finger to the hearthrug), under their accursed wheels, the great mass of men festers and breeds in darkness, darkness those others make by standing in the light. The darkness breeds and breeds. It knows no better. . . . Unless you can crawl or pander or rob you must stay in the stew you are born in. And those rich beasts above claw and clutch as though they had nothing! They grudge us our schools, they grudge us a gleam of light and air, they cheat us and then seek to forget us. . . . There is no rule, no guidance, only accidents and happy flukes. . . . Our multitudes of poverty increase, and this crew of rulers makes no provision, foresees nothing, anticipates nothing. . . ."

He paused and made a step, and stood over Kipps in a white heat of anger. Kipps nodded in a non-committal manner and looked hard and rather gloomily at his host's slipper as he talked.

"It isn't as though they had something to show for the waste they make of us, Kipps. They haven't. They are ugly and cowardly and mean. Look at their women! Painted, dyed and drugged, hiding their ugly shapes under a load of dress! There isn't a woman in the swim of society at the present time who wouldn't sell herself body and soul, who wouldn't lick the boots of a Jew or marry a nigger, rather than live decently on a hundred a year! On what would be wealth for you and me! They know it. They know we know it. . . . No one believes in them. No one believes in nobility any more. Nobody believes in kingship any more. Nobody believes there is justice in the law. . . . But people have habits, people go on in the old grooves, as long as there's work, as long

as there's weekly money. . . . It won't last, Kipps."
He coughed and paused. "Wait for the lean years,"
he cried. "Wait for the lean years." And suddenly
he fell into a struggle with his cough and spat a gout
of blood. "It's nothing," he said to Kipps' note of
startled horror.

He went on talking, and the protests of his cough
interlaced with his words, and Sid beamed in an ecstasy
of painful admiration.

"Look at the fraud they have let life become, the
miserable mockery of the hope of one's youth. What
have _I_ had? I found myself at thirteen being forced
into a factory like a rabbit into a chloroformed box.
Thirteen!—when _their_ children are babies. But even
a child of that age could see what it meant, that Hell
of a factory! Monotony and toil and contempt and
dishonour! And then death. So I fought—at
thirteen!"

Minton's "crawling up a drain pipe until you die"
echoed in Kipps' mind, but Masterman, instead of
Minton's growl, spoke in a high, indignant tenor.

"I got out at last—somehow," he said quietly,
suddenly plumping back in his chair. He went on after
a pause. "For a bit. Some of us get out by luck,
some by cunning, and crawl on to the grass, exhausted
and crippled, to die. That's a poor man's success,
Kipps. Most of us don't get out at all. I worked
all day and studied half the night, and here I am with
the common consequences. Beaten! And never once
have I had a fair chance, never once!" His lean,
clenched fist flew out in a gust of tremulous anger.
"These Skunks shut up all the university scholarships
at nineteen for fear of men like me. And then—do
nothing. . . . We're wasted for nothing. By the time
I'd learnt something the doors were locked. I thought
knowledge would do it—I did think that! I've fought
for knowledge as other men fight for bread. I've
starved for knowledge. I've turned my back on women;

I've done even that. I've burst my accursed lung. . . ."
His voice rose with impotent anger. "I'm a better
man than any ten princes alive! And I'm beaten and
wasted. I've been crushed, trampled and defiled by a
drove of hogs. I'm no use to myself or the world.
I've thrown my life away to make myself too good for
use in this huckster's scramble. If I had gone in for
business, if I had gone in for plotting to cheat my
fellow men—ah, well! It's too late. It's too late for
that, anyhow. It's too late for anything now! And I
couldn't have done it. . . . And over in New York
now there's a pet of society making a corner in wheat!

"By God!" he cried hoarsely, with a clutch of the
lean hand. "By God! If I had his throat! Even
now I might do something for the world."

He glared at Kipps, his face flushed deep, his sunken
eyes glowing with passion, and then suddenly he changed
altogether.

There was a sound of tea things rattling upon a tray
outside the door, and Sid rose to open it.

"All of which amounts to this," said Masterman,
suddenly quiet again and talking against time. "The
world is out of joint, and there isn't a soul alive who
isn't half waste or more. You'll find it the same with
you in the end, wherever your luck may take you. . . .
I suppose you won't mind my having another cigarette?"

He took Kipps' cigarette with a hand that trembled
so violently it almost missed its object, and stood up,
with something of guilt in his manner, as Mrs. Sid came
into the room.

Her eye met him and marked the flush upon his face.

"Been talking Socialism?" said Mrs. Sid, a little
severely.

§ 5

Six o'clock that day found Kipps drifting eastward
along the southward margin of Rotten Row. You
figure him a small, respectably attired figure going

slowly through a sometimes immensely difficult and always immense world. At times he becomes pensive and whistles softly; at times he looks about him. There are a few riders in the Row, a carriage flashes by every now and then along the roadway, and among the great rhododendrons and laurels and upon the greensward there are a few groups and isolated people dressed in the style Kipps adopted to call upon the Walshinghams when first he was engaged. Amid the complicated confusion of Kipps' mind was a regret that he had not worn his other things. . . .

Presently he perceived that he would like to sit down; a green chair tempted him. He hesitated at it, took possession of it, and leant back and crossed one leg over the other.

He rubbed his under lip with his umbrella handle and reflected upon Masterman and his denunciation of the world.

" Bit orf 'is 'ead, poor chap," said Kipps, and added : " I wonder."

He thought intently for a space.

" I wonder what he meant by the lean years."

The world seemed a very solid and prosperous concern just here, and well out of reach of Masterman's dying clutch. And yet——

It was curious he should have been reminded of Minton.

His mind turned to a far more important matter. Just at the end Sid had said to him, " Seen Ann?" and as he was about to answer, " You'll see a bit more of her now. She's got a place in Folkestone."

It had brought him back from any concern about the world being out of joint or anything of that sort.

Ann !

One might run against her any day.

He tugged at his little moustache.

He would like to run against Ann very much. . . .

And it would be juiced awkward if he did !

In Folkestone! It was a jolly sight too close. . . .

Then, at the thought that he might run against Ann in his beautiful evening dress on the way to the band, he fluttered into a momentary dream, that jumped abruptly into a nightmare.

Suppose he met her when he was out with Helen! "Oh, Lor'!" said Kipps. Life had developed a new complication that would go on and go on. For some time he wished with the utmost fervour that he had not kissed Ann, that he had not gone to New Romney the second time. He marvelled at his amazing forgetfulness of Helen on that occasion. Helen took possession of his mind. He would have to write to Helen, an easy off-hand letter to say that he had come to London for a day or so. He tried to imagine her reading it. He would write just such another letter to the old people, and say he had had to come up on business. That might do for *them* all right, but Helen was different. She would insist on explanations.

He wished he need never go back to Folkestone again. That would about settle the whole affair.

A passing group attracted his attention, two faultlessly dressed gentlemen and a radiantly expensive lady. They were talking, no doubt, very brilliantly. His eyes followed them. The lady tapped the arm of the left-hand gentleman with a daintily tinted glove. Swells! No end. . . .

His soul looked out upon life in general as a very small nestling might peep out of its nest. What an extraordinary thing life was, to be sure, and what a remarkable variety of people there were in it!

He lit a cigarette and speculated upon that receding group of three, and blew smoke and watched them. They seemed to do it all right. Probably they all had incomes of very much over twelve hundred a year. Perhaps not. Probably none of them suspected, as they went past, that he too was a gentleman of independent means, dressed as he was without distinction.

Of course things were easier for them. They were brought up always to dress well and do the right thing from their very earliest years; they started clear of all his perplexities; they had never got mixed up with all sorts of different people who didn't go together. If, for example, that lady there got engaged to that gentleman, she would be quite safe from any encounter with a corpulent, osculatory Uncle, or Chitterlow, or the dangerously significant eye of Pierce.

His thoughts came round to Helen.

When they were married and Cuyps, or Cuyp— Coote had failed to justify his " s "—and in that westend flat and shaken free of all these low class associations, would he and she parade here of an afternoon dressed like that? It would be rather fine to do so. If one's dress was all right.

Helen!

She was difficult to understand at times.

He blew extensive clouds of cigarette smoke.

There would be teas, there would be dinners, there would be calls. Of course he would get into the way of it.

But Anagrams were a bit stiff to begin with!

It was beastly confusing at first to know when to use your fork at dinner, and all that. Still——

He felt an extraordinary doubt whether he would get into the way of it. He was interested for a space by a girl and groom on horseback, and then he came back to his personal preoccupations.

He would have to write to Helen. What could he say to explain his absence from the Anagram Tea? She had been pretty clear she wanted him to come. He recalled her resolute face without any great tenderness. He *knew* he would look like a silly ass at that confounded tea! Suppose he shirked it and went back in time for the dinner! Dinners were beastly difficult too, but not as bad as Anagrams. The very first thing that might happen when he got back to Folkestone would be to run against Ann. Suppose, after all, he did meet Ann when he was with Helen!

What queer encounters were possible in the world!

Thank goodness, they were going to live in London!

But that brought him round to Chitterlow. The Chitterlows would be coming to London too. If they didn't get money they'd come after it; they weren't the sort of people to be choked off easily, and if they did they'd come to London to produce their play. He tried to imagine some seemly social occasion invaded by Chitterlow and his rhetoric, by his torrential thunder of self-assertion, the whole company flattened thereunder like wheat under a hurricane.

Confound and hang Chitterlow! Yet somehow, somewhen, one would have to settle accounts with him! And there was Sid! Sid was Ann's brother. He realised with sudden horror the social indiscretion of accepting Sid's invitation to dinner.

Sid wasn't the sort of chap one could snub or cut, and besides—Ann's brother! He didn't want to cut him. It would be worse than cutting Buggins and Pierce—a sight worse. And after that lunch!

It would be the next thing to cutting Ann herself. And even as to Ann!

Suppose he was with Helen or Coote! . . .

"Oh, Blow!" he said at last, and then, viciously, "*Blow!*" and so rose and flung away his cigarette end, and pursued his reluctant, dubitating way towards the really quite uncongenial splendours of the Royal Grand. . . .

And it is vulgarly imagined that to have money is to have no troubles at all!

§ 6

Kipps endured splendour at the Royal Grand Hotel for three nights and days, and then he retreated in disorder. The Royal Grand defeated and overcame and routed Kipps, not of intention, but by sheer royal grandeur, grandeur combined with an organisation for his comfort carried to excess. On his return he came upon a difficulty; he had lost the circular piece of cardboard with the number of his room, and he drifted about the hall and passages in a state of perplexity for some time, until he thought all the porters and officials in gold lace caps must be watching him and jesting to one another about him. Finally, in a quiet corner down below near the hairdresser's shop, he found a kindly-looking personage in bottle green, to whom he broached his difficulty. "I say," he said, with a pleasant smile, "I can't find my room nohow." The personage in bottle green, instead of laughing in a nasty way, as he might well have done, became extremely helpful, showed Kipps what to do, got his key, and conducted him by lift and passage to his chamber. Kipps tipped him half a crown.

Safe in his room, Kipps pulled himself together for dinner. He had learnt enough from young Walshingham to bring his dress clothes, and now he began to assume them. Unfortunately, in the excitement of his flight from his Aunt and Uncle, he had forgotten to put in his other boots, and he was some time deciding between his purple cloth slippers, with a golden marigold, and the prospect of cleaning the boots he was wearing with the towel, but finally, being a little footsore, he took the slippers.

Afterwards, when he saw the porters and waiters and the other guests catch sight of the slippers, he was sorry he had not chosen the boots. However, to make up for any want of style at that end, he had his crush hat under his arm.

He found the dining-room without excessive trouble. It was a vast and splendidly decorated place, and a number of people, evidently quite *au fait,* were dining there at little tables lit with electric, red shaded candles, gentlemen in evening dress, and ladies with dazzling, astonishing necks. Kipps had never seen evening dress in full vigour before, and he doubted his eyes. And there were also people not in evening dress, who, no doubt, wondered what noble family Kipps represented. There was a band in a decorated recess, and the band looked collectively at the purple slippers, and so lost any chance they may have had of a donation, so far as Kipps was concerned. The chief drawback to this magnificent place was the excessive space of floor that had to be crossed before you got your purple slippers hidden under a table.

He selected a little table—not the one where a rather impudent-looking waiter held a chair, but another—sat down, and finding his Gibus in his hand, decided after a moment of thought to rise slightly and sit on it. (It was discovered in his abandoned chair at a late hour by a supper party, and restored to him next day.)

He put the napkin carefully on one side, selected his soup without difficulty, "Clear, please," but he was rather floored by the presentation of a quite splendidly bound wine card. He turned it over, discovered a section devoted to whisky, and had a bright idea.

"'Ere," he said to the waiter, with an encouraging movement of his head, and then in a confidential manner, "you haven't any Old Methusaleh Three Stars, 'ave you?"

The waiter went away to inquire, and Kipps went on with his soup with an enhanced self-respect. Finally, Old Methusaleh being unobtainable, he ordered claret from about the middle of the list. "Let's 'ave some of this," he said. He knew claret was a good sort of wine.

"A half bottle?" said the waiter.

"Right you are," said Kipps.

He felt he was getting on. He leant back after his soup, a man of the world, and then slowly brought his eyes round to the ladies in evening dress on his right. . . .

He couldn't have thought it!

They were scorchers. Jest a bit of black velvet over the shoulders!

He looked again. One of them was laughing with a glass of wine half raised—wicked-looking woman she was—the other, the black-velvet one, was eating bits of bread with nervous quickness and talking fast.

He wished old Buggins could see them.

He found a waiter regarding him and blushed deeply. He did not look again for some time, and became confused about his knife and fork over the fish. Presently he remarked a lady in pink to the left of him eating the fish with an entirely different implement.

It was over the *vol au vent* that he began to go to pieces. He took a knife to it; then saw the lady in pink was using a fork only, and hastily put down his knife, with a considerable amount of rich creaminess on the blade, upon the cloth. Then he found that a fork in his inexperienced hand was an instrument of chase rather than capture. His ears became violently red, and then he looked up to discover the lady in pink glancing at him, and then smiling as she spoke to the man beside her.

He hated the lady in pink very much.

He stabbed a large piece of the *vol au vent* at last, and was too glad of his luck not to make a mouthful of it. But it was an extensive fragment, and pieces escaped him. Shirt front! " Desh it!" he said, and had resort to his spoon. His waiter went and spoke to two other waiters, no doubt jeering at him. He became very fierce suddenly. " 'Ere!" he said, gesticulating, and then, " clear this away!"

The entire dinner party on his right, the party of the ladies in advanced evening dress, looked at him. . . . He felt that everyone was watching him and making fun of him, and the injustice of this angered him. After all, they had had every advantage he hadn't. And then, when they got him there doing his best, what must they do but glance and sneer and nudge one another. He tried to catch them at it, and then took refuge in a second glass of wine.

Suddenly and extraordinarily he found himself a socialist. He did not care how close it was to the lean years when all these things would end.

Lamb came, with peas. He arrested the hand of the waiter. "No peas," he said. He knew something of the difficulty and danger of eating peas. Then, when the peas went away again he was embittered again. . . . Echoes of Masterman's burning rhetoric began to reverberate in his mind. Nice lot of people these were to laugh at anyone! Women half undressed! It was that made him so beastly uncomfortable. How could one eat one's dinner with people about him like that? Nice lot they were. He was glad he wasn't one of them, anyhow. Yes, they might look. He resolved if they looked at him again he would ask one of the men who he was staring at. His perturbed and angry face would have concerned anyone. The band by an unfortunate accident was playing truculent military music. The mental change Kipps underwent was, in its way, what psychologists call a conversion. In a few moments all Kipps' ideals were changed. He who had been "practically a gentleman," the sedulous pupil of Coote, the punctilious raiser of hats, was instantly a rebel, an outcast, the hater of everything "stuck up," the foe of Society and the social order of to-day. Here they were among the profits of their robbery, these people who might do anything with the world. . . .

"No, thenks," he said to a dish.

He addressed a scornful eye at the shoulders of the lady to his left.

Presently he was refusing another dish. He didn't like it—fussed-up food! Probably cooked by some foreigner. He finished up his wine and his bread.

"No, thenks."

"No, thenks. . . ."

He discovered the eye of a diner fixed curiously upon his flushed face. He responded with a glare. Couldn't he go without things if he liked?

"What's this?" said Kipps to a great green cone.

"Ice," said the waiter.

"I'll 'ave some," said Kipps.

He seized a fork and spoon and assailed the bombe. It cut rather stiffly. "Come up!" said Kipps, with concentrated bitterness, and the truncated summit of the bombe flew off suddenly, travelling eastward with remarkable velocity. Flop, it went upon the floor a yard away, and for a while time seemed empty.

At the adjacent table they were laughing together.

Shy the rest of the bombe at them?

Flight?

At any rate, a dignified withdrawal.

"No!" said Kipps, "no more," arresting the polite attempt of the waiter to serve him with another piece. He had a vague idea he might carry off the affair as though he had meant the ice to go on the floor—not liking ice, for example, and being annoyed at the badness of his dinner. He put both hands on the table, thrust back his chair, disengaged a purple slipper from his napkin, and rose. He stepped carefully over the prostrate ice, kicked the napkin under the table, thrust his hands deep into his pockets, and marched out —shaking the dust of the place, as it were, from his feet. He left behind him a melting fragment of ice upon the floor, his Gibus hat, warm and compressed in his chair, and in addition every social ambition he had ever entertained in the world.

§ 7

Kipps went back to Folkestone in time for the Anagram Tea. But you must not imagine that the change of heart that came to him in the dining-room of the

Royal Grand Hotel involved any change of attitude
toward this promised social and intellectual treat. He
went back because the Royal Grand was too much
for him.

Outwardly calm, or at most a little flushed and ruffled,
inwardly Kipps was a horrible tormented battleground
of scruples, doubts, shames and self-assertions during
that three days of silent, desperate grappling with the
big hotel. He did not intend the monstrosity should
beat him without a struggle, but at last he had sullenly
to admit himself overcome. The odds were terrific.
On the one hand himself—with, among other things,
only one pair of boots; on the other a vast wilderness of
rooms, covering several acres, and with over a thousand
people, staff and visitors, all chiefly occupied in looking
queerly at Kipps, in laughing at him behind his back,
in watching for difficult corners at which to confront
and perplex him, and inflict humiliations upon him.
For example, the hotel scored over its electric light.
After the dinner the chambermaid, a hard, unsympathetic young woman with a superior manner, was
summoned by a bell Kipps had rung under the impression the button was the electric light switch. "Look
'ere," said Kipps, rubbing a shin that had suffered during
his search in the dark, "why aren't there any candles or
matches?" The hotel explained and scored heavily.

"It isn't everyone is up to these things," said Kipps.

"No, it isn't," said the chambermaid with ill-concealed scorn, and slammed the door at him.

"S'pose I ought to have tipped her," said Kipps.

After that Kipps cleaned his boots with a pocket-
handkerchief and went for a long walk and got home
in a hansom, but the hotel scored again by his not
putting out his boots and so having to clean them again
in the morning. The hotel also snubbed him by bringing him hot water when he was fully dressed and looking surprised at his collar, but he got a breakfast, I must
admit, with scarcely any difficulty.

After that the hotel scored heavily by the fact that there are twenty-four hours in the day and Kipps had nothing to do in any of them. He was a little footsore from his previous day's pedestrianism, and he could make up his mind for no long excursions. He flitted in and out of the hotel several times, and it was the polite porter who touched his hat every time that first set Kipps tipping.

"What 'e wants is a tip," said Kipps.

So at the next opportunity he gave the man an unexpected shilling, and having once put his hand in his pocket, there was no reason why he should not go on. He bought a newspaper at the book-stall and tipped the boy the rest of the shilling, and then went up by the lift and tipped the man sixpence, leaving his newspaper inadvertently in the lift. He met his chambermaid in the passage and gave her half a crown. He resolved to demonstrate his position to the entire establishment in this way. He didn't like the place; he disapproved of it politically, socially, morally, but he resolved no taint of meanness should disfigure his sojourn in its luxurious halls. He went down by the lift (tipping again), and, being accosted by a waiter with his Gibus, tipped the finder half a crown. He had a vague sense that he was making a flank movement upon the hotel and buying over its staff. They would regard him as a "character," they would get to like him. He found his stock of small silver diminishing, and replenished it at the desk in the hall. He tipped a man in bottle green who looked like the man who had shown him his room the day before, and then he saw a visitor eyeing him, and doubted whether he was in this instance doing right. Finally he went out and took chance buses to their destinations, and wandered a little in remote, wonderful suburbs and returned. He lunched at a chop house in Islington, and found himself back in the Royal Grand, now unmistakably footsore and London weary, about three. He was attracted to the drawing-room by a neat placard about afternoon tea.

It occurred to him that the campaign of tipping upon which he had embarked was perhaps after all a mistake. He was confirmed in this by observing that the hotel officials were watching him, not respectfully, but with a sort of amused wonder, as if to see whom he would tip next. However, if he backed out now, they would think him an awful fool. Everyone wasn't so rich as he was. It was his way to tip. Still——

He grew more certain the hotel had scored again.

He pretended to be lost in thought and so drifted by, and having put hat and umbrella in the cloakroom went into the drawing-room for afternoon tea.

There he did get what for a time he held to be a point in his favour. The room was large and quiet at first, and he sat back restfully until it occurred to him that his attitude brought his extremely dusty boots too prominently into the light, so instead he sat up, and then people of the upper and upper middle classes began to come and group themselves about him and have tea likewise, and so revive the class animosities of the previous day.

Presently a fluffy, fair-haired lady came into prominent existence a few yards away. She was talking to a respectful, low-voiced clergyman, whom she was possibly entertaining at tea. "No," she said, "dear Lady Jane wouldn't like that!"

"Mumble, mumble, mumble," from the clergyman.

"Poor dear Lady Jane was always so sensitive," the voice of the lady sang out clear and emphatic.

A fat, hairless, important-looking man joined this group, took a chair and planted it firmly with its back in the face of Kipps, a thing that offended Kipps mightily. "Are you telling him," gurgled the fat, hairless man, "about dear Lady Jane's affliction?" A young couple, lady brilliantly attired and the man in a magnificently cut frock coat, arranged themselves to the right, also with an air of exclusion towards Kipps. "I've told him," said the gentleman in a flat, abundant voice. "My!" said the young lady, with an American smile. No doubt they all thought Kipps was out of it. A great desire to assert himself surged up in his heart. He felt he would like to cut in on the conversation in some dramatic way. A monologue something in the manner of Masterman? At any rate, abandoning that as impossible, he would like to appear self-centred and at ease. His eye, wandering over the black surfaces of a noble architectural mass close by, discovered a slot and an enamelled plaque of directions.

It was some sort of musical box! As a matter of fact, it was the very best sort of Harmonicon and specially made to the scale of the Hotel.

He scrutinised the plaque with his head at various angles and glanced about him at his neighbours.

It occurred to Kipps that he would like some music, that to inaugurate some would show him a man of taste and at his ease at the same time. He rose, read over a list of tunes, selected one haphazard, pressed his sixpence—it was sixpence!—home, and prepared for a confidential, refined little melody.

Considering the high social tone of the Royal Grand, it was really a very loud instrument indeed. It gave vent to three deafening brays and so burst the dam of silence that had long pent it in. It seemed to be chiefly full of the great-uncles of trumpets, megalo-trombones and railway brakes. It made sounds like shunting trains. It did not so much begin as blow up your counter-scarp and rush forward to storm under cover of melodious shrapnel. It had not so much an air as a *ricochette*. The music had, in short, the in-imitable quality of Sousa. It swept down upon the friend of Lady Jane and carried away something socially striking into the eternal night of the unheard; the American girl to the left of it was borne shrieking into the inaudible. "HIGH cockalorum Tootletootle tootle

loo. High cockalorum tootle lootle loo. Bump, bump,
bump—bump." Joyous, exorbitant music it was from
the gigantic nursery of the Future, bearing the hearer
along upon its torrential succession of sounds, as if he
was in a cask on Niagara. Whiroo! Yah and have
at you! The strenuous Life! Yaha! Stop! A Reprieve! A Reprieve! No! Bang! Bump!

Everybody looked round, conversation ceased and
gave place to gestures.

The friend of Lady Jane became terribly agitated.

"Can't it be stopped?" she vociferated, pointing a
gloved finger and saying something to the waiter about
"that dreadful young man."

"Ought not to be working," said the clerical friend
of Lady Jane.

The waiter shook his head at the fat, hairless gentleman. People began to move away. Kipps leant back
luxurious, and then tapped with a half-crown to pay.
He paid, tipped like a gentleman, rose with an easy
gesture, and strolled towards the door. His retreat
evidently completed the indignation of the friend of
Lady Jane, and from the door he could still discern her
gestures as asking, "Can't it be stopped?" The music
followed him into the pasage and pursued him to the
lift and only died away completely in the quiet of his
own room, and afterwards from his window he saw the
friend of Lady Jane and her party having their tea
carried out to a little table in the court.

Certainly that was a point to him. But it was his
only score; all the rest of the game lay in the hands of
the upper classes and the big hotel. And presently he
was doubting whether even this was really a point. It
seemed a trifle vulgar, come to think it over, to interrupt
people when they were talking.

He saw a clerk peering at him from the office, and
suddenly it occurred to him that the place might get
back at him tremendously over the bill.

They would probably take it out of him by charging pounds and pounds.

Suppose they charged more than he had!

The clerk had a particularly nasty face, just the face to take advantage of a vacillating Kipps.

He became aware of a man in a cap touching it, and produced his shilling automatically, but the strain was beginning to tell. It was a deuce and all of an expense —this tipping.

If the hotel chose to stick it on to the bill something tremendous, what was Kipps to do? Refuse to pay? Make a row?

If he did he couldn't fight all these men in bottle green. . . .

He went out about seven and walked for a long time, and dined at last upon a chop in the Euston Road; then he walked along to the Edgware Road and sat and rested in the Metropolitan Music Hall for a time until a trapeze performance unnerved him, and finally he came back to bed. He tipped the lift man sixpence and wished him good-night. In the silent watches of the night he reviewed the tale of the day's tipping, went over the horrors of the previous night's dinner, and heard again the triumphant bray of the harmonicon devil released from its long imprisonment. Everyone would be told about him to-morrow. He couldn't go on! He admitted his defeat. Never in their whole lives had any of these people seen such a Fool as he! Ugh! . . .

His method of announcing his withdrawal to the clerk was touched with bitterness.

"I'm going to get out of this," said Kipps, blowing windily. "Let's see what you got on my bill."

"One breakfast?" asked the clerk.

"Do I *look* as if I'd ate two? . . ."

At his departure Kipps, with a hot face, convulsive gestures and an embittered heart, tipped everyone who did not promptly and actively resist, including an absent-minded South African diamond merchant who was waiting in the hall for his wife and succumbed to old habit. He paid his cabman a four-shilling piece at Charing Cross, having no smaller change, and wished he could burn him alive. Then in a sudden reaction of economy he refused the proffered help of a porter, and carried his bag quite violently to the train.

CHAPTER THE EIGHTH

Kipps Enters Society

§ I

SUBMISSION to Inexorable Fate took Kipps to the Anagram Tea.

At any rate he would meet Helen there in the presence of other people, and be able to carry off the worst of the difficulty of explaining his little jaunt to London. He had not seen her since his last portentous visit to New Romney. He was engaged to her, he would have to marry her, and the sooner he faced her again the better. Before wild plans of turning socialist, defying the world and repudiating all calling for ever, his heart on second thoughts sank. He felt Helen would never permit anything of the sort. As for the Anagrams, he could do no more than his best and that he was resolved to do. What had happened at the Royal Grand, what had happened at New Romney, he must bury in his memory and begin again at the reconstruction of his social position. Ann, Buggins, Chitterlow, all these, seen in the matter-of-fact light of the

Folkestone train, stood just as they stood before—people
of an inferior social position who had to be eliminated
from his world. It was a bother about Ann, a bother
and a pity. His mind rested so for a space on Ann until
the memory of those Anagrams drew him away. If he
could see Coote that evening he might, he thought, be
able to arrange some sort of connivance about the
Anagrams, and his mind was chiefly busy sketching proposals for such an arrangement. It would not, of course,
be ungentlemanly cheating, but only a little mystifica-
tion. Coote very probably might drop him a hint of the
solution of one or two of the things, not enough to win
a prize, but enough to cover his shame. Or failing that
he might take a humorous, quizzical line and pretend
he was pretending to be very stupid. There were plenty
of ways out of it if one kept a sharp lookout. . . .

The costume Kipps wore to the Anagram Tea was
designed as a compromise between the strict letter of
high fashion and seaside laxity, a sort of easy, semi-state
for afternoon. Helen's first reproof had always lingered
in his mind. He wore a frock coat, but mitigated it by
a Panama hat of romantic shape with a black band,
grey gloves, but for relaxation brown button boots.
The only other man besides the clergy present, a new
doctor with an attractive wife, was in full afternoon
dress. Coote was not there.

Kipps was a little pale, but quite self-possessed, as he
approached Mrs. Bindon Botting's door. He took a
turn while some people went in, and then faced it
manfully. The door opened and revealed—Ann!

In the background through a draped doorway behind
a big fern in a great art pot the elder Miss Botting was
visible talking to two guests; the auditory background
was a froth of feminine voices. . . .

Our two young people were much too amazed to
give one another any formula of greeting, though they
had parted warmly enough. Each was already in a
state of extreme tension to meet the demands of this

great and unprecedented occasion, an Anagram Tea. "Lor'!" said Ann, her sole remark, and then the sense of Miss Botting's eye ruled her straight again. She became very pale, but she took his hat mechanically, and he was already removing his gloves. "Ann," he said in a low tone, and then "Fency!" The elder Miss Botting knew Kipps was the sort of guest who requires nursing, and she came forward vocalising charm. She said it was "Awfully jolly of him to come, awfully jolly. It was awfully difficult to get any good men!"

She handed Kipps forward, mumbling in a dazed condition, to the drawing-room, and there he encountered Helen looking unfamiliar in an unfamiliar hat. It was as if he had not met her for years.

She astonished him. She didn't seem to mind in the least his going to London. She held out a shapely hand, and smiled encouragingly. "You've faced the anagrams?" she said.

The second Miss Botting accosted them, a number of oblong pieces of paper in her hand, mysteriously inscribed. "Take an anagram," she said; "take an anagram," and boldly pinned one of these brief documents to Kipps' lapel. The letters were "Cypshi," and Kipps from the very beginning suspected this was an anagram for Cuyps. She also left a thing like a long dance programme, from which dangled a little pencil, in his hand. He found himself being introduced to people, and then he was in a corner with the short lady in a big bonnet, who was pelting him with gritty little bits of small talk that were gone before you could take hold of them and reply.

"Very hot," said this lady. "Very hot indeed—hot all the summer—remarkable year—all the years remarkable now—don't know what we're coming to—don't you think so, Mr. Kipps?"

"Oo rather," said Kipps, and wondered if Ann was still in the hall. Ann!

He ought not to have stared at her like a stuck fish

and pretended not to know her. That couldn't be right. But what *was* right?

The lady in the big bonnet proceeded to a second discharge. "Hope you're fond of anagrams, Mr. Kipps—difficult exercise—still one must do something to bring people together—better than Ludo anyhow. Don't you think so, Mr. Kipps?"

Ann fluttered past the open door. Her eyes met his in amazed inquiry. Something had got dislocated in the world for both of them. . . .

He ought to have told her he was engaged. He ought to have explained things to her. Perhaps even now he might be able to drop her a hint.

"Don't you think so, Mr. Kipps?"

"Oo rather," said Kipps for the third time.

A lady with a tired smile, who was labelled conspicuously "Wogdelenk," drifted towards Kipps' interlocutor and the two fell into conversation. Kipps found himself socially aground. He looked about him. Helen was talking to a curate and laughing. Kipps was overcome by a vague desire to speak to Ann. He was for sidling doorward.

"What are *you,* please?" said an extraordinarily bold, tall girl, and arrested him while she took down "Cypshi."

"I'm sure I don't know what it means," she explained. "I'm Sir Bubh. Don't you think anagrams are something chronic?"

Kipps made stockish noises, and the young lady suddenly became the nucleus of a party of excited friends who were forming a syndicate to guess, and barred his escape. She took no further notice of him. He found himself jammed against an occasional table and listening to the conversation of Mrs. "Wogdelenk" and his lady with the big bonnet.

"She packed her two beauties off together," said the lady in the big bonnet. "Time enough, too. Don't think much of this girl she's got as housemaid now.

Pretty, of course, but there's no occasion for a house-maid to be pretty—none whatever. And she doesn't look particularly up to her work either. Kind of 'mazed expression."

"You never can tell," said the lady labelled "Wog-delenk"; "you never can tell. My wretches are big enough, Heaven knows, and do they work? Not a bit of it! . . ."

Kipps felt dreadfully out of it with regard to all these people, and dreadfully in it with Ann.

He scanned the back of the big bonnet, and con-cluded it was an extremely ugly bonnet. It went jerk-ing forward as each short, dry sentence was snapped off at the end and a plume of osprey on it jerked exces-sively. "She hasn't guessed even one!" followed by a shriek of girlish merriment, came from the group about the tall, bold girl. They'd shriek at him presently, perhaps. Beyond thinking his own anagram might be Cuyps, he hadn't a notion. What a chatter they were all making! It was just like a summer sale! Just the sort of people who'd give a lot of trouble and swap you! And suddenly the smouldering fires of rebellion leapt to flame again. These were a rotten lot of people, and the anagrams were rotten nonsense, and he, Kipps, had been a rotten fool to come. There was Helen away there, still laughing, with her curate. Pity she couldn't marry a curate and leave him (Kipps) alone! Then he'd know what to do. He disliked the whole gathering collectively and in detail. Why were they all trying to make him one of themselves? He perceived unexpected ugliness everywhere about him. There were two great pins jabbed through the tall girl's hat, and the swirls of her hair below the brim with the minutest piece of tape tie-up showing, did not repay close examination. Mrs. "Wogdelenk" wore a sort of mumps bandage of lace, and there was another lady perfectly dazzling with beads and jewels and bits of trimming. They were all flaps and angles and

10*

flounces—these women. Not one of them looked as neat and decent a shape as Ann's clean, trim little figure. Echoes of Masterman woke up in him again. Ladies indeed! Here were all these chattering people, with money, with leisure, with every chance in the world, and all they could do was to crowd like this into a couple of rooms and jabber nonsense about anagrams.

" Could Cypshi really mean Cuyps?" floated like a dissolving wreath of mist across his mind.

Abruptly resolution stood armed in his heart. He was going to get out of this!

" 'Scuse me," he said, and began to wade neck deep through the bubbling tea party.

He was going to get out of it all!

He found himself close by Helen. " I'm orf," he said, but she gave him the briefest glance. She did not appear to hear him. " Still, Mr. Spratlingdown, you *must* admit there's a limit even to conformity," she was saying. . . .

He was in a curtained archway, and Ann was before him carrying a tray supporting several small sugar bowls.

He was moved to speech. " *What* a Lot!" he said, and then mysteriously, " I'm engaged to *her*." He indicated Helen's new hat, and became aware of a skirt he had stepped upon.

Ann stared at him helplessly, borne past in the grip of incomprehensible imperatives.

Why shouldn't they talk together?

He was in a small room, and then at the foot of the staircase in the hall. He heard the rustle of a dress, and what was conceivably his hostess was upon him.

" But you're not going, Mr. Kipps?" she said.

" I must," he said; " I got to."

" But, Mr. Kipps!"

" I must," he said. " I'm not well."

" But before the guessing! Without any tea!"

Ann appeared and hovered behind him.

" I got to go," said Kipps.

If he parleyed with her Helen might awake to his desperate attempt.

"Of course if you *must* go."

"It's something I've forgotten," said Kipps, beginning to feel regrets. "Reely I must."

Mrs. Botting turned with a certain offended dignity, and Ann in a state of flushed calm that evidently concealed much, came forward to open the door.

"I'm very sorry," he said; "I'm very sorry," half to his hostess and half to her, and was swept past her by superior social forces—like a drowning man in a mill-race—and into the Upper Sandgate Road. He half turned upon the step, and then slam went the door. . . .

He retreated along the Leas, a thing of shame and perplexity — Mrs. Botting's aggrieved astonishment uppermost in his mind. . . .

Something—reinforced by the glances of the people he was passing—pressed its way to his attention through the tumultuous disorder of his mind.

He became aware that he was still wearing his little placard with the letters "Cypshi."

"Desh it!" he said, clutching off this abomination. In another moment its several letters, their task accomplished, were scattering gleefully before the breeze down the front of the Leas.

§ 2

Kipps was dressed for Mrs. Wace's dinner half an hour before it was time to start, and he sat waiting until Coote should come to take him round. "Manners and Rules of Good Society" lay before him neglected. He had read the polished prose of the Member of the Aristocracy, on page 96, as far as—

"the acceptance of an invitation is in the eyes of
"diners out, a binding obligation which only ill-

" health, family bereavement, or some all-important
" reason justifies its being set on one side or other-
" wise evaded "—

and then he had lapsed into gloomy thoughts.

That afternoon he had had a serious talk with Helen.

He had tried to express something of the change of heart that had happened to him. But to broach the real state of the matter had been altogether too terrible for him. He had sought a minor issue. " I don't like all this Society," he had said.

" But you must *see* people," said Helen.

" Yes, but— It's the sort of people you see." He nerved himself. " I didn't think much of that lot at the Enegram Tea."

" You have to see all sorts of people if you want to see the world," said Helen.

Kipps was silent for a space and a little short of breath.

" My dear Arthur," she began, almost kindly, " I shouldn't ask you to go to these affairs if I didn't think it good for you, should I ?"

Kipps acquiesced in silence.

" You will find the benefit of it all when we get to London. You learn to swim in a tank before you go out into the sea. These people here are good enough to learn upon. They're stiff and rather silly, and dreadfully narrow and not an idea in a dozen of them, but it really doesn't matter at all. You'll soon get Savoir Faire."

He made to speak again, and found his powers of verbal expression lacking. Instead he blew a sigh.

" You'll get used to it all very soon," said Helen helpfully. . . .

As he sat meditating over that interview and over the vistas of London that opened before him, on the little flat, and teas and occasions and the constant presence of Brudderkins and all the bright prospect of his new and better life, and how he would never see Ann any more, the housemaid entered with a little package, a small, square envelope to "Arthur Kipps, Esquire."

"A young woman left this, Sir," said the housemaid, a little severely.

"Eh?" said Kipps; "what young woman?" and then suddenly began to understand.

"She looked an ordinary young woman," said the housemaid coldly.

"Ah!" said Kipps. "*That's* orlright."

He waited till the door had closed behind the girl, staring at the envelope in his hand, and then, with a curious feeling of increasing tension, tore it open. As he did so, some quicker sense than sight or touch told him its contents. It was Ann's half sixpence. And besides, not a word!

Then she must have heard him——!

He was standing with the envelope in his hand, when Coote became audible without.

Coote appeared in evening dress, a clean and radiant Coote, with large greenish white gloves and a particularly large white tie, edged with black. "For a third cousin," he presently explained. "Nace, isn't it?" He could see Kipps was pale and disturbed, and put this down to the approaching social trial. "You keep your nerve up, Kipps, my dear chap, and you'll be all right," said Coote, with a big, brotherly glove on Kipps' sleeve.

§ 3

The dinner came to a crisis so far as Kipps' emotions were concerned, with Mrs. Bindon Botting's talk about servants, but before that there had been several things of greater or smaller magnitude to perturb and disarrange his social front. One little matter that was mildly insurgent throughout the entire meal was, if I may be permitted to mention so intimate a trouble, the

behaviour of his left brace. The webbing—which was
of a cheerful scarlet silk—had slipped away from its
buckle, fastened no doubt in agitation, and had
developed a strong tendency to place itself obliquely
in the manner rather of an official decoration, athwart
his spotless front. It first asserted itself before they
went in to dinner. He replaced this ornament by a
dexterous thrust when no one was looking and thereafter the suppression of his novel innovation upon the
stereotyped sombreness of evening dress became a standing preoccupation. On the whole, he was inclined to
think his first horror excessive; at any rate no one
remarked upon it. However, you imagine him constantly throughout the evening, with one eye and one
hand, whatever the rest of him might be doing, pre-
dominantly concerned with the weak corner.

But this, I say, was a little matter. What exercised
him much more was to discover Helen quite terribly in
evening dress.

The young lady had let her imagination rove
London-ward, and this costume was perhaps an anticipation of that clever little flat not too far west which
was to become the centre of so delightful a literary and
artistic set. It was, of all the feminine costumes present,
most distinctly an evening dress. One was advised Miss
Walshingham had arms and shoulders of a type by no
means despicable, one was advised Miss Walshingham
was capable not only of dignity but charm, even a
certain glow of charm. It was, you know, her first
evening dress, a tribute paid by Walshingham finance
to her brightening future. Had she wanted keeping in
countenance, she would have had to have fallen back
upon her hostess, who was resplendent in black and
steel. The other ladies had to a certain extent compromised. Mrs. Walshingham had dressed with just a
refined little V and Mrs. Bindon Botting, except for
her dear mottled arms, confided scarcely more of her
plump charm to the world. The elder Miss Botting

stopped short of shoulders, and so did Miss Wace. But Helen didn't. She was—had Kipps had eyes to see it— a quite beautiful human figure; she knew it, and she met him with a radiant smile that had forgotten all the little difference of the afternoon. But to Kipps her appearance was the last release. With that she had become as remote, as foreign, as incredible as a wife and mate, as though the Cnidian Venus herself, in all her simple elegance, was, before witnesses, declared to be his. If, indeed, she had ever been credible as a wife and mate.

She ascribed his confusion to modest reverence, and having blazed smiling upon him for a moment turned a shapely shoulder towards him and exchanged a remark with Mrs. Bindon Botting. Ann's poor little half sixpence came against Kipps' fingers in his pocket, and he clutched at it suddenly as though it was a talisman. Then he abandoned it to suppress his Order of the Brace. He was affected by a cough. "Miss Wace tells me Mr. Revel is coming," Mrs. Botting was saying.

"Isn't it delightful?" said Helen. "We saw him last night. He's stopped on his way to Paris. He's going to meet his wife there."

Kipps' eyes rested for a moment on Helen's dazzling deltoid, and then went inquiringly, accusingly almost, to Coote's face. Where, in the presence of this terrible emergence, was the gospel of suppression now—that Furtive treatment of Religion and Politics and Birth and Death and Bathing and Babies, and "all those things" which constitutes your True Gentleman? He had been too modest even to discuss this question with his Mentor, but surely, surely this quintessence of all that is good and nice could regard these unsolicited confidences only in one way. With something between relief and the confirmation of his worst fears he perceived, by a sort of twitching of the exceptionally abundant muscles about Coote's lower jaw, in a certain deliberate avoidance of one particular direction by these pale but resolute grey eyes, by the almost convulsive grip of the ample, greenish white gloves behind him, a grip broken at times for controlling pats at the black-bordered tie and the back of that spacious head, and by a slight but increasing disposition to cough, that *Coote did not approve!*

To Kipps Helen had once supplied a delicately beautiful dream, a thing of romance and unsubstantial mystery. But this was her final materialisation, and the last thin wreath of glamour about her was dispelled. In some way (he had forgotten how and it was perfectly incomprehensible) he was bound to this dark, solid and determined young person whose shadow and suggestion he had once loved. He had to go through with the thing as a gentleman should. Still——

And when he was sacrificing Ann!

He wouldn't stand this sort of thing, whatever else he stood. . . . Should he say something about her dress to her—to-morrow?

He could put his foot down firmly. He could say, " Look 'ere. I don't care. I ain't going to stand it. See ?"

She'd say something unexpected, of course. She always did say something unexpected.

Suppose for once he overrode what she said, and simply repeated his point ?

He found these thoughts battling with certain conversational aggressions from Mrs. Wace, and then Revel arrived and took the centre of the stage.

The author of that brilliant romance, " Red Hearts a-Beating," was a less imposing man than Kipps had anticipated, but he speedily effaced that disappointment by his predominating manners. Although he lived habitually in the vivid world of London, his collar and tie were in no way remarkable, and he was neither brilliantly handsome nor curly nor long-haired. His personal appearance suggested armchairs rather than the equestrian exercises and amorous toyings and passionate intensities of his masterpiece; he was inclined to be fat, with whitish flesh and muddy-coloured straight hair, he had a rather shapeless and truncated nose and his chin was asymmetrical. One eye was more inclined to stare than the other. He might have been esteemed a little undistinguished-looking were it not for his beeswaxed moustache, which came amidst his features with a pleasing note of incongruity, and the whimsical wrinkles above and about his greater eye. His regard sought and found Helen's as he entered the room, and they shook hands presently with an air of intimacy Kipps, for no clear reason, found objectionable. He saw them clasp hands, heard Coote's characteristic cough— a sound rather more like a very, very old sheep a quarter of a mile away being blown to pieces by a small charge of gunpowder than anything else in the world—did some confused beginnings of a thought, and then they were all going in to dinner and Helen's shining bare arm lay along his sleeve. Kipps was in no state for conversation. She glanced at him, and, though he did not know it, very slightly pressed his elbow. He struggled with strange respiratory dislocations. Before them went Coote, discoursing in amiable reverberations to Mrs. Walshingham, and at the head of the procession was Mrs. Bindon Botting talking fast and brightly beside the erect military figure of little Mr. Wace. (He was not a soldier really, but he had caught a martinet bearing by living so close to Shorncliffe.) Revel came last, in charge of Mrs. Wace's queenly black and steel, politely admiring in a flute-like cultivated voice the mellow wall paper of the staircase. Kipps marvelled at everybody's self-possession.

From the earliest spoonful of soup it became evident that Revel considered himself responsible for the table talk. And before the soup was over it was almost as manifest that Mrs. Bindon Botting inclined to consider his sense of responsibility excessive. In her circle Mrs. Bindon Botting was esteemed an agreeable rattle, her

manner and appearance were conspicuously vivacious for
one so plump, and she had an almost Irish facility for
humorous description. She would keep people amused
all through an afternoon call with the story of how her
jobbing gardener had got himself married and what his
home was like, or how her favourite butt, Mr. Stigson
Warder, had all his unfortunate children taught almost
every conceivable instrument because they had the
phrenological bump of music abnormally large. The
family itself was also abnormally large. "They got to
trombones, my dear!" she would say, with her voice
coming to a climax. Usually her friends conspired to
draw her out, but on this occasion they neglected to
do so, a thing that militated against her keen desire to
shine in Revel's eyes. After a time she perceived that
the only thing for her to do was to cut in on the talk
on her own account, and this she began to do. She
made several ineffectual snatches at the general attention,
and then Revel drifted towards a topic she regarded as
particularly her own, the ordering of households.

They came to the thing through talk about localities.
"We are leaving our house in The Boltons," said Revel,
"and taking a little place at Wimbledon, and I think
of having rooms in Dane's Inn. It will be more convenient in many ways. My wife is furiously addicted
to golf and exercise of all sorts, and I like to sit about
in clubs—I haven' the strength necessary for these
hygienic proceedings—and the old arrangement suited
neither of us. And besides, no one could imagine the
demoralisation the domestics of West London have
undergone during the last three years."

"It's the same everywhere," said Mrs. Bindon
Botting.

"Very possibly it is. A friend of mine calls it the
servile tradition in decay, and regards it all as a most
hopeful phenomenon——"

"He ought to have had my last two criminals," said
Mrs. Bindon Botting.

She turned to Mrs. Wace while Revel came again a little too late with a " Possibly——"

"And I haven't told you, my dear," she said, speaking with voluble rapidity, " I'm in trouble again."

" The last girl?"

" The last girl. Before I can get a cook, my hard-won housemaid "—she paused—" chucks it."

" Panic?" asked young Walshingham.

" Mysterious grief! Everything merry as a marriage bell until my Anagram Tea! Then in the evening a portentous rigour of bearing, a word or so from my Aunt, and immediately—Floods of Tears and Notice!" For a moment her eye rested thoughtfully on Kipps, as she said : " Is there anything heartrending about Anagrams?"

"I find them so," said Revel. " I——"

But Mrs. Bindon Botting got away again. " For a time it made me quite uneasy——"

Kipps jabbed his lip with his fork rather painfully, and was recalled from a fascinated glare at Mrs. Botting to the immediate facts of dinner.

" —whether anagrams might not have offended the good domestic's Moral Code—you never can tell. We made inquiries. No. No. No. She *must* go and that's all!"

" One perceives," said Revel, " in these disorders, dimly and distantly, the last dying glow of the age of Romance. Let us suppose, Mrs. Botting, let us at least try to suppose—it is Love."

Kipps clattered with his knife and fork.

" It's love," said Mrs. Botting; " what else can it be? Beneath the orderly humdrum of our lives these romances are going on, until at last they bust up and give Notice and upset our humdrum altogether. Some fatal, wonderful soldier——"

" The passions of the common or house domestic," said Revel, and recovered possession of the table.

Upon the troubled disorder of Kipps' table manners

there had supervened a quietness, an unusual calm. For once in his life he had distinctly made up his mind on his own account. He listened no more to Revel. He put down his knife and fork and refused everything that followed. Coote regarded him with tactful concern and Helen flushed a little.

§ 4

About half-past nine that night came a violent pull at the bell of Mrs. Bindon Botting, and a young man in a dress suit, a Gibus and other marks of exalted social position stood without. Athwart his white expanse of breast lay a ruddy bar of patterned silk that gave him a singular distinction and minimised the glow of a few small stains of burgundy. His Gibus was thrust back and exposed a disorder of hair that suggested a reckless desperation. He had, in fact, burnt his boats and refused to join the ladies. Coote, in the subsequent conversation, had protested quietly, "You're going on all right, you know," to which Kipps had answered he didn't care a "Eng" about that, and so, after a brief tussle with Walshingham's detaining arm, had got away. "I got something to do," he said. "'Ome." And here he was—panting an extraordinary resolve. The door opened, revealing the pleasantly furnished hall of Mrs. Bindon Botting, lit by rose-tinted lights, and in the centre of the picture, neat and pretty in black and white, stood Ann. At the sight of Kipps her colour vanished.

"Ann," said Kipps, "I want to speak to you. I got something to say to you right away. See? I'm——"

"This ain't the door to speak to me at," said Ann.

"But, Ann! It's something special."

"You spoke enough," said Ann.

"Ann!"

"Besides. That's my door, down there. Basement. If I was caught talking at *this* door——!"

" But, Ann, *I'm*——"

" Basement after nine. Them's my hours. I'm a servant and likely to keep one. If you're calling here, what name, please? But you got your friends and I got mine, and you mustn't go talking to *me*."

" But, Ann, I want to ask you——"

Someone appeared in the hall behind Ann. " Not here," said Ann. " Don't know anyone of that name," and incontinently slammed the door in his face.

" What was that, Ann?" said Mrs. Bindon Botting's invalid Aunt.

" Ge'm a little intoxicated, Ma'am—asking for the wrong name, Ma'am."

" What name did he want?" asked the lady doubtfully.

" No name that *we* know, Ma'am," said Ann, hustling along the hall towards the kitchen stairs.

" I hope you weren't too short with him, Ann."

" No shorter than he deserved, considering 'ow he be'aved," said Ann, with her bosom heaving.

And Mrs. Bindon Botting's invalid Aunt, perceiving suddenly that this call had some relation to Ann's private and sentimental trouble, turned, after one moment of hesitating scrutiny, away.

She was an extremely sympathetic lady, was Mrs. Bindon Botting's invalid Aunt; she took an interest in the servants, imposed piety, extorted confessions and followed human nature, blushing and lying defensively, to its reluctantly revealed recesses, but Ann's sense of privacy was strong and her manner, under drawing out and encouragement, sometimes even alarming. . . .

So the poor old lady went upstairs again.

§ 5

The basement door opened and Kipps came into the kitchen. He was flushed and panting.

He struggled for speech.

"'Ere," he said, and held out two half sixpences.

Ann stood behind the kitchen table—face pale and eyes round, and now—and it simplified Kipps very much—he could see she had indeed been crying.

"Well?" she said.

"Don't you see?"

Ann moved her head slightly.

"I kep' it all these years."

"You kep' it too long."

His mouth closed and his flush died away. He looked at her. The amulet, it seemed, had failed to work.

"Ann!" he said.

"Well?"

"Ann."

The conversation still hung fire.

"Ann," he said, made a movement with his hands that suggested appeal, and advanced a step.

Ann shook her head more definitely, and became defensive.

"Look here, Ann," said Kipps. "I been a fool."

They stared into each other's miserable eyes.

"Ann," he said. "I want to marry you."

Ann clutched the table edge. "You can't," she said faintly.

He made as if to approach her around the table, and she took a step that restored their distance.

"I must," he said.

"You can't."

"I must. You *got* to marry me, Ann."

"You can't go marrying everybody. You got to marry 'er."

"I shan't."

Ann shook her head. "You're engaged to that girl. Lady, rather. You can't be engaged to me."

"I don't want to be engaged to you. I *been* engaged. I want to be married to you. See? Right away."

Ann turned a shade paler. "But what d'you mean?" she asked.

"Come right off to London and marry me.   Now."

"What d'you mean?"

Kipps became extremely lucid and earnest.

"I mean come right off and marry me now before anyone else can.   See?"

"In London?"

"In London."

They stared at one another again.   They took things for granted in the most amazing way.

"I couldn't," said Ann.   "For one thing, my month's not up for mor'n free weeks yet."

They hung before that for a moment as though it was insurmountable.

"Look 'ere, Ann!   Arst to go.   Arst to go!"

"*She* wouldn't," said Ann.

"Then come without arsting," said Kipps.

"She'd keep my box——"

"She won't."

"She will."

"She won't."

"You don't know 'er."

"Well, desh 'er—let 'er!   LET 'ER!   Who cares? I'll buy you a 'undred boxes if you'll come."

"It wouldn't be right towards Her."

"It isn't Her you got to think about, Ann.   It's me."

"And you 'aven't treated me properly," she said. "You 'aven't treated me properly, Artie.   You didn't ought to 'ave——"

"I didn't say I '*ad*," he interrupted, "did I?   Ann," he appealed, "I didn't come to arguefy.   I'm all wrong. I never said I wasn't.   It's yes or no.   Me or not. . . . I been a fool.   There!   See?   I been a fool.   Ain't that enough?   I got myself all tied up with everyone and made a fool of myself all round. . . ."

He pleaded, "It isn't as if we didn't care for one another, Ann."

She seemed impassive, and he resumed his discourse.

"I thought I wasn't likely ever to see you again, Ann. I reely did. It isn't as though I was seein' you all the time. I didn't know what I wanted, and I went and be'aved like a fool—jest as anyone might. I know what I want and I know what I don't want now.

"Ann!"

"Well?"

"Will you come? . . . Will you come? . . ."

Silence.

"If you don't answer me, Ann—I'm desprit—if you don't answer me now, if you don't say you'll come, I'll go right out now——"

He turned doorward passionately as he spoke, with his threat incomplete.

"I'll go," he said; "I 'aven't a friend in the world! I been and throwed everything away. I don't know why I done things and why I 'aven't. All I know is I can't stand nothing in the world any more." He choked. "The pier," he said.

He fumbled with the door latch, grumbling some inarticulate self-pity, as if he sought a handle, and then he had it open.

Clearly he was going.

"Artie!" said Ann sharply.

He turned about, and the two hung white and tense.

"I'll do it," said Ann.

His face began to work, he shut the door and came a step back to her, staring; his face became pitiful and then suddenly they moved together. "Artie!" she cried, "don't go!" and held out her arms, weeping.

They clung close to one another. . . .

"Oh! I *been* so mis'bel," cried Kipps, clinging to this lifebuoy; and suddenly his emotion, having no further serious work in hand, burst its way to a loud *boohoo!* His fashionable and expensive Gibus flopped off and fell and rolled and lay neglected on the floor.

"I been so mis'bel," said Kipps, giving himself vent. "Oh, I *been* so mis'bel, Ann."

"Be quiet," said Ann, holding his poor blubbering head tightly to her heaving shoulder, herself all a-quiver; "be quiet. She's there! Listenin'. She'll 'ear you, Artie, on the stairs. . . ."

§ 6

Ann's last words when, an hour later, they parted, Mrs. and Miss Bindon Botting having returned very audibly upstairs, deserve a section to themselves.

"I wouldn't do this for everyone, mind you," whispered Ann.

CHAPTER THE NINTH

The Labyrinthodon

§ 1

YOU imagine them fleeing through our complex and difficult social system as it were for life, first on foot and severally to the Folkestone Central Station, then in a first-class carriage, with Kipps' bag as sole chaperon, to Charing Cross, and then in a four-wheeler, a long, rumbling, palpitating, slow flight through the multitudinous swarming London streets to Sid. Kipps kept peeping out of the window. "It's the next corner after this, I believe," he would say. For he had a sort of feeling that at Sid's he would be immune from the hottest pursuit. He paid the cabman in a manner adequate to the occasion, and turned to his prospective brother-in-law. "Me and Ann," he said, "we're going to marry."

"But I thought——" began Sid.

Kipps motioned him towards explanations in the shop. . . .

"It's no good my arguing with you," said Sid, smiling delightedly as the case unfolded. "You done it now." And Masterman being apprised of the nature

312

of the affair descended slowly in a state of flushed congratulation.

"I thought you might find the Higher Life a bit difficult," said Masterman, projecting a bony hand. "But I never thought you'd have the originality to clear out. . . . Won't the young lady of the superior classes swear! Never mind—it doesn't matter anyhow.

"You were starting a climb," he said at dinner, "that doesn't lead anywhere. You would have clambered from one refinement of vulgarity to another and never got to any satisfactory top. There isn't a top. It's a squirrel's cage. Things are out of joint, and the only top there is a lot of blazing card-playing women and betting men—seasoned with archbishops and officials and all that sort of glossy, pandering Tosh. . . . You'd have hung on, a disconsolate, dismal little figure, somewhere up the ladder, far below even the motor-car class, while your wife larked about—or fretted because she wasn't a bit higher than she was. . . . I found it all out long ago. I've seen women of that sort. And I don't climb any more."

"I often thought about what you said last time I saw you," said Kipps.

"I wonder what I said," said Masterman in parenthesis. "Anyhow, you're doing the right and sane thing, and that's a rare spectacle. You're going to marry your equal, and you're going to take your own line, quite independently of what people up there, or people down there, think you ought or ought not to do. That's about the only course one can take nowadays with everything getting more muddled and upside down every day. Make your own little world and your own house first of all, keep that right side up whatever you do, and marry your mate. . . . That, I suppose, is what I should do—if I had a mate. . . . But people of my sort, luckily for the world, don't get made in pairs. No!

"Besides—! However—" And abruptly, taking

advantage of an interruption by Master Walt, he lapsed
into thought.

Presently he came out of his musings.

"After all," he said, "there's hope."

"What about?" said Sid.

"Everything," said Masterman.

"Where there's life there's hope," said Mrs. Sid.
"But none of you aren't eating anything like you
ought to."

Masterman lifted his glass.

"Here's to Hope!" he said. "The Light of the
World!"

Sid beamed at Kipps as who should say, "You don't
meet a character like *this* every dinner time."

"Here's to Hope," repeated Masterman. "The best
thing one can have. Hope of life—yes."

He imposed his moment of magnificent self-pity on
them all. Even young Walt was impressed.

§ 2

They spent the days before their marriage in a
number of agreeable excursions together. One day
they went to Kew by steamboat, and admired the house
full of paintings of flowers extremely; and one day they
went early to have a good long day at the Crystal
Palace, and enjoyed themselves very much indeed. They
got there so early that nothing was open inside, all the
stalls were wrappered up and all the minor exhibitions
locked and barred. They seemed the minutest creatures
even to themselves in that enormous empty aisle, and
their echoing footsteps indecently loud. They contemplated realistic groups of plaster savages, and Ann
thought they'd be queer people to have about. She
was glad there were none in this country. They
meditated upon replicas of classical statuary without
excessive comment. Kipps said, at large, it must have
been a queer world then; but Ann very properly doubted

if they really went about like that. But the place at
that early hour was lonely. One began to fancy things.
So they went out into the October sunshine of the
mighty terraces, and wandered amidst miles of stucco
tanks and about those quiet Gargantuan grounds. A
great, grey emptiness it was, and it seemed marvellous
to them, but not nearly so marvellous as it might have
seemed. "I never see a finer place, never," said Kipps,
turning to survey the entirety of the enormous glass
front with Paxton's vast image in the centre.

"What it must 'ave cost to build!" said Ann, and
left her sentence eloquently incomplete.

Presently they came to a region of caves and waterways, and amidst these waterways strange reminders of
the possibilities of the Creator. They passed under
an arch made of a whale's jaws, and discovered amidst
herbage browsing or standing unoccupied and staring as
if amazed at themselves, huge effigies of iguanodons and
deinotheria and mastodons and suchlike cattle, gloriously
done in green and gold.

"They got everything," said Kipps. "Earl's Court
isn't a patch on it."

His mind was very greatly exercised by these
monsters, and he hovered about them and returned to
them. "You'd wonder 'ow they ever got enough to
eat," he said several times.

§ 3

It was later in the day, and upon a seat in the presence
of the green and gold Labyrinthodon that looms so
splendidly above the lake, that the Kippses fell into
talk about their future. They had made a sufficient
lunch in the palace, they had seen pictures and no end
of remarkable things, and that and the amber sunlight made a mood for them, quiet and philosophical,
a haven mood. Kipps broke a contemplative silence
with an abrupt allusion to one principal preoccupation.

" I shall offer an 'pology and I shall offer 'er brother
damages. If she likes to bring an action for Breach
after that, well—I done all I can. . . . They can't
get much out of reading my letters in court, because I
didn't write none. I dessay a thousan' or two'll settle
all that, anyhow. I ain't much worried about that.
That don't worry me very much, Ann— No."

And then, " It's a lark, our marrying. It's curious
'ow things come about. If I hadn't run against you,
where should I 'ave been now? Eh? . . . Even after
we met, I didn't seem to see it like—not marrying you
I mean—until that night I came. I didn't—reely."

" I didn't neither," said Ann, with thoughtful eyes
on the water.

For a time Kipps' mind was occupied by the prettiness of her thinking face. A faint, tremulous network
of lights, reflected from the ripples of a passing duck,
played subtly over her cheek and faded away.

Ann reflected. " I s'pose things 'ad to be," she
said.

Kipps mused. " It's curious 'ow ever I got on to be
engaged to 'er."

" She wasn't suited to you," said Ann.

" Suited. No fear! That's jest it. 'Ow did it come
about?"

" I expect she led you on," said Ann.

Kipps was half-minded to assent. Then he had a
twinge of conscience. " It wasn't that, Ann," he said.
" It's curious. I don't know what it was, but it wasn't
that. I don't recollect. . . . No. . . . Life's jolly
rum; that's one thing any'ow. And I suppose I'm a
rum sort of feller. I get excited sometimes, and then
I don't seem to care *what* I do. That's about what it
was reely. Still——"

They meditated, Kipps with his arms folded and
pulling at his scanty moustache. Presently a faint
smile came over his face.

" We'll get a nice little 'ouse out 'Ithe way."

"It's 'omelier than Folkestone," said Ann.

"Jest a nice *little* 'ouse," said Kipps. "There's Hughenden, of course. But that's let. Besides being miles too big. And I wouldn't live in Folkestone again some'ow—not for anything."

"I'd like to 'ave a 'ouse of my own," said Ann. "I've often thought, being in service, 'ow much I'd like to manage a 'ouse of my own."

"You'd know all about what the servants was up to anyhow," said Kipps, amused.

"Servants! We don't want no servants," said Ann, startled.

"You'll 'ave to 'ave a servant," said Kipps. "If it's only to do the 'eavy work of the 'ouse."

"What! and not be able 'ardly to go into my own kitchen?" said Ann.

"You ought to 'ave a servant," said Kipps.

"One could easy 'ave a woman in for anything that's 'eavy," said Ann. "Besides— If I 'ad one of the girls one sees about nowadays, I should want to be taking the broom out of 'er 'and and do it all over myself. I'd manage better without 'er."

"We ought to 'ave one servant anyhow," said Kipps, "else 'ow should we manage if we wanted to go out together or anything like that?"

"I might get a *young* girl," said Ann, "and bring 'er up in my own way."

Kipps left the matter at that and came back to the house.

"There's little 'ouses going into Hythe, just the sort we want, not too big and not too small. We'll 'ave a kitching and a dining-room and a little room to sit in of a night."

"It mustn't be a 'ouse with a basement," said Ann.

"What's a basement?"

"It's a downstairs, where there's not arf enough light and everything got to be carried—up and down, up and down, all day—coals and everything. And it's got to 'ave a watertap and sink and things upstairs. You'd 'ardly believe, Artie, if you 'adn't been in service, 'ow cruel and silly some 'ouses are built—you'd think they 'ad a spite against servants the way the stairs are made."

"We won't 'ave one of that sort," said Kipps. . . .

"We'll 'ave a quiet little life. Now go out a bit—now come 'ome again. Read a book perhaps if we got nothing else to do. 'Ave old Buggins in for an evening at times. 'Ave Sid down. There's bicycles——"

"I don't fancy myself on a bicycle," said Ann.

"'Ave a trailer," said Kipps, "and sit like a lady. I'd take you out to New Romney easy as anything, jest to see the old people."

"I wouldn't mind that," said Ann.

"We'll jest 'ave a sensible little 'ouse, and sensible things. No art or anything of that sort, nothing stuck-up or anything, but jest sensible. We'll be as right as anything, Ann."

"No socialism," said Ann, starting a lurking doubt.

"No socialism," said Kipps; "just sensible, that's all."

"I dessay it's all right for them that understand it, Artie, but I don't agree with this socialism."

"I don't neither, reely," said Kipps. "I can't argue about it, but it don't seem real like to me. All the same, Masterman's a clever fellow, Ann."

"I didn't like 'im at first, Artie, but I do now—in a way. You don't understand 'im all at once."

"'E's so clever," said Kipps. "Arf the time I can't make out what 'e's up to. 'E's the cleverest chap I ever met. I never 'eard such talking. 'E ought to write a book. . . . It's a rum world, Ann, when a chap like that isn't 'ardly able to earn a living."

"It's 'is 'ealth," said Ann.

"I expect it is," said Kipps, and ceased to talk for a little while.

Then he spoke with deliberation, "Sea air might be the saving of 'im, Ann."

He glanced doubtfully at Ann, and she was looking at him even fondly.

"You think of other people a lot," said Ann. "I been looking at you sittin' there and thinking."

"I suppose I do. I suppose when one's 'appy one does."

"*You* do," said Ann.

"We shall be 'appy in that little 'ouse, Ann. Don't y' think?"

She met his eyes and nodded.

"I seem to see it," said Kipps, "sort of cosy like. 'Bout tea time and muffins, kettle on the 'ob, cat on the 'earthrug— We must get a cat, Ann—and *you* there. Eh?"

They regarded each other with appreciative eyes; and Kipps became irrelevant.

"I don't believe, Ann," he said, "I 'aven't kissed you not for 'arf an hour. Leastways not since we was in those caves."

For kissing had already ceased to be a matter of thrilling adventure for them.

Ann shook her head. "You be sensible and go on talking about Mr. Masterman," she said. . . .

But Kipps had wandered to something else. "I like the way your 'air turns back just there," he said, with an indicative finger. "It was like that, I remember, when you was a girl. Sort of wavy. I've often thought of it— . . . 'Member when we raced that time—out be'ind the church?"

Then for a time they sat idly, each following out agreeable meditations.

"It's rum," said Kipps.

"What's rum?"

"'Ow everything's 'appened," said Kipps. "Who'd 'ave thought of our being 'ere like this six weeks ago? . . . Who'd 'ave thought of my ever 'aving any money?"

His eyes went to the big Labyrinthodon. He looked

11

first carelessly, and then suddenly with a growing intimacy at its vast face.

"I'm deshed!" he murmured. Ann became interested. He laid a hand on her arm and pointed. Ann scrutinised the Labyrinthodon and then came around to Kipps' face in mute interrogation.

"Don't you see it?" said Kipps.

"See what?"

"'E's jest like old Coote."

"It's extinct," said Ann, not clearly apprehending.

"I dessay 'e is. But 'e's jest like old Coote all the same for that."

Kipps meditated on the monstrous shapes in sight. "I wonder 'ow all these old antediluvium animals *got* ex.inct," he asked. "No one couldn't possibly 'ave killed 'em."

"Why! *I* know that," said Ann. "They was overtook by the Flood. . . ."

Kipps meditated for a while. "But I thought they had to take two of everything there was——"

"Within reason they 'ad," said Ann. . . .

The Kippses left it at that.

The great green-and-gold Labyrinthodon took no notice of their conversation. It gazed with its wonderful eyes over their heads into the infinite—inflexibly calm. It might indeed have been Coote himself there, Coote the unassuming, cutting them dead. . . .

§ 4

And in due course these two simple souls married, and Venus Urania, the Goddess of Wedded Love, who is indeed a very great and noble and kindly goddess, bent down and blessed them in their union.

END OF BOOK II

BOOK III

KIPPSES

CHAPTER THE FIRST

The Housing Problem

HONEYMOONS and all things come to an end, and you see at last Mr. and Mrs. Arthur Kipps descending upon the Hythe platform—coming to Hythe to find that nice *little* house, to realise that bright dream of a home they had first talked about in the grounds of the Crystal Palace. They are a valiant couple, you perceive, but small; and the world is a large incongruous system of complex and difficult things. Kipps wears a grey suit, with a wing-poke collar and a neat, smart tie. Mrs. Kipps is the same bright and healthy little girl woman you saw in the marsh; not an inch has been added to her stature in all my voluminous narrative. Only now she wears a hat.

It is a hat very unlike the hats she used to wear on her Sundays out, a flourishing hat with feathers and buckle and bows and things. The price of that hat would take many people's breath away—it cost two guineas! Kipps chose it. Kipps paid for it. They left the shop with flushed cheeks and smarting eyes, glad to be out of range of the condescending saleswoman.

"Artie," said Ann, "you didn't ought to 'ave——"

That was all. And you know, the hat didn't suit Ann a bit. Her clothes did not suit her at all. The simple, cheap, clean brightness of her former style had given place not only to this hat, but to several other things in the same key. And out from among these things looked her pretty face, the face of a wise little child—an artless wonder struggling through a preposterous dignity.

They had bought that hat one day when they had gone to see the shops in Bond Street. Kipps had looked at the passers-by and it had suddenly occurred to him that Ann was dowdy. He had noted the hat of a very proud-looking lady passing in an electric brougham, and had resolved to get Ann the nearest thing to that.

The railway porters perceived some subtle incongruity in Ann, so did the knot of cabmen in the station doorway, the two golfers and the lady with daughters, who had also got out of the train. And Kipps, a little pale, blowing a little, not in complete possession of himself, knew that they noticed her and him. And Ann— It is hard to say just what Ann observed of these things.

"'Ere!" said Kipps to a cabman, and regretted too late a vanished "H."

"I got a trunk up there," he said to a ticket inspector, "marked A. K."

"Ask a porter," said the inspector, turning his back.

"Demn!" said Kipps, not altogether inaudibly.

§ 2

It is all very well to sit in the sunshine and talk of the house you will have, and another altogether to achieve it. We English—all the world indeed to-day— live in a strange atmosphere of neglected great issues, of insistent, triumphant petty things; we are given up to the fine littlenesses of intercourse; table manners and small correctitudes are the substance of our lives. You do not escape these things for long even by so catastrophic a proceeding as flying to London with a young lady of no wealth and inferior social position. The mists of noble emotion swirl and pass, and there you are, divorced from all your deities and grazing in the meadows under the Argus eyes of the social system, the innumerable mean judgments you feel raining upon you, upon your clothes and bearing, upon your pretensions and movements.

Our world to-day is a meanly conceived one—it is only an added meanness to conceal that fact. For one consequence, it has very few nice little houses. Such things do not come for the asking, they are not to be bought with money during ignoble times. Its houses are built on the ground of monstrously rich, shabbily extortionate landowners, by poor, parsimonious, greedy people in a mood of elbowing competition. What can you expect from such ridiculous conditions? To go house-hunting is to spy out the nakedness of this pretentious world, to see what our civilisation amounts to when you take away curtains and flounces and carpets and all the fluster and distraction of people and fittings. It is to see mean plans meanly executed for mean ends, the conventions torn aside, the secrets stripped, the substance underlying all such Chester Cootery, soiled and worn and left.

So you see our poor dear Kippses going to and fro, in Hythe, in Sandgate, in Ashford and Canterbury and Deal and Dover—at last even in Folkestone, with

" orders to view," pink and green and white and yellow orders to view, and labelled keys in Kipps' hand and frowns and perplexity upon their faces. . . . They did not clearly know what they wanted, but whatever it was they saw, they knew they did not want that. Always they found a confusing multitude of houses they could not take, and none they could. Their dreams began to turn mainly on empty, abandoned-looking rooms, with unfaded patches of paper to mark the place of vanished pictures and doors that had lost their keys. They saw rooms floored with boards that yawned apart and were splintered, skirtings eloquent of the industrious mouse, kitchens with a dead black-beetle in the empty cupboard, and a hideous variety of coal holes and dark cupboards under the stairs. They stuck their little heads through roof trap-doors and gazed at disorganised ball taps, at the black filthiness of un-stopped roofs. There were occasions when it seemed to them that they must be the victims of an elaborate con-spiracy of house agents, so bleak and cheerless is a second-hand empty house in comparison with the humblest of inhabited dwellings.

Commonly the houses were too big. They had huge windows that demanded vast curtains in mitigation, countless bedrooms, acreage of stone steps to be cleaned, kitchens that made Ann protest. She had come so far towards a proper conception of Kipps' social position as to admit the prospect of one servant—" but lor'!" she would say, "you want a manservant in this 'ouse." When the houses were not too big, then they were almost invariably the product of speculative building, of that multitudinous hasty building for the extravagant swarm of new births that was the essential disaster of the nineteenth century. The new houses Ann refused as damp, and even the youngest of these that had been in use showed remarkable signs of a sickly constitution, the plaster flaked away, the floors gaped, the paper mouldered and peeled, the doors dropped, the bricks scaled and the railings rusted, Nature in the form of spiders, earwigs, cockroaches, mice, rats, fungi and remarkable smells, was already fighting her way back. . . .

And the plan was invariably inconvenient, invariably. All the houses they saw had a common quality for which she could find no word, but for which the proper word is incivility. "They build these 'ouses," she said, "as though girls wasn't 'uman beings." Sid's social democracy had got into her blood perhaps, and anyhow they went about discovering the most remarkable inconsiderateness in the contemporary house. "There's kitching stairs to go up, Artie!" Ann would say. "Some poor girl's got to go up and down, up and down, and be tired out, jest because they haven't the sense to leave enough space to give their steps a proper rise—and no water upstairs anywhere—every drop got to be carried! It's 'ouses like this wear girls out.

"It's 'aving 'ouses built by men, I believe, makes all the work and trouble," said Ann. . . .

The Kippses, you see, thought they were looking for a reasonably simple little contemporary house, but they were looking for dreamland or 1975 A.D. or thereabouts, and it hadn't come.

§ 3

But it was a foolish thing for Kipps to begin building a house.

He did that out of an extraordinary animosity for house agents he had conceived.

Everybody hates house agents just as everybody loves sailors. It is no doubt a very wicked and unjust hatred, but the business of a novelist is not ethical principle but facts. Everybody hates house agents because they have everybody at a disadvantage. All other callings have a certain amount of give and take; the house agent simply takes. All other callings want you; your solicitor

is afraid you may change him, your doctor cannot go too
far, your novelist—if only you knew it—is mutely
abject towards your unspoken wishes; and as for your
tradespeople, milkmen will fight outside your front door
for you, and green-grocers call in tears if you discard
them suddenly; but who ever heard of a house agent
struggling to serve anyone? You want a house; you go
to him, you dishevelled and angry from travel, anxious,
inquiring; he calm, clean, inactive, reticent, quietly
doing nothing. You beg him to reduce rents, white-
wash ceilings, produce other houses, combine the
summer house of No. 6 with the conservatory of No. 4
—much he cares! You want to dispose of a house;
then he is just the same, serene, indifferent—on one
occasion I remember he was picking his teeth all the
time he answered me. Competition is a mockery among
house agents, they are all alike, you cannot wound them
by going to the opposite office, you cannot dismiss them,
you can at most dismiss yourself. They are invulnerably
placed behind mahogany and brass, too far usually even
for a sudden swift lunge with an umbrella; and to
throw away the keys they lend you instead of returning
them is larceny and punishable as such.

It was a house agent in Dover who finally decided
Kipps to build. Kipps, with a certain faltering in his
voice, had delivered his ultimatum, no basement, not
more than eight rooms, hot and cold water upstairs,
coal cellar in the house but with intervening doors to
keep dust from the scullery and so forth. He stood
blowing. "You'll have to build a house," said the
house agent, sighing wearily, "if you want all that."
It was rather for the sake of effective answer than with
any intention at the time that Kipps mumbled, "That's
about what I shall do—this goes on."

Whereupon the house agent smiled. He smiled!

When Kipps came to turn the thing over in his
mind, he was surprised to find quite a considerable
intention had germinated and was growing up in him.

After all, lots of people *have* built houses. How could there be so many if they hadn't? Suppose he "reely" did! Then he would go to the house agent and say, "'Ere, while you been getting me a sootable 'ouse, blowed if I 'aven't built one!" Go round to all of them; all the house agents in Folkestone, in Dover, Ashford, Canterbury, Margate, Ramsgate, saying that! Perhaps then they might be sorry. It was in the small hours that he awoke to a realisation that he had made up his mind in the matter.

"Ann," he said, "Ann," and also used the sharp of his elbow.

Ann was at last awakened to the pitch of an indistinct inquiry what was the matter.

"I'm going to build a house, Ann."

"Eh?" said Ann suddenly, as if awake.

"Build a house."

Ann said something incoherent about he'd better wait until the morning before he did anything of the sort, and immediately with a fine trustfulness went fast asleep again.

But Kipps lay awake for a long while building his house, and in the morning at breakfast he made his meaning clear. He had smarted under the indignities of house agents long enough, and this seemed to promise revenge—a fine revenge. "And, you know, we might reely make rather a nice little 'ouse out of it—like we want."

So resolved, it became possible for them to take a house for a year, with a basement, no service lift, blackleading to do everywhere, no water upstairs, no bathroom, vast sash windows to be cleaned from the sill, stone steps with a twist and open to the rain into the coal cellar, insufficient cupboards, unpaved path to the dustbin, no fireplace to the servant's bedroom, no end of splintery wood to scrub—in fact, a very typical English middle-class house. And having added to this house some furniture, and a languid young person with unauthentic golden hair named Gwendolen, who was engaged to a sergeant-major and had formerly been in an hotel, having " moved in " and spent some sleepless nights varied by nocturnal explorations in search of burglars, because of the strangeness of being in a house for which they were personally responsible, Kipps settled down for a time and turned himself with considerable resolution to the project of building a home.

§ 4

At first Kipps gathered advice, finding an initial difficulty in how to begin. He went into a builder's shop at Seabrook one day, and told the lady in charge that he wanted a house built. He was breathless but quite determined, and he was prepared to give his order there and then; but she temporised with him and said her husband was out, and he left without giving his name. Also he went and talked to a man in a cart who was pointed out to him by a workman as the builder of a new house near Saltwood, but he found him first sceptical and then overpoweringly sarcastic. " I suppose you build a 'ouse every 'oliday," he said, and turned from Kipps with every symptom of contempt.

Afterwards Carshot told alarming stories about builders, and shook Kipps' expressed resolution a good deal, and then Pierce raised the question whether one ought to go in the first instance to a builder at all and not rather to an architect. Pierce knew a man at Ashford whose brother was an architect, and as it is always better in these matters to get someone you know, the Kippses decided, before Pierce had gone and Carshot's warnings had resumed their sway, to apply to him. They did so—rather dubiously.

The architect who was brother of Pierce's friend appeared as a small, alert individual with a black bag and a cylindrical silk hat, and he sat at the dining-room table with his hat and his bag exactly equidistant right and left of him, and maintained a demeanour of impressive woodenness while Kipps on the hearthrug, with a quaking sense of gigantic enterprise, vacillated answers to his inquiries.   Ann held a watching brief for herself, in a position she had chosen as suitable to the occasion beside the corner of the carved oak sideboard.   They felt, in a sense, at bay.

The architect began by asking for the site, and seemed a little discomposed to discover this had still to be found.   "I thought of building just anywhere," said Kipps.   "I 'aven't made up my mind about that yet."   The architect remarked that he would have preferred to see the site in order to know where to put what he called his "ugly side," but it was quite possible of course to plan a house "in the air," on the level, "simply with back and front assumed"—if they would like to do that.   Kipps flushed slightly, and secretly hoping it would make no great difference in the fees, said a little doubtfully that he thought that would be all right.

The architect then marked off as it were the first section of his subject with a single dry cough, opened his bag, took out a spring tape measure, some hard biscuits, a metal flask, a new pair of dogskin gloves, a clockwork motor-car partially wrapped in paper, a bunch of violets, a paper of small brass screws, and finally a large, distended notebook; he replaced the other objects carefully, opened his notebook, put a pencil to his lips and said: "And what accommodation will you require?"   To which Ann, who had followed his every movement with the closest attention and a deepening dread, replied with the violent suddenness of one who has lain in wait, "Cubbuds!"

"Anyhow," she added, catching her husband's eye.

The architect wrote it down.

"And how many rooms?" he said, coming to secondary matters.

The young people regarded one another. It was dreadfully like giving an order.

"How many bedrooms, for example?" asked the architect.

"One?" suggested Kipps, inclined now to minimise at any cost.

"There's Gwendolen," said Ann.

"Visitors perhaps," said the architect, and temperately. "You never know."

"Two p'r'aps?" said Kipps. "We don't want no more than a *little* 'ouse, you know."

"But the merest shooting-box—," said the architect.

They got to six; he beat them steadily from bedroom to bedroom, the word "nursery" played across their imaginative skies—he mentioned it as the remotest possibility—and then six being reluctantly conceded, Ann came forward to the table, sat down and delivered herself of one of her prepared conditions : "'Ot and cold water," she said, "laid on to each room—any'ow."

It was an idea long since acquired from Sid.

"Yes," said Kipps, on the hearthrug, "'ot and cold water laid on to each bedroom—we've settled on that."

It was the first intimation to the architect that he had to deal with a couple of exceptional originality, and as he had spent the previous afternoon in finding three large houses in *The Builder,* which he intended to combine into an original and copyright design of his own, he naturally struggled against these novel requirements. He enlarged on the extreme expensiveness of plumbing, on the extreme expensiveness of everything not already arranged for in his scheme, and only when Ann declared she'd as soon not have the house as not have her requirements, and Kipps, blenching the while, had said he didn't mind what a thing cost him so long as he got what he wanted, did he allow a kindred originality of his own to appear beneath the acquired professionalism of his methods. He dismissed their previous talk with his paragraphic cough. "Of course," he said, "if you don't mind being unconventional——"

He explained that he had been thinking of a Queen Anne style of architecture (Ann directly she heard her name shook her head at Kipps in an aside) so far as the exterior went. For his own part, he said, he liked to have the exterior of a house in a style, not priggishly in a style, but mixed with one style uppermost; and the gables and dormers and casements of the Queen Anne style, with a little rough-cast and sham timbering here and there and perhaps a bit of an overhang diversified a house and made it interesting. The advantage of what he called a Queen Anne style was that it had such a variety of features. . . . Still, if they were prepared to be unconventional it could be done. A number of houses were now built in the unconventional style and were often very pretty. In the unconventional style one frequently had what perhaps he might call Internal Features, for example an Old English oak staircase and gallery. White rough-cast and green paint were a good deal favoured in houses of this type.

He indicated that this excursus on style was finished by a momentary use of his cough, and reopened his notebook, which he had closed to wave about in a moment of descriptive enthusiasm while expatiating on the unbridled wealth of External Features associated with Queen Anne. "Six bedrooms," he said, moistening his pencil. "One with barred windows suitable for a nursery if required."

Kipps endorsed this huskily and reluctantly.

There followed a most interesting discussion upon house building, in which Kipps played a minor part. They passed from bedrooms to the kitchen and scullery, and there Ann displayed an intelligent exactingness that won the expressed admiration of the architect. They were particularly novel upon the position of the coal cellar, which Ann held to be altogether too low in the ordinary house, necessitating much heavy carrying.

They dismissed as impracticable the idea of having coal cellar and kitchen at the top of the house, because that would involve carrying all the coal through the house, and therewith much subsequent cleaning, and for a time they dealt with a conception of a coal cellar on the ground floor with a light staircase running up outside to an exterior shoot. "It might be made a Feature," said the architect, a little doubtfully, jotting down a note of it. "It would be apt to get black, you know."

Thence they passed to the alternative of service lifts, and then by an inspiration of the architect to the possibilities of gas heating. Kipps did a complicated verbal fugue on the theme, "gas heating heats the air," with variable aspirates; he became very red and was lost to the discussion altogether for a time, though his lips kept silently moving.

Subsequently the architect wrote to say that he found in his notebook very full and explicit directions for bay windows to all rooms, for bedrooms, for water supply, lift, height of stairs and absence of twists therein, for a well-ventilated kitchen twenty feet square, with two dressers and a large box window-seat, for scullery and outhouses and offices, but nothing whatever about drawing-room, dining-room, library or study, or approximate cost, and he awaited further instructions. He presumed there would be a breakfast-room, dining-room, drawing-room, and study for Mr. Kipps, at least that was his conception, and the young couple discussed this matter long and ardently.

Ann was distinctly restrictive in this direction. "I don't see what you want a drawin'-room and a dinin' *and* a kitchen for. If we was going to let in summer —well and good. But we're not going to let. Consequently we don't want so many rooms. Then there's a 'all. What use is a 'all? It only makes work. And a study!"

Kipps had been humming and stroking his moustache since he had read the architect's letter "I think I'd like a little bit of a study—not a big one, of course, but one with a desk and book-shelves, like there was in Hughenden. I'd like that."

It was only after they had talked to the architect again and seen how scandalised he was at the idea of not having a drawing-room, that they consented to that Internal Feature. They consented to please him. "But we shan't never use it," said Ann.

Kipps had his way about a study. "When I get that study," said Kipps, "I shall do a bit of reading I've long wanted to do. I shall make a nabit of going in there and reading something an hour every day. There's Shakespeare and a lot of things a man like me ought to read. Besides, we got to 'ave *somewhere* to put the Encyclopædia. I've always thought a study was about what I've wanted all along. You can't 'elp reading if you got a study. If you 'aven't, there's nothing for it, so far's *I* can see, but treshy novels."

He looked down at Ann and was surprised to see a joyless thoughtfulness upon her face.

"Fency, Ann!" he said, not too buoyantly, "'aving a little 'ouse of our own!"

"It won't be a little 'ouse," said Ann, "not with all them rooms."

§ 5

Any lingering doubt in that matter was dispelled when it came to plans.

The architect drew three sets of plans on a transparent bluish sort of paper that smelt abominably. He painted them very nicely; brick red and ginger, and arsenic green and a leaden sort of blue, and brought them over to show our young people. The first set were very simple, with practically no External Features —"a plain style," he said it was—but it looked a big sort of house nevertheless; the second had such extras as a conservatory, bay windows of various sorts, one rough-cast gable and one half-timbered ditto in plaster, and a sort of overhung veranda, and was much more imposing; and the third was quite fungoid with External Features, and honey-combed with Internal ones; it was, he said, "practically a mansion," and altogether a very noble fruit of the creative mind of man. It was, he admitted, perhaps almost too good for Hythe; his art had run away with him and produced a modern mansion in the "best Folkestone style"; it had a central hall with a staircase, a Moorish gallery, and a Tudor stained-glass window, crenellated battlements to the leading over the portico, an octagonal bulge with octagonal bay windows, surmounted by an oriental dome of metal, lines of yellow bricks to break up the red and many other richnesses and attractions. It was the sort of house, ornate and in its dignified way voluptuous, that a city magnate might build, but it seemed excessive to the Kippses. The first plan had seven bedrooms, the second eight, the third eleven; they had, the architect explained, "worked in," as if they were pebbles in a mountaineer's boot.

"They're big 'ouses," said Ann directly the elevations were unrolled.

Kipps listened to the architect with round eyes and an exuberant caution in his manner, anxious not to commit himself further than he had done to the enterprise, and the architect pointed out the Features and other objects of interest with the scalpel belonging to a pocket manicure set that he carried. Ann watched Kipps' face and communicated with him furtively over the architect's head. "*Not so big,*" said Ann's lips.

"It's a bit big for what I meant," said Kipps, with a reassuring eye on Ann

"You won't think it big when you see it up," said the architect; "you take my word for that."

"We don't want no more than six bedrooms," said Kipps.

"Make this one a box-room, then," said the architect.

A feeling of impotence silenced Kipps for a time.

"Now which," said the architect, spreading them out, "is it to be?"

He flattened down the plans of the most ornate mansion to show it to better effect.

Kipps wanted to know how much each would cost "at the outside" which led to much alarmed signalling from Ann. But the architect could estimate only in the most general way.

They were not really committed to anything when the architect went away. Kipps had promised to think it over, that was all.

"We can't 'ave that 'ouse," said Ann.

"They're miles too big—all of them," agreed Kipps.

"You'd want— Four servants wouldn't be 'ardly enough," said Ann.

Kipps went to the hearthrug and spread himself. His tone was almost offhand. "Nex' time 'e comes," said Kipps, "I'll 'splain to him. It isn't at all the sort of thing we want. It's—it's a misunderstanding. You got no occasion to be anxious 'bout it, Ann."

"I don't see much good reely in building an 'ouse at all," said Ann.

"Oo, we *got* to build a 'ouse now we begun," said Kipps. "But now, supposin' we 'ad——"

He spread out the most modest of the three plans and scratched his cheek.

§ 6

It was unfortunate that old Kipps came over the next day.

Old Kipps always produced peculiar states of mind in his nephew, a rash assertiveness, a disposition towards display unlike his usual self. There had been great difficulty in reconciling both these old people to the Pornick mésalliance, and at times the controversy echoed in old Kipps' expressed thoughts. This perhaps it was,

and no ignoble vanity, that set the note of florid suc-
cessfulness going in Kipps' conversation whenever his
uncle appeared. Mrs. Kipps was, as a matter of fact,
not reconciled at all; she had declined all invitations
to come over on the bus, and was a taciturn hostess on
the one occasion when the young people called at the
toy shop *en route* for Mrs. Pornick. She displayed a
tendency to sniff that was clearly due to pride rather
than catarrh, and except for telling Ann she hoped she
would not feel too "stuck up" about her marriage,
confined her conversation to her nephew or the infinite.
The call was a brief one and made up chiefly of pauses,
no refreshment was offered or asked for, and Ann departed with a singularly high colour. For some reason
she would not call at the toy shop when they found
themselves again in New Romney.

But old Kipps, having adventured over and tried
the table of the new *ménage* and found it to his taste,
showed many signs of softening towards Ann. He
came again and then again. He would come over by
the bus, and except when his mouth was absolutely
full, he would give his nephew one solid and continuous mass of advice of the most subtle and disturbing description, until it was time to toddle back to the
High Street for the afternoon bus. He would walk
with him to the sea front, and commence *pourparlers*
with boatmen for the purchase of one of their boats—
"You ought to keep a boat of your own," he said,
though Kipps was a singularly poor sailor—or· he would
pursue a plan that was forming in his mind in which
he should own and manage what he called "weekly"
property in the less conspicuous streets of Hythe. The
cream of that was to be a weekly collection of rents in
person, the nearest approach to feudal splendour left
in this democratised country. He gave no hint of the
source of the capital he designed for his investment, and
at times it would appear he intended it as an occupation
for his nephew rather than himself.

But there remained something in his manner towards Ann, in the glances of scrutiny he gave her unawares, that kept Kipps alertly expansive whenever he was about. And in all sorts of ways. It was on account of old Kipps, for example, that our Kipps plunged one day, a golden plunge, and brought home a box of cummer-bundy ninepenny cigars, and substituted blue label old Methusaleh Four Stars for the common and generally satisfactory white brand.

"Some of this is whisky, my boy," said old Kipps when he tasted it, smacking critical lips.

"Saw a lot of young officery fellers coming along," said old Kipps. "You ought to join the volunteers, my boy, and get to know a few."

"I dessay I shall," said Kipps. "Later."

"They'd make you an officer, you know, 'n no time. They want officers," said old Kipps. "It isn't every-one can afford it. They'd be regular glad to 'ave you. . . . Ain't bort a dog yet?"

"Not yet, uncle. 'Ave a segar?"

"Nor a moty car?"

"Not yet, uncle."

"There's no 'urry 'bout that. And don't get one of these 'ere trashy cheap ones when you do get it, my boy. Get one as'll last a lifetime. . . . I'm surprised you don't 'ire a bit more."

"Ann don't seem to fency a moty car," said Kipps.

"Ah!" said old Kipps, "I expect not," and glanced a comment at the door. "She ain't used to going out," he said. "More at 'ome indoors."

"Fact is," said Kipps hastily, "we're thinking of building a 'ouse."

"I wouldn't do that, my boy," began old Kipps, but his nephew was routing in the chiffonier drawer amidst the plans. He got them in time to check some further comment on Ann. "Um," said the old gentleman, a little impressed by the extraordinary odour and the unusual transparency of the tracing paper Kipps put into his hands. "Thinking of building a 'ouse, are you?"

Kipps began with the most modest of the three projects.

Old Kipps read slowly through his silver-rimmed spectacles: "Plan of a 'ouse for Arthur Kipps Esquire —Um."

He didn't warm to the project all at once, and Ann drifted into the room to find him still scrutinising the architect's proposals a little doubtfully.

"We couldn't find a decent 'ouse anywhere," said Kipps, leaning against the table and assuming an off-hand note. "I didn't see why we shouldn't run up one for ourselves." Old Kipps could not help liking the tone of that.

"We thought we might see—" said Ann.

"It's a spekerlation, of course," said old Kipps, and held the plan at a distance of two feet or more from his glasses and frowned. "This isn't exactly the 'ouse I should expect you to 'ave thought of, though," he said. "Practically it's a villa. It's the sort of 'ouse a bank clerk might 'ave. 'Tisn't what I should call a gentleman's 'ouse, Artie."

"It's plain, of course," said Kipps, standing beside his uncle and looking down at this plan, which certainly did seem a little less magnificent now than it had at the first encounter.

"You mustn't 'ave it too plain," said old Kipps.

"If it's comfortable—" Ann hazarded.

Old Kipps glanced at her over his spectacles. "You ain't comfortable, my gal, in this world, not if you don't live up to your position," so putting compactly into contemporary English that fine old phrase, *noblesse oblige*. "A 'ouse of this sort is what a retired trades-man might 'ave, or some little whippersnapper of a s'liciter. But *you*——"

"Course that isn't the on'y plan," said Kipps, and tried the middle one.

But it was the third one which won over old Kipps. "Now that's a *'ouse,* my boy," he said at the sight of it.

Ann came and stood just behind her husband's shoulder while old Kipps expanded upon the desirability of the larger scheme. "You ought to 'ave a billiard-room," he said; "I don't see that, but all the rest's about right. A lot of these 'ere officers 'ere 'ud be glad of a game of billiards.

"What's all these dots?" said old Kipps.

"S'rubbery," said Kipps. "Flow'ing s'rubs."

"There's eleven bedrooms in that 'ouse," said Ann. "It's a bit of a lot, ain't it, Uncle?"

"You'll want 'em, my girl. As you get on, you'll be 'aving visitors. Friends of your 'usband's, p'r'aps, from the School of Musketry, what you want 'im to get on with. You can't never tell."

"If we 'ave a great s'rubbery," Ann ventured, "we shall 'ave to keep a gardener."

"If you don't 'ave a s'rubbery," said old Kipps, with a note of patient reasoning, "'ow are you to prevent every jackanapes that goes by, starin' into your drorin'-room winder—p'r'aps when you get someone a bit special to entertain?"

"We ain't *used* to a s'rubbery," said Ann mulishly; "we get on very well 'ere."

"It isn't what you're used to," said old Kipps, "it's what you ought to 'ave *now*." And with that Ann dropped out of the discussion.

"Study and lib'ry," old Kipps read. "That's right. I see a Tantalus the other day over Brookland, the very thing for a gentleman's study. I'll try and get over and bid for it. . . ."

By bus time old Kipps was quite enthusiastic about the house building, and it seemed to be definitely settled that the largest plan was the one decided upon.

But Ann had said nothing further in the matter.

§ 7

When Kipps returned from seeing his uncle into the bus—there always seemed a certain doubt whether that portly figure would go into the little red "Tip-Top" box—he found Ann still standing by the table, looking with an expression of comprehensive disapproval at the three plans.

"There don't seem much the matter with uncle," said Kipps, assuming the hearthrug, "spite of 'is 'eartburn. 'E 'opped up them steps like a bird."

Ann remained staring at the plans.

"You don't like them plans?" hazarded Kipps.

"No, I don't, Artie."

"We got to build somethin' now."

"But—it's a gentleman's 'ouse, Artie!"

"It's—it's a decent size, o' course."

Kipps took a flirting look at the drawing and went to the window.

"Look at the cleanin'. Free servants'll be lost in that 'ouse, Artie."

"We must 'ave servants," said Kipps.

Ann looked despondently at her future residence.

"We got to keep up our position, any'ow," said Kipps, turning towards her. "It stands to reason, Ann, we got a position. Very well! I can't 'ave you scrubbin' floors. You got to 'ave a servant and you got to manage a 'ouse. You wouldn't 'ave me ashamed——"

Ann opened her lips and did not speak.

"What?" asked Kipps.

"Nothing," said Ann, "only I did want it to be a *little* 'ouse, Artie. I wanted it to be a 'andy little 'ouse, jest for us."

Kipps' face was suddenly flushed and obstinate. He took up the curiously smelling tracings again. "I'm not a-going to be looked down upon," he said. "It's not only Uncle I'm thinking of!"

Ann stared at him.

Kipps went on. " I won't 'ave that young Walshing-ham, f'r instance, sneering and sniffing at me. Making out as if we was all wrong. I see 'im yesterday. . . . Nor Coote neether. I'm as good—we're as good—whatever's 'appened."

Silence and the rustle of plans.

He looked up and saw Ann's eyes bright with tears. For a moment the two stared at one another.

" We'll 'ave the big 'ouse," said Ann, with a gulp. " I didn't think of that, Artie."

Her aspect was fierce and resolute, and she struggled with emotion. " We'll have the big 'ouse," she repeated. " They shan't say I dragged you down wiv' me—none of them shan't say that. I've thought—I've always been afraid of that."

Kipps looked again at the plan, and suddenly the grand house had become very grand indeed. He blew.

" No, Artie, none of them shan't say that," and with something blind in her motions Ann tried to turn the plan round to her. . . .

After all, Kipps thought, there might be something to say for the milder project. . . . But he had gone so far that now he did not know how to say it.

And so the plans went out to the builders, and in a little while Kipps was committed to two thousand five hundred pounds worth of building. But then, you know, he had an income of twelve hundred a year.

§ 8

It is extraordinary what minor difficulties cluster about house-building.

" I say, Ann," remarked Kipps one day, " we shall 'ave to call this little 'ouse by a name. I was thinking of 'Ome Cottage. But I dunno whether 'Ome Cottage is quite the thing like. All these little fishermen's places are called Cottages."

" I like ' Cottage,' " said Ann.

"It's got eleven bedrooms, y'see," said Kipps. "I don't see 'ow you can call it a cottage with more bedrooms than four. Prop'ly speaking, it's a Large Villa. Prop'ly, it's almost a Big 'Ouse. Leastways a 'Ouse."

"Well," said Ann, "if you must call it Villa—Home Villa. . . . I wish it wasn't."

Kipps meditated.

"'Ow about Eureka Villa?" he said, raising his voice.

"What's Eureka?"

"It's a name," he said. "There used to be Eureka Dress Fasteners. There's lots of names, come to think of it, to be got out of a shop. There's Pyjama Villa. I remember that in the hosiery. No, come to think, that wouldn't do. But Maraposa—sort of oatmeal cloth, that was. . . . No! Eureka's better."

Ann meditated. "It seems silly like to 'ave a name that don't mean much."

"Perhaps it does," said Kipps. "Though it's what people 'ave to do."

He became meditative. "I got it!" he cried.

"Not Oreeka!" said Ann.

"No! There used to be a 'ouse at Hastings opposite our school—quite a big 'ouse it was—St. Ann's. Now *that*——"

"No," said Mrs. Kipps with decision. "Thanking you kindly, but I don't have no butcher boys making game of me. . . ."

They consulted Carshot, who suggested after some days of reflection, Waddycombe, as a graceful reminder of Kipps' grandfather; old Kipps, who was for "Upton Manor House," where he had once been second footman; Buggins, who favoured either a stern simple number, "Number One"—if there were no other houses there—or something patriotic, as "Empire Villa," and Pierce, who inclined to "Sandringham"; but in spite of all this help they were still undecided when, amidst violent perturbations of the soul, and after the most complex and difficult hagglings, wranglings, fears, muddles and goings to and fro, Kipps became the joyless owner of a freehold plot of three-eighths of an acre, and saw the turf being wheeled away from the site that should one day be his home.

CHAPTER THE
SECOND

The Callers

*T*HE Kippses sat at their midday dinner-table amidst the vestiges of rhubarb pie, and discussed two postcards the one o'clock post had brought. It was a rare bright moment of sunshine in a wet and windy day in the March that followed their marriage. Kipps was attired in a suit of brown, with a tie of fashionable green, while Ann wore one of those picturesque loose robes that are usually associated with sandals and advanced ideas. But there weren't any sandals on Ann or any advanced ideas, and the robe had come quite recently through the counsels of Mrs. Sid Pornick. "It's Art-like," said Kipps, but giving way. "It's more comfortable," said Ann. The room looked out by French windows upon a little patch of green and the Hythe parade. The parade was all shiny wet with rain, and the green-grey sea tumbled and tumbled between parade and sky.

The Kipps' furniture, except for certain chromo-lithographs of Kipps' incidental choice that struck a quiet note amidst the wall-paper, had been tactfully forced by an expert salesman, and it was in a style of mediocre elegance. There was a sideboard of carved oak that had only one fault, it reminded Kipps at times of wood-carving, and its panel of bevelled glass now reflected the back of his head. On its shelf were two books from Parsons' Library, each with a "place" marked by a slip of paper; neither of the Kippses could have told you the title of either book they read, much less the author's name. There was an ebonised overmantel set with phials and pots of brilliant colour, each duplicated by looking-glass, and bearing also a pair of Chinese jars made in Birmingham, a wedding present from Mr. and Mrs. Sidney Pornick, and several sumptuous Japanese fans. And there was a Turkey carpet of great richness. In addition to these modern exploits of Messrs. Bunt and Bubble, there were two inactive tall clocks, whose extreme dilapidation appealed to the connoisseur; a terrestrial and a celestial globe, the latter deeply indented; a number of good old iron-moulded and dusty books, and a stuffed owl wanting one (easily replaceable) glass eye, obtained by the exertions of Uncle Kipps. The table equipage was as much as possible like Mrs. Bindon Botting's, only more costly, and in addition there were green and crimson wine glasses—though the Kippses never drank wine.

Kipps turned to the more legible of his two postcards again.

"'Unavoidably prevented from seein' me to-day,' 'e says. I like 'is cheek. After I give 'im 'is start and everything."

He blew.

"'E certainly treats you a bit orf'and," said Ann.

Kipps gave vent to his dislike of young Walshingham. "He's getting too big for 'is britches," he said. "I'm beginning to wish she 'ad brought an action for breach.

Ever since 'e said she wouldn't, 'e's seemed to think I've
got no right to spend my own money."

" 'E's never liked your building the 'ouse," said Ann.

Kipps displayed wrath. "What the goodness 'as it
got to do wiv 'im?

"Overman indeed!" he added. "Overmantel! . . .
'E tries that on with me, I'll tell 'im something 'e
won't like."

He took up the second card. "Dashed if I can read
a word of it. I can jest make out Chit'low at the end
and that's all."

He scrutinised it. "It's like someone in a fit writing.
This here might be W H A T—*what*. P R I C E—
I got it! What price Harry now? It was a sort of
saying of 'is. I expect 'e's either done something or not
done something towards starting that play, Ann."

"I expect that's about it," said Ann.

Kipps grunted with effort. "I can't read the rest,"
he said at last, "nohow."

A thoroughly annoying post. He pitched the card
on the table, stood up and went to the window, where
Ann, after a momentary reconnaissance at Chitterlow's
hieroglyphics, came to join him.

"Wonder what I shall do this afternoon," said Kipps,
with his hands deep in his pockets.

He produced and lit a cigarette.

"Go for a walk, I s'pose," said Ann.

"I *been* for a walk this morning.

"S'pose I must go for another," he added, after an
interval.

They regarded the windy waste of sea for a space.

"Wonder why it is 'e won't see me," said Kipps,
returning to the problem of young Walshingham. "It's
all lies about 'is being too busy."

Ann offered no solution.

"Rain again!" said Kipps, as the lash of the little
drops stung the window.

"Oo, bother!" said Kipps, "you got to do some-

thing. Look 'ere, Ann! I'll go orf for a reg'lar tramp
through the rain, up by Saltwood, round by Newington,
over the camp, and so round and back, and see 'ow
they're getting on about the 'ouse. See? And look
'ere! you get Gwendolen to go out a bit before I come
back. If it's still rainy, she can easy go round and see
'er sister. Then we'll 'ave a bit of tea, with tea cake—
all buttery, see? Toce it ourselves, p'r'aps. Eh?"

"I dessay I can find something to do in the 'ouse,"
said Ann, considering. "You'll take your mackintosh
and leggin's, I s'pose. You'll get wet without your
mackintosh over those roads."

"Right-O," said Kipps, and went to ask Gwendolen
for his brown leggings and his other pair of boots.

§ 2

Things conspired to demoralise Kipps that afternoon.
When he got outside the house everything looked so
wet under the drive of the southwester that he abandoned
the prospect of the clay lanes towards Newington
altogether, and turned east to Folkestone along the
Seabrook digue. His mackintosh flapped about him,
the rain stung his cheek; for a time he felt a hardy
man. And then as abruptly the rain ceased and the
wind fell, and before he was through Sandgate High
Street it was a bright spring day. And there was Kipps
in his mackintosh and squeaky leggings, looking like a
fool!

Inertia carried him another mile to the Leas, and
there the whole world was pretending there had never
been such a thing as rain—ever. There wasn't a cloud
in the sky; except for an occasional puddle the asphalt
paths looked as dry as a bone. A smartly dressed man
in one of those overcoats that look like ordinary cloth
and are really most deceitfully and unfairly waterproof,
passed him and glanced at the stiff folds of his mackintosh. "Demn!" said Kipps. His mackintosh swished

against his leggings, his leggings piped and whistled over his boot-tops.

"Why do I never get anything right?" Kipps asked of a bright implacable universe.

Nice old ladies passed him, refined people with tidy umbrellas, bright, beautiful, supercilious-looking children. Of course! the right thing for such a day as this was a light overcoat and an umbrella. A child might have known that. He had them at home, but how could one explain that? He decided to turn down by the Harvey monument and escape through Clifton Gardens towards the hills. And thereby he came upon Coote.

He already felt the most abject and propitiatory of social outcasts when he came upon Coote, and Coote finished him. He passed within a yard of Coote. Coote was coming along towards the Leas, and when Kipps saw him his legs hesitated about their office and he seemed to himself to stagger about all over the footpath. At the sight of him Coote started visibly. Then a sort of *rigor vitae* passed through his frame, his jaw protruded and errant bubbles of air seemed to escape and run about beneath his loose skin. (Seemed, I say—I am perfectly well aware that there is really connective tissue in Coote as in all of us to prevent anything of the sort.) His eyes fixed themselves on the horizon and glazed. As he went by Kipps could hear his even, resolute breathing. He went by, and Kipps staggered on into a universe of dead cats and dust heaps, rind and ashes—*cut!*

It was part of the inexorable decrees of Providence that almost immediately afterwards the residuum of Kipps had to pass a very, very long and observant-looking girls' school.

Kipps recovered consciousness again on the road between Shorncliffe Station and Cheriton, though he cannot remember, indeed to this day he has never attempted to remember, how he got there. And he was back at certain thoughts suggested by his last night's novel reading, that linked up directly with the pariah-like emotions of these last encounters. The novel lay at home upon the chiffonier; it was one about society and politics—there is no need whatever to give the title or name the author—written with a heavy-handed thoroughness that overrode any possibility of resistance on the part of the Kipps mind. It had crushed all his poor edifice of ideals, his dreams of a sensible, unassuming existence, of snugness, of not caring what people said and all the rest of it, to dust; it had reinstated, squarely and strongly again, the only proper conception of English social life. There was a character in the book who trifled with Art, who was addicted to reading French novels, who dressed in a loose, careless way, who was a sorrow to his dignified, silvery-haired, politico-religious mother, and met the admonitions of bishops with a front of brass. He treated a "nice girl," to whom they had got him engaged, badly; he married beneath him—some low thing or other. And sank. . . .

Kipps could not escape the application of the case. He was enabled to see how this sort of thing looked to decent people; he was enabled to gauge the measure of the penalties due. His mind went from that to the frozen marble of Coote's visage.

He deserved it! . . .

That day of remorse! Later it found him upon the site of his building operations and surveying the disorder of preparation in a mood near to despair, his mackintosh over his arm.

Hardly anyone was at work that day—no doubt the builders were having him in some obscure manner—and the whole place seemed a dismal and depressing litter. The builder's shed, black-lettered WILKINS, BUILDER, HYTHE, looked like a stranded thing amidst a cast-up disorder of wheelbarrows and wheeling planks, and earth and sand and bricks. The foundations of the walls were trenches full of damp concrete, drying in

12

patches; the rooms—it was incredible they could ever be rooms—were shaped out as squares and oblongs of coarse, wet grass and sorrel. They looked absurdly small—dishonestly small. What could you expect? Of course the builders were having him, building too small, building all wrong, using bad materials! Old Kipps had told him a wrinkle or two. The builders were having him, young Walshingham was having him, everybody was having him! They were having him and laughing at him because they didn't respect him. They didn't respect him because he couldn't do things right. Who could respect him? . . .

He was an outcast, he had no place in the society of mankind. He had had his chance in the world and turned his back on it. He had " behaved badly "—that was the phrase. . . .

Here a great house was presently to arise, a house to be paid for, a house neither he nor Ann could manage —with eleven bedrooms, and four disrespectful servants having them all the time!

How had it all happened exactly?

This was the end of his great fortune! What a chance he had had! If he had really carried out his first intentions and stuck to things, how much better everything might have been! If he had got a tutor— that had been in his mind originally—a special sort of tutor to show him everything right; a tutor for gentlemen of neglected education! If he had read more and attended better to what Coote had said!

Coote, who had just cut him! . . .

Eleven bedrooms! What had possessed him? No one would ever come to see them, no one would ever have anything to do with them. Even his aunt cut him! His uncle treated him with a half-contemptuous sufferance. He had not a friend worth counting in the world! Buggins, Carshot, Pierce; shop assistants! The Pornicks—a low socialist lot! He stood among his foundations like a lonely figure among ruins; he stood among the ruins of his future, and owned himself a foolish and mistaken man. He saw himself and Ann living out their shameful lives in this great crazy place— as it would be—with everybody laughing secretly at them and their eleven bedrooms, and nobody approaching them—nobody nice and right that is, for ever! And Ann!

What was the matter with Ann? She'd given up going for walks lately, got touchy and tearful, been fitful with her food. Just when she didn't ought to. It was all a part of the judgment upon wrong-doing, it was all part of the social penalties that Juggernaut of a novel had brought home to his mind.

§ 3

He let himself in with his latchkey. He went moodily into the dining-room and got out the plans to look at them. He had a vague hope that there would prove to be only ten bedrooms. But he found there were still eleven. He became aware of Ann standing over him. "Look 'ere, Artie!" said Ann.

He looked up and found her holding a number of white oblongs. His eyebrows rose.

"It's Callers," said Ann.

He put his plans aside slowly and took and read the cards in silence, with a sort of solemnity. Callers. Then perhaps he wasn't to be left out of the world after all. Mrs. G. Porrett Smith, Miss Porrett Smith, Miss Mabel Porrett Smith, and two smaller cards of the Rev. G. Porrett Smith. "Lor'!" he said, "*Clergy!*"

"There was a lady," said Ann, "and two growed-up gals—all dressed up!"

"And 'im?"

"There wasn't no '*im.*"

"Not—?" He held out the little cards.

"No; there was a lady and two young ladies."

"But—these cards! Wad they go and leave these two little cards with the Rev. G. Smith on for? Not if 'e wasn't with 'em."

"'E wasn't with 'em."

"Not a little chap—-dodgin' about be'ind the others? And didn't come in?"

"I didn't see no gentleman with them at all," said Ann.

"Rum!" said Kipps. A half-forgotten experience came back to him. "*I* know," he said, waving the reverend gentleman's card; "'e give 'em the slip, that's what he'd done. Gone off while they was rapping before you let 'em in. It's a fair call, any'ow." He felt a momentary base satisfaction at his absence. "What did they talk about, Ann?"

There was a pause. "I didn't let 'em in," said Ann.

He looked up suddenly and perceived that something unusual was the matter with Ann. Her face was flushed, her eyes were red and hard.

"Didn't let 'em in?"

"No! They didn't come in at all."

He was too astonished for words.

"I answered the door," said Ann; "I'd been up-stairs 'namelling the floor. 'Ow was I to think about Callers, Artie? We ain't never 'ad Callers all the time we been 'ere. I'd sent Gwendolen out for a bref of fresh air, and there I was upstairs 'namelling that floor she done so bad, so's to get it done before she came back. I thought I'd 'namel that floor and then get tea and 'ave it quiet with you, toce and all, before she came back. 'Ow was I to think about Callers?"

She paused. "Well," said Kipps, "what then?"

"They came and rapped. 'Ow was I to know? I thought it was a tradesman or something. Never took my apron off, never wiped the 'namel off my 'ands— nothing. There they was!"

She paused again. She was getting to the disagree-able part.

"Wad they say?" said Kipps.

"She says, 'Is Mrs. Kipps at home?' See? To me."

"Yes."

"And me all painty and no cap on and nothing, neither missis nor servant like. There, Artie, I could 'a sunk through the floor with shame, I really could. I could 'ardly get my voice. I couldn't think of nothing to say but just 'Not at 'Ome,' and out of 'abit like I 'eld the tray. And they give me the cards and went, and 'ow I shall ever look that lady in the face again I don't know. . . . And that's all about it, Artie! They looked me up and down, they did, and then I shut the door on 'em."

"Goo!" said Kipps.

Ann went and poked the fire needlessly with a passion-quivering hand.

"I wouldn't 'ave 'ad that 'appen for five pounds," said Kipps. "A clergyman and all!"

Ann dropped the poker into the fender with some *éclat* and stood up and looked at her hot face in the glass. Kipps' disappointment grew. "You did ought to 'ave known better than that, Ann! You reely did."

He sat forward, cards in hand, with a deepening sense of social disaster. The plates were laid upon the table, toast sheltered under a cover at mid fender, the teapot warmed beside it, and the kettle, just lifted from the hob, sang amidst the coals. Ann glanced at him for a moment, then stooped with the kettle-holder to wet the tea.

"Tcha!" said Kipps, with his mental state developing.

"I don't see it's any use getting in a state about it now," said Ann.

"Don't you? I do. See? 'Ere's these people, good people, want to 'sociate with us, and 'ere you go and slap 'em in the face!"

"I didn't slap 'em in the face."

"You do—practically. You slams the door in their face, and that's all we see of 'em ever. I wouldn't 'ave 'ad this 'appen not for a ten-pound note."

He rounded his regrets with a grunt. For a while there was silence, save for the little stir of Ann's movements preparing the tea.

"Tea, Artie," said Ann, handing him a cup.

Kipps took it.

"I put sugar *once*," said Ann.

"Oo, dash it! Oo cares?" said Kipps, taking an extraordinarily large additional lump with fury-quivering fingers, and putting his cup with a slight excess of force on the recess cupboard. "Oo cares?

"I wouldn't 'ave 'ad that 'appen," he said, bidding steadily against accomplished things, "for twenty pounds."

He gloomed in silence through a long minute or so.

Then Ann said the fatal thing that exploded him. "Artie!" she said.

"What?"

"There's Buttud Toce down there! By your foot!"

There was a pause; husband and wife regarded one another.

"Buttud Toce!" he said. "You go and mess up them callers and then you try and stuff me up with Buttud Toce! Buttud Toce indeed! 'Ere's our first chance of knowing anyone that's at all fit to 'sociate with— Look 'ere, Ann! Tell you what it is—you got to return that call."

"Return that call!"

"Yes, you got to return that call. That's what you got to do! I know—" He waved his arm vaguely towards the miscellany of books in the recess. "It's in Manners and Rools of Good S'ity. You got to find jest 'ow many cards to leave and you got to go and leave 'em. See?"

Ann's face expressed terror. "But, Artie, 'ow *can* I?"

"'Ow *can* you? 'Ow *could* you? You got to do it, any'ow. They won't know you—not in your Bond Street 'at! If they do, they won't say nothing."

His voice assumed a note of entreaty. "You mus', Ann."

"I can't."

"You mus'."

"I can't and I won't. Anything in reason I'll do, but face those people again I can't—after what 'as 'appened."

"You won't?"

"No!"

"So there they go—orf! And we never see them again! And so it goes on! So it goes on! We don't know nobody and we *shan't* know anybody! And you won't put yourself out not a little bit, or take the trouble to find out anything 'ow it ought to be done."

Terrible pause.

"I never ought to 'ave married you, Artie, that's the troof."

"Oh! *don't* go into that."

"I never ought to 'ave married you, Artie. I'm not equal to the position. If you 'adn't said you'd drown yourself——" She choked.

"I don' see why you shouldn't *try*, Ann. *I'm* improved. Why don't you? 'Stead of which you go sending out the servant and 'namelling floors, and then when visitors come——"

"'Ow was *I* to know about y'r old visitors?" cried Ann in a wail, and suddenly got up and fled from amidst their ruined tea, the tea of which " toce, all buttery," was to be the crown and glory.

Kipps watched her with a momentary consternation. Then he hardened his heart. "Ought to 'ave known better," he said, "goin' on like that!" He remained for a space rubbing his knees and muttering. He emitted scornfully: "I carn't an' I won't." He saw her as the source of all his shames.

Presently, quite mechanically, he stooped down and lifted the flowery china cover. "Ter dash 'er Buttud Toce!" he shouted at the sight of it, and clapped the cover down again hard. . . .

When Gwendolen came back she perceived things were in a slightly unusual poise. Kipps sat by the fire in a rigid attitude reading a casually selected volume of the *Encyclopædia Britannica,* and Ann was upstairs and inaccessible—to reappear at a later stage with reddened eyes. Before the fire and still in a perfectly assimilable condition was what was evidently an untouched supply of richly buttered toast under a cracked cover.

"They've 'ad a bit of a tiff," said Gwendolen, attending to her duties in the kitchen, with her outdoor hat still on and her mouth full. "They're rummuns—if ever! My eye!"

And she took another piece of Ann's generously buttered toast.

§ 4

The Kippses spoke no more that day to one another.

The squabble about cards and buttered toast was as serious to them as the most rational of differences. It was all rational to them. Their sense of wrong burnt within them; their sense of what was owing to themselves, the duty of implacability, the obstinacy of pride. In the small hours Kipps lay awake at the nadir of unhappiness and came near groaning. He saw life as an extraordinarily desolating muddle; his futile house, his social discredit, his bad behaviour to Helen, his low marriage with Ann. . . .

He became aware of something irregular in Ann's breathing. . . .

He listened. She was awake and quietly and privately sobbing!

He hardened his heart; resolutely he hardened his heart.

And presently Ann lay still.

§ 5

The stupid little tragedies of these clipped and limited lives!

As I think of them lying unhappily there in the darkness, my vision pierces the night. See what I can see! Above them, brooding over them, I tell you there is a monster, a lumpish monster, like some great clumsy griffin thing, like the Crystal Palace labyrinthodon, like Coote, like the leaden goddess of the Dunciad, like some fat, proud flunkey, like pride, like indolence, like all that is darkening and heavy and obstructive in life. It is matter and darkness, it is the anti-soul, it is the ruling power of this land, Stupidity. My Kippses live in its shadow. Shalford and his apprenticeship system, the Hastings Academy, the ideas of Coote, the ideas of the old Kippses, all the ideas that have made Kipps what he is, all these are a part of its shadow. But for that monster they might not be groping among false ideas and hurt one another so sorely; but for that, the glowing promise of childhood and youth might have had a happier fruition, thought might have awakened in them to meet the thought of the world, the quickening sunshine of literature pierced to the substance of their souls, their lives might not have been divorced, as now they are divorced, from the apprehension of beauty that we favoured ones are given——the vision of the Grail that makes life fine for ever. I have laughed, and I laugh at these two people; I have sought to make you laugh. . . .

But I see through the darkness the souls of my Kippses as they are, as little pink strips of quivering living stuff, as things like the bodies of little, ill-nourished, ailing, ignorant children, children who feel pain, who are naughty and muddled and suffer and do not understand why. And the claw of this Beast rests upon them!

CHAPTER THE THIRD

Terminations

NEXT morning came a remarkable telegram from Folkestone. "Please come at once, urgent, Walshingham," said the telegram, and Kipps, after an agitated but still ample breakfast, departed. . . .

When he returned his face was very white and his countenance disordered. He let himself in with his latchkey and came into the dining-room where Ann sat, affecting to work at a little thing she called a bib. She heard his hat fall in the hall before he entered, as though he had missed the peg. "I got something to tell you, Ann," he said, disregarding their overnight quarrel, and went to the hearthrug and took hold of the mantel, and stared at Ann as though the sight of her was novel.

"Well?" said Ann, not looking up and working a little faster.

" 'E's gone !"

Ann looked up sharply, and her hands stopped. "*Who's* gone?" For the first time she perceived Kipps' pallor.

"Young Walshingham—I saw 'er and she tole me."

"Gone? What d'you mean?"

"Cleared out! Gone off for good!"

"What for?"

"For 'is 'ealth," said Kipps, with sudden bitterness. " 'E's been speckylating. He's speckylated our money and 'e's speckylated their money, and now 'e's took 'is 'ook. That's all about it, Ann."

"You mean?"

"I mean 'e's orf and our twenty-four fousand's orf too! And 'ere we are! Smashed up! That's all about it, Ann." He panted.

Ann had no vocabulary for such an occasion. "Oh, lor'!" she said, and sat still.

Kipps came about and stuck his hands deeply in his trouser pockets. "Speckylated every penny—lorst it all—and gorn."

Even his lips were white.

"You mean we ain't got nothin' left, Artie?"

"Not a penny! Not a bloomin' penny, Ann. No!"

A gust of passion whirled across the soul of Kipps. He flung out a knuckly fist. "If I 'ad 'im 'ere," he said, "I'd—I'd—I'd wring 'is neck for 'im. I'd—I'd—" His voice rose to a shout. He thought of Gwendolen in the kitchen, and fell to "Ugh!"

"But, Artie," said Ann, trying to grasp it, "d'you mean to say he's took our money?"

"Speckylated it!" said Kipps, with an illustrative flourish of the arm that failed to illustrate. "Bort things dear and sold 'em cheap, and played the 'ankey-pankey jackass with everything we got. That's what I mean 'e's done, Ann." He repeated this last sentence with the addition of violent adverbs.

"D'you mean to say our money's *gone*, Artie?"

"Ter-dash it, *Yes, Ann!*" swore Kipps, exploding in a shout. "Ain't I tellin' you?"

He was immediately sorry. "I didn't mean to 'oller at you, Ann," he said, "but I'm all shook up. I don't 'ardly know what I'm sayin'. Ev'ry penny. . . ."

"But, Artie——"

Kipps grunted. He went to the window and stared for a moment at a sunlit sea. "Gord!" he swore.

"I mean," he said, coming back to Ann and with an air of exasperation, "that he's 'bezzled and 'ooked it. That's what I mean, Ann."

Ann put down the bib. "But wot are we going to *do*, Artie?"

Kipps indicated ignorance, wrath and despair with one comprehensive gesture of his hands. He caught an ornament from the mantel and replaced it. "I'm going to bang about," he said, "if I ain't precious careful."

"You saw *'er*, you say?"

"Yes."

"What did she say 'xactly?" said Ann.

"Tole me to see a s'licitor—tole me to get someone to 'elp me at once. She was there in black—like she used to be—and speaking cool and careful-like. 'Elen! . . . She's precious 'ard, is 'Elen. She looked at me straight. 'It's my fault,' she said, 'I ought to 'ave warned you. . . . Only under the circumstances it was a little difficult.' Straight as anything. I didn't 'ardly say anything to 'er. I didn't seem to begin to take it in until she was showing me out. I 'adn't anything to say. Jest as well, perhaps. She talked—like a Call a'most. She said—what *was* it she said about her mother? 'My mother's overcome with grief,' she said, 'so naturally everything comes on me.'"

"And she told you to get someone to 'elp you?"

"Yes. I been to old Bean."

"O' Bean?"

"Yes. What I took my business away from!"

"What did he say?"

"He was a bit off and at first, but then 'e come round. He couldn't tell me anything till 'e knew the facts. What I know of young Walshingham, there won't be much 'elp in the facts. No!"

He reflected for a space. "It's a smash-up, Ann. More likely than not, Ann, 'e's left us over'ead in debt. We got to get out of it just 'ow we can. . . .

"We got to begin again," he went on. "'Ow, I don't know. All the way 'ome—my 'ead's been going. We got to get a living some'ow or other. 'Aving time to ourselves, and a bit of money to spend, and no hurry and worry, it's all over for ever, Ann. We was fools, Ann. We didn't know our benefits. We been caught. Gord! . . . Gord!"

He was on the verge of "banging about" again.

They heard a jingle in the passage, the large soft impact of a servant's indoor boots. As if she were a part, a mitigatory part of Fate, came Gwendolen to lay the midday meal. Kipps displayed self-control forthwith. Ann picked up the bib again and bent over it, and the Kippses bore themselves gloomily perhaps, but not despairfully, while their dependent was in the room. She spread the cloth and put out the cutlery with a slow inaccuracy, and Kipps, after a whisper to himself, went again to the window. Ann got up and put away her work methodically in the chiffonier.

"When I think," said Kipps, as soon as the door closed again behind Gwendolen, "when I think of the ole people and 'aving to tell 'em of it all—I want to smesh my 'ead against the nearest wall. Smesh my silly brains out! And Buggins—Buggins what I'd 'arf promised to start in a lill' outfitting shop in Rendezvous Street. . . ."

Gwendolen returned and restored dignity.

The midday meal spread itself slowly before them. Gwendolen, after her custom, left the door open, and Kipps closed it carefully before sitting down.

He stood for a moment, regarding the meal doubt-fully.

"I don't feel as if I could swaller a moufful," he said.

"You got to eat," said Ann. . . .

For a time they said little, and once swallowing was achieved, ate on with a sort of melancholy appetite. Each was now busy thinking.

"After all," said Kipps presently, "whatever 'appens, they can't turn us out or sell us up before nex' quarter-day. I'm pretty sure about that."

"Sell us up!" said Ann.

"I dessay we're bankrup'," said Kipps, trying to say it easily and helping himself with a trembling hand to unnecessary potatoes.

Then a long silence. Ann ceased to eat, and there were silent tears.

"More potatoes, Artie?" choked Ann.

"I couldn't," said Kipps. "No."

He pushed back his plate, which was indeed replete with potatoes, got up and walked about the room. Even the dinner-table looked distraught and unusual.

"What to do, I *don't* know," he said.

"Oh, *Lord!*" he ejaculated, and picked up and slapped down a book.

Then his eyes fell upon another postcard that had come from Chitterlow by the morning's post, and which now lay by him on the mantel-shelf. He took it up, glanced at its imperfectly legible message, and put it down.

"Delayed!" he said scornfully. "Not prodooced in the smalls. Or is it smells 'e says? 'Ow can one understand that? Any'ow 'e's 'umbugging again. . . . Somefing about the Strand. No! Well, 'e's 'ad all the money 'e'll ever get out of me! . . . I'm done."

He seemed to find a momentary relief in the dramatic effect of his announcement. He came near to a swagger of despair upon the hearthrug, and then suddenly came and sat down next to Ann and rested his chin on the knuckles of his two clenched hands.

" I been a fool, Ann," he said in a gloomy monotone. " I been a brasted fool. But it's 'ard on us, all the same. It's 'ard."

" 'Ow was you to know?" said Ann.

" I ought to 'ave known. I did in a sort of way know. And 'ere we are! I wouldn't care so much if it was myself, but it's *you,* Ann! 'Ere we are! Regular smashed up! And you——" He checked at an unspeakable aggravation of their disaster. " I knew 'e wasn't to be depended upon and there I left it! And you got to pay. . . . What's to 'appen to us all, I don't know."

He thrust out his chin and glared at fate.

" 'Ow do you know 'e's speckylated everything?" said Ann, after a silent survey of him.

" 'E 'as," said Kipps irritably, holding firm to disaster.

" She say so?"

" She don't know, of course, but you depend upon it that's it. She told me she knew something was on, and when she found 'im gone and a note lef' for her she knew it was up with 'im. 'E went by the night boat. She wrote that telegrarf off to me straight away."

Ann surveyed his features with tender, perplexed eyes; she had never seen him so white and drawn before, and her hand rested an inch or so away from his arm, The actual loss was still, as it were, afar from her. The immediate thing was his enormous distress.

" 'Ow do you know——?" she said and stopped. It would irritate him too much.

Kipps' imagination was going headlong.

" Sold up!" he emitted presently, and Ann flinched. " Going back to work, day after day—I can't stand it, Ann, I can't. And you——"

" It don't do to think of it," said Ann.

Presently he came upon a resolve. " I keep on thinking of it, and thinking of it, and what's to be

done and what's to be done. I shan't be any good
'ome s'arfernoon. It keeps on going round and round
in my 'ead and round and round. I better go for a walk
or something. I'd be no comfort to you, Ann. I should
want to 'owl and 'ammer things if I 'ung about 'ome.
My fingers is all atwitch. I shall keep on thinking 'ow
I might 'ave stopped it and callin' myself a fool. . . ."

He looked at her between pleading and shame. It
seemed like deserting her.

Ann regarded him with tear-dimmed eyes.

"You'd better do what's good for you, Artie," she
said. . . . "*I'll* be best cleaning. It's no use sending
off Gwendolen before her month, and the top room
wants turning out." She added with a sort of grim
humour: "May as well turn it out now while I got it."

"I *better* go for a walk," said Kipps. . . .

And presently our poor exploded Kipps was marching out to bear his sudden misery. Habit turned him
up the road towards his growing house, and then suddenly he perceived his direction—"Oh, lor'!"—and
turned aside and went up the steep way to the hill
crest and the Sandling Road, and over the line by that
tree-embowered Junction, and athwart the wide fields
towards Postling—a little, black, marching figure—and
so up the Downs and over the hills, whither he had
never gone before. . . .

§ 2

He came back long after dark, and Ann met him in
the passage.

"Where you been, Artie?" she asked, with a
strained note in her voice.

"I been walking and walking—trying to tire myself
out. All the time I been thinking what shall I do.
Trying to fix something up all out of nothing."

"I didn't know you meant to be out all this time."

Kipps was gripped by compunction. . . .

"I can't think what we ought to do," he said, presently.

"You can't do anything much, Artie, not till you hear from Mr. Bean."

"No; I can't do anything much. That's jest it. And all this time I keep feelin' if I don't do something the top of my 'ead'll bust. . . . Been trying to make up advertisements 'arf the time I been out—'bout finding a place, good salesman and stock-keeper, and good Manchester dresses, window-dressing—lor'! Fancy that all beginning again! . . . If you went to stay with Sid a bit—if I sent every penny I got to you—I dunno! I dunno!"

When they had gone to bed there was an elaborate attempt to get to sleep. . . . In one of their great waking pauses Kipps remarked in a muffled tone: "I didn't mean to frighten you, Ann, being out so late. I kep' on walking and walking, and some'ow it seemed to do me good. I went out to the 'illtop ever so far beyond Stanford, and sat there ever so long, and it seemed to make me better. Just looking over the marsh like, and seeing the sun set. . . ."

"Very likely," said Ann, after a long interval, "it isn't so bad as you think it is, Artie."

"It's bad," said Kipps.

"Very likely, after all, it isn't quite so bad. If there's only a little——"

There came another long silence.

"Ann," said Kipps in the quiet darkness.

"Yes," said Ann.

"Ann," said Kipps, and stopped as though he had hastily shut a door upon speech.

"I kep' thinking," he said, trying again, "I kep' thinking—after all—I been cross to you and a fool about things—about them cards, Ann; but "—his voice shook to pieces—"we 'ave been 'appy, Ann . . . some'ow . . . togever."

And with that he and then she fell into a passion of

weeping. They clung very tightly together—closer than they had been since ever the first brightness of their married days turned to the grey of common life again.

All the disaster in the world could not prevent their going to sleep at last with their poor little troubled heads close together on one pillow. There was nothing more to be done, there was nothing more to be thought. Time might go on with his mischiefs, but for a little while at least they still had one another.

§ 3

Kipps returned from his second interview with Mr. Bean in a state of strange excitement. He let himself in with his latchkey and slammed the door. "Ann!" he shouted, in an unusual note; "Ann!"

Ann replied distantly.

"Something to tell you," said Kipps; "something noo!"

Ann appeared apprehensive from the kitchen.

"Ann," he said, going before her into the little dining-room, for his news was too dignified for the passage, "very likely, Ann, o' Bean says, we shall 'ave——" He decided to prolong the suspense. "Guess!"

"I can't, Artie."

"Think of a lot of money!"

"A 'undred pounds p'r'aps?"

He spoke with immense deliberation. "Over a fousand pounds!"

Ann stared and said nothing, only went a shade whiter.

"Over, he said. A'most certainly over."

He shut the dining-room door and came forward hastily, for Ann, it was clear, meant to take this mitigation of their disaster with a complete abandonment of her self-control. She came near flopping; she fell into his arms.

"Artie," she got to at last and began to weep, clinging tightly to him.

"Pretty near certain," said Kipps, holding her. "A fousand pounds!"

"I *said*, Artie," she wailed on his shoulder with the note of accumulated wrongs, "very likely it wasn't so bad. . . ."

"There's things," he said, when presently he came to particulars, "'e couldn't touch. The noo place! It's freehold and paid for, and with the bit of building on it, there's five or six 'undred pounds p'r'aps—say worf free 'undred for safety. We can't be sold up to finish it, like we thought. O' Bean says we can very likely sell it and get money. 'E says you often get a chance to sell a 'ouse lessen 'arf done, 'specially frec'old. *Very* likely, 'e says. Then there's Hughenden. Hughenden 'asn't been mortgaged not for more than 'arf its value. There's a 'undred or so to be got on that, and the furniture, and the rent for the summer still coming in. 'E says there's very likely other things. A fousand pounds, that's what 'e said. 'E said it might even be more. . . ."

They were sitting now at the table.

"It alters everything," said Ann.

"I been thinking that, Ann, all the way 'ome. I came in the motor car. First ride I've 'ad since the smash. We needn't send off Gwendolen, leastways not till *after*. You know. We needn't turn out of 'ere—not for a long time. What we been doing for the o' people we can go on doing a'most as much. And your mother! . . . I wanted to 'oller, coming along. I pretty near run coming down the road by the hotel."

"Oh, I *am* glad we can stop 'ere and be comfortable a bit," said Ann. "I *am* glad for that."

"I pretty near told the driver on the motor—only 'e was the sort won't talk. . . . You see, Ann, we'll be able to start a shop, we'll be able to get *into* something like. All about our 'aving to go back to places and that; all that doesn't matter any more."

For a while they abandoned themselves to ejaculating transports. Then they fell talking to shape an idea to themselves of the new prospect that opened before them.

"We must start a sort of shop," said Kipps, whose imagination had been working. "It'll 'ave to be a shop."

"Drapery?" said Ann.

"You want such a lot of capital for the drapery, more'n a thousand pounds you want by a long way— to start it anything like proper."

"Well, outfitting. Like Buggins was going to do."

Kipps glanced at that for a moment, because the idea had not occurred to him. Then he came back to his prepossession.

"Well, I thought of something else, Ann," he said. "You see, I've always thought a little bookshop— It isn't like the drapery—'aving to be learnt. I thought —even before this smash-up—'ow I'd like to 'ave something to do, instead of always 'aving 'olidays always like we 'ave been 'aving."

He reflected.

"You don't know *much* about books, do you, Artie?"

"You don't want to." He illustrated. "I noticed when we used to go to that Lib'ry at Folkestone, ladies weren't anything like what they was in a draper's— if you 'aven't got *just* what they want it's 'Oh, no!' and out they go. But in a bookshop it's different. One book's very like another—after all, what is it? Something to read and done with. It's not a thing that matters like print dresses or serviettes—where you either like 'em or don't, and people judge you by. They take what you give 'em in books and lib'ries, and glad to be told *what* to. See 'ow we was—up at that lib'ry. . . ."

He paused. "You see, Ann——

"Well, I read 'n 'dvertisement the other day. I been asking Mr. Bean. It said—five 'undred pounds."

"What did?"

"Branches," said Kipps.

Ann failed to understand. "It's a sort of thing that gets up bookshops all over the country," said Kipps. "I didn't tell you, but I arst about it a bit. On'y I dropped it again. Before this smash, I mean. I'd thought I'd like to keep a shop for a lark, on'y then I thought it silly. Besides it 'ud 'ave been beneath me."

He blushed vividly. "It was a sort of projek of mine, Ann.

"On'y it wouldn't 'ave done," he added.

It was a tortuous journey when the Kippses set out to explain anything to each other. But through a maze of fragmentary elucidations and questions, their minds did presently begin to approximate to a picture of a compact, bright little shop, as a framework for themselves.

"I thought of it one day when I was in Folkestone. I thought of it one day when I was looking in at a window. I see a chap dressin' a window, and he was whistlin' reg'lar light-'earted. . . . I thought then I'd like to keep a bookshop, any'ow, jest for something to do. And when people weren't about, then you could sit and read the books. See? It wouldn't be 'arf bad. . . ."

They mused, each with elbows on table and knuckles to lips, looking with speculative eyes at each other.

"Very like we'll be 'appier than we should 'ave been with more money," said Kipps presently.

"We wasn't 'ardly suited," reflected Ann, and left her sentence incomplete.

"Fish out of water like," said Kipps. . . .

"You won't 'ave to return that call now," said Kipps, opening a new branch of the question. "That's one good thing."

"Lor'!" said Ann, "no more I shan't!"

"I don't s'pose they'd want you to, even if you did—with things as they are."

A certain added brightness came into Ann's face. "Nobody won't be able to come leaving cards on us, Artie, now, any more. We are out of *that*!"

"There isn't no necessity for us to be stuck up," said Kipps, "any more for ever! 'Ere we are, Ann, common people, with jest no position at all, as you might say, to keep up. No sev'nts, not if you don't like. No dressin' better than other people. If it wasn't we been robbed—dashed if I'd care a rap about losing that money. I b'lieve"—his face shone with the rare pleasure of paradox—"I reely b'lieve, Ann, it'll prove a savin' in the end."

§ 4

The remarkable advertisement which had fired Kipps' imagination with this dream of a bookshop opened out in the most alluring way. It was one little facet in a comprehensive scheme of transatlantic origin, which was to make our old-world methods of bookselling "sit up," and it displayed an imaginative briskness, a lucidity and promise that aroused the profoundest scepticism in the mind of Mr. Bean. To Kipps' renewed investigations it presented itself in an expository illustrated pamphlet (far too well printed, Mr. Bean thought, for a reputable undertaking) of the most convincing sort. Mr. Bean would not let him sink his capital in shares in its projected company that was to make all things new in the world of books, but he could not prevent Kipps becoming one of their associated booksellers. And so when presently it became apparent that an epoch was not to be made, and the "Associated Booksellers' Trading Union (Limited)" receded and dissolved and liquidated (a few drops) and vanished and went away to talk about something else, Kipps remained floating undamaged in this interestingly uncertain universe as an independent bookseller.

Except that it failed, the Associated Booksellers' Trading Union had all the stigmata of success. Its fault, perhaps, was that it had them all instead of only one or two. It was to buy wholesale for all its members and associates and exchange stock, having a common books-in-stock list and a common lending library, and it was to provide a uniform registered shop front to signify all these things to the intelligent passer-by. Except that it was controlled by buoyant young Over-men with a touch of genius in their arithmetic, it was, I say, a most plausible and hopeful project. Kipps went several times to London and an agent came to Hythe; Mr. Bean made some timely interventions, and then behind a veil of planks and an announcement in the High Street, the uniform registered shop front came rapidly into being. "Associated Booksellers' Trading Union," said this shop front, in a refined, artistic lettering that bookbuyers were going to value as wise men over forty value the proper label for Bern-casteler Doctor, and then, "Arthur Kipps."

Short of starting a haberdasher's shop I doubt if Kipps could have been more truly happy than during those weeks of preparation.

There is, of course, nothing on earth, and I doubt at times if there is a joy in Heaven, like starting a small haberdasher's shop. Imagine, for example, having a drawerful of tapes (one whole piece most exquisitely blocked of every possible width of tape), or, again, an army of neat, large packages, each displaying one sample of hooks and eyes. Think of your cottons, your drawer of coloured silks, the little, less, least of the compartments and thin packets of your needle drawer! Poor princes and wretched gentlefolk, mysteriously above retail trade, may taste only the faint unsatisfactory shadow of these delights with trays of stamps or butterflies. I write, of course, for those to whom these things

appeal; there are clods alive who see nothing, or next
to nothing, in spools of mercerised cotton and endless
bands of paper-set pins. I write for the wise, and as I
write I wonder that Kipps resisted haberdashery. He
did. Yet even starting a bookshop is at least twenty
times as interesting as building your own house to
your own design in unlimited space and time, or any
possible thing people with indisputable social position
and sound securities can possibly find to do. Upon that
I rest.

You figure Kipps " going to have a look to see how
the little shop is getting on," the shop that is not to
be a loss and a spending of money, but a gain. He
does not walk too fast towards it; as he comes into
view of it his paces slacken and his head goes to one
side. He crosses to the pavement opposite in order to
inspect the fascia better, already his name is adumbrated in faint white lines; stops in the middle of
the road and scrutinises imaginary details for the benefit
of his future next-door neighbour, the curiosity-shop
man, and so at last, in. . . . A smell of paint and
of the shavings of imperfectly seasoned pine-wood!
The shop is already glazed and a carpenter is busy over
the fittings for adjustable shelves in the side windows.
A painter is busy on the fixtures round about (shelving
above and drawers below), which are to accommodate
most of the stock, and the counter—the counter and
desk are done. Kipps goes inside the desk, the desk
which is to be the strategic centre of the shop, brushes
away some sawdust, and draws out the marvellous till;
here gold is to be, here silver, here copper—notes
locked up in a cash-box in the well below. Then he
leans his elbows on the desk, rests his chin on his fist
and fills the shelves with imaginary stock; books beyond
reading. Every day a man who cares to wash his hands
and read uncut pages artfully may have his cake and
eat it, among that stock. Under the counter to the
right, paper and string are to lurk ready to leap up and

embrace goods sold; on the table to the left, art publications, whatever they may prove to be! He maps it out, serves an imaginary customer, receives a dream seven and sixpence, packs, bows out. He wonders how it was he ever came to fancy a shop a disagreeable place.

"It's different," he says at last, after musing on that difficulty, "being your own."

It *is* different. . . .

Or, again, you figure Kipps with something of the air of a young sacristan, handling his brightly virginal account-book, and looking, and looking again, and then still looking, at an unparalleled specimen of copper-plate engraving, ruled money below and above bearing the words "In Account with, ARTHUR KIPPS" (loud flourishes), "The Booksellers' Trading Union" (temperate decoration). You figure Ann sitting and stitching at one point of the circumference of the light of the lamp, stitching queer little garments for some unknown stranger, and over against her sits Kipps. Before him is one of those engraved memorandum forms, a moist pad, wet with some thick and greasy greenish purple ink that is also spreading quietly but steadily over his fingers, a cross-nibbed pen for first-aid surgical assistance to the patient in his hand, a dating rubber stamp. At intervals he brings down this latter with great care and emphasis upon the paper, and when he lifts it there appears a beautiful oval design of which "Paid, Arthur Kipps, The Associated Booksellers' Trading Union," and a date, are the essential ingredients, stamped in purple ink.

Anon he turns his attention to a box of small, round, yellow labels, declaring "This book was bought from the Associated Booksellers' Trading Union." He licks one with deliberate care, sticks it on the paper before him and defaces it with great solemnity. "I can do it, Ann," he says, looking up brightly. For the Associated Booksellers' Trading Union, among other brilliant notions and inspirations, devised an ingenious system of taking back its books again in part payment for new ones within a specified period. When it failed, all sorts of people were left with these unredeemed pledges in hand.

§ 5

Amidst all this bustle and interest, all this going to and fro before they " moved in " to the High Street, came the great crisis that hung over the Kippses, and one morning in the small hours Ann's child was born. . . .

Kipps was coming to manhood swiftly now. The once rabbit-like soul that had been so amazed by the discovery of " chubes " in the human interior and so shocked by the sight of a woman's shoulder-blades, that had found shame and anguish in a mislaid Gibus and terror in an Anagram Tea, was at last facing the greater realities. He came suddenly upon the master thing in life, birth. He passed through hours of listening, hours of impotent fear in the night and in the dawn, and then there was put into his arms something most wonderful, a weak and wailing creature, incredibly, heart-stirringly soft and pitiful, with minute appealing hands that it wrung his heart to see. He held it in his arms and touched its tender cheek as if he feared his lips might injure it. And this marvel was his Son!

And there was Ann, with a greater strangeness and a greater familiarity in her quality than he had ever found before. There were little beads of perspiration on her temples and her lips, and her face was flushed, not pale as he had feared to see it. She had the look of one who emerges from some strenuous and invigorating act. He bent down and kissed her, and he had no words to say. She wasn't to speak much yet, but she stroked his arm with her hand and had to tell him one thing:

" He's over nine pounds, Artie," she whispered. " Bessie's——Bessie's wasn't no more than eight."

To have given Kipps a pound of triumph over Sid seemed to her almost to justify Nunc Dimittis. She watched his face for a moment, then closed her eyes in a kind of blissful exhaustion as the nurse, with something motherly in her manner, pushed Kipps out of the room.

§ 6

Kipps was far too much preoccupied with his own life to worry about the further exploits of Chitterlow. The man had got his two thousand; on the whole Kipps was glad he had had it rather than young Walshingham, and there was an end to the matter. As for the complicated transactions he achieved and proclaimed by mainly illegible and always incomprehensible postcards, they were like passing voices heard in the street as one goes about one's urgent concerns. Kipps put them aside and they got in between the pages of the stock and were lost for ever, and sold in with the goods to customers who puzzled over them mightily.

Then one morning as our bookseller was dusting round before breakfast, Chitterlow returned, appeared suddenly in the shop doorway.

It was the most unexpected thing in the world. The man was in evening dress, evening dress in that singularly crumpled state it assumes after the hour of dawn, and above his dishevelled red hair, a smallish Gibus hat tilted remarkably forward. He opened the door and stood, tall and spread, with one vast white glove flung out as if to display how burst a glove might be, his eyes bright, such wrinkling of brow and mouth as only an experienced actor can produce, and a singular radiance of emotion upon his whole being; an altogether astonishing spectacle.

The bell jangled for a bit, and then gave it up and was silent. For a long, long second everything was quietly attentive. Kipps was amazed to his uttermost; had he had ten times the capacity he would still have been fully amazed. "It's Chit'low!" he said at last, standing duster in hand.

But he doubted whether it was not a dream.

"Tzit!" gasped that most extraordinary person, still in an incredibly expanded attitude, and then with a slight forward jerk of the starry split glove, "Bif!"

He could say no more. The tremendous speech he had had ready vanished from his mind. Kipps stared at his facial changes, vaguely conscious of the truth of the teachings of Nisbet and Lombroso concerning men of genius.

Then suddenly Chitterlow's features were convulsed, the histrionic fell from him like a garment, and he was weeping. He said something indistinct about "Old Kipps! *Good* old Kipps! Oh, old Kipps!" and somehow he managed to mix a chuckle and a sob in the most remarkable way. He emerged from somewhere near the middle of his original attitude, a merely life-size creature. "My play, boohoo!" he sobbed, clutching at his friend's arm. "My play, Kipps (sob)! You know?"

"Well?" cried Kipps, with his heart sinking in sympathy, "it ain't——"

"No," howled Chitterlow; "no. It's a Success! My dear chap! my dear boy! oh! it's a—bu—boohoo! —a Big Success!" He turned away and wiped stream-ing tears with the back of his hand. He walked a pace or so and turned. He sat down on one of the specially designed artistic chairs of the Associated Book-sellers' Trading Union and produced an exiguous lady's handkerchief, extraordinarily belaced. He choked. "*My* play," and covered his face here and there.

He made an unsuccessful effort to control himself, and shrank for a space to the dimensions of a small and pathetic creature. His great nose suddenly came through a careless place in the handkerchief.

"I'm knocked," he said in a muffled voice, and so remained for a space—wonderful—veiled.

He made a gallant effort to wipe his tears away. " I had to tell you," he said, gulping.

" Be all right in a minute," he added, " calm," and sat still. . . .

Kipps stared in commiseration of such success. Then he heard footsteps, and went quickly to the house doorway. " Jest a minute," he said. " Don't go in the shop, Ann, for a minute. It's Chitterlow. He's a bit essited. But he'll be better in a minute. It's knocked him over a bit. You see "—his voice sank to a hushed note as one who announces death—" 'e's made a success with his play."

He pushed her back, lest she should see the scandal of another male's tears. . . .

Soon Chitterlow felt better, but for a little while his manner was even alarmingly subdued. " I *had* to come and tell you," he said. " I *had* to astonish someone. Muriel —she'll be first-rate, of course. But she's over at Dymchurch." He blew his nose with enormous noise, and emerged instantly a merely garrulous optimist.

" I expect she'll be precious glad."

" She doesn't know yet, my dear boy. She's at Dymchurch—with a friend. She's seen some of my first nights before. . . . Better out of it. . . . I'm going to her now. I've been up all night—talking to the Boys and all that. I'm a bit off it just for a bit. But—it Knocked 'em. It Knocked Everybody."

He stared at the floor and went on in a monotone. " They laughed a bit at the beginning—but nothing like a settled laugh—not until the second act—you know—the chap with the beetle down his neck. Little Chisholme did that bit to rights. Then they began— *to* rights." His voice warmed and increased. " Laughing ! It made *me* laugh ! We jumped 'em into the third act before they had time to cool. Everybody was on it. I never saw a first night go so fast. Laugh, laugh, l a u g h, L A U G H, L A U G H, L A U G H " (he howled the last repetition with stupendous violence).

Everything they laughed at. They laughed at things that we hadn't meant to be funny—not for one moment. Bif! Bizz! Curtain. A Fair Knock-Out! . . . I went on—but I didn't say a word. Chisholme did the patter. Shouting! It was like walking under Niagara—going across that stage. It was like never having seen an audience before. . . .

"Then afterwards—the Boys!"

His emotion held him for a space. "Dear old Boys!" he murmured.

His words multiplied, his importance increased. In a little while he was restored to something of his old self. He was enormously excited. He seemed unable to sit down anywhere. He came into the breakfast-room so soon as Kipps was sure of him, shook hands with Mrs. Kipps parenthetically, sat down and immediately got up again. He went to the bassinette in the corner and looked absent-mindedly at Kipps junior, and said he was glad if only for the youngster's sake. He immediately resumed the thread of his discourse. . . . He drank a cup of coffee noisily and walked up and down the room talking, while they attempted breakfast amidst the gale of his excitement. The infant slept marvellously through it all.

"You won't mind my not sitting down, Mrs. Kipps. I couldn't sit down for anyone, or I'd do it for you. It's you I'm thinking of more than anyone, you and Muriel, and all Old Pals and Good Friends. It means wealth, it means money—hundreds and thousands. . . . If you'd heard 'em, *you'd know*."

He was silent through a portentous moment while topics battled for him, and finally he burst and talked of them altogether. It was like the rush of water when a dam bursts and washes out a fair-sized provincial town; all sorts of things floated along on the swirl. For example, he was discussing his future behaviour. "I'm glad it's come now. Not before. I've had my lesson. I shall be very discreet now, trust me. We've

learnt the value of money." He discussed the possibility
of a country house, of taking a Martello tower as a
swimming-box (as one might say a shooting-box), of
living in Venice because of its artistic associations and
scenic possibilities, of a flat in Westminster, or a house
in the West End. He also raised the question of giving
up smoking and drinking, and what classes of drink were
especially noxious to a man of his constitution. But
discourses on all this did not prevent a parenthetical
computation of the probable profits on the supposition
of a thousand nights here and in America, nor did it
ignore the share Kipps was to have, nor the gladness
with which Chitterlow would pay that share, nor the
surprise and regret with which he had learnt, through
an indirect source which awakened many associations,
of the turpitude of young Walshingham, nor the distaste Chitterlow had always felt for young Walshingham and men of his type. An excursus upon Napoleon
had got into the torrent somehow and kept bobbing up
and down. The whole thing was thrown into the form
of a single complex sentence, with parenthetical and
subordinate clauses fitting one into the other like
Chinese boxes, and from first to last it never even had
an air of approaching anything in the remotest degree
partaking of the nature of a full stop.

Into this deluge came the *Daily News,* like the gleam
of light in Watts' picture, the waters were assuaged
while its sheet was opened, and it had a column, a
whole column, of praise. Chitterlow held the paper
and Kipps read over his left hand, and Ann under his
right. It made the affair more real to Kipps; it seemed
even to confirm Chitterlow against lurking doubts he
had been concealing. But it took him away. He
departed in a whirl, to secure a copy of every morning
paper, every blessed rag there is, and take them all to
Dymchurch and Muriel forthwith. It had been the
send-off the Boys had given him that had prevented
his doing as much at Charing Cross—let alone that he

only caught it by the skin of his teeth. . . . Besides which the bookstall wasn't open. His white face, lit by a vast excitement, bid them a tremendous farewell, and he departed through the sunlight, with his buoyant walk buoyant almost to the tottering pitch. His hair, as one got it sunlit in the street, seemed to have grown in the night.

They saw him stop a newsboy.

"Every blessed rag," floated to them on the notes of that gorgeous voice.

The newsboy, too, had happened on luck. Something like a faint cheer from the newsboy came down the air to terminate that transaction.

Chitterlow went on his way swinging a great budget of papers, a figure of merited success. The newsboy recovered from his emotion with a jerk, examined something in his hand again, transferred it to his pocket, watched Chitterlow for a space, and then in a sort of hushed silence resumed his daily routine. . . .

Ann and Kipps watched that receding happiness in silence, until he vanished round the bend of the road.

"I *am* glad," said Ann at last, speaking with a little sigh.

"So'm I," said Kipps, with emphasis. "For if ever a feller 'as worked and waited—it's 'im. . . ."

They went back through the shop rather thoughtfully, and after a peep at the sleeping baby, resumed their interrupted breakfast. "If ever a feller 'as worked and waited, it's 'im," said Kipps, cutting bread.

"Very likely it's true," said Ann, a little wistfully.

"What's true?"

"About all that money coming."

Kipps meditated. "I don't see why it shouldn't be," he decided, and handed Ann a piece of bread on the tip of his knife.

"But we'll keep on the shop," he said after an interval for further reflection, "all the same. . . . I 'aven't much trust in money after the things we've seen."

§ 7

That was two years ago, and as the whole world knows, the "Pestered Butterfly" is running still. It *was* true. It has made the fortune of a once declining little theatre in the Strand, night after night the great beetle scene draws happy tears from a house packed to repletion, and Kipps—for all that Chitterlow is not what one might call a business man—is almost as rich as he was in the beginning. People in Australia, people in Lancashire, Scotland, Ireland, in New Orleans, in Jamaica, in New York and Montreal, have crowded through doorways to Kipps' enrichment, lured by the hitherto unsuspected humours of the entomological drama. Wealth rises like an exhalation all over our little planet, and condenses, or at least some of it does, in the pockets of Kipps.

"It's rum," said Kipps.

He sat in the little kitchen out behind the bookshop and philosophised and smiled, while Ann gave Arthur Waddy Kipps his evening tub before the fire. Kipps was always present at this ceremony unless customers prevented; there was something in the mixture of the odours of tobacco, soap and domesticity that charmed him unspeakably.

"Chuckerdee, o' man," he said affably, wagging his pipe at his son, and thought incidentally, after the manner of all parents, that very few children could have so straight and clean a body.

"Dadda's got a cheque," said Arthur Waddy Kipps, emerging for a moment from the towel.

"'E gets 'old of everything," said Ann. "You can't say a word——"

"Dadda got a cheque," this marvellous child repeated.

"Yes, o' man, I got a cheque. And it's got to go into a bank for you, against when you got to go to school. See? So's you'll grow up knowing your way about a bit."

13

"Dadda's got a cheque," said the wonder son, and then gave his mind to making mighty splashes with his foot. Every time he splashed, laughter overcame him, and he had to be held up for fear he should tumble out of the tub in his merriment. Finally he was towelled to his toe-tips, wrapped up in warm flannel, and kissed, and carried off to bed by Ann's cousin and lady help, Emma. And then after Ann had carried away the bath into the scullery, she returned to find her husband with his pipe extinct and the cheque still in his hand.

"Two fousand pounds," he said. "It's dashed rum. Wot 'ave *I* done to get two fousand pounds, Ann?"

"What 'aven't you—not to?" said Ann.

He reflected upon this view of the case.

"I shan't never give up this shop," he said at last.

"We're very 'appy 'ere," said Ann.

"Not if I 'ad *fifty* fousand pounds."

"No fear," said Ann.

"You got a shop," said Kipps, "and you come along in a year's time and there it is. But money—look 'ow it come and goes! There's no sense in money. You may kill yourself trying to get it, and then it comes when you aren't looking. There's my 'riginal money! Where is it now? Gone! And it's took young Walshingham with it, and 'e's gone too. It's like playing skittles. 'Long comes the ball, right and left you fly, and there it is rolling away and not changed a bit. No sense in it! 'E's gone and she's gone—gone off with that chap Revel, that sat with me at dinner. Married man! And Chit'low rich! Lor'!—what a fine place that Gerrik Club is to be sure, where I 'ad lunch wiv 'im! Better'n *any* 'otel. Footmen in powder they got—not waiters, Ann—footmen! 'E's rich and me rich—in a sort of way. . . . Don't seem much sense in it, Ann, 'owever you look at it." He shook his head.

"I know one thing," said Kipps.

"What?"

"I'm going to put it in jest as many different banks as I can. See? Fifty 'ere, fifty there. 'Posit. I'm not going to 'nvest it—no fear."

"It's only frowing money away," said Ann.

"I'm 'arf a mind to bury some of it under the shop. Only I expect one 'ud always be coming down at nights to make sure it was there . . . . I don't seem to trust anyone—not with money." He put the cheque on the table corner and smiled and tapped his pipe on the grate, with his eyes on that wonderful document. "S'pose old Bean started orf," he reflected. . . . "One thing, 'e *is* a bit lame."

"'E wouldn't," said Ann; "not 'im."

"I was only joking like." He stood up, put his pipe among the candlesticks on the mantel, took up the cheque and began folding it carefully to put it back in his pocket-book.

A little bell jangled.

"Shop!" said Kipps. "That's right. Keep a shop and the shop'll keep you. That's 'ow I look at it, Ann."

He drove his pocket-book securely into his breast pocket before he opened the living-room door. . . .

But whether indeed it is the bookshop that keeps Kipps or whether it is Kipps who keeps the bookshop is just one of those commercial mysteries people of my unarithmetical temperament are never able to solve. They do very well, the dears, anyhow, thank Heaven!

The bookshop of Kipps is on the left-hand side of the Hythe High Street coming from Folkestone, between the yard of the livery stable and the shop-window full of old silver and such like things—it is quite easy to find—and there you may see him for yourself and speak to him and buy this book of him if you like. He has it in stock, I know. Very delicately I've seen to that. His name is not Kipps, of course, you must understand that, but everything else is exactly as I have told you. You can talk to him about books, about politics, about going to Boulogne, about life, and the ups and downs of life. Perhaps he will quote you Buggins—from whom, by the by, one can now buy everything a gentleman's wardrobe should contain at the little shop in Rendezvous Street, Folkestone. If you are fortunate to find Kipps in a good mood he may even let you know how he inherited a fortune " once." " Run froo it," he'll say with a not unhappy smile. " Got another afterwards—speckylating in plays. Needn't keep this shop if I didn't like. But it's something to do. . . ."

Or he may be even more intimate. " I seen some things," he said to me once. " Raver ! Life ! Why ! once I—I *'loped !* I did—reely !"

(Of course you will not tell Kipps that he *is* " Kipps," or that I have put him in this book. He hasn't the remotest suspicion of that. And you know, you never can tell how people are going to take that sort of thing. I am an old and trusted customer now, and for many amiable reasons I should prefer that things remained exactly on their present footing.)

§ 8

One early-closing evening in July they left the baby to the servant cousin, and Kipps took Ann for a row on the Hythe canal. The sun set in a mighty blaze and left a world warm, and very still. The twilight came. And there was the water, shining bright, and the sky a deepening blue, and the great trees that dipped their boughs towards the water, exactly as it had been when he paddled home with Helen, when her eyes had seemed to him like dusky stars. He had ceased from rowing and rested on his oars, and suddenly he was touched by the wonder of life, the strangeness that is a presence stood again by his side.

Out of the darknesses beneath the shallow, weedy stream of his being rose a question, a question that looked up dimly and never reached the surface. It was the question of the wonder of the beauty, the purposeless, inconsecutive beauty, that falls so strangely among the happenings and memories of life. It never reached the surface of his mind, it never took to itself substance or form; it looked up merely as the phantom of a face might look, out of deep waters, and sank again to nothingness.

"Artie," said Ann.

He woke up and pulled a stroke. "What?" he said.

"Penny for your thoughts, Artie."

He considered.

"I reely don't think I was thinking of anything," he said at last with a smile. "No."

He still rested on his oars.

"I expect," he said, "I was thinking jest what a Rum Go everything is. I expect it was something like that."

"Queer old Artie!"

"Ain't I? I don't suppose there ever was a chap quite like me before."

He reflected for just another minute.

"Oo!—I dunno," he said, and roused himself to pull.

THE HISTORY OF MR. POLLY

CHAPTER THE FIRST

Beginnings and the Bazaar

§ 1

"HOLE!" said Mr. Polly, and then for a change, and with greatly increased emphasis: "'*Ole!*" He paused, and then broke out with one of his private and peculiar idioms. "Oh! *Beastly* Silly Wheeze of a hole!"

He was sitting on a stile between two threadbare-looking fields, and suffering acutely from indigestion.

He suffered from indigestion now nearly every afternoon in his life, but as he lacked introspection he projected the associated discomfort upon the world. Every afternoon he discovered afresh that life as a whole, and every aspect of life that presented itself, was "beastly." And this afternoon, lured by the delusive blueness of a sky that was blue because the March wind was in the east, he had come out in the hope of snatching something of the joyousness of spring. The mysterious alchemy of mind and body refused, however, to permit any joyousness in the spring.

He had had a little difficulty in finding his cap before he came out. He wanted his cap—the new golf cap—and Mrs. Polly must needs fish out his old soft brown felt hat. "'*Ere's* your 'at," she said, in a tone of insincere encouragement.

He had been routing among the piled newspapers under the kitchen dresser, and had turned quite hopefully and taken the thing. He put it on. But it didn't feel right. Nothing felt right. He put a trembling hand upon the crown and pressed it on his head, and tried it askew to the right, and then askew to the left.

Then the full sense of the offered indignity came home to him. The hat masked the upper sinister quarter of his face, and he spoke with a wrathful eye regarding his wife from under the brim. In a voice thick with fury he said, "I s'pose you'd like me to wear that silly Mud Pie for ever, eh? I tell you I won't. I'm sick of it. I'm pretty near sick of everything, comes to that. . . . Hat!"

He clutched it with quivering fingers. "Hat!" he repeated. Then he flung it to the ground, and kicked it with extraordinary fury across the kitchen. It flew up against the door and dropped to the ground with its ribbon band half off.

"Shan't go out!" he said, and sticking his hands into his jacket pockets, discovered the missing cap in the right one.

There was nothing for it but to go straight up-stairs without a word, and out, slamming the shop door hard.

"Beauty!" said Mrs. Polly at last to a tremendous silence, picking up and dusting the rejected headdress. "Tantrums," she added. "I 'aven't patience." And moving with the slow reluctance of a deeply offended woman, she began to pile together the simple apparatus of their recent meal, for transportation to the scullery sink.

The repast she had prepared for him did not seem to her to justify his ingratitude. There had been the cold pork from Sunday, and some nice cold potatoes, and Rashdall's Mixed Pickles, of which he was inordinately fond. He had eaten three gherkins, two onions, a small cauliflower head, and several capers, with every appearance of appetite, and indeed with avidity; and then there had been cold suet pudding to follow, with treacle, and then a nice bit of cheese. It was the pale, hard sort of cheese he liked; red cheese he declared was indigestible. He had also had three big slices of greyish baker's bread, and had drunk the best part of the jugful of beer. . . . But there seems to be no pleasing some people.

"Tantrums!" said Mrs. Polly at the sink, struggling with the mustard on his plate, and expressing the only solution of the problem that occurred to her.

And Mr. Polly sat on the stile and hated the whole scheme of life—which was at once excessive and inadequate of him. He hated Fishbourne, he hated Fishbourne High Street, he hated his shop and his wife and his neighbours—every blessed neighbour—and with indescribable bitterness he hated himself.

"Why did I ever get in this silly Hole?" he said. "Why did I ever?"

He sat on the stile, and looked with eyes that seemed blurred with impalpable flaws at a world in which even the spring buds were wilted, the sunlight metallic, and the shadows mixed with blue-black ink.

To the moralist I know he might have served as a figure of sinful discontent, but that is because it is the habit of moralists to ignore material circumstances—if, indeed, one may speak of a recent meal as a circumstance—seeing that Mr. Polly was circum. Drink, indeed, our teachers will criticise nowadays both as regards quantity and quality, but neither church nor state nor school will raise a warning finger between a man and his hunger and his wife's catering. So on nearly every day in his life Mr. Polly fell into a violent rage and hatred against the outer world in the afternoon, and never suspected that it was this inner world to which I am with such masterly delicacy alluding, that was thus reflecting its sinister disorder upon the things without. It is a pity that some human beings are not more transparent. If Mr. Polly, for example, had been transparent, or even passably translucent, then perhaps he might have realised, from the Laocoön struggle he would have glimpsed, that indeed he was not so much a human being as a civil war.

Wonderful things must have been going on inside Mr. Polly. Oh! wonderful things. It must have been like a badly managed industrial city during a period of depression; agitators, acts of violence, strikes, the forces of law and order doing their best, rushings to and fro, upheavals, the *Marseillaise,* tumbrils, the rumble and the thunder of the tumbrils. . . .

I do not know why the east wind aggravates life to unhealthy people. It made Mr. Polly's teeth seem loose in his head, and his skin feel like a misfit, and his hair a dry stringy exasperation. . . .

Why cannot doctors give us an antidote to the east wind?

"Never have the sense to get your hair cut till it's too long," said Mr. Polly, catching sight of his shadow, "you blighted, desgenerated Paintbrush! Ugh!" and he flattened down the projecting tails with an urgent hand.

§ 2

Mr. Polly's age was exactly thirty-seven years and a half. He was a short, compact figure, and a little inclined to a localised embonpoint. His face was not unpleasing; the features fine, but a trifle too large about the lower half of his face, and a trifle too pointed about the nose to be classically perfect. The corners of his sensitive mouth were depressed. His eyes were ruddy brown and troubled, and the left one was round with more of wonder in it than its fellow. His complexion was dull and yellowish. That, as I have explained, on account of those civil disturbances. He was, in the technical sense of the word, clean-shaved, with a small fallow patch under the right ear and a cut on the chin. His brow had the little puckerings of a thoroughly discontented man, little wrinklings and lumps, particularly over his right eye, and he sat with his hands in his pockets, a little askew on the stile, and swung one leg.

"Hole!" he repeated presently.

He broke into a quavering song : " Roöötten Beëëastly Silly Hole!"

His voice thickened with rage, and the rest of his discourse was marred by an unfortunate choice of epithets.

He was dressed in a shabby black morning coat and vest; the braid that bound these garments was a little loose in places. His collar was chosen from stock and with projecting corners, what was called in those days a " wing-poke "; that and his tie, which was new and loose and rich in colouring, had been selected to encourage and stimulate customers—for he dealt in gentleman's outfitting. His golf cap, which was also from stock and aslant over his eye, gave his misery a desperate touch. He wore brown leather boots—because he hated the smell of blacking.

Perhaps after all it was not simply indigestion that troubled him.

Behind the superficialities of Mr. Polly's being moved a larger and vaguer distress. The elementary education he had acquired had left him with the impression that arithmetic was a fluky science and best avoided in practical affairs, but even the absence of bookkeeping and a total inability to distinguish between capital and interest, could not blind him for ever to the fact that the little shop in the High Street was not paying. An absence of returns, a constriction of credit, a depleted till—the most valiant resolves to keep smiling could not prevail for ever against these insistent phenomena. One might bustle about in the morning before dinner and in the afternoon after tea and forget that huge dark cloud of insolvency that gathered and spread in the background, but it was part of the desolation of these afternoon periods, those grey spaces of time after meals when all one's courage had descended to the unseen battles of the pit, that life seemed stripped to the bone and one saw with a hopeless clearness.

Let me tell the history of Mr. Polly from the cradle to these present difficulties.

" First the infant, mewling and puking in its nurse's arms."

There had been a time when two people had thought Mr. Polly the most wonderful and adorable thing in the world, and kissed his toe-nails, saying " myum, myum !" and marvelled at the exquisite softness and delicacy of his hair, had called to one another to remark the peculiar distinction with which he bubbled, had disputed whether the sound he had made was just da, da, or truly and intentionally dadda, had washed him in the utmost detail, and wrapped him up in soft warm blankets, and smothered him with kisses. A regal time that was, and four-and-thirty years ago; and a merciful forgetfulness barred Mr. Polly from ever bringing its careless luxury, its autocratic demands and instant obedience, into contrast with his present condition of life. These two people had worshipped him from the crown of his head to the soles of his exquisite feet. And also they had fed him rather unwisely, for no one had ever troubled to teach his mother anything about the mysteries of a child's upbringing—though, of course, the monthly nurse and the charwoman gave some valuable hints—and by his fifth birthday the perfect rhythms of his nice new interior were already darkened with perplexity. . . .

His mother died when he was seven. He began only to have distinctive memories of himself in the time when his education had already begun.

I remember seeing a picture of Education—in some place. I think it was Education, but quite conceivably it represented the Empire teaching her Sons, and I have a strong impression that it was a wall-painting upon some public building in Manchester or Birmingham or Glasgow, but very possibly I am mistaken about that. It represented a glorious woman, with a wise and fearless face, stooping over her children, and pointing them to far horizons. The sky displayed a pearly warmth of a summer dawn, and all the painting was marvellously bright as if with the youth and hope of the delicately beautiful children in the foreground. She was telling them, one felt, of the great prospect of life that opened before them, of the splendours of sea and mountain they might travel and see, the joys of skill they might acquire, of effort and pride of effort, and the devotions and nobilities it was theirs to achieve. Perhaps even she whispered of the warm triumphant mystery of love that comes at last to those who have patience and unblemished hearts. . . . She was reminding them of their great heritage as English children, rulers of more than one-fifth of mankind, of the obligation to do and be the best that such a pride of empire entails, of their essential nobility and knighthood, and of the restraints and charities and disciplined strength that is becoming in knights and rulers. . . .

The education of Mr. Polly did not follow this picture very closely. He went for some time to a National School, which was run on severely economical lines to keep down the rates, by a largely untrained staff; he was set sums to do that he did not understand, and that no one made him understand; he was made to read the Catechism and the Bible with the utmost industry and an entire disregard of punctuation or significance; caused to imitate writing copies and drawing copies; given object-lessons upon sealing-wax and silk-worms and potato-bugs and ginger and iron and such-like things; taught various other subjects his mind refused to entertain; and afterwards when he was about twelve, he was jerked by his parents to "finish off" in a private school of dingy aspect and still dingier pretensions, where there were no object-lessons, and the studies of bookkeeping and French were pursued (but never effectually overtaken) under the guidance of an elderly gentleman, who wore a nondescript gown and took snuff, wrote copperplate, explained nothing, and used a cane with remarkable dexterity and gusto.

Mr. Polly went into the National School at six, and he left the private school at fourteen, and by that time his mind was in much the same state that you would be in, dear reader, if you were operated upon for appendicitis by a well-meaning, boldly enterprising, but rather overworked and underpaid butcher boy, who was superseded towards the climax of the operation by a left-handed clerk of high principles but intemperate habits—that is to say it was in a thorough mess. The nice little curiosities and willingness of a child were in a jumbled and thwarted condition, hacked and cut about—the operators had left, so to speak, all their sponges and ligatures in a mangled confusion— and Mr. Polly had lost much of his natural confidence, so far as figures and sciences and languages and the possibilities of learning things were concerned. He thought of the present world no longer as a wonderland of experiences, but as geography and history, as the repeating of names that were hard to pronounce, and lists of products and populations and heights and lengths, and as lists and dates—oh! and Boredom indescribable. He thought of religion as the recital of more or less incomprehensible words that were hard to remember, and of the Divinity as of a limitless Being having the nature of a schoolmaster and making infinite rules, known and unknown, rules that were always ruthlessly enforced, and with an infinite capacity for punishment and—most horrible of all to think of—limitless powers of espial. (So to the best of his ability he did not think of that unrelenting eye.) He was uncertain about the spelling and pronunciation of most of the words in our beautiful but abundant and perplexing tongue—that especially was a pity, because words attracted him, and under happier conditions he might have used them well—he was always doubtful whether it was eight sevens or nine eights that was sixty-three (he knew no method for settling the difficulty), and he thought the merit of a drawing consisted in the care with which it was "lined in." "Lining in" bored him beyond measure.

But the indigestions of mind and body that were to play so large a part in his subsequent career were still only beginning. His liver and his gastric juice, his wonder and imagination kept up a fight against the things that threatened to overwhelm soul and body together. Outside the regions devastated by the school curriculum he was still intensely curious. He had cheerful phases of enterprise, and, about thirteen, he suddenly discovered reading and its joys. He began to read stories voraciously, and books of travel, provided they were also adventurous. He got these chiefly from the local institute, and he also "took in" irregularly, but thoroughly, one of those inspiring weeklies that dull people used to call "penny dreadfuls," admirable weeklies crammed with imagination that the cheap boys' "comics" of to-day have replaced. At fourteen, when he emerged from the valley of the shadow of education, there survived something—indeed it survived still, obscured and thwarted, at five-and-thirty—that pointed not with a visible and prevailing finger like the finger of that beautiful woman in the picture, but pointed nevertheless to the idea that there was interest and happiness in the world. Deep in the being of Mr. Polly, deep in that darkness, like a creature which has been beaten about the head and left for dead but still lives, crawled a persuasion that over and above the things that are jolly and " bits of all right," there was beauty, there was delight; that somewhere—magically inaccessible, perhaps, but still somewhere—were pure and easy and joyous states of body and mind.

He would sneak out on moonless winter nights and stare up at the stars, and afterwards find it difficult to tell his father where he had been.

He would read tales about hunters and explorers, and imagine himself riding mustangs as fleet as the wind across the prairies of Western America, or coming as a conquering and adored white man into the swarming villages of Central Africa. He shot bears with a revolver—a cigarette in the other hand—and made a necklace of their teeth and claws for the chief's beautiful young daughter. Also he killed a lion with a pointed stake, stabbing through the beast's heart as it stood over him.

He thought it would be splendid to be a diver and go down into the dark-green mysteries of the sea.

He led stormers against well-nigh impregnable forts, and died on the ramparts at the moment of victory. (His grave was watered by a nation's tears.)

He rammed and torpedoed ships, one against ten.

He was beloved by queens in barbaric lands, and reconciled whole nations to the Christian faith.

He was martyred, and took it very calmly and beautifully—but only once or twice after the Revivalist week. It did not become a habit with him.

He explored the Amazon, and found, newly exposed by the fall of a great tree, a rock of gold.

Engaged in these pursuits, he would neglect the work immediately in hand, sitting somewhat slackly on the form and projecting himself in a manner tempting to a schoolmaster with a cane. . . . And twice he had books confiscated.

Recalled to the realities of life, he would rub himself or sigh as the occasion required, and resume his attempts to write as good as copperplate. He hated writing; the ink always crept up his fingers, and the smell of ink offended him. And he was filled with unexpressed doubts. *Why* should writing slope down from right to left? *Why* should down-strokes be thick and up-strokes thin? *Why* should the handle of one's pen point over one's right shoulder?

His copy-books towards the end foreshadowed his destiny and took the form of commercial documents. "*Dear Sir,*" they ran, "*Referring to your esteemed order of the 26th ult., we beg to inform you,*" and so on.

The compression of Mr. Polly's mind and soul in the educational institutions of his time was terminated abruptly by his father between his fourteenth and fifteenth birthday. His father—who had long since forgotten the time when his son's little limbs seemed to have come straight from God's hand, and when he had kissed five minute toe-nails in a rapture of loving tenderness—remarked——

"It's time that dratted boy did something for a living."

And a month or so later Mr. Polly began that career in business that led him at last to the sole proprietorship of a bankrupt outfitter's shop—and to the stile on which he was sitting.

§ 3

Mr. Polly was not naturally interested in hosiery and gentlemen's outfitting. At times, indeed, he urged himself to a spurious curiosity about that trade, but presently something more congenial came along and checked the effort. He was apprenticed in one of those large, rather low-class establishments which sell everything from pianos and furniture to books and millinery, a department store, in fact the Port Burdock Drapery Bazaar at Port Burdock, one of the three townships that are grouped round the Port Burdock naval dockyards.

There he remained six years. He spent most of the time inattentive to business, in a sort of uncomfortable happiness, increasing his indigestion.

On the whole he preferred business to school; the hours were longer, but the tension was not nearly so great. The place was better aired, you were not kept in for no reason at all, and the cane was not employed. You watched the growth of your moustache with interest and impatience, and mastered the beginnings of social intercourse. You talked and found there were things amusing to say. Also you had regular pocket-money, and a voice in the purchase of your clothes, and presently a small salary. And there were girls! And friendship! In the retrospect Port Burdock sparkled with the facets of quite a cluster of remembered jolly times.

("Didn't save much money, though," said Mr. Polly.)

The first apprentices' dormitory was a long, bleak room with six beds, six chests of drawers and looking-glasses, and a number of boxes of wood or tin; it opened into a still longer and bleaker room of eight beds, and this into a third apartment with yellow-grained paper and American cloth tables, which was the dining-room by day and the men's sitting and smoking room after nine. Here Mr. Polly, who had been an only child, first tasted the joys of social intercourse. To begin with, there were attempts to bully him on account of his refusal to consider face-washing a diurnal duty, but two fights with the apprentices next above him established a useful reputation for choler, and the presence of girl apprentices in the shop somehow raised his standard of cleanliness to a more acceptable level. He didn't, of course, have very much to do with the feminine staff in his department, but he spoke to them casually as he traversed foreign parts of the Bazaar, or got out of their way politely, or helped them to lift down heavy boxes, and on such occasions he felt their scrutiny. Except in the course of business or at meal-times the men and women of the establishment had very little opportunity of meeting; the men were in their rooms and the girls in theirs. Yet these feminine creatures, at once so near and so remote, affected him profoundly. He would watch them going to and fro, and marvel secretly at the beauty of their hair, or the roundness of their necks, or the warm softness of their cheeks, or the delicacy of their hands. He would fall into passions for them at dinner-time, and try to show devotions by his manner of passing the bread and margarine at tea. There was a very fair-haired, fair-skinned apprentice in the adjacent haberdashery to whom he said "good morning" every morning, and for a period it seemed to him the most significant event in his day. When she said, "I do hope it will be fine to-morrow," he felt it marked an epoch. He had had no sisters, and was innately disposed to worship womankind. But he did not betray as much to Platt and Parsons.

To Platt and Parsons he affected an attitude of seasoned depravity towards the creatures. Platt and Parsons were his contemporary apprentices in departments of the drapery shop, and the three were drawn together into a close friendship by the fact that all their names began with P. They decided they were the three P's, and went about together of an evening with the bearing of desperate dogs. Sometimes when they had money they went into public houses and had drinks. Then they would become more desperate than ever, and walk along the pavement under the gas-lamps arm in arm singing. Platt had a good tenor voice and had been in a church choir, and so he led the singing. Parsons had a serviceable bellow, which roared and faded and roared again very wonderfully. Mr. Polly's share was an extraordinary lowing noise, a sort of flat recitative which he called "singing seconds." They would have sung catches if they had known how to do it, but as it was they sang melancholy music-hall songs about dying soldiers and the old folks far away.

They would sometimes go into the quieter residential

quarters of Port Burdock, where policemen and other obstacles were infrequent, and really let their voices soar like hawks, and feel very happy. The dogs of the district would be stirred to hopeless emulation, and would keep it up for long after the three P's had been swallowed up by the night. One jealous brute of an Irish terrier made a gallant attempt to bite Parsons, but was beaten by numbers and solidarity.

The three P's took the utmost interest in each other, and found no other company so good. They talked about everything in the world; and would go on talking in their dormitory after the gas was out, until the other men were reduced to throwing boots. They skulked from their departments in the slack hours of the afternoon to gossip in the packing room of the warehouse. On Sundays and Bank Holidays they went for long walks together, talking.

Platt was white-faced and dark, and disposed to undertones and mystery, and a curiosity about society and the *demi-monde*. He kept himself *au courant* by reading a penny paper of infinite suggestion called *Modern Society*. Parsons was an ampler build, already promising fatness, with curly hair and a lot of rolling, rollicking, curly features, and a large, blob-shaped nose. He had a great memory, and a real interest in literature. He knew great portions of Shakespear and Milton by heart, and would recite them at the slightest provocation. He read everything he could get hold of, and if he liked it he read it aloud; it did not matter who else liked it. At first Mr. Polly was disposed to be suspicious of this literature, but he was carried away by Parsons' enthusiasm. The three P's went to a performance of "Romeo and Juliet" at the Port Burdock Theatre Royal, and hung over the gallery fascinated. After that they made a sort of password of, "Do you bite your thumbs at Us, Sir?" To which the countersign was, "We bite our Thumbs."

For weeks the glory of Shakespear's Verona lit Mr.

Polly's life. He walked as though he carried a sword at his side and swung a mantle from his shoulders. He went through the grimy streets of Port Burdock with his eye on the first-floor windows—looking for balconies. A ladder in the yard flooded his mind with romantic ideas. Then Parsons discovered an Italian writer, whose name Mr. Polly rendered as "Bocashieu"; and after some excursions into that author's remains, the talk of Parsons became infested with the word "amours," and Mr. Polly would stand in front of his hosiery fixtures trifling with paper and string, and thinking of perennial picnics under dark olive-trees in the everlasting sunshine of Italy.

And about that time it was that all three P's adopted turn-down collars and large, loose, artistic silk ties, which they tied very much on one side, and wore with an air of defiance; and a certain swashbuckling carriage.

And then came the glorious revelation of that great Frenchman whom Mr. Polly called "Rabooloose." The three P's thought the birth-feast of Gargantua the most glorious piece of writing in the world—and I am not certain they were wrong; and on wet Sunday evenings, when there was danger of hymn-singing, they would get Parsons to read it aloud.

Towards the several members of the Y.M.C.A. who shared the dormitory, the three P's always maintained a sarcastic and defiant attitude.

"We have got a perfect right to do what we like in our corner," Platt maintained. "You do what you like in yours."

"But the language," objected Morrison, the white-faced, earnest-eyed improver, who was leading a profoundly religious life under great difficulties.

"*Language,* man!" roared Parsons; "why, it's *LITERATURE!*"

"Sunday isn't the time for Literature."

"It's the only time we've got. And besides——"

The horrors of religious controversy would begin. . . .

Mr. Polly stuck loyally by the three P's, but in the secret places of his heart he was torn. A fire of conviction burned in Morrison's eyes and spoke in his urgent, persuasive voice. He lived the better life manifestly : chaste in word and deed, industrious, studiously kindly. When the junior apprentice had sore feet and homesickness, Morrison washed the feet and comforted the heart; and he helped other men to get through with their work when he might have gone early—a superhuman thing to do. No one who has not worked for endless days of interminable hours, with scarce a gleam of rest or liberty between the toil and the sleep, can understand how superhuman. Polly was secretly a little afraid to be left alone with this man and the power of the spirit that was in him. He felt watched.

Platt, also struggling with things his mind could not contrive to reconcile, said, "That confounded hypocrite."

"He's no hypocrite," said Parsons; "he's no hypocrite, O' Man. But he's got no blessed *Joy de Vive*—that's what's wrong with him. Let's go down to the Harbour Arms and see some of those blessed old captains getting drunk."

"Short of sugar, O' Man," said Mr. Polly, slapping his trouser pocket.

"Oh, *carm* on," said Parsons; "always do it on tuppence for a bitter."

"Lemme get my Pipe on," said Platt, who had recently taken to smoking with great ferocity. "Then I'm with you."

(Pause and struggle.)

"Don't ram it down, O' Man," said Parsons, watching with knitted brows; "don't ram it down. Give it Air. Seen my stick, O' Man ? Right-o."

And, leaning on his cane, he composed himself in an attitude of sympathetic patience towards Platt's incendiary efforts.

§ 4

Jolly days of companionship they were for the incipi-ent bankrupt on the stile to look back upon.

The interminable working hours of the Bazaar had long since faded from his memory—except for one or two conspicuous rows and one or two larks—but the rare Sundays and holidays shone out like diamonds among pebbles. They shone with the mellow splendour of evening skies reflected in calm water, and athwart them all went old Parsons bellowing an interpretation of life, gesticulating, appreciating, and making appre-ciate, expounding books, talking of that mystery of his, the " Joy de Vive."

There were some particularly splendid walks on Bank Holidays. The three P's would start on Sunday morn-ing early, and find a room in some modest inn and talk themselves asleep, and return singing through the night, or having an " argy bargy " about the stars, on Monday evening. They would come over the hill out of the pleasant English countryside in which they had wan-dered and see Port Burdock spread out below, a network of interlacing street-lamps and shifting tram-lights against the black, beacon-gemmed immensity of the harbour waters.

"Back to the collar, O' Man," Parsons would say. There is no satisfactory plural to "O' Man," so he always used it in the singular.

"Don't mention it," said Platt.

And once they got a boat for the whole summer day, and rowed up past the moored ironclads and the black old hulks and the various shipping of the harbour, past a white troop-ship, and past the trim front and the slips and interesting vistas of the dockyard to the shallow channels and rocky, weedy wildernesses of the upper harbour. And Parsons and Mr. Polly had a great dis-pute and quarrel that day as to how far a big gun could shoot.

The country over the hills behind Port Burdock is all that an old-fashioned, scarcely disturbed English countryside should be. In those days the bicycle was still rare and costly, and the motor-car had yet to come and stir up rural serenities. The three P's would take footpaths haphazard across fields, and plunge into unknown winding lanes between high hedges of honeysuckle and dogrose. Greatly daring, they would follow green bridle-paths through primrose-studded undergrowths, or wander waist-deep in the bracken of beech woods. About twenty miles from Port Burdock there came a region of hop-gardens and hoast-crowned farms; and farther on, to be reached only by cheap tickets on Bank Holiday times, was a sterile ridge of very clean roads and red sandpits and pines, and gorse and heather. The three P's could not afford to buy bicycles, and they found boots the greatest item of their skimpy expenditure. They threw appearances to the winds at last, and got ready-made working-men's hobnails. There was much discussion and strong feeling over this step in the dormitory, and the three P's were held to have derogated from the dignity of the emporium.

There is no countryside like the English countryside for those who have learned to love it; its firm yet gentle lines of hill and dale, its ordered confusion of features, its deer parks and downland, its castles and stately houses, its hamlets and old churches, its farms and ricks and great barns and ancient trees, its pools and ponds and shining threads of rivers, its flower-starred hedgerows, its orchards and woodland patches, its village greens and kindly inns. Other countrysides have their pleasant aspects, but none such variety, none that shine so steadfastly throughout the year. Picardy is pink-and-white and pleasant in the blossom time; Burgundy goes on with its sunshine and wide hillsides and cramped vineyards, a beautiful tune repeated and repeated; Italy gives salitas and wayside chapels, and chestnuts and olive-orchards; the Ardennes has its woods and gorges—

Touraine and the Rhineland, the wide Campagna with its distant Apennines, and the neat prosperity and mountain backgrounds of South Germany all clamour their especial merits at one's memory. And there are the hills and fields of Virginia, like an England grown very big and slovenly, the woods and big river sweeps of Pennsylvania, the trim New England landscape, a little bleak and rather fine, like the New England mind, and the wide, rough country roads and hills and woodland of New York State. But none of these change scene and character in three miles of walking, nor have so mellow a sunlight nor so diversified a cloudland nor confess the perpetual refreshment of the strong soft winds that blow from off the sea, as our mother England does.

It was good for the three P's to walk through such a land and forget for a time that indeed they had no footing in it all, that they were doomed to toil behind counters in such places as Port Burdock for the better part of their lives. They would forget the customers and shop-walkers and department buyers and everything, and become just happy wanderers in a world of pleasant breezes and song-birds and shady trees.

The arrival at the inn was a great affair. No one, they were convinced, would take them for drapers, and there might be a pretty serving-girl or a jolly old land-lady, or what Parsons called a " bit of character " drinking in the bar.

There would always be weighty inquiries as to what they could have, and it would work out always at cold beef and pickles, or fried ham and eggs and shandy-gaff, two pints of beer and two bottles of ginger-beer foaming in a huge round-bellied jug.

The glorious moment of standing lordly in the inn doorway and staring out at the world, the swinging sign, the geese upon the green, the duck-pond, a waiting wagon, the church-tower, a sleepy cat, the blue heavens, with the sizzle of the frying audible behind one! The keen smell of the bacon! The trotting of feet bearing the repast; the click and clatter as the tableware is finally arranged! A clean white cloth! "Ready, Sir!" or "Ready, Gentlemen!" Better hearing that than "Forward, Polly! Look sharp!"

The going in! The sitting down! The falling to! "Bread, O' Man?"

"Right-o! Don't bag all the crust, O' Man."

Once a simple-mannered girl in a pink print dress stayed and talked with them as they ate; led by the gallant Parsons they professed to be all desperately in love with her, and courted her to say which she preferred of them, it was so manifest she did prefer one and so impossible to say which it was held her there, until a distant maternal voice called her away. Afterwards, as they left the inn, she waylaid them at the orchard corner and gave them, a little shyly, three yellow-green apples—and wished them to come again some day, and vanished, and reappeared looking after them as they turned the corner, waving a white handkerchief. All the rest of that day they disputed over the signs of her favour, and the next Sunday they went there again.

But she had vanished, and a mother of forbidding aspect afforded no explanations.

If Platt and Parsons and Mr. Polly live to be a hundred, they will none of them forget that girl as she stood with a pink flush upon her, faintly smiling and yet earnest, parting the branches of the hedgerows and reaching down, apple in hand. . . .

And once they went along the coast, following it as closely as possible, and so came at last to Fishbourne, that easternmost suburb of Brayling and Hampstead-on-the-Sea.

Fishbourne seemed a very jolly little place to Mr. Polly that afternoon. It has a clean sandy beach, instead of the mud and pebbles and coaly defilements of Port Burdock, a row of six bathing-machines, and a shelter on the Parade in which the three P's sat after a satisfying but rather expensive lunch that had included celery.

Rows of verandahed villas proffered apartments; they had feasted in a hotel with a porch painted white, and gay with geraniums above; and the High Street, with the old church at the head, had been full of an agreeable afternoon stillness.

" Nice little place for business," said Platt sagely from behind his big pipe.

It stuck in Mr. Polly's memory.

§ 5

Mr. Polly was not so picturesque a youth as Parsons. He lacked richness in his voice, and went about in those days with his hands in his pockets looking quietly speculative.

He specialised in slang and the misuse of English, and he played the rôle of an appreciative stimulant to Parsons. Words attracted him curiously, words rich in suggestion, and he loved a novel and striking phrase. His school training had given him little or no mastery of the mysterious pronunciation of English, and no confidence in himself. His schoolmaster indeed had been both unsound and variable. New words had terror and fascination for him; he did not acquire them, he could not avoid them, and so he plunged into them. His only rule was not to be misled by the spelling. That was no guide anyhow. He avoided every recognised phrase in the language, and mispronounced everything in order that he should be suspected of whim rather than of ignorance.

" Sesquippledan," he would say. " Sesquippledan verboojuice."

" Eh ?" said Platt.

" Eloquent Rapsodooce."

" Where ?" asked Platt.

" In the warehouse, O' Man. All among the table-cloths and blankets. Carlyle. He's reading aloud. Doing the High Froth. Spuming ! Windmilling !

Waw, waw! It's a sight worth seeing. He'll bark his blessed knuckles one of these days on the fixtures, O' Man."

He held an imaginary book in one hand and waved an eloquent gesture. "So too shall every Hero inasmuch as notwithstanding for evermore come back to Reality," he parodied the enthusiastic Parsons, "so that in fashion and thereby, upon things and not *under* things articulariously He stands."

"I should laugh if the Governor dropped on him," said Platt. "He'd never hear him coming."

"The O' Man's drunk with it—fair drunk," said Polly. "*I* never did. It's worse than when he got on to Rabooloose."

CHAPTER THE SECOND

The Dismissal of Parsons

§ 1

SUDDENLY Parsons got himself dismissed.

He got himself dismissed under circumstances of peculiar violence, that left a deep impression on Mr. Polly's mind. He wondered about it for years afterwards, trying to get the rights of the case.

Parsons' apprenticeship was over; he had reached the status of an Improver, and he dressed the window of the Manchester department. By his own standards he dressed it wonderfully. "Well, O' Man," he used to say, "there's one thing about my position here—I *can* dress a window."

And when trouble was under discussion he would hold that "little Fluffums"—which was the apprentices' name for Mr. Garvace, the senior partner and managing director of the Bazaar—would think twice before he

413

got rid of the only man in the place who could make a windowful of Manchester goods *tell*.

Then, like many a fellow artist, he fell a prey to theories.

"The art of window-dressing is in its infancy, O' Man—in its blooming Infancy. All balance and stiffness like a blessed Egyptian picture. No Joy in it, no blooming Joy! Conventional. A shop-window ought to get hold of people, *grip* 'em as they go along. It stands to reason. Grip!"

His voice would sink to a kind of quiet bellow. "*Do* they grip?"

Then, after a pause, a savage roar: "*Naw!*"

"He's got a Heavy on," said Mr. Polly. "Go it, O' Man; let's have some more of it."

"Look at old Morrison's dress-stuff windows! Tidy, tasteful, correct, I grant you, but Bleak!" He let out the word reinforced to a shout: "Bleak!"

"Bleak!" echoed Mr. Polly.

"Just pieces of stuff in rows, rows of tidy little puffs, perhaps one bit just unrolled, quiet tickets."

"Might as well be in church, O' Man," said Mr. Polly.

"A window ought to be exciting," said Parsons; "it ought to make you say, ''El-*lo!*' when you see it."

He paused, and Platt watched him over a snorting pipe.

"Rockcockyo," said Mr. Polly.

"We want a new school of window-dressing," said Parsons, regardless of the comment. "A New School! The Port Burdock school. Day after to-morrow I change the Fitzallan Street stuff. This time it's going to be a change. I mean to have a crowd or bust!"

And as a matter of fact he did both.

His voice dropped to a note of self-reproach. "I've been timid, O' Man. I've been holding myself in. I haven't done myself Justice. I've kept down the simmering, seething, teeming ideas. . . . All that's over now."

"Over," gulped Polly.

"Over for good and all, O' Man."

§ 2

Platt came to Polly, who was sorting up collar-boxes.
"O' Man's doing his Blooming Window."

"What window?"

"What he said."

Polly remembered.

He went on with his collar-boxes with his eye on
his senior, Mansfield. Mansfield was presently called
away to the counting-house, and instantly Polly shot
out by the street front door, and made a rapid transit along
the street front past the Manchester window, and so
into the silk-room door. He could not linger long, but
he gathered joy, a swift and fearful joy, from his brief
inspection of Parsons' unconscious back. Parsons had his
tail-coat off, and was working with vigour; his habit of
pulling his waistcoat straps to their utmost brought out
all the agreeable promise of corpulence in his youthful
frame. He was blowing excitedly and running his
fingers through his hair, and then moving with all the
swift eagerness of a man inspired. All about his feet
and knees were scarlet blankets, not folded, not formally
unfolded, but—the only phrase is—shied about. And a
great bar sinister of roller towelling stretched across the
front of the window on which was a ticket, and the
ticket said in bold, black letters : "*LOOK!*"

So soon as Mr. Polly got into the silk department
and met Platt he knew he had not lingered nearly
long enough outside.

"Did you see the boards at the back?" said Platt.

Mr. Polly hadn't. "The High Egrugious is fairly
On," he said, and dived down to return by devious
subterranean routes to the outfitting department.

Presently the street door opened and Platt, with an
air of intense devotion to business assumed to cover

14

his adoption of that unusual route, came in and made for the staircase down to the warehouse. He rolled up his eyes at Polly. "Oh, *Lor'!*" he said, and vanished.

Irresistible curiosity seized Polly. Should he go through the shop to the Manchester department, or risk a second transit outside?

He was impelled to make a dive at the street door.

"Where are you going?" asked Mansfield.

"Lill dog," said Polly, with an air of lucid explanation, and left him to get any meaning he could from it.

Parsons was worth the subsequent trouble. Parsons really was extremely rich. This time Polly stopped to take it in.

Parsons had made a huge asymmetrical pile of thick white-and-red blankets twisted and rolled to accentuate their woolly softness heaped up in a warm disorder, with large window tickets inscribed in blazing red letters: "Cosy Comfort at Cut Prices," and "Curl up and Cuddle below Cost." Regardless of the daylight he had turned up the electric light on that side of the window to reflect a warm glow upon the head, and behind, in pursuit of contrasted bleakness, he was now hanging long strips of grey silesia and chilly-coloured linen dustering.

It was wonderful, but——

Mr. Polly decided that it was time he went in. He found Platt in the silk department, apparently on the verge of another plunge into the exterior world. "Cosy Comfort at Cut Prices," said Polly. "Allittritions Artful Aid."

He did not dare go into the street for the third time, and he was hovering feverishly near the window when he saw the governor, Mr. Garvace—that is to say, the managing director of the Bazaar—walking along the pavement after his manner, to assure himself all was well with the establishment he guided.

Mr. Garvace was a short, stout man, with that air

of modest pride that so often goes with corpulence, choleric and decisive in manner, and with hands that looked like bunches of fingers. He was red-haired and ruddy, and after the custom of such complexions, hairs sprang from the tip of his nose. When he wished to bring the power of the human eye to bear upon an assistant, he projected his chest, knitted one brow, and partially closed the left eyelid.

An expression of speculative wonder overspread the countenance of Mr. Polly. He felt he must *see*. Yes, whatever happened, he must *see*.

"Wanttospeak to Parsons, Sir," he said to Mr. Mansfield, and deserted his post hastily, dashed through the intervening departments, and was in position behind a pile of Bolton sheeting as the governor came in out of the street.

"What on earth do you think you are doing with that window, Parsons?" began Mr. Garvace.

Only the legs of Parsons and the lower part of his waistcoat and an intervening inch of shirt were visible. He was standing inside the window on the steps, hanging up the last strip of his background from the brass rail along the ceiling. Within, the Manchester shop-window was cut off by a partition rather like the partition of an old-fashioned church pew from the general space of the shop. There was a panelled barrier, that is to say, with a little door like a pew door in it. Parsons' face appeared, staring with round eyes at his employer.

Mr. Garvace had to repeat his question.

"Dressing it, Sir—on new lines."

"Come out of it," said Mr. Garvace.

Parsons stared, and Mr. Garvace had to repeat his command.

Parsons, with a dazed expression, began to descend the steps slowly.

Mr. Garvace turned about. "Where's Morrison? Morrison!"

Morrison appeared.

"Take this window over," said Mr. Garvace, pointing his bunch of fingers at Parsons. "Take all this muddle out and dress it properly."

Morrison advanced and hesitated.

"I beg your pardon, Sir," said Parsons, with an immense politeness, "but this is *my* window."

"Take it all out," said Mr. Garvace, turning away.

Morrison advanced. Parsons shut the door with a click that arrested Mr. Garvace.

"Come out of that window," he said. "You can't dress it. If you want to play the fool with a window——"

"This window's All Right," said the genius in window-dressing, and there was a little pause.

"Open the door and go right in," said Mr. Garvace to Morrison.

"You leave that door alone, Morrison," said Parsons.

Polly was no longer even trying to hide behind the stack of Bolton sheetings. He realised he was in the presence of forces too stupendous to heed him.

"Get him out," said Mr. Garvace.

Morrison seemed to be thinking out the ethics of his position. The idea of loyalty to his employer prevailed with him. He laid his hand on the door to open it; Parsons tried to disengage his hand. Mr. Garvace joined his effort to Morrison's. Then the heart of Polly leaped, and the world blazed up to wonder and splendour. Parsons disappeared behind the partition for a moment, and reappeared instantly, gripping a thin cylinder of rolled huckaback. With this he smote at Morrison's head. Morrison's head ducked under the resounding impact, but he clung on and so did Mr. Garvace. The door came open, and then Mr. Garvace was staggering back, hand to head, his autocratic, his sacred baldness, smitten. Parsons was beyond all control —a strangeness, a marvel. Heaven knows how the artistic struggle had strained that richly endowed temperament. "Say I can't dress a window, you thundering old Humbug," he said, and hurled the huckaback at his master. He followed this up by pitching first a blanket, then an armful of silesia, then a window support out of the window into the shop. It leaped into Polly's mind that Parsons hated his own effort and was glad to demolish it. For a crowded second his attention was concentrated upon Parsons, infuriated, active, like a figure of earthquake with its coat off, shying things headlong.

Then he perceived the back of Mr. Garvace and heard his gubernatorial voice crying to no one in particular and everybody in general, "Get him out of the window. He's mad. He's dangerous. Get him out of the window."

Then a crimson blanket was for a moment over the head of Mr. Garvace, and his voice, muffled for an instant, broke out into unwonted expletive.

Then people had arrived from all parts of the Bazaar. Luck, the ledger clerk, blundered against Polly and said, "Help him!" Somerville from the silks vaulted the counter, and seized a chair by the back. Polly lost his head. He clawed at the Bolton sheeting before him, and if he could have detached a piece he would certainly have hit somebody with it. As it was he simply upset the pile. It fell away from Polly, and he had an impression of somebody squeaking as it went down. It was the sort of impression one disregards. The collapse of the pile of goods just sufficed to end his subconscious efforts to get something to hit somebody with, and his whole attention focussed itself upon the struggle in the window. For a splendid instant Parsons towered up over the active backs that clustered about the shop-window door, an active whirl of gesture, tearing things down and throwing them, and then he went under. There was an instant's furious struggle, a crash, a second crash, and the crack of broken plate glass. Then a stillness and heavy breathing.

Parsons was overpowered. . . .

Polly, stepping over scattered pieces of Bolton sheeting, saw his transfigured friend with a dark cut, that was not at present bleeding, on the forehead, one arm held by Somerville and the other by Morrison.

"You—you—you—you annoyed me," said Parsons, sobbing for breath.

§ 3

There are events that detach themselves from the general stream of occurrences and seem to partake of the nature of revelations. Such was this Parsons affair. It began by seeming grotesque; it ended disconcertingly. The fabric of Mr. Polly's daily life was torn, and beneath it he discovered depths and terrors.

Life was not altogether a lark.

The calling in of a policeman seemed at the moment a pantomime touch. But when it became manifest that Mr. Garvace was in a fury of vindictiveness, the affair took on a different complexion. The way in which the policeman made a note of everything and aspirated nothing impressed the sensitive mind of Polly profoundly. Polly presently found himself straightening up ties to the refrain of " 'E then 'It you on the 'Ead— 'Ard."

In the dormitory that night Parsons became heroic. He sat on the edge of the bed with his head bandaged, packing very slowly and insisting over and over again, "He ought to have left my window alone, O' Man. He didn't ought to have touched my window."

Polly was to go to the police-court in the morning as a witness. The terror of that ordeal almost overshadowed the tragic fact that Parsons was not only summoned for assault, but "swapped," and packing his box. Polly knew himself well enough to know he would make a bad witness. He felt sure of one fact only—namely, that " 'E then 'It 'Im on the 'Ead— 'Ard." All the rest danced about in his mind now, and how it would dance about on the morrow Heaven only knew. Would there be a cross-examination? Is it perjoocery to make a slip? People did sometimes perjuice themselves. Serious offence.

Platt was doing his best to help Parsons and inciting public opinion against Morrison. But Parsons would not hear of anything against Morrison. "He was all right, O' Man—according to his lights," said Parsons. "It isn't him I complain of."

He speculated on the morrow. "I shall 'ave to pay a fine," he said. "No good trying to get out of it. It's true I hit him. I hit him"—he paused and seemed to be seeking an exquisite accuracy. His voice sank to a confidential note—"on the head—about here."

He answered the suggestion of a bright junior apprentice in a corner of the dormitory. "What's the Good of a Cross summons," he replied, "with old Corks the chemist and Mottishead the house agent and all that lot on the Bench? Humble Pie, that's my meal to-morrow, O' Man. Humble Pie."

Packing went on for a time.

"But, Lord! what a Life it is!" said Parsons, giving his deep notes scope. "Ten-thirty-five a man trying to do his Duty, mistaken perhaps, but doing his best; ten-forty, Ruined. Ruined!" He lifted his voice to a shout: "Ruined!" and dropped it to "Like an earthquake."

"Heated altaclation," said Polly.

"Like a blooming earthquake," said Parsons, with the notes of a rising wind.

He meditated gloomily upon his future, and a colder chill invaded Polly's mind. "Likely to get another crib, ain't I?—with assaulted the guv'nor on my reference. . . . I suppose, though, he won't give me refs. Hard enough to get a crib at the best of times," said Parsons.

"You ought to go round with a show, O' Man," said Mr. Polly.

Things were not so dreadful in the police-court as

Mr. Polly had expected. He was given a seat with other witnesses against the wall of the court, and after an interesting larceny case Parsons appeared and stood, not in the dock, but at the table. By that time Mr. Polly's legs, which had been tucked up at first under his chair out of respect to the court, were extended straight before him, and his hands were in his trousers pockets. He was inventing names for the four magistrates on the bench, and had got to "the Grave and Reverend Signor with the palatial Boko," when his thoughts were recalled to gravity by the sound of his name. He rose with alacrity, and was fielded by an expert policeman from a brisk attempt to get into the vacant dock. The clerk to the Justices repeated the oath with incredible rapidity.

"Right-o," said Mr. Polly, but quite respectfully, and kissed the book.

His evidence was simple and quite audible after one warning from the superintendent of police to "speak up." He tried to put in a good word for Parsons by saying he was "naturally of a choleraic disposition," but the start and the slow grin of enjoyment upon the face of "the Grave and Reverend Signor with the palatial Boko" suggested that the word was not so good as he had thought it. The rest of the bench was frankly puzzled, and there were hasty consultations.

"You mean 'E 'as a 'Ot temper," said the presiding magistrate.

"I mean 'E 'as a 'Ot temper," replied Polly, magically incapable of aspirates for the moment.

"You don't mean 'E ketches cholera?"

"I mean—he's easily put out."

"Then why can't you say so?" said the presiding magistrate.

Parsons was bound over.

He came for his luggage while every one was in the shop, and Garvace would not let him invade the business to say good-bye. When Mr. Polly went upstairs for margarine and bread and tea, he slipped on into the dormitory at once to see what was happening further in the Parsons case. But Parsons had vanished. There was no Parsons, no trace of Parsons. His cubicle was swept and garnished. For the first time in his life Polly had a sense of irreparable loss.

A minute or so after Platt dashed in.

"Ugh!" he said, and then discovered Polly. Polly was leaning out of the window, and did not look round. Platt went up to him.

"He's gone already," said Platt. "Might have stopped to say good-bye to a chap."

There was a little pause before Polly replied. He thrust his finger into his mouth and gulped.

"Bit on that beastly tooth of mine," he said, still not looking at Platt. "It's made my eyes water something chronic. Any one might think I'd been Piping my Eye, by the look of me."

CHAPTER THE THIRD

Cribs

PORT BURDOCK was never the same place for Mr. Polly after Parsons had left it. There were no chest notes in his occasional letters, and little of the " Joy de Vive " got through by them. Parsons had gone, he said, to London, and found a place as warehouseman in a cheap outfitting shop near St. Paul's Churchyard, where references were not required. It became apparent as time passed that new interests were absorbing him. He wrote of Socialism and the rights of man, things that had no appeal for Mr. Polly. He felt strangers had got hold of his Parsons, were at work upon him, making him into some one else, something less picturesque. . . . Port Burdock became a dreariness full of faded memories of Parsons, and work a bore. Platt revealed himself alone as a tiresome companion, obsessed by romantic ideas about intrigues and vices and " society women."

Mr. Polly's depression manifested itself in a general

slackness. A certain impatience in the manner of Mr. Garvace presently got upon his nerves. Relations were becoming strained. He asked for a rise of salary to test his position, and gave notice to leave when it was refused.

It took him two months to place himself in another situation, and during that time he had quite a disagreeable amount of loneliness, disappointment, anxiety, and humiliation.

He went at first to stay with a married cousin who had a house at Easewood. His widowed father had recently given up the music and bicycle shop (with the post of organist at the parish church) that had sustained his home, and was living upon a small annuity as a guest of his cousin, and growing a little tiresome on account of some mysterious internal discomfort that the local practitioner diagnosed as imagination. He had aged with unusual rapidity and become excessively irritable, but the cousin's wife was a born manager, and contrived to get along with him. Our Mr. Polly's status was that of a guest pure and simple; but after a fortnight of congested hospitality, in which he wrote nearly a hundred variants :

Sir,—Reffering to your advt. in the " Christian World " for an Improver in Gents' outfitting, I beg to submit myself for the situation. Have had six years' experience. . . .

and upset a penny bottle of ink over a toilet cover and the bedroom carpet, his cousin took him for a walk and pointed out the superior advantages of apartments in London from which to swoop down upon the briefly yawning vacancy.

" Helpful," said Mr. Polly; "very helpful, O' Man, indeed. I might have gone on here for weeks," and packed.

He got a room in an institution that was partly a

benevolent hostel for men in his circumstances and partly a high-minded but forbidding coffee-house, and a centre for Pleasant Sunday Afternoons. Mr. Polly spent a critical but pleasant Sunday afternoon in a back seat inventing such phrases as :

" Soulful Owner of the Exorbiant Largenial Development." An Adam's Apple being in question.

" Earnest Joy."

" Exultant, Urgent Loogoobuosity."

A manly young curate, marking and misunderstanding his preoccupied face and moving lips, came and sat by him and entered into conversation with the idea of making him feel more at home. The conversation was awkward and disconnected for a minute or so, and then suddenly a memory of the Port Burdock Bazaar occurred to Mr. Polly, and with a baffling whisper of " Lill dog," and a reassuring nod, he rose up and escaped, to wander out relieved and observant into the varied London streets.

He found the collection of men he met waiting about in wholesale establishments in Wood Street and St. Paul's Churchyard (where they interview the buyers who have come up from the country) interesting and stimulating, but far too strongly charged with the suggestion of his own fate to be really joyful. There were men in all degrees between confidence and distress, and in every stage between extravagant smartness and the last stages of decay. There were sunny young men full of an abounding and elbowing energy before whom the soul of Polly sank into hate and dismay. " Smart Juniors," said Polly to himself, " full of Smart Juniosity. The Shoveacious Cult." There were hungry-looking individuals of thirty-five or so, that he decided must be " Proletelerians "—he had often wanted to find some one who fitted that attractive word. Middle-aged men, " too old at Forty," discoursed in the waiting-rooms on the outlook in the trade; it had never been so bad, they said, while Mr. Polly wondered if " De-juiced" was a permissible epithet. There were men with an overweening sense of their importance, manifestly annoyed and angry to find themselves still disengaged, and inclined to suspect a plot, and men so faint-hearted one was terrified to imagine their behaviour when it came to an interview. There was a fresh-faced young man with an unintelligent face who seemed to think himself equipped against the world beyond all misadventure by a collar of exceptional height, and another who introduced a note of gaiety by wearing a flannel shirt and a check suit of remarkable virulence. Every day Mr. Polly looked round to mark how many of the familiar faces had gone, and the deepening anxiety (reflecting his own) on the faces that remained, and every day some new type joined the drifting shoal. He realised how small a chance his poor letter from Easewood ran against this hungry cluster of competitors at the fountainhead.

At the back of Mr. Polly's mind while he made his observations was the disagreeable flavour of the dentist's parlour. At any moment his name might be shouted, and he might have to haul himself into the presence of some fresh specimen of employer, and to repeat once more his passionate protestation of interest in the business, his possession of capacity for zeal—zeal on behalf of any one who would pay him a salary of twenty-six pounds a year.

The prospective employer would unfold his ideals of the employee. "I want a smart, willing young man, thoroughly willing, who won't object to take trouble. I don't want a slacker, the sort of fellow who has to be pushed up to his work and held there. I've got no use for him."

At the back of Mr. Polly's mind, and quite beyond his control, the insubordinate phrasemaker would be proffering such combinations as "Chubby Chops," or "Chubby Charmer," as suitable for the gentleman, very much as a hat salesman proffers hats.

"I don't think you'd find much slackness about *me,* Sir," said Mr. Polly brightly, trying to disregard his deeper self.

"I want a young man who means getting on."

"Exactly, Sir. Excelsior."

"I beg your pardon?"

"I said excelsior, Sir. It's a sort of motto of mine. From Longfellow. Would you want me to serve through?"

The chubby gentleman explained and reverted to his ideals, with a faint air of suspicion. "Do *you* mean getting on?" he asked.

"I hope so, Sir," said Mr. Polly.

"Get on or get out, eh?"

Mr. Polly made a rapturous noise, nodded appreciation, and said indistinctly, "*Quite* my style."

"Some of my people have been with me twenty years," said the employer. "My Manchester buyer came to me as a boy of twelve. You're a Christian?"

"Church of England," said Mr. Polly.

"H'm," said the employer, a little checked. "For good all round business work, I should have preferred a Baptist. Still——"

He studied Mr. Polly's tie, which was severely neat and businesslike, as became an aspiring outfitter. Mr. Polly's conception of his own pose and expression was rendered by that uncontrollable phrase-monger at the back as "Obsequies Deference."

"I am inclined," said the prospective employer in a conclusive manner, "to look up your references."

Mr. Polly stood up abruptly.

"Thank you," said the employer and dismissed him.

"Chump chops! How about chump chops?" said the phrasemonger with an air of inspiration.

"I hope then to hear from you, Sir," said Mr. Polly in his best salesman manner.

"If everything is satisfactory," said the prospective employer.

§ 2

A man whose brain devotes its hinterland to making odd phrases and nicknames out of ill-conceived words, whose conception of life is a lump of auriferous rock to which all the value is given by rare veins of un-businesslike joy, who reads Boccaccio and Rabelais and Shakespear with gusto, and uses " Stertoraneous Shover " and " Smart Junior " as terms of bitterest opprobrium, is not likely to make a great success under modern business conditions. Mr. Polly dreamt always of picturesque and mellow things, and had an instinctive hatred of the strenuous life. He would have resisted the spell of ex-President Roosevelt, or General Baden Powell, or Mr. Peter Keary, or the late Dr. Samuel Smiles quite easily—I doubt if even Mr. St. Loe Strachey could have inspired him; and he loved Falstaff and Hudibras and coarse laughter, and the Old England of Washington Irving and the memory of Charles the Second's courtly days. His progress was necessarily slow. He did not get rises; he lost situations; there was something in his eye employers did not like; he would have lost his places oftener if he had not been at times an exceptionally brilliant salesman, rather carefully neat, and a slow but very fair window-dresser.

He went from situation to situation, he invented a great wealth of nicknames, he conceived enmities and made friends—but none so richly satisfying as Parsons. He was frequently, but mildly and discursively, in love; and sometimes he thought of that girl who had given him a yellow-green apple. He had an idea amounting to a flattering certainty whose youthful freshness it was had stirred her to self-forgetfulness. And sometimes he thought of Fishbourne sleeping prosperously in the sun. And he had moods of discomfort and lassitude and ill-temper, due to the beginnings of indigestion.

Various forces and suggestions came into his life and swayed him for longer and shorter periods.

He went to Canterbury and came under the influence of Gothic architecture. There was a blood affinity between Mr. Polly and the Gothic; in the Middle Ages he would, no doubt, have sat upon a scaffolding and carved out penetrating and none-too-flattering portraits of church dignitaries upon the capitals; and when he strolled, with his hands behind his back, along the cloisters behind the cathedral, and looked at the rich grass-plot in the centre, he had the strangest sense of being at home——far more than he had ever been at home before. "Portly capons," he used to murmur to himself, under the impression that he was naming a characteristic type of medieval churchman.

He liked to sit in the nave during the service, and look through the great gates at the candles and choristers, and listen to the organ-sustained voices, but the transepts he never penetrated because of the charge for admission. The music and the long vista of the fretted roof filled him with a vague and mystical happiness that he had no words, even mispronounced words, to express. But some of the smug monuments in the aisles got a wreath of epithets; "metrorious urnfuls," "funererial claims," "dejected angelosity," for example. He wandered about the precincts, and speculated about the people who lived in the ripe and cosy houses of grey stone that cluster there so comfortably. Through green doors in high stone walls he caught glimpses of level lawns and blazing flower-beds; mullioned windows revealed shaded reading-lamps and disciplined shelves of brown bound books. Now and then a dignitary in gaiters would pass him ("Portly capon"), or a drift of white-robed choir-boys cross a distant arcade and vanish in a doorway, or the pink and cream of some girlish dress flit like a butterfly across the cool still spaces of the place. Particularly he responded to the ruined arches of the Benedictine's Infirmary and the view of Bell Harry Tower from the school-building. He was stirred to read the "Canterbury Tales," but he could not get on with Chaucer's old-fashioned English, it fatigued his attention, and he would have given all the story-telling very readily for a few adventures on the road. He wanted these nice people to live more and yarn less. He appreciated the wife of Bath very keenly. He would have liked to have known that woman.

At Canterbury too, he first, to his knowledge, saw Americans.

His shop did a good class trade in Westgate Street, and he would see them go by on the way to stare at Chaucer's "Chequers" and then turn down Mercery Lane to Prior Goldstone's gate. It impressed him that they were always in a kind of quiet hurry, and very determined and methodical people—much more so than any English he knew.

"Cultured Rapacacity," he tried.

"Vorocious Return to the Heritage."

He would expound them incidentally to his attendant apprentices. He had overheard a little lady putting her view to a friend near the Christchurch gate. The accent and intonation had hung in his memory, and he would reproduce them more or less accurately. "Now, does this Marlowe monument really and truly *matter?*" he had heard the little lady inquire. "We've no time for sideshows and second-rate stunts, Mamie. We want just the Big Simple Things of the place, just the Broad Elemental Canterbury Prahposition. What is it saying to us? I want to get right hold of that, and then have tea in the very room where Chaucer did, and hustle to get that four-eighteen train back to London. . . ."

He would go over these specious phrases, finding them full of an indescribable flavour. "Just the Broad Elemental Canterbury Prahposition," he would repeat. . . .

He would try to imagine Parsons confronted with Americans. For his own part, he knew himself to be altogether inadequate. . . .

Canterbury was the most congenial situation Mr. Polly ever found during these wander years, albeit a very desert so far as companionship went.

§ 3

It was after Canterbury that the universe became really disagreeable to Mr. Polly. It was brought home to him not so much vividly as with a harsh ungainly insistence that he was a failure in his trade. It was not the trade he ought to have chosen, though what trade he ought to have chosen was by no means clear.

He made great but irregular efforts, and produced a forced smartness that, like a cheap dye, refused to stand sunshine. He acquired a sort of parsimony also, in which acquisition he was helped by one or two phases of absolute impecuniosity. But he was hopeless in competition against the naturally gifted, the born hustlers, the young men who meant to get on.

He left the Canterbury place very regretfully. He and another commercial gentleman took a boat one Sunday afternoon at Sturry-on-the-Stour, when the wind was in the west, and sailed it very happily eastward for an hour. They had never sailed a boat before, and it seemed a simple and wonderful thing to do. When they turned, they found the river too narrow for tacking, and the tide running out like a sluice. They battled back to Sturry in the course of six hours (at a shilling the first hour and sixpence for each hour afterwards), rowing a mile in an hour and a half or so, until the turn of the tide came to help them, and then they had a night walk to Canterbury, and found themselves remorselessly locked out.

The Canterbury employer was an amiable, religious-spirited man, and he would probably not have dismissed Mr. Polly if that unfortunate tendency to phrase things had not shocked him. "A Tide's a Tide, Sir," said Mr. Polly, feeling that things were not so bad. "I've no lune-attic power to alter *that*."

It proved impossible to explain to the Canterbury employer that this was not a highly disrespectful and blasphemous remark.

"And besides, what good are you to me this morning, do you think?" said the Canterbury employer; "with your arms pulled out of their sockets?"

So Mr. Polly resumed his observations in the Wood Street warehouses once more, and had some dismal times. The shoal of fish waiting for the crumbs of employment seemed larger than ever.

He took counsel with himself. Should he "chuck" the outfitting? It wasn't any good for him now, and presently, when he was older and his youthful smartness had passed into the dulness of middle age, it would be worse. What else could he do?

He could think of nothing. He went one night to a music-hall and developed a vague idea of a comic performance; the comic men seemed violent rowdies, and not at all funny; but when he thought of the great pit of the audience yawning before him, he realised that his was an altogether too delicate talent for such a use. He was impressed by the charm of selling vegetables by auction in one of those open shops near London Bridge, but admitted upon reflection his general want of technical knowledge. He made some inquiries about emigration, but none of the colonies were in want of shop assistants without capital. He kept up his attendance in Wood Street.

He subdued his ideal of salary by the sum of five pounds a year, and was taken into a driving establishment in Clapham, which dealt chiefly in ready-made suits, fed its assistants in an underground dining-room, and kept open until twelve on Saturdays. He found it hard to be cheerful there. His fits of indigestion became worse, and he began to lie awake at night and think.   Sunshine and laughter seemed things lost for ever; picnics, and shouting in the moonlight.

The chief shop-walker took a dislike to him and nagged him.   "Nar, then, Polly!"   "Look alive, Polly!" became the burden of his days.   "As Smart a chap as you could have," said the chief shop-walker, "but no *Zest*.   No *Zest!*   No *Vim!*   What's the matter with you?"

During his night vigils Mr. Polly had a feeling. . . . A young rabbit must have very much the feeling when, after a youth of gambolling in sunny woods and furtive jolly raids upon the growing wheat and exciting triumphant bolts before ineffectual casual dogs, it finds itself at last for a long night of floundering effort and perplexity in a net—for the rest of its life.

He could not grasp what was wrong with him.   He made enormous efforts to diagnose his case.   Was he really just a "lazy slacker" who ought to "buck up"? He couldn't find it in him to believe it.   He blamed his father a good deal—it is what fathers are for—in putting him to a trade he wasn't happy to follow, but he found it impossible to say what he ought to have followed.   He felt there had been something stupid about his school, but just where that came in he couldn't say.   He made some perfectly sincere efforts to "buck up" and "shove" ruthlessly.   But that was infernal— impossible.   He had to admit himself miserable with all the misery of a social misfit, and with no clear prospect of more than the most incidental happiness ahead of him.   And for all his attempts at self-reproach and self-discipline he felt at bottom that he wasn't at fault.

As a matter of fact all the elements of his troubles had been adequately diagnosed by a certain high-browed, spectacled gentleman living at Highbury, wearing a gold pince-nez, and writing for the most part in the beautiful library of the Climax Club.   This gentleman did not know Mr. Polly personally, but he had dealt with him generally as "one of those ill-adjusted units that abound in a society that has failed to develop a collective intelligence and a collective will for order commensurate with its complexities."

But phrases of that sort had no appeal for Mr. Polly.

CHAPTER THE FOURTH

Mr. Polly an Orphan

THEN a great change was brought about in the life of Mr. Polly by the death of his father. His father died suddenly—the local practitioner still clung to his theory that it was imagination he suffered from, but compromised in the certificate with the appendicitis that was then so fashionable—and Mr. Polly found himself heir to a debatable number of pieces of furniture in the house of his cousin near Easewood Junction, a family Bible, an engraved portrait of Garibaldi and a bust of Mr. Gladstone, an invalid gold watch, a gold locket formerly belonging to his mother, some minor jewellery and bric-à-brac, a quantity of nearly valueless old clothes, and an insurance policy and money in the bank amounting altogether to the sum of three hundred and fifty-five pounds.

Mr. Polly had always regarded his father as an immortal, as an eternal fact; and his father, being of a reserved nature in his declining years, had said nothing

436

about the insurance policy. Both wealth and bereavement therefore took Mr. Polly by surprise, and found him a little inadequate. His mother's death had been a childish grief and long forgotten, and the strongest affection in his life had been for Parsons. An only child of sociable tendencies turns his back a good deal upon home; and the aunt who had succeeded his mother was an economist and furniture-polisher, a knuckle-rapper and sharp silencer : no friend for a slovenly little boy. He had loved other little boys and girls transitorily; none had been frequent and familiar enough to strike deep roots in his heart; and he had grown up with a tattered and dissipated affectionateness that was becoming wildly shy. His father had always been a stranger, an irritable stranger with exceptional powers of intervention and comment, and an air of being disappointed about his off-spring. It was shocking to lose him; it was like an un-expected hole in the universe, the writing of "Death" upon the sky; but it did not at first tear Mr. Polly's heart-strings so much as rouse him to a pitch of vivid attention.

He came down to the cottage at Easewood in response to an urgent telegram, and found his father already dead. His Cousin Johnson received him with much solemnity, and ushered him upstairs to look at a stiff, straight, shrouded form with a face unwontedly quiet and, it seemed by reason of its pinched nostrils, scornful.

"Looks peaceful," said Mr. Polly, disregarding the scorn to the best of his ability.

"It was a merciful relief," said Mr. Johnson.

There was a pause.

"Second—second Departed I've ever seen—not counting mummies," said Mr. Polly, feeling it necessary to say something.

"We did all we could."

"No doubt of it, O' Man," said Mr. Polly.

A second long pause followed, and then, to Mr. Polly's great relief, Johnson moved towards the door.

Afterwards Mr. Polly went for a solitary walk in the evening light, and as he walked, suddenly his dead father became real to him. He thought of things far away down the perspective of memory—of jolly moments when his father had skylarked with a wildly excited little boy; of a certain annual visit to the Crystal Palace pantomime, full of trivial glittering incidents and wonders; of his father's dread back while customers were in the old, minutely known shop. It is curious that the memory which seemed to link him nearest to the dead man was the memory of a fit of passion. His father had wanted to get a small sofa up the narrow winding staircase from the little room behind the shop to the bedroom above, and it had jammed. For a time his father had coaxed, and then groaned like a soul in torment, and given way to blind fury; had sworn, kicked, and struck at the offending piece of furniture, and finally, with an immense effort, wrenched it upstairs, with considerable incidental damage to lath and plaster and one of the casters. That moment when self-control was altogether torn aside, the shocked discovery of his father's perfect humanity, had left a singular impression on Mr. Polly's queer mind. It was as if something extravagantly vital had come out of his father and laid a warmly passionate hand upon his heart. He remembered that now very vividly, and it became a clue to endless other memories that had else been dispersed and confusing.

A weakly, wilful being, struggling to get obdurate things round impossible corners—in that symbol Mr. Polly could recognise himself and all the trouble of humanity.

He hadn't had a particularly good time, poor old chap; and now it was all over—finished. . . .

Johnson was the sort of man who derives great satisfaction from a funeral; a melancholy, serious, practical-minded man of five-and-thirty, with great powers of advice. He was the up-line ticket clerk at Easewood

Junction, and felt the responsibilities of his position.
He was naturally thoughtful and reserved, and greatly
sustained in that by an innate rectitude of body and an
overhanging and forward inclination of the upper part
of his face and head. He was pale but freckled, and his
dark grey eyes were deeply set. His highest interest
was cricket, but he did not take that lightly. His chief
holiday was to go to a cricket-match, which he did as
if he was going to church; and he watched critically,
applauded sparingly, and was darkly offended by any
unorthodox play. His convictions upon all subjects
were taciturnly inflexible. He was an obstinate player
of draughts and chess, and an earnest and persistent
reader of the *British Weekly*. His wife was a pink,
short, wilfully smiling, managing, ingratiating, talkative
woman who was determined to be pleasant, and take a
bright, hopeful view of everything, even when it was
not really bright and hopeful. She had large, blue,
expressive eyes and a round face, and she always spoke
of her husband as Harold. She addressed sympathetic
and considerate remarks about the deceased to Mr. Polly
in notes of brisk encouragement. " He was really quite
cheerful at the end," she said several times, with con-
gratulatory gusto; "quite cheerful."

She made dying seem almost agreeable.

Both these people were resolved to treat Mr. Polly
very well, and to help his exceptional incompetence in
every possible way; and after a simple supper of ham
and bread and cheese and pickles and cold apple tart
and small beer had been cleared away, they put him
into the armchair almost as though he was an invalid,
and sat on chairs that made them look down upon him,
and opened a directive discussion of the arrangements
for the funeral. After all, a funeral is a distinct social
opportunity, and rare when you have no family and
few relations, and they did not want to see it spoiled
and wasted.

" You'll have a hearse, of course," said Mrs. Johnson;

"not one of them combinations, with the driver sitting on the coffin. Disrespectful, I think they are. I can't fancy how people can bring themselves to be buried in combinations." She flattened her voice in a manner she used to intimate æsthetic feeling. "I *do* like them glass hearses," she said. "So refined and nice they are."

"Podger's hearse you'll have," said Johnson conclusively; "it's the best in Easewood."

"Everything that's right and proper," said Mr. Polly.

"Podger's ready to come and measure at any time," said Johnson.

"Then you'll want a mourner's carriage or two, according to whom you're going to invite," said Mr. Johnson.

"Didn't think of inviting anyone," said Mr. Polly.

"Oh, you'll *have* to ask a few friends," said Mr. Johnson. "You can't let your father go to his grave without asking a few friends."

"Funerial baked meats, like," said Mr. Polly.

"Not baked; but of course you'll have to give them something. Ham and chicken's very suitable. You don't want a lot of cooking, with the ceremony coming into the middle of it. I wonder who Alfred ought to invite, Harold? Just the immediate relations. One doesn't want a Great Crowd of People, and one doesn't want not to show respect."

"But he hated our relations—most of them."

"He's not hating them *now*," said Mr. Johnson; "you may be sure of that. It's just because of that I think they ought to come, all of them—even your Aunt Mildred."

"Bit vulturial, isn't it?" said Mr. Polly, unheeded.

"Wouldn't be more than twelve or thirteen people if they *all* came," said Mr. Johnson.

"We could have everything put out ready in the back room, and the gloves and whisky in the front room; and while we were all at the—ceremony, Bessie could bring it all into the front room on a tray, and put it out nice and proper. There'd have to be whisky, and sherry-or-port for the ladies. . . ."

"Where'll you get your mourning?" asked Johnson abruptly.

Mr. Polly had not yet considered this by-product of sorrow. "Haven't thought of it yet, O' Man."

A disagreeable feeling spread over his body, as though he was blackening as he sat. He hated black garments.

"I suppose I must *have* mourning," he said.

"*Well!*" said Johnson, with a solemn smile.

"Got to see it through," said Mr. Polly indistinctly.

"If I were you," said Johnson, "I should get ready-made trousers. That's all you really want. And a black satin tie, and a top hat with a deep mourning band. And gloves."

"Jet cuff-links he ought to have—as chief mourner," said Mrs. Johnson.

"Not obligatory," said Johnson.

"It shows respect," said Mrs. Johnson.

"It shows respect, of course," said Johnson.

And then Mrs. Johnson went on with the utmost gusto to the details of the "casket," while Mr. Polly sat more and more deeply and droopingly into the arm-chair, assenting with a note of protest to all they said. After he had retired for the night he remained for a long time perched on the edge of the sofa, which was his bed, staring at the prospect before him. "Chasing the o' man about to the last," he said.

He hated the thought and elaboration of death as a healthy animal must hate it. His mind struggled with unwonted social problems.

"Got to put 'em away somehow, I suppose," said Mr. Polly. "Wish I'd looked him up a bit more while he was alive."

§ 2

Bereavement came to Mr. Polly before the realisation of opulence and its anxieties and responsibilities. That only dawned upon him on the morrow—which chanced to be Sunday—as he walked with Johnson before church time about the tangle of struggling building enterprise that constituted the rising urban district of Easewood. Johnson was off duty that morning, and devoted the time very generously to the admonitory discussion of Mr. Polly's worldly outlook.

" Don't seem to get the hang of the business somehow," said Mr. Polly. ".Too much blooming humbug in it for my way of thinking."

" If I were you," said Mr. Johnson, " I should push for a first-class place in London—take almost nothing and live on my reserves. That's what I should do."

" Come the Heavy," said Mr. Polly.

" Get a better-class reference."

There was a pause. " Think of investing your money?" asked Johnson.

" Hardly got used to the idea of having it yet, O' Man."

" You'll have to do something with it. Give you nearly twenty pounds a year if you invest it properly."

" Haven't seen it yet in that light," said Mr. Polly defensively.

" There's no end of things you could put it into."

" It's getting it out again I shouldn't feel sure of. I'm no sort of Fiancianier. Sooner back horses."

" I wouldn't do that if I were you."

" Not my style, O' Man."

" It's a nest-egg," said Johnson.

Mr. Polly made an indeterminate noise.

" There's building societies," Johnson threw out in a speculative tone. Mr. Polly, with detached brevity, admitted there were.

"You might lend it on mortgage," said Johnson.
"Very safe form of investment."

"Shan't think anything about it—not till the o'
man's underground," said Mr. Polly, with an inspiration.

They turned a corner that led towards the junction.

"Might do worse," said Johnson, "than put it into
a small shop."

At the moment this remark made very little appeal
to Mr. Polly. But afterwards it developed. It fell into
his mind like some obscure seed and germinated.

"These shops aren't in a bad position," said Johnson.

The row he referred to gaped in the late painful stage
in building before the healing touch of the plasterer
assuages the roughness of the brickwork. The space for
the shop yawned an oblong gap below, framed above by
an iron girder; "Windows and fittings to suit tenant,"
a board at the end of the row promised; and behind was
the door space and a glimpse of stairs going up to the
living room above. "Not a bad position," said Johnson, and led the way into the establishment. "Room
for fixtures there," he said, pointing to the blank wall.

The two men went upstairs to the little sitting-room
(or best bedroom it would have to be) above the shop.
Then they descended to the kitchen below.

"Rooms in a new house always look a bit small," said
Johnson.

They came out of the house again by the prospective
back door, and picked their way through builder's litter
across the yard space to the road again. They drew
nearer the junction to where a pavement and shops
already open and active formed the commercial centre
of Easewood. On the opposite side of the way the side
door of a flourishing little establishment opened, and a
man and his wife and a small boy in a sailor suit came
into the street. The wife was a pretty woman in
brown, with a floriferous straw hat, and the group was
altogether very Sundayfied and shiny and spic and span.
The shop itself had a large plate-glass window whose

contents were now veiled by a buff blind on which was inscribed in scrolly letters : "Rymer, Pork Butcher and Provision Merchant," and then with voluptuous elaborations, "The World Famed Easewood Sausage."

Greetings were exchanged between Mr. Johnson and this distinguished comestible.

"Off to church already?" said Johnson.

"Walking across the fields to Little Dorington," said Mr. Rymer.

"Very pleasant walk," said Johnson.

"Very," said Mr. Rymer.

"Hope you'll enjoy it," said Mr. Johnson.

"That chap's done well," said Johnson, *sotto voce,* as they went on. "Came here with nothing—practically, four years ago. And as thin as a lath. Look at him now!

"He's worked hard, of course," said Johnson, improving the occasion.

Thought fell between the cousins for a space.

"Some men can do one thing," said Johnson, "and some another. . . . For a man who sticks to it there's a lot to be done in a shop."

§ 3

All the preparations for the funeral ran easily and happily under Mrs. Johnson's skilful hands. On the eve of the sad occasion she produced a reserve of black sateen, the kitchen steps, and a box of tin tacks, and decorated the house with festoons and bows of black in the best possible taste. She tied up the knocker with black crape, and put a large bow over the corner of the steel engraving of Garibaldi, and swathed the bust of Mr. Gladstone that had belonged to the deceased with inky swathings. She turned round the two vases that had views of Tivoli and the Bay of Naples, so that these rather brilliant landscapes were hidden and only the plain blue enamel showed, and she anticipated the long contemplated purchase of a table-cloth for the front room, and substituted a violet-purple cover for the now very worn and faded raptures and roses in plushette that had hitherto done duty there. Everything that loving consideration could do to impart a dignified solemnity to her little home was done.

She had released Mr. Polly from the irksome duty of issuing invitations, and as the moments of assembly drew near she sent him and Mr. Johnson out into the narrow, long strip of garden at the back of the house, to be free to put a finishing touch or so to her preparations. She sent them out together because she had a queer little persuasion at the back of her mind that Mr. Polly wanted to bolt from his sacred duties, and there was no way out of the garden except through the house.

Mr. Johnson was a steady, successful gardener, and particularly good with celery and peas. He walked slowly along the narrow path down the centre, pointing out to Mr. Polly a number of interesting points in the management of peas, wrinkles neatly applied and difficulties wisely overcome, and all that he did for the comfort and propitiation of that fitful but rewarding vegetable. Presently a sound of nervous laughter and raised voices from the house proclaimed the arrival of the earlier guests, and the worst of that anticipatory tension was over.

When Mr. Polly re-entered the house he found three entirely strange young women with pink faces, demonstrative manners, and emphatic mourning engaged in an incoherent conversation with Mrs. Johnson. All three kissed him with great gusto after the ancient English fashion. " These are your Cousins Larkins," said Mrs. Johnson. " That's Annie " (unexpected hug and smack), " that's Miriam " (resolute hug and smack), " and that's Minnie " (prolonged hug and smack).

" Right-o," said Mr. Polly, emerging a little crumpled and breathless from the hearty introduction. " I see."

"Here's Aunt Larkins," said Mrs. Johnson, as an elderly and stouter edition of the three young women appeared in the doorway.

Mr. Polly backed rather faint-heartedly, but Aunt Larkins was not to be denied. Having hugged and kissed her nephew resoundingly, she gripped him by the wrists and scanned his features. She had a round, sentimental, freckled face. "I should 'ave known 'im anywhere," she said, with fervour.

"Hark at Mother!" said the cousin called Annie. "Why, she's never set eyes on him before."

"I should 'ave known 'im anywhere," said Mrs. Larkins, "for Lizzie's child. You've got her eyes! It's a Resemblance! And as for never seeing 'im—I've *dandled* him, Miss Imperence. I've dandled him."

"You couldn't dandle him now, Ma!" Miss Annie remarked, with a shriek of laughter.

All the sisters laughed at that. "The things you say, Annie!" said Miriam, and for a time the room was full of mirth.

Mr. Polly felt it incumbent upon him to say something. "*My* dandling days are over," he said.

The reception of this remark would have convinced a far more modest character than Mr. Polly that it was extremely witty.

Mr. Polly followed it up by another one almost equally good. "My turn to dandle," he said, with a sly look at his aunt, and convulsed everyone.

"Not me," said Mrs. Larkins, taking his point, "*thank* you," and achieved a climax.

It was queer, but they seemed to be easy people to get on with anyhow. They were still picking little ripples and giggles of mirth from the idea of Mr. Polly dandling Aunt Larkins when Mr. Johnson, who had answered the door, ushered in a stooping figure, who was at once hailed by Mrs. Johnson as "Why! Uncle Pentstemon!" Uncle Pentstemon was rather a shock. His was an aged rather than venerable figure. Time had removed the hair from the top of his head and distributed a small dividend of the plunder in little bunches carelessly and impartially over the rest of his features; he was dressed in a very big, old frock-coat and a long, cylindrical top-hat, which he had kept on; he was very much bent, and he carried a rush basket, from which protruded coy intimations of the lettuces and onions he had brought to grace the occasion. He hobbled into the room, resisting the efforts of Johnson to divest him of his various encumbrances, halted, and surveyed the company with an expression of profound hostility, breathing hard. Recognition quickened in his eyes.

"*You* here?" he said to Aunt Larkins, and then, "You *would* be. . . . These your gals?"

"They are," said Aunt Larkins, "and better gals——"

"That Annie?" asked Uncle Pentstemon, pointing a horny thumb-nail.

"Fancy your remembering her name!"

"She mucked up my mushroom bed, the baggage!" said Uncle Pentstemon ungenially, "and I give it to her to rights. Trounced her I did—fairly. *I* remember her. Here's some green stuff for you, Grace. Fresh it is, and wholesome. I shall be wanting the basket back, and mind you let me have it. . . . Have you nailed him down yet? Ah! You always was a bit in front of what was needful."

His attention was drawn inward by a troublesome tooth, and he sucked at it spitefully. There was something potent about this old man that silenced every one for a moment or so. He seemed a fragment from the ruder agricultural past of our race, like a lump of soil among things of paper. He put his packet of earthy vegetables very deliberately on the new violet table-cloth, removed his hat carefully, and dabbled his brow, and wiped out his hat brim with an abundant crimson-and-yellow pocket-handkerchief.

15

"I'm glad you were able to come, Uncle," said Mrs. Johnson.

"Oh, I came," said Uncle Pentstemon.   "I *came*."

He turned on Mrs. Larkins.   "Gals in service?" he asked.

"They aren't, and they won't be," said Mrs. Larkins.

"No," he said, with infinite meaning, and turned his eye on Mr. Polly.

"You Lizzie's boy?" he said.

Mr. Polly was spared much self-exposition by the tumult occasioned by further arrivals.

"Ah! here's May Punt!" said Mrs. Johnson, and a small woman dressed in the borrowed mourning of a large woman, and leading a very small, fair-haired, sharp-nosed, observant little boy—it was his first funeral—appeared, closely followed by several friends of Mrs. Johnson, who had come to swell the display of respect, and who left only vague, confused impressions upon Mr. Polly's mind. (Aunt Mildred, who was an unexplained family scandal, had declined Mrs. Johnson's hospitality to the relief of every one who understood — as Mrs. Johnson intimated — though who understood, and what, as my head master used to say, Mr. Polly could form no idea.)

Everybody was in profound mourning, of course— mourning in the modern English style, with the dyer's handiwork only too apparent, and hats and jackets of the current cut. There was very little crape, and the costumes had none of the goodness and specialisation and genuine enjoyment of mourning for mourning's sake that a similar Continental gathering would have displayed. Still that congestion of strangers in black sufficed to stun and confuse Mr. Polly's impressionable mind. It seemed to him much more extraordinary than anything he had expected.

"Now, gals," said Mrs. Larkins, "see if you can help," and the three daughters became confusingly active between the front room and the back.

"I hope every one'll take a glass of sherry and a biscuit," said Mrs. Johnson. "We don't stand on ceremony," and a decanter appeared in the place of Uncle Pentstemon's vegetables.

Uncle Pentstemon had refused to be relieved of his hat; he sat stiffly down on a chair against the wall, with that venerable head-dress between his feet, watching the approach of any one jealously. "Don't you go squashing my hat," he said. Conversation became confused and general. Uncle Pentstemon addressed himself to Mr. Polly.

"You're a little chap," he said; "a puny little chap. I never did agree to Lizzie marrying him, but I suppose bygones must be bygones now. I suppose they made you a clerk or something."

"Outfitter," said Mr. Polly.

"I remember. Them girls pretend to be dressmakers."

"They *are* dressmakers," said Mrs. Larkins across the room.

"I *will* take a glass of sherry," he remarked; and then mildly to Mr. Polly, "They 'old to it, you see."

He took the glass Mrs. Johnson handed him, and poised it critically between a horny finger and thumb. "You'll be paying for this," he said to Mr. Polly. "Here's *to* you. . . . Don't you go treading on my hat, young woman. You brush your skirts against it and you take a shillin' off its value. It ain't the sort of 'at you see nowadays."

He drank noisily.

The sherry presently loosened everybody's tongue, and the opening coldness passed.

"There ought to have been a *post-mortem,*" Polly heard Mrs. Punt remarking to one of Mrs. Johnson's friends, and Miriam and another were lost in admiration of Mrs. Johnson's decorations. "So very nice and refined," they were both repeating at intervals.

The sherry and biscuits were still being discussed when Mr. Podger, the undertaker, arrived, a broad, cheerfully sorrowful, clean-shaven little man, accompanied by a melancholy-faced assistant. He conversed for a time with Johnson in the passage outside. The sense of his business stilled the rising waves of chatter and carried off every one's attention in the wake of his heavy footsteps to the room above.

§ 4

Things crowded upon Mr. Polly. Every one, he noticed, took sherry with a solemn avidity, and a small portion was administered sacramentally even to the Punt boy. There followed a distribution of black kid gloves, and much trying-on and humouring of fingers. "*Good* gloves," said one of Mrs. Johnson's friends. "There's a little pair there for Willie," said Mrs. Johnson triumphantly. Every one seemed gravely content with the amazing procedure of the occasion. Presently Mr. Podger was picking Mr. Polly out as Chief Mourner to go with Mrs. Johnson, Mrs. Larkins, and Annie in the first mourning carriage.

"Right-o," said Mr. Polly, and repented instantly of the alacrity of the phrase.

"There'll have to be a walking-party," said Mrs. Johnson cheerfully. "There's only two coaches. I dare say we can put in six in each, but that leaves three over."

There was a generous struggle to be pedestrian, and the two other Larkin girls, confessing coyly to tight new boots and displaying a certain eagerness, were added to the contents of the first carriage.

"It'll be a squeeze," said Annie.

"*I* don't mind a squeeze," said Mr. Polly.

He decided privately that the proper phrase for the result of that remark was " Hysterial catechunations."

Mr. Podger re-entered the room from a momentary

supervision of the bumping business that was now proceeding down the staircase.

"Bearing up," he said cheerfully, rubbing his hands together. "Bearing up!"

That stuck very vividly in Mr. Polly's mind, and so did the close-wedged drive to the churchyard, bunched in between two young women in confused dull and shiny black, and the fact that the wind was bleak and that the officiating clergyman had a cold, and sniffed between his sentences. The wonder of life! The wonder of everything! What had he expected that this should all be so astoundingly different?

He found his attention converging more and more upon the Larkins cousins. The interest was reciprocal. They watched him with a kind of suppressed excitement and became risible with his every word and gesture. He was more and more aware of their personal quality. Annie had blue eyes, and a red, attractive mouth, a harsh voice, and a habit of extreme liveliness that even this occasion could not suppress; Minnie was fond, extremely free about the touching of hands and such-like endearments; Miriam was dark and quieter than her sisters and regarded him earnestly. Mrs. Larkins was very happy in her daughters, and they had the naïve affectionateness of those who see few people and find a strange cousin a wonderful outlet. Mr. Polly had never been very much kissed, and it made his mind swim. He did not know for the life of him whether he liked or disliked all or any of the Larkins cousins. It was rather attractive to make them laugh anyhow; they laughed at anything.

There they were tugging at his mind, and the funeral tugging at his mind too, and the sense of himself as Chief Mourner in a brand-new silk hat with a broad mourning band. He watched the ceremony and missed his responses, and strange feelings twisted at his heartstrings.

§ 5

Mr. Polly walked back to the house because he wanted to be alone. Miriam and Minnie would have accompanied him, but finding Uncle Pentstemon beside the Chief Mourner they went on in front.

"You're wise," said Uncle Pentstemon.

"Glad you think so," said Mr. Polly, rousing himself to talk.

"I likes a bit of walking before a meal," said Uncle Pentstemon, and made a kind of large hiccup. "That sherry rises," he remarked. "Grocer's stuff, I expect."

He went on to ask how much the funeral might be costing, and seemed pleased to find Mr. Polly didn't know.

"In that case," he said impressively, "it's pretty certain to cost more'n you expect, my boy."

He meditated for a time. "I've seen a mort of undertakers," he declared; "a mort of undertakers."

The Larkins girls attracted his attention.

"Lets lodgin's and chars," he commented. "Least-ways she goes out to cook dinners. And *look* at 'em! Dressed up to the nines. If it ain't borryd clothes, that is. And they goes out to work at a factory!"

"Did you know my father much, Uncle Pentstemon?" asked Mr. Polly.

"Couldn't stand Lizzie throwin' herself away like that," said Uncle Pentstemon, and repeated his hiccup on a larger scale.

"That *weren't* good sherry," said Uncle Pentstemon, with the first note of pathos Mr. Polly had detected in his quavering voice.

The funeral in the rather cold wind had proved wonderfully appetising, and every eye brightened at the sight of the cold collation that was now spread in the front room. Mrs. Johnson was very brisk, and Mr. Polly, when he re-entered the house, found the party sitting down.

"Come along, Alfred," cried the hostess cheerfully. "We can't very well begin without you. Have you got the bottled beer ready to open, Bessie? Uncle, you'll have a drop of whisky, I expect."

"Put it where I can mix for myself; I can't bear wimmin's mixing," said Uncle Pentstemon, placing his hat very carefully out of harm's way on the bookcase.

There were two cold boiled chickens, which Johnson carved with great care and justice, and a nice piece of ham, some brawn, and a steak-and-kidney pie, a large bowl of salad and several sorts of pickles, and afterwards some cold apple tart, jam roll, and a good piece of Stilton cheese, lots of bottled beer, some lemonade for the ladies, and milk for Master Punt: a very bright and satisfying meal. Mr. Polly found himself seated between Mrs. Punt, who was much preoccupied with Master Punt's table manners, and one of Mrs. Johnson's school friends, who was exchanging reminiscences with Mrs. Johnson of school-days and news of how various common friends had changed and married. Opposite him was Miriam and another of the early Johnson circle, and also he had brawn to carve, and there was hardly room for the helpful Bessie to pass behind his chair, so that altogether his mind would have been amply distracted from any mortuary broodings, even if a wordy warfare about the education of the modern young woman had not sprung up between Uncle Pentstemon and Mrs. Larkins, and threatened for a time, in spite of a word or so in season from Johnson, to wreck all the harmony of the sad occasion.

The general effect was after this fashion:

First an impression of Mrs. Punt on the right, speaking in a refined undertone: "You didn't, I suppose, Mr. Polly, think to 'ave your poor dear father *post-mortemed?*"

Lady on the left side, breaking in: "I was just reminding Grace of the dear dead days beyond recall."

Attempted reply to Mrs. Punt: "Didn't think of it

for a moment. Can't give you a piece of this brawn, can I?"

Fragment from the left: "Grace and Beauty they used to call us, and we used to sit at the same desk."

Mrs. Punt, breaking out suddenly: "Don't *swaller* your fork, Willie—You see, Mr. Polly, I used to have a young gentleman, a medical student, lodging with me——"

Voice from down the table with a large softness: "'Am, Elfred? I didn't give you very much 'am."

Bessie became evident at the back of Mr. Polly's chair, struggling wildly to get past. Mr. Polly did his best to be helpful. "Can you get past? Lemme sit forward a bit. Urr-oo! Right-o!"

Lady to the left going on valiantly and speaking to every one who cared to listen, while Mrs. Johnson beamed beside her: "There she used to sit as bold as brass, and the fun she used to make of things no one *could* believe—knowing her now. She used to make faces at the mistress through the——"

Mrs. Punt, keeping steadily on: "The contents of the stummik at any rate *ought* to be examined."

Voice of Mrs. Johnson: "Elfrid, pass the mustid down."

Miriam, leaning across the table: "Elfrid!"

"Once she got us all kept in. The whole school!"

Miriam, more insistently: "Elfrid!"

Uncle Pentstemon, raising his voice defiantly: "Trounce 'er again I would if she did as much now. That I would. Dratted mischief!"

Miriam, catching Mr. Polly's eye: "Elfrid! This lady knows Canterbury. I been telling her you been there."

Mr. Polly: "Glad you know it."

The lady, shouting: "I like it."

Mrs. Larkins, raising her voice: "I won't 'ave my girls spoken of, not by nobody, old *or* young."

POP! imperfectly located.

Mr. Johnson, at large : "*Ain't* the beer up! It's the 'eated room."

Bessie : "'Scuse me, Sir, passing so soon again, but—" Rest inaudible. Mr. Polly, accommodating himself : "Urr-oo! Right? Right-o!"

The knives and forks, probably by some secret common agreement, clash and clatter together, and drown every other sound.

"Nobody 'ad the least idea 'ow 'E died—nobody. . . . Willie, don't *golp* so. You ain't in a 'urry, are you? You don't want to ketch a train, or anything— golping like that!"

"D'you remember, Grace, 'ow one day we 'ad writing lesson . . ."

"Nicer girls no one ever 'ad— though I say it who shouldn't."

Mrs. Johnson, in a shrill, clear, hospitable voice : "Harold, won't Mrs. Larkins 'ave a teeny bit more fowl?"

Mr. Polly was rising to the situation. "Or some brawn, Mrs. Larkins?" Catching Uncle Pentstemon's eye : "Can't send *you* some brawn, Sir?"

"Elfrid!"

Loud hiccup from Uncle Pentstemon, momentary consternation, followed by giggle from Annie.

The narration at Mr. Polly's elbow pursued a quiet but relentless course. "Directly the new doctor came in, he said, 'Everything must be took out and put in spirits—everything.'"

Willie—audible ingurgitation.

The narration on the left was flourishing up to a climax. "Ladies, she sez, dip their pens *in* their ink and keep their noses out of it."

"Elfrid!" persuasively.

"Certain people may cast snacks at other people's daughters, never having had any of their own, though two poor souls of wives dead and buried through their goings on——"

Johnson, ruling the storm: "We don't want old scores dug up on such a day as this——"

"Old scores you may call them, but worth a dozen of them that put them to their rest, poor dears."

"Elfrid!" with a note of remonstrance.

"If you choke yourself, my lord, not another mouthful do you 'ave. No nice puddin'! Nothing!"

"And kept us in, she did, every afternoon for a week!"

It seemed to be the end, and Mr. Polly replied, with an air of being profoundly impressed, "Really!"

"Elfrid!" a little disheartened.

"And then they 'ad it! They found he'd swallowed the very key to unlock the drawer——"

"Then don't let people go casting snacks!"

"*Who's* casting snacks?"

"Elfrid! This lady wants to know, 'ave the Prossers left Canterbury?"

"No wish to make myself disagreeable, not to God's 'umblest worm——"

"Alf, you aren't very busy with that brawn up there!"

And so on for the hour.

The general effect upon Mr. Polly at the time was at once confusing and exhilarating; but it led him to eat copiously and carelessly, and long before the end, when after an hour and a quarter a movement took the party, and it pushed away its cheese-plates and rose sighing and stretching from the remains of the repast, little streaks and bands of dyspeptic irritation and melancholy were darkening the serenity of his mind.

He stood between the mantel-shelf and the window —the blinds were up now—and the Larkins sisters clustered about him. He battled with the oncoming depression, and forced himself to be extremely facetious about two noticeable rings on Annie's hand. "They ain't real," said Annie coquettishly. "Got 'em out of a prize packet."

"Prize packet in trousers, I expect," said Mr. Polly, and awakened inextinguishable laughter.

"Oh, the Things you say!" said Minnie, slapping his shoulder.

Something he had quite extraordinarily forgotten came into his head.

"Bless my heart!" he cried, suddenly serious.

"What's the matter?" asked Johnson.

"Ought to have gone back to shop three days ago. They'll make no end of a row!"

"Lor', you *are* a treat!" said Cousin Annie, and screamed with laughter at a delicious idea. "You'll get the Chuck," she said.

Mr. Polly made a convulsive grimace at her.

"I'll die!" she said. "I don't believe you care a bit."

Feeling a little disorganised by her hilarity and a shocked expression that had come to the face of Cousin Miriam, he made some indistinct excuse and went out through the back room and scullery into the little garden. The cool air and a very slight drizzle of rain was a relief—anyhow. But the black mood of the replete dyspeptic had come upon him. His soul darkened hopelessly. He walked with his hands in his pockets down the path between the rows of exceptionally cultured peas, and unreasonably, overwhelmingly, he was smitten by sorrow for his father. The heady noise and muddle and confused excitement of the feast passed from him like a curtain drawn away. He thought of that hot and angry and struggling creature who had tugged and sworn so foolishly at the sofa upon the twisted staircase, and who was now lying still and hidden at the bottom of a wall-sided, oblong pit, beside the heaped gravel that would presently cover him. The stillness of it! the wonder of it! the infinite reproach! Hatred for all these people—all of them—possessed Mr. Polly's soul.

"Hen-witted gigglers," said Mr. Polly.

He went down to the fence, and stood with his hands on it, staring away at nothing. He stayed there for what seemed a long time. From the house came a sound of raised voices that subsided, and then Mrs. Johnson calling for Bessie.

"Gowlish gusto," said Mr. Polly. "Jumping it in. Funererial Games. Don't hurt him, of course. Doesn't matter to *him*. . . ."

Nobody missed Mr. Polly for a long time.

When at last he reappeared among them his eye was almost grim, but nobody noticed his eye. They were looking at watches, and Johnson was being omniscient about trains. They seemed to discover Mr. Polly afresh just at the moment of parting, and said a number of more or less appropriate things. But Uncle Pentstemon was far too worried about his rush basket, which had been carelessly mislaid, he seemed to think with larcenous intentions, to remember Mr. Polly at all. Mrs. Johnson had tried to fob him off with a similar but inferior basket—his own had one handle mended with string according to a method of peculiar virtue and inimitable distinction known only to himself—and the old gentleman had taken her attempt as the gravest reflection upon his years and intelligence. Mr. Polly was left very largely to the Larkins trio. Cousin Minnie became shameless, and kept kissing him good-bye—and then finding out it wasn't time to go. Cousin Miriam seemed to think her silly, and caught Mr. Polly's eye sympathetically. Cousin Annie ceased to giggle, and lapsed into a nearly sentimental state. She said with real feeling that she had enjoyed the funeral more than words could tell.

CHAPTER THE
FIFTH

Romance

§ 1

MR. POLLY returned to Clapham from the
funeral celebrations prepared for trouble, and took his
dismissal in a manly spirit.

"You've merely antiseparated me by a hair," he said
politely.

And he told them in the dormitory that he meant
to take a little holiday before his next crib, though a
certain inherited reticence suppressed the fact of the
legacy.

"You'll do that all right," said Ascough, the head
of the boot-shop. "It's quite the fashion just at
present. Six Weeks in Wonderful Wood Street.
They're running excursions. . . ."

"A little holiday"; that was the form his sense of
wealth took first—it made a little holiday possible.
Holidays were his life, and the rest merely adulterated
living. And now he might take a little holiday and
have money for railway fares and money for meals, and

459

money for inns. But— He wanted someone to take the holiday with.

For a time he cherished a design of hunting up Parsons, getting him to throw up his situation, and going with him to Stratford-on-Avon and Shrewsbury, and the Welsh mountains and the Wye, and a lot of places like that, for a really gorgeous, careless, illimitable old holiday of a month. But, alas! Parsons had gone from the St. Paul's Churchyard outfitter's long ago, and left no address.

Polly tried to think he would be almost as happy wandering alone, but he knew better. He had dreamt of casual encounters with delightfully interesting people by the wayside—even romantic encounters. Such things happened in Chaucer and "Bocashiew"; they happened with extreme facility in Mr. Richard le Gallienne's very detrimental book, "The Quest of the Golden Girl," which he had read at Canterbury; but he had no confidence they would happen in England—to him.

When, a month later, he came out of the Clapham side door at last into the bright sunshine of a fine London day, with a dazzling sense of limitless freedom upon him, he did nothing more adventurous than order the cabman to drive to Waterloo, and there take a ticket to Easewood.

He wanted—what *did* he want most in life? I think his distinctive craving is best expressed as fun—fun in companionship. He had already spent a pound or two upon three select feasts to his fellow assistants, sprat suppers they were, and there had been a great and very successful Sunday pilgrimage to Richmond, by Wandsworth and Wimbledon's open common, a trailing garrulous company walking about a solemnly happy host, to wonderful cold meat and salad at the Roebuck, a bowl of punch, punch! and a bill to correspond; but now it was a week-day, and he went down to Easewood with his bag and portmanteau in a solitary compartment, and looked out of the window upon a world in which every possible congenial seemed either toiling in a situation or else looking for one with a gnawing and hopelessly preoccupying anxiety. He stared out of the window at the exploitation roads of suburbs and rows of houses all very much alike, either emphatically and impatiently TO LET, or full of rather busy unsocial people. Near Wimbledon he had a glimpse of golf-links, and saw two elderly gentlemen, who, had they chosen, might have been gentlemen of grace and leisure, addressing themselves to smite hunted little white balls great distances with the utmost bitterness and dexterity. Mr. Polly could not understand them.

Every road, he remarked as freshly as though he had never observed it before, was bordered by inflexible palings or iron fences or severely disciplined hedges. He wondered if perhaps abroad there might be beautifully careless, unenclosed highroads. Perhaps after all the best way of taking a holiday is to go abroad.

He was haunted by the memory of what was either a half-forgotten picture or a dream; a carriage was drawn up by the wayside and four beautiful people, two men and two women graciously dressed, were dancing a formal ceremonious dance, full of bows and curtseys, to the music of a wandering fiddler they had encountered. They had been driven one way and he walking another—a happy encounter with this obvious result. They might have come straight out of happy Theleme, whose motto is : " Do what thou wilt." The driver had taken his two sleek horses out; they grazed unchallenged; and he sat on a stone clapping time with his hands while the fiddler played. The shade of the trees did not altogether shut out the sunshine, the grass in the wood was lush and full of still daffodils, the turf they danced on was starred with daisies.

Mr. Polly, dear heart! firmly believed that things like that could and did happen—somewhere. Only it puzzled him that morning that he never saw them happening. Perhaps they happened south of Guildford! Perhaps they happened in Italy. Perhaps they ceased to happen a hundred years ago. Perhaps they happened just round the corner——on week-days when all good Mr. Pollys are safely shut up in shops. And so dreaming of delightful impossibilities until his heart ached for them, he was rattled along in the suburban train to Johnson's discreet home and the briskly stimulating welcome of Mrs. Johnson.

§ 2

Mr. Polly translated his restless craving for joy and leisure into Harold Johnsonese by saying that he meant to look about him for a bit before going into another situation. It was a decision Johnson very warmly approved. It was arranged that Mr. Polly should occupy his former room and board with the Johnsons in consideration of a weekly payment of eighteen shillings. And the next morning Mr. Polly went out early and reappeared with a purchase, a safety bicycle which he proposed to study and master in the sandy lane below the Johnsons' house. But over the struggles that preceded his mastery it is humane to draw a veil.

And also Mr. Polly bought a number of books; Rabelais for his own, and "The Arabian Nights," the works of Sterne, a pile of "Tales from Blackwood," cheap in a second-hand book-shop, the plays of William Shakespear, a second-hand copy of Belloc's "Path to Rome," an odd volume of "Purchas his Pilgrimes" and "The Life and Death of Jason."

"Better get yourself a good book on bookkeeping," said Johnson, turning over perplexing pages.

A belated spring, to make up for lost time, was now advancing with great strides. Sunshine and a stirring wind were poured out over the land, fleets of towering clouds sailed upon urgent tremendous missions across the blue sea of heaven, and presently Mr. Polly was riding a little unstably along unfamiliar Surrey roads, wondering always what was round the next corner, and marking the blackthorn and looking out for the first white flower-buds of the may. He was perplexed and distressed, as indeed are all right-thinking souls, that there is no may in early May.

He did not ride at the even pace sensible people use, who have marked out a journey from one place to another, and settled what time it will take them. He rode at variable speeds, and always as though he was looking for something that missing left life attractive still, but a little wanting in significance. And sometimes he was so unreasonably happy he had to whistle and sing, and sometimes he was incredibly, but not at all painfully, sad. His indigestion vanished with air and exercise, and it was quite pleasant in the evening to stroll about the garden with Johnson and discuss plans for the future. Johnson was full of ideas. Moreover, Mr. Polly had marked the road that led to Stamton, that rising popular suburb; and as his bicycle legs grew strong his wheel, with a sort of inevitableness, carried him towards a row of houses in a back street in which his Larkins cousins made their home together.

He was received with great enthusiasm.

The street was a dingy little street, a *cul-de-sac* of very small houses in a row, each with an almost flattened bow window and a blistered brown door with a black knocker. He poised his bright new bicycle against the window, and knocked and stood waiting, and felt himself in his straw hat and black serge suit a very pleasant and prosperous-looking figure. The door was opened by Cousin Miriam. She was wearing a bluish print dress that brought out a kind of sallow warmth in her skin, and although it was nearly four o'clock in the afternoon her sleeves were tucked up, as if for some domestic task, above her elbows, showing her rather slender but very shapely yellowish arms. The loosely pinned bodice confessed a delicately rounded neck.

For a moment she regarded him with suspicion and a faint hostility, and then recognition dawned in her eyes.

"Why!" she said, "it's Cousin Elfrid!"

"Thought I'd look you up," he said.

"Fancy you coming to see us like this!" she answered.

They stood confronting one another for a moment, while Miriam collected herself for the unexpected emergency.

"Exploratious menanderings," said Mr. Polly, indicating the bicycle.

Miriam's face betrayed no appreciation of the remark.

"Wait a moment," she said, coming to a rapid decision, "and I'll tell Ma."

She closed the door on him abruptly, leaving him a little surprised in the street. "Ma!" he heard her calling, and a swift speech followed, the import of which he didn't catch. Then she reappeared. It seemed but an instant, but she was changed; the arms had vanished into sleeves, the apron had gone, a certain pleasing disorder of the hair had been at least reproved.

"I didn't mean to shut you out," she said, coming out upon the step. "I just told Ma. How are you, Elfrid? You *are* looking well. I didn't know you rode a bicycle. Is it a new one?"

She leaned upon his bicycle. "Bright it is!" she said. "What a trouble you must have to keep it clean!"

Mr. Polly was aware of a rustling transit along the passage, and of the house suddenly full of hushed but strenuous movement.

"It's plated mostly," said Mr. Polly.

"What d'you carry in that little bag thing?" she asked, and then branched off to: "We're all in a mess to-day, you know. It's my cleaning-up day to-day. I'm not a bit tidy, I know, but I *do* like to 'ave a go in at things now and then. *They'd* leave everything, I believe. If I let 'em. . . . You got to take us as you find us, Elfrid. Mercy we wasn't all out." She paused. She was talking against time. "I *am* glad to see you again," she repeated.

"Couldn't keep away," said Mr. Polly gallantly. "Had to come over and see my pretty cousins again."

Miriam did not answer for a moment. She coloured deeply. "You *do say* things!" she said.

She stared at Mr. Polly, and his unfortunate sense of fitness made him nod his head towards her, regard her firmly with a round brown eye, and add impressively: "I don't say *which* of them."

Her answering expression made him realise for an instant the terrible dangers he trifled with. Avidity flared up in her eyes. Minnie's voice came happily to dissolve the situation.

"'Ello, Elfrid!" she said from the door-step.

Her hair was just passably tidy, and she was a little effaced by a red blouse, but there was no mistaking the genuine brightness of her welcome.

He was to come in to tea, and Mrs. Larkins, exuberantly genial in a floriferous but dingy flannel dressing-gown appeared to confirm that. He brought in his bicycle and put it in a narrow, empty, dingy passage, and every one crowded into a small, untidy kitchen, whose table had been hastily cleared of the débris of the midday repast.

"You must come in 'ere," said Mrs. Larkins, "for Miriam's turning out the front room. I never did see such a girl for cleanin' up. Miriam's 'Oliday's a scrub. You've caught us on the 'Op, as the sayin' is, but Welcome all the same. Pity Annie's at work to-day; she won't be 'ome till seven."

Miriam put chairs and attended to the fire; Minnie edged up to Mr. Polly and said, "I *am* glad to see you again, Elfrid," with a warm contiguous intimacy that betrayed a broken tooth. Mrs. Larkins got out tea-things, and descanted on the noble simplicity of their

lives, and how he "mustn't mind our simple ways."
They enveloped Mr. Polly with a geniality that intoxicated his amiable nature; he insisted upon helping
to lay the things, and created enormous laughter by
pretending not to know where plates and knives and
cups ought to go. "Who'm I going to sit next?" he
said, and developed voluminous amusement by attempts
to arrange the plates so that he could rub elbows with
all three. Mrs. Larkins had to sit down in the windsor
chair by the grandfather clock (which was dark with
dirt, and not going) to laugh at her ease at his well-
acted perplexity.

They got seated at last, and Mr. Polly struck a vein
of humour in telling them how he learned to ride the
bicycle. He found the mere repetition of the word
"wabble" sufficient to produce almost inextinguishable
mirth.

"No foreseeing little accidentulous misadventures,"
he said, "none whatever."

(Giggle from Minnie.)

"Stout elderly gentleman—shirt-sleeves—large straw
waste-paper basket sort of hat—starts to cross the road
—going to the oil-shop—prodic refreshment of oil-
can——"

"Don't say you run 'im down," said Mrs. Larkins,
gasping. "Don't say you run 'im down, Elfrid!"

"Run 'im down! Not me, Madam; I never run
anything down. Wabble. Ring the bell. Wabble,
wabble——"

(Laughter and tears.)

"No one's going to run him down. Hears the bell!
Wabble. Gust of wind. Off comes the hat smack into
the wheel. Wabble. *Lord! what's* going to happen?
Hat across the road, old gentleman after it, bell, shriek.
He ran into me. Didn't ring his bell, hadn't *got* a
bell—just ran into me. Over I went clinging to his
venerable head. Down he went with me clinging to
him. Oil-can blump, blump into the road."

(Interlude while Minnie is attended to for crumb in the windpipe.)

"Well, what happened to the old man with the oil-can?" said Mrs. Larkins.

"We sat about among the debreece and had a bit of an argument. I told him he oughtn't to come out wearing such a dangerous hat—flying at things. Said if he couldn't control his hat, he ought to leave it at home. High old jawbacious argument we had, I tell you. 'I tell you, Sir—' 'I tell *you*, Sir.' Waw-waw-waw. Infuriacious. But that's the sort of thing that's constantly happening, you know—on a bicycle. People run into you, hens, and cats, and dogs, and things. Everything seems to have its mark on you; everything."

"*You* never run into anything."

"Never, Swelpme," said Mr. Polly very solemnly.

"Never, 'E say!" squealed Minnie. "Hark at 'im!" and relapsed into a condition that urgently demanded back-thumping. "Don't be so silly," said Miriam, thumping hard.

Mr. Polly had never been such a social success before. They hung upon his every word—and laughed. What a family they were for laughter! And he loved laughter. The background he apprehended dimly; it was very much the sort of background his life had always had. There was a threadbare table-cloth on the table, and the slop-basin and teapot did not go with the cups and saucers, the plates were different again, the knives worn down, the butter lived in a greenish glass dish of its own. Behind was a dresser hung with spare and miscellaneous crockery, with a work-box and an untidy work-basket; there was an ailing musk-plant in the window, and the tattered and blotched wall-paper was covered by bright-coloured grocers' almanacs. Feminine wrappings hung from pegs upon the door, and the floor was covered with a varied collection of fragments of oilcloth. The windsor chair he sat in was unstable—and presently afforded material for humour.

"Steady, old nag," he said; "Whoa, my friskiacious palfrey!"

"The things he says! You never know what he won't say next!"

§ 3

."You ain't talkin' of goin'!" cried Mrs. Larkins.

"Supper at eight."

"Stay to supper with *us,* now you *'ave* come over," said Mrs. Larkins, with corroborating cries from Minnie. "'Ave a bit of a walk with the gals, and then come back to supper. You might all go and meet Annie while I straighten up, and lay things out."

"You're not to go touching the front room, mind," said Miriam.

"*Who's* going to touch yer front room?" said Mrs. Larkins, apparently forgetful for the moment of Mr. Polly.

Both girls dressed with some care while Mrs. Larkins sketched the better side of their characters, and then the three young people went out to see something of Stamton. In the streets their risible mood gave way to a self-conscious propriety that was particularly evident in Miriam's bearing. They took Mr. Polly to the Stamton wreckery-ation ground—that at least was what they called it—with its handsome custodian's cottage, its asphalt paths, its Jubilee drinking-fountain, its clumps of wallflowers and daffodils, its charmingly artistic notice-boards with green borders and "art" lettering, and so to the new cemetery and a distant view of the Surrey hills, and round by the gas-works to the canal, to the factory that presently disgorged a surprised and radiant Annie.

"'El-*lo!*" said Annie.

It is very pleasant to every properly constituted mind to be a centre of amiable interest for one's fellow creatures; and when one is a young man conscious of becoming mourning and a certain wit, and the fellow creatures are three young and ardent and sufficiently expressive young women who dispute for the honour of walking by one's side, one may be excused a secret exaltation. They did dispute.

"I'm going to 'ave 'im now," said Annie. "You two've been 'aving 'im all the safternoon. Besides, I've got something to say to 'im."

She had something to say to him. It came presently.

"I say," she said abruptly, "I *did* get them rings out of a prize packet."

"What rings?" asked Mr. Polly.

"What you saw at your poor father's funeral. You made out they meant something. They didn't— straight."

"Then some people have been very remiss about their chances," said Mr. Polly, understanding.

"They haven't had any chances," said Annie. "I don't believe in making oneself too free with people."

"Nor me," said Mr. Polly.

"I may be a bit larky and cheerful in my manner," Annie admitted. "But it don't *mean* anything. I ain't that sort."

"Right-o," said Mr. Polly.

§ 4

It was past ten when Mr. Polly found himself riding back towards Easewood in a broad moonlight and with a little Japanese lantern dangling from his handle-bar, making a fiery circle of pinkish light on and round-about his front wheel. He was mightily pleased with himself and the day. There had been four-ale to drink at supper mixed with ginger beer, very free and jolly in a jug. No shadow fell upon the agreeable excitement of his mind until he faced the anxious and reproachful face of Johnson, who had been sitting up for him, smoking and trying to read the odd volume of "Purchas his Pilgrimes"—about the monk who went into Sarmatia and saw those limitless Tartar carts that carried tents.

"Not had an accident, Elfrid?" said Johnson.

The weakness of Mr. Polly's character came out in his reply.

"Not much," he said. "Pedal got a bit loose in Stamton, O' Man. Couldn't ride it; so I looked up the cousins while I waited."

"Not the Larkins lot?"

"Yes."

Johnson yawned hugely, and asked for and was given friendly particulars.

"Well," he said, "better get to bed. I been reading that book of yours; rum stuff. Can't make it out quite. Quite out of date, I should say, if you asked me."

"That's all right, O' Man," said Mr. Polly.

"Not a bit of use for anything that I can see."

"Not a bit."

"See any shops in Stamton?"

"Nothing to speak of," said Mr. Polly. "Goo'-night, O' Man."

Before and after this brief conversation his mind ran on his cousins very warmly and prettily in the vein of high spring. Mr. Polly had been drinking at the poisoned fountains of English literature, fountains so unsuited to the needs of a decent clerk or shopman, fountains charged with the dangerous suggestion that it becomes a man of gaiety and spirit to make love gallantly and rather carelessly. It seemed to him that evening to be handsome and humorous and practicable to make love to all his cousins. It wasn't that he liked any of them particularly, but he liked something about them. He liked their youth and femininity, their resolute high spirits, and their interest in him.

They laughed at nothing and knew nothing, and Minnie had lost a tooth, and Annie screamed and shouted; but they were interesting, intensely interesting.

And Miriam wasn't so bad as the others. He had kissed them all, and had been kissed in addition several times by Minnie—" oscoolatory exercises."

He buried his nose in his pillow and went to sleep —to dream of anything rather than getting on in the world, as a sensible young man in his position ought to have done.

§ 5

And now Mr. Polly began to lead a double life. With the Johnsons he professed to be inclined, but not so conclusively inclined as to be inconvenient, to get a shop for himself—to be, to use the phrase he preferred, "looking for an opening." He would ride off in the afternoon upon that research, remarking that he was going to "cast a strategical eye" on Chertsey or Weybridge. But if not all roads, still a great majority of them led by however devious ways to Stamton, and to laughter and increasing familiarity. Relations developed with Annie and Minnie and Miriam. Their various characters were increasingly interesting. The laughter became perceptibly less abundant, something of the fizz had gone from the first opening, still these visits remained wonderfully friendly and upholding. Then back he would come to grave and evasive discussions with Johnson.

Johnson was really anxious to get Mr. Polly "into something." His was a reserved, honest character, and he would really have preferred to see his lodger doing things for himself than receiving his money for housekeeping. He hated waste, anybody's waste, much more than he desired profit. But Mrs. Johnson was all for Mr. Polly's loitering. She seemed much the more human and likeable of the two to Mr. Polly.

He tried at times to work up enthusiasm for the various avenues to well-being his discussion with Johnson opened. But they remained disheartening prospects. He imagined himself wonderfully smartened up, acquiring style and value in a London shop; but the picture was stiff and unconvincing. He tried to rouse himself to enthusiasm by the idea of his property increasing by leaps and bounds, by twenty pounds a year or so, let us say, each year, in a well-placed little shop, the corner shop Johnson favoured. There was a certain picturesque interest in imagining cutthroat economies, but his heart told him there would be little in practising them.

And then it happened to Mr. Polly that real Romance came out of dreamland into his life, intoxicated and gladdened him with sweet beautiful suggestions—and left him. She came and left him as that dear lady leaves so many of us, alas! not sparing him one jot or one tittle of the hollowness of her retreating aspect.

It was all the more to Mr. Polly's taste that the thing should happen as things happen in books.

In a resolute attempt not to get to Stamton that day, he had turned due southward from Easewood towards a country where the abundance of bracken jungles, lady's smock, stitchwort, bluebells, and grassy stretches by the wayside under shady trees does much to compensate the lighter type of mind for the absence of promising "openings." He turned aside from the road, wheeled his machine along a faintly marked attractive trail through bracken until he came to a heap of logs against a high old stone wall with a damaged coping and wallflower plants already gone to seed. He sat down, balanced the straw hat on a convenient lump of wood, lit a cigarette, and abandoned himself to agreeable musings and the friendly observation of a cheerful little brown-and-grey bird his stillness presently encouraged to approach him.

"This is All Right," said Mr. Polly softly to the little brown-and-grey bird. "Business—later."

He reflected that he might go on in this way for four or five years, and then be scarcely worse off than he had been in his father's lifetime.

"Vile Business," said Mr. Polly.

Then Romance appeared. Or to be exact, Romance became audible.

Romance began as a series of small but increasingly vigorous movements on the other side of the wall, then a voice murmuring, then as a falling of little fragments on the other side and as ten pink finger-tips, scarcely apprehended before Romance became startlingly and emphatically a leg, remained for a time a fine, slender, actively struggling limb, brown-stockinged, and wearing a brown toe-worn shoe, and then. . . . A handsome, red-haired girl wearing a short dress of blue linen was sitting astride the wall, panting, considerably disarranged by her climbing, and as yet unaware of Mr. Polly. . . .

His fine instincts made him turn his head away and assume an attitude of negligent contemplation, with his ears and mind alive to every sound behind him.

"Goodness!" said a voice, with a sharp note of surprise.

Mr. Polly was on his feet in an instant. "Dear me! Can I be of any assistance?" he said, with deferential gallantry.

"I don't know," said the young lady, and regarded him calmly with clear blue eyes. "I didn't know there was any one here," she added.

"Sorry," said Mr. Polly, "if I am intrudacious. I didn't know you didn't want me to be here."

She reflected for a moment on the word.

"It isn't that," she said, surveying him. "I oughtn't to get over the wall," she explained. "It's out of bounds; at least in term time. But this being holidays——"

Her manner placed the matter before him.

"Holidays is different," said Mr. Polly.

"I don't want to actually *break* the rules," she said.

"Leave them behind you," said Mr. Polly, with a catch of the breath, "where they are safe." And marvelling at his own wit and daring, and indeed trembling within himself, he held out a hand for her.

She brought another brown leg from the unknown, and arranged her skirt with a dexterity altogether feminine.

"I think I'll stay on the wall," she decided. "So long as some of me's in bounds——"

She continued to regard him with an irresistible smile of satisfaction. Mr. Polly smiled in return.

"You bicycle?" she said.

Mr. Polly admitted the fact, and she said she did too.

"All my people are in India," she explained. "It's beastly rot—I meant it's frightfully dull being left here alone."

"All *my* people," said Mr. Polly, "are in heaven!"

"I say!"

"Fact," said Mr. Polly. "Got nobody."

"And that's why——" She checked her artless comment on his mourning. "I say," she said in a sympathetic voice, "I am sorry. I really am. Was it a fire, or a ship—or something?"

Her sympathy was very delightful. He shook his head. "The ordinary tables of mortality," he said. "First one, and then another."

Behind his outward melancholy, delight was dancing wildly.

"Are *you* lonely?" asked the girl.

Mr. Polly nodded.

"I was just sitting there in melancholic rectrospectatiousness," he said, indicating the logs; and again a swift thoughtfulness swept across her face.

"There's no harm in our talking," she reflected.

"It's a kindness. Won't you get down?"

She reflected, and surveyed the turf below and the scene around, and him.

"I'll stay on the wall," she said, "if only for bounds' sake."

She certainly looked quite adorable on the wall. She had a fine neck and pointed chin that was particularly admirable from below, and pretty eyes and fine eye-

brows are never so pretty as when they look down upon
one. But no calculation of that sort, thank Heaven,
was going on beneath her ruddy shock of hair.

§ 6

"Let's talk," she said, and for a time they were both
tongue-tied.

Mr. Polly's literary proclivities had taught him that
under such circumstances a strain of gallantry was demanded. And something in his blood repeated that
lesson.

"You make me feel like one of those old knights,"
he said, "who rode about the country looking for
dragons and beautiful maidens and chivalresque adventures."

"Oh!" she said. "Why?"

"Beautiful maiden," he said.

She flushed under her freckles with the quick bright
flush those pretty red-haired people have. "Nonsense!"
she said.

"You are. I'm not the first to tell you that. A
beautiful maiden imprisoned in an enchanted school."

"*You* wouldn't think it enchanted."

"And here am I—clad in steel. Well, not exactly,
but my fiery war-horse is, anyhow. Ready to absquatulate all the dragons, and rescue you."

She laughed, a jolly laugh, that showed delightfully
gleaming teeth. "I wish you could *see* the dragons,"
she said, with great enjoyment. Mr. Polly felt they
were a sun's distance from the world of every day.

"Fly with me!" he dared.

She stared for a moment, and then went off into
peals of laughter. "You *are* funny!" she said. "Why,
I haven't known you five minutes."

"One doesn't—in this medevial world. My mind
is made up, anyhow."

He was proud and pleased with his joke, and quick

to change his key neatly. "I wish one could," he said.

"I wonder if people ever did."

"If there were people like you."

"We don't even know each other's names," she remarked, with a descent to matters of fact.

"Yours is the prettiest name in the world."

"How do you know?"

"It must be—anyhow."

"It *is* rather pretty, you know. It's Christabel."

"What did I tell you?"

"And yours?"

"Poorer than I deserve. It's Alfred."

"*I* can't call you Alfred."

"Well, Polly."

"It's a girl's name!"

For a moment he went out of tune. "I wish it was," he said, and could have bitten out his tongue at the Larkins sound of it.

"I shan't forget it," she remarked consolingly.

"I say," she said, in the pause that followed, "why are you riding about the country on a bicycle?"

"I'm doing it because I like it."

She sought to estimate his social status on her limited basis of experience. He stood leaning with one hand against the wall, looking up at her and tingling with daring thoughts. He was a littleish man, you must remember, but neither mean-looking nor unhandsome in those days, sunburnt by his holiday and now warmly flushed. He had an inspiration to simple speech that no practised trifler with love could have bettered. "There *is* love at first sight," he said, and said it sincerely.

She stared at him with eyes round and big with excitement.

"I think," she said slowly, and without any signs of fear or retreat, "I ought to get back over the wall."

"It needn't matter to you," he said; "I'm just a

nobody. But I know you are the best and most beautiful thing I've ever spoken to." His breath caught against something. "No harm in telling you that," he said.

"I should have to go back if I thought you were serious," she said after a pause, and they both smiled together.

After that they talked in a fragmentary way for some time. The blue eyes surveyed Mr. Polly with kindly curiosity from under a broad, finely modelled brow, much as an exceptionally intelligent cat might survey a new sort of dog. She meant to find out all about him. She asked questions that riddled the honest knight in armour below, and probed ever nearer to the hateful secret of the shop and his normal servitude. And when he made a flourish and mispronounced a word, a thoughtful shade passed like the shadow of a cloud across her face.

"Boom!" came the sound of a gong.

"Lordy!" cried the girl, and flashed a pair of brown legs at him and was gone.

Then her pink finger-tips reappeared, and the top of her red hair. "Knight," she cried from the other side of the wall. "Knight there!"

"Lady!" he answered.

"Come again to-morrow."

"At your command. But——"

"Yes?"

"Just one finger."

"What do you mean?"

"To kiss."

The rustle of retreating footsteps and silence. . . .

But after he had waited next day for twenty minutes she reappeared, a little out of breath with the effort to surmount the wall, and head first this time. And it seemed to him she was lighter and more daring and altogether prettier than the dreams and enchanted memories that had filled the interval.

§ 7

From the first to last their acquaintance lasted ten days, but into that time Mr. Polly packed ten years of dreams.

" He don't seem," said Johnson, " to take a serious interest in anything. That shop at the corner's bound to be snapped up if he don't look out."

The girl and Mr. Polly did not meet on every one of those ten days; one was Sunday and she could not come, and on the eighth the school reassembled and she made vague excuses. All their meetings amounted to this, that she sat on the wall, more or less in bounds as she expressed it, and let Mr. Polly fall in love with her and try to express it below. She sat in a state of irresponsible exaltation, watching him, and at intervals prodding a vivisecting point of encouragement into him, with that strange passive cruelty which is natural and proper in her sex and age.

And Mr. Polly fell in love, as though the world had given way beneath him and he had dropped through into another, into a world of luminous clouds and of a desolate, hopeless wilderness of desiring and of wild valleys of unreasonable ecstasy, a world whose infinite miseries were finer and in some inexplicable way sweeter than the purest gold of the daily life, whose joys— they were indeed but the merest remote glimpses of joy —were brighter than a dying martyr's vision of heaven. Her smiling face looked down upon him out of the sky, her careless pose was the living body of life. It was senseless, it was utterly foolish, but all that was best and richest in Mr. Polly's nature broke like a wave and foamed up at the girl's feet, and died, and never touched her. And she sat on the wall and marvelled at him, and was amused, and once, suddenly moved and wrung by his pleading, she bent down rather shame-facedly and gave him a freckled, tennis-blistered little paw to kiss. And she looked into his eyes and suddenly felt a perplexity, a curious swimming of the mind that made her recoil and stiffen, and wonder afterwards and dream. . . .

And then with some instinct of self-protection she went and told her three best friends, great students of character all, of this remarkable phenomenon she had discovered on the other side of the wall.

"Look here," said Mr. Polly, "I'm wild for the love of you! I can't keep up this gesticulatious game any more. I'm not a Knight. Treat me as a human man. You may sit up there smiling, but I'd die in torments to have you mine for an hour. I'm nobody and nothing. But look here! Will you wait for me five years? You're just a girl yet, and it wouldn't be hard."

"Shut up!" said Christabel, in an aside he did not hear, and something he did not see touched her hand.

"I've always been just dilletentytating about till now, but I could work. I've just woke up. Wait till I've got a chance with the money I've got."

"But you haven't got much money!"

"I've got enough to take a chance with, some sort of chance. I'd find a chance. I'll do that, anyhow. I'll go away. I mean what I say. I'll stop trifling and shirking. If I don't come back it won't matter. If I do——"

Her expression had become uneasy. Suddenly she bent down towards him.

"Don't!" she said in an undertone.

"Don't—what?"

"Don't go on like this! You're different. Go on being the knight who wants to kiss my hand as his— what did you call it?" The ghost of a smile curved her face. "Gurdrum!"

"But——"

Then through a pause they both stared at each other, listening.

16

A muffled tumult on the other side of the wall asserted itself.

"Shut *up,* Rosie!" said a voice.

"I tell you I will see! I can't half hear. Give me a leg up!"

"You Idiot! He'll see you. You're spoiling everything."

The bottom dropped out of Mr. Polly's world. He felt as people must feel who are going to faint.

"You've got some one—" he said, aghast.

She found life inexpressible to Mr. Polly. She addressed some unseen hearers. "You filthy little Beasts!" she cried, with a sharp note of agony in her voice, and swung herself back over the wall and vanished. There was a squeal of pain and fear, and a swift, fierce altercation.

For a couple of seconds he stood agape.

Then a wild resolve to confirm his worse sense of what was on the other side of the wall made him seize a log, put it against the stones, clutch the parapet with insecure fingers, and lug himself to a momentary balance on the wall.

Romance and his goddess had vanished.

A red-haired girl with a pigtail was wringing the wrist of a schoolfellow, who shrieked with pain and cried, "Mercy! mercy! O-o-o! Christabel!"

"You Idiot!" cried Christabel. "You giggling Idiot!"

Two other young ladies made off through the beech trees from this outburst of savagery.

Then the grip of Mr. Polly's fingers gave, and he hit his chin against the stones and slipped clumsily to the ground again, scraping his cheek against the wall, and hurting his shin against the log by which he had reached the top. Just for a moment he crouched against the wall.

He swore, staggered to the pile of logs, and sat down.

He remained very still for some time, with his lips pressed together.

"Fool!" he said at last. "You Blithering Fool!" and began to rub his shin as though he had just discovered his bruises.

Afterwards he found his face was wet with blood —which was none the less red stuff from the heart because it came from slight abrasions.

CHAPTER THE SIXTH

Miriam

§ 1

IT is an illogical consequence of one human being's ill-treatment that we should fly immediately to another, but that is the way with us. It seemed to Mr. Polly that only a human touch could assuage the smart of his humiliation. Moreover, it had, for some undefined reason, to be a feminine touch, and the number of women in his world was limited.

He thought of the Larkins family—the Larkins whom he had not been near now for ten long days. Healing people they seemed to him now—healing, simple people. They had good hearts, and he had neglected them for a mirage. If he rode over to them he would be able to talk bosh, and laugh, and forget the whirl of memories and thoughts that was spinning round and round so unendurably in his brain.

"Law!" said Mrs. Larkins, "come in! You're quite a stranger, Elfrid!"

"Been seeing to business," said the unveracious Polly.

"None of 'em ain't at 'ome, but Miriam's just out to do a bit of shopping. Won't let me shop, she won't, because I'm so keerless. She's a wonderful manager, that girl. Minnie's got some work at the carpet place. 'Ope it won't make 'er ill again. She's the loving delikit sort, is Minnie. . . . Come into the front parlour. It's a bit untidy, but you got to take us as you find us. Wot you been doing to your face?"

"Bit of a scraze with the bicycle," said Mr. Polly.

"'Ow?"

"Trying to pass a carriage on the wrong side, and he drew up and ran me against a wall."

Mrs. Larkins scrutinised it. "You ought to 'ave some one look after your scrazes," she said. "That's all red and rough. It ought to be cold-creamed. Bring your bicycle into the passage and come in."

She "straightened up a bit." That is to say, she increased the dislocation of a number of scattered articles, put a work-basket on the top of several books, swept two or three dogs'-eared numbers of *The Lady's Own Novelist* from the table into the broken armchair, and proceeded to sketch together the tea-things with various such interpolations as: "Law, if I ain't forgot the butter!" All the while she talked of Annie's good spirits and cleverness with her millinery, and of Minnie's affection, and Miriam's relative love of order and management. Mr. Polly stood by the window uneasily, and thought how good and sincere was the Larkins' tone. It was well to be back again.

"You're a long time finding that shop of yours," said Mrs. Larkins.

"Don't do to be too precipitous," said Mr. Polly.

"No," said Mrs. Larkins, "once you got it you got it. Like choosing a 'usband. You better see you got it good. I kept Larkins 'esitating two years, I did, until I felt sure of him. A 'ansom man 'e was, as you can see by the looks of the girls, but 'ansom is as 'ansom does. You'd like a bit of jam to your tea, I expect?

I 'ope they'll keep *their* men waiting when the time comes. I tell them if they think of marrying, it only shows they don't know when they're well off. Here's Miriam!"

Miriam entered with several parcels in a net, and a peevish expression. "Mother," she said, "you might 'ave prevented my going out with the net with the broken handle. I've been cutting my fingers with the string all the way 'ome." Then she discovered Mr. Polly and her face brightened.

"'Ello, Elfrid!" she said. "Where you been all this time?"

"Looking round," said Mr. Polly.

"Found a shop?"

"One or two likely ones. But it takes time."

"You've got the wrong cups, Mother."

She went into the kitchen, disposed of her purchases, and returned with the right cups. "What you done to your face, Elfrid?" she asked, and came and scrutinised his scratches. "All rough it is."

He repeated his story of the accident, and she was sympathetic in a pleasant, homely way.

"You *are* quiet to-day," she said, as they sat down to tea.

"Meditations," said Mr. Polly.

Quite by accident he touched her hand on the table, and she answered his touch.

"Why not?" thought Mr. Polly, and looking up, caught Mrs. Larkins' eye and flushed guiltily. But Mrs. Larkins, with unusual restraint, said nothing. She made a grimace, enigmatical, but in its essence friendly.

Presently Minnie came in with some vague grievance against the manager of the carpet-making place about his method of estimating piece-work. Her account was redundant, defective, and highly technical, but redeemed by a certain earnestness. "I'm never within sixpence of what I reckon to be," she said. "It's a bit too 'ot." Then Mr. Polly, feeling that he was being conspicuously dull, launched into a description of the shop he was looking for and the shops he had seen. His mind warmed up as he talked.

"Found your tongue again," said Mrs. Larkins.

He had. He began to embroider the subject and work upon it. For the first time it assumed picturesque and desirable qualities in his mind. It stimulated him to see how readily and willingly they accepted his sketches. Bright ideas appeared in his mind from nowhere. He was suddenly enthusiastic.

"When I get this shop of mine I shall have a cat. Must make a home for a cat, you know."

"What, to catch the mice?" said Mrs. Larkins.

"No—sleep in the window. A venerable signor of a cat. Tabby. Cat's no good if it isn't a tabby. Cat I'm going to have, and a canary! Didn't think of that before, but a cat and a canary seem to go, you know. Summer weather I shall sit at breakfast in the little room behind the shop, sun streaming in the window to rights, cat on a chair, canary singing, and—Mrs. Polly. . . ."

"'Ello!" said Mrs. Larkins.

"Mrs. Polly frying an extra bit of bacon. Bacon singing, cat singing, canary singing, kettle singing. Mrs. Polly——"

"But who's Mrs. Polly going to be?" said Mrs. Larkins.

"Figment of imagination, M'am," said Mr. Polly. "Put in to fill up picture. No face to figure—as yet. Still, that's how it will be, I can assure you. I think I must have a bit of garden. Johnson's the man for a garden, of course," he said, going off at a tangent, "but I don't mean a fierce sort of garden. Earnest industry. Anxious moments. Fervous digging. Shan't go in for that sort of garden, M'am. No! Too much Backache for me. My garden will be just a patch of 'sturtiums and sweetpea. Red-bricked yard, clothes-line. Trellis put up in odd time. Humorous wind-vane. Creeper up the back of the house."

"Virginia creeper?" asked Miriam.

"Canary creeper," said Mr. Polly.

"You *will* 'ave it nice," said Miriam desirously.

"Rather," said Mr. Polly. "Ting-a-ling-a-ling. Shop!"

He straightened himself up, and they all laughed.

"Smart little shop," he said. "Counter. Desk. All complete. Umbrella-stand. Carpet on the floor. Cat asleep on the counter. Ties and hose on a rail over the counter. All right."

"I wonder you don't set about it right off," said Miriam.

"Mean to get it exactly right, M'am," said Mr. Polly.

"Have to have a Tom-cat," said Mr. Polly, and paused for an expectant moment. "Wouldn't do to open shop one morning, you know, and find the window full of kittens. Can't sell kittens. . . ."

When tea was over he was left alone with Minnie for a few minutes, and an odd intimation of an incident occurred that left Mr. Polly rather scared and shaken. A silence fell between them—an uneasy silence. He sat with his elbows n the table looking at her. All the way from Easewood to Stamton his erratic imagination had been running upon neat ways of proposing marriage. I don't know why it should have done, but it had. It was a kind of secret exercise that had not had any definite aim at the time, but which now recurred to him with extraordinary force. He couldn't think of anything in the world that wasn't the gambit to a proposal. It was almost irresistibly fascinating to think how immensely a few words from him would excite and revolutionise Minnie. She was sitting at the table with a work-basket among the tea-things, mending a glove in order to avoid her share of clearing away.

"I like cats," said Minnie, after a thoughtful pause. "I'm always saying to Mother, I wish we 'ad a cat. But we couldn't 'ave a cat 'ere—not with no yard."

"Never had a cat myself," said Mr. Polly. "No!"

"I'm fond of them," said Minnie.

"I like the look of them," said Mr. Polly. "Can't exactly call myself fond."

"I expect I shall get one some day. When about you get your shop."

"I shall have my shop all right before long," said Mr. Polly. "Trust me. Canary-bird and all."

She shook her head. "I shall get a cat first," she said. "You never mean anything you say."

"Might get 'em together," said Mr. Polly, with his sense of a neat thing outrunning his discretion.

"Why! 'ow do you mean?" said Minnie, suddenly alert.

"Shop and cat thrown in," said Mr. Polly in spite of himself, and his head swam, and he broke out into a cold sweat as he said it.

He found her eyes fixed on him with an eager expression. "Mean to say——?" she began, as if for verification. He sprang to his feet, and turned to the window. "Little dog!" he said, and moved doorward hastily. "Eating my bicycle tyre, I believe," he explained. And so escaped.

He saw his bicycle in the hall and cut it dead.

He heard Mrs. Larkins in the passage behind him as he opened the front door.

He turned to her. "Thought my bicycle was on fire," he said. "Outside. Funny fancy! All right reely. Little dog outside. . . . Miriam ready?"

"What for?"

"To go and meet Annie."

Mrs. Larkins stared at him. "You're stopping for a bit of supper!"

"If I may," said Mr. Polly.

"You're a rum 'un," said Mrs. Larkins, and called: "Miriam!"

Minnie appeared at the door of the room looking

16*

infinitely perplexed. "There ain't a little dog anywhere, Elfrid," she said.

Mr. Polly passed his hand over his brow. "I had a
most curious sensation. Felt exactly as though something was up somewhere. That's why I said Little Dog.
All right now."

He bent down and pinched his bicycle tyre.

"You was saying something about a cat, Elfrid," said
Minnie.

"Give you one," he answered, without looking up.
"The very day my shop is opened."

He straightened himself up and smiled reassuringly.
"Trust me," he said.

§ 2

When, after imperceptible manœuvres by Mrs.
Larkins, he found himself starting circuitously through
the inevitable recreation-ground with Miriam to meet
Annie, he found himself quite unable to avoid the
topic of the shop that had now taken such a grip upon
him. A sense of danger only increased the attraction.
Minnie's persistent disposition to accompany them had
been crushed by a novel and violent and pungently
expressed desire on the part of Mrs. Larkins to see her
do something in the house sometimes. . . .

"You really think you'll open a shop?" said Miriam.

"I hate cribs," said Mr. Polly, adopting a moderate
tone. "In a shop there's this drawback and that, but
one *is* one's own Master."

"That wasn't all talk?"

"Not a bit of it."

"After all," he went on, "a little shop needn't be
so bad."

"It's a 'ome," said Miriam.

"It's a home."

Pause.

"There's no need to keep accounts and that sort of

thing if there's no assistant. I dare say I could run a
shop all right if I wasn't interfered with."

"I should like to see you in your shop," said Miriam.
"I expect you'd keep everything tremendously neat."

The conversation flagged.

"Let's sit down on one of those seats over there past
that notice-board," said Miriam, "where we can see
those blue flowers."

They did as she suggested, and sat down in a corner
where a triangular bed of stock and delphinium
brightened the asphalted traceries of the recreation-
ground.

"I wonder what they call those flowers," she said.
"I always like them. They're handsome."

"Delphicums and larkspurs," said Mr. Polly.
"They used to be in the park at Port Burdock.

"Floriferous corner," he added approvingly.

He put an arm over the back of the seat, and
assumed a more comfortable attitude. He glanced at
Miriam, who was sitting in a lax, thoughtful pose,
with her eyes on the flowers. She was wearing her old
dress. She had not had time to change, and the blue
tones of her old dress brought out a certain warmth in
her skin, and her pose exaggerated whatever was
feminine in her rather lean and insufficient body, and
rounded her flat chest delusively. A little line of light
lay across her profile. The afternoon was full of transfiguring sunshine, children were playing noisily in the
adjacent sand-pit, some Judas-trees were abloom in the
villa gardens that bordered the recreation-ground, and
all the place was bright with touches of young summer
colour. It all merged with the effect of Miriam in Mr.
Polly's mind.

Her thought found speech. "One did ought to be
happy in a shop," she said, with a note of unusual
softness in her voice.

It seemed to him that she was right. One did ought
to be happy in a shop. Folly not to banish dreams that

made one ache of townless woods and bracken tangles and red-haired linen-clad figures sitting in dappled sunshine upon grey and crumbling walls and looking queenly down on one with clear blue eyes. Cruel and foolish dreams they were, that ended in one's being laughed at and made a mock of. There was no mockery here.

"A shop's such a respectable thing to be," said Miriam thoughtfully.

"*I* could be happy in a shop," he said.

His sense of effect had made him pause.

"If I had the right company," he added.

She became very still.

Mr. Polly swerved a little from the conversational ice-run upon which he had embarked.

"I'm not such a blooming Geezer," he said, "as not to be able to sell goods a bit. One has to be nosey over one's buying, of course. But I shall do all right."

He stopped, and felt falling, falling through the aching silence that followed.

"If you get the right company," said Miriam.

"I shall get that all right."

"You don't mean you've got someone——?"

He found himself plunging.

"I've got someone in my eye this minute," he said.

"Elfrid!" she said, turning to him. "You don't mean——"

Well, *did* he mean? "I do!" he said.

"Not reely!" She clenched her hands to keep still.

He took the conclusive step.

"Well, you and me, Miriam, in a little shop, with a cat and a canary——" He tried too late to get back to a hypothetical note. "Just suppose it!"

"You mean," said Miriam, "you're in love with me, Elfrid?"

What possible answer can a man give to such a question but "Yes!"

Regardless of the public park, the children in the

sand-pit, and every one, she bent forward and seized his shoulder and kissed him on the lips. Something lit up in Mr. Polly at the touch. He put an arm about her and kissed her back, and felt an irrevocable act was sealed. He had a curious feeling that it would be very satisfying to marry and have a wife—only somehow he wished it wasn't Miriam. Her lips were very pleasant to him, and the feel of her in his arm.

They recoiled a little from each other, and sat for a moment flushed and awkwardly silent. His mind was altogether incapable of controlling its confusions.

"I didn't dream," said Miriam, "you cared— Sometimes I thought it was Annie, sometimes Minnie——"

"Always I liked you better than them," said Mr. Polly.

"I loved you, Elfrid," said Miriam, "since ever we met at your poor father's funeral. Leastways I *would* have done if I had thought— You didn't seem to mean anything you said.

"I can't believe it!" she added.

"Nor I," said Mr. Polly.

"You mean to marry me and start that little shop?"

"Soon as ever I find it," said Mr. Polly.

"I had no more idea when I came out with you——"

"Nor me."

"It's like a dream."

They said no more for a little while.

"I got to pinch myself to think it's real," said Miriam. "What they'll do without me at 'ome I can't imagine. When I tell them——"

For the life of him Mr. Polly could not tell whether he was fullest of tender anticipations or regretful panic.

"Mother's no good at managing—not a bit. Annie don't care for housework, and Minnie's got no 'ead for it. What they'll do without me I can't imagine."

"They'll have to do without you," said Mr. Polly, sticking to his guns.

A clock in the town began striking.

"Lor'!" said Miriam, "we shall miss Annie, sitting 'ere and love-making."

She rose and made as if to take Mr. Polly's arm. But Mr. Polly felt that their condition must be nakedly exposed to the ridicule of the world by such a linking, and evaded her movement.

Annie was already in sight before a flood of hesitation and terrors assailed Mr. Polly.

"Don't tell any one yet a bit," he said.

"Only Mother," said Miriam firmly.

§ 3

Figures are the most shocking things in the world. The pettiest little squiggles of black, looked at in the right light; and yet consider the blow they can give you upon the heart. You return from a careless holiday abroad, and turn over the page of a newspaper, and against the name of the distant, vague-conceived railway, in mortgages upon which you have embarked the bulk of your capital, you see, instead of the familiar, persistent 95–6 (varying at most to 93 *ex div.*), this slightly richer arrangement of marks $76\frac{1}{2}$–$78\frac{1}{2}$.

It is like the opening of a pit just under your feet.

So, too, Mr. Polly's happy sense of limitless resources was obliterated suddenly by a vision of this tracery:

"298"

instead of the

"350"

he had come to regard as the fixed symbol of his affluence.

It gave him a disagreeable feeling about the diaphragm, akin in a remote degree to the sensation he had when the perfidy of the red-haired schoolgirl became plain to him. It made his brow moist.

"Going down a Vorterex," he whispered.

By a characteristic feat of subtraction he decided that he must have spent sixty-two pounds.

"Funererial baked meats," he said, recalling possible items.

The happy dream in which he had been living, of long, warm days, of open roads, of limitless, unchecked hours, of infinite time to look about him, vanished like a thing enchanted. He was suddenly back in the hard old economic world, that exacts work, that limits range, that discourages phrasing and dispels laughter. He saw Wood Street and its fearful suspenses yawning beneath his feet.

And also he had promised to marry Miriam, and on the whole rather wanted to.

He was distraught at supper. Afterwards, when Mrs. Johnson had gone to bed with a slight headache, he opened a conversation with Johnson.

"It's about time, O' Man, I saw about doing something," he said. "Riding about and looking at shops all very debonairious, O' Man, but it's time I took one for keeps."

"What did I tell you?" said Johnson.

"How do you think that corner shop of yours will figure out?" Mr. Polly asked.

"You're really meaning it?"

"If it's a practable proposition, O' Man. Assuming it's practable, what's your idea of the figures?"

Johnson went to the chiffonier, got out a letter, and tore off the back sheet. "Let's figure it out," he said, with solemn satisfaction. "Let's see the lowest you could do it on."

He squared himself to the task, and Mr. Polly sat beside him like a pupil, watching the evolution of the grey, distasteful figures that were to dispose of his little hoard.

"What running expenses have we got to provide for?" said Johnson, wetting his pencil. "Let's have them first. Rent? . . ."

At the end of an hour of hideous speculations, Johnson decided, "It's close; but you'll have a chance."

"M'm," said Mr. Polly. "What more does a brave man want?"

"One thing you can do quite easily. I've asked about it."

"What's that, O' Man?" said Mr. Polly.

"Take the shop without the house above it."

"I suppose I might put my head in to mind it," said Mr. Polly, "and get a job with my body."

"Not exactly that. But I thought you'd save a lot if you stayed on here—being all alone, as you are."

"Never thought of that, O' Man," said Mr. Polly, and reflected silently upon the needlessness of Miriam.

"We were talking of eighty pounds for stock," said Johnson. "Of course seventy-five is five pounds less, isn't it? Not much else we can cut."

"No," said Mr. Polly.

"It's very interesting, all this," said Johnson, folding up the half-sheet of paper and unfolding it. "I wish sometimes I had a business of my own instead of a fixed salary. You'll have to keep books, of course."

"One wants to know where one is."

"I should do it all by double entry," said Johnson. "A little troublesome at first, but far the best in the end."

"Lemme see that paper," said Mr. Polly, and took it with the feeling of a man who takes a nauseating medicine, and scrutinised his cousin's neat figures with listless eyes.

"Well," said Johnson, rising and stretching, "Bed! Better sleep on it, O' Man."

"Right-o!" said Mr. Polly, without moving; but indeed he could as well have slept upon a bed of thorns.

He had a dreadful night. It was like the end of the

annual holiday, only infinitely worse. It was like a
newly arrived prisoner's backward glance at the trees
and heather through the prison gates. He had to go
back to harness, and he was as fitted to go in harness as
the ordinary domestic cat. All night Fate, with the
quiet complacency, and indeed at times the very face
and gestures, of Johnson, guided him towards that un-
desired establishment at the corner near the station.
"O Lord!" he cried, "I'd rather go back to cribs. I
should keep my money, anyhow." Fate never winced.

"Run away to sea," whispered Mr. Polly; but he
knew he wasn't man enough. "Cut my blooming
throat."

Some braver strain urged him to think of Miriam,
and for a little while he lay still. . . .

"Well, O' Man?" said Johnson, when Mr. Polly
came down to breakfast, and Mrs. Johnson looked up
brightly. Mr. Polly had never felt breakfast so unattractive before.

"Just a day or so more, O' Man, to turn it over in
my mind," he said.

"You'll get the place snapped up," said Johnson.

There were times in those last few days of coyness
with his destiny when his engagement seemed the most
negligible of circumstances; and times—and these happened for the most part at nights, after Mrs. Johnson
had indulged everybody in a Welsh rarebit—when it
assumed so sinister and portentous an appearance as to
make him think of suicide. And there were times too
when he very distinctly desired to be married, now that
the idea had got into his head, at any cost. Also he
tried to recall all the circumstances of his proposal time
after time, and never quite succeeded in recalling what
had brought the thing off. He went over to Stamton
with a becoming frequency, and kissed all his cousins,
and Miriam especially, a great deal, and found it very
stirring and refreshing. They all appeared to know;
and Minnie was tearful but resigned. Mrs. Larkins met

him, and indeed enveloped him, with unwonted warmth, and there was a big pot of household jam for tea. And he could not make up his mind to sign his name to anything about the shop, though it crawled nearer and nearer to him, though the project had materialised now to the extent of a draft agreement, with the place for his signature indicated in pencil.

One morning, just after Mr. Johnson had gone to the station, Mr. Polly wheeled his bicycle out into the road, went up to his bedroom, packed his long white night-dress, a comb, and a tooth-brush in a manner that was as offhand as he could make it, informed Mrs. Johnson, who was manifestly curious, that he was "off for a day or two to clear his head," and fled forthright into the road, and mounting, turned his wheel towards the tropics and the equator and the south coast of England, and indeed more particularly to where the little village of Fishbourne slumbers and sleeps.

When he returned, four days later, he astonished Johnson beyond measure by remarking, so soon as the shop project was reopened, "I've took a little contraption at Fishbourne, O' Man, that I fancy suits me better."

He paused, and then added in a manner if possible even more offhand, "Oh, and I'm going to have a bit of a nuptial over at Stamton—with one of the Larkins cousins."

"Nuptial!" said Johnson.

"Wedding-bells, O' Man. Benedictine collapse."

On the whole Johnson showed great self-control. "It's your own affair, O' Man," he said, when things had been more clearly explained; "and I hope you won't feel sorry when it's too late."

But Mrs. Johnson was first of all angrily silent, and then reproachful. "I don't see what we've done to be made fools of like this," she said. "After all the trouble we've 'ad to make you comfortable and see after you—out late, and sitting up, and everything; and then

you go off as sly as sly, without a word, an' get a shop
behind our backs, as though you thought we meant to
steal your money. I 'aven't patience with such deceit-
fulness, and I didn't think it of you, Elfrid. And now
the letting season's 'arf gone by, and what I shall do
with that room of yours I've no idea. Frank is frank,
and fair play fair play; so *I* was told, any'ow, when I
was a girl. Just as long as it suits you to stay 'ere you
stay 'ere, and then it's off and no thank you whether
we like it or not. Johnson's too easy with you. 'E
sits there and doesn't say a word; and night after night
'e's been adding up and subtracting, and multiplying
and dividing, and suggesting and thinkin' for you,
instead of seeing to his own affairs."

She paused for breath.

" Unfortunate amoor," said Mr. Polly apologetically
and indistinctly. " Didn't expect it myself."

§ 4

Mr. Polly's marriage followed with a certain inevitableness.

He tried to assure himself that he was acting upon
his own forceful initiative, but at the back of his mind
was the completest realisation of his powerlessness to
resist the gigantic social forces he had set in motion.
He had got to marry under the will of society, even
as in times past it had been appointed for other sunny
souls under the will of society that they should be led
out by serious and unavoidable fellow creatures and
ceremoniously drowned or burnt or hanged. He would
have preferred infinitely a more observant and less conspicuous rôle, but the choice was no longer open to him.
He did his best to play his part, and he procured some
particularly neat check trousers to do it in. The rest
of his costume, except for some bright yellow gloves, a
grey-and-blue mixture tie, and that the broad crape
band was changed for a livelier piece of silk, were the

things he had worn at the funeral of his father.   So nearly akin are human joy and sorrow.

The Larkins sisters had done wonders with grey sateen.   The idea of orange-blossom and white veils had been abandoned reluctantly on account of the expense of the cabs.   A novelette in which the heroine had stood at the altar in "a modest going-away dress" had materially assisted this decision.   Miriam was frankly tearful, and so, indeed, was Annie, but with laughter as well to carry it off.   Mr. Polly heard Annie say something vague about never getting a chance because of Miriam always sticking about at home like a cat at a mouse-hole, that became, as people say, food for thought.   Mrs. Larkins was from the first flushed, garrulous, and wet and smeared by copious weeping; an incredibly soaked and crumpled and used-up pocket-handkerchief never left the clutch of her plump red hand.   "Goo' girls all of them," she kept on saying in a tremulous voice; "such Goo'-Goo'-Goo' girls!" She wetted Mr. Polly dreadfully when she kissed him. Her emotion affected the buttons down the back of her bodice, and almost the last filial duty Miriam did before entering on her new life was to close that gaping orifice for the eleventh time.   Her bonnet was small and ill-balanced, black adorned with red roses, and first it got over her right eye until Annie told her of it, and then she pushed it over her left eye and looked ferocious for a space, and after that baptismal kissing of Mr. Polly the delicate millinery took fright and climbed right up to the back part of her head and hung on there by a pin, and flapped piteously at all the larger waves of emotion that filled the gathering.   Mr. Polly became more and more aware of that bonnet as time went on, until he felt for it like a thing alive.   Towards the end it had yawning fits.

The company did not include Mrs. Johnson, but Johnson came with a pervading surreptitiousness and backed against walls and watched Mr. Polly with doubt and speculation in his large grey eye, and whistled noiselessly and doubtfully on the edge of things. He was, so to speak, to be best man *sotto voce*. A sprinkling of girls in gay hats from Miriam's place of business appeared in church, great nudgers all of them, but only two came on afterwards to the house. Mrs. Punt brought her son with his ever-widening mind—it was his first wedding; and a Larkins uncle, a Mr. Voules, a licensed victualler, very kindly drove over in a high-hung dog-cart from Sommershill with a plump, well-dressed wife, to give the bride away. One or two total strangers drifted into the church and sat down observantly in distant seats.

This sprinkling of people seemed only to enhance the cool brown emptiness of the church, the rows and rows of empty pews, disengaged Prayer-Books, and abandoned hassocks. It had the effect of a preposterous misfit. Johnson consulted with a thin-legged short-skirted verger about the disposition of the party. The officiating clergy appeared distantly in the doorway of the vestry putting on his surplice, and relapsed into a contemplative cheek-scratching that was manifestly habitual. Before the bride arrived, Mr. Polly's sense of the church found an outlet in whispered criticisms of ecclesiastical architecture with Johnson. "Early Norman arches, eh?" he said, "or Perpendicular."

"Can't say," said Johnson.

"Telessated pavements all right."

"It's well laid anyhow."

"Can't say I admire the altar. Scrappy rather with those flowers."

He coughed behind his hand and cleared his throat. At the back of his mind he was speculating whether flight at this eleventh hour would be criminal or merely reprehensible bad taste. A murmur from the nudgers announced the arrival of the bridal party.

The little procession from the remote door became one of the enduring memories of Mr. Polly's life. The verger had bustled to meet it and arrange it according to tradition and morality. In spite of Mrs. Larkins' impassioned " Don't take her from me yet !" he made Miriam go first with Mr. Voules, the bridesmaids followed, and then himself, hopelessly unable to disentangle himself from the whispering maternal anguish of Mrs. Larkins. Mrs. Voules, a compact, rounded woman with a square, expressionless face, imperturbable dignity, and a dress of considerable fashion, completed the procession.

Mr. Polly's eyes fell first upon the bride; the sight of her filled him with a curious stir of emotion. Alarm, desire, affection, respect—and a queer element of reluctant dislike, all played their part in that complex eddy. The grey dress made her a stranger to him, made her stiff and commonplace; she was not even the rather drooping form that had caught his facile sense of beauty when he had proposed to her in the recreation-ground. There was something, too, that did not please him in the angle of her hat; it was, indeed, an ill-conceived hat with large, aimless rosettes of pink and grey. Then his mind passed to Mrs. Larkins and the bonnet that was to gain such a hold upon him; it seemed to be flag-signalling as she advanced, and to the two eager, unrefined sisters he was acquiring.

A freak of fancy set him wondering where and when in the future a beautiful girl with red hair might march along some splendid aisle— Never mind ! He became aware of Mr. Voules.

He became aware of Mr. Voules as a watchful, blue eye of intense forcefulness. It was the eye of a man who has got hold of a situation. He was a fat, short, red-faced man, clad in tight-fitting tail-coat of black-and-white check, with a coquettish bow tie under the lowest of a number of crisp little red chins. He held the bride under his arm with an air of invincible championship, and his free arm flourished a grey top-hat of an equestrian type. Mr. Polly instantly learnt from

that eye that Mr. Voules knew all about his longing for
flight.   Its azure-rimmed pupil glowed with disciplined
resolution.   It said : " I've come to give this girl away,
and give her away I will.   I'm here now, and things
have to go on all right.   So don't think of it any more "
—and Mr. Polly didn't.   A faint phantom of a certain
" lill dog " that had hovered just beneath the threshold
of consciousness vanished into black impossibility.   Until
the conclusive moment of the service was attained the
eye of Mr. Voules watched Mr. Polly relentlessly, and
then instantly he relieved guard, and blew his nose
into a voluminous and richly patterned handkerchief,
and sighed and looked round for the approval and sympathy of Mrs. Voules, and nodded to her brightly, like
one who has always foretold a successful issue to things.
Mr. Polly felt at last like a marionette that has dropped
off its wire.   But it was long before that release arrived.

He became aware of Miriam breathing close to him.

" Hallo !" he said, and feeling that was clumsy and
would meet the eye's disapproval : " Grey dress—suits
you no end."

Miriam's eyes shone under her hat-brim.

" Not reely !" she whispered.

" You're all right," he said, with the feeling of the
eye's observation and criticism stiffening his lips.   He
cleared his throat.

The verger's hand pushed at him from behind.
Some one was driving Miriam towards the altar-rail
and the clergyman.   " We're in for it," said Mr. Polly
to her sympathetically.   " Where?   Here?   Right-o."

He was interested for a moment or so in something
indescribably habitual in the clergyman's pose.   What
a lot of weddings he must have seen !   Sick he must be
of them !

" Don't let your attention wander," said the eye.

" Got the ring ?" whispered Johnson.

" Pawned it yesterday," answered Mr. Polly, with
an attempt at lightness, and then had a dreadful moment

under that pitiless scrutiny while he felt in the wrong waistcoat pocket. . . .

The officiating clergy sighed deeply, began, and married them wearily and without any hitch.

"D'bloved we gath'd gether sighto' Gard 'n face this con'gation join gather Man Wom Ho Mat'mony whichis on'bl state stooted by Gard in times mans in'cency. . . ."

Mr. Polly's thoughts wandered wide and far, and once again something like a cold hand touched his heart, and he saw a sweet face in sunshine under the shadow of trees.

Some one was nudging him. It was Johnson's finger diverting his eyes to the crucial place in the Prayer-Book to which they had come.

"Wiltou lover, cumfer, oner keeper sickness and health? . . ."

"*Say, 'I will.'*"

Mr. Polly moistened his lips. "I will," he said hoarsely.

Miriam, nearly inaudible, answered some similar demand.

Then the clergyman said : "Who gi's Wom mad' this man?"

"Well, *I'm* doing that," said Mr. Voules in a refreshingly full voice, and looking round the church.

"Pete arf me," said the clergyman to Mr. Polly. "Take thee Mirum wed wife——"

"Take thee Mi'm wed' wife," said Mr. Polly.

"Have hold this day ford."

"Have hold this day ford."

"Betworse, richypoo'."

"Bet worse, richypoo'. . . ."

Then came Miriam's turn.

"Lego hands," said the clergyman, "gothering? No! On book. So! Here! Pete arf me 'wis ring Ivy wed.'"

"Wis ring Ivy wed——"

So it went on, blurred and hurried, like the momentary vision of a very beautiful thing seen through the smoke of a passing train. . . .

"Now, my boy," said Mr. Voules at last, gripping Mr. Polly's elbow tightly, "you've got to sign the registry and there you are! Done!"

Before him stood Miriam, a little stiffly, the hat with a slight rake across her forehead, and a kind of questioning hesitation in her face. Mr. Voules urged him past her.

It was astounding. She was his wife!

And for some reason Miriam and Mrs. Larkins were sobbing, and Annie was looking grave. Hadn't they, after all, wanted him to marry her? Because if that was the case——!

He became aware for the first time of the presence of Uncle Pentstemon in the background but approaching, wearing a tie of a light mineral-blue colour, and grinning and sucking enigmatically and judicially round his principal tooth.

§ 5

It was in the vestry that the force of Mr. Voules' personality began to show at its true value. He seemed to open out, like the fisherman's Ginn from the pot, and spread over everything directly the restraints of the ceremony were at an end.

"Ceremony," he said to the clergyman, "excellent, excellent." He also shook hands with Mrs. Larkins, who clung to him for a space, and kissed Miriam on the cheek. "First kiss for me," he said, "anyhow."

He led Mr. Polly to the register by the arm, and then got chairs for Mrs. Larkins and his wife. He then turned on Miriam. "Now, young people," he said. "One! or *I* shall again."

"That's right," said Mr. Voules. "Same again, Miss."

Mr. Polly was overcome with modest confusion, and turning, found a refuge from this publicity in the arms of Mrs. Larkins. Then in a state of profuse moisture he was assaulted and kissed by Annie and Minnie, who were immediately kissed upon some indistinctly stated grounds by Mr. Voules, who then kissed the entirely impassive Mrs. Voules, and smacked his lips and remarked, "Home again safe and sound." Then, with a strange harrowing cry Mrs. Larkins seized upon and bedewed Miriam with kisses. Annie and Minnie kissed each other, and Johnson went abruptly to the door of the vestry and stared into the church, no doubt with ideas of sanctuary in his mind. "Like a bit of a kiss round sometimes," said Mr. Voules, and made a kind of hissing noise with his teeth, and suddenly smacked his hands together with great *éclat* several times. Meanwhile the clergyman scratched his cheek with one hand and fiddled the pen with the other, and the verger coughed protestingly.

"The dog-cart's just outside," said Mr. Voules. "No walking home to-day for the bride, M'am."

"Not going to drive us?" cried Annie.

"The happy pair, Miss. Your turn soon."

"Get out!" said Annie. "I shan't marry—ever."

"You won't be able to help it. You'll have to do it, just to disperse the crowd." Mr. Voules laid his hand on Mr. Polly's shoulder. "The bridegroom gives his arm to the bride. Hands across, and down the middle. Prump, Prump, Perump-pump-pump-pump-perump."

Mr. Polly found himself and the bride leading the way towards the western door.

Mrs. Larkins passed close to Uncle Pentstemon, sobbing too earnestly to be aware of him. "Such a goo'-goo'-goo' girl," she sobbed.

"Didn't think I'd come, did you?" said Uncle Pentstemon; but she swept past him, too busy with the expression of her feelings to observe him.

"She didn't think I'd come, I lay," said Uncle

Pentstemon, a little foiled, but effecting an auditory lodgment upon Johnson.

"I don't know," said Johnson, uncomfortable. "I suppose you were asked. How are you getting on?"

"I was *arst*," said Uncle Pentstemon, and brooded for a moment.

"I goes about seeing wonders," he added, and then in a sort of enhanced undertone. "One of 'er girls gettin' married. That's what I means by wonders. Lord's goodness! Wow!"

"Nothing the matter?" asked Johnson.

"Got it in the back for a moment. Going to be a change of weather, I suppose," said Uncle Pentstemon. "I brought 'er a nice present, too, what I got in this passel. Vallyble old tea-caddy that uset' be my mother's. What I kep' my baccy in for years and years —till the hinge at the back got broke. It ain't been no use to me particular since, so thinks I, drat it! I may as well give it to 'er as not. . . ."

Mr. Polly found himself emerging from the western door.

Outside, a crowd of half a dozen adults and about fifty children had collected, and hailed the approach of the newly wedded couple with a faint, indeterminate cheer. All the children were holding something in little bags, and his attention was caught by the expression of vindictive concentration upon the face of a small, big-eared boy in the foreground. He didn't for the moment realise what these things might import. Then he received a stinging handful of rice in the ear, and a great light shone.

"Not yet, you young fool," he heard Mr. Voules saying behind him, and then a second handful spoke against his hat.

"Not yet," said Mr. Voules, with increasing emphasis, and Mr. Polly became aware that he and Miriam were the focus of two crescents of small boys, each with the light of massacre in his eyes and a grubby fist clutching into a paper bag for rice, and that Mr. Voules was warding off probable discharges with a large red hand.

The dog-cart was in charge of a loafer, and the horse and the whip were adorned with white favours, and the back seat was confused, but not untenable, with hampers. "Up we go," said Mr. Voules. "Old birds in front and young ones behind." An ominous group of ill-restrained rice-throwers followed them up as they mounted.

"Get your handkerchief for your face," said Mr. Polly to his bride, and took the place next the pavement with considerable heroism, held on, gripped his hat, shut his eyes, and prepared for the worst. "Off!" said Mr. Voules, and a concentrated fire came stinging Mr. Polly's face.

The horse shied, and when the bridegroom could look at the world again it was manifest the dog-cart had just missed an electric tram by a hair's breadth, and far away outside the church railings the verger and Johnson were battling with an active crowd of small boys for the life of the rest of the Larkins family. Mrs. Punt and her son had escaped across the road, the son trailing and stumbling at the end of a remorseless arm; but Uncle Pentstemon, encumbered by the tea-caddy, was the centre of a little circle of his own, and appeared to be dratting them all very heartily. Remoter, a policeman approached with an air of tranquil unconsciousness.

"Steady, you idiot, stead-y!" cried Mr. Voules; and then over his shoulder, "I brought that rice. I like old customs.—Whoa! stead-y."

The dog-cart swerved violently, and then, evoking a shout of groundless alarm from a cyclist, took a corner, and the rest of the wedding-party was hidden from Mr. Polly's eyes.

§ 6

" We'll get the stuff into the house before the old
gal comes along," said Mr. Voules, " if you'll hold the
hoss."

" How about the key?" asked Mr. Polly.

" I got the key, coming."

And while Mr. Polly held the sweating horse and
dodged the foam that dripped from its bit, the house
absorbed Miriam and Mr. Voules altogether. Mr.
Voules carried in the various hampers he had brought
with him and finally closed the door behind him.

For some time Mr. Polly remained alone with his
charge in the little blind alley outside the Larkins' house,
while the neighbours scrutinised him from behind their
blinds. He reflected that he was a married man, that
he must look very like a fool, that the head of a horse
is a silly shape and its eye a bulger; he wondered what
the horse thought of him, and whether it really liked
being held and patted on the neck, or whether it only
submitted out of contempt. Did it know he was
married? Then he wondered if the clergyman had
thought him much of an ass, and whether the individual
lurking behind the lace curtains of the front room next
door was a man or a woman. A door opened over the
way, and an elderly gentleman in a kind of embroidered
fez appeared smoking a pipe, with a quiet, satisfied
expression. He regarded Mr. Polly for some time with
mild but sustained curiosity. Finally he called : " Hi!"

" Hallo!" said Mr. Polly.

" You needn't 'old that 'orse," said the old gentleman.

" Spirited beast," said Mr. Polly. " And "—with
some faint analogy to ginger beer in his mind—" he's
up to-day."

" 'E won't turn 'isself round," said the old gentleman, " any'ow. And there ain't no way through for
him to go."

" *Verbum sap.*," said Mr. Polly, and abandoned the horse and turned to the door. It opened to him just as Mrs. Larkins, on the arm of Johnson, followed by Annie, Minnie, two friends, Mrs. Punt and her son, and at a slight distance Uncle Pentstemon, appeared round the corner.

" They're coming," he said to Miriam, and put an arm about her and gave her a kiss.

She was kissing him back, when they were startled violently by the shying of two empty hampers into the passage. Then Mr. Voules appeared holding a third.

" Here! you'll have plenty of time for that presently," he said; " get these hampers away before the old girl comes. I got a cold collation here to make her sit up. My eye!"

Miriam took the hampers, and Mr. Polly, under compulsion from Mr. Voules, went into the little front room. A profuse pie and a large ham had been added to the modest provision of Mrs. Larkins, and a number of select-looking bottles shouldered the bottle of sherry and the bottle of port she had got to grace the feast. They certainly went better with the iced wedding-cake in the middle. Mrs. Voules, still impassive, stood by the window regarding these things with faint approval.

" Makes it look a bit thicker, eh?" said Mr. Voules, and blew out both his cheeks, and smacked his hands together violently several times. " Surprise the old girl no end."

He stood back and smiled and bowed with arms extended as the others came clustering at the door.

" Why, Un-cle Voules!" cried Annie, with a rising note.

It was his reward.

And then came a great wedging and squeezing and crowding into the little room. Nearly every one was hungry, and eyes brightened at the sight of the pie and the ham and the convivial array of bottles. "Sit down, every one," cried Mr. Voules. "Leaning against anything counts as sitting, and makes it easier to shake down the grub!"

The two friends from Miriam's place of business came into the room among the first, and then wedged themselves so hopelessly against Johnson in an attempt to get out again to take off their things up-stairs, that they abandoned the attempt. Amid the struggle Mr. Polly saw Uncle Pentstemon relieve himself of his parcel by giving it to the bride. "Here!" he said, and handed it to her. "Weddin'-present," he explained, and added with a confidential chuckle, "*I* never thought I'd 'ave to give one—ever."

"Who says steak-and-kidney pie?" bawled Mr. Voules. "Who says steak-and-kidney pie? You 'ave a drop of old Tommy, Martha. That's what you want to steady you. . . .

"Sit down, every one, and don't all speak at once. Who says steak-and-kidney pie? . . ."

"Vocificeratious," whispered Mr. Polly. "Convivial vocificerations."

"Bit of 'am with it," shouted Mr. Voules, poising a slice of ham on his knife. "Any one 'ave a bit of 'am with it? Won't that little man of yours, Mrs. Punt —won't 'e 'ave a bit of 'am? . . .

"And now, ladies and gentlemen," said Mr. Voules, still standing and dominating the crammed roomful, "now you got your plates filled, and something I can warrant you good in your glasses, wot about drinking the 'ealth of the bride?"

"Eat a bit fust," said Uncle Pentstemon, speaking with his mouth full, amidst murmurs of applause. "Eat a bit fust."

So they did, and the plates clattered and the glasses clinked.

Mr. Polly stood shoulder to shoulder with Johnson for a moment. "In for it," said Mr. Polly cheeringly.

"Cheer up, O' Man, and peck a bit. No reason why *you* shouldn't eat, you know."

The Punt boy stood on Mr. Polly's boots for a minute, struggling violently against the compunction of Mrs. Punt's grip.

"Pie," said the Punt boy, "Pie!"

"You sit 'ere and 'ave 'am, my lord!" said Mrs. Punt, prevailing. "Pie you can't 'ave and you won't."

"Lor' bless my heart, Mrs. Punt!" protested Mr. Voules, "let the boy 'ave a bit if he wants it—wedding and all!"

"You 'aven't 'ad 'im sick on your 'ands, Uncle Voules," said Mrs. Punt. "Else you wouldn't want to humour his fancies as you do. . . ."

"I can't help feeling it's a mistake, O' Man," said Johnson, in a confidential undertone. "I can't help feeling you've been Rash. Let's hope for the best."

"Always glad of good wishes, O' Man," said Mr. Polly. "You'd better have a drink or something. Anyhow, sit down to it."

Johnson subsided gloomily, and Mr. Polly secured some ham and carried it off, and sat himself down on the sewing-machine on the floor in the corner to devour it. He was hungry, and a little cut off from the rest of the company by Mrs. Voules' hat and back, and he occupied himself for a time with ham and his own thoughts. He became aware of a series of jangling concussions on the table. He craned his neck, and discovered that Mr. Voules was standing up and leaning forward over the table in the manner distinctive of after-dinner speeches, tapping upon the table with a black bottle. "Ladies and gentlemen," said Mr. Voules, raising his glass solemnly in the empty desert of sound he had made, and paused for a second or so. "Ladies and gentlemen—the Bride." He searched his mind for some suitable wreath of speech, and brightened at last with discovery. "Here's luck to her!" he said at last.

"Here's Luck!" said Johnson hopelessly but resolutely, and raised his glass. Everybody murmured, "Here's Luck."

"Luck!" said Mr. Polly, unseen in his corner, lifting a forkful of ham.

"That's all right," said Mr. Voules, with a sigh of relief at having brought off a difficult operation. "And now, who's for a bit more pie?"

For a time conversation was fragmentary again. But presently Mr. Voules rose from his chair again, and produced a silence by renewed hammering; he had subsided with a contented smile after his first oratorical effort. "Ladies and gents," he said, "fill up for a second toast: the happy Bridegroom!" He stood for half a minute searching his mind for the apt phrase that came at last in a rush. "Here's (hic) luck to *him,*" said Mr. Voules.

"Luck to him!" said every one; and Mr. Polly, standing up behind Mrs. Voules, bowed amiably, amidst enthusiasm.

"He may say what he likes," said Mrs. Larkins, "he's *got* luck. That girl's a treasure of treasures, and always has been ever since she tried to nurse her own little sister being but three at the time and fell the full flight of stairs from top to bottom, no hurt that any outward eye 'as ever seen but always ready and helping, always tidying and busy. A treasure I must say, and a treasure I will say, giving no more than her due. . . ."

She was silenced altogether by a rapping sound that would not be denied. Mr. Voules had been struck by a fresh idea, and was standing up and hammering with the bottle again.

"The third Toast, ladies and gentlemen," he said; "fill up, please. The Mother of the Bride. I—er . . . Uoo . . . 'Ere! . . . Ladies and gem, 'Ere's Luck to 'er! . . ."

§ 7

The dingy little room was stuffy and crowded to its utmost limit, and Mr. Polly's skies were dark with the sense of irreparable acts. Everybody seemed noisy and greedy, and doing foolish things. Miriam, still in that unbecoming hat—for presently they had to start off to the station together—sat just beyond Mrs. Punt and her son, doing her share in the hospitalities, and ever and again glancing at him with a deliberately encouraging smile. Once she leant over the back of the chair to him and whispered cheeringly, "Soon be together now." Next to her sat Johnson, profoundly silent, and then Annie, talking vigorously to a friend. Uncle Pentstemon was eating voraciously opposite, but with a kindling eye for Annie. Mrs. Larkins sat next Mr. Voules. She was unable to eat a mouthful, she declared, it would choke her; but ever and again Mr. Voules wooed her to swallow a little drop of liquid refreshment.

There seemed a lot of rice upon everybody, in their hats and hair and the folds of their garments.

Presently Mr. Voules was hammering the table for the fourth time in the interests of the Best Man. . . .

All feasts come to an end at last, and the break-up of things was precipitated by alarming symptoms on the part of Master Punt. He was taken out hastily after a whispered consultation; and since he had got into the corner between the fireplace and the cupboard, that meant every one moving to make way for him. Johnson took the opportunity to say, "Well, so long," to any one who might be listening, and disappeared. Mr. Polly found himself smoking a cigarette and walking up and down outside in the company of Uncle Pentstemon, while Mr. Voules replaced bottles in hampers, and prepared for departure, and the womenkind of the party crowded up-stairs with the bride. Mr. Polly felt taciturn, but the events of the day had stirred the mind of Uncle Pentstemon to

speech. And so he spoke, discursively and disconnectedly, a little heedless of his listener, as wise old
men will.

"They do say," said Uncle Pentstemon, "one
funeral makes many. This time it's a wedding. But
it's all very much of a muchness. . . .

"'Am *do* get in my teeth nowadays," said Uncle
Pentstemon, "I can't understand it. 'Tisn't like there
was nubblicks or strings or such in 'am. It's a plain
food, sure-ly.

"You *got* to get married," said Uncle Pentstemon,
resuming his discourse. "That's the way of it. Some
has. Some hain't. I done it long before I was your
age. It hain't for me to blame you. You can't 'elp
being the marrying sort any more than me. It's
nat'ral—like poaching, or drinking, or wind on the
stummik. You can't 'elp it, and there you are! As
for the good of it, there ain't no particular good in it
as I can see. It's a toss-up. The hotter come, the
sooner cold; but they all gets tired of it sooner or
later. . . . I hain't no grounds to complain. Two
I've 'ad and buried, and might 'ave 'ad a third, and
never no worrit with kids—never. . . .

"You done well not to 'ave the big gal. I will say
that for ye. She's a gad-about grinny, she is, if ever
was. A gad-about grinny. Mucked up my mush-
room-bed to rights, she did, and I 'aven't forgot it.
Got the feet of a centipede, she 'as—all over everything, and neither with your leave nor by your leave.
Like a stray 'en in a pea-patch. Cluck! cluck! Trying to laugh it off. *I* laughed 'er off, I did. Dratted
lumpin' baggage! . . ."

For a while he mused malevolently upon Annie,
and routed out a reluctant crumb from some coy
sitting-out place in his tooth.

"Wimmin's a toss-up," said Uncle Pentstemon.
"Prize packets they are, and you can't tell what's in
'em till you took 'em 'ome and undone 'em. Never

was a bachelor married yet that didn't buy a pig in a poke. Never! Marriage seems to change the very natures in 'em through and through. You can't tell what they won't turn into—nohow.

"I seen the nicest girls go wrong," said Uncle Pentstemon, and added with unusual thoughtfulness, "Not that I mean *you* got one of that sort."

He sent another crumb on to its long home with a sucking, encouraging noise.

"The wust sort's the grizzler," Uncle Pentstemon resumed. "If ever I'd 'ad a grizzler, I'd up and 'it 'er on the 'ead with sumpthin' pretty quick. I don't think I *could* abide a grizzler," said Uncle Pentstemon. "I'd liefer 'ave a lump-about like that other gal. I would indeed. I lay I'd make 'er stop laughing after a bit for all 'er airs. And mind where her clumsy great feet went. . . .

"A man's got to tackle 'em, whatever they be," said Uncle Pentstemon, summing up the shrewd observation of an old-world lifetime. "Good or bad," said Uncle Pentstemon, raising his voice fearlessly, "a man's got to tackle 'em."

§ 8

At last it was time for the two young people to catch the train for Waterloo *en route* for Fishbourne. They had to hurry, and as a concluding glory of matrimony they travelled second class, and were seen off by all the rest of the party except the Punts, Master Punt being now beyond any question unwell.

"Off!" The train moved out of the station.

Mr. Polly remained waving his hat and Mrs. Polly her handkerchief until they were hidden under the bridge. The dominating figure to the last was Mr. Voules. He had followed them along the platform, waving the equestrian grey hat and kissing his hand to the bride.

They subsided into their seats.

"Got a compartment to ourselves, anyhow," said Mrs. Polly, after a pause.

Silence for a moment.

"The rice 'e must 'ave bought. Pounds and pounds!"

Mr. Polly felt round his collar at the thought.

"Ain't you going to kiss me, Elfrid, now we're alone together?"

He roused himself to sit forward, hands on knees, cocked his hat over one eye, and assumed an expression of avidity becoming to the occasion.

"Never!" he said. "Ever!" and feigned to be selecting a place to kiss with great discrimination.

"Come here," he said, and drew her to him.

"Be careful of my 'at," said Mrs. Polly, yielding awkwardly.

CHAPTER THE SEVENTH

The Little Shop at Fishbourne

§ 1

FOR fifteen years Mr. Polly was a respectable shop-keeper in Fishbourne.

Years they were in which every day was tedious, and when they were gone it was as if they had gone in a flash. But now Mr. Polly had good looks no more. He was, as I have described him in the beginning of this story, thirty-seven, and fattish in a not very healthy way, dull and yellowish about the complexion, and with discontented wrinkles round his eyes. He sat on the stile above Fishbourne and cried to the heavens above him: "Oh, Roöötten Beëeastly Silly Hole!" And he wore a rather shabby black morning coat and vest, and his tie was richly splendid, being from stock, and his golf cap aslant over one eye.

Fifteen years ago, and it might have seemed to you that the queer little flower of Mr. Polly's imagination might be altogether withered and dead, and with no living seed left in any part of him. But, indeed, it still lived as an insatiable hunger for bright and delight-ful experiences for the gracious aspect of things, for beauty. He still read books when he had a chance—books that told of glorious places abroad and glorious times, that wrung a rich humour from life, and contained the delight of words freshly and expressively grouped. But, alas! there are not many such books, and for the newspapers and the cheap fiction that abounded more and more in the world, Mr. Polly had little taste. There was no epithet in them. And there was no one to talk to, as he loved to talk. And he had to mind his shop.

It was a reluctant little shop from the beginning.

He had taken it to escape the doom of Johnson's choice, and because Fishbourne had a hold upon. his imagination. He had disregarded the ill-built, cramped rooms behind it in which he would have to lurk and live, and the relentless limitations of its dimensions, the inconvenience of an underground kitchen that must necessarily be the living-room in winter—the narrow yard behind giving upon the yard of the Royal Fishbourne Hotel—the tiresome sitting and waiting for custom, the restricted prospects of trade. He had visualised himself and Miriam first as at breakfast on a clear, bright, winter morning, amidst a tremendous smell of bacon, and then as having muffins for tea. He had also thought of sitting on the beach on Sunday afternoons, and of going for a walk in the country behind the town and picking marguerites and poppies. But, in fact, Miriam and he were usually extremely cross at breakfast, and it did not run to muffins at tea. And she didn't think it looked well, she said, to go trapesing about the country on Sundays.

It was unfortunate that Miriam never took to the house from the first. She did not like it when she saw it, and liked it less as she explored it. "There's too many stairs," she said, "and the coal being indoors will make a lot of work."

"Didn't think of that," said Mr. Polly, following her round.

"It'll be a hard house to keep clean," said Miriam.

"White paint's all very well in its way," said Miriam, "but it shows the dirt something fearful. Better 'ave 'ad it nicely grained."

"There's a kind of place here," said Mr. Polly, "where we might have some flowers in pots."

"Not me," said Miriam. "I've 'ad trouble enough with Minnie and 'er musk. . . ."

They stayed for a week in a cheap boarding-house before they moved in. They had bought some furniture in Stamton, mostly second-hand, but with new cheap cutlery and china and linen, and they supplemented this from the Fishbourne shops. Miriam, relieved from the hilarious associations of home, developed a meagre and serious quality of her own, and went about with knitted brows pursuing some ideal of "'aving everything right." Mr. Polly gave himself to the arrangement of the shop with a certain zest, and whistled a great deal, until Miriam appeared and said that it went through her head. So soon as he had taken the shop he had filled the window with aggressive posters, announcing in no measured terms that he was going to open; and, now he was getting his stuff put out, he was resolved to show Fishbourne what window-dressing could do. He meant to give them boater straws, imitation Panamas, bathing-dresses with novelties in stripes, light flannel shirts, summer ties, and ready-made flannel trousers for men, youths, and boys. Incidentally he watched the small fishmonger over the way, and had a glimpse of the china-dealer next door, and wondered if a friendly nod would be out of place. And on the first Sunday in this new life he and Miriam arrayed themselves with great care, he in his wedding-funeral hat and coat and she in her going-away dress, and went processionally to church— a more respectable-looking couple you could hardly imagine—and looked about them.

Things began to settle down next week into their

places. A few customers came, chiefly for bathing-suits and hat-guards, and on Saturday night the cheapest straw hats and ties, and Mr. Polly found himself more and more drawn towards the shop door and the social charm of the street. He found the china-dealer unpacking a crate at the edge of the pavement, and remarked that it was a fine day. The china-dealer gave a reluctant assent, and plunged into the crate in a manner that presented no encouragement to a loquacious neighbour.

"Zealacious commerciality," whispered Mr. Polly to that unfriendly back view. . . .

§ 2

Miriam combined earnestness of spirit with great practical incapacity. The house was never clean nor tidy, but always being frightfully disarranged for cleaning or tidying up, and she cooked because food had to be cooked, and with a sound moralist's entire disregard of the quality or the consequences. The food came from her hands done rather than improved, and looking as uncomfortable as savages clothed under duress by a missionary with a stock of out-sizes. Such food is too apt to behave resentfully, rebel, and work Obi. She ceased to listen to her husband's talk from the day she married him, and ceased to unwrinkle the kink in her brow at his presence, giving herself up to mental states that had a quality of preoccupation. And she developed an idea, for which, perhaps, there was legitimate excuse, that he was lazy. He seemed to stand about a great deal, to read—an indolent habit—and presently to seek company for talking. He began to attend the bar-parlour of the God's Providence Inn with some frequency, and would have done so regularly in the evening if cards, which bored him to death, had not arrested conversation. But the perpetual foolish variation of the permutations and combinations of two-

17*

and-fifty cards taken five at a time, and the meagre surprises and excitements that ensue, had no charm for Mr. Polly's mind, which was at once too vivid in its impressions and too easily fatigued.

It was soon manifest the shop paid only in the most exacting sense, and Miriam did not conceal her opinion that he ought to bestir himself and " do things," though what he was to do was hard to say. You see, when you have once sunken your capital in a shop you do not very easily get it out again. If customers will not come to you cheerfully and freely, the law sets limits upon the compulsion you may exercise. You cannot pursue people about the streets of a watering-place, compelling them either by threats or importunity to buy flannel trousers. Additional sources of income for a tradesman are not always easy to find. Wintershed, at the bicycle and gramophone shop to the right, played the organ in the church, and Clamp of the toy-shop was pew-opener and so forth; Gambell, the greengrocer, waited at table and his wife cooked, and Carter, the watchmaker, left things to his wife while he went about the world winding clocks; but Mr. Polly had none of these arts, and wouldn't, in spite of Miriam's quietly persistent protests, get any other. And on summer evenings he would ride his bicycle about the country, and if he discovered a sale where there were books, he would as often as not waste half the next day in going again to acquire a job lot of them haphazard, and bring them home tied about with string, and hide them from Miriam under the counter in the shop. That is a heart-breaking thing for any wife with a serious investigatory turn of mind to discover. She was always thinking of burning these finds, but her natural turn for economy prevailed with her.

The books he read during those fifteen years! He read everything he got except theology, and, as he read, his little unsuccessful circumstances vanished and the wonder of life returned to him; the routine of reluctant getting up, opening shop, pretending to dust it with zest, breakfasting with a shop egg underdone or overdone, or a herring raw or charred, and coffee made Miriam's way, and full of little particles, the return to the shop, the morning paper, the standing, standing at the door saying "How do!" to passers-by, or getting a bit of gossip, or watching unusual visitors, all these things vanished as the auditorium of a theatre vanishes when the stage is lit. He acquired hundreds of books at last—old, dusty books, books with torn covers and broken covers, fat books whose backs were naked string and glue—an inimical litter to Miriam.

There was, for example, the voyages of La Perouse, with many careful, explicit woodcuts and the frankest revelations of the ways of the eighteenth-century sailor-man, homely, adventurous, drunken, incontinent, and delightful, until he floated, smooth and slow, with all sails set and mirrored in the glassy water, until his head was full of the thought of shining, kindly, brown-skinned women, who smiled at him and wreathed his head with unfamiliar flowers. He had, too, a piece of a book about the lost palaces of Yucatan, those vast terraces buried in primordial forest, of whose makers there is now no human memory. With La Perouse he linked "The Island Nights' Entertainments," and it never palled upon him that in the dusky stabbing of the "Island of Voices" something poured over the stabber's hands ".like warm tea." Queer, incommunicable joy it is, the joy of the vivid phrase that turns the statement of the horridest fact to beauty.

And another book which had no beginning for him was the second volume of the travels of the Abbés Huc and Gabet. He followed those two sweet souls from their lessons in Thibetan under Sandura the Bearded (who called them donkeys, to their infinite benefit, and stole their store of butter) through a hundred misadventures to the very heart of Lhasa; and it was a thirst in him that was never quenched to find the other volume and whence they came, and who in fact they were. He read Fenimore Cooper and "Tom Cringle's Log" side by side with Joseph Conrad, and dreamt of the many-hued humanity of the East and West Indies until his heart ached to see those sun-soaked lands before he died. Conrad's prose had a pleasure for him that he was never able to define, a peculiar, deep-coloured effect. He found, too, one day, among a pile of soiled sixpenny books at Port Burdock, to which place he sometimes rode on his aging bicycle, Bart Kennedy's "A Sailor Tramp," all written in vivid jerks, and had for ever after a kindlier and more understanding eye for every burly rough who slouched through Fishbourne High Street. Sterne he read with a wavering appreciation and some perplexity, but except for the "Pickwick Papers," for some reason that I do not understand, he never took at all kindly to Dickens. Yet he liked Lever, and Thackeray's "Catherine," and all Dumas until he got to the "Vicomte de Bragelonne." I am puzzled by his insensibility to Dickens, and I record it, as a good historian should, with an admission of my perplexity. It is much more understandable that he had no love for Scott. And I suppose it was because of his ignorance of the proper pronunciation of words that he infinitely preferred any prose to any metrical writing.

A book he browsed over with a recurrent pleasure was Waterton's "Wanderings in South America." He would even amuse himself by inventing descriptions of other birds in the Watertonian manner, new birds that he invented, birds with peculiarities that made him chuckle when they occurred to him. He tried to make Rusper, the ironmonger, share this joy with him. He read Bates, too, about the Amazon; but when he discovered that you could not see one bank from the other, he lost, through some mysterious action of the soul that again I cannot understand, at least a tithe of the pleasure he had taken in that river. But he read all

sorts of things; a book of old Keltic stories collected by
Joyce charmed him, and Mitford's "Tales of Old
Japan," and a number of paper-covered volumes,
"Tales from Blackwood," he had acquired at Easewood,
remained a stand-by. He developed a quite considerable acquaintance with the plays of William Shakespear,
and in his dreams he wore cinque cento or Elizabethan
clothes, and walked about a stormy, ruffling, taverning,
teeming world. Great land of sublimated things, thou
World of Books, happy asylum, refreshment, and refuge
from the world of every day! . . .

The essential thing of those fifteen long years of
shopkeeping is Mr. Polly, well athwart the counter of
his rather ill-lit shop, lost in a book, or rousing himself with a sigh to attend to business.

And meanwhile he got little exercise; indigestion
grew with him until it ruled all his moods; he fattened
and deteriorated physically, great moods of distress
invaded and darkened his skies, little things irritated
him more and more, and casual laughter ceased in him.
His hair began to come off until he had a large bald
space at the back of his head. Suddenly, one day it
came to him—forgetful of those books and all he had
lived and seen through them—that he had been in his
shop for exactly fifteen years, that he would soon be
forty, and that his life during that time had not been
worth living, that it had been in apathetic and feebly
hostile and critical company, ugly in detail and mean
in scope, and that it had brought him at last to an
outlook utterly hopeless and grey.

§ 3

I have already had occasion to mention, indeed I
have quoted, a certain high-browed gentleman living
at Highbury, wearing a golden *pince-nez,* and writing
for the most part in that very beautiful room, the
library of the Climax Club. There he wrestles with

what he calls "social problems" in a bloodless but at times, I think one must admit, an extremely illuminating manner. He has a fixed idea that something called a collective "intelligence" is wanted in the world, which means in practice that you and I and every one have to think about things frightfully hard and pool the results, and obliged ourselves to be shamelessly and persistently clear and truthful, and support and respect (I suppose) a perfect horde of professors and writers and artists and ill-groomed, difficult people, instead of using our brains in a moderate and sensible manner to play golf and bridge (pretending a sense of humour prevents our doing anything else with them), and generally taking life in a nice, easy, gentlemanly way, confound him! Well, this dome-headed monster of intellect alleges that Mr. Polly was unhappy entirely through that.

"A rapidly complicating society," he writes, "which, as a whole, declines to contemplate its future or face the intricate problems of its organisation, is in exactly the position of a man who takes no thought of dietary or regimen, who abstains from baths and exercise and gives his appetites free play. It accumulates useless and aimless lives, as a man accumulates fat and morbid products in his blood; it declines in its collective efficiency and vigour, and secretes discomfort and misery. Every phase of its evolution is accompanied by a maximum of avoidable distress and inconvenience and human waste. . . .

"Nothing can better demonstrate the collective dulness of our community, the crying need for a strenuous, intellectual renewal, than the consideration of that vast mass of useless, uncomfortable, under-educated, under-trained, and altogether pitiable people we contemplate when we use that inaccurate and misleading term, the Lower Middle Class. A great proportion of the lower middle class should properly be assigned to the unemployed and the unemployable. They are only not that, because the possession of some small hoard of money, savings during a period of wage-earning, an insurance policy or such like capital, prevents a direct appeal to the rates. But they are doing little or nothing for the community in return for what they consume; they have no understanding of any relation of service to the community; they have never been trained nor their imaginations touched to any social purpose. A great proportion of small shopkeepers, for example, are people who have, through the inefficiency that comes from inadequate training and sheer aimlessness, or through improvements in machinery or the drift of trade, been thrown out of employment, and who set up in needless shops as a method of eking out the savings upon which they count. They contrive to make sixty or seventy per cent. of their expenditure, the rest is drawn from the shrinking capital. Essentially their lives are failures, not the sharp and tragic failure of the labourer who gets out of work and starves, but a slow, chronic process of consecutive small losses which may end, if the individual is exceptionally fortunate, in an impoverished deathbed before actual bankruptcy or destitution supervenes. Their chances of ascendant means are less in their shops than in any lottery that was ever planned. The secular development of transit and communications has made the organisation of distributing businesses upon large and economical lines inevitable; except in the chaotic confusions of newly opened countries, the day when a man might earn an independent living by unskilled, or practically unskilled, retailing has gone for ever. Yet every year sees the melancholy procession towards petty bankruptcy and imprisonment for debt go on, and there is no statesmanship in us to avert it. Every issue of every trade journal has its four or five columns of abridged bankruptcy proceedings, nearly every item in which means the final collapse of another struggling family upon the resources of the community, and continually a fresh supply of superfluous artisans and shop-assistants, coming out of employment with savings or 'help' from relations, of widows with a husband's insurance money, of the ill-trained sons of parsimonious fathers, replaces the fallen in the ill-equipped, jerry-built shops that everywhere abound. . . ."

I quote these fragments from a gifted if unpleasant contemporary for what they are worth. I feel this has to come in here as the broad aspect of this History. I come back to Mr. Polly, sitting upon his gate and swearing in the east wind, and so returning I have a sense of floating across unbridged abysses between the general and the particular. There, on the one hand, is the man of understanding seeing clearly—I suppose he sees clearly—the big process that dooms millions of lives to thwarting and discomfort and unhappy circumstances, and giving us no help, no hint, by which we may get that better "collective will and intelligence" which would dam that stream of human failure; and on the other hand, Mr. Polly, sitting on his gate, untrained, unwarned, confused, distressed, angry, seeing nothing except that he is, as it were, netted in greyness and discomfort—with life dancing all about him; Mr. Polly with a capacity for joy and beauty at least as keen and subtle as yours or mine.

§ 4

I have hinted that our Mother England had equipped Mr. Polly for the management of his internal concerns no whit better than she had for the direction of his external affairs. With a careless generosity she affords her children a variety of foods unparalleled in the world's history, including many condiments and preserved preparations novel to the human economy. And Miriam did the cooking. Mr. Polly's system, like a confused and ill-governed democracy, had been brought to a state of perpetual clamour and disorder, demanding now evil and unsuitable internal satisfactions such as pickles and vinegar and the crackling on pork, and now vindictive external expressions such as war and bloodshed throughout the world. So that Mr. Polly had been led into hatred and a series of disagreeable quarrels with his landlord, his wholesalers, and most of his neighbours.

Rumbold, the china-dealer next door, seemed hostile from the first for no apparent reason, and always unpacked his crates with a full back to his new neighbour, and from the first Mr. Polly resented and hated that uncivil breadth of expressionless humanity, wanted to prod it, kick it, satirise. But you cannot satirise a back, if you have no friend to nudge while you do it.

At last Mr. Polly could stand it no longer. He approached and prodded Rumbold.

"'Ello!" said Rumbold, suddenly erect and turned about.

"Can't we have some other point of view?" said Mr. Polly. "I'm tired of the end elevation."

"Eh?" said Mr. Rumbold, frankly puzzled.

"Of all the vertebracious animals man alone raises his face to the sky, O' Man. Well, why avert it?"

Rumbold shook his head with a helpless expression.

"Don't like so much Arreary Pensy."

Rumbold, distressed, in utter obscurity.

"In fact, I'm sick of your turning your back on me, see?"

A great light shone on Rumbold. "*That's* what you're talking about!" he said.

"That's it," said Polly.

Rumbold scratched his ear with the three strawy jampots he held in his hand. "Way the wind blows, I expect," he said. "But what's the fuss?"

"No fuss!" said Mr. Polly. "Passing remark. I don't like it, O' Man, that's all."

"Can't help it, if the wind blows my stror," said Mr. Rumbold, still far from clear about it.

"It isn't ordinary civility," said Mr. Polly.

"Got to unpack 'ow it suits me. Can't unpack with the stror blowing into one's eyes."

"Needn't unpack like a pig rooting for truffles, need you?"

"Truffles?"

"Needn't unpack like a pig."

Mr. Rumbold apprehended something.

"Pig!" he said, impressed. "You calling me a pig?"

"It's the side I seem to get of you."

"'Ere," said Mr. Rumbold, suddenly fierce, and shouting and making his points with gesticulated jampots, "you go indoors. I don't want no row with you, and I don't want you to row with me. I don't know what you're after, but I'm a peaceful man—teetotaller, too, and a good thing if *you* was. See? You go indoors!"

"You mean to say— I'm asking you civilly to stop unpacking—with your back to me."

"Pig ain't civil and you ain't sober. You go indoors and lemme go on unpacking. You—you're excited."

"D'you mean——!" Mr. Polly was foiled.

He perceived an immense solidity about Rumbold.

"Get back to your shop and lemme get on with my business," said Mr. Rumbold. "Stop calling me pig. See? Sweep your pavemint."

"I came here to make a civil request."

"You came 'ere to make a row. I don't want no truck with you. See? I don't like the looks of you. See? And I can't stand 'ere all day arguing. See?"

Pause of mutual inspection.

It occurred to Mr. Polly that probably he was to some extent in the wrong.

Mr. Rumbold, blowing heavily, walked past him, deposited the jampots in his shop with an immense affectation that there was no Mr. Polly in the world, returned, turned a scornful back on Mr. Polly, and dived to the interior of the crate. Mr. Polly stood baffled. Should he kick this solid mass before him? Should he administer a resounding kick?

No!

He plunged his hands deeply into his trousers pockets, began to whistle, and returned to his own doorstep with an air of profound unconcern. There, for a time, to the tune of " Men of Harlech," he contemplated the receding possibility of kicking Mr. Rumbold hard. It would be splendid—and for the moment satisfying. But he decided not to do it. For indefinable reasons he could not do it. He went indoors and straightened up his dress ties very slowly and thoughtfully. Presently he went to the window and regarded Mr. Rumbold obliquely. Mr. Rumbold was still unpacking. . . .

Mr. Polly had no human intercourse thereafter with Rumbold for fifteen years. He kept up a Hate.

There was a time when it seemed as if Rumbold might go, but he had a meeting of his creditors and then went on unpacking as before, obtusely as ever.

§ 5

Hinks, the saddler, two shops farther down the street, was a different case. Hinks was the aggressor—practically.

Hinks was a sporting man in his way, with that taste for checks in costume and tight trousers which is, under Providence, so mysteriously and invariably associated with equestrian proclivities. At first Mr. Polly took to him as a character, became frequent in the God's Providence Inn under his guidance, stood and was stood drinks, and concealed a great ignorance of horses until Hinks became urgent for him to play billiards or bet.

Then Mr. Polly took to evading him, and Hinks ceased to conceal his opinion that Mr. Polly was in reality a softish sort of flat.

He did not, however, discontinue conversation with

Mr. Polly. He would come along to him whenever he appeared at his door and converse about sport and women and fisticuffs and the pride of life with an air of extreme initiation, until Mr. Polly felt himself the faintest underdeveloped simulacrum of man that had ever hovered on the verge of non-existence.

So he invented phrases for Hinks' clothes, and took Rusper, the ironmonger, into his confidence upon the weaknesses of Hinks. He called him the "chequered Careerist," and spoke of his patterned legs as "shivery shakys." Good things of this sort are apt to get round to people.

He was standing at his door one day, feeling bored, when Hinks appeared down the street, stood still, and regarded him with a strange, malignant expression for a space.

Mr. Polly waved a hand in a rather belated salutation.

Mr. Hinks spat on the pavement and appeared to reflect. Then he came towards Mr. Polly portentously and paused, and spoke between his teeth in an earnest, confidential tone.

"You been flapping your mouth about me, I'm told," he said.

Mr. Polly felt suddenly spiritless. "Not that I know of," he answered.

"Not that you know of, be blowed! You been flapping your mouth."

"Don't see it," said Mr. Polly.

"Don't see it, be blowed! You go flapping your silly mouth about me, and I'll give you a poke in the eye. See?"

Mr. Hinks regarded the effect of this coldly but firmly, and spat again.

"Understand me?" he inquired.

"Don't recollect," began Mr. Polly.

"Don't recollect, be blowed! You flap your mouth a damn sight too much. This place gets more of your mouth than it wants. . . . Seen this?"

And Mr. Hinks, having displayed a freckled fist of extraordinary size and pugginess in an ostentatiously familiar manner to Mr. Polly's close inspection by sight or smell, turned it about this way and that, shaking it gently for a moment or so, replaced it carefully in his pocket as if for future use, receded slowly and watchfully for a pace, and then turned away as if to other matters, and ceased to be, even in outward seeming, a friend.

§ 6

Mr. Polly's intercourse with all his fellow-tradesmen was tarnished sooner or later by some such adverse incident, until not a friend remained to him, and loneliness made even the shop door terrible. Shops bankrupted all about him, and fresh people came, and new acquaintances sprang up, but sooner or later a discord was inevitable—the tension under which these badly-fed, poorly-housed, bored and bothered neighbours lived made it inevitable. The mere fact that Mr. Polly had to see them every day, that there was no getting away from them, was in itself sufficient to make them almost unendurable to his frettingly active mind.

Among other shopkeepers in the High Street there was Chuffles, the grocer, a small, hairy, silently intent polygamist, who was given rough music by the youth of the neighbourhood because of a scandal about his wife's sister, and who was nevertheless totally uninteresting, and Tonks, the second grocer, an old man with an older, very enfeebled wife, both submerged by piety. Tonks went bankrupt, and was succeeded by a branch of the National Provision Company, with a young manager exactly like a fox, except that he barked. The toy and sweetstuff shop was kept by an old woman of repellent manners, and so was the little fish shop at the end of the street. The Berlinwool shop; having gone bankrupt, became a newspaper shop, then fell to a haberdasher in consumption, and finally to a stationer;

the three shops at the end of the street wallowed in and out of insolvency in the hands of a bicycle repairer and dealer, a gramophone dealer, a tobacconist, a six-penny-halfpenny bazaar keeper, a shoemaker, a greengrocer, and the exploiter of a cinematograph peep-show—but none of them supplied friendship to Mr. Polly.

These adventurers in commerce were all more or less distraught souls, driving without intelligible comment before the gale of fate. The two milkmen of Fishbourne were brothers who had quarrelled about their father's will and started in opposition to each other. One was stone deaf and no use to Mr. Polly, and the other was a sporting man with a natural dread of epithet, who sided with Hinks. So it was all about him; on every hand, it seemed, were uncongenial people, uninteresting people, or people who conceived the deepest distrust and hostility towards him—a magic circle of suspicious, preoccupied, and dehumanised humanity. So the poison in his system poisoned the world without.

But Boomer, the wine merchant, and Tashingford, the chemist, be it noted, were fraught with pride, and held themselves to be a cut above Mr. Polly. They never quarrelled with him, preferring to bear themselves from the outset as though they had already done so.

As his internal malady grew upon Mr. Polly, and he became more and more a battle-ground of fermenting foods and warring juices, he came to hate the very sight, as people say, of every one of these neighbours. There they were, every day and all the days, just the same, echoing his own stagnation. They pained him all round the top and back of his head; they made his legs and arms weary and spiritless. The air was tasteless by reason of them. He lost his human kindliness.

In the afternoons he would hover in the shop, bored to death with his business and his home and Miriam, and yet afraid to go out because of his inflamed and magnified dislike and dread of these neighbours. He could not bring himself to go out and run the gauntlet of the observant windows and the cold and estranged eyes.

One of his last friendships was with Rusper, the ironmonger. Rusper took over Worthington's shop about three years after Mr. Polly opened. He was a tall, lean, nervous, convulsive man, with an upturned, backthrown, oval head, who read newspapers and the *Review of Reviews* assiduously, had belonged to a Literary Society somewhere once, and had some defect of the palate that at first gave his lightest word a charm and interest for Mr. Polly. It caused a peculiar clinking sound, as though he had something between a giggle and a gas-meter at work in his neck.

His literary admirations were not precisely Mr. Polly's literary admirations; he thought books were written to enshrine Great Thoughts, and that art was pedagogy in fancy dress; he had no sense of phrase or epithet or richness of texture, but still he knew there were books. He did know there were books, and he was full of large, windy ideas of the sort he called "Modern (kik) Thought," and seemed needlessly and helplessly concerned about "(kik) the Welfare of the Race."

Mr. Polly would dream about that (kik) at nights.

It seemed to that undesirable mind of his that Rusper's head was the most egg-shaped head he had ever seen; the similarity weighed upon him, and when he found an argument growing warm with Rusper he would say, "Boil it some more, O' Man; boil it harder!" or "Six minutes at least," allusions Rusper could never make head or tail of, and got at last to disregard as a part of Mr. Polly's general eccentricity. For a long time that little tendency threw no shadow over their intercourse, but it contained within it the seeds of an ultimate disruption.

Often during the days of this friendship Mr. Polly would leave his shop and walk over to Mr. Rusper's establishment and stand in his doorway and inquire, "Well, O' Man, how's the Mind of the Age working?" and get quite an hour of it; and sometimes Mr. Rusper would come into the outfitter's shop with "Heard the (kik) latest?" and spend the rest of the morning.

Then Mr. Rusper married; and he married, very inconsiderately, a woman who was totally uninteresting to Mr. Polly. A coolness grew between them from the first intimation of her advent. Mr. Polly couldn't help thinking when he saw her that she drew her hair back from her forehead a great deal too tightly, and that her elbows were angular. His desire not to mention these things in the apt terms that welled up so richly in his mind made him awkward in her presence, and that gave her an impression that he was hiding some guilty secret from her. She decided he must have a bad influence upon her husband, and she made it a point to appear whenever she heard him talking to Rusper.

One day they became a little heated about the German peril.

"I lay (kik) they'll invade us," said Rusper.

"Not a bit of it. William's not the Xerxiacious sort."

"You'll see, O' Man."

"Just what I shan't do."

"Before (kik) five years are out."

"Not it."

"Yes."

"No."

"Yes."

"Oh, boil it hard!" said Mr. Polly.

Then he looked up and saw Mrs. Rusper standing behind the counter, half hidden by a trophy of spades and garden shears and a knife-cleaning machine, and by her expression he knew instantly that she understood.

The conversation paled, and presently Mr. Polly withdrew.

After that estrangement increased steadily.

Mr. Rusper ceased altogether to come over to the outfitter's, and Mr. Polly called upon the ironmonger only with the completest air of casualty. And everything they said to each other led now to flat contradiction and raised voices. Rusper had been warned in vague and alarming terms that Mr. Polly insulted and made game of him, he couldn't discover exactly where; and so it appeared to him now that every word of Mr. Polly's might be an insult meriting his resentment, meriting it none the less because it was masked and cloaked.

Soon Mr. Polly's calls upon Mr. Rusper ceased also; and then Mr. Rusper, pursuing incomprehensible lines of thought, became afflicted with a specialised shortsightedness that applied only to Mr. Polly. He would look in other directions when Mr. Polly appeared, and his large, oval face assumed an expression of conscious serenity and deliberate happy unawareness that would have maddened a far less irritable person than Mr. Polly. It evoked a strong desire to mock and ape, and produced in his throat a cough of singular scornfulness, more particularly when Mr. Rusper also assisted with an assumed unconsciousness that was all his own.

Then one day Mr. Polly had a bicycle accident.

His bicycle was now very old, and it is one of the concomitants of a bicycle's senility that its free-wheel should one day obstinately cease to be free. It corresponds to that epoch in human decay when an old gentleman loses an incisor tooth. It happened just as Mr. Polly was approaching Mr. Rusper's shop, and the untoward chance of a motor-car trying to pass a wagon on the wrong side gave Mr. Polly no choice but to get on to the pavement and dismount. He was always accustomed to take his time and step off his left pedal at its lowest point, but the jamming of the free-wheel gear made that lowest moment a transitory one, and the pedal was lifting his foot for another revolution before he realised what had happened. Before he could dismount according to his habit the pedal had to make a revolution, and before it could make a revolution Mr. Polly found himself among the various sonorous things with which Mr. Rusper adorned the front of his shop —zinc dustbins, household pails, lawn mowers, rakes, spades, and all manner of clattering things. Before he got among them he had one of those agonising moments of helpless wrath and suspense that seem to last ages, in which one seems to perceive everything and think of nothing but words that are better forgotten. He sent a column of pails thundering across the doorway, and dismounted with one foot in a sanitary dustbin, amidst an enormous uproar of falling ironmongery.

" Put all over the place!" he cried, and found Mr. Rusper emerging from his shop with the large tranquillities of his countenance puckered to anger, like the frowns in the brow of a reefing sail. He gesticulated speechlessly for a moment.

" (kik) Jer doing?" he said at last.

" Tin mantraps!" said Mr. Polly.

" Jer (kik) doing?"

" Dressing all over the pavement as though the blessed town belonged to you! Ugh!"

And Mr. Polly, in attempting a dignified movement, realised his entanglement with the dustbin for the first time. With a low, embittering expression, he kicked his foot about in it for a moment very noisily, and finally sent it thundering to the kerb. On its way it struck a pail or so. Then Mr. Polly picked up his bicycle and proposed to resume his homeward way. But the hand of Mr. Rusper arrested him.

" Put it (kik) all (kik) back (kik)."

" Put it (kik) back yourself."

" You got (kik) put it back."

" Get out of the (kik) way."

Mr. Rusper laid one hand on the bicycle handle,

and the other gripped Mr. Polly's collar urgently. Whereupon Mr. Polly said " Leggo!" and again " D'you *hear?* Leggo!" and then drove his elbow with considerable force into the region of Mr. Rusper's mid-riff. Whereupon Mr. Rusper, with a loud, impassioned cry resembling " Woo kik " more than any other com-bination of letters, released the bicycle handles, seized Mr. Polly by the cap and hair, and bore his head and shoulders downwards. Thereat Mr. Polly, emitting such words as every one knows and nobody prints, butted his utmost into the concavity of Mr. Rusper, entwined a leg about him, and, after terrific moments of swaying instability, fell headlong beneath him amidst the bicycle and pails. There on the pavement these inexpert children of a pacific age, untrained in arms and uninured to violence, abandoned themselves to amateurish and absurd efforts to hurt and injure one another—of which the most palpable consequences were dusty backs, ruffled hair, and torn and twisted collars. Mr. Polly by accident got his finger into Mr. Rusper's mouth, and strove earnestly for some time to prolong that aperture in the direction of Mr. Rusper's ear before it occurred to Mr. Rusper to bite him (and even then he didn't bite very hard), while Mr. Rusper concen-trated his mind almost entirely on an effort to rub Mr. Polly's face on the pavement. (And their positions bristled with chances of the deadliest sort!) They did'n't, from first to last, draw blood.

Then it seemed to each of them that the other had become endowed with many hands and several voices and great accessions of strength. They submitted to fate and ceased to struggle. They found themselves torn apart and held up by outwardly scandalised and inwardly delighted neighbours, and invited to explain what it was all about.

" Got to (kik) puttem all back," panted Mr. Rusper, in the expert grasp of Hinks " Merely asked him to (kik) puttem all back."

Mr. Polly was under restraint of little Clamp of the toyshop, who was holding his hands in a complex and uncomfortable manner that he afterwards explained to Wintershed was a combination of something romantic called "Jiu-jitsu" and something else still more romantic called the "Police Grip."

"Pails," explained Mr. Polly, in breathless fragments. "All over the road. Pails. Bungs up the street with his pails. Look at them!"

"Deliber (kik) lib (kik) liberately rode into my goods (kik). Constantly (kik) annoying me (kik)!" said Mr. Rusper.

They were both tremendously earnest and reasonable in their manner. They wished every one to regard them as responsible and intellectual men acting for the love of right and the enduring good of the world. They felt they must treat this business as a profound and publicly significant affair. They wanted to explain and orate and show the entire necessity of everything they had done. Mr. Polly was convinced he had never been so absolutely correct in all his life as when he planted his foot in the sanitary dustbin, and Mr. Rusper considered his clutch at Mr. Polly's hair as the one faultless impulse in an otherwise undistinguished career. But it was clear in their minds they might easily become ridiculous if they were not careful, if for a second they stepped over the edge of the high spirit and pitiless dignity they had hitherto maintained. At any cost they perceived they must not become ridiculous.

Mr. Chuffles, the scandalous grocer, joined the throng about the principal combatants, mutely, as became an outcast, and with a sad, distressed, helpful expression picked up Mr. Polly's bicycle. Gambell's summer errand-boy, moved by example, restored the dustbin and pails to their self-respect.

"'E ought—'e ought (kik) pick them up," protested Mr. Rusper.

"What's it all about?" said Mr. Hinks for the third

time, shaking Mr. Rusper gently. "'As 'e been calling you names?"

"Simply ran into his pails—as any one might," said Mr. Polly, "and out he comes and scrags me."

"(kik) Assault!" said Mr. Rusper.

"He assaulted *me*," said Mr. Polly.

"Jumped (kik) into my dus'bin," said Mr. Rusper. "That assault? Or isn't it?"

"You better drop it," said Mr. Hinks.

"Great pity they can't be'ave better, both of 'em," said Mr. Chuffles, glad for once to find himself morally unassailable.

"Any one see it begin?" said Mr. Wintershed.

"*I* was in the shop," said Mrs. Rusper suddenly, from the doorstep, piercing the little group of men and boys with the sharp horror of a woman's voice. "If a witness is wanted, I suppose I've got a tongue. I suppose I got a voice in seeing my own husband injured. My husband went out and spoke to Mr. Polly, who was jumping off and on his bicycle all among our pails and things, and immediately 'E butted him in the stomach—immediately—most savagely—butted him. Just after his dinner, too, and him far from strong. I could have screamed. But Rusper caught hold of him right away, I will say that for Rusper——"

"I'm going," said Mr. Polly suddenly, releasing himself from the Anglo-Japanese grip and holding out his hands for his bicycle.

"Teach you (kik) to leave things alone," said Mr. Rusper, with an air of one who has given a lesson.

The testimony of Mrs. Rusper continued relentlessly in the background.

"You'll hear of me through a summons," said Mr. Polly, preparing to wheel his bicycle.

"(kik) Me too," said Mr. Rusper.

Some one handed Mr. Polly a collar. "This yours?"

Mr. Polly investigated his neck. "I suppose it is. Any one seen a tie?"

A small boy produced a grimy strip of spotted blue silk.

"Human life isn't safe with you," said Mr. Polly as a parting shot.

"(kik) Yours isn't," said Mr. Rusper.

And they got small satisfaction out of the Bench, which refused altogether to perceive the relentless correctitude of the behaviour of either party, and reproved the eagerness of Mrs. Rusper—speaking to her gently, firmly but exasperatingly as "My Good Woman," and telling her to "Answer the Question! Answer the Question!"

"Seems a Pity," said the chairman, when binding them over to keep the peace, "you can't behave like Respectable Tradesmen. Seems a Great Pity. Bad Example to the Young and all that. Don't do any Good to the town, don't do any Good to yourselves, don't do any manner of Good, to have all the Tradesmen in the Place scrapping about the Pavement of an Afternoon. Think we're letting you off very easily this time, and hope it will be a Warning to you. Don't expect men of your position to come up before us. Very Regrettable Affair. Eh?"

He addressed the latter enquiry to his two colleagues.

"Exactly, exactly," said the colleague to the right.

"Err (kik)," said Mr. Rusper.

§ 7

But the disgust that overshadowed Mr. Polly's being as he sat upon the stile had other and profounder justification than his quarrel with Rusper and the indignity of appearing before the county bench. He was, for the first time in his business career, short with his rent for the approaching quarter day; and, so far as he could trust his own handling of figures, he was sixty or seventy pounds on the wrong side of solvency. And that was the outcome of fifteen years of passive endurance of dulness throughout the best years of his life. What would Miriam say when she learned this, and was invited to face the prospect of exile—Heaven knows what sort of exile—from their present home? She would grumble and scold and become limply unhelpful, he knew, and none the less so because he could not help things. She would say he ought to have worked harder, and a hundred such exasperating, pointless things. Such thoughts as these require no aid from undigested cold pork and cold potatoes and pickles to darken the soul, and with these aids his soul was black indeed.

"May as well have a bit of a walk," said Mr. Polly at last, after nearly intolerable meditations, and sat round and put a leg over the stile.

He remained still for some time before he brought over the other leg.

"Kill myself," he murmured at last.

It was an idea that came back to his mind nowadays with a continually increasing attractiveness, more particularly after meals. Life, he felt, had no further happiness for him. He hated Miriam, and there was no getting away from her, whatever might betide. And for the rest, there was toil and struggle, toil and struggle with a falling heart and dwindling courage, to sustain that dreary duologue. "Life's insured," said Mr. Polly; "place is insured. I don't see it does any harm to her or any one."

He stuck his hands in his pockets. "Needn't hurt much," he said. He began to elaborate a plan.

He found it was quite interesting elaborating his plan. His countenance became less miserable and his pace quickened.

There is nothing so good in all the world for melancholia as walking, and the exercise of the imagination in planning something presently to be done, and soon the wrathful wretchedness had vanished from Mr. Polly's face. He would have to do the thing secretly and elaborately, because otherwise there might be difficulties about the life insurance. He began to scheme how he could circumvent that difficulty. . . .

He took a long walk, for, after all, what is the good of hurrying back to shop when you are not only insolvent but very soon to die? His dinner and the east wind lost their sinister hold upon his soul, and when at last he came back along the Fishbourne High Street his face was unusually bright and the craving hunger of the dyspeptic was returning. So he went into the grocer's and bought a ruddily decorated tin of a brightly pink fish-like substance known as " Deep Sea Salmon." This he was resolved to consume, regardless of cost, with vinegar and salt and pepper as a relish to his supper.

He did, and since he and Miriam rarely talked, and Miriam thought honour and his recent behaviour demanded a hostile silence, he ate fast and copiously and soon gloomily. He ate alone, for she refrained, to mark her sense of his extravagance. Then he prowled into the High Street for a time, thought it an infernal place, tried his pipe and found it foul and bitter, and retired wearily to bed.

He slept for an hour or so, and then woke up to the contemplation of Miriam's hunched back and the riddle of life, and this bright and attractive idea of ending for ever and ever and ever all the things that were locking him in, this bright idea that shone like a baleful star above all the reek and darkness of his misery. . . .

CHAPTER THE EIGHTH

Making an End to Things

§ 1

MR. POLLY designed his suicide with considerable care and a quite remarkable altruism.

His passionate hatred for Miriam vanished directly the idea of getting away from her for ever became clear in his mind. He found himself full of solicitude then for her welfare. He did not want to buy his release at her expense. He had not the remotest intention of leaving her unprotected, with a painfully dead husband and a bankrupt shop on her hands. It seemed to him that he could contrive to secure for her the full benefit of both his life insurance and his fire insurance if he managed things in a tactful manner. He felt happier than he had done for years. scheming out this undertaking, albeit it was, perhaps, a larger and sombrerer kind of happiness than had fallen to his lot before. It amazed him to think he had endured his monotony of misery and failure for so long.

But there were some queer doubts and questions in the dim, half-lit background of his mind that he had very resolutely to ignore.

543   18

"Sick of it," he had to repeat to himself aloud to keep his determination clear and firm. His life was a failure; there was nothing more to hope for but unhappiness. Why shouldn't he?

His project was to begin the fire with the stairs that led from the ground floor to the underground kitchen and scullery. This he would soak with paraffin, and assist with firewood and paper and a brisk fire in the coal cellar underneath. He would smash a hole or so in the stairs to ventilate the blaze, and have a good pile of boxes and paper, and a convenient chair or so, in the shop above. He would have the paraffin can upset, and the shop lamp, as if awaiting refilling, at convenient distances in the scullery ready to catch. Then he would smash the house lamp on the staircase —a fall with that in his hand was to be the ostensible cause of the blaze—and he would cut his throat at the top of the kitchen stairs, which would then become his funeral pyre. He would do all this on Sunday evening while Miriam was at church, and it would appear that he had fallen downstairs with the lamp and been burned to death. There was really no flaw whatever that he could see in the scheme. He was quite sure he knew how to cut his throat, deep at the side and not to saw at the windpipe, and he was reasonably sure it wouldn't hurt him very much. And then everything would be at an end.

There was no particular hurry to get the thing done, of course, and meanwhile he occupied his mind with possible variations of the scheme. . . .

It needed a particularly dry and dusty east wind, a Sunday dinner of exceptional virulence, a conclusive letter from Konk, Maybrick, Ghool, and Gabitas, his principal and most urgent creditors, and a conversation with Miriam, arising out of arrears of rent and leading on to mutual character sketching, before Mr. Polly could be brought to the necessary pitch of despair to carry out his plans. He went for an embittering walk, and came back to find Miriam in a bad temper over the tea things, with the brewings of three-quarters of an hour in the pot and hot buttered muffins gone leathery. He sat eating in silence with his resolution made.

"Coming to church?" said Miriam after she had cleared away.

"Rather. I got a lot to be grateful for," said Mr. Polly.

"You got what you deserve," said Miriam.

"Suppose I have," said Mr. Polly, and went and stared out of the back window at a despondent horse in the hotel yard.

He was still standing there when Miriam came downstairs dressed for church. Something in his immobility struck home to her. "You'd better come to church than mope," she said.

"I shan't mope," he answered.

She remained still. Her presence irritated him. He felt that in another moment he should say something absurd to her, make some last appeal for that understanding she had never been able to give. "Oh! *go* to church," he said.

In another moment the outer door slammed upon her. "Good riddance!" said Mr. Polly.

He turned about. "I've had my whack," he said. He reflected. "I don't see she'll have any cause to holler," he said. "Beastly Home! Beastly Life!"

For a space he remained thoughtful. "Here goes!" he said at last.

§ 2

For twenty minutes Mr. Polly busied himself about the house, making his preparations very neatly and methodically.

He opened the attic windows, in order to make sure of a good draught through the house, and drew down the blinds at the back and shut the kitchen door to conceal his arrangements from casual observation. At the end he would open the door on the yard and so make a clean, clear draught right through the house. He hacked at, and wedged off, the tread of a stair. He cleared out the coals from under the staircase, and built a neat fire of firewood and paper there; he splashed about paraffin and arranged the lamps and can even as he had designed, and made a fine, inflammable pile of things in the little parlour behind the shop. "Looks pretty arsonical," he said, as he surveyed it all. "Wouldn't do to have a caller now. Now for the stairs!"

"Plenty of time," he assured himself, and took the lamp which was to explain the whole affair, and went to the head of the staircase between the scullery and the parlour. He sat down in the twilight, with the unlit lamp beside him, and surveyed things. He must light the fire in the coal cellar under the stairs, open the back door, then come up them very quickly and light the paraffin puddles on each step, then sit down here again and cut his throat. He drew his razor from his pocket and felt the edge. It wouldn't hurt much, and in ten minutes he would be indistinguishable ashes in the blaze.

And this was the end of life for him!

The end! And it seemed to him now that life had never begun for him, never! It was as if his soul had been cramped and his eyes bandaged from the hour of his birth. Why had he lived such a life? Why had he submitted to things, blundered into things? Why had he never insisted on the things he thought beautiful and the things he desired, never sought them, fought for them, taken any risk for them, died rather than abandon them? They were the things that mattered. Safety did not matter. A living did not matter unless there were things to live for. . . .

He had been a fool, a coward and a fool; he had been fooled, too, for no one had ever warned him to take a firm hold upon life, no one had ever told him of the littleness of fear or pain or death. But what was the good of going through it now again? It was over and done with.

The clock in the back parlour pinged the half-hour. "Time!" said Mr. Polly, and stood up.

For an instant he battled with an impulse to put it all back, hastily, guiltily, and abandon this desperate plan of suicide for ever.

But Miriam would smell the paraffin!

"No way out this time, O' Man," said Mr. Polly, and went slowly downstairs, matchbox in hand.

He paused for five seconds, perhaps, to listen to noises in the yard of the Royal Fishbourne Hotel before he struck his match. It trembled a little in his hand. The paper blackened, and an edge of blue flame ran outward and spread. The fire burned up readily, and in an instant the wood was crackling cheerfully.

Some one might hear. He must hurry.

He lit a pool of paraffin on the scullery floor, and instantly a nest of wavering blue flame became agog for prey. He went up the stairs three steps at a time, with one eager blue flicker in pursuit of him. He seized the lamp at the top. "Now!" he said, and flung it smashing. The chimney broke, but the glass receiver stood the shock and rolled to the bottom, a potential bomb. Old Rumbold would hear that and wonder what it was. . . . He'd know soon enough!

Then Mr. Polly stood hesitating, razor in hand, and then sat down. He was trembling violently, but quite unafraid.

He drew the blade lightly under one ear. "Lord!" but it stung like a nettle!

Then he perceived a little blue thread of flame running up his leg. It arrested his attention, and for a moment he sat, razor in hand, staring at it. It must be paraffin. On his trousers that had caught fire on the stairs. Of course his legs were wet with paraffin! He smacked the flicker with his hand to put it out, and felt his leg burn as he did so. But his trousers still charred and glowed. It seemed to him necessary that he must put this out before he cut his throat. He put down the razor beside him to smack with both hands very eagerly. And as he did so a thin, tall, red flame came up through the hole in the stairs he had made and stood still, quite still, as it seemed, and looked at him. It was a strange-looking flame, a flattish, salmon colour, redly streaked. It was so queer and quiet-mannered that the sight of it held Mr. Polly agape.

"Whuff!" went the can of paraffin below, and boiled over with stinking white fire. At the outbreak, the salmon-coloured flames shivered and ducked and then doubled and vanished, and instantly all the staircase was noisily ablaze.

Mr. Polly sprang up and backwards, as though the uprushing tongues of fire were a pack of eager wolves.

"Good Lord!" he cried, like a man who wakes up from a dream.

He swore sharply, and slapped again at a recrudescent flame upon his leg.

"What the Deuce shall I do? I'm soaked with the confounded stuff!"

He had nerved himself for throat-cutting, but this was fire!

He wanted to delay things, to put the fire out for a moment while he did his business. The idea of arresting all this hurry with water occurred to him.

There was no water in the little parlour and none in the shop. He hesitated for a moment whether he should not run upstairs to the bedroom and get a ewer of water to throw on the flames. At this rate Rumbold's would be ablaze in five minutes. Things were going all too fast for Mr. Polly. He ran towards the staircase door, and its hot breath pulled him up sharply. Then he dashed out through the shop. The catch of the front door was sometimes obstinate; it was now, and instantly he became frantic. He rattled and stormed and felt the parlour already ablaze behind him. In another moment he was in the High Street with the door wide open.

The staircase behind him was crackling now like horsewhips and pistol-shots.

He had a vague sense that he wasn't doing as he had proposed, but the chief thing was his sense of that uncontrolled fire within. What was he going to do? There was the fire-brigade station next door but one.

The Fishbourne High Street had never seemed so empty.

Far off, at the corner by the God's Providence Inn, a group of three stiff hobbledehoys in their black, neat clothes conversed intermittently with Taplow, the policeman.

"Hi!" bawled Mr. Polly to them. "Fire! Fire!" and, struck by a horrible thought, he thought of Rumbold's deaf mother-in-law upstairs, began to bang and kick and rattle with the utmost fury at Rumbold's shop door.

"Hi!" he repeated, "Fire!"

§ 3

That was the beginning of the great Fishbourne fire, which burned its way sideways into Mr. Rusper's pile of crates and straw, and backwards to the petrol and stabling of the Royal Fishbourne Hotel, and spread from that basis until it seemed half Fishbourne would be ablaze. The east wind, which had been gathering in strength all that day, fanned the flames; everything was dry and ready, and the little shed beyond Rumbold's, in which the local fire brigade kept its manual, was alight before the Fishbourne fire-hose could be saved from disaster. In a marvellously short time a great column of black smoke, shot with red streamers, rose out of the middle of the High Street, and all Fishbourne was alive with excitement.

Much of the more respectable elements of Fishbourne society was in church or chapel; many, however, had been tempted by the blue sky and the hard freshness of spring to take walks inland, and there had been the usual disappearance of loungers and conversationalists from the beach and the back streets when, at the hour of six, the shooting of the bolts and the turning of keys had ended the British Ramadan, that weekly interlude of drought our law imposes. The youth of the place were scattered on the beach or playing in backyards, under threat if their clothes were dirtied; and the adolescent were disposed in pairs among the more secluded corners to be found upon the outskirts of the place. Several godless youths, seasick, but fishing steadily, were tossing upon the sea in old Tarbold the infidel's boat, and the Clamps were entertaining cousins from Port Burdock. Such few visitors as Fishbourne could boast in the spring were at church or on the beach. To all these that column of smoke did in a manner address itself. "Look here!" it said, "this, within limits, is your affair; what are you going to do?"

The three hobbledehoys, had it been a week-day and they in working-clothes, might have felt free to act, but the stiffness of black was upon them, and they simply moved to the corner by Rusper's to take a better view of Mr. Polly beating at his door. The policeman was a young, inexpert constable with far too lively a sense of the public-house. He put his head inside the Private Bar, to the horror of every one there. But there was no breach of the law, thank Heaven! "Polly's and Rumbold's on fire!" he said, and vanished again. A window opened in the top-story over Boomer's shop, and Boomer, captain of the fire brigade, appeared, staring out with a blank expression. Still staring, he began to fumble with his collar and tie; manifestly he had to put on his uniform. Hinks' dog, which had been lying on the pavement outside Wintershed's, woke up, and having regarded Mr. Polly suspiciously for some time, growled nervously and went round the corner into Granville Alley. Mr. Polly continued to beat and kick at Rumbold's door.

Then the public-houses began to vomit forth the less desirable elements of Fishbourne society; boys and men were moved to run and shout, and more windows went up as the stir increased. Tashingford, the chemist, appeared at his door, in shirt-sleeves and an apron, with his photographic plate-holders in his hand. And then, like a vision of purpose, came Mr. Gambell, the green-grocer, running out of Gayford's alley and buttoning on his jacket as he ran. His great brass fireman's helmet was on his head, hiding it all but the sharp nose, the firm mouth, the intrepid chin. He ran straight to the fire station and tried the door, and turned about and met the eye of Boomer still at his upper window. "The key!" cried Mr. Gambell, "the key!"

Mr. Boomer made some inaudible explanation about his trousers and half a minute.

"Seen old Rumbold?" cried Mr. Polly, approaching Mr. Gambell.

"Gone over Downford for a walk," said Mr. Gambell. "He told me! But look 'ere! We 'aven't got the key!"

"Lord!" said Mr. Polly, and regarded the china shop with open eyes. He knew the old woman must be there alone. He went back to the shop front, and stood surveying it in infinite perplexity. The other activities in the street did not interest him. A deaf old lady somewhere upstairs there! Precious moments passing! Suddenly he was struck by an idea, and vanished from public vision into the open door of the Royal Fishbourne Tap.

And now the street was getting crowded, and people were laying their hands to this and that.

Mr. Rusper had been at home reading a number of

18*

tracts upon Tariff Reform, during the quiet of the wife's absence in church, and trying to work out the application of the whole question to ironmongery. He heard a clattering in the street, and for a time disregarded it, until a cry of "Fire!" drew him to the window. He pencil-marked the tract of Chiozza Money's that he was reading side by side with one by Mr. Holt Schooling, made a hasty note, "Bal of Trade say 12,000,000," and went to look out. Instantly he opened the window and ceased to believe the Fiscal Question the most urgent of human affairs.

"Good (kik) Gud!" said Mr. Rusper.

For now the rapidly spreading blaze had forced the partition into Mr. Rumbold's premises, swept across his cellar, clambered his garden wall by means of his well-tarred mushroom shed, and assailed the engine-house. It stayed not to consume, but ran as a thing that seeks a quarry. Polly's shop and upper parts were already a furnace, and black smoke was coming out of Rumbold's cellar gratings. The fire in the engine-house showed only as a sudden rush of smoke from the back, like something suddenly blown up. The fire brigade, still much under strength, were now hard at work in front of the latter building. They had got the door open all too late; they had rescued the fire-escape and some buckets, and were now lugging out their manual, with the hose already a dripping mass of molten, flaring, stinking rubber. Boomer was dancing about and swearing and shouting; this direct attack upon his apparatus outraged his sense of chivalry. His subordinates hovered in a disheartened state about the rescued fire-escape, and tried to piece Boomer's comments into some tangible instructions.

"Hi!" said Rusper from the window. "(kik) What's up?"

Gambell answered him out of his helmet. "Hose!" he cried. "Hose gone!"

"I (kik) got hose," cried Rusper.

He had. He had a stock of several thousand feet of garden hose of various qualities and calibres, and now, he felt, was the time to use it. In another moment his shop door was open, and he was hurling pails, garden syringes, and rolls of garden hose out upon the pavement. "(kik) Undo it!" he cried to the gathering crowd in the roadway.

They did. Presently a hundred ready hands were unrolling and spreading and tangling up and twisting and hopelessly involving Mr. Rusper's stock of hose, sustained by an unquenchable assurance that presently it would in some manner contain and convey water; and Mr. Rusper on his knees, kiking violently, became incredibly busy with wire and brass junctions and all sorts of mysteries.

"Fix it to the (kik) bathroom tap!" said Mr. Rusper.

Next door to the fire station was Mantell and Throbsons', the little Fishbourne branch of that celebrated firm, and Mr. Boomer, seeking in a teeming mind for a plan of action, had determined to save this building. "Some one telephone to the Port Burdock and Hampstead-on-Sea fire brigades," he cried to the crowd, and then to his fellows: "Cut away the woodwork of the fire station!" and so led the way into the blaze with a whirling hatchet that effected wonders of ventilation in no time.

But it was not, after all, such a bad idea of his. Mantell and Throbsons' was separated from the fire station in front by a covered glass passage, and at the back the roof of the big outhouse sloped down to the fire station leads. The sturdy longshoremen, who made up the bulk of the fire brigade, assailed the glass roof of the passage with extraordinary gusto, and made a smashing of glass that drowned for a time the rising uproar of the flames.

A number of willing volunteers started off to the new telephone office in obedience to Mr. Boomer's request, only to be told, with cold official politeness by the young lady at the exchange, that all that had been done on her initiative ten minutes ago. She parleyed with these heated enthusiasts for a space, and then returned to the window.

And, indeed the spectacle was well worth looking at. The dusk was falling, and the flames were showing brilliantly at half a dozen points. The Royal Fishbourne Hotel Tap, which adjoined Mr. Polly to the west, was being kept wet by the enthusiastic efforts of a string of volunteers with buckets of water, and above, at a bathroom window, the little German waiter was busy with a garden hose. But Mr. Polly's establishment looked more like a house afire than most houses on fire contrive to look from start to finish. Every window showed eager flickering flames, and flames like serpents' tongues were licking out of three large holes in the roof, which was already beginning to fall in. Behind, larger and abundantly spark-shot gusts of fire rose from the fodder that was now getting alight in the Royal Fishbourne Hotel stables. Next door to Mr. Polly, Mr. Rumbold's house was disgorging black smoke from the gratings that protected its underground windows, and smoke and occasional shivers of flame were also coming out of its first-floor windows. The fire station was better alight at the back than in front, and its woodwork burned pretty briskly with peculiar greenish flickerings, and a pungent flavour. In the street an inaggressively disorderly crowd clambered over the rescued fire-escape, and resisted the attempts of the three local constables to get it away from the danger of Mr. Polly's tottering façade; a cluster of busy forms danced and shouted and advised on the noisy and smashing attempt to cut off Mantell and Throbsons' from the fire station that was still in effectual progress. Further, a number of people appeared to be destroying interminable red and grey snakes under the heated direction of Mr. Rusper—it was as if the High Street had a plague of worms; and beyond again, the more timid and less active crowded in front of an accumulation of arrested traffic. Most of the men were in Sabbatical black, and this, and the white and starched quality of the women and children in their best clothes, gave a note of ceremony to the whole affair.

For a moment the attention of the telephone clerk was held by the activities of Mr. Tashingford, the chemist, who, regardless of every one else, was rushing across the road hurling fire grenades into the fire station and running back for more, and then her eyes lifted to the slanting outhouse roof that went up to a ridge behind the parapet of Mantell and Throbsons'. An expression of incredulity came into the telephone operator's eyes, and gave place to hard activity. She flung up the window and screamed out, "Two people on the roof up there! Two people on the roof!"

§ 4

Her eyes had not deceived her. Two figures, which had emerged from the upper staircase window of Mr. Rumbold's and had got, after a perilous paddle in his cistern, on to the fire station, were now slowly but resolutely clambering up the outhouse roof towards the back of the main premises of Messrs. Mantell and Throbsons'. They clambered slowly, and one urged and helped the other, slipping and pausing ever and again amidst a constant trickle of fragments of broken tile.

One was Mr. Polly, with his hair wildly disordered, his face covered with black smudges and streaked with perspiration, and his trouser legs scorched and blackened; the other was an elderly lady, quietly but becomingly dressed in black with small white frills at her neck and wrists, and a Sunday cap of écru lace enlivened with a black velvet bow. Her hair was brushed back from her wrinkled brow and plastered down tightly, meeting in a small knob behind; her wrinkled mouth bore that expression of supreme resolution common with the toothless aged. She was shaky, not with fear, but with the vibrations natural to her years, and she spoke with a slow, quavering firmness.

"I don't mind scrambling," she said with piping inflexibility, "but I can't jump, and I won't jump."

"Scramble, old lady, then, scramble!" said Mr. Polly, pulling her arm. "It's one up and two down on these blessed tiles."

"It's not what I'm used to," she said.

"Stick to it," said Mr. Polly. "Live and learn," and got to the ridge and grasped at her arm to pull her after him.

"I can't jump, mind ye," she repeated, pressing her lips together. "And old ladies like me mustn't be hurried."

"Well, let's get as high as possible, anyhow," said Mr. Polly, urging her gently upwards. "Shinning up a waterspout in your line? Near as you'll get to Heaven."

"I *can't* jump," she said. "I can do anything but jump."

"Hold on," said Mr. Polly, "while I give you a boost. That's—wonderful."

"So long as it isn't jumping. . . ."

The old lady grasped the parapet above, and there was a moment of intense struggle.

"Urup!" said Mr. Polly. "Hold on! Gollys! where's she gone to? . . ."

Then an ill-mended, wavering, yet very reassuring spring-side boot appeared for an instant.

"Thought perhaps there wasn't any roof there!" he explained, scrambling up over the parapet beside her.

"I've never been out on a roof before," said the old lady. "I'm all disconnected. It's very bumpy. Especially that last bit. Can't we sit here for a bit and rest? I'm not the girl I used to be."

"You sit here ten minutes," shouted Mr. Polly, "and

you'll pop like a roast chestnut. Don't understand me?
Roast Chestnut! ROAST CHESTNUT! POP!
There ought to be a limit to deafness. Come on round
to the front and see if we can find an attic window.
Look at this smoke!"

"Nasty!" said the old lady, her eyes following his
gesture, puckering her face into an expression of great
distaste.

"Come on!"

"Can't hear a word you say."

He pulled her arm. "Come on!"

She paused for a moment to relieve herself of a series
of entirely unexpected chuckles. "Sich goings on!"
she said. "I never did! Where's he going now?"
and came along behind the parapet to the front of the
drapery establishment.

Below, the street was now fully alive to their presence, and encouraged the appearance of their heads by
shouts and cheers. A sort of free fight was going on
round the fire-escape, order represented by Mr. Boomer
and the very young policeman, and disorder by some
partially intoxicated volunteers with views of their own
about the manipulation of the apparatus. Two or three
lengths of Mr. Rusper's garden hose appeared to have
twined themselves round the ladder. Mr. Polly
watched the struggle with a certain impatience, and
glanced ever and again over his shoulder at the increasing volume of smoke and steam that was pouring up
from the burning fire station. He decided to break an
attic window and get in, and so try and get down
through the shop. He found himself in a little bedroom, and returned to fetch his charge. For some time
he could not make her understand his purpose.

"Got to come at once!" he shouted.

"I hain't 'ad sich a time for years!" said the old
lady.

"We'll have to get down through the house!"

"Can't do no jumping," said the old lady. "No!"

She yielded reluctantly to his grasp.

She stared over the parapet. "Runnin' and scurrying about like black beetles in a kitchen," she said.

"We've got to hurry."

"Mr. Rumbold 'E's a very Quiet man. 'E likes everything Quiet. He'll be surprised to see me 'ere! Why! there 'E is!" She fumbled in her garments mysteriously, and at last produced a wrinkled pocket-handkerchief and began to wave it.

"Oh, come ON!" cried Mr. Polly, and seized her.

He got her into the attic, but the staircase, he found, was full of suffocating smoke, and he dared not venture below the next floor. He took her into a long dormitory, shut the door on those pungent and pervasive fumes, and opened the window, to discover the fire-escape was now against the house, and all Fishbourne boiling with excitement as an immensely helmeted and active and resolute little figure ascended. In another moment the rescuer stared over the window-sill, heroic but just a trifle self-conscious and grotesque.

"Lawks-a-mussy!" said the old lady. "Wonders and Wonders! Why! it's Mr. Gambell! 'Iding 'is 'ead in that thing! I *never* did!"

"Can we get her out?" said Mr. Gambell. "There's not much time."

"He might git stuck in it."

"*You'll* get stuck in it," said Mr. Polly; "come along!"

"Not for jumpin' I don't," said the old lady, understanding his gestures rather than his words. "Not a bit of it. I bain't no good at jumping, and I *wun't.*"

They urged her gently but firmly towards the window.

"You lemme do it my own way," said the old lady at the sill. . . .

"I could do it better if 'e'd take it off."

"Oh! *carm* on!"

"It's wuss than Carter's stile," she said, "before they mended it—with a cow looking at you."

Mr. Gambell hovered protectingly below. Mr. Polly steered her aged limbs from above. An anxious crowd below babbled advice and did its best to upset the fire-escape. Within, streamers of black smoke were pouring up through cracks in the floor. For some seconds the world waited while the old lady gave herself up to reckless mirth again. "Sich times!" she said. "Poor Rumbold!"

Slowly they descended, and Mr. Polly remained at the post of danger, steadying the long ladder, until the old lady was in safety below and sheltered by Mr. Rumbold (who was in tears) and the young policeman from the urgent congratulations of the crowd. The crowd was full of an impotent passion to participate. Those nearest wanted to shake her hand, those remoter cheered.

"The fust fire I was ever in, and likely to be my last. It's a scurryin', 'urryin' business, but I'm real glad I haven't missed it," said the old lady, as she was borne rather than led towards the refuge of the Temperance Hotel.

Also she was heard to remark: "'E was saying something about 'ot chestnuts. *I* haven't 'ad no 'ot chestnuts."

Then the crowd became aware of Mr. Polly awkwardly negotiating the top rungs of the fire-escape. "'Ere 'e comes!" proclaimed a voice; and Mr. Polly descended into the world again out of the conflagration he had lit to be his funeral-pyre, moist, excited, and tremendously alive, amidst a tempest of applause. As he got lower and lower, the crowd howled like a pack of dogs at him. Impatient men, unable to wait for him, seized and shook his descending boots, and so brought him to earth with a run. He was rescued with difficulty from an enthusiast who wished to slake at his own expense and to his own accompaniment a thirst altogether heroic. He was hauled into the Temperance Hotel and flung like a sack, breathless and helpless, into the tear-wet embrace of Miriam.

§ 5

With the dusk and the arrival of some county constabulary, and first one and presently two other fire engines from Port Burdock and Hampstead-on-Sea, the local talent of Fishbourne found itself forced back into a secondary, less responsible, and more observant rôle. I will not pursue the story of the fire to its ashes, nor will I do more than glance at the unfortunate Mr. Rusper, a modern Laocoön, vainly trying to retrieve his scattered hose amidst the tramplings and rushings of the Port Burdock experts.

In a small sitting-room of the Fishbourne Temperance Hotel a little group of Fishbourne tradesmen sat and conversed in fragments, and anon went to the window and looked out upon the smoking desolation of their houses across the way, and anon sat down again. They and their families were the guests of old Lady Bargrave, who had displayed the utmost sympathy and interest in their misfortunes. She had taken several people into her own house at Everdean, had engaged the Temperance Hotel as a temporary refuge, and personally superintended the housing of Mantell and Throbsons' homeless assistants. The Temperance Hotel became and remained extremely noisy and congested with people sitting about anywhere, conversing in fragments, and totally unable to get themselves to bed. The manager was an old soldier, and, following the best traditions of the service, saw that every one had hot cocoa. Hot cocoa seemed to be about everywhere, and it was no doubt very heartening and sustaining to every one. When the manager detected any one disposed to be drooping or pensive, he exhorted that person at once to drink further hot cocoa and maintain a stout heart.

The hero of the occasion, the centre of interest, was Mr. Polly. For he had not only caused the fire by upsetting a lighted lamp, scorching his trousers and narrowly escaping death, as indeed he had now explained in detail about twenty times, but he had further thought at once of that amiable but helpless old lady next door, had shown the utmost decision in making his way to her over the yard wall of the Royal Fishbourne Hotel, and had rescued her with persistence and vigour, in spite of the levity natural to her years. Every one thought well of him and was anxious to show it, more especially by shaking his hand painfully and repeatedly. Mr. Rumbold, breaking a silence of nearly fifteen years, thanked him profusely, said that he had never understood him properly, and declared he ought to have a medal. There seemed to be a widely diffused idea that Mr. Polly ought to have a medal. Hinks thought so. He declared, moreover, and with the utmost emphasis, that Mr. Polly had a crowded and richly decorated interior—or words to that effect. There was something apologetic in this persistence; it was as if he regretted past intimations that Mr. Polly was internally defective and hollow. He also said that Mr. Polly was a "white man," albeit, as he developed it, with a liver of the deepest chromatic satisfactions.

Mr. Polly wandered centrally through it all, with his face washed and his hair carefully brushed and parted, looking modest and more than a little absent-minded, and wearing a pair of black dress trousers belonging to the manager of the Temperance Hotel—a larger man than himself in every way.

He drifted up-stairs to his fellow-tradesmen, and stood for a time staring into the littered street, with its pools of water and extinguished gas lamps. His companions in misfortune resumed a fragmentary, disconnected conversation. They touched now on one aspect of the disaster and now on another, and there were intervals of silence. More or less empty cocoa cups were distributed over the table, mantelshelf, and piano, and in the middle of the table was a tin of biscuits, into which Mr. Rumbold, sitting round-shouldered, dipped ever and again in an absentminded way, and munched like a distant shooting of coals. It added to the solemnity of the affair that nearly all of them were in their black Sunday clothes; little Clamp was particularly impressive and dignified in a wide open frock-coat, a Gladstone-shaped paper collar, and a large white-and-blue tie. They felt that they were in the presence of a great disaster, the sort of disaster that gets into the papers, and is even illustrated by blurred photographs of the crumbling ruins. In the presence of that sort of disaster all honourable men are lugubrious and sententious.

And yet it is impossible to deny a certain element of elation. Not one of those excellent men but was already realising that a great door had opened, as it were, in the opaque fabric of destiny, that they were to get their money again that had seemed sunken for ever beyond any hope in the deeps of retail trade. Life was already in their imagination rising like a Phœnix from the flames.

"I suppose there'll be a public subscription," said Mr. Clamp.

"Not for those who're insured," said Mr. Wintershed.

"I was thinking of them assistants from Mantell and Throbsons'. They must have lost nearly everything."

"They'll be looked after all right," said Mr. Rumbold. "Never fear."

Pause.

"*I'm* insured," said Mr. Clamp with unconcealed satisfaction. "Royal Salamander."

"Same here," said Mr. Wintershed.

"Mine's the Glasgow Sun," Mr. Hinks remarked. "Very good company."

"You insured, Mr. Polly?"

"He deserves to be," said Rumbold.

"Ra—ther," said Hinks. "Blowed if he don't. Hard lines it *would* be—if there wasn't something for him."

"Commercial and General," answered Mr. Polly over his shoulder, still staring out of the window. "Oh! I'm all right."

The topic dropped for a time, though manifestly it continued to exercise their minds.

"It's cleared me out of a lot of old stock," said Mr. Wintershed; "that's one good thing."

The remark was felt to be in rather questionable taste, and still more so was his next comment.

"Rusper's a bit sick it didn't reach '*im*."

Every one looked uncomfortable, and no one was willing to point the reason why Rusper should be a bit sick.

"Rusper's been playing a game of his own," said Hinks. "Wonder what he thought he was up to! Sittin' in the middle of the road with a pair of tweezers he was, and about a yard of wire—mending somethin'. Wonder he warn't run over by the Port Burdock engine."

Presently a little chat sprang up upon the causes of fires, and Mr. Polly was moved to tell for the one-and twentieth time how it had happened. His story had now become as circumstantial and exact as the evidence of a police witness. "Upset the lamp," he said. "I'd just lighted it. I was going upstairs, and my foot slipped against where one of the treads was a bit rotten, and down I went. Thing was aflare in a moment! . . . ."

He yawned at the end of the discussion, and moved doorward.

"So long," said Mr. Polly.

"Good-night," said Mr. Rumbold. "You played a brave man's part! If you don't get a medal——"

He left an eloquent pause.

"'Ear, 'ear!" said Mr. Wintershed and Mr. Clamp.

"Goo-night, O' Man," said Mr. Hinks.

"Goo'-night, All," said Mr. Polly. . . .

He went slowly upstairs. The vague perplexity common to popular heroes pervaded his mind. He entered the bedroom and turned up the electric light. It was quite a pleasant room, one of the best in the Temperance Hotel, with a nice clean flowered wall-paper, and a very large looking-glass. Miriam appeared to be asleep, and her shoulders were humped up under the clothes in a shapeless, forbidding lump that Mr. Polly had found utterly loathsome for fifteen years. He went softly over to the dressing-table and surveyed himself thoughtfully. Presently he hitched up the trousers. "Miles too big for me," he remarked. "Funny not to have a pair of breeches of one's own. . . . Like being born again. Naked came I into the world."

Miriam stirred and rolled over, and stared at him.

"Hallo!" she said.

"Hallo."

"Come to bed?"

"It's three."

Pause while Mr. Polly disrobed slowly.

"I been thinking," said Miriam. "It isn't going to be so bad after all. We shall get your insurance. We can easy begin all over again."

"H'm," said Mr. Polly.

She turned her face away from him and reflected.

"Get a better house," said Miriam, regarding the wallpaper pattern. "I've always 'ated them stairs."

Mr. Polly removed a boot.

"Choose a better position where there's more doing," murmured Miriam. . . .

"Not half so bad," she whispered. . . .

"You *wanted* stirring up," she said, half asleep. . . .

It dawned upon Mr. Polly for the first time that he had forgotten something.

He ought to have cut his throat!

The fact struck him as remarkable, but as now no longer of any particular urgency. It seemed a thing far off in the past, and he wondered why he had not thought of it before. Odd thing life is! If he had done it he would never have seen this clean and agreeable apartment with the electric light. . . . His thoughts wandered into a question of detail. Where could he have put down the razor? Somewhere in the little room behind the shop, he supposed, but he could not think where more precisely. Anyhow, it didn't matter now.

He undressed himself calmly, got into bed, and fell asleep almost immediately.

CHAPTER THE NINTH

The Potwell Inn

§ 1

*B*UT when a man has once broken through the paper walls of everyday circumstance, those unsubstantial walls that hold so many of us securely prisoned from the cradle to the grave, he has made a discovery. If the world does not please you, *you can change it*. Determine to alter it at any price, and you can change it altogether. You may change it to something sinister and angry, to something appalling, but it may be you will change it to something brighter, something more agreeable, and at the worst something much more interesting. There is only one sort of man who is absolutely to blame for his own misery, and that is the man who finds life dull and dreary. There are no circumstances in the world that determined action cannot alter, unless, perhaps, they are the walls of a prison cell, and even those will dissolve and change, I am told, into the in-

566

firmary compartment, at any rate, for the man who can fast with resolution. I give these things as facts and information, and with no moral intimations. And Mr. Polly, lying awake at nights, with a renewed indigestion, with Miriam sleeping sonorously beside him, and a general air of inevitableness about his situation, saw through it, understood there was no inevitable any more, and escaped his former despair.

He could, for example, " clear out."

It became a wonderful and alluring phrase to him—" Clear out !"

Why had he never thought of clearing out before?

He was amazed and a little shocked at the unimaginative and superfluous criminality in him that had turned old, cramped, and stagnant Fishbourne into a blaze and new beginnings. (I wish from the bottom of my heart I could add that he was properly sorry.) But something constricting and restrained seemed to have been destroyed by that flare. *Fishbourne wasn't the world.* That was the new, the essential fact of which he had lived so lamentably in ignorance. Fishbourne, as he had known it and hated it, so that he wanted to kill himself to get out of it, *wasn't the world.*

The insurance money he was to receive made everything humane and kindly and practicable. He would "clear out" with justice and humanity. He would take exactly twenty-one pounds, and all the rest he would leave to Miriam. That seemed to him absolutely fair. Without him, she could do all sorts of things—all the sorts of things she was constantly urging him to do. . . .

And he would go off along the white road that led to Garchester, and on to Crogate and so to Tunbridge Wells, where there was a Toad Rock he had heard of but never seen. (It seemed to him this must needs be a marvel.) And so to other towns and cities. He would walk and loiter by the way, and sleep in inns at night, and get an odd job here and there, and talk to strange people.

Perhaps he would get quite a lot of work, and prosper; and if he did not do so he would lie down in front of a train, or wait for a warm night and then fall into some smooth, broad river. Not so bad as sitting down to a dentist—not nearly so bad. And he would never open a shop any more.

So the possibilities of the future presented themselves to Mr. Polly as he lay awake at night.

It was springtime, and in the woods, so soon as one got out of reach of the sea wind, there would be anemones and primroses.

§ 2

A month later a leisurely and dusty tramp, plump equatorially and slightly bald, with his hands in his pockets and his lips puckered to a contemplative whistle, strolled along the river bank between Uppingdon and Potwell. It was a profusely budding spring day, and greens such as God had never permitted in the world before in human memory (though, indeed, they come every year and we forget) were mirrored vividly in a mirror of equally unprecedented brown. For a time the wanderer stopped and stood still, and even the thin whistle died away from his lips as he watched a water-vole run to and fro upon a little headland across the stream. The vole plopped into the water, and swam and dived, and only when the last ring of its disturbance had vanished did Mr. Polly resume his thoughtful course to nowhere in particular.

For the first time in many years he had been leading a healthy human life, living constantly in the open air, walking every day for eight or nine hours, eating sparingly, accepting every conversational opportunity, not even disdaining the discussion of possible work. And beyond mending a hole in his coat, that he had made while negotiating barbed wire, with a borrowed needle and thread in a lodging-house, he had done no real work at all. Neither had he worried about business nor about times and seasons. And for the first time in his life he had seen the Aurora Borealis.

So far, the holiday had cost him very little. He had arranged it on a plan that was entirely his own. He had started with four five-pound notes and a pound divided into silver, and he had gone by train from Fishbourne to Ashington. At Ashington he had gone to the post office, obtained a registered letter envelope, and sent his four five-pound notes with a short, brotherly note addressed to himself at Gilhampton Post Office. He sent this letter to Gilhampton for no other reason in the world than that he liked the name of Gilhampton and the rural suggestion of its containing county, which was Sussex; and having so despatched it, he set himself to discover, mark down, and walk to Gilhampton, and so recover his resources. And having got to Gilhampton at last, he changed a five-pound note, bought four pound postal orders, and repeated his manœuvre with nineteen pounds.

After a lapse of fifteen years he rediscovered this interesting world, about which so many people go incredibly blind and bored. He went along country roads while all the birds were piping and chirruping and cheeping and singing, and looked at fresh new things, and felt as happy and irresponsible as a boy with an unexpected half-holiday. And if ever the thought of Miriam returned to him, he controlled his mind. He came to country inns and sat for unmeasured hours talking of this and that to those sage carters who rest for ever in the taps of country inns, while the big, sleek, brass-jingling horses wait patiently outside with their wagons. He got a job with some van people who were wandering about the country with swings and a steam roundabout, and remained with them three days, until one of their dogs took a violent dislike to him, and made his duties unpleasant. He talked to tramps and wayside labourers. He snoozed under hedges by day, and in outhouses and hayricks at night, and once, but only once, he slept in a casual ward. He felt as the etiolated grass and daisies must do when you move the garden roller away to a new place.

He gathered a quantity of strange and interesting memories.

He crossed some misty meadows by moonlight and the mist lay low on the grass, so low that it scarcely reached above his waist, and houses and clumps of trees stood out like islands in a milky sea, so sharply defined was the upper surface of the mist-bank. He came nearer and nearer to a strange thing that floated like a boat upon this magic lake, and behold, something moved at the stern, and a rope was whisked at the prow, and it had changed into a pensive cow, drowsy-eyed, regarding him. . . .

He saw a remarkable sunset in a new valley near Maidstone, a very red and clear sunset, a wide redness under a pale, cloudless heaven, and with the hills all round the edge of the sky a deep purple blue and clear and flat, looking exactly as he had seen mountains painted in pictures. He seemed transported to some strange country, and would have felt no surprise if the old labourer he came upon leaning silently over a gate had addressed him in an unfamiliar tongue.

Then one night, just towards dawn, his sleep upon a pile of brushwood was broken by the distant rattle of a racing motor-car breaking all the speed regulations, and as he could not sleep again, he got up and walked into Maidstone as the day came. He had never been abroad in a town at four o'clock in his life before, and the stillness of everything in the bright sunrise impressed him profoundly. At one corner was a startling police-man, standing up in a doorway quite motionless like a waxen image. Mr. Polly wished him "good-morning" unanswered, and went down to the bridge over the Medway, and sat on the parapet, very still and thoughtful, watching the town awaken, and wondering what he should do if it didn't, if the world of men never woke again. . . .

One day he found himself going along a road, with a wide space of sprouting bracken and occasional trees on either side, and suddenly this road became strangely and perplexingly familiar. "Lord!" he said, and turned about and stood. "It can't be."

He was incredulous, then left the road and walked along a scarcely perceptible track to the left, and came in half a minute to an old lichenous stone wall. It seemed exactly the bit of wall he had known so well. It might have been but yesterday he was in that place; there remained even a little pile of wood. It became absurdly the same wood. The bracken, perhaps, was not so high, and most of its fronds were still coiled up, that was all. Here he had stood, it seemed, and there she had sat and looked down upon him. Where was she now, and what had become of her? He counted the years back, and marvelled that beauty should have called to him with so imperious a voice—and signified nothing.

He hoisted himself with some little difficulty to the top of the wall, and saw far off under the beech trees two schoolgirls—small, insignificant, pigtailed creatures, with heads of blond and black, with their arms twined about each other's necks, no doubt telling each other the silliest secrets.

But that girl with the red hair—was she a countess? was she a queen? Children, perhaps? Had sorrow dared to touch her?

Had she forgotten altogether? . . . .

A tramp sat by the roadside, thinking, and it seemed to the man in the passing motor-car he must needs be plotting for another pot of beer. But, as a matter of fact, what the tramp was saying to himself over and over again was a variant upon a well-known Hebrew word.

"Itchabod," the tramp was saying in the voice of one who reasons on the side of the inevitable. "It's Fair Itchabod, O' Man. There's no going back to things like that."

§ 3

It was about two o'clock in the afternoon, one hot day in May, when Mr. Polly, unhurrying and serene, came upon that broad bend of the river to which the little lawn and garden of the Potwell Inn run down. He stopped at the sight of the place and surveyed its deep tiled roof, nestling under big trees—you never get a decently big, decently shaped tree by the sea-side—its sign towards the roadway, its sun-blistered green bench and tables, its shapely white windows and its row of upshooting hollyhock plants in the garden. A hedge separated the premises from a buttercup-yellow meadow, and beyond stood three poplars in a group against the sky, three exceptionally tall, graceful, and harmonious poplars. It is hard to say what there was about them that made them so beautiful to Mr. Polly, but they seemed to him to touch a pleasant scene with a distinction almost divine. He stood admiring them quietly for a long time.

At last the need for coarser æsthetic satisfactions arose in him.

"Provinder," he whispered, drawing near to the inn. "Cold sirloin, for choice. And nutbrown brew and wheaten bread."

The nearer he came to the place the more he liked it. The windows on the ground floor were long and low, and they had pleasing red blinds. The green tables outside were agreeably ringed with memories of former drinks, and an extensive grape vine spread level branches across the whole front of the place. Against the wall was a broken oar, two boat-hooks, and the stained and faded red cushions of a pleasure-boat.

One went up three steps to the glass-panelled door and peeped into a broad, low room with a bar and a beer-engine, behind which were many bright and helpful-looking bottles against mirrors, and great and little pewter measures, and bottles fastened in brass wire upside down, with their corks replaced by taps, and a white china cask labelled " Shrub," and cigar boxes, and boxes of cigarettes, and a couple of Toby jugs and a beautifully coloured hunting scene framed and glazed, showing the most elegant people taking Piper's Cherry Brandy, and cards such as the law requires about the dilution of spirits and the illegality of bringing children into bars, and satirical verses about swearing and asking for credit, and three very bright, red-cheeked wax apples, and a round-shaped clock.

But these were the mere background to the really pleasant thing in the spectacle, which was quite the plumpest woman Mr. Polly had ever seen, seated in an armchair in the midst of all these bottles and glasses and glittering things, peacefully and tranquilly, and without the slightest loss of dignity, asleep. Many people would have called her a fat woman, but Mr. Polly's innate sense of epithet told him from the outset that plump was the word. She had shapely brows and a straight, well-shaped nose, kind lines and contentment about her mouth, and beneath it the jolly chins clustered like chubby little cherubim about the feet of an Assumptioning Madonna. Her plumpness was firm and pink and wholesome, and her hands, dimpled at every joint, were clasped in front of her; she seemed, as it were, to embrace herself with infinite confidence and kindliness, as one who knew herself good in substance, good in essence, and would show her gratitude to God by that ready acceptance of all that He had given her. Her head was a little on one side, not much, but just enough to speak of trustfulness, and rob her of the stiff effect of self-reliance. And she slept.

" *My* sort," said Mr. Polly, and opened the door

very softly, divided between the desire to enter and come nearer, and an instinctive indisposition to break slumbers so manifestly sweet and satisfying.

She awoke with a start, and it amazed Mr. Polly to see swift terror flash into her eyes. Instantly it had gone again.

" Law ! " she said, her face softening with relief. " I thought you was Jim."

" I'm never Jim," said Mr. Polly.

" You've got his sort of hat."

" Ah ! " said Mr. Polly, and leaned over the bar.

" It just came into my head you was Jim," said the plump lady, dismissed the topic and stood up. " I believe I was having forty winks," she said, " if all the truth was told. What can I do for you ? "

" Cold meat ? " said Mr. Polly.

" There *is* cold meat," the plump woman admitted. " And room for it."

The plump woman came and leaned over the bar and regarded him judicially but kindly. " There's some cold boiled beef," she said, and added, " A bit of crisp lettuce ? "

" New mustard," said Mr. Polly.

" And a tankard ! "

" A tankard."

They understood each other perfectly.

" Looking for work ? " asked the plump woman.

" In a way," said Mr. Polly.

They smiled like old friends.

Whatever the truth may be about love, there is certainly such a thing as friendship at first sight. They liked each other's voices, they liked each other's way of smiling and speaking.

" It's such beautiful weather this spring," said Mr. Polly, explaining everything.

" What sort of work do you want ? " she asked.

" I've never properly thought that out," said Mr. Polly. " I've been looking round—for ideas."

"Will you have your beef in the tap or outside? That's the tap."

Mr. Polly had a glimpse of an oaken settle. "In the tap will be handier for you," he said.

"Hear that?" said the plump lady.

"Hear what?"

"Listen."

Presently the silence was broken by a distant howl— "Oooooover!" "Eh?" she said.

He nodded.

"That's the ferry. And there isn't a ferryman."

"Could I?"

"Can you punt?"

"Never tried."

"Well—pull the pole out before you reach the end of the punt, that's all. Try."

Mr. Polly went out again into the sunshine.

At times one can tell so much so briefly. Here are the facts then—bare. He found a punt and a pole, got across to the steps on the opposite side, picked up an elderly gentleman in an alpaca jacket and a pith helmet, cruised with him vaguely for twenty minutes, conveyed him tortuously into the midst of a thicket of forget-me-not spangled sedges, splashed some waterweed over him, hit him twice with the punt pole, and finally landed him, alarmed but abusive, in treacherous soil at the edge of a hay meadow about forty yards down-stream, where he immediately got into difficulties with a noisy, aggressive little white dog that was guarding a jacket.

Mr. Polly returned in a complicated manner, but with perfect dignity, to his moorings.

He found the plump woman rather flushed and tearful, and seated at one of the green tables outside.

"I been laughing at you," she said.

"What for?" asked Mr. Polly.

"I ain't 'ad such a laugh since Jim come 'ome. When you 'it 'is 'ead, it 'urt my side."

"It didn't hurt his head—not particularly."

"Did you charge him anything?"

"Gratis," said Mr. Polly. "I never thought of it."

The plump woman pressed her hands to her sides and laughed silently for a space. "You ought to 'ave charged 'im Sumpthing," she said. "You better come and have your cold meat before you do any more puntin'. You and me'll get on together."

Presently she came and stood watching him eat. "You eat better than you punt," she said; and then, "I dessay you could learn to punt."

"Wax to receive and marble to retain," said Mr. Polly. "This beef is a Bit of All Right, Ma'm. I could have done different if I hadn't been punting on an empty stomach. There's a leer feeling as the pole goes in——"

"I've never held with fasting," said the plump woman.

"You want a ferryman?"

"I want an odd man about the place."

"I'm odd all right. What's the wages?"

"Not much, but you get tips and pickings. I've a sort of feeling it would suit you."

"I've a sort of feeling it would. What's the duties? Fetch and carry? Ferry? Garden? Wash bottles? *Ceteris paribus?*"

"That's about it," said the fat woman.

"Give me a trial."

"I've more than half a mind. Or I wouldn't have said anything about it. I suppose you're all right. You've got a sort of half-respectable look about you. I suppose you 'aven't *done* anything?"

"Bit of Arson," said Mr. Polly, as if he jested.

"So long as you haven't the habit," said the plump woman.

"My first time, Ma'm," said Mr. Polly, munching his way through an excellent big leaf of lettuce. "And my last."

" It's all right if you haven't been to Prison," said the plump woman. "It isn't what a man's happened to do makes 'im bad. We all happen to do things at times. It's bringing it home to him and spoiling his self-respect does the mischief. You don't *look* a wrong 'un. 'Ave you been to prison?"

" Never."

" Nor a Reformatory? Nor any Institution?"

" Not me. Do I *look* reformed?"

" Can you paint and carpenter a bit?"

" Ripe for it."

" Have a bit of cheese?"

" If I might."

And the way she brought the cheese showed Mr. Polly that the business was settled in her mind.

He spent the afternoon exploring the premises of the Potwell Inn and learning the duties that might be expected of him, such as Stockholm tarring fences, digging potatoes, swabbing out boats, helping people land, embarking, landing, and time-keeping for the hirers of two rowing boats and one Canadian canoe, bailing out the said vessels and concealing their leaks and defects from prospective hirers, persuading inexperienced hirers to start down-stream rather than up, repairing rowlocks and taking inventories of returning boats with a view to supplementary charges, cleaning boots, sweeping chimneys, house painting, cleaning windows, sweeping out and sanding the Tap and Bar, cleaning pewter, washing glasses, turpentining woodwork, whitewashing generally, plumbing and engineering, repairing locks and clocks, waiting and tapster's work generally, beating carpets and mats, cleaning bottles and saving corks, taking into the cellar, moving, tapping, and connecting beer-casks with their engines, blocking and destroying wasps' nests, doing forestry with several trees, drowning superfluous kittens, dog-fancying as required, assisting in the rearing of ducklings and the care of various poultry, bee-keeping, stabling, baiting and grooming horses and asses, cleaning and "garing" motor-cars and bicycles, inflating tyres and repairing punctures, recovering the bodies of drowned persons from the river as required, and assisting people in trouble in the water, first-aid and sympathy, improvising and superintending a bathing station for visitors, attending inquests and funerals in the interests of the establishment, scrubbing floors and all the ordinary duties of a scullion, the Ferry, chasing hens and goats from the adjacent cottages out of the garden, making up paths and superintending drainage, gardening generally, delivering bottled beer and soda-water siphons in the neighbourhood, running miscellaneous errands, removing drunken and offensive persons from the premises by tact or muscle, as occasion required, keeping in with the local policeman, defending the premises in general and the orchard in particular from nocturnal depredators. . . .

"Can but try it," said Mr. Polly towards tea-time. "When there's nothing else on hand I suppose I might do a bit of fishing."

§ 4

Mr. Polly was particularly charmed by the ducklings. They were piping about among the vegetables in the company of their foster mother, and as he and the plump woman came down the garden path the little creatures mobbed them, and ran over their boots and in between Mr. Polly's legs, and did their best to be trodden upon and killed after the manner of ducklings all the world over. Mr. Polly had never been near young ducklings before, and their extreme blondness and the delicate completeness of their feet and beaks filled him with admiration. It is open to question whether there is anything more friendly in the world than a very young duckling. It was with the utmost difficulty that he tore himself away to practise punting, with the plump woman coaching from the bank. Punting, he found, was difficult but not impossible, and towards four o'clock he succeeded in conveying a second passenger across the sundering flood from the inn to the unknown.

As he returned, slowly indeed, but now one might almost say surely, to the peg to which the punt was moored, he became aware of a singularly delightful human being awaiting him on the bank. She stood with her legs very wide apart, her hands behind her back, and her head a little on one side, watching his gestures with an expression of disdainful interest. She had black hair and brown legs and a buff short frock and very intelligent eyes. And when he had reached a sufficient proximity she remarked, " Hallo !"

" Hallo," said Mr. Polly, and saved himself in the nick of time from disaster.

" Silly," said the young lady, and Mr. Polly lunged nearer.

" What are you called ?"

" Polly."

" Liar !"

" Why ?"

" I'm Polly."

" Then I'm Alfred. But I meant to be Polly."

" I was first."

" All right. I'm going to be the ferryman."

" I see. You'll have to punt better."

" You should have seen me early in the afternoon."

" I can imagine it . . . I've seen the others."

" What others ?" Mr. Polly had landed now and was fastening up the punt.

" What Uncle Jim has scooted."

" Scooted ?"

" He comes and scoots them. He'll scoot you, too, I expect."

A mysterious shadow seemed to fall athwart the sunshine and pleasantness of the Potwell Inn.

" I'm not a scooter," said Mr. Polly.

"Uncle Jim is."

She whistled a little flatly for a moment, and threw small stones at a clump of meadowsweet that sprang from the bank. Then she remarked:

"When Uncle Jim comes back he'll cut your insides out. . . . P'r'aps, very likely, he'll let me see."

There was a pause.

"*Who's* Uncle Jim?" Mr. Polly asked in a faded voice.

"Don't know who Uncle Jim is! He'll show you. He's a scorcher, is Uncle Jim. He only came back just a little time ago, and he's scooted three men. He don't like strangers about, don't Uncle Jim. He *can* swear. He's going to teach me soon as I can whissle properly."

"Teach you to swear!" cried Mr. Polly, horrified.

"*And* spit," said the little girl proudly. "He says I'm the gamest little beast he ever came across—ever."

For the first time in his life it seemed to Mr. Polly that he had come across something sheerly dreadful. He stared at the pretty thing of flesh and spirit in front of him, lightly balanced on its stout little legs and looking at him with eyes that had still to learn the expression of either disgust or fear.

"I say," said Mr. Polly. "How old are you?"

"Nine," said the little girl.

She turned away and reflected. Truth compelled her to add one other statement.

"He's not what I should call handsome, not Uncle Jim," she said. "But he's a Scorcher and no Mistake. . . . Gramma don't like him."

§ 5

Mr. Polly found the plump woman in the big bricked kitchen lighting a fire for tea. He went to the root of the matter at once.

"I say," he asked, "who's Uncle Jim?"

The plump woman blanched and stood still for a moment. A stick fell out of the bundle in her hand unheeded. "That little granddaughter of mine been saying things?" she asked faintly.

"Bits of things," said Mr. Polly.

"Well, I suppose I must tell you sooner or later. He's—It's Jim. He's the Drorback to this place, that's what he is. The Drorback. I hoped you mightn't hear so soon. . . . Very likely he's gone."

"*She* don't seem to think so."

"'E 'asn't been near the place these two weeks and more," said the plump woman.

"But who is he?"

"I suppose I got to tell you," said the plump woman.

"She says he scoots people," Mr. Polly remarked after a pause.

"He's my own sister's son." The plump woman watched the crackling fire for a space. "I suppose I got to tell you," she repeated.

She softened towards tears. "I try not to think of it, and night and day he's haunting me. I try not to think of it. I've been for easy-going all my life. But I'm that worried and afraid, with death and ruin threatened and evil all about me! I don't know what to do! My own sister's son, and me a widow woman and 'elpless against his doin's!"

She put down the sticks she held upon the fender, and felt for her handkerchief. She began to sob and talk quickly.

"I wouldn't mind nothing else half so much if he'd leave that child alone. But he goes talking to her— if I leave her a moment he's talking to her, teaching her Words, and giving her ideas!"

"That's a Bit Thick," said Mr. Polly.

"Thick!" cried the plump woman; "it's 'orrible! And what am I to do? He's been here three times now, six days, and a week, and a part of a week, and I pray to God night and day he may never come again.

Praying! Back he's come, sure as fate. He takes my money and he takes my things. He won't let no man stay here to protect me or do the boats or work the ferry. The ferry's getting a scandal. They stand and shout and scream and use language. . . . If I complain they'll say I'm helpless to manage here, they'll take away my licence, out I shall go—and it's all the living I can get—and he knows it, and he plays on it, and he don't care. And here I am. I'd send the child away, but I got nowhere to send the child. I buys him off when it comes to that, and back he comes, worse than ever, prowling round and doing evil. And not a soul to help me. Not a soul! I just hoped there might be a day or so. Before he comes back again. I was just hoping— I'm the sort that hopes."

Mr. Polly was reflecting on the flaws and drawbacks that seem to be inseparable from all the more agreeable things of life.

"Biggish sort of man, I expect?" asked Mr. Polly, trying to get the situation in all its bearings.

But the plump woman did not heed him. She was going on with her fire-making, and retailing in disconnected fragments the fearfulness of Uncle Jim.

"There was always something a bit wrong with him," she said; "but nothing you mightn't have hoped for, not till they took him, and carried him off, and reformed him. . . .

"He was cruel to the hens and chickings, it's true, and stuck a knife into another boy; but then I've seen him that nice to a cat, nobody could have been kinder. I'm sure he didn't do no 'arm to that cat whatever any one tries to make out of it. I'd never listen to that. . . . It was that Reformatory ruined him. They put him along of a lot of London boys full of ideas of wickedness, and because he didn't mind pain—and he don't, I *will* admit, try as I would—they made him think himself a hero. Them boys laughed at the teachers they set over them, laughed and mocked at

them—and I don't suppose they *was* the best teachers
in the world; I don't suppose, and I don't suppose any
one sensible does suppose that every one who goes to be
a teacher or a chaplain or a warder in a Reformatory
Home goes and changes right away into an Angel of
Grace from Heaven—and, oh Lord! Where was I?"

"What did they send him to the Reformatory for?"

"Playing truant and stealing. He stole right enough
—stole the money from an old woman, and what was
I to do when it came to the trial, but say what I knew.
And him like a viper a-looking at me—more like a viper
than a human boy. He leans on the bar and looks at
me. 'All right, Aunt Flo,' he says; just that, and
nothing more. Time after time I've dreamt of it, and
now he's come. 'They've Reformed me,' he says, 'and
made me a devil, and devil I mean to be to you. So
out with it,' he says."

"What did you give him last time?" asked Mr.
Polly.

"Three golden pounds," said the plump woman.
"'That won't last very long,' he says. 'But there
ain't no hurry. I'll be back in a week about.' If I
wasn't one of the hoping sort——"

She left the sentence unfinished.

Mr. Polly reflected. "What sort of a size is he?"
he asked. "I'm not one of your Herculaceous sort, if
you mean that. Nothing very wonderful bicepitally."

"You'll scoot," said the plump woman, with conviction rather than bitterness. "You'd better scoot
now, and I'll try and find some money for him to go
away again when he comes. It ain't reasonable to
expect you to do anything but scoot. But I suppose
it's the way of a woman in trouble to try and get help
from a man, and hope and hope."

"How long's he been about?" asked Mr. Polly,
ignoring his own outlook.

"Three months it is come the seventh since he come
in by that very back door—and I hadn't set eyes on

19*

him for seven long years. He stood in the door watchin' me, and suddenly he let off a yelp—like a dog, and there he was grinning at the fright he'd given me. 'Good old Aunty Flo,' he says, 'ain't you deelighted to see me,' he says, 'now I'm Reformed?'"

The plump lady went to the sink and filled the kettle.

"I never did like 'im," she said, standing at the sink. "And seeing him there, with his teeth all black and broken— P'r'aps I didn't give him much of a welcome at first. Not what would have been kind to him. 'Lord!' I said, 'it's Jim.'

"'It's Jim,' he said. 'Like a bad shillin'—like a damned bad shilling. Jim and trouble. You all of you wanted me Reformed, and now you got me Reformed. I'm a Reformatory Reformed Character, warranted all right, and turned out as such. Ain't you going to ask me in, Aunty dear?'"

"'Come in,' I said. 'I won't have it said I wasn't ready to be kind to you!'

"He comes in and shuts the door. Down he sits in that chair. 'I come to torment you,' he says, 'you old Sumpthing!' and begins at me. . . . No, 'uman being could ever have been called such things before. It made me cry out. 'And now,' he says, 'just to show I ain't afraid of 'urting you,' he says, and ups and twists my wrist."

Mr. Polly gasped.

"I could stand even his vi'lence," said the plump woman, "if it wasn't for the child."

Mr. Polly went to the kitchen window and surveyed his namesake, who was away up the garden path, with her hands behind her back, and wisps of black hair in disorder about her little face, thinking, thinking profoundly, about ducklings.

"You two oughtn't to be left." he said.

The plump woman stared at his back with hard hope in her eyes.

"I don't see that it's *my* affair," said Mr. Polly.

The plump woman resumed her business with the kettle.

"I'd like to have a look at him before I go," said Mr. Polly, thinking aloud, and added, "somehow. Not my business, of course."

"Lord!" he cried, with a start, at a noise in the bar, "who's that?"

"Only a customer," said the plump woman.

§ 6

Mr. Polly made no rash promises, and thought a great deal.

"It seems a sort of Crib," he said, and added, "for a chap who's looking for Trouble."

But he stayed on, and did various things out of the list I have already given, and worked the ferry, and it was four days before he saw anything of Uncle Jim. And so resistant is the human mind to things not yet experienced, that he could easily have believed in that time that there was no such person in the world as Uncle Jim. The plump woman, after her one outbreak of confidences, ignored the subject, and little Polly seemed to have exhausted her impressions in her first communication, and engaged her mind now, with a simple directness, in the study and subjugation of the new human being Heaven had sent into her world. The first unfavourable impression of his punting was soon effaced; he could nickname ducklings very amusingly, create boats out of wooden splinters, and stalk and fly from imaginary tigers in the orchard, with a convincing earnestness that was surely beyond the power of any other human being. She conceded at last that he should be called Mr. Polly, in honour of her, Miss Polly, even as he desired.

Uncle Jim turned up in the twilight.

Uncle Jim appeared with none of the disruptive violence Mr. Polly had dreaded. He came quite softly.

Mr. Polly was going down the lane behind the church, that led to the Potwell Inn, after posting a letter to the lime-juice people at the post office. He was walking slowly, after his habit, and thinking discursively. With a sudden tightening of the muscles he became aware of a figure walking noiselessly beside him.

His first impression was of a face singularly broad above, and with a wide, empty grin as its chief feature below, of a slouching body and dragging feet.

"'Arf a mo'," said the figure, as if in response to his start, and speaking in a hoarse whisper. "'Arf a mo', mister. You the noo bloke at the Potwell Inn?"

Mr. Polly felt evasive. "S'pose I am," he replied hoarsely, and quickened his pace.

"'Arf a mo'," said Uncle Jim, taking his arm. "We ain't doing a (sanguinary) Marathon. It ain't a (decorated) cinder track. I want a word with you, mister. See?"

Mr. Polly wriggled his arm free and stopped. "Whad is it?" he asked, and faced the terror.

"I jest want a (decorated) word wiv you. See? —just a friendly word or two. Just to clear up any blooming errors. That's all I want. No need to be so (richly decorated) proud, if you *are* the noo bloke at Potwell Inn. Not a bit of it. See?"

Uncle Jim was certainly not a handsome person. He was short, shorter than Mr. Polly, with long arms and lean, big hands; a thin and wiry neck stuck out of his grey flannel shirt, and supported a big head that had something of the snake in the convergent lines of its broad, knobby brow, meanly proportioned face, and pointed chin. His almost toothless mouth seemed a cavern in the twilight. Some accident had left him with one small and active, and one large and expressionless reddish eye, and wisps of straight hair strayed from under the blue cricket cap he had pulled down obliquely over the latter. He spat between his teeth, and wiped his mouth untidily with the soft side of his fist.

"You got to blurry well shift," he said. "See?"

"Shift!" said Mr. Polly. "How?"

"'Cos the Potwell Inn's *my* beat. See?"

Mr. Polly had never felt less witty. "How's it your beat?" he asked.

Uncle Jim thrust his face forward and shook his open hand, bent like a claw, under Mr. Polly's nose. "Not your blooming business," he said. "You got to shift."

"S'pose I don't," said Mr. Polly.

"You got to shift."

The tone of Uncle Jim's voice became urgent and confidential.

"You don't know who you're up against," he said. "It's a kindness I'm doing to warn you. See? I'm just one of those blokes who don't stick at things, see? I don't stick at nuffin."

Mr. Polly's manner became detached and confidential —as though the matter and the speaker interested him greatly, but didn't concern him over much. "What do you think you'll do?" he asked.

"If you don't clear out?"

"Yes."

"*Gaw!*" said Uncle Jim. "You'd better! *'Ere!*"

He gripped Mr. Polly's wrist with a grip of steel, and in an instant Mr. Polly understood the relative quality of their muscles. He breathed, an uninspiring breath, into Mr. Polly's face.

"What *won't* I do," he said, "once I start in on you?"

He paused, and the night about them seemed to be listening. "I'll make a mess of you," he said, in his hoarse whisper. "I'll do you—injuries. I'll 'urt you. I'll kick you ugly, see? I'll 'urt you in 'orrible ways— 'orrible ugly ways. . . ."

He scrutinised Mr. Polly's face.

"You'll cry," he said, "to see yourself. See? Cry, you will."

"You got no right," began Mr. Polly.

"Right!" his note was fierce. "Ain't the old woman me aunt?"

He spoke still closelier. "I'll make a gory mess of you. I'll cut bits orf you——"

He receded a little. "I got no quarrel with *you*," he said.

"It's too late to go to-night," said Mr. Polly.

"I'll be round to-morrer—'bout eleven. See? And if I finds you——"

He produced a blood-curdling oath.

"H'm," said Mr. Polly, trying to keep things light. "We'll consider your suggestions."

"You better," said Uncle Jim, and suddenly, noiselessly, was going.

His whispering voice sank until Mr. Polly could hear only the dim fragments of sentences. "'Orrible things to you—'Orrible things . . . Kick yer Ugly. . . . Cut yer—liver out . . . spread it all about, I will. . . . See? I don't care a dead rat one way or the uvver."

And with a curious twisting gesture of the arm, Uncle Jim receded until his face was a still, dim thing that watched, and the black shadows of the hedge seemed to have swallowed up his body altogether.

§ 7

Next morning about half-past ten Mr. Polly found himself seated under a clump of fir-trees by the roadside, and about three miles and a half from the Potwell Inn. He was by no means sure whether he was taking a walk to clear his mind, or leaving that threat-marred Paradise for good and all. His reason pointed a lean, unhesitating finger along the latter course.

For, after all, the thing was not *his* quarrel.

That agreeable, plump woman—agreeable, motherly, comfortable as she might be—wasn't his affair; that child with the mop of black hair, who combined so magically the charm of mouse and butterfly and flitting bird, who was daintier than a flower and softer than a peach, was no concern of his. Good Heavens! What were they to him? Nothing! . . .

Uncle Jim, of course, *had* a claim, a sort of claim.

If it came to duty and chucking up this attractive, indolent, observant, humorous, tramping life, there were those who had a right to him, a legitimate right, a prior claim on his protection and chivalry.

Why not listen to the call of duty and go back to Miriam now? . . . .

He had had a very agreeable holiday. . . .

And while Mr. Polly sat thinking these things as well as he could, he knew that if only he dared to look up, the Heavens had opened, and the clear judgment on his case was written across the sky.

He knew—he knew now as much as a man can know of life. He knew he had to fight or perish.

Life had never been so clear to him before. It had always been a confused, entertaining spectacle. He had responded to this impulse and that, seeking agreeable and entertaining things, evading difficult and painful things. Such is the way of those who grow up to a life that has neither danger nor honour in its texture. He had been muddled and wrapped about and entangled, like a creature born in the jungle who has never seen sea or sky. Now he had come out of it suddenly into a great exposed place. It was as if God and Heaven waited over him and all the earth was expectation.

"Not my business," said Mr. Polly, speaking aloud. "Where the devil do I come in?"

And again, with something between a whine and a snarl in his voice, "Not my blasted business!"

His mind seemed to have divided itself into several compartments, each with its own particular discussion busily in progress, and quite regardless of the others. One was busy with the detailed interpretation of the phrase, "Kick yer ugly." There's a sort of French wrestling in which you use and guard against feet. Watch the man's eye, and as his foot comes up, grip, and over he goes—at your mercy, if you use the advantage rightly. But how do you use the advantage rightly?

When he thought of Uncle Jim the inside feeling of his body faded away rapidly to a blank discomfort. . . .

"Old cadger! She hadn't no business to drag me into her quarrels. Ought to go to the police and ask for help. Dragging me into a quarrel that don't concern me.

"Wish I'd never set eyes on the rotten inn!"

The reality of the case arched over him like the vault of the sky, as plain as the sweet blue heaven above and the wide spread of hill and valley about him. Man comes into life to seek and find his sufficient beauty, to serve it, to win and increase it, to fight for it, to face anything and dare anything for it, counting death as nothing so long as the dying eyes still turn to it. And fear and dulness and indolence and appetite, which, indeed, are no more than fear's three crippled brothers, who make ambushes and creep by night, are against him, to delay him, to hold him off, to hamper and beguile and kill him in that quest. He had but to lift his eyes to see all that, as much a part of his world as the driving clouds and the bending grass; but he kept himself downcast, a grumbling, inglorious, dirty, fattish little tramp, full of dreams and quivering excuses.

"Why the hell was I ever born?" he said, with the truth almost winning him.

What do you do when a dirty man, who smells, gets you down and under, in the dirt and dust, with a knee below your diaphragm, and a large hairy hand squeezing your windpipe tighter and tighter in a quarrel that isn't, properly speaking, yours?

"If I had a chance against him—" protested Mr. Polly.

"It's no Good, you see," said Mr. Polly.

He stood up as though his decision was made, and was for an instant struck still by doubt.

There lay the road before him, going this way to the east, and that to the west.

Westward, one hour away now, was the Potwell Inn. Already things might be happening there. . . .

Eastward was the wise man's course, a road dipping between hedges to a hop garden and a wood, and presently, no doubt, reaching an inn, a picturesque church, perhaps, a village, and fresh company. The wise man's course. Mr. Polly saw himself going along it, and tried to see himself going along it with all the self applause a wise man feels. But somehow it wouldn't come like that. The wise man fell short of happiness for all his wisdom. The wise man had a paunch, and round shoulders, and red ears, and excuses. It was a pleasant road, and why the wise man should not go along it merry and singing, full of summer happiness, was a miracle to Mr. Polly's mind. But, confound it! the fact remained; the figure went slinking—slinking was the only word for it—and would not go otherwise than slinking. He turned his eyes westward as if for an explanation, and if the figure was no longer ignoble, the prospect was appalling.

"One kick in the stummick would settle a chap like me," said Mr. Polly.

"O God!" cried Mr. Polly, and lifted his eyes to heaven, and said for the last time in that struggle, "It—isn't—my—affair!"

And so saying, he turned his face towards the Potwell Inn.

He went back, neither halting nor hastening in his pace after this last decision, but with a mind feverishly busy.

"If I get killed I get killed, and if he gets killed I get hung. Don't seem just somehow.

"Don't suppose I shall *frighten* him off."

§ 8

The private war between Mr. Polly and Uncle Jim for the possession of the Potwell Inn fell naturally into three chief campaigns. There was, first of all, the great campaign which ended in the triumphant eviction of Uncle Jim from the inn premises; there came next, after a brief interval, the futile invasions of the premises by Uncle Jim that culminated in the Battle of the Dead Eel; and, after some months of involuntary truce, there was the last supreme conflict of the Night Surprise. Each of these campaigns merits a section to itself.

Mr. Polly re-entered the inn discreetly.

He found the plump woman seated in her bar, her eyes astare, her face white and wet with tears. "O God!" she was saying over and over again—"O God!" The air was full of a spirituous reek, and on the sanded boards in front of the bar were the fragments of a broken bottle, and an overturned glass.

She turned her despair at the sound of his entry, and despair gave place to astonishment.

"You come back!" she said.

"Ra-ther," said Mr. Polly.

"He's—he's mad drunk and looking for her."

"Where is she?"

"Locked upstairs."

"Haven't you sent to the police?"

"No one to send."

"I'll see to it," said Mr. Polly. "Out this way?" She nodded.

He went to the crinkly paned window and peered out. Uncle Jim was coming down the garden path towards the house, his hands in his pockets, and singing hoarsely. Mr. Polly remembered afterwards, with pride and amazement, that he felt neither faint nor rigid. He glanced round him, seized a bottle of beer by the neck as an improvised club, and went out by the garden door. Uncle Jim stopped, amazed. His brain did not instantly rise to the new posture of things. "You!" he cried, and stopped for a moment. "You—*scoot!*"

"*Your* job," said Mr. Polly, and advanced some paces.

Uncle Jim stood swaying with wrathful astonishment, and then darted forward with clutching hands. Mr. Polly felt that if his antagonist closed, he was lost, and smote with all his force at the ugly head before him. Smash went the bottle, and Uncle Jim staggered, half stunned by the blow, and blinded with beer.

The lapses and leaps of the human mind are for ever mysterious. Mr. Polly had never expected that bottle to break. In an instant he felt disarmed and helpless. Before him was Uncle Jim, infuriated and evidently still coming on, and for defence was nothing but the neck of a bottle.

For a time our Mr. Polly has figured heroic. Now comes the fall again; he sounded abject terror; he dropped that ineffectual scrap of glass and turned and fled round the corner of the house.

"Bolls!" came the thick voice of the enemy behind him, as one who accepts a challenge, and bleeding but indomitable, Uncle Jim entered the house.

"Bolls!" he said, surveying the bar. "Fightin' with bolls! I'll showim fightin' with bolls!" •

Uncle Jim had learned all about fighting with bottles in the Reformatory Home. Regardless of his terror-stricken aunt, he ranged among the bottled beer and succeeded, after one or two failures, in preparing two bottles to his satisfaction by knocking off the bottom, and gripping them dagger-wise by the necks. So prepared, he went forth again to destroy Mr. Polly.

Mr. Polly, freed from the sense of urgent pursuit, had halted beyond the raspberry canes, and rallied his courage. The sense of Uncle Jim victorious in the house restored his manhood. He went round by the out-houses to the riverside, seeking a weapon, and found an old paddle boat-hook. With this he smote Uncle

Jim as he emerged by the door of the tap. Uncle Jim, blaspheming dreadfully, and with dire stabbing intimations in either hand, came through the splintering paddle like a circus rider through a paper hoop, and once more Mr. Polly dropped his weapon and fled.

A careless observer, watching him sprint round and round the inn in front of the lumbering and reproachful pursuit of Uncle Jim, might have formed an altogether erroneous estimate of the issue of the campaign. Certain compensating qualities of the very greatest military value were appearing in Mr. Polly, even as he ran; if Uncle Jim had strength and brute courage, and the rich toughening experience a Reformatory Home affords, Mr. Polly was nevertheless sober, more mobile, and with a mind now stimulated to an almost incredible nimbleness. So that he not only gained on Uncle Jim, but thought what use he might make of this advantage. The word "strategious" flamed red across the tumult of his mind. As he came round the house for the third time, he darted suddenly into the yard, swung the door to behind himself, and bolted it, seized the zinc pig's pail that stood by the entrance to the kitchen, and had it neatly and resonantly over Uncle Jim's head, as he came belatedly in round the outhouse on the other side. One of the splintered bottles jabbed Mr. Polly's ear—at the time it seemed of no importance—and then Uncle Jim was down and writhing dangerously and noisily upon the yard tiles, with his head still in the pig pail, and his bottle gone to splinters, and Mr. Polly was fastening the kitchen door against him.

"Can't go on like this for ever," said Mr. Polly, whooping for breath, and selecting a weapon from among the brooms that stood behind the kitchen door.

Uncle Jim was losing his head. He was up and kicking the door, and bellowing unamiable proposals and invitations, so that a strategist emerging silently by the tap door could locate him without difficulty, steal upon him unawares, and——!

But before that felling blow could be delivered, Uncle Jim's ear had caught a footfall, and he turned. Mr. Polly quailed, and lowered his broom——a fatal hesitation.

"*Now* I got you!" cried Uncle Jim, dancing forward in a disconcerting zigzag.

He rushed to close, and Mr. Polly stopped him featly, as if it were a miracle, with the head of the broom across his chest. Uncle Jim seized the broom with both hands. "Lea go," he said, and tugged. Mr. Polly shook his head, tugged, and showed pale, compressed lips. Both tugged. Then Uncle Jim tried to get round the end of the broom; Mr. Polly circled away. They began to circle about one another, both lugging hard, both intensely watchful of the slightest initiative on the part of the other. Mr. Polly wished brooms were longer——twelve or thirteen feet, for example; Uncle Jim was clearly for shortness in brooms. He wasted breath in saying what was to happen shortly——sanguinary, oriental, soul-blenching things—— when the broom no longer separated them. Mr. Polly thought he had never seen an uglier person. Suddenly Uncle Jim flashed into violent activity, but alcohol slows movement, and Mr. Polly was equal to him. Then Uncle Jim tried jerks, and, for a terrible instant, seemed to have the broom out of Mr. Polly's hands. But Mr. Polly recovered it with the clutch of a drowning man. Then Uncle Jim drove suddenly at Mr. Polly's midriff; but again Mr. Polly was ready, and swept him round in a circle. Then suddenly a wild hope filled Mr. Polly. He saw the river was very near, the post to which the punt was tied not three yards away. With a wild yell he sent the broom home under his antagonist's ribs. "Wooosh!" he cried, as the resistance gave.

"Oh! *Gaw!*" said Uncle Jim, going backward helplessly, and Mr. Polly thrust hard, and abandoned the broom to the enemy's despairing clutch.

Splash! Uncle Jim was in the water, and Mr. Polly

had leaped like a cat aboard the ferry punt, and grasped the pole.

Up came Uncle Jim spluttering and dripping. "You (unprofitable matter, and printing it might lead to a Censorship of Novels)—You know I got a weak chess!"

The pole took him in the throat and drove him backwards and downwards.

"Lea go!" cried Uncle Jim, staggering, and with real terror in his once awful eyes.

Splash! Down he fell backwards into a frothing mass of water, with Mr. Polly jabbing at him. Under water he turned round and came up again, as if in flight towards the middle of the river. Directly his head reappeared, Mr. Polly had him between his shoulders and under again, bubbling thickly. A hand clutched and disappeared.

It was stupendous! Mr. Polly had discovered the heel of Achilles. Uncle Jim had no stomach for cold water. The broom floated away, pitching gently on the swell. Mr. Polly, infuriated by victory, thrust Uncle Jim under again, and drove the punt round on its chain, in such a manner, that when Uncle Jim came up for the fourth time—and now he was nearly out of his depth, too buoyed up to walk, and apparently nearly helpless—Mr. Polly, fortunately for them both, could not reach him.

Uncle Jim made the clumsy gestures of those who struggle insecurely in the water. "Keep out," said Mr. Polly. Uncle Jim, with a great effort, got a footing, emerged until his arm-pits were out of water, until his waistcoat buttons showed, one by one, till scarcely two remained, and made for the camp-sheeting.

"Keep out!" cried Mr. Polly, and leaped off the punt and followed the movements of his victim along the shore.

"I tell you I got a weak chess," said Uncle Jim moistly. "I 'ate worter. This ain't fair fightin'."

"Keep out!" said Mr. Polly.

"This ain't fair fightin'," said Uncle Jim, almost weeping, and all his terrors had gone.

"Keep out!" said Mr. Polly, with an accurately poised pole.

"I tell you I got to land, you Fool," said Uncle Jim, with a sort of despairing wrathfulness, and began moving down-stream.

"You keep out," said Mr. Polly in parallel movement. "Don't you ever land on this place again! . . ."

Slowly, argumentatively, and reluctantly, Uncle Jim waded down-stream. He tried threats, he tried persuasion, he even tried a belated note of pathos; Mr. Polly remained inexorable, if in secret a little perplexed as to the outcome of the situation. "This cold's getting to my marrer!" said Uncle Jim.

"You want cooling. You keep out in it," said Mr. Polly.

They came round the bend into sight of Nicholson's ait, where the backwater runs down to the Potwell Mill. And there, after much parley and several feints, Uncle Jim made a desperate effort, and struggled into clutch of the overhanging osiers on the island, and so got out of the water, with the mill-stream between them. He emerged dripping and muddy and vindictive. "By *Gaw!*" he said. "I'll skin you for this!"

"You keep off, or I'll do worse to you," said Mr. Polly.

The spirit was out of Uncle Jim for the time, and he turned away to struggle through the osiers towards the mill, leaving a shining trail of water among the green-grey stems.

Mr. Polly returned slowly and thoughtfully to the inn, and suddenly his mind began to bubble with phrases. The plump woman stood at the top of the steps that led up to the inn door, to greet him.

"Law!" she cried, as he drew near, "'asn't 'e killed you?"

"Do I look it?" said Mr. Polly.

"But where's Jim?"

"Gone off."

"'E was mad drunk and dangerous!"

"I put him in the river," said Mr. Polly. "That toned down his alcolaceous frenzy! I gave him a bit of a doing altogether."

"Hain't he 'urt you?"

"Not a bit of it!"

"Then what's all that blood beside your ear?"

Mr. Polly felt. "Quite a cut! Funny how one overlooks things! Heated moments! He must have done that when he jabbed about with those bottles. Hallo, Kiddy! You venturing downstairs again?"

"Ain't he killed you?" asked the little girl.

"Well!"

"I wish I'd seen more of the fighting."

"Didn't you?"

"All I saw was you running round the house, and Uncle Jim after you."

There was a little pause. "I was leading him on," said Mr. Polly.

"Some one's shouting at the ferry," she said.

"Right-o. But you won't see any more of Uncle Jim for a bit. We've been having a conversazione about that."

"I believe it *is* Uncle Jim," said the little girl.

"Then he can wait," said Mr. Polly shortly.

He turned round and listened for the words that drifted across from the little figure on the opposite bank. So far as he could judge, Uncle Jim was making an appointment for the morrow. Mr. Polly replied with a defiant movement of the punt pole. The little figure was convulsed for a moment, and then went on its way upstream—fiercely.

So it was the first campaign ended in an insecure victory.

§ 9

The next day was Wednesday, and a slack day for the Potwell Inn. It was a hot, close day full of the murmuring of bees. One or two people crossed by the ferry; an elaborately-equipped fisherman stopped for cold meat and dry ginger ale in the bar parlour; some haymakers came and drank beer for an hour; and afterwards sent jars and jugs by a boy to be replenished; that was all. Mr. Polly had risen early, and was busy about the place meditating upon the probable tactics of Uncle Jim. He was no longer strung up to the desperate pitch of the first encounter. He was grave and anxious. Uncle Jim had shrunken, as all antagonists that are boldly faced shrink, after the first battle, to the negotiable, the vulnerable. Formidable he was, no doubt, but not invincible. He had, under Providence, been defeated once, and he might be defeated altogether.

Mr. Polly went about the place considering the militant possibilities of pacific things—pokers, copper-sticks, garden implements, kitchen knives, garden nets, barbed wire, oars, clothes'-lines, blankets, pewter pots, stockings, and broken bottles. He prepared a club with a stocking and a bottle inside, upon the best East End model. He swung it round his head once, broke an outhouse window with a flying fragment of glass, and ruined the stocking beyond all darning. He developed a subtle scheme, with the cellar flap as a sort of pitfall; but he rejected it finally because (a) it might entrap the plump woman, and (b) he had no use whatever for Uncle Jim in the cellar. He determined to wire the garden that evening, burglar fashion, against the possibilities of a night attack.

Towards two o'clock in the afternoon three young men arrived in a capacious boat from the direction of Lammam, and asked permission to camp in the paddock. It was given all the more readily by Mr. Polly because he perceived in their proximity a possible check upon the self-expression of Uncle Jim. But he did not foresee, and no one could have foreseen, that Uncle Jim, stealing craftily upon the Potwell Inn in the late afternoon, armed with a large rough-hewn stake, would have mistaken the bending form of one of those campers—who was pulling a few onions by permission in the garden—for Mr. Polly's, and crept upon it swiftly and silently, and smitten its wide invitation unforgettably and unforgivably. It was an error impossible to explain; the resounding whack went up to Heaven, the cry of amazement, and Mr. Polly emerged from the inn, armed with the frying-pan he was cleaning, to take this reckless assailant in the rear. Uncle Jim, realising his error, fled blaspheming into the arms of the other two campers, who were returning from the village with butcher's meat and groceries. They caught him, they smacked his face with steak and punched him with a bursting parcel of lump sugar, they held him though he bit them, and their idea of punishment was to duck him. They were hilarious, strong young stockbrokers' clerks, Territorials, and seasoned boating men; they ducked him as though it was romping and all that Mr. Polly had to do was to pick up lumps of sugar for them and wipe them on his sleeve and put them on a plate, and explain that Uncle Jim was a notorious bad character, and not quite right in his head.

" Got a regular Obsession the Missis is his Aunt," said Mr. Polly, expanding it. " Perfect noosance he is."

But he caught a glance of Uncle Jim's eye as he receded before the campers' urgency that boded ill for him, and in the night he had a disagreeable idea that perhaps his luck might not hold for the third occasion.

That came soon enough. So soon, indeed, as the campers had gone.

Thursday was the early closing day at Lammam, and, next to Sunday, the busiest part of the week at the Potwell Inn. Sometimes as many as six boats all at once would be moored against the ferry punt and hiring row-boats. People could either have a complete tea, a complete tea with jam, cake, and eggs, a kettle of boiling water and find the rest, or Refreshments *à la carte* as they chose. They sat about, but usually the boiling water-ers had a delicacy about using the tables, and grouped themselves humbly on the ground. The complete tea-ers with jam and eggs got the best tablecloth, on the table nearest the steps that led up to the glass-panelled door.

The groups about the lawn were very satisfying to Mr. Polly's sense of amenity. To the right were the complete tea-ers, with everything heart could desire; then a small group of three young men in remarkable green and violet and pale blue shirts, and two girls in mauve and yellow blouses, with common teas and gooseberry jam, at the green clothless table; then, on the grass down by the pollard willow, a small family of hot-water-ers with a hamper, a little troubled by wasps in their jam from the nest in the tree, and all in mourning, but happy otherwise; and on the lawn to the right a ginger beer lot of 'prentices without their collars, and very jocular and happy. The young people in the rainbow shirts and blouses formed the centre of interest; they were under the leadership of a gold-spectacled senior with a fluting voice and an air of mystery; he ordered everything, and showed a peculiar knowledge of the qualities of the Potwell jams, preferring gooseberry with much insistence. Mr. Polly watched him, christened him the "benifluous influence," glanced at the 'prentices, and went inside and down into the cellar in order to replenish the stock of stone ginger beer, which the plump woman had allowed to run low during the pre-occupations of the campaign. It was in the cellar that he first became aware of the return of Uncle Jim. He became aware of him as a voice, a voice not only hoarse but thick, as voices thicken under the influence of alcohol.

"Where's that muddy-faced mongrel?" cried Uncle

Jim. "Let 'im come out to me! Where's that blighted wisp with the punt pole—I got a word to say to 'im. Come out of it, you pot-bellied chunk of dirtiness, you! Come out and 'ave your ugly face wiped. I got a Thing for you. . . . *'Ear* me?"

"''E's 'iding, that's what 'E's doing," said the voice of Uncle Jim, dropping for a moment to sorrow, and then with a great increment of wrathfulness: "Come out of my nest, you blinking cuckoo, you, or I'll cut your silly insides out! Come out of it, you pock-marked Rat! Stealing another man's 'ome away from 'im! Come out and look me in the face, you squinting son of a Skunk! . . ."

Mr. Polly took the ginger beer and went thoughtfully upstairs to the bar.

"''E's back," said the plump woman as he appeared. "I knew 'e'd come back."

"I heard him," said Mr. Polly, and looked about. "Just gimme the old poker handle that's under the beer-engine."

The door opened softly, and Mr. Polly turned quickly. But it was only the pointed nose and intelligent face of the young man with the gilt spectacles and the discreet manner. He coughed, and the spectacles fixed Mr. Polly.

"I say," he said with quiet earnestness, "there's a chap out here seems to *want* some one."

"Why don't he come in?" said Mr. Polly.

"He seems to want you out there."

"What's he want?"

"I think," said the spectacled young man after a thoughtful moment, "he appears to have brought you a present of fish."

"Isn't he shouting?"

"He *is* a little boisterous."

"He'd better come in."

The manner of the spectacled young man intensified. "I wish you'd come out and persuade him to go away," he said. "His language—isn't quite the thing—ladies."

"It never was," said the plump woman, her voice charged with sorrow.

Mr. Polly moved towards the door and stood with his hand on the handle. The gold-spectacled face disappeared.

"Now, my man," came his voice from outside, "be careful what you're saying——"

"OO in all the World and Hereafter are you to call me me man?" cried Uncle Jim, in the voice of one astonished and pained beyond endurance, and added scornfully, "You gold-eyed Geezer, you!"

"Tut, tut!" said the gentleman in gilt glasses. "Restrain yourself!"

Mr. Polly emerged, poker in hand, just in time to see what followed. Uncle Jim in his shirt-sleeves, and a state of ferocious decolletage, was holding something—yes!—a dead eel by means of a piece of newspaper about its tail, holding it down and back and a little sideways in such a way as to smite with it upward and hard. It struck the spectacled gentleman under the jaw with a peculiar dead thud, and a cry of horror came from the two seated parties at the sight. One of the girls shrieked piercingly, "Horace!" and every one sprang up. The sense of helping numbers came to Mr. Polly's aid.

"Drop it!" he cried, and came down the steps waving his poker and thrusting the spectacled gentleman before him, as heretofore great heroes were wont to wield the ox-hide shield.

Uncle Jim gave ground suddenly, and trod upon the foot of a young man in a blue shirt, who immediately thrust at him violently with both hands.

"Lea go!" howled Uncle Jim. "That's the Chap I'm looking for!" and pressing the head of the spectacled gentleman aside, smote hard at Mr. Polly.

But at the sight of this indignity inflicted upon the spectacled gentleman a woman's heart was stirred, a pink parasol drove hard and true at Uncle Jim's wiry neck, and at the same moment the young man in the blue shirt sought to collar him, and lost his grip again.

"Suffragettes!" gasped Uncle Jim, with the ferrule at his throat. "Everywhere!" and aimed a second more successful blow at Mr. Polly.

"Wup!" said Mr. Polly.

But now the jam and egg party was joining in the fray. A stout, yet still fairly able-bodied gentleman in white and black checks inquired: "What's the fellow up to? Ain't there no police here?" And it was evident that once more public opinion was rallying to the support of Mr. Polly.

"Oh, come on then, all the LOT of you!" cried Uncle Jim, and backing dexterously, whirled the eel round in a destructive circle. The pink sunshade was torn from the hand that gripped it, and whirled athwart the complete but unadorned tea-things on the green table.

"Collar him! Some one get hold of his collar!" cried the gold-spectacled gentleman, retreating up the steps to the inn door as if to rally his forces.

"Stand clear, you blessed mantel ornaments!" cried Uncle Jim. "Stand clear!" and retired backing, staving off attack by means of the whirling eel.

Mr. Polly, undeterred by a sense of grave damage done to his nose, pressed the attack in front, the two young men in violet and blue skirmished on Uncle Jim's flanks, the man in white and black checks sought still further outflanking possibilities, and two of the apprentice boys ran for oars. The gold-spectacled gentleman, as if inspired, came down the wooden steps again, seized the tablecloth of the jam and egg party, lugged it from under the crockery with inadequate precautions against breakage, and advanced with compressed lips, curious lateral crouching movements, swift flashings of his glasses, and a general suggestion of bull-fighting in his pose and gestures. Uncle Jim was kept busy, and unable to plan his retreat with any strategic soundness. He was moreover manifestly a little nervous about the river in his rear. He gave ground in a curve, and so came right across the rapidly abandoned camp of the family in mourning, crunching teacups under his heel, oversetting the teapot, and finally tripping backwards over the hamper. The eel flew out at a tangent from his hand, and became a mere looping relic on the sward.

"Hold him!" cried the gentleman in spectacles. "Collar him!" and, moving forward with extraordinary promptitude, wrapped the best tablecloth about Uncle Jim's arms and head. Mr. Polly grasped his purpose instantly, the man in checks was scarcely slower, and in another moment Uncle Jim was no more than a bundle of smothered blasphemy, and pair of wildly active legs.

"Duck him!" panted Mr. Polly, holding on to the earthquake. "Bes' thing—duck him."

The bundle was convulsed by paroxysms of anger and protest. One boot got the hamper and sent it ten yards.

"Go in the house for a clothes'-line, some one," said the gentleman in gold spectacles. "He'll get out of this in a moment."

One of the apprentices ran.

"Bird-nets in the garden," shouted Mr. Polly. "In the garden."

The apprentice was divided in his purpose.

And then suddenly Uncle Jim collapsed, and became a limp, dead-seeming thing under their hands. His arms were drawn inward, his legs bent up under his person, and so he lay.

"Fainted!" said the man in checks, relaxing his grip.

"A fit, perhaps," said the man in spectacles.

"Keep hold!" said Mr. Polly, too late.

For suddenly Uncle Jim's arms and legs flew out like springs released. Mr. Polly was tumbled backwards, and fell over the broken teapot, and into the arms of the father in mourning. Something struck his head—

dazingly. In another second Uncle Jim was on his feet, and the tablecloth enshrouded the head of the man in checks. Uncle Jim manifestly considered he had done all that honour required of him; and against overwhelming numbers, and the possibility of reiterated duckings, flight is no disgrace.

Uncle Jim fled.

Mr. Polly sat up, after an interval of indeterminate length, among the ruins of an idyllic afternoon. Quite a lot of things seemed scattered and broken, but it was difficult to grasp it all at once. He stared between the legs of the people. He became aware of a voice speaking slowly and complainingly.

"Some one ought to pay for those tea-things," said the father in mourning. "We didn't bring them 'ere to be danced on, not by no manner of means."

§ 10

There followed an anxious peace for three days, and then a rough man in a blue jersey, in the intervals of trying to choke himself with bread and cheese and pickled onions, broke abruptly into information.

"Jim's lagged again, Missus," he said.

"What!" said the landlady. "Our Jim?"

"Your Jim," said the man; and after an absolutely necessary pause for swallowing, added, "Stealing a 'atchet."

He did not speak for some moments, and then he replied to Mr. Polly's inquiries: "Yes, a 'atchet. Down Lammam way—night before last."

"What'd 'e steal a 'atchet for?" asked the plump woman.

"'E said 'e wanted a 'atchet."

"I wonder what he wanted a hatchet for," said Mr. Polly thoughtfully.

"I dessay 'e 'ad a use for it," said the gentleman in the blue jersey, and he took a mouthful that amounted to conversational suicide. There was a prolonged pause in the little bar, and Mr. Polly did some rapid thinking.

He went to the window and whistled. "I shall stick it," he whispered at last. "'Atchets or no 'atchets."

He turned to the man with the blue jersey, when he thought him clear for speech again. "How much did you say they'd given him?" he asked.

"Three munce," said the man in the blue jersey, and refilled anxiously, as if alarmed at the momentary clearness of his voice.

§ 11

Those three months passed all too quickly—months of sunshine and warmth, of varied novel exertion in the open air, of congenial experiences, of interest and wholesome food and successful digestion; months that browned Mr. Polly and hardened him, and saw the beginnings of his beard; months marred only by one anxiety, an anxiety Mr. Polly did his utmost to suppress. The day of reckoning was never mentioned, it is true, by either the plump woman or himself, but the name of Uncle Jim was written in letters of glaring silence across their intercourse. As the term of that respite drew to an end, his anxiety increased, until at last it trenched upon his well-earned sleep. He had some idea of buying a revolver. He compromised upon a small and very foul and dirty rook rifle, which he purchased in Lammam under a pretext of bird scaring, and loaded carefully and concealed under his bed from the plump woman's eye.

September passed away, October came.

And at last came that night in October whose happenings it is so difficult for a sympathetic historian to drag out of their proper nocturnal indistinctness into the clear hard light of positive statement. A novelist should present characters, not vivisect them publicly. . . .

20

The best, the kindliest, if not the justest course, is surely to leave untold such things as Mr. Polly would manifestly have preferred untold.

Mr. Polly has declared that when the cyclist discovered him he was seeking a weapon that should make a conclusive end to Uncle Jim. That declaration is placed before the reader without comment.

The gun was certainly in the possession of Uncle Jim at that time, and no human being but Mr. Polly knows how he got hold of it.

The cyclist was a literary man named Warspite, who suffered from insomnia; he had risen and come out of his house near Lamman just before the dawn, and he discovered Mr. Polly partially concealed in the ditch by the Potwell churchyard wall. It is an ordinary dry ditch full of nettles, and overgrown with elder and dog-rose, and in no way suggestive of an arsenal. It is the last place in which a sensible man would look for a gun. And he says that when he dismounted to see why Mr. Polly was allowing only the latter part of his person to show (and that, it would seem, by inadvertency), Mr. Polly merely raised his head and advised him to "Look out!" and added, "He's let fly at me twice already."

He came out under persuasion, and with gestures of extreme caution. He was wearing a white cotton nightgown of the type that has now been so extensively superseded by pyjama sleeping suits, and his legs and feet were bare, and much scratched and torn, and very muddy.

Mr. Warspite takes that exceptionally lively interest in his fellow-creatures which constitutes so much of the distinctive and complex charm of your novelist all the world over, and he at once involved himself generously in the case. The two men returned at Mr. Polly's initiative across the churchyard to the Potwell Inn, and came upon the burst and damaged rook rifle near the new monument to Sir Samuel Harpon at the corner by the yew.

"That must have been his third go," said Mr. Polly. "It sounded a bit funny."

The sight inspirited him greatly, and he explained further that he had fled to the churchyard on account of the cover afforded by tombstones from the flight of small shot. He expressed anxiety for the fate of the landlady of the Potwell Inn and her grandchild, and led the way with enhanced alacrity along the lane to that establishment.

They found the doors of the house standing open, the bar in some disorder—several bottles of whisky were afterwards found to be missing—and Blake, the village policeman, rapping patiently at the open door. He entered with them. The glass in the bar had suffered severely, and one of the mirrors was starred from a blow from a pewter pot. The till had been forced and ransacked, and so had the bureau in the minute room behind the bar.

An upper window was opened, and the voice of the landlady became audible making inquiries. They went out and parleyed with her. She had locked herself upstairs with the little girl, she said, and refused to descend until she was assured that neither Uncle Jim nor Mr. Polly's gun was anywhere on the premises. Mr. Blake and Mr. Warspite proceeded to satisfy themselves with regard to the former condition, and Mr. Polly went to his room in search of garments more suited to the brightening dawn. He returned immediately with a request that Blake and Mr. Warspite would "just come and look." They found the apartment in a state of extraordinary confusion, the bed-clothes in a ball in the corner, the drawers all open and ransacked, the chair broken, the lock of the door forced and broken, one door panel slightly scorched and perforated by shot, and the window wide open. None of Mr. Polly's clothes were to be seen, but some garments which had apparently once formed part of a stoker's workaday outfit, two brownish-yellow halves of a shirt, and an unsound pair of boots, were scattered on the floor. A faint smell of gunpowder still hung in the air, and two or three books Mr. Polly had recently acquired had been shied with some violence under the bed. Mr. Warspite looked at Mr. Blake, and then both men looked at Mr. Polly. "That's *his* boots," said Mr. Polly.

Blake turned his eyes to the window. "Some of these tiles 'ave just got broken," he observed.

"I got out of the window and slid down the scullery tiles," Mr. Polly answered, omitting much, they both felt, from his explanation. . . .

"Well, we better find 'im and 'ave a word with 'im," said Blake. "That's about my business now."

§ 12

But Uncle Jim had gone altogether. . . .

He did not return for some days. That, perhaps, was not very wonderful. But the days lengthened to weeks, and the weeks to months, and still Uncle Jim did not recur. A year passed, and the anxiety of him became less acute, a second healing year followed the first. One afternoon about thirty months after the Night Surprise the plump woman spoke of him.

"I wonder what's become of Jim," she said.

"*I* wonder sometimes," said Mr. Polly.

CHAPTER THE TENTH

Miriam Revisited

§ 1

ONE summer afternoon, about five years after his first coming to the Potwell Inn, Mr. Polly found himself sitting under the pollard willow, fishing for dace. It was a plumper, browner, and healthier Mr. Polly altogether than the miserable bankrupt with whose dyspeptic portrait our novel opened. He was fat, but with the fatness more generally diffused, and the lower part of his face was touched to gravity by a small, square beard. Also he was balder.

It was the first time he had found leisure to fish, though from the very outset of his Potwell career he had promised himself abundant indulgence in the pleasures of fishing. Fishing, as the golden page of English literature testifies, is a meditative and retrospective pursuit, and the varied page of memory, disregarded so long for sake of the teeming duties I have already enumerated,

611

began to unfold itself to Mr. Polly's consideration. Speculation about Uncle Jim died for want of material, and gave place to a reckoning of the years and months that had passed since his coming to Potwell, and that to a philosophical review of his life. He began to think about Miriam, remotely and impersonally. He remembered many things that had been neglected by his conscience during the busier times, as, for example, that he had committed arson and deserted a wife. For the first time he looked these long-neglected facts in the face.

It is disagreeable to think one has committed arson, because it is an action that leads to jail. Otherwise I do not think there was a grain of regret for that in Mr. Polly's composition. But deserting Miriam was in a different category. Deserting Miriam was mean.

This is a history and not a glorification of Mr. Polly, and I tell of things as they were with him. Apart from the disagreeable twinge arising from the thought of what might happen if he was found out, he had not the slightest remorse about that fire. Arson, after all, is an artificial crime. Some crimes are crimes in themselves, would be crimes without any law, the cruelties, mockery, the breaches of faith that astonish and wound, but the burning of things is in itself neither good nor bad. A large number of houses deserve to be burned, most modern furniture, an overwhelming majority of pictures and books—one might go on for some time with the list. If our community was collectively anything more than a feeble idiot, it would burn most of London and Chicago, for example, and build sane and beautiful cities in the place of these pestilential heaps of rotten private property. I have failed in presenting Mr. Polly altogether if I have not made you see that he was in many respects an artless child of Nature, far more untrained, undisciplined, and spontaneous than an ordinary savage. And he was really glad, for all that little drawback of fear, that he had had the courage to set fire to his house, and fly, and come to the Potwell Inn.

But he was not glad he had left Miriam. He had seen Miriam cry once or twice in his life, and it had always reduced him to abject commiseration. He now imagined her crying. He perceived in a perplexed way that he had made himself responsible for her life. He forgot how she had spoiled his own. He had hitherto rested in the faith that she had over a hundred pounds of insurance money, but now, with his eye meditatively upon his float, he realised a hundred pounds does not last for ever. His conviction of her incompetence was unflinching; she was bound to have fooled it away somehow by this time. And then!

He saw her humping her shoulders, and sniffing in a manner he had always regarded as detestable at close quarters, but which now became harrowingly pitiful.

"Damn!" said Mr. Polly, and down went his float, and he flicked a victim to destruction, and took it off the hook.

He compared his own comfort and health with Miriam's imagined distress.

"Ought to have done something for herself," said Mr. Polly, re-baiting his hook. "She was always talking of doing things. Why couldn't she?"

He watched the float oscillating gently towards quiescence.

"Silly to begin thinking about her," he said. "Damn silly!"

But once he had begun thinking about her he had to go on.

"Oh, blow!" cried Mr. Polly presently, and pulled up his hook, to find another fish had just snatched at it in the last instant. His handling must have made the poor thing feel itself unwelcome.

He gathered his things together and turned towards the house.

All the Potwell Inn betrayed his influence now, for here, indeed, he had found his place in the world. It looked brighter, so bright, indeed, as to be almost skittish, with the white and green paint he had lavished upon it. Even the garden palings were striped white and green, and so were the boats; for Mr. Polly was one of those who find a positive sensuous pleasure in the laying on of paint. Left and right were two large boards, which had done much to enhance the inn's popularity with the lighter-minded variety of pleasure-seekers. Both marked innovations. One bore in large letters the single word "Museum," the other was as plain and laconic with "Omlets." The spelling of the latter word was Mr. Polly's own; but when he had seen a whole boatload of men, intent on Lammam for lunch, stop open-mouthed, and stare, and grin, and come in and ask in a marked sarcastic manner for "omlets," he perceived that his inaccuracy had done more for the place than his utmost cunning could have contrived. In a year or so the inn was known both up and down the river by its new name of "Omlets," and Mr. Polly, after some secret irritation, smiled, and was content. And the fat woman's omelettes were things to remember.

(You will note I have changed her epithet. Time works upon us all.)

She stood upon the steps as he came towards the house, and smiled at him richly.

"Caught many?" she asked.

"Got an idea," said Mr. Polly. "Would it put you out very much if I went off for a day or two for a bit of a holiday? There won't be much doing now until Thursday."

§ 2

Feeling recklessly secure behind his beard, Mr. Polly surveyed the Fishbourne High Street once again. The north side was much as he had known it, except that the name of Rusper had vanished. A row of new shops replaced the destruction of the great fire. Mantell and Throbsons' had risen again upon a more flamboyant pattern, and the new fire station was in the Swiss Teutonic style, with much red paint; next door, in the place of Rumbold's, was a branch of the Colonial Tea Company, and then a Salmon and Gluckstein Tobacco Shop, and then a little shop that displayed sweets, and professed a "Tea Room Upstairs." He considered this as a possible place in which to prosecute inquiries about his lost wife, wavering a little between it and the God's Providence Inn down the street. Then his eye caught the name over the window. "'Polly,' he read, '& Larkins.' Well, I'm—astonished!"

A momentary faintness came upon him. He walked past, and down the street, returned, and surveyed the shop again.

He saw a middle-aged, rather untidy woman standing behind the counter, who for an instant he thought might be Miriam terribly changed, and then recognised as his sister-in-law Annie, filled out, and no longer hilarious. She stared at him without a sign of recognition as he entered the shop.

"Can I have tea?" said Mr. Polly.

"Well," said Annie, "you *can*. But our Tea Room's upstairs. . . . My sister's been cleaning it out—and it's a bit upset."

"It *would* be," said Mr. Polly softly.

"I beg your pardon?" said Annie.

"I said *I* didn't mind. Up here?"

"I dare say there'll be a table," said Annie, and followed him up to a room whose conscientious disorder was intensely reminiscent of Miriam.

"Nothing like turning everything upside down when you're cleaning," said Mr. Polly cheerfully.

"It's my sister's way," said Annie impartially. "She's gone out for a bit of air, but I dare say she'll be back soon to finish. It's a nice light room when it's tidy. Can I put you a table over there?"

"Let *me*," said Mr. Polly, and assisted.

He sat down by the open window and drummed on

the table and meditated on his next step, while Annie vanished to get his tea. After all, things didn't seem so bad with Miriam. He tried over several gambits in imagination.

"Unusual name," he said, as Annie laid a cloth before him.

Annie looked interrogation.

"Polly. Polly and Larkins. Real, I suppose?"

"Polly's my sister's name. She married a Mr. Polly."

"Widow, I presume?" said Mr. Polly.

"Yes. This five years—come October."

"Lord!" said Mr. Polly, in unfeigned surprise.

"Found drowned he was. There was a lot of talk in the place."

"Never heard of it," said Mr. Polly. "I'm a stranger—rather."

"In the Medway near Maidstone it was. He must have been in the water for days. Wouldn't have known him, my sister wouldn't, if it hadn't been for the name sewn in his clothes. All whitey and eat away he was."

"Bless my heart! Must have been rather a shock for her."

"It *was* a shock," said Annie, and added darkly, "But sometimes a shock's better than a long agony."

"No doubt," said Mr. Polly.

He gazed with a rapt expression at the preparations before him. "So I'm drowned," something was saying inside him. "Life insured?" he asked.

"We started the tea-rooms with it," said Annie.

Why, if things were like this, had remorse and anxiety for Miriam been implanted in his soul? No shadow of an answer appeared.

"Marriage is a lottery," said Mr. Polly.

"*She* found it so," said Annie. "Would you like some jam?"

"I'd like an egg," said Mr. Polly. "I'll have two.

I've got a sort of feeling— As though I wanted keeping up. . . . Wasn't particularly good sort, this Mr. Polly?"

"He was a *wearing* husband," said Annie. "I've often pitied my sister. He was one of that sort———"

"Dissolute?" suggested Mr. Polly faintly.

"No," said Annie judiciously, "not exactly dissolute. Feeble's more the word. Weak, 'E was. Weak as water. 'Ow long do you like your eggs boiled?"

"Four minutes exactly," said Mr. Polly.

"One gets talking," said Annie.

"One does," said Mr. Polly, and she left him to his thoughts.

What perplexed him was his recent remorse and tenderness for Miriam. Now he was back in her atmosphere, all that had vanished, and the old feeling of helpless antagonism returned. He surveyed the piled furniture, the economically managed carpet, the unpleasant pictures on the wall. Why had he felt remorse? Why had he entertained this illusion of a helpless woman crying aloud in the pitiless darkness for him? He peered into the unfathomable mysteries of the heart, and ducked back to a smaller issue. *Was* he feeble? Hang it! He'd known feebler people by far.

The eggs came up. Nothing in Annie's manner invited a resumption of the discussion.

"Business brisk?" he ventured to ask.

Annie reflected. "It is," she said, "and it isn't. It's like that."

"Ah!" said Mr. Polly, and squared himself to his egg. "Was there an inquest on that chap?"

"What chap?"

"What was his name?—Polly?"

"Of course."

"You're sure it was him?"

"What you mean?"

Annie looked at him hard, and suddenly his soul was black with terror.

" Who else could it have been—in the very clo'es 'E wore?"

" Of course," said Mr. Polly, and began his egg. He was so agitated that he only realised its condition when he was half-way through it, and Annie safely downstairs.

" Lord!" he said, reaching out hastily for the pepper. " One of Miriam's! Management! I haven't tasted such an egg for five years. . . . Wonder where she gets them! Picks them out, I suppose."

He abandoned it for its fellow.

Except for a slight mustiness, the second egg was very palatable indeed. He was getting to the bottom of it as Miriam came in. He looked up. " Nice afternoon," he said, at her stare, and perceived she knew him at once by the gesture and the voice. She went white, and shut the door behind her. She looked as though she was going to faint. Mr. Polly sprang up quickly, and handed her a chair. " My God!" she whispered, and crumpled up, rather than sat down.

" It's *you*," she said.

" No," said Mr. Polly very earnestly, " it isn't. It just looks like me. That's all."

" I *knew* that man wasn't you—all along. I tried to think it was. I tried to think perhaps the water had altered your wrists and feet, and the colour of your hair."

" Ah!"

" I'd always feared you'd come back."

Mr. Polly sat down by his egg. " I haven't come back," he said very earnestly. " Don't you think it."

" 'Ow we'll pay back the Insurance now, I *don't* know."

She was weeping. She produced a handkerchief, and covered her face.

" Look here, Miriam," said Mr. Polly. " I haven't come back, and I'm not coming back. I'm—I'm a Visitant from Another World. You shut up about me, and I'll shut up about myself. I came back because I thought you might be hard up, or in trouble, or some silly thing like that. Now, I see you again—I'm satisfied. I'm satisfied completely. See? I'm going to absquatulate, see? Hey Presto, right away."

He turned to his tea for a moment, finished his cup noisily, stood up.

"Don't you think you're going to see me again," he said, "for you ain't."

He moved to the door.

"That *was* a tasty egg," he said, hovered for a second, and vanished. . . .

Annie was in the shop.

"The missus has had a bit of a shock," he remarked. "Got some sort of fancy about a ghost. Can't make it out quite. So long!"

And he had gone.

§ 3

Mr. Polly sat beside the fat woman at one of the little green tables at the back of the Potwell Inn, and struggled with the mystery of life. It was one of those evenings serenely luminous, amply and atmospherically still, when the river bend was at its best. A swan floated against the dark green masses of the further bank, the stream flowed broad and shining to its destiny, with scarce a ripple—except where the reeds came out from the headland, and the three poplars rose clear and harmonious against the sky of green and yellow. It was as if everything lay securely within a great, warm, friendly globe of crystal sky. It was as safe and enclosed and fearless as a child that has still to be born. It was an evening full of quality of tranquil, unqualified assurance. Mr. Polly's mind was filled with the persuasion that indeed all things whatsoever must need be satisfying and complete. It was incredible that life had ever done more than seemed to jar, that there could be any shadow in life save such velvet softnesses as made the setting for that silent swan, or any murmur but the ripple of the water as it swirled round the chained and gently swaying punt. And the mind of Mr. Polly, exalted and made tender by this atmosphere, sought gently, but sought, to draw together the varied memories that came drifting, half submerged, across the circle of his mind.

He spoke in words that seemed like a bent and broken stick thrust suddenly into water, destroying the mirror of the shapes they sought. " Jim's not coming back again ever," he said. " He got drowned five years ago."

" Where?" asked the fat woman, surprised.

" Miles from here. In the Medway. Away in Kent."

" Lor'!" said the fat woman.

" It's right enough," said Mr. Polly.

" How d'you know?"

" I went to my home."

" Where?"

" Don't matter. I went and found out. He'd been in the water some days. He'd got my clothes, and they'd said it was me."

" They?"

" It don't matter. I'm not going back to them."

The fat woman regarded him silently for some time. Her expression of scrutiny gave way to a quiet satisfaction. Then her brown eyes went to the river.

" Poor Jim," she said. " 'E 'adn't much Tact—ever."

She added mildly, " I can't 'ardly say I'm sorry."

" Nor me," said Mr. Polly, and got a step nearer the thought in him. " But it don't seem much good his having been alive, does it?"

" 'E wasn't much good," the fat woman admitted. " Ever."

" I suppose there were things that were good to him," Mr. Polly speculated. " They weren't *our* things."

His hold slipped again. "I often wonder about life," he said weakly.

He tried again. "One seems to start in life," he said, "expecting something. And it doesn't happen. And it doesn't matter. One starts with ideas that things are good and things are bad—and it hasn't much relation to what *is* good and what *is* bad. I've always been the skeptaceous sort, and it's always seemed rot to me to pretend men know good from evil. It's just what I've *never* done. No Adam's apple stuck in *my* throat, Ma'am. I don't own to it."

He reflected.

"I set fire to a house—once."

The fat woman started.

"I don't feel sorry for it. I don't believe it was a bad thing to do—any more than burning a toy, like I did once when I was a baby. I nearly killed myself with a razor. Who hasn't?—anyhow gone as far as thinking of it? Most of my time I've been half dreaming. I married like a dream almost. I've never really planned my life, or set out to live. I happened; things happened to me. It's so with every one. Jim couldn't help himself. I shot at him, and tried to kill him. I dropped the gun and he got it. He very nearly had me. I wasn't a second too soon—ducking. . . . Awkward—that night was. . . . Ma'am. . . . But I don't blame him—come to that. Only I don't see what it's all up to. . . .

"Like children playing about in a nursery. Hurt themselves at times. . . .

"There's something that doesn't mind us," he resumed presently. "It isn't what we try to get that we get, it isn't the good we think we do is good. What makes us happy isn't our trying, what makes others happy isn't our trying. There's a sort of character people like, and stand up for, and a sort they won't. You got to work it out, and take the consequences. . . . Miriam was always trying."

"Who was Miriam?" asked the fat woman.

"No one you know. But she used to go about with her brows knit, trying not to do whatever she wanted to do—if ever she did want to do anything——"

He lost himself.

"You can't help being fat," said the fat woman, after a pause, trying to get up to his thoughts.

"*You* can't," said Mr. Polly.

"It helps, and it hinders."

"Like my upside down way of talking."

"The magistrates wouldn't 'ave kept on the licence to me if I 'adn't been fat. . . ."

"Then what have we done," said Mr. Polly, "to get an evening like this? Lord! Look at it!" He sent his arm round the great curve of the sky.

"If I was a nigger or an Italian I should come out here and sing. I whistle sometimes, but, bless you, it's singing I've got in my mind. Sometimes I think I live for sunsets."

"I don't see that it does you any good always looking at sunsets, like you do," said the fat woman.

"Nor me. But I do. Sunsets and things I was made to like."

"They don't help you," said the fat woman thoughtfully.

"Who cares?" said Mr. Polly.

A deeper strain had come to the fat woman. "You got to die some day," she said.

"Some things I can't believe," said Mr. Polly suddenly, "and one is your being a skeleton. . . ." He pointed his hand towards the neighbour's hedge. "Look at 'em—against the yellow—and they're just stingin' nettles. Nasty weeds—if you count things by their uses. And no help in the life hereafter. But just look at the look of them!"

"It isn't only looks," said the fat woman.

"Whenever there's signs of a good sunset, and I'm

not too busy," said Mr. Polly, "I'll come and sit out here."

The fat woman looked at him with eyes in which contentment struggled with some obscure reluctant protest, and at last turned them slowly to the black nettle pagodas against the golden sky.

"I wish we could," she said.

"I will."

The fat woman's voice sank nearly to the inaudible.

"Not always," she said.

Mr. Polly was some time before he replied. "Come here always, when I'm a ghost," he replied.

"Spoil the place for others," said the fat woman, abandoning her moral solicitudes for a more congenial point of view.

"Not my sort of ghost wouldn't," said Mr. Polly, emerging from another long pause. "I'd be a sort of diaphalous feeling — just mellowish and warmish like. . . ."

They said no more, but sat on in the warm twilight, until at last they could scarcely distinguish each other's faces. They were not so much thinking, as lost in a smooth, still quiet of the mind. A bat flitted by.

"Time we was going in, O' Party," said Mr. Polly, standing up. "Supper to get. It's as you say, we can't sit here for ever."

BEALBY

CHAPTER THE FIRST

Young Bealby goes to Shonts

§ 1

THE cat is the offspring of a cat and the dog of a dog, but butlers and lady's maids do not reproduce their kind. They have other duties.

So their successors have to be sought among the prolific, and particularly among the prolific on great estates. Such are gardeners, but not undergardeners; gamekeepers and coachmen, but not lodge people because their years are too great and their lodges too small. And among those to whom this opportunity of entering service came was young Bealby who was the stepson of Mr. Darling, the gardener of Shonts.

Every one knows the glories of Shonts. Its façades. Its two towers. The great marble pond. The terraces where the peacocks walk and the lower lake with the black-and-white swans. The great park and the avenue. The view of the river winding away across the blue

627

country. And of the Shonts Velasquez—but that is now in America. And the Shonts Rubens, which is in the National Gallery. And the Shonts porcelain. And the Shonts past history; it was a refuge for the old faith; it had priests' holes and secret passages. And how at last the Marquis had to let Shonts to the Laxtons—the Peptonised Milk and Baby Soother people—for a long term of years. It was a splendid chance for any boy to begin his knowledge of service in so great an establishment, and only the natural perversity of human nature can explain the violent objection young Bealby took to anything of the sort. He did. He said he did not want to be a servant, and that he would not go and be a good boy and try his very best in that state of life to which it had pleased God to call him at Shonts. On the contrary.

He communicated these views suddenly to his mother as she was preparing a steak and kidney pie in the bright little kitchen of the gardener's cottage. He came in with his hair all ruffled and his face hot and distinctly dirty, and his hands in his trousers pockets in the way he had been repeatedly told not to.

"Mother," he said, "I'm not going to be a steward's boy at the house anyhow, not if you tell me to, not till you're blue in the face. So that's all about it."

This delivered he remained panting, having no further breath left in him.

His mother was a thin firm woman. She paused in her rolling of the dough until he had finished, and then she made a strong broadening sweep of the rolling-pin, and remained facing him, leaning forward on that implement with her head a little on one side.

"You will do," she said, "whatsoever your father has said you will do."

"'E isn't my father," said young Bealby.

His mother gave a snapping nod of the head expressive of extreme determination.

"Anyhow I ain't going to do it," said young Bealby,

and feeling the conversation was difficult to sustain he moved towards the staircase door with a view to slamming it.

"You'll do it," said his mother, "right enough."

"You see whether I do," said young Bealby, and then got in his door-slam rather hurriedly because of steps outside.

Mr. Darling came in out of the sunshine a few moments later. He was a large, many-pocketed, earthy-whiskered man with a clean-shaven determined mouth, and he carried a large pale cucumber in his hand.

"I tole him," he said.

"What did he say?" asked his wife.

"Nuthin," said Mr. Darling.

"'E says 'e won't," said Mrs. Darling.

Mr. Darling regarded her thoughtfully for a moment.

"I never see such a boy," said Mr. Darling. "Why —'e's *got* to."

§ 2

But young Bealby maintained an obstinate fight against the inevitable.

He had no gift of lucid exposition. "I ain't going to be a servant," he said. "I don't see what right people have making a servant of me."

"You got to be something," said Mr. Darling.

"Everybody's got to be something," said Mrs. Darling.

"Then let me be something else," said young Bealby.

"*I* dessay you'd like to be a gentleman," said Mr. Darling.

"I wouldn't mind," said young Bealby.

"You got to be what your opportunities give you," said Mr. Darling.

Young Bealby became breathless. "Why shouldn't I be an engine-driver?" he asked.

"All oily," said his mother. "And getting yourself

killed in an accident. And got to pay fines. You'd *like* to be an engine-driver."

"Or a soldier."

"Oo!—a Swaddy!" said Mr. Darling derisively.

"Or the sea."

"With that weak stummik of yours," said Mrs. Darling.

"Besides which," said Mr. Darling, "it's been arranged for you to go up to the 'ouse the very first of next month. And your box and everything ready."

Young Bealby became very red in the face. "I won't go," he said very faintly.

"You will," said Mr. Darling, "if I 'ave to take you by the collar and the slack of your breeches to get you there."

§ 3

The heart of young Bealby was a coal of fire within his breast as—unassisted—he went across the dewy park up to the great house whither his box was to follow him.

He thought the world a "rotten show."

He also said, apparently to two does and a fawn, "If you think I'm going to stand it, you know, you're JOLLY-well mistaken."

I do not attempt to justify his prejudice against honourable usefulness in a domestic capacity. He had it. Perhaps there is something in the air of Highbury, where he had spent the past eight years of his life, that leads to democratic ideals. It is one of those new places where estates seem almost forgotten. Perhaps too there was something in the Bealby strain. . . .

I think he would have objected to any employment at all. Hitherto he had been a remarkably free boy with a considerable gusto about his freedom. Why should that end? The little village mixed school had been a soft job for his Cockney wits, and for a year and a half he had been top boy. Why not go on being top boy?

Instead of which, under threats, he had to go across

the sunlit corner of the park, through that slanting morning sunlight which had been so often the prelude to golden days of leafy wanderings! He had to go past the corner of the laundry where he had so often played cricket with the coachman's boys (already swallowed up into the working world), he had to follow the laundry wall to the end of the kitchen and there, where the steps go down and underground, he had to say farewell to the sunlight, farewell to childhood, boyhood, freedom. He had to go down and along the stone corridor to the pantry, and there he had to ask for Mr. Mergleson. He paused on the top step, and looked up at the blue sky across which a hawk was slowly drifting. His eyes followed the hawk out of sight beyond a cypress bough, but indeed he was not thinking about the hawk, he was not seeing the hawk; he was struggling with a last wild impulse of his ferial nature. "Why not sling it?" his ferial nature was asking. "Why not even now—*do a bunk?*"

It would have been better for him perhaps and better for Mr. Mergleson and better for Shonts if he had yielded to the whisper of the Tempter. But his heart was heavy within him, and he had no provisions. And never a penny. One can do but a very little bunk on an empty belly! "Must" was written all over him. He went down the steps.

The passage was long and cool and at the end of it was a swing door. Through that and then to the left, he knew one had to go, past the still-room and so to the pantry. The maids were at breakfast in the still-room with the door open. The grimace he made in passing was intended rather to entertain than to insult, and anyhow a chap must do something with his face. And then he came to the pantry and into the presence of Mr. Mergleson.

Mr. Mergleson was in his shirt-sleeves and generally dishevelled, having an early cup of tea in an atmosphere full of the bleak memories of overnight. He was an ample man with a large nose, a vast under lip and mutton-chop side-whiskers. His voice would have suited a succulent parrot. He took out a gold watch from his waistcoat pocket and regarded it. "Ten minutes past seven, young man," he said, "isn't seven o'clock."

Young Bealby made no articulate answer.

"Just stand there for a minute," said Mr. Mergleson, "and when I'm at libbuty I'll run through your duties." And almost ostentatiously he gave himself up to the enjoyment of his cup of tea.

Three other gentlemen in deshabille sat at table with Mr. Mergleson. They regarded young Bealby with attention, and the youngest, a red-haired bare-faced youth in shirt-sleeves and a green apron, was moved to a grimace that was clearly designed to echo the scowl on young Bealby's features.

The fury that had been subdued by a momentary awe of Mr. Mergleson revived and gathered force. Young Bealby's face became scarlet, his eyes filled with tears and his mind with the need for movement. After all— he wouldn't stand it. He turned round abruptly and made for the door.

"Where'n earth you going to?" cried Mr. Mergleson.

"He's shy!" cried the second footman.

"Steady on!" cried the first footman and had him by the shoulder in the doorway.

"Lemme *go!*" howled the new recruit, struggling. "I won't be a blooming servant. I won't."

"Here!" cried Mr. Mergleson, gesticulating with his teaspoon, "Bring 'im to the end of the table there. What's this about a blooming servant?"

Bealby suddenly blubbering was replaced at the end of the table.

"May I ask what's this about a blooming servant?" asked Mr. Mergleson.

Sniff and silence.

"Did I understand you to say that you ain't going to be a blooming servant, young Bealby?"

"Yes," said young Bealby.

"Thomas," said Mr. Mergleson, "just smack 'is 'ed. Smack it rather 'ard. . . ."

Things too rapid to relate occurred. "So you'd *bite,* would you?" said Thomas. . . .

"Ah!" said Mr. Mergleson. "*Got* 'im! That one!" . . .

"Just smack 'is 'ed once more," said Mr. Mergleson. . . .

"And now you just stand there, young man, until I'm at libbuty to attend to you further," said Mr. Mergleson, and finished his tea slowly and eloquently. . . .

The second footman rubbed his shin thoughtfully.

"If I got to smack 'is 'ed much," he said, "'e'd better change into his slippers."

"Take him to 'is room," said Mr. Mergleson getting up. "See 'e washes the grief and grubbiness off 'is face in the handwash at the end of the passage and make him put on his slippers. Then show 'im 'ow to lay the table in the steward's room."

§ 4

The duties to which Bealby was introduced struck him as perplexingly various, undesirably numerous, uninteresting and difficult to remember, and also he did not try to remember them very well because he wanted to do them as badly as possible, and he thought that forgetting would be a good way of starting at that. He was beginning at the bottom of the ladder; to him it fell to wait on the upper servants, and the green baize door at the top of the service staircase was the limit of his range. His room was a small wedge-shaped apartment under some steps leading to the servants' hall, lit by a window that did not open and that gave upon the underground passage. He received his instructions in a state of crumpled mutinousness, but for a day his desire to be remarkably impossible was more than counterbalanced by his respect for the large able hands of the four men servants, his seniors, and by a disinclination to be returned too promptly to the gardens. Then in a tentative manner he broke two plates, and got his head smacked by Mr. Mergleson himself. Mr. Mergleson gave a staccato slap quite as powerful as Thomas's but otherwise different. The hand of Mr. Mergleson was large and fat and he got his effects by dash, Thomas's was horny and lingered. After that young Bealby put salt in the teapot in which the housekeeper made tea. But that, he observed, she washed out with hot water before she put in the tea. It was clear that he had wasted his salt, which ought to have gone into the kettle.

Next time——the kettle.

Beyond telling him his duties almost excessively nobody conversed with young Bealby during the long hours of his first day in service. At midday dinner in the servants' hall, he made one of the kitchen-maids giggle by pulling faces intended to be delicately suggestive of Mr. Mergleson, but that was his nearest approach to disinterested human intercourse.

When the hour for retirement came——" Get out of it. Go to bed, you dirty little Kicker," said Thomas. " We've had about enough of you for one day "—— young Bealby sat for a long time on the edge of his bed weighing the possibilities of arson and poison. He wished he had some poison. Some sort of poison with a mediæval manner, poison that hurts before it kills. Also he produced a small penny pocketbook with a glazed black cover and blue edges. He headed one page of this " Mergleson " and entered beneath it three black crosses. Then he opened an account to Thomas, who was manifestly destined to be his principal creditor. Bealby was not a forgiving boy. At the village school they had been too busy making him a good Churchman to attend to things like that. There were a lot of crosses for Thomas.

And while Bealby made these sinister memoranda
downstairs Lady Laxton—for Laxton had bought a
baronetcy for twenty thousand down to the party
funds and a tip to the whip over the Peptonised Milk
flotation—Lady Laxton, a couple of floors above
Bealby's ruffled head, mused over her approaching
week-end party. It was an important week-end party.
The Lord Chancellor of England was coming. Never
before had she had so much as a member of the Cabinet
at Shonts. He was coming, and do what she would
she could not help but connect it with her very strong
desire to see the master of Shonts in the clear scarlet of
a Deputy Lieutenant. Peter would look so well in that.
The Lord Chancellor was coming and to meet him and
to circle about him there were Lord John Woodenhouse
and Slinker Bond, there were the Countess of Barracks
and Mrs. Rampound Pilby, the novelist, with her
husband Rampound Pilby, there was Professor Timbre,
the philosopher, and there were four smaller (though
quite good) people who would run about very satisfactorily among the others. (At least she thought they
would run about very satisfactorily among the others,
not imagining any evil of her cousin Captain Douglas.)

All this good company in Shonts filled Lady Laxton
with a pleasant realisation of progressive successes, but
at the same time one must confess that she felt a certain
diffidence. In her heart of hearts she knew she had not
made this party. It had happened to her. How it might
go on happening to her she did not know, it was beyond
her control. She hoped very earnestly that everything
would pass off well.

The Lord Chancellor was as big a guest as any she
had had. One must grow as one grows, but still—
being easy and friendly with him would be, she knew,
a tremendous effort. Rather like being easy and friendly
with an elephant. She was not good at conversation.
The task of interesting people taxed her and puzzled
her. . . .

It was Slinker Bond, the whip, who had arranged the whole business—after, it must be confessed, a hint from Sir Peter. Laxton had complained that the government were neglecting this part of the country. "They ought to show up more than they do in the county," said Sir Peter and added almost carelessly, "I could easily put anybody up at Shonts." There were to be two select dinner parties and a large but still select Sunday lunch to let in the countryside to the spectacle of the Laxtons taking their (new) proper place at Shonts. . . .

It was not only the sense of her own deficiencies that troubled Lady Laxton; there were also her husband's excesses. He had—it was no use disguising it—rather too much the manner of an employer. He had a way of getting, how could one put it?—*confident* at dinner, and Mergleson seemed to *delight* in filling up his glass. Then he would contradict a good deal. . . . She felt that Lord Chancellors, however, are the sort of men one doesn't contradict. . . .

Then the Lord Chancellor was said to be interested in philosophy—a difficult subject. She had got Timbre to talk to him upon that. Timbre was a professor of philosophy at Oxford, so that was sure to be all right. But she wished she knew one or two good safe things to say in philosophy herself. She had long felt the need of a secretary and now she felt it more than ever. If she had a secretary she could just tell him what it was she wanted to talk about, and he could get her one or two of the right books and mark the best passages and she could learn it all up.

She feared—it was a worrying fear—that Laxton would say right out and very clearly in the week-end that he didn't believe in philosophy. He had a way of saying he "didn't believe in" large things like that, art, philanthropy, novels, and so on. Sometimes he said, "I don't believe in all this"—art or whatever it was. She had watched people's faces when he had said it and she had come to the conclusion that saying you

don't believe in things isn't the sort of thing people say
nowadays. It was wrong somehow. But she did not
want to tell Laxton directly that it was wrong. He
would remember if she did, but he had a way of taking
such things rather badly at the time. . . . She hated
him to take things badly.

" If one could invent some little hint," she whispered
to herself.

She had often wished she was better at hints.

She was, you see, a gentlewoman, modest, kindly.
Her people were quite good people. Poor of course.
But she was not clever, she was anything but clever.
And the wives of these captains of industry need to be
very clever indeed if they are to escape a magnificent
social isolation. They get the titles and the big places
and all that sort of thing; people don't at all intend to
isolate them, but there is nevertheless an inadvertent
avoidance. . . .

Even as she uttered these words, "If one could invent
some little hint," Bealby down there less than forty
feet away through the solid floor below her feet and a
little to the right was wetting his stump of pencil as
wet as he could in order to insure a sufficiently emphatic
fourteenth cross on the score-sheet of the doomed
Thomas. Most of the other thirteen marks were done
with such hard breathing emphasis that the print of
them went more than half-way through that little blue-
edged book.

§ 5

The arrival of the week-end guests impressed Bealby
at first merely as a blessed influence that withdrew the
four men servants into that unknown world on the other
side of the green-baize door, but then he learned that
it also involved the appearance of five new persons,
two valets and three maids, for whom places had to be
laid in the steward's room. Otherwise Lady Laxton's

social arrangements had no more influence upon the mind of Bealby than the private affairs of the Emperor of China. There was something going on up there, beyond even his curiosity. All he heard of it was a distant coming and going of vehicles and some slight talk to which he was inattentive while the coachman and grooms were having a drink in the pantry—until these maids and valets appeared. They seemed to him to appear suddenly out of nothing, like slugs after rain, black and rather shiny, sitting about inactively and quietly consuming small matters. He disliked them and they regarded him without affection or respect.

Who cared? He indicated his feeling towards them as soon as he was out of the steward's room by a gesture of the hand and nose venerable only by reason of its antiquity.

He had things more urgent to think about than strange valets and maids. Thomas had laid hands on him, jeered at him, inflicted shameful indignities on him, and he wanted to kill Thomas in some frightful manner. (But if possible unobtrusively.)

If he had been a little Japanese boy this would have been an entirely honourable desire. It would have been Bushido and all that sort of thing. In the gardener's stepson however it is—undesirable. . . .

Thomas, on the other hand, having remarked the red light of revenge in Bealby's eye and being secretly afraid, felt that his honour was concerned in not relaxing his persecutions. He called him "Kicker" and when he did not answer to that name, he called him "Snorter," "Bleater," "Snooks," and finally tweaked his ear. Then he saw fit to assume that Bealby was deaf and that ear-tweaking was the only available method of address. This led on to the convention of a sign language whereby ideas were communicated to Bealby by means of painful but frequently quite ingeniously symbolical freedoms with various parts of his person. Also Thomas affected to discover uncleanliness in

Bealby's head, and succeeded after many difficulties in putting it into a sinkful of lukewarm water.

Meanwhile young Bealby devoted such scanty time as he could give to reflection to debating whether it was better to attack Thomas suddenly with a carving-knife or throw a lighted lamp. The large pantry inkpot of pewter might be effective in its way, he thought, but he doubted whether in the event of a charge it had sufficient stopping power. He was also curiously attracted by a long two-pronged toasting-fork that hung at the side of the pantry fireplace. It had *reach*. . . .

Over all these dark thoughts and ill-concealed emotions Mr. Mergleson prevailed, large yet speedy, speedy yet exact, parroting orders and making plump gestures, performing duties and seeing that duties were performed.

Matters came to a climax late on Saturday night at the end of a trying day, just before Mr. Mergleson went round to lock up and turn out the lights.

Thomas came into the pantry close behind Bealby, who, greatly belated through his own inefficiency, was carrying a tray of glasses from the steward's room, applied an ungentle hand to his neck, and ruffled up his back hair in a smart and painful manner. At the same time Thomas remarked, " Burrrrh !"

Bealby stood still for a moment and then put down his tray on the table and, making peculiar sounds as he did so, resorted very rapidly to the toasting-fork. . . . He got a prong into Thomas's chin at the first prod.

How swift are the changes of the human soul ! At the moment of his thrust young Bealby was a primordial savage; so soon as he saw this incredible piercing of Thomas's chin—for all the care that Bealby had taken it might just as well have been Thomas's eye—he moved swiftly through the ages and became a simple Christian child. He abandoned violence and fled.

The fork hung for a moment from the visage of Thomas like a twisted beard of brass, and then rattled on the ground.

Thomas clapped his hand to his chin and discovered blood.

"You little——!" He never found the right word (which perhaps is just as well), instead he started in pursuit of Bealby.

Bealby in his sudden horror of his own act—and Thomas—fled headlong into the passage and made straight for the service stairs that went up into a higher world. He had little time to think. Thomas with a red-smeared chin appeared in pursuit. Thomas the avenger. Thomas really roused. Bealby shot through the green-baize door and the pursuing footman pulled up only just in time not to follow him.

Only just in time. He had an instinctive instant anxious fear of great dangers. He heard something, a sound as though the young of some very large animal had squeaked feebly. He had a glimpse of something black and white—and large. . . .

Then something, some glass thing, smashed.

He steadied the green-baize door which was wabbling on its brass hinges, controlled his panting breath, and listened.

A low rich voice was—ejaculating. It was not Bealby's voice, it was the voice of some substantial person being quietly but deeply angry. They were the ejaculations restrained in tone but not in quality of a ripe and well-stored mind—no boy's thin stuff.

Then very softly Thomas pushed open the door just widely enough to see, and as instantly let it fall back into place.

Very gently and yet with an alert rapidity he turned about and stole down the service stairs.

His superior officer appeared in the passage below.

"Mr. Mergleson," he cried, "I say—Mr. Mergleson."

"What's up?" said Mr. Mergleson.

"He's gone!"

"Who?"

" Bealby."

" Home ?" This almost hopefully.

" No."

" Where ?"

" Up there! I think he ran against somebody."

Mr. Mergleson scrutinised his subordinate's face for a second. Then he listened intently; both men listened intently.

" Have to fetch him out of that," said Mr. Mergleson, suddenly preparing for brisk activity.

Thomas bent lower over the banisters.

" *The Lord Chancellor!*" he whispered with white lips and a sideways gesture of his head.

" What about 'im ?" said Mergleson arrested by something in the manner of Thomas.

Thomas's whisper became so fine that Mr. Mergleson drew nearer to catch it. Thomas repeated the last remark. " He's just through there—on the landing—cursing and swearing—'orrible things—more like a mad turkey than a human being."

" Where's Bealby ?"

" He must almost 'ave run into 'im," said Thomas after consideration.

" But now—where is he ?"

Thomas pantomimed infinite perplexity.

Mr. Mergleson reflected and decided upon his line. He came up the service staircase, lifted his chin and with an air of meek officiousness went through the green door. There was no one now on the landing, there was nothing remarkable on the landing except a broken tumbler, but half-way up the grand staircase stood the Lord Chancellor. Under one arm the great jurist carried a soda-water siphon and he grasped a decanter of whisky in his hand. He turned sharply at the sound of the green-baize door and bent upon Mr. Mergleson the most terrible eyebrows that ever surely adorned a legal visage. He was very red in the face and savage-looking.

"Was it *you*," he said with a threatening gesture of the decanter, and his voice betrayed a noble indignation, "was it *you* who slapped me behind?"

"Slapped you behind, me lord?"

"Slapped me *behind*. Don't I speak—plainly?"

"I—such a libbuty, me lord!"

"Idiot! I ask you a plain question——"

With almost inconceivable alacrity Mr. Mergleson rushed up three steps, leaped forward and caught the siphon as it slipped from his lordship's arm.

He caught it, but at a price. He overset and, clasping it in his hands, struck his lordship first with the siphon on the left shin and then butted him with a face that was still earnestly respectful in the knees. His lordship's legs were driven sideways, so that they were no longer beneath his centre of gravity. With a monosyllabic remark of a topographical nature his lordship collapsed upon Mr. Mergleson. The decanter flew out of his grasp and smashed presently with emphasis upon the landing below. The siphon escaping from the wreckage of Mr. Mergleson and drawn no doubt by a natural affinity, rolled noisily from step to step in pursuit of the decanter. . . .

It was a curious little procession that hurried down the great staircase of Shonts that night. First the whisky like a winged harbinger with the pedestrian siphon in pursuit. Then the great lawyer gripping the great butler by the tails of his coat and punching furiously. Then Mr. Mergleson trying wildly to be respectful—even in disaster. First the Lord Chancellor dived over Mr. Mergleson grappling as he passed, then Mr. Mergleson, attempting explanations, was pulled backwards over the Lord Chancellor; then again the Lord Chancellor was for a giddy but vindictive moment uppermost; a second rotation and they reached the landing.

Bang! There was a deafening report——

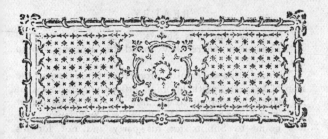

CHAPTER THE SECOND

A Week-end at Shonts

§ 1

THE week-end visit is a form of entertainment peculiar to Great Britain. It is a thing that could have been possible only in a land essentially aristocratic and mellow, in which even the observance of the Sabbath has become mellow. At every London terminus on a Saturday afternoon the outgoing trains have an unusually large proportion of first-class carriages, and a peculiar abundance of rich-looking dressing-bags provokes the covetous eye. A discreet activity of valets and maids mingles with the stimulated alertness of the porters. One marks celebrities in gay raiment. There is an indefinable air of distinction upon platform and bookstall. Sometimes there are carriages reserved for especially privileged parties. There are greetings.

"And so *you* are coming too!"

643

"No, this time it is Shonts."

"The place where they found the Rubens. Who has it now?" . . .

Through this cheerfully prosperous throng went the Lord Chancellor with his high nose, those eyebrows of his which he seemed to be able to furl or unfurl at will, and his expression of tranquil self-sufficiency. He was going to Shonts for his party and not for his pleasure, but there was no reason why that should appear upon his face. He went along preoccupied, pretending to see nobody, leaving to others the disadvantage of the greetings. In his right hand he carried a small important bag of leather. Under his left arm he bore a philosophical work by Doctor MacTaggart, three illustrated papers, *The Fortnightly Review,* the day's *Times, The Hibbert Journal, Punch* and two blue books. His lordship never quite knew the limits set to what he could carry under his arm. His man, Candler, followed therefore at a suitable distance with several papers that had already been dropped, alert to retrieve any further losses.

At the large bookstall they passed close by Mrs. Rampound Pilby, who according to her custom was feigning to be a member of the general public and was asking the clerk about her last book. The Lord Chancellor saw Rampound Pilby hovering at hand and deftly failed to catch his eye. He loathed the Rampound Pilbys. He speculated for a moment what sort of people could possibly stand Mrs. Pilby's vast pretensions—even from Saturday to Monday. One dinner-party on her right hand had glutted him for life. He chose a corner seat, took possession of both it and the seat opposite it in order to have somewhere to put his feet, left Candler to watch over and pack in his hand luggage, and went high up the platform, remaining there with his back to the world—rather like a bigger more aquiline Napoleon—in order to evade the great novelist.

In this he was completely successful.

He returned however to find Candler on the verge of a personal conflict with a very fair young man in grey. He was so fair as to be almost an albino, except that his eyes were quick and brown; he was blushing the brightest pink and speaking very rapidly.

"These two places," said Candler, breathless with the badness of his case, "are engaged."

"Oh ve-*very* well," said the very fair young man, with his eyebrows and moustache looking very pale by contrast, "have it so. But do permit me to occupy the middle seat of the carriage. With a residuary interest in the semi-gentleman's place."

"You little know, young man, *whom* you are calling a semi-gentleman," said Candler, whose speciality was grammar.

"Here he is!" said the young gentleman.

"Which place will you have, my lord?" asked Candler, abandoning his case altogether.

"Facing," said the Lord Chancellor slowly unfurling the eyebrows and scowling at the young man in grey.

"Then I'll have the other," said the very fair young man talking very glibly. He spoke with a quick low voice, like one who forces himself to keep going. "You see," he said, addressing the great jurist with the extreme familiarity of the courageously nervous, "I've gone into this sort of thing before. First, mind you, I have a fair look for a vacant corner. I'm not the sort to spoil sport. But if there isn't a vacant corner I look for traces of a semi-gentleman. A semi-gentleman is one who has a soft cap and not an umbrella—his friend in the opposite seat has the umbrella—or he has an umbrella and not a soft cap, or a waterproof and not a bag, or a bag and not a waterproof. And a half-interest in a rug. That's what I call a semi-gentleman. You see the idea. Sort of divided beggar. Nothing in any way offensive."

" Sir," said the Lord Chancellor, interrupting in a voice of concentrated passion, " I don't care a *rap* what you call a semi-gentleman. *Will* you get out of my way?"

" Just as you please," said the very fair young man, and going a few paces from the carriage door he whistled for the boy with the papers. He was bearing up bravely.

"*Pink 'un?*" said the very fair young gentleman almost breathlessly. "*Black and White?* What's all these others? *Athenæum? Sporting and Dramatic?* Right O. And—eh? What? Do I *look* the sort that buys a *Spectator?* You don't know. Do I wear galoshes? My dear boy, where's your *savoir faire?*"

§ 2

The Lord Chancellor was a philosopher and not easily perturbed. His severe manner was consciously assumed and never much more than skin-deep. He had already furled his eyebrows and dismissed his vis-à-vis from his mind before the train started. He turned over *The Hibbert Journal,* and read in it with a large tolerance.

Dimly on the outskirts of his consciousness the very fair young man hovered, as a trifling annoyance, as something pink and hot rustling a sheet of a discordant shade of pink, as something that got in the way of his legs and whistled softly some trivial cheerful air, just to show how little it cared. Presently, very soon, this vague trouble would pass out of his consciousness altogether. . . .

The Lord Chancellor was no mere amateur of philosophy. His activities in that direction were a part of his public reputation. He lectured on religion and æsthetics. He was a fluent Hegelian. He spent his holidays, it was understood, in the Absolute—at any rate in Germany. He would sometimes break into philosophy at dinner-tables and particularly over the dessert, and be more luminously incomprehensible while still apparently sober than almost any one. An article in the *Hibbert* caught and held his attention. It attempted to define a new and doubtful variety of Infinity. You know of course that there are many sorts and species of Infinity, and that the Absolute is just the king among Infinities as the lion is king among the beasts. . . .

" I say," said a voice coming out of the world of Relativity and coughing the cough of those who break a silence, " *You* aren't going to Shonts, are you?"

The Lord Chancellor returned slowly to earth.

" Just seen your label," said the very fair young man. " You see,—*I'm* going to Shonts."

The Lord Chancellor remained outwardly serene. He reflected for a moment. And then he fell into that snare which is more fatal to great lawyers and judges perhaps than to any other class of men, the snare of the crushing repartee. . One had come into his head now—a beauty.

" Then we shall meet there," he said in his suavest manner.

" Well—rather."

" It would be a great pity," said the Lord Chancellor with an effective blandness, using a kind of wry smile that he employed to make things humorous, " it would be a great pity, don't you think, to anticipate that pleasure?"

And having smiled the retort well home with his head a little on one side, he resumed with large leisurely movements the reading of his *Hibbert Journal.*

" Got me there," said the very fair young man belatedly, looking boiled to a turn, and after a period of restlessness settled down to an impatient perusal of *Black and White.*

" There's a whole blessed week-end of course," the

21*

young man remarked presently without looking up from his paper and apparently pursuing some obscure meditations. . . .

A vague uneasiness crept into the Lord Chancellor's mind as he continued to appear to peruse. Out of what train of thought could such a remark arise? His weakness for crushing retort had a little betrayed him. . . .

It was however only when he found himself upon the platform of Chelsome, which as every one knows is the station for Shonts, and discovered Mr. and Mrs. Rampound Pilby upon the platform looking extraordinarily like a national monument and its custodian, that the Lord Chancellor began to realise that he was in the grip of fate, and that the service he was doing his party by week-ending with the Laxtons was likely to be not simply joyless but disagreeable.

Well anyhow he had MacTaggart, and he could always work in his own room. . . .

§ 3

By the end of dinner the Lord Chancellor was almost at the end of his large but clumsy endurance; he kept his eyebrows furled only by the most strenuous relaxation of his muscles, and within he was a sea of silent blasphemies. All sorts of little things had accumulated. . . .

He exercised an unusual temperance with the port and old brandy his host pressed upon him, feeling that he dared not relax lest his rage had its way with him. The cigars were quite intelligent at any rate, and he smoked and listened with a faintly perceptible disdain to the conversation of the other men. At any rate Mrs. Rampound Pilby was out of the room. The talk had arisen out of a duologue that had preceded the departure of the ladies, a duologue of Timbre's, about apparitions and the reality of the future life. Sir Peter Laxton, released from the eyes of his wife, was at liberty to say he did not believe in all this stuff; it was just thought transference and fancy and all that sort of thing. His declaration did not arrest the flow of feeble instances and experiences into which such talk invariably degenerates. His lordship remained carelessly attentive, his eyebrows unfurled but drooping, his cigar upward at an acute angle; he contributed no anecdotes, content now and then to express himself compactly by some brief sentence of pure Hegelian—much as a Mahometan might spit.

"Why! come to that, they say Shonts is haunted," said Sir Peter. "I suppose we could have a ghost here in no time if I chose to take it on. Rare place for a ghost too."

The very fair young man of the train had got a name now and was Captain Douglas. When he was not blushing too brightly he was rather good-looking. He was a distant cousin of Lady Laxton. He impressed the Lord Chancellor as unabashed. He engaged people in conversation with a cheerful familiarity that excluded only the Lord Chancellor, and even at the Lord Chancellor he looked ever and again. He pricked up his ears at the mention of ghosts, and afterwards when the Lord Chancellor came to think things over, it seemed to him that he had caught a curious glance of the Captain's bright little brown eye.

"What sort of ghost, Sir Peter? Chains? Eh? No?"

"Nothing of the sort, it seems. I don't know much about it, I wasn't sufficiently interested. No, sort of spook that bangs about and does you a mischief. What's its name? Plundergeist?"

"Poltergeist," the Lord Chancellor supplied carelessly in the pause.

"Runs its hand over your hair in the dark. Taps your shoulder. All nonsense. But we don't tell the servants. Sort of thing I don't believe in. Easily explained,—what with panelling and secret passages and priests' holes and all that."

"Priests' holes!" Douglas was excited.

"Where they hid. Perfect rabbit-warren. There's one going out from the drawing-room alcove. Quite a good room in its way. But you know,"—a note of wrath crept into Sir Peter's voice,—"they didn't treat me fairly about these priests' holes. I ought to have had a sketch and a plan of these priests' holes. When a chap is given possession of a place, he ought to be given possession. Well! I don't know where half of them are myself. That's not possession. Else we might refurnish them and do them up a bit. I guess they're pretty musty."

Captain Douglas spoke with his eye on the Lord Chancellor. "Sure there isn't a murdered priest in the place, Sir Peter?" he asked.

"Nothing of the sort," said Sir Peter. "I don't believe in these priests' holes. Half of 'em never had priests in 'em. It's all pretty tidy rot I expect—come to the bottom of it. . . ."

The conversation did not get away from ghosts and secret passages until the men went to the drawing-room. If it seemed likely to do so Captain Douglas pulled it back. He seemed to delight in these silly particulars; the sillier they were the more he was delighted.

The Lord Chancellor was a little preoccupied by one of those irrational suspicions that will sometimes afflict the most intelligent of men. Why did Douglas want to know all the particulars about the Shonts ghosts? Why every now and then did he glance with that odd expression at one's face—a glance half appealing and half amused? Amused! It was a strange fancy, but the Lord Chancellor could almost have sworn that the young man was laughing at him. At dinner he had had that feeling one has at times of being talked about; he had glanced along the table to discover

the Captain and a rather plain woman, that idiot
Timbre's wife she probably was, with their heads
together looking up at him quite definitely and both
manifestly pleased by something Douglas was telling
her. . . .

What was it Douglas had said in the train? Something like a threat. But the exact words had slipped
the Lord Chancellor's memory. . . .

The Lord Chancellor's preoccupation was just sufficient to make him a little unwary. He drifted into
grappling distance of Mrs. Rampound Pilby. Her voice
caught him like a lasso and drew him in.

"Well, and *how* is Lord Moggeridge now?" she
asked.

What on earth is one to say to such an impertinence?

She was always like that. She spoke to a man of the
calibre of Lord Bacon as though she was speaking to a
schoolboy home for the holidays. She had an invincible
air of knowing all through everybody. It gave confidence to her work rather than charm to her manner.

"Do you still go on with your philosophy?" she
said.

"No," shouted the Lord Chancellor, losing all self-
control for the moment and waving his eyebrows about
madly, "No, I go *off* with it."

"For your vacations? Ah, Lord Moggeridge, how
I envy you great lawyers your long vacations. *I*—
never get a vacation. Always we poor authors are pursued by our creations, sometimes it's typescript, sometimes it's proofs. Not that I really complain of proofs.
I confess to a weakness for proofs. Sometimes alas!
it's criticism. Such *undiscerning* criticism! . . ."

The Lord Chancellor began to think very swiftly of
some tremendous lie that would enable him to escape
at once without incivility from Lady Laxton's drawing-
room. Then he perceived that Mrs. Rampound Pilby
was asking him: "Is that *the* Captain Douglas, or his
brother who's in love with the actress woman?"

The Lord Chancellor made no answer. What he thought was : " Great Silly Idiot! How should I know ?"

" I think it must be *the* one—the one who had to leave Portsmouth in disgrace because of the ragging scandal. He did nothing there, they say, but organise practical jokes. Some of them were quite subtle practical jokes. He's a cousin of our hostess; that perhaps accounts for his presence. . . ."

The Lord Chancellor's comment betrayed the drift of his thoughts. " He'd better not try that sort of thing on here," he said. " I abominate—clowning."

Drawing-room did not last very long. Even Lady Laxton could not miss the manifest gloom of her principal guest, and after the good-nights and barley-water and lemonade on the great landing Sir Peter led Lord Moggeridge by the arm—he hated being led by the arm—into the small but still spacious apartment that was called the study. The Lord Chancellor was now very thirsty; he was not used to abstinence of any sort; but Sir Peter's way of suggesting a drink roused such a fury of resentment in him that he refused tersely and conclusively. There was nobody else in the study but Captain Douglas, who seemed to hesitate upon the verge of some familiar address, and Lord Woodenhouse, who was thirsty too, and held a vast tumbler of whisky and soda, with a tinkle of ice in it, on his knee in a way annoying to a parched man. The Lord Chancellor helped himself to a cigar and assumed the middle of the fireplace with an air of contentment, but he could feel the self-control running out of the heels of his boots.

Sir Peter after a quite unsuccessful invasion of his own hearthrug—the Lord Chancellor stood like a rock —secured the big arm-chair, stuck his feet out towards his distinguished guest and resumed a talk that he had been holding with Lord Woodenhouse about firearms. Mergleson had as usual been too attentive to his master's glass, and the fine edge was off Sir Peter's deference. "I always have carried firearms," he said, "and I always shall. Used properly they are a great protection. Even in the country how are you to know who you're going to run up against—anywhen?"

"But you might shoot and hit something," said Douglas.

"Properly used, I said—properly used. Whipping out a revolver and shooting *at* a man, that's not properly used. Almost as bad as pointing it at him—which is pretty certain to make him fly straight at you. If he's got an ounce of pluck. But *I* said properly used and I *mean* properly used."

The Lord Chancellor tried to think about that article on Infinities, while appearing to listen to this fool's talk. He despised revolvers. Armed with such eyebrows as his it was natural for him to despise revolvers.

"Now, I've got some nice little barkers upstairs," said Sir Peter. "I'd almost welcome a burglar, just to try them."

"If you shoot a burglar," said Lord Woodenhouse abruptly, with a gust of that ill-temper that was frequent at Shonts towards bedtime, "when he's not attacking you, it's murder."

Sir Peter held up an offensively pacifying hand. "I know *that*," he said, "you needn't tell me *that*."

He raised his voice a little to increase his already excessive accentuations. "*I* said properly used."

A yawn took the Lord Chancellor unawares and he caught it dexterously with his hand. Then he saw Douglas hastily pull at his blonde moustache to conceal a smile—grinning ape! What was there to smile at? The man had been smiling all the evening.

Up to something.

"Now let me *tell* you," said Sir Peter, "let me *tell* you the proper way to use a revolver. You whip it out and *instantly* let fly at the ground. You should never let any one see a revolver ever before they hear it—see? You let fly at the ground first off, and the concussion stuns them. It doesn't stun you. You expect it, *they* don't. See? There you are—five shots left, master of the situation."

"I think, Sir Peter, I'll bid you good-night," said the Lord Chancellor, allowing his eye to rest for one covetous moment on the decanter and struggling with the devil of pride.

Sir Peter made a gesture of extreme friendliness from his chair, expressive of the Lord Chancellor's freedom to do whatever he pleased at Shonts. "I may perhaps tell you a little story that happened once in Morocco."

"My eyes won't keep open any longer," said Captain Douglas suddenly, with a whirl of his knuckles into his sockets, and stood up.

Lord Woodenhouse stood up too.

"You see," said Sir Peter, standing also but sticking to his subject and his hearer. "This was when I was younger than I am now, you must understand, and I wasn't married. Just mooching about a bit, between business and pleasure. Under such circumstances one goes into parts of a foreign town where one wouldn't go if one was older and wiser. . . ."

Captain Douglas left Sir Peter and Woodenhouse to it.

He emerged on the landing and selected one of the lighted candlesticks upon the table. "Lord!" he whispered. He grimaced in soliloquy and then perceived the Lord Chancellor regarding him with suspicion and disfavour from the ascending staircase. He attempted ease. For the first time since the train incident he addressed Lord Moggeridge.

"I gather, my lord, you don't believe in ghosts?" he said.

"No, sir," said the Lord Chancellor, "I don't."

"They won't trouble me to-night."

"They won't trouble any of us."

"Fine old house anyhow," said Captain Douglas.

The Lord Chancellor disdained to reply. He went on his way upstairs.

§ 4

When the Lord Chancellor sat down before the thoughtful fire in the fine old panelled room assigned to him he perceived that he was too disturbed to sleep. This was going to be an infernal week-end. The worst week-end he had ever had. Mrs. Rampound Pilby maddened him; Timbre, who was a Pragmatist—which stands in the same relation to a Hegelian that a small dog does to a large cat—exasperated him; he loathed Laxton, detested Rampound Pilby and feared—as far as he was capable of fearing anything—Captain Douglas. There was no refuge, no soul in the house to whom he could turn for consolation and protection from these others. Slinker Bond could talk only of the affairs of the party, and the Lord Chancellor, being Lord Chancellor, had lost any interest in the affairs of the party; Woodenhouse could talk of nothing. The women were astonishingly negligible. There were practically no pretty women. There ought always to be pretty *young* women for a Lord Chancellor, pretty young women who can at least seem to listen. . . .

And he was atrociously thirsty.

His room was supplied only with water—stuff you use to clean your teeth—and nothing else. . . .

No good thinking about it. . . .

He decided that the best thing he could do to compose himself before turning in would be to sit down at the writing-table and write a few sheets of Hegelian— about that Infinity article in *The Hibbert*. There is indeed no better consolation for a troubled mind than the Hegelian exercises; they lift it above—everything. He took off his coat and sat down to this beautiful amusement, but he had scarcely written a page before his thirst became a torment. He kept thinking of that great tumbler Woodenhouse had held—sparkling, golden, cool—and stimulating.

What he wanted was a good stiff whisky and a cigar, one of Laxton's cigars, the only good thing in his entertainment so far.

And then Philosophy.

Even as a student he had been a worker of the Teutonic type—never abstemious.

He thought of ringing and demanding these comforts, and then it occurred to him that it was a little late to ring for things. Why not fetch them from the study himself? . . .

He opened his door and looked out upon the great staircase. It was a fine piece of work, that staircase. Low, broad, dignified. . . .

There seemed to be nobody about. The lights were still on. He listened for a little while, and then put on his coat and went with a soft swiftness that was still quite dignified downstairs to the study, the study redolent of Sir Peter.

He made his modest collection.

Lord Moggeridge came nearer to satisfaction as he emerged from the study that night at Shonts than at any other moment during this ill-advised week-end. In his pocket were four thoroughly good cigars. In one hand he held a cut-glass decanter of whisky. In the other a capacious tumbler. Under his arm, with that confidence in the unlimited portative power of his arm that nothing could shake, he had tucked the siphon. His soul rested upon the edge of tranquillity like a bird that has escaped the fowler. He was already composing his next sentence about that new variety of Infinity. . . .

Then something struck him from behind and impelled him forward a couple of paces. It was something hairy, something in the nature, he thought afterwards, of a worn broom. And also there were two other things softer and a little higher on each side. . . .

Then it was he made that noise like the young of some large animal.

He dropped the glass in a hasty attempt to save the siphon. . . .

"What in the name of Heavens——?" he cried, and found himself alone.

"Captain Douglas!"

The thought leaped to his mind.

But indeed it was not Captain Douglas. It was Bealby. Bealby in panic flight from Thomas. And how was Bealby to know that this large, richly laden man was the Lord Chancellor of England? Never before had Bealby seen any one in evening dress except a butler, and so he supposed this was just some larger, finer kind of butler that they kept upstairs. Some larger, finer kind of butler blocking the path of escape. Bealby had taken in the situation with the rapidity of a hunted animal. The massive form blocked the door to the left. . . .

In the playground of the village school Bealby had been pre-eminent for his dodging; he moved as quickly as a lizard. His little hands, his head, poised with the skill of a practised butter, came against that mighty back, and then Bealby had dodged into the study. . . .

But it seemed to Lord Moggeridge, staggering over his broken glass and circling about defensively, that this fearful indignity could come only from Captain Douglas. Foolery. . . . Blup, blup. . . . Sham Poltergeist. Imbeciles. . . .

He said as much, believing that this young man and possibly confederates were within hearing; he said as much—hotly. He went on to remarks of an unphilosophical tendency about Captain Douglas generally, and about army officers, practical joking, Laxton's hospitalities, Shonts. . . . Thomas, you will remember, heard him. . . .

Nothing came of it. No answer, not a word of apology.

At last in a great dudgeon and with a kind of wariness about his back, the Lord Chancellor, with things more spoiled for him than ever, went on his way upstairs.

When the green-baize door opened behind him, he turned like a shot, and a large foolish-faced butler appeared. Lord Moggeridge with a sceptre-like motion of the decanter very quietly and firmly asked him a simple question and then, then the lunatic must needs leap up three stairs and dive suddenly and upsettingly at his legs.

Lord Moggeridge was paralysed with amazement. His legs were struck from under him. He uttered one brief topographical cry.

(To Sir Peter unfortunately it sounded like "Help!")

For a few seconds the impressions that rushed upon Lord Moggeridge were too rapid for adequate examination. He had a compelling fancy to kill butlers. Things culminated in a pistol-shot. And then he found himself sitting on the landing beside a disgracefully dishevelled man servant, and his host was running downstairs to them with a revolver in his hand.

On occasion Lord Moggeridge could produce a tremendous voice. He did so now. For a moment he stared panting at Sir Peter, and then emphasised by a pointing finger came the voice. Never had it been so charged with emotion.

"What does this *mean,* you, sir?" he shouted. "What does this mean?"

It was exactly what Sir Peter had intended to say.

§ 5

Explanations are detestable things.

And anyhow it isn't right to address your host as "You, sir."

§ 6

Throughout the evening the persuasion had grown in Lady Laxton's mind that all was not going well with the Lord Chancellor. It was impossible to believe he was enjoying himself. But she did not know how to give things a turn for the better. Clever women would have known, but she was so convinced she was not clever that she did not even try.

Thing after thing had gone wrong.

How was she to know that there were two sorts of philosophy—quite different? She had thought philosophy was philosophy. But it seemed that there were these two sorts, if not more; a round large sort that talked about the Absolute and was scornfully superior and rather irascible, and a jabby-pointed sort that called people " Tender " or " Tough," and was generally much too familiar. To bring them together was just mixing trouble. There ought to be little books for hostesses explaining these things. . . .

Then it was extraordinary that the Lord Chancellor, who was so tremendously large and clever, wouldn't go and talk to Mrs. Rampound Pilby, who was also so tremendously large and clever. Repeatedly Lady Laxton had tried to get them into touch with one another. Until at last the Lord Chancellor had said distinctly and deliberately, when she had suggested his going across to the eminent writer, " God forbid !" Her dream of a large clever duologue that she could afterwards recall with pleasure was altogether shattered. She thought the Lord Chancellor uncommonly hard to please. These weren't the only people for him. Why couldn't he " chat party secrets " with Slinker Bond or say things to Lord Woodenhouse? You could say anything you liked to Lord Woodenhouse. Or talk with Mr. Timbre. Mrs. Timbre had given him an excellent opening; she had asked, wasn't it a dreadful anxiety always to have the Great Seal to mind? He had simply *grunted*. . . . And then why did he keep on looking so *dangerously* at Captain Douglas? . . .

Perhaps to-morrow things would take a turn for the better. . . .

One can at least be hopeful. Even if one is not *clever* one can be that. . . .

From such thoughts as these it was that this unhappy hostess was roused by a sound of smashing glass, a rumpus, and a pistol-shot.

She stood up, she laid her hand on her heart, she said "*Oh!*" and gripped her dressing-table for support. . . .

After a long time and when it seemed that it was now nothing more than a hubbub of voices, in which her husband's could be distinguished clearly, she crept out very softly upon the upper landing.

She perceived her cousin, Captain Douglas, looking extremely fair and frail and untrustworthy in a much too gorgeous kimono dressing-gown of embroidered Japanese silk. "I can assure you, my lord," he was saying in a strange high-pitched deliberate voice, "on my word of honour as a soldier, on my word of honour as a soldier, that I know absolutely nothing about it."

"Sure it wasn't all imagination, my lord?" Sir Peter asked with his inevitable infelicity. . . .

She decided to lean over the balustrading and ask very quietly and clearly:

"Lord Moggeridge, please! is anything the matter?"

§ 7

All human beings are egotists, but there is no egotism to compare with the egotism of the very young.

Bealby was so much the centre of his world that he was incapable of any interpretation of this shouting and uproar, this smashing of decanters and firing of pistol-shots, except in reference to himself. He supposed it to be a Hue and Cry. He supposed that he was being hunted—hunted by a pack of great butlers hounded on by the irreparably injured Thomas. The thought of upstairs gentlefolks passed quite out of his mind. He snatched up a faked Syrian dagger that lay, in the capacity of a paper-knife, on the study-table, concealed himself under the chints valance of a sofa, adjusted its rumpled skirts neatly, and awaited the issue of events.

For a time events did not issue. They remained talking noisily upon the great staircase. Bealby could not hear what was said, but most of what was said appeared to be flat contradiction.

"Perchance," whispered Bealby to himself, gathering courage, "perchance we have eluded them. . . . A breathing space. . . ."

At last a woman's voice mingled with the others and seemed a little to assuage them. . . .

Then it seemed to Bealby that they were dispersing to beat the house for him. "Good-night *again* then," said some one.

That puzzled him, but he decided it was a "blind." He remained very, very still.

He heard a clicking in the apartment—the blue parlour it was called—between the study and the dining-room. Electric light?

Then some one came into the study. Bealby's eye was as close to the ground as he could get it. He was breathless, he moved his head with an immense circumspection. The valance was translucent but not transparent, below it there was a crack of vision, a strip of carpet, the castors of chairs. Among these things he perceived feet—not ankles, it did not go up to that, but just feet. Large flattish feet. A pair. They stood still, and Bealby's hand lighted on the hilt of his dagger.

The person above the feet seemed to be surveying the room—or reflecting.

"Drunk! . . . Old fool's either drunk or mad! That's about the truth of it," said a voice.

Mergleson! Angry, but parroty and unmistakable.

The feet went across to the table and there were faint sounds of refreshment, discreetly administered. Then a moment of profound stillness. . . .

" Ah !" said the voice at last, a voice renewed.

Then the feet went to the passage door, halted in the doorway. There was a double click. The lights went out. Bealby was in absolute darkness.

Then a distant door closed and silence followed upon the dark. . . .

Mr. Mergleson descended to a pantry ablaze with curiosity.

"The Lord Chancellor's going dotty," said Mr. Mergleson replying to the inevitable question. " *That's* what's up. . . ."

" I tried to save the blessed siphon," said Mr. Mergleson pursuing his narrative, " and 'e sprang on me like a leppard. I suppose 'e thought I wanted to take it away from 'im. 'E'd broke a glass already. *'Ow,*—I *don't* know. There it was, lying on the landing. . . ."

" 'Ere's where 'e bit my 'and," said Mr. Mergleson. . . .

A curious little side-issue occurred to Thomas. " Where's young Kicker all this time?" he asked.

" Lord !" said Mr. Mergleson, " all them other things, they clean drove 'im out of my 'ed. I suppose 'e's up there, hiding somewhere. . . ."

He paused. His eye consulted the eye of Thomas.

" 'E's got be'ind a curtain or something," said Mr. Mergleson. . . .

" Queer where 'e can 'ave got to," said Mr. Mergleson. . . .

" Can't be bothered about 'im," said Mr. Mergleson.

" I expect he'll sneak down to 'is room when things are quiet," said Thomas, after reflection.

" No good going and looking for 'im now," said Mr. Mergleson. " Things upstairs,—they *got* to settle down. . . ."

But in the small hours Mr. Mergleson awakened and thought of Bealby and wondered whether he was in bed. This became so great an uneasiness that about the hour of dawn he got up and went along the passage to Bealby's compartment. Bealby was not there and his bed had not been slept in.

That sinister sense of gathering misfortunes which comes to all of us at times in the small hours, was so strong in the mind of Mr. Mergleson that he went on and told Thomas of this disconcerting fact. Thomas woke with difficulty and rather crossly, but sat up at last, alive to the gravity of Mr. Mergleson's mood.

"If 'e's found hiding about upstairs after all this upset," said Mr. Mergleson, and left the rest of the sentence to a sympathetic imagination.

"Now it's light," said Mr. Mergleson after a slight pause, "I think we better just go round and 'ave a look for 'im. Both of us."

So Thomas clad himself provisionally, and the two men-servants went upstairs very softly and began a series of furtive sweeping movements—very much in the spirit of Lord Kitchener's historical sweeping movements in the Transvaal—through the stately old rooms in which Bealby must be lurking. . . .

§ 8

Man is the most restless of animals. There is an incessant urgency in his nature. He never knows when he is well off. And so it was that Bealby's comparative security under the sofa became presently too irksome to be endured. He seemed to himself to stay there for ages, but, as a matter of fact, he stayed there only twenty minutes. Then with eyes tempered to the darkness he first stuck out an alert attentive head, then crept out and remained for the space of half a minute on all fours surveying the indistinct blacknesses about him.

Then he knelt up. Then he stood up. Then with

arms extended and cautious steps he began an exploration of the apartment.

The passion for exploration grows with what it feeds upon. Presently Bealby was feeling his way into the blue parlour and then round by its shuttered and curtained windows to the dining-room. His head was now full of the idea of some shelter, more permanent, less pervious to housemaids than that sofa. He knew enough now of domestic routines to know that upstairs in the early morning was much routed about by housemaids. He found many perplexing turns and corners, and finally got into the dining-room fireplace where it was very dark, and kicked against some fire-irons. That made his heart beat fast for a time. Then, groping on past it, he found in the darkness what few people could have found in the day, the stud that released the panel that hid the opening of the way that led to the priest hole. He felt the thing open, and halted perplexed. In that corner there wasn't a ray of light. For a long time he was trying to think what this opening could be, and then he concluded it was some sort of back way from downstairs. . . . Well, anyhow it was all exploring. With an extreme gingerliness he got himself through the panel. He closed it almost completely behind him.

Careful investigation brought him to the view that he was in a narrow passage of brick or stone that came in a score of paces to a spiral staircase going both up and down. Up this he went, and presently breathed cool night air and had a glimpse of stars through a narrow slit-like window almost blocked by ivy. Then— what was very disagreeable—something scampered.

When Bealby's heart recovered he went on up again.

He came to the priest hole, a capacious cell six feet square with a bench bed and a little table and chair. It had a small door upon the stairs that was open and a niche cupboard. Here he remained for a time. Then restlessness made him explore a cramped passage, he had to crawl along it for some yards, that came presently into a curious space with wood on one side and stone on the other. Then ahead, most blessed thing! he saw light.

He went blundering towards it and then stopped appalled. From the other side of this wooden wall to the right of him had come a voice.

"Come in!" said the voice. A rich masculine voice that seemed scarcely two yards away.

Bealby became rigid. Then after a long interval he moved—as softly as he could.

The voice soliloquised.

Bealby listened intently, and then when all was still again crept forward two paces more towards the gleam. It was a peephole.

The unseen speaker was walking about. Bealby listened, and the sound of his beating heart mingled with the pad, pad, of slippered footsteps. Then with a brilliant effort his eye was at the chink. All was still again. For a time he was perplexed by what he saw, a large pink shining dome, against a deep greenish-grey background. At the base of the dome was a kind of interrupted hedge, brown and leafless. . . .

Then he realised that he was looking at the top of a head and two enormous eyebrows. The rest was hidden. . . .

Nature surprised Bealby into a penetrating sniff.

"Now," said the occupant of the room, and suddenly he was standing up—Bealby saw a long hairy neck sticking out of a dressing-gown—and walking to the side of the room. "I won't stand it," said the great voice, "I won't stand it. Ape's foolery!"

Then the Lord Chancellor began rapping at the panelling about his apartment.

"Hollow! It all sounds hollow."

Only after a long interval did he resume his writing. . . .

All night long that rat behind the wainscot troubled the Lord Chancellor. Whenever he spoke, whenever he moved about it was still; whenever he composed himself to write it began to rustle and blunder. Again and again it sniffed—an annoying kind of sniff. At last the Lord Chancellor gave up his philosophical relaxation and went to bed, turned out the lights and attempted sleep, but this only intensified his sense of an uneasy, sniffing presence close to him. When the light was out it seemed to him that this Thing, whatever it was, instantly came into the room and set the floor creaking and snapping. A Thing perpetually attempting something and perpetually thwarted. . . .

The Lord Chancellor did not sleep a wink. The first feeble infiltration of day found him sitting up in bed, wearily wrathful. . . . And now surely some one was going along the passage outside!

A great desire to hurt somebody very much seized upon the Lord Chancellor. Perhaps he might hurt that dismal *farceur* upon the landing! No doubt it was Douglas sneaking back to his own room after the night's efforts.

The Lord Chancellor slipped on his dressing-gown of purple silk. Very softly indeed did he open his bedroom door and very warily peep out. He heard the soft pad of feet upon the staircase.

He crept across the broad passage to the beautiful old balustrading. Down below he saw Mergleson—Mergleson again!—in a shameful deshabille—going like a snake, like a slinking cat, like an assassin, into the door of the study. Rage filled the great man's soul. Gathering up the skirts of his dressing-gown he started in a swift yet noiseless pursuit.

He followed Mergleson through the little parlour and into the dining-room, and then he saw it all! There was a panel open, and Mergleson very cautiously going in. Of course! They had got at him through the priest hole. They had been playing on his nerves. All night they had been doing it—no doubt in relays. The whole house was in this conspiracy.

With his eyebrows spread like the wings of a fighting-cock the Lord Chancellor in five vast noiseless strides had crossed the intervening space and gripped the butler by his collarless shirt as he was disappearing. It was like a hawk striking a sparrow. Mergleson felt himself clutched, glanced over his shoulder and, seeing that fierce familiar face again close to his own, pitiless, vindictive, lost all sense of human dignity and yelled like a lost soul. . . .

§ 9

Sir Peter Laxton was awakened from an uneasy sleep by the opening of the dressing-room door that connected his room with his wife's.

He sat up astonished and stared at her white face, its pallor exaggerated by the cold light of dawn.

"Peter," she said, "I'm sure there's something more going on."

"Something more going on?"

"Something—shouting and swearing."

"You don't mean——?"

She nodded. "The Lord Chancellor," she said, in an awe-stricken whisper. "He's at it again. Downstairs in the dining-room."

Sir Peter seemed disposed at first to receive this quite passively. Then he flashed into extravagant wrath. "I'm *damned*," he cried, jumping violently out of bed, "if I'm going to stand this! Not if he was a hundred Lord Chancellors! He's turning the place into a bally lunatic asylum. *Once*—one might excuse. But to start it again. . . . *What's that?*"

They both stood still listening. Faintly yet quite distinctly came the agonised cry of some imperfectly educated person—"'Elp!"

"Here! Where's my trousers?" cried Sir Peter. "He's murdering Mergleson. There isn't a moment to lose."

§ 10

Until Sir Peter returned Lady Laxton sat quite still just as he had left her on his bed, aghast.

She could not even pray.

The sun had still to rise; the room was full of that cold weak inky light, light without warmth, knowledge without faith, existence without courage, that creeps in before the day. She waited. . . . In such a mood women have waited for massacre. . . .

Downstairs a raucous shouting. . . .

She thought of her happy childhood upon the Yorkshire wolds, before the idea of week-end parties had entered her mind. The heather. The little birds. Kind things. A tear ran down her cheek. . . .

§ 11

Then Sir Peter stood before her again, alive still, but breathless and greatly ruffled.

She put her hands to her heart. She would be brave. "Yes," she said. "Tell me."

"He's as mad as a hatter," said Sir Peter.

She nodded for more. She knew that.

"Has he—*killed* any one?" she whispered.

"He looked uncommonly like trying," said Sir Peter.

She nodded, her lips tightly compressed.

"Says Douglas will either have to leave the house or he does."

"But—Douglas!"

"I know, but he won't hear a word."

"But *why* Douglas?"

"I tell you he's as mad as a hatter. Got persecution mania. People tapping and bells ringing under his pillow all night—that sort of idea. . . . And furious, I tell you—he frightened me. He was *awful*. He's given Mergleson a black eye. Hit him, you know. With

his fist. Caught him in the passage to the priest hole—
how they got there *I* don't know—and went for him
like a madman."

"But what has Douglas done?"

"*I don't know.* I asked him, but he won't listen.
He's just off his head. . . . Says Douglas has got the
whole household trying to work a ghost on him. I tell
you—he's off his nut."

Husband and wife looked at each other. . . .

"Of course if Douglas didn't mind just going off to
oblige me," said Sir Peter at last. . . .

"It might calm him," he explained. . . . "You
see, it's all so infernally awkward. . . ."

"Is he back in his room?"

"Yes. Waiting for me to decide about Douglas.
Walking up and down."

For a little while their minds remained prostrate and
inactive.

"I'd been so looking forward to the lunch," she said
with a joyless smile. "The county——"

She could not go on.

"You know," said Sir Peter, "one thing—I'll see to
it myself. I won't have him have a single drop of liquor
more. If we have to search his room."

"What I shall say to him at breakfast," she said, "I
don't know."

Sir Peter reflected. "There's no earthly reason why
you should be brought into it at all. Your line is to
know nothing about it. *Show* him you know nothing
about it. Ask him—ask him if he's had a good
night. . . ."

CHAPTER THE THIRD

The Wanderers

NEVER had the gracious eastward face of Shonts
looked more beautiful than it did on the morning of
the Lord Chancellor's visit. It glowed as translucent
as amber lit by flames, its two towers were pillars of
pearl gold. It looked over its slopes and parapets upon
a great valley of mist-barred freshness through which
the distant river shone like a snake of light. The south-
west façade was still in the shadow, and the ivy hung
from it darkly greener than the greenest green. The
stained-glass windows of the old chapel reflected the
sunrise as though lamps were burning inside. Along
the terrace a pensive peacock trailed his sheathed splendours through the dew.

Amidst the ivy was a fuss of birds.

And presently there was pushed out from amidst the
ivy at the foot of the eastward tower a little brownish
buff thing, that seemed as natural there as a squirrel or a

rabbit. It was a head—a ruffled human head. It remained still for a moment contemplating the calm spaciousness of terrace and garden and countryside. Then it emerged farther and rotated and surveyed the house above it. Its expression was one of alert caution. Its natural freshness and innocence were a little marred by an enormous transverse smudge, a bar sinister of smut, and the elfin delicacy of the left ear was festooned with a cobweb—probably a genuine antique. It was the face of Bealby.

He was considering the advisability of leaving Shonts —for good.

Presently his decision was made. His hands and shoulders appeared following his head, and then a dusty but undamaged Bealby was running swiftly towards the corner of the shrubbery. He crouched lest at any moment that pursuing pack of butlers should see him and give tongue. In another moment he was hidden from the house altogether, and rustling his way through a thicket of budding rhododendra. After those dirty passages the morning air was wonderfully sweet—but just a trifle hungry.

Grazing deer saw Bealby fly across the park, stared at him for a time with great gentle unintelligent eyes, and went on feeding.

They saw him stop ever and again. He was snatching at mushrooms, that he devoured forthwith as he sped on.

On the edge of the beech-woods he paused and glanced back at Shonts.

Then his eyes rested for a moment on the clump of trees through which one saw a scrap of the head gardener's cottage, a bit of the garden wall. . . .

A physiognomist might have detected a certain lack of self-confidence in Bealby's eyes.

But his spirit was not to be quelled. Slowly, joylessly perhaps, but with a grave determination, he raised his hand to his face and extended his fingers in that prehistoric gesture by which youth, since ever there was

22

youth, has asserted the integrity of its soul against established and predominant things.

"*Ketch* me!" said Bealby.

§ 2

Bealby left Shonts about half-past four in the morning. He went westward because he liked the company of his shadow and was amused at first by its vast length. By half past eight he had covered ten miles, and he was rather bored by his shadow. He had eaten nine raw mushrooms, two green apples and a quantity of unripe blackberries. None of these things seemed quite at home in him. And he had discovered himself to be wearing slippers. They were stout carpet slippers, but still they were slippers—and the road was telling on them. At the ninth mile the left one began to give on the outer seam. He got over a stile into a path that ran through the corner of a wood, and there he met a smell of frying bacon that turned his very soul to gastric juice.

He stopped short and sniffed the air—and the air itself was sizzling.

"Oh Krikey," said Bealby, manifestly to the Spirit of the World. "This is a bit too strong. I wasn't thinking much before."

Then he saw something bright yellow and bulky just over the hedge.

From this it was that the sound of frying came.

He went to the hedge, making no effort to conceal himself. Outside a great yellow caravan with dainty little windows stood a largish dark woman in a deerstalker hat, a short brown skirt, a large white apron and spatterdashes (among other things) frying bacon and potatoes in a frying-pan. She was very red in the face, and the frying-pan was spitting at her as frying-pans do at a timid cook. . . .

Quite mechanically Bealby scrambled through the hedge and drew nearer this divine smell. The woman scrutinised him for a moment, and then blinking and averting her face went on with her cookery.

Bealby came quite close to her and remained, noting the bits of potato that swam about in the pan, the jolly curling of the rashers, the dancing of the bubbles, the hymning splash and splutter of the happy fat. . . .

(If it should ever fall to my lot to be cooked, may I be fried with potatoes and butter. May I be fried with potatoes and good butter made from the milk of the cow. God send I am spared boiling; the prison of the pot, the rattling lid, the evil darkness, the greasy water. . . .)

"I suppose," said the lady prodding with her fork at the bacon, "I suppose you call yourself a Boy."

"Yes, Miss," said Bealby.

"Have you ever fried?"

"I could, Miss."

"Like this?"

"Better."

"Just lay hold of this handle—for it's scorching the skin off my face I am." She seemed to think for a moment and added, "entirely."

In silence Bealby grasped that exquisite smell by the handle, he took the fork from her hand and put his hungry eager nose over the seething mess. It wasn't only bacon; there were onions, onions giving it—an *edge!* It cut to the quick of appetite. He could have wept with the intensity of his sensations.

A voice almost as delicious as the smell came out of the caravan window behind Bealby's head.

"*Ju*-dy!" cried the voice.

"Here!—I mean—it's here I am," said the lady in the deerstalker.

"Judy—you didn't take my stockings for your own by any chance?"

The lady in the deerstalker gave way to delighted horror. "Sssh, Mavourneen!" she cried—she was one of that large class of amiable women who are more Irish than they need be—"there's a Boy here!"

§ 3

There was indeed an almost obsequiously industrious and obliging Boy. An hour later he was no longer *a* Boy but *the* Boy, and three friendly women were regarding him with a merited approval.

He had done the frying, renewed a waning fire with remarkable skill and despatch, reboiled a neglected kettle in the shortest possible time, laid almost without direction a simple meal, very exactly set out campstools and cleaned the frying-pan marvellously. Hardly had they taken their portions of that appetising savouriness, than he had whipped off with that implement, gone behind the caravan, busied himself there, and returned with the pan—glittering bright. Himself if possible brighter. One cheek indeed shone with an animated glow.

"But wasn't there some of the bacon and stuff left?" asked the lady in the deerstalker.

"I didn't think it was wanted, Miss," said Bealby. "So I cleared it up."

He met understanding in her eye. He questioned her expression.

"Mayn't I wash up for you, Miss?" he asked to relieve the tension.

He washed up, swiftly and cleanly. He had never been able to wash up to Mr. Mergleson's satisfaction before, but now he did everything Mr. Mergleson had ever told him. He asked where to put the things away and he put them away. Then he asked politely if there was anything else he could do for them. Questioned, he said he liked doing things. "You haven't," said the lady in the deerstalker; "a taste for cleaning boots?"

Bealby declared he had.

"Surely," said a voice that Bealby adored, "'tis an angel from heaven."

He had a taste for cleaning boots! This was an

extraordinary thing for Bealby to say. But a great change had come to him in the last half-hour. He was violently anxious to do things, any sort of things, servile things, for a particular person. He was in love.

The owner of the beautiful voice had come out of the caravan, she had stood for a moment in the doorway before descending the steps to the ground and the soul of Bealby had bowed down before her in instant submission. Never had he seen anything so lovely. Her straight, slender body was sheathed in blue; fair hair a little tinged with red poured gloriously back from her broad forehead, and she had the sweetest eyes in the world. One hand lifted her dress from her feet; the other rested on the lintel of the caravan door. She looked at him and smiled.

So for two years she had looked and smiled across the footlights to the Bealby in mankind. She had smiled now on her entrance out of habit. She took the effect upon Bealby as a foregone conclusion.

Then she had looked to make sure that everything was ready before she descended.

"How good it smells, Judy!" she had said.

"I've had a helper," said the woman who wore spats.

That time the blue-eyed lady had smiled at him quite definitely. . . .

The third member of the party had appeared unobserved; the irradiations of the beautiful lady had obscured her. Bealby discovered her about. She was bareheaded; she wore a simple grey dress with a Norfolk jacket, and she had a pretty, clear white profile under black hair. She answered to the name of "Winnie." The beautiful lady was Madeleine. They made little obscure jokes with each other and praised the morning ardently. "This is the best place of all," said Madeleine.

"All night," said Winnie, "not a single mosquito."

None of these three ladies made any attempt to conceal the sincerity of their hunger or their appreciation of Bealby's assistance. How good a thing is appreciation! Here he was doing with joy and pride and an eager excellence, the very services he had done so badly under the cuffings of Mergleson and Thomas. . . .

§ 4

And now Bealby, having been regarded with approval for some moments and discussed in tantalising undertones, was called upon to explain himself.

"Boy," said the lady in the deerstalker, who was evidently the leader and still more evidently the spokeswoman of the party, "come here."

"Yes, Miss." He put down the boot he was cleaning on the caravan step.

"In the first place, know by these presents, I am a married woman."

"Yes, Miss."

"And Miss is not a seemly mode of address for me."

"No, Miss. I mean——" Bealby hung for a moment and by the happiest of accidents, a scrap of his instruction at Shonts came up in his mind. "No," he said, "your—ladyship."

A great light shone on the spokeswoman's face. "Not yet, my child," she said, "not yet. He hasn't done his duty by me. I am—a simple Mum."

Bealby was intelligently silent.

"Say—Yes, Mum."

"Yes, Mum," said Bealby, and everybody laughed very agreeably.

"And now," said the lady, taking pleasure in her words, "know by these presents—— By-the-by, what is your name?"

Bealby scarcely hesitated. "Dick Maltravers, Mum," he said and almost added, "The Dauntless Daredevil of the Diamond-fields Horse," which was the second title.

"Dick will do," said the lady who was called Judy,

and added suddenly and very amusingly : "You may keep the rest."

(These were the sort of people Bealby liked. The *right* sort.)

"Well, Dick, we want to know, have you ever been in service?"

It was sudden. But Bealby was equal to it. "Only for a day or two, Miss—I mean, Mum—just to be useful."

"*Were* you useful?"

Bealby tried to think whether he had been, and could recall nothing but he face of Thomas with the fork hanging from it. "I did my best, Mum," he said impartially.

"And all that is over?"

"Yes, Mum."

"And you're at home again and out of employment?"

"Yes, Mum."

"Do you live near here?"

"No—leastways, not very far."

"With your father?"

"Stepfather, Mum. I'm a Norfan."

"Well, how would you like to come with us for a few days and help with things? Seven-and-sixpence a week."

Bealby's face was eloquent.

"Would your stepfather object?"

Bealby considered. "I don't think he would," he said.

"You'd better go round and ask him."

"I—suppose—yes," he said.

"And get a few things."

"Things, Mum?"

"Collars and things. You needn't bring a great box for such a little while."

"Yes, Mum. . . ."

He hovered rather undecidedly.

"Better run along now. Our man and horse will be

coming presently. We shan't be able to wait for you long. . . ."

Bealby assumed a sudden briskness and departed.

At the gate of the field he hesitated almost imperceptibly and then directed his face to the Sabbath stillness of the village.

Perplexity corrugated his features. The stepfather's permission presented no difficulties, but it was more difficult about the luggage.

A voice called after him.

"Yes, Mum?" he said attentive and hopeful. Perhaps—somehow—they wouldn't want luggage.

"You'll want boots. You'll have to walk by the caravan, you know. You'll want some good stout boots."

"All right, Mum," he said with a sorrowful break in his voice. He waited a few moments but nothing more came. He went on—very slowly. He had forgotten about the boots.

That defeated him. . . .

It is hard to be refused permission to Paradise for the want of a hand-bag and a pair of walking-boots. . . .

§ 5

Bealby was by no means certain that he was going back to that caravan. He wanted to do so quite painfully, but——

He'd just look a fool going back without boots and—nothing on earth would reconcile him to the idea of looking a fool in the eyes of that beautiful woman in blue.

"Dick," he whispered to himself despondently, "Daredevil Dick!" (A more miserable-looking face you never set eyes on.) "It's all up with your little schemes, Dick my boy. You *must* get a bag—and nothing on earth will get you a bag."

He paid little heed to the village through which he wandered. He knew there were no bags there. Chance rather than any volition of his own guided him down a side path that led to the nearly dry bed of a little rivulet, and there he sat down on some weedy grass under a group of willows. It was an untidy place that needed all the sunshine of the morning to be tolerable; one of those places where stinging nettles take heart and people throw old kettles, broken gallipots, jaded gravel, grass cuttings, rusty rubbish, old boots——

For a time Bealby's eyes rested on the objects with an entire lack of intere t.

Then he was reminded of his not so very remote childhood when he had found an old boot and made it into a castle. . . .

Presently he got up and walked across to the rubbish heap and surveyed its treasures with a quickened intelligence. He picked up a widowed boot and weighed it in his hand.

He dropped it abruptly, turned about and hurried back into the village street.

He had ideas, two ideas, one for the luggage and one for the boots. . . . If only he could manage it. Hope beat his great pinions in the heart of Bealby.

Sunday! The shops were shut. Yes, that was a fresh obstacle. He'd forgotten that.

The public-house stood bashfully open, the shy uninviting openness of Sunday morning before closing time, but public-houses alas! at all hours are forbidden to little boys. And besides he wasn't likely to get what he wanted in a public-house; he wanted a shop, a general shop. And here before him was the general shop—and its door ajar! His desire carried him over the threshold. The Sabbatical shutters made the place dark and cool, and the smell of bacon and cheese and chandleries, the very spirit of grocery, calm and unhurried, was cool and Sabbatical too, as if it sat there for the day in its best clothes. And a pleasant woman was talking over the counter to a thin and worried one who carried a bundle.

Their intercourse had a flavour of emergency and

they both stopped abruptly at the appearance of Bealby.

His desire, his craving was now so great that it had altogether subdued the natural wiriness of his appearance. He looked meek, he looked good, he was swimming in propitiation and tender with respect. He produced an effect of being much smaller. He had got nice eyes. His movements were refined and his manners perfect.

" Not doing business to day, my boy," said the pleasant woman.

" Oh, *please* 'm," he said from his heart.

" Sunday, you know."

" Oh, *please* 'm. If you could just give me a nold sheet of paper 'm, please."

" What for ?" asked the pleasant woman.

" Just to wrap something up 'm."

She reflected and natural goodness had its way with her.

" A nice *big* bit ?" said the woman.

" Please 'm."

" Would you like it brown ?"

" Oh, *please* 'm."

" And you got some string ?"

" Only cottony stuff," said Bealby, disembowelling a trouser pocket. " Wiv knots. But I dessay I can manage."

" You'd better have a bit of good string with it, my dear," said the pleasant woman, whose generosity was now fairly on the run. " Then you can do your parcel up nice and tidy. . . ."

§ 6

The white horse was already in the shafts of the caravan and William, a deaf and clumsy man of uncertain age and a vast sharp nosiness, was lifting in the basket of breakfast gear and grumbling in undertones at the wickedness and unfairness of travelling on Sunday, when Bealby returned to gladden three waiting women.

"Ah!" said the inconspicuous lady, "I knew he'd come."

"Look at his poor little precious parsivel," said the actress.

Regarded as luggage it was rather pitiful, a knobby, brown-paper parcel about the size—to be perfectly frank —of a tin can, two old boots and some grass, very carefully folded and tied up,—and carried gingerly.

"But—" the lady in the deerstalker began and then paused.

"Dick," she said, as he came nearer, "where's your boots?"

"Oh, please, Mum," said the dauntless one, "they was away being mended. My stepfather thought perhaps you wouldn't mind if I didn't have boots. He said perhaps I might be able to get some more boots out of my salary. . . ."

The lady in the deerstalker looked alarmingly uncertain and Bealby controlled infinite distresses.

"Haven't you got a mother, Dick?" asked the beautiful voice suddenly. Its owner abounded in such spasmodic curiosities.

"She—last year . . ." Matricide is a painful business at any time. And just as you see, in spite of every effort you have made, the jolliest lark in the world slipping out of your reach. And the sweet voice so sorry for him! So sorry! Bealby suddenly veiled his face with his elbow and gave way to honourable tears. . . .

A simultaneous desire to make him happy, help him to forget his loss, possessed three women. . . .

"That'll be all right, Dick," said the lady in the deerstalker patting his shoulder. "We'll get you some boots to-morrow. And to-day you must sit up beside William and spare your feet. You'll have to go to the inns with him. . . ."

"It's wonderful, the elasticity of youth," said the inconspicuous lady five minutes later. "To see that boy now, you'd never imagine he'd had a sorrow in the world."

"Now get up there," said the lady who was the leader. "We shall walk across the fields and join you later. You understand where you are to wait for us, William?"

She came nearer and shouted, "You understand, William?"

William nodded ambiguously. "'Ent a *Vool*," he said.

The ladies departed. "*You'll* be all right, Dick," cried the actress kindly.

He sat up where he had been put, trying to look as Orphan Dick as possible after all that had occurred.

§ 7

"Do you know the wind on the heath—have you lived the Gypsy life? Have you spoken, wanderers yourselves, with ' Romany chi and Romany chal' on the wind-swept moors at home or abroad? Have you tramped the broad highways, and, at close of day, pitched your tent near a running stream and cooked your supper by starlight over a fire of pine-wood? Do you know the dreamless sleep of the wanderer at peace with himself and all the world?"

For most of us the answer to these questions of the Amateur Camping Club is in the negative.

Yet every year the call of the road, the Borrovian glamour, draws away a certain small number of the imaginative from the grosser comforts of a complex civilisation, takes them out into the tents and caravans and intimate communion with Nature and, incidentally, with various ingenious appliances designed to meet the needs of cooking in a breeze. It is an adventure to which high spirits and great expectations must be brought, it is an experience in proximity which few friendships survive—and altogether very great fun.

The life of breezy freedom resolves itself in practice chiefly into washing up and an anxious search for permission to camp. One learns how rich and fruitful our world can be in bystanders, and how easy it is to forget essential groceries. . . .

The heart of the joy of it lies in its perfect detachment. There you are in the morning sunlight under the trees that overhang the road going whither you will. Everything you need you have. Your van creaks along at your side. You are outside inns, outside houses, a home, a community, an *imperium in imperio*. At any moment you may draw out of the traffic upon the wayside grass and say, "Here—until the owner catches us at it—is home!" At any time—subject to the complaisance of William and your being able to find him—you may inspan and go onward. The world is all before you. You taste the complete yet leisurely insouciance of the snail.

And two of those three ladies had other satisfactions to supplement their pleasures. They both adored Madeleine Philips. She was not only perfectly sweet and lovely but she was known to be so; she had that most potent charm for women, prestige. They had got her all to themselves. They could show now how false is the old idea that there is no friendship nor conversation among women. They were full of wit and pretty things for one another and snatches of song in between. And they were free too from their "menfolk." They were doing without them. Dr. Bowles, the husband of the lady in the deerstalker, was away in Ireland, and Mr. Geedge, the lord of the inconspicuous woman, was golfing at Sandwich. And Madeleine Philips, it was understood, was only too glad to shake herself free from the crowd of admirers that hovered about her like wasps about honey. . . .

Yet after three days each one had thoughts about the need of helpfulness and more particularly about washing-up, that were better left unspoken, that were indeed conspicuously unspoken beneath their merry give and take, like a black and silent river flowing beneath a bridge of ivory. And each of them had a curious feeling in the midst of all this fresh free behaviour, as though the others were not listening sufficiently, as though something of the effect of them was being wasted. Madeleine's smiles became rarer; at times she was almost impassive, and Judy preserved nearly all her wit and verbal fireworks for the times when they passed through villages. . . . Mrs. Geedge was less visibly affected. She had thoughts of writing a book about it all, telling in the gayest, most provocative way, full of the quietest quaintest humour, just how jolly they had been. Menfolk would read it. This kept a little thin smile upon her lips. . . .

As an audience William was tough stuff. He pretended deafness; he never looked. He did not want to look. He seemed always to be holding his nose in front of his face to prevent his observation—as men pray into their hats at church. But once Judy Bowles overheard a phrase or so in his private soliloquy. " Pack o' wimmin," William was saying. " Dratted petticoats. *Dang* 'em. That's what I say to 'um. *Dang* 'em !"

As a matter of fact, he just fell short of saying it to them. But his manner said it. . . .

You begin to see how acceptable an addition was young Bealby to this company. He was not only helpful, immensely helpful, in things material, a vigorous and at first a careful washer-up, an energetic bootpolisher, a most serviceable cleaner and tidier of things, but he was also belief and support. Undisguisedly he thought the caravan the loveliest thing going, and its three mistresses the most wonderful of people. His alert eyes followed them about full of an unstinted admiration and interest, he pricked his ears when Judy opened her mouth, handed things to Mrs. Geedge. He made no secret about Madeleine. When she spoke to him, he lost his breath, he reddened and was embarrassed. . . .

They went across the fields saying that he was the luckiest of finds. It was fortunate his people had been so ready to spare him. Judy said boys were a race very cruelly maligned; see how *willing* he was! Mrs. Geedge said there was something elfin about Bealby's little face; Madeleine smiled at the thought of his quaint artlessness. She knew quite clearly that he'd die for her. . . .

§ 8

There was a little pause as the ladies moved away.

Then William spat and spoke in a note of irrational bitterness.

"Brasted Voolery," said William and then loudly and fiercely, "Cam up y' ode Runt you."

At these words the white horse started into a convulsive irregular redistribution of its feet, the caravan strained and quivered into motion and Bealby's wanderings as a caravanner began.

For a time William spoke no more and Bealby scarcely regarded him. The light of strange fortunes and deep enthusiasm was in Bealby's eyes. . . .

"One Thing," said William, "they don't 'ave the Sense to lock anythink up—Whatever."

Bealby's attention was recalled to the existence of his companion.

William's face was one of those faces that give one at first the impression of a solitary and very conceited nose. The other features are entirely subordinated to that salient effect. One sees them later. His eyes were small and uneven, his mouth apparently toothless, thin-lipped and crumpled, with the upper lip falling over the other in a manner suggestive of a meagre firmness mixed with appetite. When he spoke he made a faint slobbering sound. "Everyfink," he said, "behind there."

He became confidential. "I been *in* there. I larked about wiv their Fings.

"They got some choc'late," he said, lusciously. "Oo Fine!

"All sorts of Fings."

He did not seem to expect any reply from Bealby.

"We going far before we meet 'em?" asked Bealby.

William's deafness became apparent.

His mind was preoccupied by other ideas. One wicked eye came close to Bealby's face. "We going to 'ave a bit of choc'late," he said in a wet desirous voice.

He pointed his thumb over his shoulder at the door. "*You* get it," said William with reassuring nods and the mouth much pursed and very oblique.

Bealby shook his head.

"It's in a little dror, under 'er place where she sleeps."

Bealby's head-shake became more emphatic.

"*Yus,* I tell you," said William.

"No," said Bealby.

"Choc'late I tell you," said William and ran the tongue of appetite round the rim of his toothless mouth.

"Don't want choc'late," said Bealby, thinking of a large lump of it.

"Go on," said William. "Nobody won't see you. . . .

"*Go* it!" said William. . . .

"You're afraid," said William. . . .

"Here, *I'll* go," said William, losing self-control. "You just 'old these reins."

Bealby took the reins. William got up and opened the door of the caravan. Then Bealby realised his moral responsibility—and, leaving the reins, clutched William firmly by his baggy nether garments. They were elderly garments, much sat upon. "Don't be a Vool," said William, struggling. "Leago my slack."

Something partially gave way and Williams' head came round to deal with Bealby.

"What you mean pullin' my cloes orf me?

"That,"—he investigated. "Take me a Nour to sew up."

"I ain't going to steal," shouted Bealby into the ear of William.

"Nobody arst you to steal——"

"Nor you neither," said Bealby.

The caravan bumped heavily against a low garden wall, skidded a little and came to rest. William sat down suddenly. The white horse after a period of confusion with its legs, tried the flavour of some over-hanging lilac branches and was content.

"Gimme those reins," said William. "You be the Brastedest Young Vool. . . .

"Sittin' 'ere," said William presently, "chewin' our teeth, when we might be eatin' choc'late. . . .

"I 'ent got no use for *you*," said William, "blowed if I 'ave. . . ."

Then the thought of his injuries returned to him.

"I'd make you sew 'em up yourself, darned if I woun't—on'y you'd go running the brasted needle into me. . . . Nour's work there is—by the feel of it. . . . Mor'n nour. . . . Gooddbe done, too. . . . All I got. . . ."

"I'll give you Sumpfin you little Beace 'fore I done wi' you."

"I wouldn't steal 'er choc'lates," said young Bealby. "Not if I was starving."

"Eh?" shouted William.

"*Steal!*" shouted Bealby.

"I'll steal ye, 'fore I done with ye," said William. "Tearin' my cloes for me. . . . Oh! Cam *up* y' old Runt. We don't want *you* to stop and lissen. Cam *up* I tell you!"

§ 9

They found the ladies rather, it seemed, by accident than design, waiting upon a sandy common rich with purple heather and bordered by woods of fir and spruce. They had been waiting some time and it was clear that the sight of the yellow caravan relieved an accumulated anxiety. Bealby rejoiced to see them. His soul glowed with the pride of chocolate resisted and William overcome. He resolved to distinguish himself over the preparation of the midday meal. It was a pleasant little island of green they chose for their midday pitch, a little patch of emerald turf amidst the purple, a patch already doomed to removal, as a bare oblong and a pile of rolledup turves witnessed. This pile and a little bank of heather and bramble promised shelter from the breeze, and down the hill a hundred yards away was a spring and a built-up pool. This spot lay perhaps fifty yards away from the high road and one reached it along a rutty track which had been made by the turf cutters. And overhead was the glorious sky of an English summer, with great clouds like sunlit, white-sailed ships, the Constable sky. The white horse was hobbled and turned out to pasture among the heather, and William was sent off to get congenial provender at the nearest publichouse. "William!" shouted Mrs. Bowles as he departed, shouting confidentially into his ear, "Get your clothes mended!"

"Eh?" said William.

"Mend your clothes."

"Yah! 'E did that," said William viciously with a movement of self-protection and so went.

Nobody watched him go. Almost sternly they set to work upon the luncheon preparation as William receded. "William," Mrs. Bowles remarked, as she bustled with the patent cooker, putting it up wrong way round so that afterwards it collapsed, "William—takes offence. Sometimes I think he takes offence almost too often. . . . Did you have any difficulty with him, Dick?"

"It wasn't anything, Miss," said Bealby meekly.

Bealby was wonderful with the fire-lighting, and except that he cracked a plate in warming it, quite admirable as a cook. He burned his fingers twice—and liked doing it; he ate his portion with instinctive modesty on the other side of the caravan, and he washed up as Mr. Mergleson had always instructed him to do. Mrs. Bowles showed him how to clean knives and forks by sticking them into the turf. A little to his surprise these ladies lit and smoked cigarettes. They sat about and talked perplexingly. Clever stuff. Then he had to get water from the neighbouring brook and boil the kettle for an early tea. Madeleine produced a charmingly bound little book and read in it, the other two professed themselves anxious for the view from a neighbouring hill. They produced their sensible spiked Swiss walking-sticks such as one does not see in England; they seemed full of energy. " You go," Madeleine had said, " while I and Dick stay here and make tea. I've walked enough to-day. . . ."

So Bealby, happy to the pitch of ecstasy, first explored the wonderful interior of the caravan—there was a dresser, a stove, let-down chairs and tables and all manner of things—and then nursed the kettle to the singing stage on the patent cooker while the beautiful lady reclined close at hand on a rug.

" Dick !" she said.

He had forgotten he was Dick.

" Dick !"

He remembered his personality with a start. " Yes, Miss !" He knelt up, with a handful of twigs in his hand and regarded her.

" Well, Dick," she said.

He remained flushed adoration. There was a little pause and the lady smiled at him an unaffected smile.

" What are you going to be, Dick, when you grow up ?"

" I don't know, Miss. I've wondered."

" What would you like to be ?"

" Something abroad. Something—so that you could see things."

"A soldier?"

"Or a sailor, Miss."

"A sailor sees nothing but the sea."

"I'd rather be a sailor than a common soldier, Miss."

"You'd like to be an officer?"

"Yes, Miss—only——"

"One of my very best friends is an officer," she said, a little irrelevantly it seemed to Bealby.

"I'd be a Norficer like a shot," said Bealby, "if I 'ad 'arf a chance, Miss."

"Officers nowadays," she said, "have to be very brave, able men."

"I know, Miss," said Bealby modestly.

The fire required attention for a little while. . . .

The lady turned over on her elbow. "What do you think you are *likely* to be, Dick?" she asked.

He didn't know.

"What sort of man is your stepfather?"

Bealby looked at her. "He isn't much," he said.

"What is he?"

Bealby hadn't the slightest intention of being the son of a gardener. "'E's a law-writer."

"What! in that village."

"'E 'as to stay there for 'is 'ealth, Miss," he said. "Every summer. 'Is 'ealth is very pre-precocious, Miss. . . ."

He fed his fire with a few judiciously administered twigs.

"What was your own father, Dick?"

With that she opened a secret door into Bealby's imagination. All stepchildren have those dreams. With him they were so frequent and vivid that they had long since become a kind of second truth. He coloured a little and answered with scarcely an interval for reflection. "'E passed as Mal-travers," he said.

"Wasn't that his name?"

"I don't rightly know, Miss. There was always something kep' from me. My mother used to say, 'Artie,' she used to say : ' there's things that some day you must know, things that concern you. Things about your farver. But poor as we are now and struggling. . . . Not yet. . . . Some day you shall know truly—*who you are.*' That was 'ow she said it, Miss."

"And she died before she told you?"

He had almost forgotten that he had killed his mother that very morning. "Yes, Miss," he said.

She smiled at him and something in her smile made him blush hotly. For a moment he could have believed she understood. And indeed she did understand, and it amused her to find this boy doing what she herself had done at times, what indeed she felt it was still in her to do. She felt that most delicate of sympathies, the sympathy of one rather over-imaginative person for another. But her next question dispelled his doubt of her though it left him red and hot. She asked it with a convincing simplicity.

"Have you any idea, Dick, have you any guess or suspicion, I mean, who it is you really are?"

"I wish I had, Miss," he said. "I suppose it doesn't matter, really—but one can't help wondering. . . ."

How often he had wondered in his lonely wanderings through that dear city of day-dreams where all the people one knows look out of windows as one passes and the roads are paved with pride ! How often had he decided and changed and decided again !

§ 10

Now suddenly a realisation of intrusion shattered this conversation. A third person stood over the little encampment, smiling mysteriously and waving a cleek in a slow hieratic manner through the air.

"De licious lill' corn'," said the newcomer in tones of benediction.

He met their inquiring eyes with a luxurious smile, "Licious," he said, and remained swaying insecurely

and failing to express some imperfectly apprehended
deep meaning by short peculiar movements of the
cleek.

He was obviously a golfer astray from some adjacent
course—and he had lunched.

" Mighty Join you," he said, and then very distinctly
in a full large voice, " Miss Malleleine Philps." These
are the penalties of a public and popular life.

" He's *drunk,*" the lady whispered. " Get him to go
away, Dick. I can't endure drunken men."

She stood up and Bealby stood up. He advanced in
front of her, slowly, with his nose in the air, extraordinarily like a small terrier smelling at a strange dog.

" I said Mighty Join-you," the golfer repeated. His
voice was richly excessive. He was a big heavy man
with a short-cropped moustache, a great deal of neck and
dewlap and a solemn expression.

" Prup. Be'r. Introzuze m'self," he remarked. He
tried to indicate himself by waving his hand towards
himself but finally abandoned the attempt as impossible.
" Ma' Goo' Soch'l Poshishun," he said.

Bealby had a disconcerting sense of retreating footsteps behind him. He glanced over his shoulder and
saw Miss Philips standing at the foot of the steps that
led up to the fastne ses of the caravan. " Dick," she
cried with a sharp note of alarm in her voice, " get rid
of that man."

A moment after Bealby heard the door shut and a
sound of a key in its lock. He concealed his true feelings by putting his arms akimbo, sticking his legs wider
apart and contemplating the task before him with his
head a little on one side. He was upheld by the
thought that the yellow caravan had a window looking
upon him. . . .

The newcomer seemed to consider the ceremony of
introduction completed. " I done care for goff," he
said, almost vaingloriously.

He waved his cleek to express his preference.

" Natua," he said with a satisfaction that bordered on fatuity.

He prepared to come down from the little turfy crest on which he stood to the encampment.

" 'Ere!" said Bealby. " This is Private."

The golfer indicated by solemn movements of the cleek that this was understood but that other considerations overrode it.

" You— You got to go!" cried Bealby in a breathless squeak. " You get out of here."

The golfer waved an arm as who should say, " You do not understand but I forgive you," and continued to advance towards the fire. And then Bealby, at the end of his tact, commenced hostilities.

He did so because he felt he had to do something and he did not know what else to do.

" Wan' nothin' but frenly conversation sushus custm'ry webred peel," the golfer was saying, and then a large fragment of turf hit him in the neck, burst all about him and stopped him abruptly.

He remained for some lengthy moments too astonished for words. He was not only greatly surprised but he chose to appear even more surprised than he was. In spite of the brown-black mould upon his cheek and brow and a slight displacement of his cap, he achieved a sort of dignity. He came slowly to a focus upon Bealby, who stood by the turf pile grasping a second missile. The cleek was extended sceptrewise.

" Replace the—Divot."

" You go orf," said Bealby. " I'll chuck it if you don't. I tell you fair."

" Replace the—Divot," roared the golfer again in a voice of extraordinary power.

" You—you go!" said Bealby.

" Am I t'ask you. Third time. Reshpect—Roos. . . . Replace the Divot."

It struck him fully in the face.

He seemed to emerge through the mould. He was

blinking but still dignified. " Tha'—was intentional," he said.

He seemed to gather himself together. . . .

Then suddenly and with a surprising nimbleness he discharged himself at Bealby. He came with astonishing swiftness. He got within a foot of him. Well it was for Bealby that he had learned to dodge in the village playground. He went down under the golfer's arm and away round the end of the stack, and the golfer with his force spent in concussion remained for a time clinging to the turf pile and apparently trying to remember how he got there. Then he was reminded of recent occurrences by a shrill small voice from the other side of the stack.

" You gow away!" said the voice. " Can't you see you're annoying a lady? You gow away."

" Nowish—'noy anyone. Pease wall wirl."

But this was subterfuge. He meant to catch that boy.

Suddenly and rather brilliantly he turned the flank of the turf pile, and only a couple of loose turfs at the foot of the heap upset his calculations. He found himself on all fours on ground from which it was difficult to rise. But he did not lose heart. " Boy—hic—scow," he said, and became for a second rush a nimble quadruped.

Again he got quite astonishingly near to Bealby, and then in an instant was on his feet and running across the encampment after him. He succeeded in kicking over the kettle and the patent cooker without any injury to himself or loss of pace, and succumbed only to the sharp turn behind the end of the caravan and the steps. He hadn't somehow thought of the steps. So he went down rather heavily. But now the spirit of a fine man was roused. Regardless of the scream from inside that had followed his collapse, he was up and in pursuit almost instantly. Bealby only escaped the swiftness of his rush by jumping the shafts and going away across the front of the caravan to the turf pile again. The golfer tried to jump the shafts too, but he was not equal to that. He did in a manner jump. But it was almost as much diving as jumping. And there was something in it almost like the curveting of a Great Horse. . . .

When Bealby turned at the crash, the golfer was already on all fours again and trying very busily to crawl out between the shaft and the front wheel. He would have been more successful in doing this if he had not begun by putting his arm through the wheel. As it was he was trying to do too much; he was trying to crawl out at two points at once and getting very rapidly annoyed at his inability to do so. The caravan was shifting slowly forward. . . .

It was manifest to Bealby that getting this man to go was likely to be a much more lengthy business than he had supposed.

He surveyed the situation for a moment and then, realising the entanglement of his opponent, he seized a camp-stool by one leg, went round by the steps and attacked the prostrate enemy from the rear with effectual but inconclusive fury.

He hammered. . . .

"Steady on, young man," said a voice and he was seized from behind. He turned—to discover himself in the grip of a second golfer. . . .

Another! Bealby fought in a fury of fear. . . .

He bit an arm—rather too tweedy to feel much—and got in a couple of shinners—alas! that they were only slippered shinners!—before he was overpowered. . . .

A cuffed, crumpled, disarmed and panting Bealby found himself watching the careful extraction of the first golfer from the front wheel. Two friends assisted that gentleman with a reproachful gentleness, and his repeated statements that he was all right seemed to re-assure him gently. Altogether there were now four golfers in the field, counting the pioneer.

"He was after this devil of a boy," said the one who held Bealby.

"Yes, but how did he get here?" asked a second friend.

"Feel better now?" said the third, helping the first comer to his uncertain feet. "Let me have your cleek o'man. . . . You won't want your cleek. . . ."

Across the heather, lifting their heads a little, came Mrs. Bowles and Mrs. Geedge returning from their walk. They were wondering whoever their visitors could be.

And then like music after a dispute came Madeleine Philips, a beautiful blue-robed thing, coming slowly with a kind of wonder on her face, out of the caravan and down the steps. Instinctively everybody turned to her. The drunkard with a gesture released himself from his supporter and stood erect. His cap was replaced upon him—obliquely. His cleek had been secured.

"I heard a noise," said Madeleine lifting her pretty chin and speaking in her sweetest tones.

She looked her inquiries. . . .

She surveyed the three sober men with a practised eye. She chose the tallest, a fair, serious-looking young man standing conveniently at the drunkard's elbow.

"Will you please take your friend away?" she said, indicating the offender with her beautiful white hand.

"Simly," he said in a slightly subdued voice. "Simly coring."

Everybody tried for a moment to understand him.

"Look here, old man, you've got no business here," said the fair young man. "You'd better come back to the club-house."

The drunken man stuck to his statement. "Simly coring," he said a little louder.

"I *think*," said a little bright-eyed man with a very cheerful yellow vest, "I *think* he's apologising. I *hope* so."

The drunken man nodded his head. That among other matters.

The tall young man took his arm but he insisted on

his point. "Simly coring," he said with emphasis. "If
—if—done*wan*' me to cor. Notome. Nottot. . . .
Mean' say. Nottot tat-toem. Nottotome. Orny way
—sayin' notome. No wish 'trude. No wish 'all."

"Well then, you see, you'd better come away."

"I *ars*' you—are you *tome?* Miss—Miss Pips." He
appealed to Miss Philips.

"If you'd answer him—" said the tall young man.

"No, sir," she said with great dignity and the pretty
chin higher than ever. "I am *not* at home."

"Nuthin' more t'say then," said the drunken man,
and with a sudden stoicism he turned away.

"Come," he said, submitting to support.

"Simly orny arfnoon cor," he said generally and permitted himself to be led off.

"Orny frenly cor. . . ."

For some time he was audible as he receded explaining in a rather condescending voice, the extreme social
correctness of his behaviour. Just for a moment or so
there was a slight tussle, due to his desire to return and
leave cards. . . .

He was afterwards seen to be distributing a small
handful of visiting cards amidst the heather with his
free arm, rather in the manner of a paper chase—but
much more gracefully. . . .

Then decently and in order he was taken out of
sight. . . .

§ 11

Bealby had been unostentatiously released by his
captor as soon as Miss Philips appeared, and the two
remaining golfers now addressed themselves to the three
ladies in regret and explanation.

The man who had held Bealby was an aquiline grey-
clad person with a cascade moustache and wrinkled eyes
and for some obscure reason he seemed to be amused;
the little man in the yellow vest however was quite

earnest and serious enough to make up for him. He was one of those little fresh-coloured men whose faces stick forward openly. He had open projecting eyes, an open mouth, his cheeks were frank to the pitch of ostentation, his cap was thrust back from his exceptionally open forehead. He had a chest and a stomach. These, too, he held out. He would have held out anything. His legs leaned forward from the feet. It was evidently impossible for a man of his nature to be anything but clean shaved. . . .

"Our fault entirely," he said. "Ought to have looked after him. Can't say how sorry and ashamed we are. Can't say how sorry we are he caused you any inconvenience."

"Of course," said Mrs. Bowles, "our boy-servant ought not to have pelted him."

"He didn't exactly *pelt* him, dear," said Madeleine. . . .

"Well, anyhow our friend ought not to have been off his chain. It was our affair to look after him and we didn't. . . ."

"You see," the open young man went on, with the air of lucid explanation, "he's our worst player. And he got round in a hundred and twenty-seven. And beat—somebody. And—it's upset him. It's not a bit of good disguising that we've been letting him drink. . . . We have. To begin with we encouraged him. . . . We oughtn't to have let him go. But we thought a walk alone might do him good. And some of us were a bit off him. Fed up rather. You see he'd been singing. Would go on singing. . . ."

He went on to propitiations. "Anything the club can do to show how we regret. . . . If you would like to pitch later on in our rough beyond the pine-woods. . . . You'd find it safe and secluded. . . . Custodian—most civil man. Get you water or anything you wanted. Especially after all that has happened. . . ."

Bealby took no further part in these concluding politenesses. He had a curious feeling in his mind that perhaps he had not managed this affair quite so well as he might have done. He ought to have been more tactful like, more persuasive. He was a fool to have started chucking. . . . Well, well. He picked up the overturned kettle and went off down the hill to get water. . . .

What had she thought of him? . . .

In the meantime one can at least boil kettles.

§ 12

One consequence of this little incident of the rejoicing golfer was that the three ladies were no longer content to dismiss William and Bealby at nightfall and sleep unprotected in the caravan. And this time their pitch was a lonely one with only the golf club-house within call. They were inclined even to distrust the golf club. So it was decided, to his great satisfaction, that Bealby should have a certain sleeping-sack Mrs. Bowles had brought with her and that he should sleep therein between the wheels.

This sleeping-sack was to have been a great feature of the expedition, but when it came to the test Judy could not use it. She had not anticipated that feeling of extreme publicity the open air gives one at first. It was like having all the world in one's bedroom. Every night she had relapsed into the caravan.

Bealby did not mind what they did with him so long as it meant sleeping. He had had a long day of it. He undressed sketchily and wriggled into the nice woolly bag and lay for a moment listening to the soft bumpings that were going on overhead. *She* was there. He had the instinctive confidence of our sex in women, and here were three of them. He had a vague idea of getting out of his bag again and kissing the under side of the van that held this dear beautiful creature. . . .

He didn't. . . .

Such a lot of things had happened that day—and the day before. He had been going without intermission, it seemed now for endless hours. He thought of trees, roads, dew-wet grass, frying-pans, pursuing packs of gigantic butlers hopelessly at fault—no doubt they were hunting now—chinks and crannies, tactless missiles flying, bursting missiles it was vain to recall. He stared for a few seconds through the wheel spokes at the dancing, crackling fire of pine-cones which it had been his last duty to replenish, stared and blinked much as a little dog might do, and then he had slipped away altogether into the world of dreams. . . .

§ 13

In the morning he was extraordinarily hard to wake. . . .

"Is it after sleeping all day ye'd be?" cried Judy Bowles, who was always at her most Irish about breakfast-time.

CHAPTER THE FOURTH

The Unobtrusive Parting

§ 1

MONDAY was a happy day for Bealby.

The caravan did seventeen miles and came to rest at last in a sloping field outside a cheerful little village set about a green on which was a long tent professing to be a theatre.

At the first stopping-place that possessed a general shop Mrs. Bowles bought Bealby a pair of boots. Then she had a bright idea. "Got any pocket money, Dick?" she asked.

She gave him half a crown, that is to say she gave him two shillings and sixpence, or five sixpences or thirty pennies—according as you choose to look at it—in one large undivided shining coin.

Even if he had not been in love here surely was incentive to a generous nature to help and do distinguished services. He dashed about doing things. The little accident on Sunday had warned him to be careful of the plates, and the only flaw upon a perfect day's

701

service was the dropping of an egg on its way to the frying-pan for supper. It remained where it fell and there presently he gave it a quiet burial. There was nothing else to be done with it. . . .

All day long at intervals Miss Philips smiled at him and made him do little services for her. And in the evening, after the custom of her great profession when it keeps holiday, she insisted on going to the play. She said it would be the loveliest fun. She went with Mrs. Bowles because Mrs. Geedge wanted to sit quietly in the caravan and write down a few little things while they were still fresh in her mind. And it wasn't in the part of Madeleine Philips not to insist that both William and Bealby must go too; she gave them each a shilling— though the prices were sixpence, threepence, twopence and a penny—and Bealby saw his first real play.

It was called " Brothers in Blood or the Gentleman Ranker." There was a poster—which was only very slightly justified by the performance—of a man in khaki with a bandaged head proposing to sell his life dearly over a fallen comrade.

One went to the play through an open and damaged field gate and across trampled turf. Outside the tent were two paraffin flares illuminating the poster and a small cluster of the impecunious young. Within on grass that was worn and bleached were benches, a gathering audience, a piano played by an offhand lady and a drop scene displaying the Grand Canal, Venice. The Grand Canal was invested by a crowded multitude of zealous and excessive reflections of the palaces above and by peculiar crescentic black boats floating entirely out of water and having no reflections at all. The off-hand lady gave a broad impression of the Wedding March in " Lohengrin " and the back seats assisted by a sort of gastric vocalisation called humming and by whistling between the teeth. Madeleine Philips evidently found it tremendous fun, even before the curtain rose.

And then—illusion. . . .

The scenery was ridiculous, it waved about, the actors and actresses were surely the most pitiful of their tribe and every invention in the play impossible, but the imagination of Bealby like the lovingkindness of God made no difficulties, it rose up and met and embraced and gave life to all these things. It was a confused story in the play, everybody was more or less somebody else all the way through, and it got more confused in Bealby's mind, but it was clear from the outset that there was vile work afoot, nets spread and sweet simple people wronged. And never were sweet and simple people quite so sweet and simple. There was the wrongful brother who was weak and wicked and the rightful brother who was vindictively, almost viciously good, and there was an ingrained villain who was a baronet, a man who wore a frock-coat and a silk hat and carried gloves and a stick in every scene and upon all occasions—that sort of man. He looked askance, always. There was a dear simple girl, with a vast sweet smile, who was loved according to their natures by the wrongful and the rightful brother, and a large wicked red-clad, lip-biting woman whose passions made the crazy little stage quiver. There was a comic butler—very different stuff from old Mergleson—who wore an evening coat and plaid trousers and nearly choked Bealby. Why weren't all butlers like that? Funny. And there were constant denunciations. Always there were denunciations going on or denunciations impending. That took Bealby particularly. Never surely in all the world were bad people so steadily and thoroughly scolded and told what. Everybody hissed them; Bealby hissed them. And when they were told what, he applauded. And yet they kept on with their wickedness to the very curtain. They retired—askance to the end. Foiled but pursuing. "A time will come," they said.

There was a moment in the distresses of the heroine when Bealby dashed aside a tear. And then at last

23

most wonderfully it all came right. The company lined up and hoped that Bealby was satisfied. Bealby wished he had more hands. His heart seemed to fill his body. Oh *prime! prime!* . . .

And out he came into the sympathetic night. But he was no longer a trivial Bealby, his soul was purged, he was a strong and silent man, ready to explode into generous repartee or nerve himself for high endeavour. He slipped off in the opposite direction from the caravan because he wanted to be alone for a time and *feel*. He was in a sphere of glorious illusion. . . .

He was quite sure that he had been wronged. Not to be wronged is to forgo the first privilege of goodness. He had been deeply wronged by a plot—all those butlers were in the plot or why should they have chased him— he was much older than he really was, if it had been kept from him, and in truth he was a rightful earl. " Earl Shonts," he whispered! and indeed, why not? And Madeleine too had been wronged; she had been reduced to wander in this uncomfortable caravan; this Gypsy Queen; she had been brought to it by villains, the same villains who had wronged Bealby. . . .

Out he went into the night, the kindly consenting summer night, where there is nothing to be seen or heard that will contradict these delicious wonderful persuasions.

He was so full of dreams that he strayed far away along the dark country lanes and had at last the utmost difficulty in finding his way back to the caravan. And when ultimately he got back after hours and hours of heroic existence it did not even seem that they had missed him. It did not seem that he had been away half an hour.

§ 2

Tuesday was not so happy a day for Bealby as Monday. Its shadows began when Mrs. Bowles asked him in a friendly tone when it was clean-collar day.

He was unready with his answer.

"And don't you ever use a hair-brush, Dick?" she asked. "I'm sure now there's one in your parcel."

"I do use it *sometimes,* Mum," he admitted.

"And I've never detected you with a tooth-brush yet. Though that perhaps is extreme. And Dick—soap? I think you'd better be letting me give you a cake of soap."

"I'd be very much obliged, Mum."

"I hardly dare hint, Dick, at a clean handkerchief. Such things are known."

"If you wouldn't mind—when I've got the breakfast things done, Mum. . . ."

The thing worried him all through breakfast. He had not expected personalities from Mrs. Bowles. More particularly personalities of this kind. He felt he had to think hard.

He affected modesty after he had cleared away breakfast, and carried off his little bundle to a point in the stream which was masked from the encampment by willows. With him he also brought that cake of soap. He began by washing his handkerchief, which was bad policy because that left him no dry towel but his jacket. He ought, he perceived, to have secured a dish-cloth or a newspaper. (This he must remember on the next occasion.) He did over his hands and the more exposed parts of his face with soap and jacket. Then he took off and examined his collar. It certainly was pretty bad. . . .

"Why!" cried Mrs. Bowles when he returned, "that's still the same collar."

"They all seem to've got crumpled, 'm," said Bealby.

"But are they all as dirty?"

"I'd some blacking in my parcel," said Bealby, "and it got loose, Mum. I'll have to get another collar when we come to a shop."

It was a financial sacrifice, but it was the only way, and when they came to the shop Bealby secured a very nice collar indeed, high with pointed turn-down corners, so that it cut his neck all round, jabbed him under the chin and gave him a proud upcast carriage of the head that led to his treading upon and very completely destroying a stray plate while preparing lunch. But it was more of a man's collar, he felt, than anything he had ever worn before. And it cost sixpence halfpenny, six dee and a half.

(I should have mentioned that while washing up the breakfast things he had already broken the handle off one of the breakfast-cups. Both these accidents deepened the cloud upon his day.)

And then there was the trouble of William. William having meditated upon the differences between them for a day had now invented an activity. As Bealby sat beside him behind the white horse he was suddenly and frightfully pinched. *Gee!* One wanted to yelp.

"Choc'late," said William through his teeth and very savagely. "*Now* then."

After William had done that twice Bealby preferred to walk beside the caravan. Thereupon William whipped up the white horse and broke records and made all the crockery sing together and forced the pace until he was spoken to by Mrs. Bowles. . . .

It was upon a Bealby thus depressed and worried that the rumour of impending "men-folk" came. It began after the party had stopped for letters at a village post-office; there were not only letters but a telegram, that Mrs. Bowles read with her spats far apart and her head on one side. "Ye'd like to know about it," she said waggishly to Miss Philips, "and you just shan't."

She then went into her letters.

"You've got some news," said Mrs. Geedge.

"I have that," said Mrs. Bowles, and not a word more could they get from her.

"I'll keep my news no longer," said Mrs. Bowles, lighting her cigarette after lunch as Bealby hovered about clearing away the banana-skins and suchlike vestiges of dessert. "To-morrow night as ever is, if so be we get to Winthorpe-Sutbury, there'll be Men among us."

"But Tom's not coming?" said Mrs. Geedge.

"He asked Tim to tell me to tell you."

"And you've kept it these two hours, Judy."

"For your own good and peace of mind. But now the murther's out. Come they will, your Man and my Man, pretending to a pity because they can't do without us. But like the self-indulgent monsters they are, they must needs stop at some grand hotel, Redlake he calls it, the Royal, on the hill above Winthorpe-Sutbury. The Royal! The very name describes it. Can't you see the lounge, girls, with its white cane chairs? And saddlebacks! No other hotel it seems is good enough for them, and we if you please are asked to go in and have—what does the man call it—the 'comforts of decency'—and let the caravan rest for a bit."

"Tom promised me I should run wild as long as I chose," said Mrs. Geedge, looking anything but wild.

"They're after thinking we've had enough of it," said Mrs. Bowles.

"It sounds like that."

"Sure I'd go on like this for ever," said Judy. "'Tis the Man and the House and all of it that oppresses me. Vans for Women. . . ."

"Let's not go to Winthorpe-Sutbury," said Madeleine.

(The first word of sense Bealby had heard.)

"Ah!" said Mrs. Bowles archly, "who knows but what there'll be a Man for you? Some sort of Man anyhow."

(Bealby thought that a most improper remark.)

"I want no man."

"Ah!"

"Why do you say *Ah* like that?"

"Because I mean *Ah* like that."

"Meaning?"

"Just that."

Miss Philips eyed Mrs. Bowles and Mrs. Bowles eyed Miss Philips.

"Judy," she said, "you've got something up your sleeve."

"Where it's perfectly comfortable," said Mrs. Bowles.

And then quite maddeningly, she remarked, "Will you be after washing up presently, Dick?" and looked at him with a roguish quiet over her cigarette. It was necessary to disabuse her mind at once of the idea that he had been listening. He took up the last few plates and went off to the washing-place by the stream. All the rest of that conversation *had* to be lost.

Except that as he came back for the Hudson's soap he heard Miss Philips say, "Keep your old Men. I'll just console myself with Dick, my dears. Making such a Mystery!"

To which Mrs. Bowles replied darkly, "She *little* knows. . . ."

A kind of consolation was to be got from that. . . . But what was it she little knew? . . .

§ 3

The men-folk when they came were nothing so terrific to the sight as Bealby had expected. And thank Heaven there were only two of them and each assigned. Something he perceived was said about some one else, he couldn't quite catch what, but if there was to have been some one else, at any rate there now wasn't. Professor Bowles was animated and Mr. Geedge was gracefully cold, they kissed their wives but not offensively, and there was a chattering pause while Bealby walked on beside the caravan. They were on the bare road that runs along the high ridge above Winthorpe-Sutbury, and the men had walked to meet them from some hotel or other—Bealby wasn't clear about that—by the golf-links. Judy was the life and soul of the encounter, and all for asking the men what they meant by intruding upon three independent women who, sure-alive, could very well do without them. Professor Bowles took her pretty calmly, and seemed on the whole to admire her.

Professor Bowles was a compact little man wearing spectacles with alternative glasses, partly curved, partly flat, he was hairy and dressed in that sort of soft tweedy stuff that ravels out—he seemed to have been sitting among thorns—and baggy knickerbockers with straps and very thick stockings and very sensible, open-air, in fact quite mountainous, boots. And yet though he was short and stout and active he had a kind of authority about him, and it was clear that for all her persuasiveness his wife merely ran over him like a creeper without making any great difference to him. "I've found," he said, "the perfect place for your encampment." She had been making suggestions. And presently he left the ladies and came hurrying after the caravan to take control.

He was evidently a very controlling person.

"Here, you get down," he said to William. "That poor beast's got enough to pull without *you*."

And when William mumbled he said, "Hey?" in such a shout that William for ever after held his peace.

"Where d'you come from, you boy, you?" he asked suddenly, and Bealby looked to Mrs. Bowles to explain.

"Great silly collar you've got," said the Professor, interrupting her reply. "Boy like this ought to wear a wool shirt. Dirty too. Take it off, boy. It's choking you. Don't you *feel* it?"

Then he went on to make trouble about the tackle William had rigged to contain the white horse.

"This harness makes me sick," said Professor Bowles. "It's worse than Italy. . . ."

"Ah!" he cried and suddenly darted off across the
turf, going inelegantly and very rapidly, with peculiar
motions of the head and neck as he brought first the flat
and then the curved surface of his glasses into play.
Finally he dived into the turf, remained scrabbling on
all fours for a moment or so, became almost still for the
fraction of a minute and then got up and returned to his
wife, holding in an exquisite manner something that
struggled between his finger and his thumb.

"That's the third to-day," he said triumphantly.
"They swarm here. It's a migration."

Then he resumed his penetrating criticism of the
caravan outfit.

"That boy," he said suddenly with his glasses oblique,
"hasn't taken off his collar yet."

Bealby revealed the modest secrets of his neck and
pocketed the collar.

Mr. Geedge did not appear to observe Bealby. He
was a man of the super-aquiline type with a nose like a
rudder, he held his face as if it was a hatchet in a procession, and walked with the dignity of a man of
honour. You could see at once he was a man of
honour. Inflexibly, invincibly he was a man of honour.
You felt that anywhen, in a fire, in an earthquake, in a
railway accident when other people would be running
about and doing things he would have remained—a man
of honour. It was his pride rather than his vanity to be
mistaken for Sir Edward Grey. He now walked along
with Miss Philips and his wife behind the disputing
Bowleses, and discoursed in deep sonorous tones about
the healthiness of healthy places and the stifling feeling
one had in towns when there was no air.

§ 4

The Professor was remarkably active when at last the
point he had chosen for the encampment was reached.
Bealby was told to "look alive" twice, and William was

assigned to his genius and species: "The man's an absolute idiot," was the way the Professor put it. William
just shot a glance at him over his nose.

The place certainly commanded a wonderful view.
It was a turfy bank protected from the north and south
by bushes of yew and the beech-bordered edge of a chalk-
pit; it was close beside the road, a road which went
steeply down the hill into Winthorpe-Sutbury, with that
intrepid decision peculiar to the hill roads of the south
of England. It looked indeed as though you could throw
the rinse of your teacups into the Winthorpe-Sutbury
street; as if you could jump and impale yourself upon
the church spire. The hills bellied out east and west and
carried hangers, and then swept round to the west in a
long level succession of projections, a perspective that
merged at last with the general horizon of hilly blue-
nesses, amidst which Professor Bowles insisted upon a
"sapphire glimpse" of sea. "The Channel," said Professor Bowles, as though that made it easier for them.
Only Mr. Geedge refused to see even that mitigated
version of the sea. There was something perhaps bluish
and level, but he was evidently not going to admit it
was sea until he had paddled in it and tested it in every
way known to him. . . .

"Good *Lord!*" cried the Professor. "What's the
man doing now?"

William stopped the struggles and confidential dis-
couragements he was bestowing upon the white horse
and waited for a more definite reproach.

"Putting the caravan alongside to the sun! Do you
think it will ever get cool again? And think of the
blaze of the sunset—through the glass of that door!"

William spluttered. "If I put'n t'other way—goo
runnin' down t'hill like," said William.

"Imbecile!" cried the Professor. "Put something
under the wheels. *Here!*" He careered about and
produced great grey fragments of a perished yew-tree.
"Now, then," he said. "Head up-hill."

23*

William did his best.

" Oh! *not* like that! Here, *you!*"

Bealby assisted with obsequious enthusiasm.

It was some time before the caravan was adjusted to the complete satisfaction of the Professor. But at last it was done, and the end door gaped at the whole prospect of the Weald with the steps hanging out idiotically like a tongue. The hind wheels were stayed up very cleverly by lumps of chalk and chunks of yew, living and dead, and certainly the effect of it was altogether taller and better. And then the preparations for the midday cooking began. The Professor was full of acute ideas about camping and cooking, and gave Bealby a lively but instructive time. There was no stream handy, but William was sent off to the hotel to fetch a garden water-cart that the Professor with infinite foresight had arranged should be ready.

The Geedges held aloof from these preparations— they were unassuming people; Miss Philips concentrated her attention upon the Weald—it seemed to Bealby a little discontentedly, as if it was unworthy of her—and Mrs. Bowles hovered, smoking cigarettes, over her husband's activities, acting great amusement.

" You see it pleases me to get Himself busy," she said. " You'll end a Camper yet, Darlint, and us in the hotel."

The Professor answered nothing, but seemed to plunge deeper into practicality.

Under the urgency of Professor Bowles Bealby stumbled and broke a glass jar of marmalade over some fried potatoes, but otherwise did well as a cook's assistant. Once things were a little interrupted by the Professor going off to catch a cricket, but whether it was the right sort of cricket or not he failed to get it. And then with three loud reports—for a moment Bealby thought the mad butlers from Shonts were upon him with firearms—Captain Douglas arrived and got off his motorbicycle and left it by the roadside. His machine accounted for his delay, for those were the early days of motor-bicycles. It also accounted for a black smudge under one of his bright little eyes. He was fair and flushed, dressed in oilskins and a helmet-shaped cap and great gauntlets that made him, in spite of the smudge, look strange and brave and handsome like a Crusader—only that he was clad in oilskin and not steel, and his moustache was smaller than those of Crusaders were—and when he came across the turf to the encampment Mrs. Bowles and Mrs. Geedge both set up a cry of "A-*Ah!*" and Miss Philips turned an accusing face upon those two ladies. Bealby knelt with a bunch of knives and forks in his hand laying the cloth for lunch, and when he saw Captain Douglas approaching Miss Philips, he perceived clearly that that lady had already forgotten her lowly adorer, and his little heart was smitten with desolation. This man was arrayed like a chivalrous god, and how was a poor Bealby, whose very collar, his one little circlet of manhood, had been reft from him, how was he to compete with this tremendousness? In that hour the ambition for mechanism, the passion for leather and oilskin was sown in Bealby's heart.

"I told you not to come near me for a month," said Madeleine, but her face was radiant.

"These motor-bicycles—very difficult to control," said Captain Douglas, and all the little golden-white hairs upon his sunlit cheek glittered in the sun.

"And besides," said Mrs. Bowles, "it's all nonsense."

The Professor was in a state of arrested administration; the three others were frankly audience to a clearly understood scene.

"You ought to be in France."

"I'm not in France."

"I sent you into exile for a month," and she held out a hand for the Captain to kiss.

He kissed it.

Someday, somewhere, it was written in the book of destiny Bealby should also kiss hands. It was a lovely thing to do.

"Month! It's been years!" said the Captain. "Years and years."

"Then you ought to have come back before," she replied, and the Captain had no answer ready. . . .

§ 5

When William arrived with the water-cart, he brought also further proofs of the Professor's organising ability. He brought various bottles of wine, red Burgundy and sparkling hock, two bottles of cider, and peculiar and meritorious waters; he brought tinned things for *hors d'œuvre;* he brought some luscious pears.

When he had a moment with Bealby behind the caravan he repeated thrice in tones of hopeless sorrow, "They'll eat um all. I *knows* they'll eat um all." And then plumbing a deeper tone of woe, "Ef they *don't* they'll count um. Ode Goggles'll bag um. . . . 'E's a *bagger,* 'e is."

It was the brightest of luncheons that was eaten that day in the sunshine and spaciousness above Winthorpe-Sutbury. Every one was gay, and even the love-lorn Bealby, who might well have sunk into depression and lethargy, was galvanised into an activity that was almost cheerful by flashes from the Professor's glasses.

They talked of this and that; Bealby hadn't much time to attend, though the laughter that followed various sallies from Judy Bowles was very tantalising, and it had come to the pears before his attention wasn't so much caught as felled by the word "Shonts." . . .

It was as if the sky had suddenly changed to vermilion. *All these people were talking of Shonts!* . . .

"Went there," said Captain Douglas, "in perfect good faith. Wanted to fill up Lucy's little party. One doesn't go to Shonts nowadays for idle pleasure. And then—I get ordered out of the house, absolutely Told to Go."

(This man had been at Shonts!)

"That was on Sunday morning?" said Mrs. Geedge.

"On Sunday morning," said Mrs. Bowles suddenly, "we were almost within sight of Shonts."

(This man had been at Shonts even at the time when Bealby was there!)

"Early on Sunday morning. Told to go. I was fairly flabbergasted. What the deuce is a man to do? Where's he to go? Sunday? One doesn't go to places, Sunday morning. There I'd been sleeping like a lamb all night and suddenly in came Laxton and said, 'Look here, you know,' he said, 'you've got to oblige me and pack your bag and go. Now.' 'Why?' said I. 'Because you've driven the Lord Chancellor stark staring mad!'"

"But how?" asked the Professor almost angrily, "how? I don't see it. Why should he ask you to go?"

"*I* don't know!" cried Captain Douglas.

"Yes, but—!" said the Professor, protesting against the unreasonableness of mankind.

"I'd had a word or two with him in the train. Nothing to speak of. About occupying two corner seats—always strikes me as a cad's trick—but on my honour I didn't rub it in. And then he got it into his head we were laughing at him at dinner—we were a bit, but only the sort of thing one says about any one—way he works his eyebrows and all that—and then he thought I was ragging him. . . . I *don't* rag people. Got it so strongly he made a row that night. Said I'd made a ghost slap him on his back. Hang it!—what *can* you say to a thing like that? In my room all the time."

"You suffer for the sins of your brother," said Mrs. Bowles.

"Heavens!" cried the Captain, "I never thought of that! Perhaps he mistook me. . . ."

He reflected for a moment and continued his narrative. "Then in the night, you know, he heard noises."

"They always do," said the Professor nodding confirmation.

"Couldn't sleep."

"A sure sign," said the Professor.

"And finally he sallied out in the early morning, caught the butler in one of the secret passages——"

"How did the butler get into the secret passage?"

"Going round, I suppose. Part of his duties. . . . Anyhow he gave the poor beggar an awful doing—awful—*brutal*—black eye—all that sort of thing; man much too respectful to hit back. Finally declared I'd been getting up a kind of rag—squaring the servants to help and so forth. . . . Laxton, I fancy, half believed it. . . . Awkward thing, you know, having it said about that you ragged the Lord Chancellor. Makes a man seem a sort of mischievous idiot. Injures a man. Then going away, you see, seems a kind of admission. . . ."

"Why did you go?"

"Lucy," said the Captain compactly. "Hysterics."

"Shonts would have burst," he added, "if I hadn't gone."

Madeleine was helpful. "But you'll have to do *something* further," she said.

"What is one to *do?*" squealed the Captain.

"The sooner you get the Lord Chancellor certified a lunatic," said the Professor soundly, "the better for your professional prospects."

"He went on pretty bad after I'd gone."

"You've heard?"

"Two letters. I picked 'em up at Wheatley Post Office this morning. You know he hadn't done with that butler. Actually got out of his place and scruffed the poor devil at lunch. Shook him like a rat, she says. Said the man wasn't giving him anything to drink—nice story, eh? Anyhow he scruffed him until things got broken. . . .

"I had it all from Minnie Timbre—you know, used to be Minnie Flax." He shot a propitiatory glance at

Madeleine. "Used to be neighbours of ours you know, in the old time. Half the people, she says, didn't know what was happening. Thought the butler was apoplectic and that old Moggeridge was helping him stand up. Taking off his collar. It was Laxton thought of saying it was a fit. Told everybody, she says. Had to tell 'em Something, I suppose. But she saw better, and she thinks a good many others did. Laxton ran 'em both out of the room. Nice scene for Shonts, eh? Thundering awkward for poor Lucy. Not the sort of thing the county expected. Has her both ways. Can't go to a house where the Lord Chancellor goes mad. One alternative. Can't go to a house where the butler has fits. That's the other. See the dilemma? . . .

"I've got a letter from Lucy too. It's here"—he struggled—"See? Eight sheets—pencil. No Joke for a man to read that. And she writes worse than any decent, self-respecting, illiterate woman, has a right to do. Quivers. Like writing in a train. Can't read half of it. But *she's* got something about a boy on her mind. Mad about a boy. Have I taken away a boy? They've lost a boy. Took him in my luggage, I suppose. She'd better write to the Lord Chancellor. Likely as not he met him in some odd corner and flew at him. Smashed him to atoms. Dispersed him. Anyhow they've lost a boy."

He protested to the world. "*I* can't go hunting lost boys for Lucy. I've done enough coming away as I did. . . ."

Mrs. Bowles held out an arresting cigarette.

"What sort of boy was lost?" she asked.

"*I* don't know. Some little beast of a boy. I dare say she'd only imagined it. Whole thing been too much for her."

"Read that over again," said Mrs. Bowles, "about losing a boy. We've found one."

"That *little* chap?"

"We found that boy"—she glanced over her

shoulder, but Bealby was nowhere to be seen — "on Sunday morning near Shonts. He strayed into us like a lost kitten."

"But I thought you said you knew his father, Judy," objected the Professor.

"Didn't verify," said Mrs. Bowles shortly, and then to Captain Douglas, "Read over again what Lady Laxton says about him. . . ."

§ 6

Captain Douglas struggled with the difficulties of his cousin's handwriting.

Everybody drew together over the fragments of the dessert with an eager curiosity, and helped to weigh Lady Laxton's rather dishevelled phrases. . . .

§ 7

"We'll call the principal witness," said Mrs. Bowles at last, warming to the business. "Dick!"

"Di-ick!"

"*Dick!*"

The Professor got up and strolled round behind the caravan. Then he returned. "No boy there."

"He *heard!*" said Mrs. Bowles in a large whisper and making round wonder-eyes.

"She *says*," said Douglas, "that the chances are he's got into the secret passages. . . ."

The Professor strolled out to the road and looked up it and then down upon the roofs of Winthorpe-Sutbury. "No," he said. "He's mizzled."

"He's only gone away for a bit," said Mrs. Geedge. "He does sometimes after lunch. He'll come back to wash up."

"He's probably taking a snooze among the yew bushes before facing the labours of washing up," said Mrs.

Bowles. "He *can't* have mizzled. You see—in there—He can't by any chance have taken his luggage!"

She got up and clambered—with a little difficulty because of its piled-up position, into the caravan. "It's all right," she called out of the door. "His little parsivel is still here."

Her head disappeared again.

"I don't think he'd go away like this," said Madeleine. "After all, what is there for him to go to—even if he is Lady Laxton's missing boy? . . ."

"I don't believe he heard a word of it," said Mrs. Geedge. . . .

Mrs. Bowles reappeared, with a curious-looking brown-paper parcel in her hand. She descended carefully. She sat down by the fire and held the parcel on her knees. She regarded it and her companions waggishly and lit a fresh cigarette. "Our link with Dick," she said, with the cigarette in her mouth.

She felt the parcel, she poised the parcel, she looked at it more and more waggishly. "I *wonder*," she said.

Her expression became so waggish that her husband knew she was committed to behaviour of the utmost ungentlemanliness. He had long ceased to attempt restraint in these moods. She put her head on one side and tore open the corner of the parcel just a little way.

"A tin can," she said in a stage whisper.

She enlarged the opening. "Blades of grass," she said.

The Professor tried to regard it humorously. "Even if you have ceased to be decent you can still be frank. . . . I think now, my dear, you might just straightforwardly undo the parcel."

She did. Twelve unsympathetic eyes surveyed the evidences of Bealby's utter poverty.

"He's coming," cried Madeleine suddenly.

Judy re-packed hastily, but it was a false alarm.

"I said he'd mizzled," said the Professor.

"And without washing up!" wailed Madeleine. "I couldn't have thought it of him. . . ."

§ 8

But Bealby had not "mizzled," although he was conspicuously not in evidence about the camp. There was neither sight nor sound of him for all the time they sat about the vestiges of their meal. They talked of him and of topics arising out of him, and whether the Captain should telegraph to Lady Laxton, "Boy practically found."

"I'd rather just find him," said the Captain, "and anyhow until we get hold of him we don't know it's her particular boy."

Then they talked of washing up and how detestable it was. And suddenly the two husbands, seeing their advantage, renewed their proposals that the caravanners should put up at the golf-links hotel, and have baths and the comforts of civilisation for a night or so—and anyhow walk thither for tea. And as William had now returned—he was sitting on the turf afar off smoking a nasty-looking short clay pipe—they rose up and departed. But Captain Douglas and Miss Philips for some reason did not go off exactly with the others but strayed apart, straying away more and more into a kind of solitude. . . .

First the four married people and then the two lovers disappeared over the crest of the downs. . . .

§ 9

For a time except for its distant sentinel the caravan seemed absolutely deserted, and then a clump of bramble against the wall of the old chalk-pit became agitated and a small, rueful, disillusioned, white-smeared little Bealby crept back into the visible universe again. His heart was very heavy.

The time had come to go.

And he did not want to go. He had loved the caravan. He had adored Madeleine.

He would go, but he would go beautifully—touchingly.

He would wash up before he went, he would make everything tidy, he would leave behind him a sense of irreparable loss. . . .

With a mournful precision he set about this undertaking. If Mergleson could have seen him Mergleson would have been amazed. . . .

He made everything look wonderfully tidy.

Then in the place where she had sat, lying on her rug, he found her favourite book, a small volume of Swinburne's poems very beautifully bound. Captain Douglas had given it to her.

Bealby handled it with a kind of reverence. So luxurious it was, so unlike the books in Bealby's world, so altogether of her quality. . . .

Strange forces prompted him. For a time he hesitated. Then decision came with a rush. He selected a page, drew the stump of a pencil from his pocket, wetted it very wet and, breathing hard, began to write that traditional message, "Farewell. Remember Art Bealby."

To this he made an original addition: "I washt up before I went."

Then he remembered that so far as this caravan went he was not Art Bealby at all. He renewed the wetness of his pencil and drew black lines athwart the name of Art Bealby until it was quite unreadable; then across this again and pressing still deeper so that the subsequent pages re-echoed it he wrote these singular words, "Ed rightful Earl Shonts." Then he was ashamed, and largely obliterated this by still more forcible strokes. Finally above it all plainly and nakedly he wrote "Dick Maltravers. . . ."

He put down the book with a sigh and stood up.

Everything was beautifully in order. But could he

not do something yet? There came to him the idea
of wreathing the entire camping-place with boughs of
yew. It would look lovely—and significant. He set
to work. At first he toiled zealously, but yew is tough
to get and soon his hands were painful. He cast about
for some easier way, and saw beneath the hind wheels
of the caravan great green boughs—one particularly a
splendid long branch. . . . It seemed to him that it
would be possible to withdraw this branch from the
great heap of sticks and stones that stayed up the hind
wheels of the caravan. It seemed to him that that was
so. He was mistaken, but that was the idea.

He set to work to do it. It was rather more difficult
to manage than he had supposed; there were unexpected
ramifications, wider resistances. Indeed the thing seemed
rooted.

Bealby was a resolute youngster at bottom.

He warmed to his task. . . . He tugged harder and
harder. . . .

§ 10

How various is the quality of humanity!

About Bealby there was ever an imaginative touch;
he was capable of romance, of gallantries, of devotion.
William was of a grosser clay, slave of his appetites, a
materialist. Such men as William drive one to believe
in born inferiors, in the existence of a lower sort, in the
natural inequality of men.

While Bealby was busy at his gentle task of repara-
tion, a task foolish perhaps and not too ably conceived,
but at any rate morally gracious, William had no thought
in the world but the satisfaction of those appetites that
the consensus of all mankind has definitely relegated to
the lower category. And which Heaven has relegated to
the lower region of our frame. He came now slinking
towards the vestiges of the caravanners' picnic, and no
one skilled in the interpretation of the human physi-

ognomy could have failed to read the significance of the tongue tip that drifted over his thin oblique lips. He came so softly towards the encampment that Bealby did not note him. Partly William thought of remnants of food but chiefly he was intent to drain the bottles. Bealby had stuck them all neatly in a row a little way up the hill. There was a cider-bottle with some heel-taps of cider, William drank that; then there was nearly half a bottle of hock and William drank that, then there were the drainings of the Burgundy and Apollinaris. It was all drink to William.

And after he had drained each bottle William winked at the watching angels and licked his lips, and patted the lower centres of his being with a shameless base approval. Then fired by alcohol, robbed of his last vestiges of self-control, his thoughts turned to the delicious chocolates that were stored in a daintily be-ribboned box in the little drawers beneath the sleeping-bunk of Miss Philips. There was a new brightness in his eye, a spot of pink in either cheek. With an expression of the lowest cunning he reconnoitred Bealby.

Bealby was busy about something at the back end of the caravan, tugging at something.

With swift stealthy movements of an entirely graceless sort, William got up into the front of the caravan.

Just for a moment he hesitated before going in. He craned his neck to look round the side at the unconscious Bealby, wrinkled the vast nose into an unpleasant grimace and then—a crouching figure of appetite—he crept inside.

Here they were! He laid his hand in the drawer, halted listening. . . .

What was that? . . .

Suddenly the caravan swayed. He stumbled, and fear crept into his craven soul. The caravan lurched. It was moving. . . . Its hind wheels came to the ground with a crash. . . .

He took a step doorward and was pitched sideways

and thrown upon his knees. . . . Then he was hurled against the dresser and hit by a falling plate. A cup fell and smashed and the caravan seemed to leap and bound. . . .

Through the little window he had a glimpse of yew bushes hurrying upward. The caravan was going downhill. . . .

"Lummy!" said William, clutching at the bunks to hold himself upright. . . .

"Ca'arnt be that drink!" said William, aspread and aghast. . . .

He attempted the door.

"Crikey! Here! Hold on! My shin! . . . 'Tis thut Brasted Vool of a Boy!"

". . ." said William. ". . . ——— . . ."

"████████ ███████ ███████ "

"████████ "

"██████████████ "

"████████ ████████ "

§ 11

The caravan party soon came to its decision. They would stay the night in the hotel. And so as soon as they had had some tea they decided to go back and make William bring the caravan and all the ladies' things round to the hotel. With characteristic eagerness Professor Bowles led the way.

And so it was Professor Bowles who first saw the release of the caravan. He barked. One short sharp bark. "Whup!" he cried, and very quickly, "Whatstheboydoing?"

Then quite a different style of noise, with the mouth open : "Wha—hoop!"

Then he set off running very fast down towards the caravan, waving his arms and shouting as he ran, "Yaaps! You *Idiot*. Yaaps!"

The others were less promptly active.

Down the slope they saw Bealby, a little struggling active Bealby, tugging away at a yew branch until the caravan swayed with his efforts, and then—then there was a movement as though the thing tossed its head and reared, and a smash as the heap of stuff that stayed up its hind wheels collapsed. . . .

It plunged like a horse with a dog at its heels, it lurched sideways, and then with an air of quiet deliberation started down the grass slope to the road and Winthorpe-Sutbury. . . .

Professor Bowles sped in pursuit like the wind, and Mrs. Bowles after a gasping moment set off after her lord, her face round and resolute. Mr. Geedge followed at a more dignified pace, making the only really sound suggestion that was offered on the occasion. "Hue! Stop it!" cried Mr. Geedge, for all the world like his great prototype at the Balkan Conference. And then like a large languid pair of scissors he began to run. Mrs. Geedge after some indefinite moments decided to see the humour of it all, and followed her husband in a fluttering rush, emitting careful little musical giggles as she ran, giggles that she had learned long ago from a beloved schoolfellow. Captain Douglas and Miss Philips were some way behind the others, and the situation had already developed considerably before they grasped what was happening. Then obeying the instincts of a soldier the Captain came charging to support the others, and Miss Madeleine Philips after some wasted gestures realised that nobody was looking at her, and sat down quietly on the turf until this paralysing state of affairs should cease.

The caravan remained the centre of interest.

Without either indecent haste or any complete pause it pursued its way down the road towards the tranquil village below. Except for the rumbling of its wheels and an occasional concussion it made very little sound; once or twice there was a faint sound of breaking crockery from its interior and once the phantom of an angry yell, but that was all.

There was an effect of discovered personality about the thing. This vehicle which had hitherto been content to play a background part, a yellow patch amidst the scenery, was now revealing an individuality. It was purposeful and touched with a suggestion of playfulness, at once kindly and human; it had its thoughtful instants, its phases of quick decision, yet never once did it altogether lose a certain mellow dignity. There was nothing servile about it; never for a moment for example did it betray its blind obedience to gravitation. It was rather as if it and gravitation were going hand in hand. It came out into the road, butted into the bank, swept round, meditated for a full second, and then headed down-hill, shafts foremost, going quietly faster and faster and swaying from bank to bank. The shafts went before it like arms held out. . . .

It had a quality—as if it were a favourite elephant running to a beloved master from whom it had been over-long separated. Or a slightly intoxicated and altogether happy yellow guinea-pig making for some coveted food. . . .

At a considerable distance followed Professor Bowles, a miracle of compact energy, running so fast that he seemed only to touch the ground at very rare intervals. . . .

And then, dispersedly, in their order and according to their natures, the others. . . .

There was fortunately very little on the road.

There was a perambulator containing twins, whose little girl guardian was so lucky as to be high up on the bank gathering blackberries.

A ditcher, ditching.

A hawker lost in thought.

His cart, drawn by a poor little black screw of a pony and loaded with the cheap flawed crockery that is so popular among the poor.

A dog asleep in the middle of the village street. . . .

Amidst this choice of objects the caravan displayed a whimsical humanity. It reduced the children in the perambulator to tears, but passed. It might have reduced them to a sort of red-currant jelly. It lurched heavily towards the ditcher and spared him, it chased the hawker up the bank, it whipped off a wheel from the cart of crockery (which after an interval of astonishment fell like a vast objurgation) and then it directed its course with a grim intentness towards the dog.

It just missed the dog.

He woke up not a moment too soon. He fled with a yelp of dismay.

And then the caravan careered on a dozen yards farther, lost energy and—the only really undignified thing in its whole career—stood on its head in a wide wet ditch. It did this with just the slightest lapse into emphasis. *There!* It was as if it gave a grunt—and perhaps there was the faintest suggestion of William in that grunt—and then it became quite still. . . .

For a time the caravan seemed finished and done. Its steps hung from its upper end like the tongue of a tired dog. Except for a few minute noises as though it was scratching itself inside, it was as inanimate as death itself.

But up the hill road the twins were weeping, the hawker and the ditcher were saying raucous things, the hawker's pony had backed into a ditch and was taking ill-advised steps, for which it was afterwards to be sorry, amidst the stock-in-trade, and Professor Bowles, Mrs. Bowles, Mr. Geedge, Captain Douglas and Mrs. Geedge were running—running—one heard the various patter of their feet.

And then came signs of life at the upward door of the caravan, a hand, an arm, an active investigating leg seeking a hold, a large nose, a small intent vicious eye; in fact—William.

William maddened.

Professor Bowles had reached the caravan. With a startling agility he clambered up by the wheels and step and confronted the unfortunate driver. It was an occasion for mutual sympathy rather than anger, but the Professor was hasty, efficient and unsympathetic with the lower classes, and William's was an ill-regulated temperament.

"You consummate *ass!*" began Professor Bowles. . . .

When William heard Professor Bowles say this, incontinently he smote him in the face, and when Professor Bowles was smitten in the face he grappled instantly and very bravely and resolutely with William.

For a moment they struggled fearfully, they seemed to be endowed instantaneously with innumerable legs, and then suddenly they fell through the door of the caravan into the interior, their limbs seemed to whirl for a wonderful instant and then they were swallowed up. . . .

The smash was tremendous. You would not have thought there was nearly so much in the caravan still left to get broken. . . .

A healing silence. . . .

At length smothered noises of still inadequate adjustment within. . . .

The village population in a state of scared delight appeared at a score of points and converged upon the catastrophe. Sounds of renewed dissension between William and the Professor inside the rearing yellow bulk, promised further interests and added an element of mystery to this manifest disaster.

§ 12

As Bealby, still grasping his great branch of yew, watched these events, a sense of human futility invaded his youthful mind. For the first time he realised the gulf between intention and result. He had meant so well. . . .

He perceived it would be impossible to explain. . . .

The thought of even attempting to explain things to Professor Bowles was repellent to him. . . .

He looked about him with round despairful eyes. He selected a direction which seemed to promise the maximum of concealment with the minimum of conversational possibility, and in that direction and without needless delay he set off, eager to turn over an entirely fresh page in his destiny as soon as possible. . . .

To get away;—the idea possessed all his being.

From the crest of the downs a sweet voice floated after his retreating form and never overtook him.

" Di—ick!"

§ 13

Then presently Miss Philips arose to her feet, gathered her skirts in her hand, and with her delicious chin raised and an expression of countenance that was almost business-like, descended towards the gathering audience below. She wore wide flowing skirts and came down the hill in Artemisian strides.

It was high time that somebody looked at her.

CHAPTER THE FIFTH

The Seeking of Bealby

§ 1

ON the same Monday evening that witnessed Bealby's first experience of the theatre, Mr. Mergleson, the house steward of Shonts, walked slowly and thoughtfully across the corner of the park between the laundry and the gardens. His face was much recovered from the accidents of his collision with the Lord Chancellor, resort to raw meat in the kitchen had checked the development of his injuries, and only a few contusions on the side of his face were more than faintly traceable. And suffering had on the whole rather ennobled than depressed his bearing. He had a black eye, but it was not, he felt, a common black eye. It came from high quarters and through no fault of Mr. Mergleson's own. He carried it well. It was a fruit of duty rather than the outcome of wanton pleasure-seeking or misdirected passion.

He found Mr. Darling in profound meditation over some peach-trees against the wall. They were not doing so well as they ought to do, and Mr. Darling was engaged in wondering why.

"Good evening, Mr. Darling," said Mr. Mergleson.

Mr. Darling ceased rather slowly to wonder and turned to his friend. "Good evening, Mr. Mergleson," he said. "I don't quite like the look of these here peaches, *blowed* if I do."

Mr. Mergleson glanced at the peaches and then came to the matter that was nearest his heart.

"You 'aven't I suppose seen anything of your stepson these last two days, Mr. Darling?"

"Naturally *not*," said Mr. Darling, putting his head on one side and regarding his interlocutor. "Naturally not,—I've left that to you, Mr. Mergleson."

"Well, that's what's awkward," said Mr. Mergleson, and then, with a forced easiness, "You see, I ain't seen 'im either."

"No!"

"No. I lost sight of 'im "—Mr. Mergleson appeared to reflect—"late on Sattiday night."

"'Ow's that, Mr. Mergleson?"

Mr. Mergleson considered the difficulties of lucid explanation. "We missed 'im," said Mr. Mergleson, simply regarding the well-weeded garden path with a calculating expression and then lifting his eyes to Mr. Darling's with an air of great candour. "And we continue to miss him."

"*Well!*" said Mr. Darling. "That's rum."

"Yes," said Mr. Mergleson.

"It's decidedly rum," said Mr. Darling.

"We thought 'e might be 'iding from 'is work. Or cut off 'ome."

"You didn't send down to ask."

"We was too busy with the week-end people. On the 'ole we thought if 'e 'ad cut 'ome, on the 'ole 'e wasn't a very serious loss. 'E got in the way at times. . . . And there was one or two things 'appened—. . . Now that they're all gone and 'e 'asn't turned up— Well,

I came down, Mr. Darling, to arst you. Where's 'e gone?"

"'E ain't come 'ere," said Mr. Darling surveying the garden.

"I 'arf expected 'e might and I 'arf expected 'e mightn't," said Mr. Mergleson with the air of one who had anticipated Mr. Darling's answer but hesitated to admit as much.

The two gentlemen paused for some seconds and regarded each other searchingly.

"Where's 'e *got* to?" said Mr. Darling.

"Well," said Mr. Mergleson, putting his hands where the tails of his short jacket would have been if it hadn't been short and looking extraordinarily like a parrot in its more thoughtful moods, "to tell you the truth, Mr. Darling, I've 'ad a dream about 'im——and it worries me. I got a sort of ideer of 'im as being in one of them secret passages. 'Iding away. There was a guest, well, I say it with all respec' but *anyone* might 'ave 'id from 'im. . . . S'morning soon as the week-end 'ad cleared up and gone 'ome, me and Thomas went through them passages as well as we could. Not a trace of 'im. But I still got that ideer. 'E was a wriggling, climbing, enterprising sort of boy."

"I've checked 'im for it once or twice," said Mr. Darling with the red light of fierce memories gleaming for a moment in his eyes.

"'E might even," said Mr. Mergleson, "well, very likely 'ave got 'imself jammed in one of them secret passages. . . ."

"Jammed," repeated Mr. Darling.

"Well—got 'imself somewhere where 'e can't get out. I've 'eard tell there's walled-up dungeons."

"They say," said Mr. Darling, "there's underground passages to the Abbey ruins—three good mile away."

"Orkward," said Mr. Mergleson. . . .

"Drat 'is eyes!" said Mr. Darling, scratching his head. "What does 'e mean by it?"

"We can't leave 'im there," said Mr. Mergleson.

"I knowed a young devil once what crawled up a culvert," said Mr. Darling. "'Is father 'ad to dig 'im out like a fox. . . . Lord! 'ow 'e walloped 'im for it."

"Mistake to 'ave a boy in so young," said Mr. Mergleson.

"It's all very awkward," said Mr. Darling, surveying every aspect of the case. "You see—— 'Is Mother sets a most estrordinary value on 'im. Most estrordinary."

"I don't know whether she oughtn't to be told," said Mr. Mergleson. "I was thinking of that."

Mr. Darling was not the sort of man to meet trouble half-way. He shook his head at that. "Not yet, Mr. Mergleson. I don't think yet. Not until everything's been tried. I don't think there's any need to give her needless distress,—none whatever. If you don't mind I think I'll come up to-night—nineish say—and 'ave a talk to you and Thomas about it—a quiet talk. Best to begin with a *quiet* talk. It's a dashed rum go, and me and you we got to think it out a bit."

"That's what *I* think," said Mr. Mergleson with unconcealed relief at Mr. Darling's friendliness. "That's exactly the light, Mr. Darling, in which it appears to me. Because you see—if 'e's all right and in the 'ouse, why doesn't 'e come for 'is vittels?"

§ 2

In the pantry that evening the question of telling someone was discussed further. It was discussed over a number of glasses of Mr. Mergleson's beer. For, following a sound tradition, Mr. Mergleson brewed at Shonts, and sometimes he brewed well and sometimes he brewed ill, and sometimes he brewed weak and sometimes he brewed strong, and there was no monotony in the cups at Shonts. This was sturdy stuff and suited Mr. Darling's mood, and ever and again with an author's natural weakness and an affectation of an abstraction Mr. Mergleson took the jug out empty and brought it back foaming.

Henry, the second footman, was disposed to a forced hopefulness so as not to spoil the evening, but Thomas was sympathetic and distressed. The red-haired youth made cigarettes with a little machine, licked them and offered them to the others, saying little, as became him. Etiquette deprived him of an unproffered beer, and Mr. Mergleson's inattention completed what etiquette began.

"I can't bear to think of the poor little beggar, stuck head foremost into some cobwebby cranny, blowed if I can," said Thomas, getting help from the jug.

"He was an interesting kid," said Thomas in a tone that was frankly obituary. "He didn't like his work, one could see that, but he was lively—and I tried to help him along all I could, when I wasn't too busy myself."

"There was something sensitive about him," said Thomas.

Mr. Mergleson sat with his arms loosely thrown out over the table.

"What we got to do is to tell someone," he said, "I don't see 'ow I can put off telling 'er ladyship—after to-morrow morning. And then—'eaven 'elp us!"

"Course *I* got to tell *my* missis," said Mr. Darling, and poured in a preoccupied way, some running over.

"We'll go through them passages again now before we go to bed," said Mr. Mergleson, "as far as we can. But 'there's 'oles and chinks on'y a boy could get through."

"*I* got to tell the missis," said Mr. Darling. "That's what's worrying me. . . ."

As the evening wore on there was a tendency on the part of Mr. Darling to make this the refrain of his discourse. He sought advice. "'Ow'd you tell the missis?" he asked Mr. Mergleson, and emptied a glass to control his impatience before Mr. Mergleson replied.

"I shall tell 'er ladyship, just simply, the fact. I shall say, 'Your ladyship, here's my boy gone and we don't know where.' And as she arsts me questions so shall I give particulars."

Mr. Darling reflected and then shook his head slowly.

"'Ow'd *ju* tell the missis?" he asked Thomas.

"Glad I haven't got to," said Thomas. "*Poor* little beggar!"

"Yes, but 'ow *would* you tell 'er?" Mr. Darling said, varying the accent very carefully.

"I'd go to 'er and I'd pat her back and I'd say 'Bear up,' see, and when she asked what for, I'd just tell her what for—gradual like."

"You don't know the missis," said Mr. Darling. "Henry, 'ow'd *ju* tell 'er?"

"Let 'er find out," said Henry. "Wimmin do."

Mr. Darling reflected, and decided that too was unworkable.

"'Ow'd *you?*" he asked with an air of desperation of the red-haired youth.

The red-haired youth remained for a moment with his tongue extended, licking the gum of a cigarette paper, and his eyes on Mr. Darling. Then he finished the cigarette slowly, giving his mind very carefully to the question he had been honoured with. "I think," he said, in a low serious voice, "I should say, just simply, 'Mary'—or 'Susan'—or whatever her name is."

"Tilda," supplied Mr. Darling.

"'Tilda,' I should say, 'The Lord gave and the Lord 'ath taken away. Tilda!—'e's gone.' Somethin' like that!"

The red-haired boy cleared his throat. He was rather touched by his own simple eloquence.

Mr. Darling reflected on this with profound satisfaction for some moments. Then he broke out almost querulously, "Yes, but brast him!—*where's* 'e gone?"

"Anyhow," said Mr. Darling, "I ain't going to tell 'er not till the morning. I ain't going to lose my night's

24

rest if I *'ave* lost my stepson. Nohow. Mr. Mergleson, I *must* say, I don't think I ever *'ave* tasted better beer. Never. It's—it's famous beer."

He had some more. . . .

On his way back through the moonlight to the gardens Mr. Darling was still unsettled as to the exact way of breaking things to his wife. He had come out from the house a little ruffled because of Mr. Mergleson's opposition to a rather good idea of his that he should go about the house and "holler for 'im a bit. He'd know my voice you see. Ladyship wouldn't mind. Very likely 'sleep by now." But the moonlight dispelled his irritation.

How was he to tell his wife? He tried various methods to the listening moon.

There was for example the offhand newsy way. "You know tha' boy yours?" Then a pause for the reply. Then, "'E's toley dis'peared."

Only there are difficulties about the word totally.

Or the distressed impersonal manner. "Dre'fle thing happen'd. Dre'fle thing. Tha' poo' lill' chap, Artie— toley dis'peared."

Totally again.

Or the personal intimate note. "Dunno wha' you'll say t' me, Tilda, when you hear whattogottasay. Thur'ly bad news. Seems they los' our Artie up there—clean los' 'im. Can't fine 'im nowhere 'tall."

Or the authoritative kindly. "Tilda—you go' control yourself. Go' show whadyou made of. Our boy— 'e's—hic—*los*'."

Then he addressed the park at large with a sudden despair. "Don' care wha' I say, she'll blame it on to me. I *know* 'er!"

After that the enormous pathos of the situation got hold of him. "Poor lill' chap," he said. "Poor lill' fell'," and shed a few natural tears.

"Loved 'im jessis mione son."

As the circumambient night made no reply he repeated the remark in a louder, almost domineering tone. . . .

He spent some time trying to climb the garden wall because the door did not seem to be in the usual place. (Have to inquire about that in the morning. Difficult to see everything is all right when one is so bereaved.) But finally he came on the door round a corner.

He told his wife merely that he intended to have a peaceful night, and took off his boots in a defiant and intermittent manner.

The morning would be soon enough.

She looked at him pretty hard, and he looked at her ever and again, but she never made a guess at it.

Bed.

§ 3

So soon as the week-enders had dispersed and Sir Peter had gone off to London to attend to various matters affecting the peptonising of milk and the distribution of baby soothers about the habitable globe, Lady Laxton went back to bed and remained in bed until midday on Tuesday. Nothing short of complete rest and the utmost kindness from her maid would, she felt, save her from a nervous breakdown of the most serious description. The festival had been stormy to the end. Sir Peter's ill-advised attempts to deprive Lord Moggeridge of alcohol had led to a painful struggle at lunch, and this had been followed by a still more unpleasant scene between host and guest in the afternoon. "This is an occasion for tact," Sir Peter had said, and had gone off to tackle the Lord Chancellor, leaving his wife to the direst, best-founded apprehensions. For Sir Peter's tact was a thing by itself, a mixture of misconception, recrimination and familiarity that was rarely well received. . . .

She had had to explain to the Sunday dinner party that his lordship had been called away suddenly. "Something connected with the Great Seal," Lady Laxton had whispered in a discreet mysterious whisper.

One or two simple hearers were left with the persuasion
that the Great Seal had been taken suddenly unwell—
and probably in a slightly indelicate manner.   Thomas
had to paint Mergleson's eye with grease-paint left over
from some private theatricals.   It had been a patched-up
affair altogether, and before she retired to bed that night
Lady Laxton had given way to her accumulated tensions
and wept.

There was no reason whatever why to wind up the
day Sir Peter should have stayed in her room for an
hour saying what he thought of Lord Moggeridge.   She
felt she knew quite well enough what he thought of
Lord Moggeridge, and on these occasions he always used
a number of words that she did her best to believe, as a
delicately brought-up woman, were unfamiliar to her
ears. . . .

So on Monday, as soon as the guests had gone, she
went to bed again and stayed there, trying as a good
woman should to prevent herself thinking of what the
neighbours could be thinking—and saying—of the whole
affair, by studying a new and very circumstantial pamphlet by Bishop Fowle on social evils, turning over the
moving illustrations of some recent antivivisection
literature and re-reading the accounts in the morning
papers of a colliery disaster in the north of England.

To such women as Lady Laxton, brought up in an
atmosphere of refinement that is almost colourless and
living a life troubled only by small social conflicts and
the minor violence of Sir Peter, blameless to the point
of complete uneventfulness, and secure and comfortable
to the point of tedium, there is something amounting to
fascination in the wickedness and sufferings of more
normally situated people, there is a real attraction and
solace in the thought of pain and stress; and as her access
to any other accounts of vice and suffering was restricted
she kept herself closely in touch with the more explicit
literature of the various movements for human moralisa-
tion that distinguish our age, and responded eagerly and

generously to such painful catastrophes as enliven it.
The counterfoils of her cheque-book witnessed to her
gratitude for these vicarious sensations. She figured herself to herself in her day dreams as a calm and white
and shining intervention checking and reproving amuse-
ments of an undesirable nature, and earning the tearful
blessings of the mangled bye-products of industrial
enterprise.

There is a curious craving for entire reality in the
feminine composition, and there were times when in
spite of these feasts of particulars, she wished she could
come just a little nearer to the heady dreadfulnesses of
life than simply writing a cheque against it. She would
have liked to have actually *seen* the votaries of evil blench
and repent before her contributions, to have herself
unstrapped and revived and pitied some doomed and
chloroformed victim of the so-called " scientist," to have
herself participated in the stretcher and the hospital and
humanity made marvellous by enlistment under the red-
cross badge. But Sir Peter's ideals of womanhood were
higher than his language, and he would not let her soil
her refinement with any vision of the pain and evil in
the world. " Sort of woman they want up there is a
Trained Nurse," he used to say when she broached the
possibility of *going* to some famine or disaster. " *You*
don't want to go prying, old girl. . . ."

She suffered, she felt, from repressed heroism. If
ever she was to shine in disaster that disaster, she felt,
must come to her, she might not go to meet it, and
so you realise how deeply it stirred her, how it
brightened her and uplifted her to learn from Mr.
Mergleson's halting statements that perhaps, that probably, that almost certainly, a painful and tragical thing
was happening even now within the walls of Shonts,
that there was urgent necessity for action—if anguish
was to be witnessed before it had ended and life saved.

She clasped her hands; she surveyed her large servitor
with agonised green-grey eyes.

"Something must be done at once," she said. "Everything possible must be done. Poor little Mite!"

"Of course, my lady, 'e *may* 'ave run away!"

"Oh no!" she cried, "he hasn't run away. He hasn't run away. How can you be so *wicked,* Mergleson? Of course he hasn't run away. He's there now. And it's too dreadful."

She became suddenly very firm and masterful. The morning's colliery tragedy inspired her imagination.

"We must get pick-axes," she said. "We must organise search parties. Not a moment is to be lost, Mergleson—not a moment. . . . Get the men in off the roads. Get everyone you can. . . ."

And not a moment was lost. The road men were actually at work in Shonts before their proper dinner-hour was over.

They did quite a lot of things that afternoon. Every passage attainable from the dining-room opening was explored, and where these passages gave off chinks and crannies they were opened up with a vigour which Lady Laxton had greatly stimulated by an encouraging presence and liberal doses of whisky. Through their efforts a fine new opening was made into the library from the wall near the window, a hole big enough for a man to fall through, because one did, and a great piece of stonework was thrown down from the Queen Elizabeth tower exposing the upper portion of the secret passage to the light of day. Lady Laxton herself and the head housemaid went round the panelling with a hammer and a chisel, and called out "Are you there?" and attempted an opening wherever it sounded hollow. The sweep was sent for to go up the old chimneys outside the present flues. Meanwhile Mr. Darling had been set with several of his men to dig for, discover, pick up and lay open the underground passage or disused drain, whichever it was, that was known to run from the corner of the laundry towards the old ice-house, and that was supposed to reach to the Abbey ruins. After some bold exploratory excavations this channel was located and a report sent at once to Lady Laxton.

It was this and the new and alarming scar on the Queen Elizabeth tower that brought Mr. Beaulieu Plummer post-haste from the estate office up to the house. Mr. Beaulieu Plummer was the Marquis of Cranberry's estate agent, a man of great natural tact, and charged among other duties with the task of seeing that the Laxtons did not make away with Shonts during the period of their tenancy. He was a sound compact little man, rarely out of extreme riding breeches and gaiters, and he wore glasses, that now glittered with astonishment as he approached Lady Laxton and her band of spade workers.

At his approach Mr. Darling attempted to become invisible, but he was unable to do so.

"Lady Laxton," Mr. Beaulieu Plummer appealed, "may I ask——?"

"Oh, Mr. Beaulieu Plummer, I'm so *glad* you've come. A little boy—suffocating! I can hardly *bear* it."

"Suffocating!" cried Mr. Beaulieu Plummer, "*where?*" and was in a confused manner told.

He asked a number of questions that Lady Laxton found very tiresome. But how did she *know* the boy was in the secret passages? Of course she knew; was it likely she would do all this if she didn't know? But mightn't he have run away? How could he when he was in the secret passages? But why not first scour the countryside? By which time he would be smothered and starved and dead! . . .

They parted with a mutual loss of esteem, and Mr. Beaulieu Plummer, looking very serious indeed, ran as fast as he could straight to the village telegraph-office. Or to be more exact he walked until he thought himself out of sight of Lady Laxton and then he took to his

heels and ran. He sat for some time in the parlour
post-office spoiling telegraph forms, and composing tele-
grams to Sir Peter Laxton and Lord Cranberry.

He got these off at last, and then drawn by an irresistible fascination went back to the park and watched
from afar the signs of fresh activities on the part of
Lady Laxton.

He saw men coming from the direction of the stables
with large rakes. With these they dragged the ornamental waters.

Then a man with a pick-axe appeared against the
skyline and crossed the roof in the direction of the clock
tower, bound upon some unknown but probably highly
destructive mission.

Then he saw Lady Laxton going off to the gardens.
She was going to console Mrs. Darling in her trouble.
This she did through nearly an hour and a half. And
on the whole it seemed well to Mr. Beaulieu Plummer
that so she should be occupied. . . .

It was striking five when a telegraph boy on a bicycle
came up from the village with a telegram from Sir Peter
Laxton.

"Stop all proceedings absolutely," it said, "until I
get to you."

Lady Laxton's lips tightened at the message. She was
back from much weeping with Mrs. Darling and altogether finely strung. Here she felt was one of those
supreme occasions when a woman must assert herself.
"A matter of life or death," she wired in reply, and to
show herself how completely she overrode such dictation
as this, she sent Mr. Mergleson down to the village
public-house with orders to engage anyone he could find
there for an evening's work on an extraordinarily liberal
overtime scale.

After taking this step the spirit of Lady Laxton
quailed. She went and sat in her own room and
quivered. She quivered but she clenched her delicate
fist.

She would go through with it, come what might, she would go on with the excavation all night if necessary, but at the same time she began a little to regret that she had not taken earlier steps to demonstrate the improbability of Bealby having simply run away. She set to work to repair this omission. She wrote off to the Superintendent of Police in the neighbouring town, to the nearest magistrate, and then on the off-chance to various of her week-end guests, including Captain Douglas. If it was true that he had organised the annoyance of the Lord Chancellor (and though she still rejected that view she did now begin to regard it as a permissible hypothesis), then he might also know something about the mystery of this boy's disappearance.

Each letter she wrote she wrote with greater fatigue and haste than its predecessor and more illegibly.

Sir Peter arrived long after dark. He cut across the corner of the park to save time, and fell into one of the trenches that Mr. Darling had opened. This added greatly to the *éclat* with which he came into the hall.

Lady Laxton withstood him for five minutes and then returned abruptly to her bedroom and locked herself in, leaving the control of the operations in his hands. . . .

"If he's not in the house," said Sir Peter, "all this is thunderin' foolery, and if he's in the house he's dead. If he's dead he'll smell in a bit and then'll be the time to look for him. Somethin' to go upon instead of all this blind hacking the place about. No wonder they're threatenin' proceedings. . . ."

§ 4

Upon Captain Douglas Lady Laxton's letter was destined to have a very distracting effect. Because as he came to think it over, as he came to put her partly illegible allusions to secret passages and a missing boy side by side with his memories of Lord Moggeridge's

24*

accusations and the general mystery of his expulsion from
Shonts, it became more and more evident to him that he
had here something remarkably like a clue, something
that might serve to lift the black suspicion of irreverence
and levity from his military reputation. And he had
already got to the point of suggesting to Miss Philips
that he ought to follow up and secure Bealby forthwith,
before ever they came over the hill crest to witness the
disaster to the caravan.

Captain Douglas, it must be understood, was a young
man at war within himself.

He had been very nicely brought up, first in a charming English home, then in a preparatory school for
selected young gentlemen, then in a good set at Eton,
then at Sandhurst, where the internal trouble had begun
to manifest itself. Afterwards the Bistershires.

There were three main strands in the composition
of Captain Douglas. In the first place and what was
peculiarly his own quality was the keenest interest in
the *why* of things and the *how* of things and the general
mechanism of things. He was fond of clocks, curious
about engines, eager for science; he had a quick brain
and nimble hands. He read Jules Verne and liked to
think about going to the stars and making flying
machines and submarines—in those days when everybody knew quite certainly that such things were impossible. His brain teemed with larval ideas that only
needed air and light to become active full-fledged
ideas. There he excelled most of us. In the next
place—but this second strand was just a strand that
most young men have—he had a natural keen interest
in the other half of humanity, he thought them lovely,
interesting, wonderful, and they filled him with warm
curiosities and set his imagination cutting the prettiest
capers. And in the third place, and there again he was
ordinarily human, he wanted to be liked, admired,
approved, well thought of. . . . And so constituted he
had passed through the educational influence of that

English home, that preparatory school, the good set at Eton, the Sandhurst discipline, the Bistershire mess. . . .

Now the educational influence of the English home, the preparatory school, the good set at Eton and Sandhurst in those days—though Sandhurst has altered a little since—was all to develop that third chief strand of his being to the complete suppression of the others, to make him look well and unobtrusive, dress well and unobtrusively, behave well and unobtrusively, carry himself well, play games reasonably well, do nothing else well, and in the best possible form. And the two brothers Douglas, who were both really very much alike, did honestly do their best to be such plain and simple gentlemen as our country demands, taking pretentious established things seriously, and not being odd or intelligent—in spite of those insurgent strands.

But the strands were in them. Below the surface the disturbing impulses worked and at last forced their way out. . . .

In one Captain Douglas, as Mrs. Rampound Pilby told the Lord Chancellor, the suppressed ingenuity broke out in disconcerting mystifications and practical jokes that led to a severance from Portsmouth, in the other the pent-up passions came out before the other ingredients in an uncontrollable devotion to the obvious and challenging femininity of Miss Madeleine Philips. . . . His training had made him proof against ordinary women, deaf as it were to their charms, but she—she had penetrated. And impulsive forces that have been pent up go with a bang when they go. . . .

The first strand in the composition of Captain Douglas has still to be accounted for, the sinister strain of intelligence and inventiveness and lively curiosity. On that he had kept a warier hold. So far that had not been noted against him. He had his motor bicycle it is true at a time when motor bicycles were on the verge of the caddish; to that extent a watchful eye might have found him suspicious; that was all that showed. I wish I could add it was all that there was, but other things—other things were going on. Nobody knew about them. But they were going on more and more.

He read books.

Not decent fiction, not official biographies about other fellows' fathers and all the old anecdotes brought up to date and so on, but books with ideas,—you know, philosophy, social philosophy, scientific stuff, all that rot. *The sort of stuff they read in mechanics' institutes.*

He thought. He could have controlled it. But he did not attempt to control it. He *tried* to think. He knew perfectly well that it wasn't good form, but a vicious attraction drew him on.

He used to sit in his bedroom-study at Sandhurst, with the door locked, and write down on a bit of paper what he really believed and why. He would cut all sorts of things to do this. He would question things no properly trained English gentleman ever questions.

And—he experimented.

This you know was long before the French and American aviators. It was long before the coming of that emphatic lead from abroad without which no well-bred English mind permits itself to stir. In the darkest secrecy he used to make little models of cane and paper and elastic in the hope that somehow he would find out something about flying. Flying—that dream! He used to go off by himself to lonely places and climb up as high as he could and send these things fluttering earthward. He used to moon over them and muse about them. If anyone came upon him suddenly while he was doing these things, he would sit on his model, or pretend it didn't belong to him or clap it into his pocket, whichever was most convenient, and assume the vacuous expression of a well-bred gentleman at leisure—and so far nobody had caught him. But it was a dangerous practice.

And finally, and this now is the worst and last thing to tell of his eccentricities, he was keenly interested in the science of his profession and intensely ambitious.

He thought—though it wasn't his business to think, the business of a junior officer is to obey and look a credit to his regiment—that the military science of the British army was not nearly so bright as it ought to be, and that if big trouble came there might be considerable scope for an inventive man who had done what he could to keep abreast with foreign work, and a considerable weeding out of generals whose promotion had been determined entirely by their seniority, amiability and unruffled connubial felicity. He thought that the field artillery would be found out—there was no good in making a fuss about it beforehand—that no end of neglected dodges would have to be picked up from the enemy, that the transport was feeble, and a health service—other than surgery and ambulance—an unknown idea; but he saw no remedy but experience. So he worked hard in secret; he worked almost as hard as some confounded foreigner might have done; in the belief that after the first horrid smash-up there might be a chance to do things.

Outwardly of course he was sedulously all right. But he could not quite hide the stir in his mind. It broke out upon his surface in a chattering activity of incompleted sentences which he tried to keep as decently silly as he could. He had done his utmost hitherto to escape the observation of the powers that were. His infatuation for Madeleine Philips had at any rate distracted censorious attention from these deeper infamies. . . .

And now here was a crisis in his life. Through some idiotic entanglement manifestly connected with this missing boy, he had got tarred by his brother's brush and was under grave suspicion for liveliness and disrespect.

The thing might be his professional ruin. And he

loved the suppressed possibilities of his work beyond measure.

It was a thing to make him absent-minded even in the company of Madeleine.

§ 5

Not only were the first and second strands in the composition of Captain Douglas in conflict with all his appearances and pretensions, but they were also in conflict with one another.

He was full of that concealed resolve to do and serve and accomplish great things in the world. That was surely purpose enough to hide behind an easy-going unpretending gentlemanliness. But he was also tremendously attracted by Madeleine Philips, more particularly when she was not there.

A beautiful woman may be the inspiration of a great career. This however he was beginning to find was not the case with himself. He had believed it at first and written as much and said as much, and said it very variously and gracefully. But becoming more and more distinctly clear to his intelligence was the fact that the reverse was the case. Miss Madeleine Philips was making it very manifest to Captain Douglas that she herself was a career; that a lover with any other career in view need not—as the advertisements say—apply.

And the time she took up!

The distress of being with her!

And the distress of *not* being with her!

She was such a proud and lovely and entrancing and distressing being to remember, and such a vain and difficult thing to be with.

She knew clearly that she was made for love, for she had made herself for love, and she went through life like its empress with all mankind and numerous women at her feet. And she had an ideal of the lover who should win her which was like an oleographic copy of a Laszlo portrait of Douglas greatly magnified. He was to rise rapidly to great things, he was to be a conqueror and administrator, while attending exclusively to her. And incidentally she would gather desperate homage from all other men of mark, and these attentions would be an added glory to her love for him. At first Captain Douglas had been quite prepared to satisfy all these requirements. He had met her at Shorncliffe, for her people were quite good military people, and he had worshipped his way straight to her feet. He had made the most delightfully simple and delicate love to her. He had given up his secret vice of thinking for the writing of quite surprisingly clever love-letters, and the little white paper models had ceased for a time to flutter in lonely places.

And then the thought of his career returned to him from a new aspect, as something he might lay at her feet. And once it had returned to him it remained with him.

" Some day," he said, " and it may not be so very long, some of those scientific chaps will invent flying. Then the army will have to take it up, you know."

" I should *love*," she said, " to soar through the air."

He talked one day of going on active service. How would it affect them if he had to do so? It was a necessary part of a soldier's lot.

" But I should come too!" she said. " I should come with you."

" It might not be altogether convenient," he said, for already he had learned that Madeleine Philips usually travelled with quite a large number of trunks and considerable impressiveness.

" Of course," she said, " it would be splendid! How could I let you go alone? You would be the great general and I should be with you always."

" Not always very comfortable," he suggested.

" Silly boy!—I shouldn't mind *that!* How little you know me! Any hardship!"

"A woman—if she isn't a nurse———"

"I should come dressed as a man. I would be your groom. . . ."

He tried to think of her dressed as a man, but nothing on earth could get his imagination any further than a vision of her dressed as a Principal Boy. She was so delightfully and valiantly not virile; her hair would have flowed, her body would have moved, a richly fluent femininity—visible through any disguise.

§ 6

That was in the opening stage of the controversy between their careers. In those days they were both acutely in love with each other. Their friends thought the spectacle quite beautiful; they went together so well. Admirers, fluttered with the pride of participation, asked them for week-ends together; those theatrical week-ends that begin on Sunday morning and end on Monday afternoon. She confided widely.

And when at last there was something like a rupture it became the concern of a large circle of friends.

The particulars of the breach were differently stated. It would seem that looking ahead he had announced his intention of seeing the French army manœuvres just when it seemed probable that she would be out of an engagement.

"But I ought to see what they are doing," he said. "They're going to try those new dirigibles."

Then should she come?

He wanted to whisk about. It wouldn't be any fun for her. They might get landed at nightfall in any old hole. And besides people would talk— Especially as it was in France. One could do unconventional things in England one couldn't in France. Atmosphere was different.

For a time after that halting explanation she maintained a silence. Then she spoke in a voice of deep feeling. She perceived, she said, that he wanted his freedom. She would be the last person to hold a reluctant lover to her side. He might go—to *any* manœuvres. He might go if he wished round the world. He might go away from her for ever. She would not detain him, cripple him, hamper a career she had once been assured she inspired. . . .

The unfortunate man torn between his love and his profession protested that he hadn't meant *that*.

Then what *had* he meant?

He realised he had meant something remarkably like it, and he found great difficulty in expressing these fine distinctions. . . .

She banished him from her presence for a month, said he might go to his manœuvres—with her blessing. As for herself, that was her own affair. Some day perhaps he might know more of the heart of a woman. . . . She choked back tears—very beautifully, and military science suddenly became a trivial matter. But she was firm. He wanted to go. He must go. For a month anyhow.

He went sadly. . . .

Into this opening breach rushed friends. It was the inestimable triumph of Judy Bowles to get there first. To begin with, Madeleine confided in her and then, availing herself of the privilege of a distant cousinship, she commanded Douglas to tea in her Knightsbridge flat and had a good straight talk with him. She liked good straight talks with honest young men about their love affairs; it was almost the only form of flirtation that the Professor, who was a fierce tough undiscriminating man upon the essentials of matrimony, permitted her. And there was something peculiarly gratifying about Douglas's complexion. Under her guidance he was induced to declare that he could not live without Madeleine, that her love was the heart of his life, without it he was nothing and with it he could conquer the world. . . . Judy permitted herself great protestations on behalf of Madeleine, and Douglas was worked up to the pitch of kissing her intervening hand. He had little silvery hairs, she saw, all over his temples. And he was such a simple perplexed dear. It was a rich beautiful afternoon for Judy.

And then in a very obvious way Judy, who was already deeply in love with the idea of a caravan tour and the "wind on the heath" and the "Gipsy life" and the "open road" and all the rest of it, worked this charming little difficulty into her scheme, utilized her reluctant husband to arrange for the coming of Douglas, confided in Mrs. Geedge. . . .

And Douglas went off with his perplexities. He gave up all thought of France, week-ended at Shonts instead, to his own grave injury, returned to London unexpectedly by a Sunday train, packed for France and started. He reached Rheims on Monday afternoon. And then the image of Madeleine which always became more beautiful and mysterious and commanding with every mile he put between them would not let him go on. He made unconvincing excuses to the *Daily Excess* military expert with whom he was to have seen things—"There's a woman in it, my boy, and you're a fool to go," said the *Daily Excess* man, "but of course you'll go, and I for one don't blame you—." He hurried back to London and was at Judy's trysting-place even as Judy had anticipated.

And when he saw Madeleine standing in the sunlight, pleased and proud and glorious, with a smile in her eyes and trembling on her lips, with a strand or so of her beautiful hair and a streamer or so of delightful blue fluttering in the wind about her gracious form, it seemed to him for the moment that leaving the manœuvres and coming back to England was quite a right and almost a magnificent thing to do.

§ 7

This meeting was no exception to their other meetings.

The coming to her was a crescendo of poetical desire, the sight of her a climax and then—an accumulation of irritations.

He had thought being with her would be pure delight, and as they went over the down straying after the Bowles and the Geedges towards the Redlake Hotel he already found himself rather urgently asking her to marry him, and being annoyed by what he regarded as her evasiveness.

He walked along with the restrained movement of a decent Englishman, he seemed as it were to gesticulate only through his clenched teeth, and she floated beside him, in a blue dress that with a wonderful foresight she had planned for breezy uplands on the basis of Botticelli's *Primavera*. He was urging her to marry him soon; he needed her, he could not live in peace without her. It was not at all what he had come to say; he could not recollect that he had come to say anything, but now that he was with her it was the only thing he could find to say to her.

"But, my dearest boy," she said, "how are we to marry? What is to become of *your* career and *my* career?"

"I've *left* my career!" cried Captain Douglas with the first clear note of irritation in his voice.

"Oh! don't let us quarrel," she cried. "Don't let us talk of all those *distant* things. Let us be happy. Let us enjoy just this lovely day and the sunshine and the freshness and the beauty. . . . Because you know we are snatching these days. We have so few days together. Each—each must be a gem. . . . Look, dear, how the breeze sweeps through these tall dry stems that stick up everywhere—low broad ripples."

She was a perfect work of art, abolishing time and obligations.

For a time they walked in silence. Then Captain Douglas said, " All very well—beauty and all that— but a fellow likes to know where he is."

She did not answer immediately and then she said, " I believe you are angry because you have come away from France."

" Not a bit of it," said the Captain stoutly. " I'd come away from anywhere to be with you."

" I wonder," she said.

" Well,—haven't I ?"

" I wonder if you ever are with me. . . . Oh!—I know you *want* me. I know you desire me. But the real thing, the happiness,—love. What is anything to love—anything at all ?"

In this strain they continued until their footsteps led them through the shelter of a group of beeches. And there the gallant Captain sought expression in deeds. He kissed her hand, he sought her lips. She resisted softly.

" No," she said, " only if you love me with all your heart."

Then suddenly, wonderfully, conqueringly she yielded him her lips.

" Oh!" she sighed presently, " if only you understood."

And leaving speech at that enigma she kissed again. . . .

But you see now how difficult it was under these mystically loving conditions to introduce the idea of a prompt examination and dispatch of Bealby. Already these days were consecrated. . . .

And then Bealby vanished—going seaward. . . .

Even the crash of the caravan disaster did little to change the atmosphere. In spite of a certain energetic quality in the Professor's direction of the situation— he was a trifle embittered because his thumb was

sprained and his knee bruised rather badly and he had
a slight abrasion over one ear and William had bitten
his calf—the general disposition was to treat the affair
hilariously. Nobody seemed really hurt except William,
—the Professor was not so much hurt as annoyed—
and William's injuries though striking were all superficial, a sprained jaw and grazes and bruises and little
things like that; everybody was heartened up to the
idea of damages to be paid for; and neither the internal
injuries to the caravan nor the hawker's estimate of
his stock-in-trade proved to be as great as one might
reasonably have expected. Before sunset the caravan
was safely housed in the Winthorpe-Sutbury public-
house, William had found a congenial corner in the
bar parlour, where his account of an inside view of the
catastrophe and his views upon Professor Bowles were
much appreciated, the hawker had made a bit extra by
carting all the luggage to the Redlake Royal Hotel,
and the caravanners and their men folk had loitered
harmoniously back to this refuge. Madeleine had
walked along the road beside Captain Douglas and his
motor bicycle, which he had picked up at the now
desolate encampment.

"It only remains," she said, "for that thing to get
broken."

"But I may want it," he said.

"No," she said, "Heaven has poured us together
and now He has smashed the vessels. At least He has
smashed one of the vessels. And look!—like a great
shield, there is the moon. It's the Harvest Moon,
isn't it?"

"No," said the Captain, with his poetry running
away with him. "It's the Lovers' Moon."

"It's like a benediction rising over our meeting."

And it was certainly far too much like a benediction
for the Captain to talk about Bealby.

That night was a perfect night for lovers, a night
flooded with a kindly radiance, so that the warm

mystery of the centre of life seemed to lurk in every shadow, and hearts throbbed instead of beating and eyes were stars. After dinner everyone found wraps and slipped out into the moonlight; the Geedges vanished like moths; the Professor made no secret that Judy was transfigured for him. Night works these miracles. The only other visitors there, a brace of couples, resorted to the boats upon the lake.

Two enormous waiters removing the coffee cups from the small tables upon the veranda heard Madeleine's beautiful voice for a little while, and then it was stilled. . . .

§ 8

The morning found Captain Douglas in a state of reaction. He was anxious to explain quite clearly to Madeleine how necessary it was that he should go in search of Bealby forthwith. He was beginning to realise now just what a chance in the form of Bealby had slipped through his fingers. He had dropped Bealby, and now the thing to do was to pick up Bealby again before he was altogether lost. Her professional life unfortunately had given Miss Philips the habit of never rising before midday, and the Captain had to pass the time as well as he could until the opportunity for his explanation came.

A fellow couldn't go off without an explanation. . . .

He passed the time with Professor Bowles upon the golf-links.

The Professor was a first-rate player and an unselfish one; he wanted all other players to be as good as himself. He would spare no pains to make them so. If he saw them committing any of the many errors into which golfers fall he would tell them of it and tell them why it was an error, and insist upon showing them just how to avoid it in future. He would point out any want of judgment, and not confine himself as so many professional golf teachers do merely to the stroke. After a time he found it necessary to hint to the Captain that nowadays a military man must accustom himself to self-control. The Captain kept Pishing and Tushing and presently, it was only too evident, swearing softly; his play got jerky, his strokes were forcible without any real strength, once he missed the globe altogether and several times he sliced badly. The eyes under his light eyelashes were wicked little things.

He remembered that he had always detested golf.

And the Professor. He had always detested the Professor.

And his caddie; at least he would have always detested his caddie if he had known him long enough. His caddie was one of those maddening boys with no expression at all. It didn't matter what he did or failed to do, there was the silly idiot with his stuffed face, unmoved. Really of course overjoyed—but apparently unmoved. . . .

"Why did I play it that way?" the Captain repeated. "Oh! because I like to play it that way."

"*Well,*" said the Professor. "It isn't a recognised way anyhow. . . ."

Then came a moment of evil pleasure.

He sliced. Old Bowles sliced. For once in a while he'd muffed something. Always teaching others and here he was slicing! Why, sometimes the Captain didn't slice! . . .

He'd got out of that neatly enough. Luck! He'd get the hole yet. What a bore it all was! . . .

Why couldn't Madeleine get up at a decent hour to see a fellow? Why must she lie in bed when she wasn't acting? If she had got up all this wouldn't have happened. The shame of it! Here he was, an able-bodied capable man in the prime of life and the morning of a day playing this blockhead's game——!

Yes—blockhead's game!

"You play the like," said the Professor.

"*Rather,*" said the Captain and addressed himself to his stroke.

"That's not your ball," said the Professor.

"Similar position," said the Captain.

"You know, you might *win* this hole," said the Professor.

"Who cares?" said the Captain under his breath, and putted extravagantly.

"That saves me," said the Professor and went down from a distance of twelve yards.

The Captain, full of an irrational resentment, did his best to halve the hole and failed.

"You ought to put in a week at nothing but putting," said the Professor. "It would save you at least a stroke a hole. I've noticed that on almost every green, if I haven't beaten you before I pull up in the putting."

The Captain pretended not to hear and said a lot of rococo things inside himself.

It was Madeleine who had got him in for this game. A beautiful healthy girl ought to get up in the mornings. Mornings and beautiful healthy girls are all the same thing really. She ought to be *dewy*—positively dewy. . . . There she must be lying, warm and beautiful in bed—like Catherine the Great or somebody of that sort. No. It wasn't right. All very luxurious and so on, but not *right*. She ought to have understood that he was bound to fall a prey to the Professor if she didn't get up. Golf! Here he was, neglecting his career; hanging about on these *beastly* links, all the sound men away there in France—it didn't do to think of it!—and he was playing this retired tradesman's consolation!

(Beastly the Professor's legs looked from behind. The uglier a man's legs are the better he plays golf. It's almost a law.)

That's what it was, a retired tradesman's consolation. A decent British soldier has no more business to be playing golf than he has to be dressing dolls. It's a game at once worthless and exasperating. If a man isn't perfectly fit he cannot play golf, and when he is perfectly fit he ought to be doing a man's work in the world. If ever anything deserved the name of vice, if ever anything was pure, unforgivable dissipation, surely golf was that thing. . . .

And meanwhile that boy was getting more and more start. Anyone with a ha'porth of sense would have been up at five and after that brat—might have had him bagged and safe and back to lunch. *Ass* one was at times!

"You're here, sir," said the caddie.

The Captain perceived he was in a nasty place, open green ahead but with some tumbled country near at hand and to the left, a rusty old gravel pit, furze at the sides, water at the bottom. Nasty attractive hole of a place. Sort of thing one gets into. He must pull himself together for this. After all, having undertaken to play a game one must play the game. If he hit the infernal thing, that is to say the ball, if he hit the ball so that if it didn't go straight it would go to the right rather—clear of the hedge it wouldn't be so bad to the right. Difficult to manage. Best thing was to think hard of the green ahead, a long way ahead,—with just the slightest deflection to the right. Now then,—heels well down, club up, a good swing, keep your eye on the ball, keep your eye on the ball, keep your eye on the ball just where you mean to hit it—far below there and a little to the right—and *don't* worry. . . .

Rap.

"In the pond, I *think,* sir."

"The water would have splashed if it had gone in the pond," said the Professor. "It must be over there in the wet sand. You hit it pretty hard, I thought."

Search. The caddie looked as though he didn't care whether he found it or not. *He* ought to be interested. It was his profession, not just his game. But nowadays everybody had this horrid disposition towards slacking. A Tired generation we are. The world is too much with us. Too much to think about, too much to do, Madeleines, army manœuvres, angry lawyers, lost boys—let alone such exhausting foolery as this game. . . .

" *Got* it sir!" said the caddie.

" Where?"

" Here, sir! Up in the bush, sir!"

It was resting in the branches of a bush two yards above the slippery bank.

" I doubt if you can play it," said the Professor, " but it will be interesting to try."

The Captain scrutinized the position. " I can play it," he said.

" You'll slip, I'm afraid," said the Professor.

They were both right. Captain Douglas drove his feet into the steep slope of rusty sand below the bush, held his iron a little short and wiped the ball up and over and as he found afterwards out of the rough. All eyes followed the ball except his. The Professor made sounds of friendly encouragement. But the Captain was going—going. He was on all fours, he scrabbled handfuls of prickly gorse, of wet sand. His feet, his ankles, his calves slid into the pond. How much more? No. He'd reached the bottom. He proceeded to get out again as well as he could. Not so easy. The bottom of this pond sucked at him. . . .

When at last he rejoined the other three his hands were sandy red, his knees were sandy red, his feet were of clay, but his face was like the face of a little child. Like the face of a little fair child after it has been boiled red in its bath and then dusted over with white powder. His ears were the colour of roses, Lancaster roses. And his eyes too had something of the angry wonder of a little child distressed. . . .

" I was afraid you'd slip into the pond," said the Professor.

" I didn't," said the Captain.

" ! "

" I just got in to see how deep it was and cool my feet—I hate warm feet."

He lost that hole but he felt a better golfer now, his anger he thought was warming him up so that he would presently begin to make strokes by instinct and do remarkable things unawares. After all there is something in the phrase " getting one's blood up." If only the Professor wouldn't dally so with his ball and let one's blood get down again. Tap!—the Professor's ball went soaring. Now for it. The Captain addressed himself to his task, altered his plans rather hastily, smote and topped the ball.

The least one could expect was a sympathetic silence. But the Professor thought fit to improve the occasion.

" You'll never drive," said the Professor, " you'll never drive with that *irritable* jerk in the middle of the stroke. You might just as well smack the ball without raising your club. If you think——"

The Captain lost his self-control altogether.

" Look here," he said, " if *you* think that *I* care a single rap about how I hit the ball, if you think that I really want to win and do well at this beastly silly elderly childish game——"

He paused on the verge of ungentlemanly language.

" If a thing's worth doing at all," said the Professor after a pause for reflection, " it's worth doing well."

" Then it isn't worth doing at all. As this hole gives you the game—if you don't mind——"

The Captain's hot moods were so rapid that already he was acutely ashamed of himself.

" Oh *certainly* if you wish it," said the Professor.

With a gesture the Professor indicated the altered situation to the respectful caddies, and the two gentlemen turned their faces towards the hotel.

For a time they walked side by side in silence, the caddies following with hushed expressions.

"Splendid weather for the French manœuvres," said the Captain presently in an off-hand tone, "that is to say if they are getting this weather."

"At present there is a series of high-pressure systems over the whole of Europe north of the Alps," said the Professor. "It is as near set fair as Europe can be."

"Fine weather for tramps and wanderers," said the Captain after a further interval.

"There's a drawback to everything," said the Professor. "But it's very lovely weather."

§ 9

They got back to the hotel about half-past eleven and the Captain went and had an unpleasant time with one of the tyres of his motor bicycle which had got down in the night. In replacing the tyre he pinched the top of one of his fingers rather badly. Then he got the ordnance map of the district and sat at a green table in the open air in front of the hotel windows and speculated on the probable flight of Bealby. He had been last seen going south by east. That way lay the sea, and all boy fugitives go naturally for the sea.

He tried to throw himself into the fugitive's mind and work out just exactly the course Bealby *must* take to the sea.

For a time he found this quite an absorbing occupation.

Bealby probably had no money or very little money. Therefore he would have to beg or steal. He wouldn't go to the workhouse because he wouldn't know about the workhouse, respectable poor people never know anything about the workhouse, and the chances were he would be both too honest and too timid to steal. He'd beg. He'd beg at front doors because of dogs and things and he'd probably go along a high road. He'd be more likely to beg from houses than from passers-by because a door is at first glance less formidable than a pedestrian and more accustomed to being addressed. And he'd try isolated cottages rather than the village street doors, an isolated wayside cottage is so much more confidential. He'd ask for food—not money. All that seemed pretty sound.

Now this road on the map—into it he was bound to fall and along it he would go begging. No other? . . . No.

In the fine weather he'd sleep out. And he'd go—ten, twelve, fourteen—thirteen, thirteen miles a day.

So now, he ought to be about here. And to-night,—here.

To-morrow at the same pace,—here.

But suppose he got a lift! . . .

He'd only get a slow lift if he got one at all. It wouldn't make much difference in the calculation. . . .

So if to-morrow one started and went on to these cross roads marked *Inn,* just about twenty-six miles it must be by the scale, and beat round it one ought to get something in the way of tidings of Mr. Bealby. Was there any reason why Bealby shouldn't go on south by east and seaward?" . . .

None.

And now there remained nothing to do but to explain all this clearly to Madeleine. And why didn't she come down? Why didn't she come down?

But when one got Bealby what would one do with him?

Wring the truth out of him—half by threats and half by persuasion. Suppose after all he hadn't any connection with the upsetting of Lord Moggeridge? He had. Suppose he hadn't? He had. He had. He had.

And when one had the truth?

Whisk the boy right up to London and confront the Lord Chancellor with the facts. But suppose he wouldn't be confronted with the facts? He was a touchy old sinner. . . .

For a time Captain Douglas baulked at this difficulty. Then suddenly there came into his head the tall figure, the long moustaches of that kindly popular figure, his adopted uncle Lord Chickney. Suppose he took the boy straight to Uncle Chickney, told him the whole story. Even the Lord Chancellor would scarcely refuse ten minutes to General Lord Chickney. . . .

The clearer the plans of Captain Douglas grew the more anxious he became to put them before Madeleine —clearly and convincingly. . .

Because first he had to catch his boy. . . .

Presently as Captain Douglas fretted at the continued eclipse of Madeleine, his thumb went into his waistcoat pocket and found a piece of paper. He drew it out and looked at it. It was a little piece of stiff note-paper cut into the shape of a curved V rather after the fashion of a soaring bird. It must have been there for months. He looked at it. His care-wrinkled brow relaxed. He glanced over his shoulder at the house and then held this little scrap high over his head and let go. It descended with a slanting flight curving round to the left, and then came about and swept down to the ground to the right. . . . Now why did it go like that? As if it changed its mind. He tried it again. Same result. . . . Suppose the curvature of the wings was a little greater? Would it make a more acute or a less acute angle? He did not know. . . . Try it.

He felt in his pocket for a piece of paper, found Lady Laxton's letter, produced a stout pair of nail scissors in a sheath from his waistcoat pocket, selected a good clear sheet, and set himself to cut out his improved V. . . .

As he did so his eyes were on V number one, on the ground. It would be interesting to see if this thing turned about to the left again. If in fact it would go on zig-zagging. It ought he felt to do so. But to test that one ought to release it from some higher point so as to give it a longer flight. Stand on the chair? . .

Not in front of the whole rotten hotel. And there was a beastly looking man in a green apron coming out of the house,—the sort of man who looks at you. He might come up and watch; these fellows are equal to anything of that sort. Captain Douglas replaced his scissors and scraps in his pockets, leaned back with an affectation of boredom, got up, lit a cigarette—sort of thing the man in the green apron would think all right —and strolled off towards a clump of beech trees, beyond which were bushes and a depression. There perhaps one might be free from observation. Just try these things for a bit. That point about the angle was a curious one; it made one feel one's ignorance not to know that.

§ 10

The ideal King has a careworn look, he rules, he has to do things, but the ideal Queen is radiant happiness, tall and sweetly dignified, simply she has to be things. And when at last towards midday Queen Madeleine dispelled the clouds of the morning and came shining back into the world that waited outside her door, she was full of thankfulness for herself and for the empire that was given her. She knew she was a delicious and wonderful thing, she knew she was well done, her hands, the soft folds of her dress as she held it up, the sweep of her hair from her forehead pleased her, she lifted her chin but not too high for the almost unenvious homage in the eyes of the housemaid on the staircase. Her descent was well timed for the lunch gathering of the hotel guests; there was "*Ah!*—here she comes at last!" and there was her own particular court out upon the veranda before the entrance, Geedge and the Professor and Mrs. Bowles—and Mrs. Geedge coming acrosss the lawn,—and the lover?

She came on down and out into the sunshine. She betrayed no surprise. The others met her with flattering greetings that she returned smilingly. But the lover——?

He was not there!

It was as if the curtain had gone up on almost empty stalls.

He ought to have been worked up and waiting tremendously. He ought to have spent the morning in writing a poem to her or in writing a delightful poetical love-letter she could carry away and read, or in wandering alone and thinking about her. He ought to be feeling now like the end of a vigil. He ought to be standing now, a little in the background and with that pleasant flush of his upon his face and that shy, subdued, reluctant look that was so infinitely more flattering than any boldness of admiration. And then she would go towards him, for she was a giving type, and hold out both hands to him, and he, as though he couldn't help it, in spite of all his British reserve, would take one and hesitate—which made it all the more marked—and kiss it. . . .

Instead of which he was just not there. . . .

No visible disappointment dashed her bravery. She knew that at the slightest flicker Judy and Mrs. Geedge would guess and that anyhow the men would guess nothing. "I've rested," she said, "I've rested delightfully. What have you all been doing?"

Judy told of great conversations, Mr. Geedge had been looking for trout in the stream, Mrs. Geedge with a thin little smile said she had been making a few notes and—she added the word with deliberation—"observations," and Professor Bowles said he had had a round of golf with the Captain. "And he lost?" asked Madeleine.

"He's careless in his drive and impatient at the greens," said the Professor modestly.

"And then?"

"He vanished," said the Professor, recognizing the true orientation of her interest.

There was a little pause and Mrs. Geedge said, " You know——" and stopped short.

Interrogative looks focussed upon her.

" It's so odd," she said.

Curiosity increased.

" I suppose one ought not to say," said Mrs. Geedge, " and yet—why shouldn't one ? "

" Exactly," said Professor Bowles and everyone drew a little nearer to Mrs. Geedge.

" One can't help being amused," she said. " It was so—extraordinary."

" Is it something about the Captain ? " asked Madeleine.

" Yes. You see,—he didn't see me."

" Is he—is he writing poetry ? " Madeleine was much entertained and relieved at the thought. That would account for everything. The poor dear ! He hadn't been able to find some rhyme !

But one gathered from the mysterious airs of Mrs. Geedge that he was not writing poetry. " You see," she said, " I was lying out there among the bushes, just jotting down a few little things,—and he came by. And he went down into the hollow out of sight. . . . And what do you think he is doing ? You'd never guess. He's been at it for twenty minutes."

They didn't guess.

" He's playing with bits of paper—oh ! like a kitten plays with dead leaves. He throws them up—and they flutter to the ground—and then he pounces on them."

" But——" said Madeleine. And then very brightly, " Let's go and see ! "

She was amazed. She couldn't understand. She hid it under a light playfulness, that threatened to become distraught. Even when presently, after a very careful stalking of the dell under the guidance of Mrs. Geedge, with the others in support, she came in sight of him, she still found him incredible. There was her lover, her devoted lover, standing on the top bar of a fence, his

25

legs wide apart and his body balanced with difficulty, and in his fingers poised high was a scrap of paper. This was the man who should have been waiting in the hall with feverish anxiety. His fingers released the little model and down it went drifting. . . .

He seemed to be thinking of nothing else in the world. She might never have been born. . . .

Some noise, some rustle, caught his ear. He turned his head quickly, guiltily, and saw her and her companions.

And then he crowned her astonishment. No love-light leaped to his eyes; he uttered no cry of joy. Instead he clutched wildly at the air, shouted, "Oh, *damn!*" and came down with a complicated inelegance on all fours upon the ground.

He was angry with her—angry; she could see that he was extremely angry.

§ 11

So it was that the incompatibilities of man and woman arose again in the just recovering love-dream of Madeleine Philips. But now the discord was far more evident than it had been at the first breach.

Suddenly her dear lover, her flatterer, her worshipper, had become a strange averted man. He scrabbled up two of his paper scraps before he came towards her, still with no love-light in his eyes. He kissed her hand as if it was a matter of course and said almost immediately: "I've been hoping for you all the endless morning. I've had to amuse myself as best I can."

His tone was resentful. He spoke as if he had a claim upon her, upon her attentions. As if it wasn't entirely upon his side that obligations lay.

She resolved that shouldn't deter her from being charming.

And all through the lunch she was as charming as she could be, and under such treatment that rebellious ruffled quality vanished from his manner, vanished so completely that she could wonder if it had really been evident at any time. The alert servitor returned.

She was only too pleased to forget the disappointment of her descent and forgive him, and it was with a puzzled incredulity that she presently saw his " difficult " expression returning. It was an odd little knitting of the brows, a faint absent-mindedness, a filming of the brightness of his worship. He was just perceptibly indifferent to the charmed and charming things he was saying.

It seemed best to her to open the question herself. " Is there something on your mind, Dot?"

" Dot " was his old school nickname.

" Well no—not exactly on my mind. But— It's a bother of course. There's that confounded boy. . . ."

" Were you trying some sort of divination about him? With those pieces of paper?"

" No. That was different. That was—just something else. But you see that boy— Probably clear up the whole of the Moggeridge bother—and you know it *is* a bother. Might turn out beastly awkward. . . ."

It was extraordinarily difficult to express. He wanted so much to stay with her and he wanted so much to go.

But all reason, all that was expressible, all that found vent in words and definite suggestions was on the side of an immediate pursuit of Bealby. So that it seemed to her he wanted and intended to go much more definitely that he actually did.

That divergence of purpose flawed a beautiful afternoon, cast chill shadows of silences over their talk, arrested endearments. She was irritated. About six o'clock she urged him to go; she did not mind, anyhow she had things to see to, letters to write, and she left him with an effect of leaving him for ever. He went and overhauled his motor bicycle thoroughly, and then an aching dread of separation from her arrested him.

Dinner, the late June sunset and the moon seemed to bring them together again. Almost harmoniously he was able to suggest that he should get up very early the next morning, pursue and capture Bealby and return for lunch.

"You'd get up at dawn!" she cried. "But how perfectly Splendid the midsummer dawn must be."

Then she had an inspiration. "Dot!" she cried, "I will get up at dawn also and come with you. . . . Yes, but as you say he cannot be more than thirteen miles away we'd catch him warm in his little bed somewhere. And the freshness! The dewy freshness!"

And she laughed her beautiful laugh and said it would be "Such *Fun!*" entering as she supposed into his secret desires and making the most perfect of reconciliations. They were to have tea first, which she would prepare with the caravan lamp and kettle. Mrs. Geedge would hand it over to her.

She broke into song. "A Hunting we will go—ooh," she sang. "A Hunting we will go. . . ."

But she could not conquer the churlish underside of the Captain's nature even by such efforts. She threw a glamour of vigour and fun over the adventure, but some cold streak in his composition was insisting all the time that as a boy hunt the attempt failed. Various delays in her preparations prevented a start before half-past seven, he let that weigh with him, and when sometimes she clapped her hands and ran—and she ran like a deer, and sometimes she sang, he said something about going at an even pace.

At a quarter-past one Mrs. Geedge observed them returning. They were walking abreast and about six feet apart, they bore themselves grimly after the manner of those who have delivered ultimata and they conversed no more. . . .

In the afternoon Madeleine kept her own room exhausted, and Captain Douglas sought opportunities of speaking to her in vain. His face expressed distress and perplexity, with momentary lapses into wrathful resolution, and he evaded Judy and her leading questions and talked about the weather with Geedge. He declined a proposal of the Professor's to go round the links, with especial reference to his neglected putting. "You ought to, you know," said the Professor.

About half-past three and without any publication of his intention, Captain Douglas departed upon his motor bicycle. . . .

Madeleine did not reappear until dinner-time, and then she was clad in lace and gaiety that impressed the naturally very good observation of Mrs. Geedge as unreal.

§ 12

The Captain, a confusion of motives that was as it were a mind returning to chaos, started upon his motor bicycle. He had seen tears in her eyes. Just for one instant, but certainly they were tears. Tears of vexation. Or sorrow? (Which is the worse thing for a lover to arouse, grief or resentment?) But this boy must be caught, because if he was not caught a perpetually developing story of imbecile practical joking upon eminent and influential persons would eat like a cancer into the Captain's career. And if his career was spoiled what sort of thing would he be as a lover? Not to mention that he might never get a chance then to try flying for military purposes. . . . So anyhow, anyhow this boy must be caught. But quickly, for women's hearts are tender, they will not stand exposure to hardship. There is a kind of unreasonableness natural to goddesses. Unhappily this was an expedition needing wariness, deliberation, and one brought to it a feverish hurry to get back. There must be self-control. There must be patience. Such occasions try the soldierly quality of a man. . . .

It added nothing to the Captain's self-control that after he had travelled ten miles he found he had for-

gotten his quite indispensable map and had to return
for it. Then he was seized again with doubts about
his inductions and went over them again, sitting by the
roadside. (There must be patience.) . . . He went
on at a pace of thirty-five miles an hour to the Inn he
had marked upon his map as Bealby's limit for the
second evening. It was a beastly little inn, it stewed
tea for the Captain atrociously, and it knew nothing of
Bealby. In the adjacent cottages also they had never
heard of Bealby. Captain Douglas revised his deduc-
tions for the third time and came to the conclusion
that he had not made a proper allowance for Wednesday
afternoon. Then there was all Thursday, and the
longer, lengthening part of Friday. He might have
done thirty miles or more already. And he might have
crossed this corner—inconspicuously.

Suppose he hadn't after all come along this road!

He had a momentary vision of Madeleine with eyes
brightly tearful. "You left me for a Wild Goose
Chase," he fancied her saying. . . .

One must stick to one's job. A soldier more particularly must stick to his job. Consider Balaclava. . . .

He decided to go on along this road and try the
incidental cottages that his reasoning led him to suppose
were the most likely places at which Bealby would ask
for food. It was a business demanding patience and
politeness.

So a number of cottagers, for the greater part they
were elderly women past the fiercer rush and hurry of
life, grandmothers and ancient dames or wives at leisure
with their children away at the Council schools, had a
caller that afternoon. Cottages are such lonely places in
the daytime that even district visitors and canvassers are
godsends, and only tramps ill-received. Captain Douglas
ranked high in the scale of visitors. There was something about him, his fairness, a certain handsomeness, his
quick colour, his active speech, which interested women
at all times, and now an indefinable flow of romantic

excitement conveyed itself to his interlocutors. He encountered the utmost civility everywhere, doors at first tentatively ajar opened wider at the sight of him, and there was a kindly disposition to enter into his troubles lengthily and deliberately. They listened attentively to his demands, and before they testified to Bealby's sustained absence from their perception they would for the most part ask numerous questions in return. They wanted to hear the Captain's story, the reason for his research, the relationship between himself and the boy, they wanted to feel something of the sentiment of the thing. After that was the season for negative facts. Perhaps when everything was stated they might be able to conjure up what he wanted. He was asked in to have tea twice, for he looked not only pink and dusty but dry, and one old lady said that years ago she had lost just such a boy as Bealby seemed to be—"Ah! not in the way *you* have lost him"—and she wept, poor old dear! and was only comforted after she had told the Captain three touching but extremely lengthy and detailed anecdotes of Bealby's vanished prototype.

(Fellow cannot rush away, you know; still all this sort of thing, accumulating, means a confounded lot of delay.)

And then there was a deaf old man. . . . A very, very tiresome deaf old man who said at first he *had* seen Bealby. . . .

After all the old fellow was deaf. . . .

The sunset found the Captain on a breezy common forty miles away from the Redlake Royal Hotel, and by this time he knew that fugitive boys cannot be trusted to follow the lines even of the soundest inductions. This business meant a search.

Should he pelt back to Redlake and start again more thoroughly on the morrow?

A moment of temptation.

If he did he knew she wouldn't let him go.

No!

NO!

He must make a sweeping movement through the country to the left, trying up and down the roads that, roughly speaking, radiated from Redlake between the twenty-fifth and the thirty-fifth milestone. . . .

It was night and high moonlight when at last the Captain reached Crayminster, that little old town decayed to a village, in the Crays valley. He was hungry, dispirited, quite unsuccessful, and here he resolved to eat and rest for the night.

He would have a meal, for by this time he was ravenous, and then go and talk in the bar or the tap about Bealby.

Until he had eaten he felt he could not endure the sound of his own voice repeating what had already become a tiresome stereotyped formula : " You haven't I suppose seen or heard anything during the last two days of a small boy—little chap of about thirteen—wandering about? He's a sturdy, resolute little fellow with a high colour, short wiry hair, rather dark. . . ."

The White Hart at Crayminster after some negotiations produced mutton cutlets and Australian hock. As he sat at his meal in the small ambiguous respectable dining-room of the inn—adorned with framed and glazed beer advertisements, crinkled paper fringes and insincere sporting prints—he became aware of a murmurous confabulation going on in the bar parlour. It must certainly, he felt, be the bar parlour. . . .

He could not hear distinctly, and yet it seemed to him that the conversational style of Crayminster was abnormally rich in expletive. And the tone was odd. It had a steadfast quality of commination.

He brushed off a crumb from his jacket, lit a cigarette and stepped across the passage to put his hopeless questions.

The talk ceased abruptly at his appearance.

It was one of those deep-toned bar parlours that are so infinitely more pleasant to the eye than the tawdry decorations of the genteel accommodation. It was brown with a trimming of green paper hops and it had a mirror and glass shelves sustaining bottles and tankards. Six or seven individuals were sitting about the room. They had a numerous effect. There was a man in very light floury tweeds, with a floury bloom on his face and hair and an anxious depressed expression. He was clearly a baker. He sat forward as though he nursed something precious under the table. Next him was a respectable-looking, regular-featured, fair man with a large head, and a ruddy-faced butcher-like individual smoked a clay pipe by the side of the fireplace. A further individual with an alert intrusive look might have been a grocer's assistant associating above himself.

"Evening," said the Captain.

"Evening," said the man with the large head guardedly.

The Captain came to the hearthrug with an affectation of ease.

"I suppose," he began, "that you haven't any of you seen anything of a small boy, wandering about. He's a little chap about thirteen. Sturdy, resolute-looking little fellow with a high colour, short wiry hair, rather dark. . . ."

He stopped short arrested by the excited movements of the butcher's pipe and by the changed expressions of the rest of the company.

"We—we seen 'im," the man with the big head managed to say at last.

"We seen 'im all right," said a voice out of the darkness beyond the range of the lamp.

The baker with the melancholy expression interjected, "I don't care if I don't ever see 'im again."

"Ah!" said the Captain, astonished to find himself suddenly beyond hoping on a hot fresh scent. "Now all that's very interesting. Where did you see him?"

"Thunderin' vicious little varmint," said the butcher. "Owdacious."

25*

"Mr. Benshaw," said the voice from the shadows, "'E's arter 'im now with a shot gun loaded up wi' oats. 'E'll pepper 'im if 'e gets 'im, Bill will, you bet your 'at. And serve 'im jolly well right *tew*."

"I doubt," said the baker, "I doubt if I'll ever get my stummik—not thoroughly proper again. It's a Blow I've 'ad. 'E give me a Blow. Oh! Mr. 'Orrocks, *could* I trouble you for another thimbleful of brandy? Just a thimbleful neat. It eases the ache. . . ."

CHAPTER THE SIXTH

Bealby and the Tramp

§ 1

BEALBY was loth to leave the caravan party even
when by his own gross negligence it had ceased to be a
caravan party. He made off regretfully along the crest
of the hills through bushes of yew and box until the
clamour of the disaster was no longer in his ears. Then
he halted for a time and stood sorrowing and listening,
and then turned up by a fence along the border of a
plantation and so came into a little overhung road.

His ideas of his immediate future were vague in the
extreme. He was a receptive expectation. Since his
departure from the gardener's cottage circumstances had
handed him on. They had been interesting but unstable circumstances. He supposed they would still
hand him on. So far as he had any definite view about
his intentions it was that he was running away to sea.
And that he was getting hungry.

It was also, he presently discovered, getting dark very
gently and steadily. And the overhung road, after some

777

tortuosities expired suddenly upon the bosom of a great grey empty common with distant mysterious hedges.

It seemed high time to Bealby that something happened of a comforting nature.

Always hitherto something or someone had come to his help when the world grew dark and cold, and given him supper and put him or sent him to bed. Even when he had passed a night in the interstices of Shonts he had known there was a bed at quite a little distance under the stairs. If only that loud Voice hadn't shouted curses whenever he moved he would have gone to it. But as he went across this common in the gloaming it became apparent that this amiable routine was to be broken. For the first time he realised the world could be a homeless world.

And it had become very still.

Disagreeably still, and full of ambiguous shadows.

That common was not only an unsheltered place, he felt, but an unfriendly place, and he hurried to a gate at the farther end. He kept glancing to the right and to the left. It would be pleasanter when he had got through that gate and shut it after him.

In England there are no grey wolves.

Yet at times one thinks of wolves, grey wolves, the colour of twilight and running noiselessly, almost noiselessly, at the side of their prey for quite a long time before they close in on it.

In England, I say, there are no grey wolves.

Wolves were extinguished in the reign of Edward the Third; it was in the histories, and since then no free wolf has trod the soil of England; only menagerie captives.

Of course there may be *escaped* wolves!

Now the gate!—sharp through it and slam it behind you, and a brisk run and so into this plantation that slopes downhill. This is a sort of path, vague, but it must be a path. Let us hope it is a path.

What was that among the trees?

It stopped, surely it stopped, as Bealby stopped. Pump, pump— Of course! that was one's heart.

Nothing there! Just fancy. Wolves live in the open; they do not come into woods like this. And besides, there are no wolves. And if one shouts—even if it is but a phantom voice one produces, they go away. They are cowardly things—really. Such as there aren't.

And there is the power of the human eye.

Which is why they stalk you and watch you and evade you when you look, and creep and creep and creep behind you!

Turn sharply.

Nothing.

How this stuff rustled under the feet! In woods at twilight, with innumerable things darting from trees and eyes watching you everywhere, it would be pleasanter if one could walk without making quite such a row. Presently surely, Bealby told himself, he would come out on a high road and meet other people and say "Good-night" as they passed. Jolly other people they would be, answering "Good-night." He was now going at a moistening trot. It was getting darker and he stumbled against things.

When you tumble down wolves leap. Not of course that there *are* any wolves.

It was stupid to keep thinking of wolves in this way. Think of something else. Think of things beginning with a B. Beautiful things, boys, beads, butterflies, bears. The mind stuck at bears. *Are there such things as long grey bears?* Ugh! Almost endless, noiseless bears? . . .

It grew darker until at last the trees were black. The night was swallowing up the flying Bealby and he had a preposterous persuasion that it had teeth and would begin at the back of his legs. . . .

§ 2

" Hi!" cried Bealby weakly, hailing the glow of the fire out of the darkness of the woods above.

The man by the fire peered at the sound, he had been listening to the stumbling footsteps for some time, and he answered nothing.

In another minute Bealby had struggled through the hedge into the visible world and stood regarding the man by the fire. The phantom wolves had fled beyond Sirius. But Bealby's face was pale still from the terrors of the pursuit and altogether he looked a smallish sort of small boy.

" Lost?" said the man by the fire.

" Couldn't find my way," said Bealby.

" Anyone with you?"

" No."

The man reflected. " Tired?"

" Bit."

" Come and sit down by the fire and rest yourself."

" I won't 'urt you," he added as Bealby hesitated.

So far in his limited experience Bealby had never seen a human countenance lit from behind by a flickering red flame. The effect he found remarkable rather than pleasing. It gave him the most active and unstable countenance Bealby had ever seen. The nose seemed to be in active oscillation between Pug and Roman, the eyes jumped out of black caves and then went back into them, the more permanent features appeared to be a vast triangle of neck and chin. The tramp would have impressed Bealby as altogether inhuman if it had not been for the smell of cooking he diffused. There were onions in it and turnips and pepper—mouth-watering constituents, testimonials to virtue. He was making a stew in an old can that he had slung on a cross stick over brisk fire of twigs that he was constantly replenishing.

" I won't 'urt you, darn you," he repeated. " Come

and sit down on these leaves here for a bit and tell me all abart it."

Bealby did as he was desired. "I got lost," he said, feeling too exhausted to tell a good story.

The tramp, examined more closely, became less pyrotechnic. He had a large loose mouth, a confused massive nose, much long fair hair, a broad chin with a promising beard and spots—a lot of spots. His eyes looked out of deep sockets and they were sharp little eyes. He was a lean man. His hands were large and long and they kept on with the feeding of the fire as he sat and talked to Bealby. Once or twice he leaned forward and smelled the pot judiciously, but all the time the little eyes watched Bealby very closely.

"Lose yer collar?" said the tramp.

Bealby felt for his collar. "I took it orf," he said.

"Come far?"

"Over there," said Bealby.

"Where?"

"Over there."

"What place?"

"Don't know the name of it."

"Then it ain't your 'ome?"

"No."

"You've run away," said the man.

"P'raps I 'ave," said Bealby.

"P'raps you 'ave! Why p'raps? You *'ave?* What's the good of telling lies about it? When d'you start?"

"Monday," said Bealby.

The tramp reflected. "Had about enough of it?"

"Dunno," said Bealby truthfully.

"Like some soup?"

"Yes."

"'Ow much?"

"I could do with a lot," said Bealby.

"Ah yah! I didn't mean that. I meant, 'ow much for some? 'Ow much will you pay for a nice, nice 'arf can of soup? I ain't a darn charity. See?"

" Tuppence," said Bealby.

The tramp shook his head slowly from side to side and took out the battered iron spoon he was using to stir the stuff and tasted the soup lusciously. It was—jolly good soup and there were potatoes in it.

" Thrippence," said Bealby.

" 'Ow much you got?" asked the tramp.

Bealby hesitated perceptibly. " Sixpence," he said weakly.

" It's sixpence," said the tramp. " Pay up."

" 'Ow big a can?" asked Bealby.

The tramp felt about in the darkness behind him and produced an empty can with a jagged mouth that had once contained, the label witnessed—I quote, I do not justify—" *Deep Sea Salmon*." " That," he said, " and this chunk of bread. . . . Right enough?"

" You *will* do it?" said Bealby.

" Do I look a swindle?" cried the tramp, and suddenly a lump of the abundant hair fell over one eye in a singularly threatening manner. Bealby handed over the sixpence without further discussion. " I'll treat you fairly, you see," said the tramp, after he had spat on and pocketed the sixpence, and he did as much. He decided that the soup was ready to be served and he served it with care. Bealby began at once. " There's a nextry onion," said the tramp, throwing one over. " It didn't cost me much and I gives it you for nothin'. That's all right, eh? Here's 'ealth!"

Bealby consumed his soup and bread meekly with one eye upon his host. He would, he decided, eat all he could and then sit a little while, and then get this tramp to tell him the way to—anywhere else. And the tramp wiped soup out of his can with gobbets of bread very earnestly and meditated sagely on Bealby.

" You better pal in with me, matey, for a bit," he said at last. " You can't go nowhere else—not to-night."

" Couldn't I walk perhaps to a town or sumpthing?"

" These woods ain't safe."

" 'Ow d'you mean?"

" Ever 'eard tell of a gurrillia?—sort of big black monkey thing."

" Yes," said Bealby faintly.

" There's been one loose abät 'ere—oh week or more. Fact. And if you wasn't a grown up man quite and going along in the dark, well—'e might say something *to* you. . . . Of course 'e wouldn't do nothing where there was a fire or a man—but a little chap like you. I wouldn't like to let you do it, 'strewth I wouldn't. It's risky. Course I don't want to *keep* you. There it is. You go if you like. But I'd rather you didn't. 'Onest."

" Where'd he come from?" asked Bealby.

" M'nagery," said the tramp.

" 'E very near bit through the fist of a chap that tried to stop 'im," said the tramp.

Bealby after weighing tramp and gorilla very carefully in his mind decided he wouldn't, and drew closer to the fire—but not too close—and the conversation deepened.

§ 3

It was a long and rambling conversation and the tramp displayed himself at times as quite an amiable person. It was a discourse varied by interrogations, and as a thread of departure and return it dealt with the life of the road and with life at large and—life, and with matters of " must " and " may."

Sometimes and more particularly at first Bealby felt as though a ferocious beast lurked in the tramp and peered out through the fallen hank of hair and might leap out upon him, and sometimes he felt the tramp was large and fine and gay and amusing, more particularly when he lifted his voice and his bristling chin. And ever and again the talker became a nasty creature and a disgusting

creature, and his red-lit face was an ugly creeping
approach that made Bealby recoil. And then again he
was strong and wise. So the unstable needle of a boy's
moral compass spins.

The tramp used strange terms. He spoke of the
"deputy" and the "doss-house," of the "spike" and
"padding the hoof," of "screevers" and "tarts" and
"copper's narks." To these words Bealby attached such
meanings as he could, and so the things of which the
tramp talked floated unsurely into his mind and again
and again he had to readjust and revise his interpreta-
tions. And through these dim and fluctuating veils a
new side of life dawned upon his consciousness, a side
that was strange and lawless and dirty—in every way
dirty—and dreadful and—attractive. That was the
queer thing about it, that attraction. It had humour.
For all its squalor and repulsiveness it was lit by defiance
and laughter, bitter laughter perhaps but laughter. It
had a gaiety that Mr. Mergleson for example did not
possess, it had a penetration, like the penetrating quality
of onions or acids or asafœtida, that made the memory
of Mr. Darling insipid.

The tramp assumed from the outset that Bealby had
"done something" and run away, and some mysterious
etiquette prevented his asking directly what was the
nature of his offence. But he made a number of insidious soundings. And he assumed that Bealby was
taking to the life of the road and that, until good cause
to the contrary appeared, they were to remain together.
"It's a tough life," he said, "but it has its points, and
you got a toughish look about you."

He talked of roads and the quality of roads and
countryside. This was a good countryside; it wasn't
overdone and there was no great hostility to wanderers
and sleeping out. Some roads—the London to Brighton
for example—if a chap struck a match somebody came
running. But here unless you went pulling the hay-
stacks about too much they left you alone. And they

weren't such dead nuts on their pheasants, and one had a chance of an empty cowshed. "If I've spotted a shed or anything with a roof to it I stay out," said the tramp, "even if it's raining cats and dogs. Otherwise it's the doss'ouse or the 'spike.' It's the rain is the worst thing—getting wet. You haven't been wet yet, not if you only started Monday. Wet—with a chilly wind to drive it. Gaw! I been blown out of a holly hedge. You *would* think there'd be protection in a holly hedge. . . .

"Spike's the last thing," said the tramp, "I'd rather go bare-gutted to a doss-'ouse anywhen. Gaw!— you've not 'ad your first taste of the spike yet."

But it wasn't heaven in the doss-houses. He spoke of several of the landladies in strange but it would seem unflattering terms. "And there's always such a blamed lot of washing going on in a doss-'ouse. Always washing they are! One chap's washing 'is socks and another's washing 'is shirt. Making a steam drying it. Disgustin'. Carn't see what they want with it all. Bänd to git dirty again. . . ."

He discoursed of spikes, that is to say of workhouses, and of masters. "And then," he said with revolting yet alluring adjectives, "there's the bath.

"That's the worst side of it," said the tramp. . . . "'Owever it doesn't always rain, and if it doesn't rain, well, you can keep yourself dry."

He came back to the pleasanter aspects of the nomadic life. He was all for the outdoor style. "Ain't we comfortable 'ere?" he asked. He sketched out the simple larcenies that had contributed and given zest to the evening's meal. But it seemed there were also doss-houses that had the agreeable side. "Never been in one!" he said. "But where you been sleeping since Monday?"

Bealby described the caravan in phrases that seemed suddenly thin and anæmic to his ears.

"You hit it lucky," said the tramp. "If a chap's a

kid he strikes all sorts of luck of that sort. Now ef *I* come up against three ladies travellin' in a van—think they'd arst me in? Not it!"

He dwelt with manifest envy on the situation and the possibilities of the situation for some time. "You ain't dangerous," he said; "that's where you get in. . . ."

He consoled himself by anecdotes of remarkable good fortunes of a kindred description. Apparently he sometimes travelled in the company of a lady named Izzy Berners—"a fair scorcher, been a regular, slap-up circus actress." And there was also "good old Susan." It was a little difficult for Bealby to see the point of some of these flashes because of a tendency on the part of the tramp while his thoughts turned on these matters to adopt a staccato style of speech, punctuated by brief, darkly significant guffaws. There grew in the mind of Bealby a vision of the doss-house as a large crowded place, lit by a great central fire, with much cooking afoot and much jawing and disputing going on, and then "me and Izzy sailed in. . . ."

The fire sank, the darkness of the woods seemed to creep nearer. The moonlight pierced the trees only in long beams that seemed to point steadfastly at unseen things, it made patches of ashen light that looked like watching faces. Under the tramp's direction Bealby skirmished round and got sticks and fed the fire until the darkness and thoughts of a possible gorilla were driven back for some yards and the tramp pronounced the blaze a "fair treat." He had made a kind of bed of leaves which he now invited Bealby to extend and share, and lying feet to the fire he continued his discourse.

He talked of stealing and cheating by various endearing names; he made these enterprises seem adventurous and facetious; there was it seemed a peculiar sort of happy find one came upon called a "flat," that it was not only entertaining but obligatory to swindle. He made fraud seem so smart and bright at times that Bealby found it difficult to keep a firm grasp on the fact that it was—fraud. . . .

Bealby lay upon the leaves close up to the prone body of the tramp, and his mind and his standards became confused. The tramp's body was a dark but protecting ridge on one side of him; he could not see the fire beyond his toes but its flickerings were reflected by the tree stems about them, and made perplexing sudden movements that at times caught his attention and made him raise his head to watch them. . . . Against the terrors of the night the tramp had become humanity, the species, the moral basis. His voice was full of consolation; his topics made one forget the watchful silent circumambient. Bealby's first distrusts faded. He began to think the tramp a fine, brotherly, generous fellow. He was also growing accustomed to a faint something—shall I call it an olfactory bar—that had hitherto kept them apart. The monologue ceased to devote itself to the elucidation of Bealby; the tramp was lying on his back with his fingers interlaced beneath his head and talking not so much to his companion as to the stars and the universe at large. His theme was no longer the wandering life simply but the wandering life as he had led it, and the spiritedness with which he had led it and the real and admirable quality of himself. It was that soliloquy of consolation which is the secret preservative of innumerable lives.

He wanted to make it perfectly clear that he was a tramp by choice. He also wanted to make it clear that he was a tramp and no better because of the wicked folly of those he had trusted and the evil devices of enemies. In the world that contained those figures of spirit, Isobel Berners and Susan, there was also it seemed a bad and spiritless person, the tramp's wife, who had done him many passive injuries. It was clear she did not appreciate her blessings. She had been much to blame. "Anybody's opinion is better than 'er

'usband's," said the tramp. "Always 'as been." Bealby
had a sudden memory of Mr. Darling saying exactly
the same thing of his mother. "She's the sort," said
the tramp, "what would rather go to a meetin' than a
music 'all. She'd rather drop a shilling down a crack
than spend it on anything decent. If there was a choice
of jobs going she'd ask which 'ad the lowest pay and
the longest hours and she'd choose *that*. She'd feel
safer. She was born scared. When there wasn't anything else to do she'd stop at 'ome and scrub the floors.
Gaw! it made a chap want to put the darn' pail over
'er 'ed, so's she'd get enough of it. . . ."

"I don't hold with all this crawling through life and
saying *Please*," said the tramp. "I say it's *my* world
just as much as it's *your* world. You may have your
'orses and carriages, your 'ouses and country places and
all that, and you may think Gawd sent me to run abart
and work for you; but *I* don't. See?"

Bealby saw.

"I seek my satisfactions just as you seek your satisfactions, and if you want to get me to work you've jolly
well got to make me. I don't choose to work. I choose
to keep on my own and a bit loose, and take my chance
where I find it. You got to take your chances in this
world. Sometimes they come bad and sometimes they
come good. And very often you can't tell which it is
when they 'ave come. . . ."

Then he fell questioning Bealby again and then he
talked of the immediate future. He was beating for the
seaside. "Always something doing," he said. "You
got to keep your eye on for cops; those seaside benches,
they're 'ot on tramps—give you a month for begging
soon as look at you—but there's flats dropping sixpences thick as flies on a sore 'orse. You want a pal
there for all sorts of jobs. You're just the chap for it,
matey. Saw it soon's ever I set eyes on you. Then
you can 'ave fun. . . ."

He made projects. . . .

Finally he became more personal and very flattering.
"Now you and me," he said, suddenly shifting himself quite close to Bealby, "we're going to be downright pals. I've took a liking to you. Me and you are
going to pal together. See?"

He breathed into Bealby's face and laid a hand on his
knee and squeezed it, and Bealby, on the whole, felt
honoured by his protection. . . .

§ 4

In the unsympathetic light of a bright and pushful
morning the tramp was shorn of much of his overnight
glamour. It became manifest that he was not merely
offensively unshaven but extravagantly dirty. It was
not ordinary rural dirt. During the last few days he
must have had dealings of an intimate nature with
coal. He was taciturn and irritable, he declared that
this sleeping out would be the death of him, and the
breakfast was only too manifestly wanting in the
comforts of a refined home. He seemed a little less
embittered after breakfast, he became even faintly
genial, but he remained unpleasing. A distaste for the
tramp arose in Bealby's mind, and as he walked on
behind his guide and friend, he revolved schemes of unobtrusive detachment.

Far be it from me to accuse Bealby of ingratitude.
But it is true that that same disinclination which made
him a disloyal assistant to Mr. Mergleson was now
affecting his comradeship with the tramp. And he was
deceitful. He allowed the tramp to build projects in
the confidence of his continued adhesion, he did not
warn him of the defection he meditated. But on the
other hand Bealby had acquired from his mother an
effective horror of stealing. And one must admit, since
the tramp admitted it, that the man stole.

And another little matter had at the same time

estranged Bealby from the tramp and linked the two of them together. The attentive reader will know that Bealby had exactly two shillings and twopence-half-penny when he came down out of the woods to the fireside. He had Mrs. Bowles' half-crown and the balance of Madeleine Philips' theatre shilling, minus six-pence-halfpenny for a collar and sixpence he had given the tramp for the soup overnight. But all this balance was now in the pocket of the tramp. Money talks and the tramp had heard it. He had not taken it away from Bealby, but he had obtained it in this manner: "We two are pals," he said, "and one of us had better be Treasurer. That's Me. I know the ropes better. So hand over what you got there, matey."

And after he had pointed out that a refusal might lead to Bealby's evisceration the transfer occurred. Bealby was searched, kindly but firmly. . . .

It seemed to the tramp that this trouble had now blown over completely.

Little did he suspect the rebellious and treacherous thoughts that seethed in the head of his companion. Little did he suppose that his personal appearance, his manners, his ethical flavour—nay, even his physical flavour—were being judged in a spirit entirely un-amiable. It seemed to him that he had obtained youthful and subservient companionship, companionship that would be equally agreeable and useful; he had adopted a course that he imagined would cement the ties between them; he reckoned not with ingratitude. "If anyone arsts you who I am, call me uncle," he said. He walked along, a little in advance, sticking his toes out right and left in a peculiar wide pace that character-ised his walk, and revolving schemes for the happiness and profit of the day. To begin with—great draughts of beer. Then tobacco. Later perhaps, some bread and cheese for Bealby. "You can't come in 'ere," he said at the first public-house. "You're under age, me boy. It ain't my doing, matey; it's 'Erbert Samuel.

You blame 'im. 'E don't objec' to you going to work
for any other Mr. Samuel there may 'appen to be abart
or anything of that sort, that's good for you, that is;
but 'e's most particular you shouldn't go into a public-
'ouse. So you just wait outside 'ere. *I'll* 'ave my eye
on you."

"You going to spend my money?" asked Bealby.

"I'm going to ration the party," said the tramp.

"You—you got no right to spend my money," said
Bealby.

"I— 'Ang it— I'll get you some acid drops," said
the tramp in tones of remonstrance. "I tell you,
blame you,—it's 'Erbert Samuel. I can't 'elp it! I
can't fight against the lor."

"You 'aven't any right to spend my money," said
Bealby.

"*Down't* cut up crusty. 'Ow can *I* 'elp it?"

"I'll tell a policeman. You gimme back my money
and lemme go."

The tramp considered the social atmosphere. It did
not contain a policeman. It contained nothing but a
peaceful kindly corner public-house, a sleeping dog and
the back of an elderly man digging.

The tramp approached Bealby in a confidential
manner. "Oo's going to believe you?" he said. "And
besides, 'ow did you come by it?"

Moreover. "*I* ain't going to spend *your* money. I
got money of my own. *'Ere!* See?" And suddenly
before the dazzled eyes of Bealby he held and instantly
withdrew three shillings and two coppers that seemed
familiar. He had had a shilling of his own. . . .

Bealby waited outside. . . .

The tramp emerged in a highly genial mood, with
acid drops, and a short clay pipe going strong. "'Ere,"
he said to Bealby with just the faintest flavour of
magnificence over the teeth-held pipe and handed over
not only the acid drops but a virgin short clay. "Fill,"
he said, proffering the tobacco. "It's yours jus' much

as it's mine. Be'r not let 'Erbert Samuel see you though; that's all. 'E's got a lor abart it."

Bealby held his pipe in his clenched hand. He had already smoked—once. He remembered it quite vividly still, although it had happened six months ago. Yet he hated not using that tobacco. "No," he said, "I'll smoke later."

The tramp replaced the screw of red Virginia in his pocket with the air of one who has done the gentlemanly thing. . . .

They went on their way, an ill-assorted couple.

All day Bealby chafed at the tie and saw the security in the tramp's pocket vanish. They lunched on bread and cheese and then the tramp had a good sustaining drink of beer for both of them, and after that they came to a common where it seemed agreeable to repose. And after a due meed of repose in a secluded hollow among the gorse the tramp produced a pack of exceedingly greasy cards and taught Bealby to play Euchre. Apparently the tramp had no distinctive pockets in his tail coat, the whole lining was one capacious pocket. Various knobs and bulges indicated his cooking tin, his feeding tin, a turnip and other unknown properties. At first they played for love and then they played for the balance in the tramp's pocket. And by the time Bealby had learned Euchre thoroughly, that balance belonged to the tramp. But he was very generous about it and said they would go on sharing just as they had done. And then he became confidential. He scratched about in the bagginess of his garment and drew out a little dark blade of stuff, like a flint implement, regarded it gravely for a moment and held it out to Bealby. "Guess what this is."

Bealby gave it up.

"Smell it."

It smelled very nasty. One familiar smell indeed there was with a paradoxical sanitary quality that he did not quite identify, but that was a mere basis for a complex reek of acquisitions. " What is it ?" said Bealby.

" *Soap !*"

" But what's it for ?"

" I thought you'd ask that. . . . What's soap usually for ?"

" Washing," said Bealby guessing wildly.

The tramp shook his head. " Making a foam," he corrected. " That's what I has my fits with. See ? I shoves a bit in my mouth and down I goes and I rolls about. Making a sort of moaning sound. Why, I been given brandy often—neat brandy. . . . It isn't always a cert—nothing's absolutely a cert. I've 'ad some let-downs. . . . Once I was bit by a nasty little dog— that brought me to pretty quick, and once I 'ad an old gentleman go through my pockets. ' Poor chap !' 'e ses, ' very likely 'e's destitoot, let's see if 'e's *got* any-thing.' . . . I'd got all sorts of things, I didn't want *'im* prying about. But I didn't come-to sharp enough to stop 'im. Got me into trouble that did. . . ."

" It's an old lay," said the tramp, " but it's astonish-ing 'ow it'll go in a quiet village. Sort of amuses 'em. Or dropping suddenly in front of a bicycle party. Lot of them old tricks are the best tricks, and there ain't many of 'em Billy Bridget don't know. That's where you're lucky to 'ave met me, matey. Billy Bridget's a 'ard man to starve. And I know the ropes. I know what you *can* do and what you can't do. And I got a feeling for a policeman—same as some people 'ave for cats. I'd know if one was 'idden in the room."

He expanded into anecdotes and the story of various encounters in which he shone. It was amusing and it took Bealby on his weak side. Wasn't he the Champion Dodger of the Chelsome playground ?

The tide of talk ebbed. " Well," said the tramp, " time we was up and doing. . . ."

They went along shady lanes and across an open park, and they skirted a breezy common from which they could see the sea. And among other things that the tramp said was this, "Time we began to forage a bit."

He turned his large observant nose to the right of him and the left.

§ 5

Throughout the afternoon the tramp discoursed upon the rights and wrongs of property, in a way that Bealby found very novel and unsettling. The tramp seemed to have his ideas about owning and stealing arranged quite differently from those of Bealby. Never before had Bealby thought it possible to have them arranged in any other than the way he knew. But the tramp contrived to make most possession seem unrighteous and honesty a code devised by those who have for those who haven't. "They've just got hold of it," he said. "They want to keep it to themselves. . . . Do I look as though I'd stole much of anybody's? It isn't me got 'old of this land and sticking up my notice boards to keep everybody off. It isn't me spends my days and nights scheming 'ow I can get 'old of more and more of the stuff. . . .

"I don't *envy* it 'em," said the tramp. "Some 'as one taste and some another. But when it comes to making all this fuss because a chap who *isn't* a schemer 'elps 'imself to a mäthful,—well, it's Rot. . . .

"It's them makes the rules of the game and nobody ever arst me to play it. I don't blame 'em, mind you. Me and you might very well do the same. But brast me if I see where the sense of *my* keeping the rules comes in. This world ought to be a share out. Gawd meant it to be a share out. And me and you—we been done out of our share. That justifies us."

"It isn't right to steal," said Bealby.

"It isn't right to steal—certainly. It isn't right— but it's universal. Here's a chap here over this fence, ask 'im where 'e got 'is land. Stealing! What you call stealing, matey, *I* call restitootion. You ain't probably never even 'eard of socialism."

"I've 'eard of socialists right enough. Don't believe in Gawd and 'aven't no morality."

"Don't you believe it. Why!—'Arf the socialists are parsons. What I'm saying *is* socialism—practically. *I'm* a socialist. I know all abät socialism. There isn't nothing you can tell me abät socialism. Why!—for three weeks I was one of these here Anti-Socialist speakers. Paid for it. And I tell you there ain't such a thing as property left; it's all a blooming old pinch. Lords, commons, judges, all of them they're just a crew of brasted old fences and the lawyers getting in the stuff. Then you talk to me of stealing! *Stealing!*"

The tramp's contempt and his long intense way of saying "stealing" were very unsettling to a sensitive mind.

They bought some tea and grease in a village shop and the tramp made tea in his old tin with great dexterity, and then they gnawed bread on which two ounces of margarine had been generously distributed. "Live like fighting cocks, we do," said the tramp wiping out his simple cuisine with the dragged-out end of his shirt sleeve. "And if I'm not very much mistaken we'll sleep to-night on a nice bit of hay. . . ."

But these anticipations were upset by a sudden temptation, and instead of a starry summer comfort the two were destined to spend a night of suffering and remorse.

A green lane lured them off the road, and after some windings led them past a field of wire-netted enclosures containing a number of perfect and conceited-looking hens close beside a little cottage, a vegetable garden and some new elaborate outhouses. It was manifestly a poultry farm, and something about it gave the tramp the conviction that it had been left, that nobody was at home.

These realisations are instinctive, they leap to the

mind. He knew it, and an ambition to know further what was in the cottage came with the knowledge. But it seemed to him desirable that the work of exploration should be done by Bealby. He had thought of dogs, and it seemed to him that Bealby might be unembarrassed by that idea. So he put the thing to Bealby. "Let's have a look round 'ere," he said. "You go in and see what's abät. . . ."

There was some difference of opinion. "I don't ask you to take anything," said the tramp. . . . "Nobody won't catch you. . . . I tell you nobody won't catch you. . . . I tell you there ain't nobody here to catch you. . . . Just for the fun of seeing in. I'll go up by them outhouses. And I'll see nobody comes. . . . Ain't afraid to go up a garden path, are you? . . . I tell you, I don't want you to steal. . . . You ain't got much guts to funk a thing like that. . . . I'll be abät too. . . . Thought you'd be the very chap for a bit of scouting. . . . Well, if you ain't afraid you'd do it. . . . Well, why didn't you say you'd do it at the beginning? . . ."

Bealby went through the hedge and up a grass track between poultry runs, made a cautious inspection of the outhouses and then approached the cottage. Everything was still. He thought it more plausible to go to the door than peep into the window. He rapped. Then after an interval of stillness he lifted the latch, opened the door and peered into the room. It was a pleasantly furnished room, and before the empty summer fireplace a very old white man was sitting in a chints-covered armchair, lost it would seem in painful thought. He had a peculiar grey shrunken look, his eyes were closed, a bony hand with the shiny texture of alabaster gripped the chair arm. . . . There was something about him that held Bealby quite still for a moment.

And this old gentleman behaved very oddly.

His body seemed to crumple into his chair, his hands slipped down from the arms, his head nodded forwards and his mouth and eyes seemed to open together. And he made a snoring sound. . . .

For a moment Bealby remained rigidly agape and then a violent desire to rejoin the tramp carried him back through the hen-runs. . . .

He tried to describe what he had seen.

"Asleep with his mouth open," said the tramp. "Well, that ain't anything so wonderful. You *got* anything? That's what I want to know. . . . Did anyone ever see such a boy? 'Ere! I'll go. . . .

"You keep a look out here," said the tramp.

But there was something about that old man in there, something so strange and alien to Bealby, that he could not remain alone in the falling twilight. He followed the cautious advances of the tramp towards the house. From the corner by the outhouses he saw the tramp go and peer in at the open door. He remained for some time peering; his head hidden from Bealby. . . .

Then he went in. . . .

Bealby had an extraordinary desire that somebody else would come. His soul cried out for help against some vaguely apprehended terror. And in the very moment of his wish came its fulfilment. He saw advancing up the garden path a tall woman in a blue serge dress, hatless and hurrying and carrying a little package—it was medicine—in her hand. And with her came a big black dog. At the sight of Bealby the dog came forward barking, and Bealby after a moment's hesitation turned and fled.

The dog was quick. But Bealby was quicker. He went up the netting of a hen-run and gave the dog no more than an ineffectual snap at his heels. And then dashing from the cottage door came the tramp. Under one arm was a brass-bound workbox and in the other was a candlestick and some smaller articles. He did not instantly grasp the situation of his treed companion, he was too anxious to escape the tall woman, and then with a yelp of dismay he discovered himself between

woman and dog. All too late he sought to emulate
Bealby. The workbox slipped from under his arm,
the rest of his plunder fell from him, for an uneasy
moment he was clinging to the side of the swaying
hen-run and then it had caved in and the dog had
got him.

The dog bit, desisted and then finding itself confronted by two men retreated. Bealby and the tramp
rolled and scrambled over the other side of the collapsed
netting into a parallel track and were half-way to the
hedge before the dog,—but this time in a less vehement
fashion,—resumed his attack.

He did not close with them again and at the hedge
he halted altogether and remained hacking the gloaming
with his rage.

The woman it seemed had gone into the house,
leaving the tramp's scattered loot upon the field of
battle.

"This means mizzle," said the tramp, leading the
way at a trot.

Bealby saw no other course but to follow.

He had a feeling as though the world had turned
against him. He did not dare to think what he was
thinking of the events of these crowded ten minutes.
He felt he had touched something dreadful; that the
twilight was full of accusations. . . . He feared and
hated the tramp now, but he perceived something had
linked them as they had not been linked before. Whatever it was they shared it.

§ 6

They fled through the night; it seemed to Bealby for
interminable hours. At last when they were worn out
and footsore they crept through a gate and found an
uncomfortable cowering-place in the corner of a field.

As they went they talked but little, but the tramp
kept up a constant muttering to himself. He was

troubled by the thought of hydrophobia. " I know I'll
'ave it," he said, " I know I'll get it."

Bealby after a time ceased to listen to his companion. His mind was preoccupied. He could think
of nothing but that very white man in the chair and
the strange manner of his movement.

" Was 'e awake when you saw 'im?" he asked at last.

" Awake—who?"

" That old man."

For a moment or so the tramp said nothing.

" 'E wasn't awake, you young silly," he said at last.

" But—wasn't he?"

" Why!—don't you know! 'E'd croaked,—popped
off the 'ooks—very moment you saw 'im."

For a moment Bealby's voice failed him.

Then he said quite faintly, " You mean—he'd—
Was dead?"

" Didn't you know?" said the tramp.   " Gaw!
What a kid you are!"

In that manner it was Bealby first saw a dead man.
Never before had he seen anyone dead.   And after
that for all the night the old white man pursued him,
with strange slowly-opening eyes, and a head on one
side and his mouth suddenly and absurdly agape. . . .

All night long that white figure presided over seas
of dark dismay. It seemed always to be there, and
yet Bealby thought of a score of other painful things.
For the first time in his life he asked himself, " Where
am I going? What am I drifting to?" The world beneath the old man's dominance was a world of prisons.

Bealby believed he was a burglar, and behind the
darkness he imagined the outraged law already seeking
him. And the terrors of his associate reinforced his
own.

He tried to think what he should do in the morning.
He dreaded the dawn profoundly. But he could not
collect his thoughts because of the tramp's incessant
lapses into grumbling lamentation. Bealby knew he

26

had to get away from the tramp, but now he was too
weary and alarmed to think of running away as a possible expedient. And besides there was the matter of
his money. And beyond the range of the tramp's voice
there were darknesses which to-night at least might
hold inconceivable forms of lurking evil. But could
he not appeal to the law to save him? Repent. Was
there not something called turning King's Evidence?

The moon was no comfort that night. Across it
there passed with incredible slowness a number of
jagged little black clouds, blacker than any clouds
Bealby had ever seen before. They were like velvet
palls, lined with snowy fur. There was no end to
them. And one at last most horribly gaped slowly and
opened a mouth. . . .

§ 7

At intervals there would be uncomfortable movements and the voice of the tramp came out of the darkness beside Bealby lamenting his approaching fate and
discoursing—sometimes with violent expressions—on
watch-dogs.

"I know I shall 'ave 'idrophobia," said the tramp.
"I've always 'ad a disposition to 'idrophobia. Always
a dread of water—and now it's got me.

"Think of it!—keeping a beast to set at a 'uman
being. Where's the brotherhood of it? Where's the
law and the humanity? Getting a animal to set at a
brother man. And a poisoned animal, a animal with
death in his teeth. And a 'orrible death too. Where's
the sense and brotherhood?

"Gaw! when I felt 'is teeth coming through my
träsers—!

"Dogs oughtn't to be allowed. They're a noosance
in the towns and a danger in the country. They
oughtn't to be allowed anywhere—not till every
blessed 'uman being 'as got three square meals a day.

Then if you like, keep a dog. And see 'e's a clean dog. . . .

"Gaw! if I'd been a bit quicker up that 'en roost——!

"I ought to 'ave landed him a kick.

"It's a man's duty to 'urt a dog. When 'e sees a dog 'e ought to 'urt 'im. It's a natural 'atred. If dogs were what they ought to be, if dogs understood 'ow they're situated, there wouldn't be a dog go for a man ever.

"And if one did they'd shoot 'im. . . .

"After this if ever I get a chance to land a dog a oner with a stone I'll land 'im one. I been too sorft with dogs. . . ."

Towards dawn Bealby slept uneasily, to be awakened by the loud snorting curiosity of three lively young horses. He sat up in a blinding sunshine and saw the tramp looking very filthy and contorted, sleeping with his mouth wide open and an expression of dismay and despair on his face.

§ 8

Bealby took his chance to steal away next morning while the tramp was engaged in artificial epilepsy.

"I feel like fits this morning," said the tramp. "I could do it well. I want a bit of human kindness again. After that brasted dog.

"I expect soon I'll 'ave the foam all right withat any soap."

They marked down a little cottage before which a benevolent-looking spectacled old gentleman in a large straw hat and a thin alpaca jacket was engaged in budding roses. Then they retired to prepare. The tramp handed over to Bealby various compromising possessions, which might embarrass an afflicted person under the searching hands of charity. There was for example the piece of soap after he had taken sufficient for his immediate needs, there was ninepence in money, there were the pack of cards with which they had played Euchre, a key or so and some wires, much assorted string, three tins, a large piece of bread, the end of a composite candle, a box of sulphur matches, list slippers, a pair of gloves, a clasp knife, sundry grey rags. They all seemed to have the distinctive flavour of the tramp.

"If you do a bunk with these," said the tramp. "By Gawd——"

He drew his finger across his throat.

(King's Evidence.)

Bealby from a safe distance watched the beginnings of the fit, and it impressed him as a thoroughly nasty kind of fit. He saw the elderly gentleman hurry out of the cottage and stand for a moment looking over his little green garden gate, surveying the sufferings of the tramp with an expression of intense yet discreet commiseration. Then suddenly he was struck by an idea, he darted in among his rose bushes and reappeared with a big watering-can and an enormous syringe. Still keeping the gate between himself and the sufferer he loaded his syringe very carefully and deliberately. . . .

Bealby would have liked to see more, but he felt his moment had come. Another instant and it might be gone again. Very softly he dropped from the gate on which he was sitting and made off like a running partridge along the hedge of the field.

Just for a moment did he halt—at a strange sharp yelp that came from the direction of the little cottage. Then his purpose of flight resumed its control of him.

He would strike across country for two or three miles, then make for the nearest police station and give himself up. (Loud voices. Was that the tramp murdering the benevolent old gentleman in the straw hat, or was it the benevolent old gentleman in the straw hat murdering the tramp? No time to question. Onward, Onward!) The tramp's cans rattled in his pocket. He drew one out, hesitated a moment and flung it away and then sent its two companions after it. . . .

He found his police station upon the road between Someport and Crayminster, a little peaceful rural station, a mere sunny cottage with a blue and white label and a notice board covered with belated bills about the stealing of pheasants' eggs. And another bill——

It was headed MISSING and the next most conspicuous words were £5 REWARD and the next ARTHUR BEALBY.

He was fascinated. So swift, so terribly swift is the law. Already they knew of his burglary, of his callous participation in the robbing of a dead man. Already the sleuths were upon his trail. So surely did his conscience strike to this conclusion that even the carelessly worded offer of a reward that followed his description conveyed no different intimation to his mind. " To whomsoever will bring him back to Lady Laxton, at Shonts near Chelsmore," so it ran.

" And out of pocket expenses."

And even as Bealby read this terrible document, the door of the police station opened and a very big pink young policeman came out and stood regarding the world in a friendly, self-approving manner. He had innocent, happy, blue eyes; thus far he had had much to do with order and little with crime; and his rosebud mouth would have fallen open, had not discipline already closed it and set upon it the beginnings of a resolute expression that accorded ill with the rest of his open freshness. And when he had surveyed the sky and the distant hills and the little rose bushes that occupied the leisure of the force, his eyes fell upon Bealby. . . .

Indecision has ruined more men than wickedness. And when one has slept rough and eaten nothing and one is conscious of a marred unclean appearance, it is hard to face one's situations. What Bealby had intended to do was to go right up to a policeman and say to him, simply and frankly: "I want to turn King's Evidence, please. I was in that burglary where there was a dead old man and a workbox and a woman and a dog. I was led astray by a bad character and I did not mean to do it. And really it was him that did it and not me."

But now his tongue clove to the roof of his mouth, he felt he could not speak, could not go through with it. His heart had gone down into his feet. Perhaps he had caught the tramp's constitutional aversion to the police. He affected not to see the observant figure in the doorway. He assumed a slack careless bearing like one who reads by chance idly. He lifted his eyebrows to express unconcern. He pursed his mouth to whistle but no whistle came. He stuck his hands into his pockets, pulled up his feet as one pulls up plants by the roots and strolled away.

He quickened his stroll as he supposed by imperceptible degrees. He glanced back and saw that the young policeman had come out of the station and was reading the notice. And as the young policeman read he looked ever and again at Bealby like one who checks off items.

Bealby quickened his pace and then, doing his best to suggest by the movements of his back a mere boyish levity quite unconnected with the law, he broke into a trot.

Then presently he dropped back into a walking pace, pretended to see something in the hedge, stopped and took a sidelong look at the young policeman.

He was coming along with earnest strides, every movement of his suggested a stealthy hurry!

Bealby trotted and then becoming almost frank about it, ran. He took to his heels.

From the first it was not really an urgent chase; it was a stalking rather than a hunt, because the young policeman was too young and shy and lacking in confidence really to run after a boy without any definite warrant for doing so. When anyone came along he would drop into a smart walk and pretend not to be looking at Bealby but just going somewhere briskly. And after two miles of it he desisted, and stood for a time watching a heap of mangold wurzel directly and the disappearance of Bealby obliquely, and then when Bealby was quite out of sight he turned back thoughtfully towards his proper place.

On the whole he considered he was well out of it. He might have made a fool of himself. . . .

And yet,—five pounds reward!

CHAPTER THE SEVENTH

The Battle of Crayminster

§ 1

BEALBY was beginning to realise that running away from one's situation and setting up for oneself is not so easy and simple a thing as it had appeared during those first days with the caravan. Three things he perceived had arisen to pursue him, two that followed in the daylight, the law and the tramp, and a third that came back at twilight, the terror of the darkness. And within there was a hollow faintness, for the afternoon was far advanced and he was extremely hungry. He had dozed away the early afternoon in the weedy corner of a wood. But for his hunger I think he would have avoided Crayminster.

Within a mile of that place he had come upon the "Missing" notice again, stuck to the end of a barn. He had passed it askance, and then with a sudden inspiration returned and torn it down. Somehow with the daylight his idea of turning King's Evidence against the tramp had weakened. He no longer felt sure.

Mustn't one wait and be asked first to turn King's Evidence?

Suppose they said he had merely confessed. . . .

The Crayminster street had a picturesque nutritious look. Half-way down it was the White Hart with cyclist club signs on its walls and geraniums over a white porch, and beyond a house being built and already at the roofing pitch. To the right was a baker's shop diffusing a delicious suggestion of buns and cake, and to the left a little comfortable sweetstuff window and a glimpse of tables and a board : "Teas." Tea! He resolved to break into his ninepence boldly and generously. Very likely they would boil him an egg for a penny or so. Yet on the other hand if he just had three or four buns, soft new buns. He hovered towards the baker's shop and stopped short. That bill was in the window!

He wheeled about sharply and went into the sweet-stuff shop and found a table with a white cloth and a motherly little woman in a large cap. Tea? He could have an egg and some thick bread-and-butter and a cup of tea for fivepence. He sat down respectfully to await her preparations.

But he was uneasy.

He knew quite well that she would ask him questions. For that he was prepared. He said he was walking from his home in London to Someport to save the fare. "But you're so dirty!" said the motherly little woman. "I sent my luggage by post, ma'am, and I lost my way and didn't get it. And I don't much mind ma'am, if you don't. Not washing. . . ."

All that he thought he did quite neatly. But he wished there was not that bill in the baker's window opposite and he wished he hadn't quite such a hunted feeling. A faint claustrophobia affected him. He felt the shop might be a trap. He would be glad to get into the open again. Was there a way out behind if, for example, a policeman blocked the door? He hovered to the entrance while his egg was boiling, and then when he saw a large fat baker surveying the world with

26*

an afternoon placidity upon his face, he went back
and sat by the table. He wondered if the baker had
noted him.

He had finished his egg; he was drinking his tea
with appreciative noises, when he discovered that the
baker *had* noted him. Bealby's eyes, at first inanely
open above the tilting teacup, were suddenly riveted on
something that was going on in the baker's window.
From where he sat he could see that detestable bill,
and then slowly feeling about for it, he beheld a hand
and a floury sleeve. The bill was drawn up and
vanished, and then behind a glass shelf of fancy bread
and a glass shelf of buns something pink and indistinct
began to move jerkily. . . . It was a human face and
it was trying to peer into the little refreshment shop
that sheltered Bealby. . . .

Bealby's soul went faint.

He had one inadequate idea. "Might I go out," he
said, "by your back way?"

"There isn't a back way," said the motherly little
woman. "There's a yard——"

"If I might," said Bealby and was out in it.

No way at all! High walls on every side. He was
back like a shot in the shop, and now the baker was
half-way across the road. "Fivepence," said Bealby,
and gave the little old woman sixpence. "Here," she
cried, "take your penny!"

He did not wait. He darted out of the door.

The baker was all over the way of escape. He extended arms that seemed abnormally long and with a
weak cry Bealby found himself trapped. Trapped,
but not hopelessly. He knew how to do it. He had
done it in milder forms before, but now he did it with
all his being. Under the diaphragm of the baker
smote Bealby's hard little head, and instantly he was
away running up the quiet sunny street. Man when
he assumed the erect attitude made a hostage of his
belly. It is a proverb among the pastoral Berbers of

the Atlas mountains that the man who extends his
arms in front of an angry ram is a fool.

It seemed probable to Bealby that he would get
away up the street. The baker was engaged in
elaborately falling backward, making the most of sitting
down in the road, and the wind had been knocked out
of him so that he could not shout. He emitted "Stop
him!" in large whispers. Away ahead there were only
three builder's men sitting under the wall beyond the
White Hart, consuming tea out of their tea-cans. But
the boy who was trimming the top of the tall privet
hedge outside the doctor's saw the assault of the baker
and incontinently uttered the shout that the baker
could not. Also he fell off his steps with great alacrity
and started in pursuit of Bealby. A young man from
anywhere—perhaps the grocer's shop—also started for
Bealby. But the workmen were slow to rise to the
occasion. Bealby could have got past them. And
then, abruptly at the foot of the street ahead, the tramp
came into view, a battered disconcerting figure. His
straw-coloured hat which had recently been wetted
and dried in the sun was a swaying mop. The sight of
Bealby seemed to rouse him from some disagreeable
meditations. He grasped the situation with a terrible
quickness. Regardless of the wisdom of the pastoral
Berbers he extended his arms and stood prepared to
intercept.

Bealby thought at the rate of a hundred thoughts
to the minute. He darted sideways and was up the
ladder and among the beams and rafters of the unfinished roof before the pursuit had more than begun.
"Here, come off that," cried the foreman builder, only
now joining in the hunt with any sincerity. He came
across the road while Bealby regarded him wickedly
from the rafters above. Then as the good man made
to ascend Bealby got him neatly on the hat—it was a
bowler hat—with a tile. This checked the advance.
There was a disposition to draw a little off and look up

at Bealby. One of the younger builders from the opposite sidewalk got him very neatly in the ribs with a stone. But two other shots went wide, and Bealby shifted to a more covered position behind the chimney-stack.

From here however he had a much less effective command of the ladder, and he perceived that his tenure of the new house was not likely to be a long one.

Below men parleyed. "Who *is* 'e?" asked the foreman builder. "Where'd 'e come from?"

"'E's a brasted little thief," said the tramp. "'E's one of the wust characters on the road."

The baker was recovering his voice now. "There's a reward out for 'im," he said, "and 'e butted me in the stummick."

"'Ow much reward?" asked the foreman builder.

"Five pound for the man who catches him."

"'Ere!" cried the foreman builder in an arresting voice to the tramp. "Just stand away from that ladder. . . ."

Whatever else Bealby might or might not be, one thing was very clear about him and that was that he was a fugitive. And the instinct of humanity is to pursue fugitives. Man is a hunting animal, inquiry into the justice of a case is an altogether later accretion to his complex nature, and that is why, whatever you are or whatever you do you should never let people get you on the run. There is joy in the mere fact of hunting, the sight of a scarlet coat and a hound will brighten a whole village, and now Crayminster was rousing itself like a sleeper who wakes to sunshine and gay music. People were looking out of windows and coming out of shops, a policeman appeared and heard the baker's simple story, a brisk hatless young man in a white apron and with a pencil behind his ear became prominent. Bealby, peeping over the ridge of the roof, looked a thoroughly dirty and unpleasant little creature to all these people. The only spark of human sympathy for him below was in the heart of the little old woman in the cap who had given him his breakfast. She surveyed the roof of the new house from the door of her shop, she hoped Bealby wouldn't hurt himself up there, and she held his penny change clutched in her hand in her apron pocket with a vague idea that perhaps presently if he ran past she could very quickly give it him.

§ 2

Considerable delay in delivering the assault on the house was caused by the foreman's insistence that he alone should ascend the ladder to capture Bealby. He was one of those regular-featured men with large heads who seem to have inflexible backbones, he was large and fair and full with a sweetish chest voice, and in all his movements authoritative and deliberate. Whenever he made to ascend he discovered that people were straying into his building, and he had to stop and direct his men how to order them off. Inside his large head he was trying to arrange everybody to cut off Bealby's line of retreat without risking that anybody but himself should capture the fugitive. It was none too easy and it knitted his brows. Meanwhile Bealby was able to reconnoitre the adjacent properties and to conceive plans for a possible line of escape. He also got a few tiles handy against when the rush up the ladder came. At the same time two of the younger workmen were investigating the possibility of getting at him from inside the house. There was still no staircase, but there were ways of clambering. They had heard about the reward and they knew that they must do this before the foreman realised their purpose, and this a little retarded them. In their pockets they had a number of stones, ammunition in reserve, if it came again to throwing.

Bealby was no longer fatigued nor depressed; anxiety for the future was lost in the excitement of the present, and his heart told him that, come what might, getting on to the roof was an extraordinarily good dodge.

And if only he could bring off a certain jump he had in mind, there were other dodges. . . .

In the village street an informal assembly of leading citizens, a little recovered now from their first nervousness about flying tiles, discussed the problem of Bealby. There was Mumby, the draper and vegetarian, with the bass voice and the big black beard. He advocated the fire engine. He was one of the volunteer fire brigade and never so happy as when he was wearing his helmet. He had come out of his shop, at the shouting. Schocks the butcher, and his boy were also in the street; Schocks's yard with its heap of manure and fodder bounded the new house on the left. Rymell the vet emerged from the billiard-room of the White Hart, and with his head a little on one side was watching Bealby and replying inattentively to the baker, who was asking him a number of questions that struck him as irrelevant. All the White Hart people were in the street.

"I suppose, Mr. Rymell," said the baker, "there's a mort of dangerous things in a man's belly round about 'is Stummick?"

"Tiles," said Mr. Rymell. "Loose bricks. It wouldn't do if he started dropping those."

"I was saying, Mr. Rymell," said the baker after a pause for digestion, "is a man likely to be injured badly by a Blaw in his stummick?"

Mr. Rymell stared at him for a moment with unresponsive eyes. "More likely to get you in the head," he said, and then, "Here! What's that fool of a carpenter going to do?"

The tramp was hovering on the outskirts of the groups of besiegers, vindictive but dispirited. He had been brought to from his fit and given a shilling by the old gentleman, but he was dreadfully wet between his shirt—he wore a shirt, under three waistcoats and a coat—and his skin, because the old gentleman's method of revival had been to syringe him suddenly with cold water. It had made him weep with astonishment and misery. Now he saw no advantage in claiming Bealby publicly. His part, he felt, was rather a waiting one. What he had to say to Bealby could be best said without the assistance of a third person. And he wanted to understand more of this talk about a reward. If there was a reward out for Bealby——

"That's not a bad dodge!" said Rymell, changing his opinion of the foreman suddenly as that individual began his ascent of the ladder with a bricklayer's hod carried shield-wise above his head. He went up with difficulty and slowly because of the extreme care he took to keep his head protected. But no tiles came. Bealby had discovered a more dangerous attack developing inside the house and was already in retreat down the other side of the building.

He did a leap that might have hurt him badly, taking off from the corner of the house and jumping a good twelve feet on to a big heap of straw in the butcher's yard. He came down on all fours and felt a little jarred for an instant, and then he was up again and had scrambled up by a heap of manure to the top of the butcher's wall. He was over that and into Maccullum's yard next door before anyone in the front of the new house had realised that he was in flight. Then one of the two workmen who had been coming up inside the house saw him from the oblong opening that was some day to be the upstairs bedroom window, and gave tongue.

It was thirty seconds later and after Bealby had vanished from the butcher's wall that the foreman, still clinging to his hod, appeared over the ridge of the roof. At the workmen's shout the policeman who, with the preventive disposition of his profession, had hitherto been stopping anyone from coming into the unfinished house, turned about and ran out into its brick and plaster and timber-littered backyard, whereupon the crowd in the street realising that the quarry had gone away and no longer restrained, came pouring partly through the house and partly round through the butcher's gate into his yard.

Bealby had had a check.

He had relied upon the tarred felt roof of the mushroom shed of Maccullum the tailor and breeches-maker to get him to the wall that gave upon Mr. Benshaw's strawberry fields, and he had not seen from his roof above the ramshackle glazed outhouse which Maccullum called his workroom and in which four industrious tailors were working in an easy déshabillé. The roof of the shed was the merest tarred touchwood, it had perished as felt long ago, it collapsed under Bealby, he went down into a confusion of mushrooms and mushroom bed, he blundered out trailing mushrooms and spawn and rich matter, he had a ninefoot wall to negotiate and only escaped by a hair's-breadth from the clutch of a little red-slippered man who came dashing out from the workroom. But by a happy use of the top of the dustbin he did just get away over the wall in time, and the red-slippered tailor who was not good at walls was left struggling to imitate an ascent that had looked easy enough until he came to try it.

For a moment the little tailor struggled alone, and then both Maccullum's domain and the butcher's yard next door and the narrow patch of space behind the new house, were violently injected with a crowd of active people, all confusedly on the Bealby trail. Someone, he never knew who, gave the little tailor a leg-up and then his red slippers twinkled over the wall and he was leading the hunt into the market gardens of Mr. Benshaw. A collarless colleague in list slippers and conspicuous braces followed. The policeman, after he had completed the wreck of Mr. Maccullum's mushroom shed, came next, and then Mr. Maccullum, with no sense of times and seasons, anxious to have a discussion at once upon the question of this damage.

Mr. Maccullum was out of breath and he never got farther with this projected conversation than " Here !" This was repeated several times as opportunity seemed to offer. The remaining tailors got to the top of the wall more sedately with the help of the Maccullum kitchen steps and dropped; Mr. Schocks followed breathing hard, and then a fresh jet of humanity came squirting into the gardens through a gap in the fence at the back of the building site. This was led by the young workman who had first seen Bealby go away. Hard behind him came Rymell, the vet, the grocer's assistant, the doctor's page-boy and, less briskly, the baker. Then the tramp. Then Mumby and Schocks's boy. Then a number of other people. The seeking of Bealby had assumed the dimensions of a Hue and Cry.

The foreman with the large head and the upright back was still on the new roof; he was greatly distressed at the turn things had taken and shouted his claims to a major share in the capture of Bealby, mixed with his opinions of Bealby and a good deal of mere swearing, to a sunny but unsympathetic sky. . . .

§ 3

Mr. Benshaw was a small holder, a sturdy English yeoman of the new school. He was an Anti-Socialist, a self-helper, an independent-spirited man. He had a steadily growing banking account and a plain but sterile wife, and he was dark in complexion and so erect in his bearing as to seem a little to lean backward. Usually he wore a sort of grey gamekeeper's suit with brown gaiters (except on Sundays when the coat was black), he was addicted to bowler hats that accorded ill with his large grave grey-coloured face, and he was altogether a very sound young man. His bowler hats did but accentuate that. He had no time for vanities, even the vanity of dressing consistently. He went into the nearest shop and just bought the cheapest hat he could, and so he got hats designed for the youthful and giddy, hats with flighty crowns and flippant bows and amorous brims that undulated attractively to set off flushed and foolish young faces. It made his unrelenting mask look rather like the Puritans under the Stuart monarchy.

He was a horticulturist rather than a farmer. He had begun his career in cheap lodgings with a field of early potatoes and cabbages, supplemented by employment, but with increased prosperity his area of cultivation had extended and his methods intensified. He now grew considerable quantities of strawberries, raspberries, celery, seakale, asparagus, early peas, late peas and onions, and consumed more stable manure than any other cultivator within ten miles of Crayminster. He was beginning to send cut flowers to London. He had half an acre of glass and he was rapidly extending it. He had built himself a cottage on lines of austere economy, and a bony-looking dwelling-house for some of his men. He also owned a number of useful sheds of which tar and corrugated iron were conspicuous features. His home was furnished with the utmost respectability, and notably joyless even in a countryside where gaiety is regarded as an impossible quality in furniture. He was already in a small local way a mortgagee. Good fortune had not turned the head of Mr. Benshaw nor robbed him of the feeling that he was a particularly deserving person, entitled to a preferential treatment from a country which in his plain unsparing way he felt that he enriched.

In many ways he thought that the country was careless of his needs. And in none more careless than in the laws relating to trespass. Across his dominions ran three footpaths, and one of these led to the public elementary school. That he should have to maintain this latter—and if he did not keep it in good order the children spread out and made parallel tracks among his cultivations—seemed to him a thing almost intolerably unjust. He mended it with cinders, acetylene refuse, which he believed and hoped to be thoroughly bad for boots, and a peculiarly slimy chalky clay, and he put on a board at each end "Keep to the footpaths, Trespassers will be prosecuted, by Order," which he painted himself to save expense when he was confined indoors by the influenza. Still more unjust it would be, he felt, for him to spend money upon effective fencing, and he could find no fencing cheap enough and ugly enough and painful enough and impossible enough to express his feelings in the matter. Every day the children streamed to and fro, marking how his fruits ripened and his produce became more esculent. And other people pursued these tracks, many Mr. Benshaw was convinced went to and fro through his orderly crops who had no business whatever, no honest business, to pass that way. Either, he concluded, they did it to annoy him, or they did it to injure him. This continual invasion aroused in Mr. Benshaw all that stern anger against unrighteousness latent in our race which more than any other single force has made America and the Empire what they are to-day. Once already he had been robbed—a raid upon his raspberries—and he felt convinced that at any time he might be robbed again. He had made representations to the local authority to get the footpaths closed, but in vain. They defended themselves with the paltry excuse that the children would then have to go nearly a mile round to the school.

It was not only the tyranny of these footpaths that offended Mr. Benshaw's highly developed sense of Individual Liberty. All round his rather straggling dominions his neighbours displayed an ungenerous indisposition to maintain their fences to his satisfaction. In one or two places, in abandonment of his clear rights in the matter, he had at his own expense supplemented these lax defences with barbed wire. But it was not a very satisfactory sort of barbed wire. He wanted barbed wire with extra spurs like a fighting cock; he

wanted barbed wire that would start out after nightfall and attack passers-by. This boundary trouble was
universal; in a way it was worse than the footpaths,
which after all only affected the Cage Fields where his
strawberries grew. Except for the yard and garden
walls of Maccullum and Schocks and that side, there
was not really a satisfactory foot of enclosure all round
Mr. Benshaw. One the one side rats and people's dogs
and scratching cats came in, on the other side rabbits.
The rabbits were intolerable, and recently there had
been a rise of nearly thirty per cent. in the price of
wire netting.

Mr. Benshaw wanted to hurt rabbits; he did not
want simply to kill them, he wanted so to kill them as
to put the fear of death into the burrows. He wanted
to kill them so that scared little furry survivors with
their tails as white as ghosts would go lolloping home
and say, " I say, you chaps, we'd better shift out of this.
We're up against a Strong Determined Man. . . ."

I have made this lengthy statement of Mr. Benshaw's economic and moral difficulties in order that the
reader should understand the peculiar tension that
already existed upon this side of Crayminster. It has
been necessary to do so now because in a few seconds
there will be no further opportunity for such preparations. There had been trouble, I may add very hastily,
about the shooting of Mr. Benshaw's gun; a shower of
small shot had fallen out of the twilight upon the
umbrella and basket of old Mrs. Frobisher. And only
a week ago an unsympathetic bench after a hearing of
over an hour and in the face of overwhelming evidence
had refused to convict little Lucy Mumby, aged eleven,
of stealing fruit from Mr. Benshaw's fields. She had
been caught red-handed. . . .

At the very moment that Bealby was butting the
baker in the stomach, Mr. Benshaw was just emerging
from his austere cottage after a wholesome but inex-
pensive high tea in which he had finished up two left-

over cold sausages, and he was considering very deeply the financial side of a furious black fence that he had at last decided should pen in the school children from further depredations. It should be of splintery tarred deal, and high, with well-pointed tops studded with sharp nails, and he believed that by making the path only two feet wide, a real saving of ground for cultivation might be made and a very considerable discomfort for the public arranged, to compensate for his initial expense. The thought of a narrow lane which would in winter be characterised by an excessive sliminess and from which there would be no lateral escape was pleasing to a mind by no means absolutely restricted to considerations of pounds, shillings and pence. In his hand after his custom he carried a hoe, on the handle of which feet were marked so that it was available not only for destroying the casual weed but also for purposes of measurement. With this he now checked his estimate, and found that here he would reclaim as much as three feet of trodden waste, here a full two.

Absorbed in these calculations, he heeded little the growth of a certain clamour from the backs of the houses bordering on the High Street. It did not appear to concern him, and Mr. Benshaw made it almost ostentatiously his rule to mind his own business. His eyes remained fixed on the lumpy, dusty sun-baked track, that with an intelligent foresight he saw already transformed into a deterrent slough of despond for the young. . . .

Then quite suddenly the shouting took on a new note. He glanced over his shoulder almost involuntarily and discovered that after all this uproar was his business. Amazingly his business. His mouth assumed a Cromwellian fierceness. His grip tightened on his hoe. That anyone should dare! But it was impossible!

His dominions were being invaded with a peculiar boldness and violence.

Ahead of everyone else and running with wild wavings of the arms across his strawberries was a small and very dirty little boy. He impressed Mr. Benshaw merely as a pioneer. Some thirty yards behind him was a collarless, short-sleeved man in red slippers running with great effrontery, and behind him another still more denuded lunatic, also in list slippers and with braces—braces of inconceivable levity. And then Wiggs, the policeman, hotly followed by Mr. Maccullum. Then more distraught tailors and Schocks the butcher. But a louder shout heralded the main attack and Mr. Benshaw turned his eyes—already they were slightly blood-shot eyes—to the right and saw, pouring through the broken hedge, a disorderly crowd, Rymell whom he had counted his friend, the grocer's assistant, the doctor's boy, some strangers—Mumby!

At the sight of Mumby, Mr. Benshaw leaped at a conclusion. He saw it all. The whole place was rising against him; they were asserting some infernal new right-of-way. Mumby—Mumby had got them to do it. All the fruits of fifteen years of toil, all the care and accumulation of Mr. Benshaw's prime, were to be trampled and torn to please a draper's spite! . . .

Sturdy yeoman as Mr. Benshaw was he resolved instantly to fight for his liberties. One moment he paused to blow the powerful police whistle he carried in his pocket, and then rushed forward in the direction of the hated Mumby, the leader of trespassers, the parent and abetter and defender of the criminal Lucy. He took the hurrying panting man almost unawares, and with one wild sweep of the hoe felled him to the earth. Then he staggered about and smote again, but not quite in time to get the head of Mr. Rymell.

This whistle he carried was part of a systematic campaign he had developed against trespassers and fruit stealers. He and each of his assistants carried one, and at the first shrill note—it was his rule—everyone seized on any weapon that was handy and ran to pursue and capture. All his assistants were extraordinarily prompt in responding to these alarms, which were often the only break in long days of strenuous and strenuously directed toil. So now with an astonishing promptitude and animated faces men appeared from sheds and greenhouses and distant patches of culture hastening to the assistance of their dour employer.

It says much for the amiable relations that existed between employers and employed in those days before Syndicalism became the creed of the younger workers that they did hurry to his assistance.

But many rapid things were to happen before they came into action. For first a strange excitement seized upon the tramp. A fantastic delusive sense of social rehabilitation took possession of his soul. Here he was pitted against a formidable hoe-wielding man, who for some inscrutable reason was resolved to cover the retreat of Bealby. And all the world, it seemed, was with the tramp and against this hoe-wielder. All the tremendous forces of human society against which the tramp had struggled for so many years, whose power he knew and feared as only the outlaw can, had suddenly come into line with him. Across the strawberries to the right there was even a policeman hastening to join the majority, a policeman closely followed by a tradesman of the blackest, most respectable quality. The tramp had a vision of himself as a respectable man heroically leading respectable people against outcasts. He dashed the lank hair from his eyes, waved his arms laterally and then with a loud strange cry flung himself towards Mr. Benshaw. Two pairs of super-imposed coat-tails flapped behind him. And then the hoe whistled through the air and the tramp fell to the ground like a sack.

But now Schocks's boy had grasped his opportunity. He had been working discreetly round behind Mr. Benshaw and as the hoe smote he leaped upon that hero's back and seized him about the neck with both

arms and bore him staggering to the ground, and
Rymell, equally quick, and used to the tackling of formidable creatures, had snatched and twisted away the
hoe and grappled Mr. Benshaw almost before he was
down. The first of Mr. Benshaw's helpers to reach
the fray found the issue decided, his master held down
conclusively and a growing circle trampling down a
wide area of strawberry plants about the panting
group. . . .

Mr. Mumby more frightened than hurt was already
sitting up, but the tramp with a glowing wound upon
his cheekbone and an expression of astonishment in his
face, lay low and pawed the earth.

"What d'you mean," gasped Mr. Rymell, "hitting
people about with that hoe?"

"What d'you mean," groaned Mr. Benshaw, "running across my strawberries?"

"We were going after that boy."

"Pounds and pounds worth of damage.   Mischief
and wickedness. . . . Mumby!"

Mr. Rymell, suddenly realising the true values of
the situation, released Mr. Benshaw's hands and knelt
up. "Look here, Mr. Benshaw," he said, "you seem
to be under the impression we are trespassing."

Mr. Benshaw struggling into a sitting position was
understood to inquire with some heat what Mr. Rymell
called it. Schocks's boy picked up the hat with the
erotic brim and handed it to the horticulturist silently
and respectfully.

"We were not trespassing," said Mr. Rymell. "We
were following up that boy. *He* was trespassing if you
like. . . . By the bye,—where *is* the boy? Has anyone caught him?"

At the question attention which had been focussed
upon Mr. Benshaw and his hoe, came round. Across
the field in the direction of the sunlit half-acre of
glass the little tailor was visible standing gingerly and
picking up his red slippers for the third time—they

would come off in that loose good soil, everybody else had left the trail to concentrate on Mr. Benshaw—and Bealby— Bealby was out of sight. He had escaped, clean got away.

"What boy?" asked Mr. Benshaw.

"Ferocious little beast who's fought us like a rat. Been committing all sorts of crimes about the country. Five pounds reward for him."

"Fruit stealing?" asked Mr. Benshaw.

"Yes," said Mr. Rymell, chancing it.

Mr. Benshaw reflected slowly. His eyes surveyed his trampled crops. "Goooooooooooooo *Lord!*" he cried. "Look at those strawberries!" His voice gathered violence. "And that lout there!" he said. "Why!—he's lying on them! That's the brute who went for me!"

"You got him a pretty tidy one aside the head!" said Maccullum.

The tramp rolled over on some fresh strawberries and groaned pitifully.

"He's hurt," said Mr. Mumby.

The tramp flopped and lay still.

"Get some water!" said Rymell, standing up.

At the word water, the tramp started convulsively, rolled over and sat up with a dazed expression.

"No water," he said weakly. "No more water," and then catching Mr. Benshaw's eye he got rather quickly to his feet.

Everybody who wasn't already standing was getting up, and everyone now was rather carefully getting himself off any strawberry plant he had chanced to find himself smashing in the excitement of the occasion.

"That's the man that started in on me," said Mr. Benshaw. "What's he doing here? Who is he?"

"Who are *you,* my man? What business have you to be careering over this field?" asked Mr. Rymell.

"I was only 'elping," said the tramp.

"Nice help," said Mr. Benshaw.

" I thought that boy was a thief or something."

" And so you made a rush at me."

" I didn't exactly—sir— I thought you was 'elping 'im."

".You be off anyhow," said Mr. Benshaw. "Whatever you thought."

" Yes, you be off!" said Mr. Rymell.

" That's the way, my man," said Mr. Benshaw. " We haven't any jobs for you. The sooner we have you out of it the better for everyone. Get right on to the path and keep it." And with a desolating sense of exclusion the tramp withdrew. "There's pounds and pounds worth of damage here," said Mr. Benshaw. " This job'll cost me a pretty penny. Look at them berries there. Why they ain't fit for jam! And all done by one confounded boy." An evil light came into Mr. Benshaw's eyes. "You leave him to me and my chaps. If he's gone up among those sheds there— we'll settle with him. Anyhow there's no reason why my fruit should be trampled worse than it has been. Fruit stealer, you say, he is?"

" They live on the country this time of year," said Mr. Mumby.

" And catch them doing a day's work picking!" said Mr. Benshaw. " I know the sort."

" There's a reward of five pounds for 'im already," said the baker. . . .

§ 4

You perceive how humanitarian motives may sometimes defeat their own end, and how little Lady Laxton's well-intentioned handbills were serving to rescue Bealby. Instead they were turning him into a scared and hunted animal. In spite of its manifest impossibility he was convinced that the reward and this pursuit had to do with his burglary of the poultry farm, and that his capture would be but the preliminary to prison, trial and sentence. His one remaining idea was to get away. But his escape across the market gardens had left him so blown and spent, that he was obliged to hide up for a time in this perilous neighbourhood, before going on. He saw a disused-looking shed in the lowest corner of the gardens behind the green-houses and by doubling sharply along a hedge he got to it unseen. It was not disused—nothing in Mr. Benshaw's possession ever was absolutely disused, but it was filled with horticultural lumber, with old calcium carbide tins, with broken wheelbarrows and damaged ladders awaiting repair, with some ragged wheeling planks and surplus rolls of roofing felt. At the back were some unhinged shed doors leaning against the wall, and between them Bealby tucked himself neatly and became still, glad of any respite from the chase.

He would wait for twilight and then get away across the meadows at the back and then go— He didn't know whither. And now he had no confidence in the wild world any more. A qualm of home-sickness for the compact little gardener's cottage at Shonts, came to Bealby. Why, as a matter of fact, wasn't he there now?

He ought to have tried more at Shonts.

He ought to have minded what they told him and not have taken up a toasting-fork against Thomas. Then he wouldn't now have been a hunted burglar with a reward of five pounds on his head and nothing in his pocket but threepence and a pack of greasy playing cards, a box of sulphur matches and various objectionable sundries, none of which were properly his own.

If only he could have his time over again!

Such wholesome reflections occupied his thoughts until the onset of the dusk stirred him to departure. He crept out of his hiding place and stretched his limbs which had got very stiff, and was on the point

of reconnoitring from the door of the shed when he
became aware of stealthy footsteps outside.

With the quickness of an animal he shot back into
his hiding-place. The footsteps had halted. For a
long time it seemed the unseen waited listening. Had
he heard Bealby?

Then someone fumbled with the door of the shed,
it opened and there was a long pause of cautious
inspection.

Then the unknown had shuffled into the shed and
sat down on a heap of matting.

" *Gaw!* " said a voice.

The tramp's!

"If ever I struck a left-handed Mascot it was that
boy," said the tramp. "The little *swine!*"

For the better part of two minutes he went on from
this mild beginning to a descriptive elaboration of
Bealby. For the first time in his life Bealby learned
how unfavourable was the impression he might leave
on a fellow-creature's mind.

"Took even my matches!" cried the tramp, and
tried this statement over with variations.

"First that old fool with his syringe!" The tramp's
voice rose in angry protest. "Here's a chap dying
epilepsy on your doorstep and all you can do is to
squirt cold water at him! Cold water! Why you
might *kill* a man doing that! And then say you'd
thought'd bring 'im ränd! Bring 'im ränd! You be
jolly glad I didn't stash your silly face in. You [mis-
begotten] old fool! What's a shilling for wetting a
man to 'is skin? Wet through I was. Running inside
my shirt,—dripping. . . . And then the blooming
boy clears!

"*I* don't know what boys are coming to!" cried the
tramp. "These board schools it is. Gets 'old of
everything 'e can and bunks! Gaw! if I get my 'ands
on 'im, I'll show 'im. I'll——"

For some time the tramp revelled in the details, for

the most part crudely surgical, of his vengeance upon
Bealby. . . .

"Then there's that dog bite. 'Ow do I know 'ow
that's going to turn ät? If I get 'idrophobia, blowed
if I don't *bite* some of 'em. 'Idrophobia. Screaming
and foaming. Nice death for a man—my time o' life!
Bark I shall. Bark and bite.

"And this is your world," said the tramp. "This
is the world you put people into and expect 'em to be
'appy. . .   .

"I'd like to bite that dough-faced fool with the silly
'at. I'd enjoy biting *'im*. I'd spit it out, but I'd
bite it right enough. Wiping abät with 'is 'O. *Gaw!*
Get off my ground! Be orf with you. Slash. 'E
ought to be shut up.

"Where's the justice of it?" shouted the tramp.
"Where's the right and the sense of it? What 'ave
I done that I should always get the under side? Why
should *I* be stuck on the under side of everything?
There's worse men than me in all sorts of positions.
. . . Judges there are. 'Orrible Kerecters. Minis-
ters and people. I've read abät 'em in the papers. . . .

"It's we tramps are the scapegoats. Somebody's got
to suffer so as the police can show a face. Gaw! Some
of these days I'll do something. . . . I'll do something. You'll drive me too far with it. I tell
you——"

He stopped suddenly and listened. Bealby had
creaked.

"Gaw! What can one do?" said the tramp after
a long interval.

And then complaining more gently, the tramp
began to feel about to make his simple preparations
for the night.

"'Unt me out of this I expect," said the tramp.
"And many sleeping in feather beds that ain't fit to
'old a candle to me. Not a hordinary farthing
candle. . . ."

§ 5

The subsequent hour or so was an interval of tedious tension for Bealby.

After vast spaces of time he was suddenly aware of three vertical threads of light. He stared at them with mysterious awe, until he realised that they were just the moonshine streaming through the cracks of the shed.

The tramp tossed and muttered in his sleep.

Footsteps?

Yes—Footsteps.

Then voices.

They were coming along by the edge of the field, and coming and talking very discreetly.

"Ugh!" said the tramp and then softly, "What's that?" Then he too became noiselessly attentive.

Bealby could hear his own heart beating.

The men were now close outside the shed. "He wouldn't go in there," said Mr. Benshaw's voice. "He wouldn't dare. Anyhow we'll go up by the glass first. I'll let him have the whole barrel-full of oats if I get a glimpse of him. If he's gone away they'd have caught him in the road. . . ."

The footsteps receded. There came a cautious rustling on the part of the tramp and then his feet padded softly to the door of the shed. He struggled to open it, and then with a jerk got it open a few inches; a great bar of moonlight leaped and lay still across the floor of the shed. Bealby advanced his head cautiously until he could see the black obscure indications of the tramp's back as he peeped out.

"Now," whispered the tramp, and opened the door wider. Then he ducked his head down and had darted out of sight, leaving the door open behind him.

Bealby questioned whether he should follow. He came out a few steps and then went back at a shout from away up the garden. "There he goes," shouted a voice, "in the shadow of the hedge."

"Look out, Jim!"—*Bang*—and a yelp.

"Stand away! I've got another barrel!" *Bang*.

Then silence for a time, and then the footsteps coming back.

"That ought to teach him," said Mr. Benshaw. "First time I got him fair, and I think I peppered him a bit the second. Couldn't see very well, but I heard him yell. He won't forget that in a hurry. Not him. There's nothing like oats for fruit-stealers. Jim, just shut that door, will you? That's where he was hiding. . . ."

It seemed a vast time to Bealby before he ventured out into the summer moonlight, and a very pitiful and outcast little Bealby he felt himself to be.

He was beginning to realise what it means to go beyond the narrow securities of human society. He had no friends, no friends at all. . . .

He caught at and arrested a sob of self-pity.

Perhaps after all it was not so late as Bealby had supposed. There were still lights in some of the houses and he had the privilege of seeing Mr. Benshaw going to bed with pensive deliberation. Mr. Benshaw wore a flannel nightshirt and said quite a lengthy prayer before extinguishing his candle. Then suddenly Bealby turned nervously and made off through the hedge. A dog had barked.

At first there were nearly a dozen lighted windows in Crayminster. They went out one by one. He hung for a long time with a passionate earnestness on the sole surviving one, but that too went at last. He could have wept when at last it winked out. He came down into the marshy flats by the river, but he did not like the way in which the water sucked and swirled in the vague moonlight; also he suddenly discovered a great white horse standing quite still in the misty grass not thirty yards away; so he went up to and crossed

the high road and wandered up the hillside towards
the allotments, which attracted him by reason of the
sociability of the numerous tool sheds. In a hedge
near at hand a young rabbit squealed sharply and was
stilled. Why?

Then something like a short snake scrabbled by very
fast through the grass.

Then he thought he saw the tramp stalking him
noiselessly behind some currant bushes. That went
on for some time, but came to nothing.

Then nothing pursued him, nothing at all. The gap,
the void, came after him. The bodiless, the faceless,
the formless; these are evil hunters in the night. . . .

What a cold still *watching* thing moonlight can
be! . . .

He thought he would like to get his back against
something solid and found near one of the sheds a little
heap of litter. He sat down against good tarred boards,
assured at least that whatever came must come in front.
Whatever he did, he was resolved, he would not shut
his eyes.

That would be fatal. . . .

He awoke in broad daylight amidst a cheerful uproar
of birds.

§ 6

And then again flight and pursuit were resumed.

As Bealby went up the hill away from Crayminster
he saw a man standing over a spade and watching his
retreat, and when he looked back again presently this
man was following. It was Lady Laxton's five pound
reward had done the thing for him.

He was half minded to surrender and have done with
it, but gaol he knew was a dreadful thing of stone and
darkness. He would make one last effort. So he beat
along the edge of a plantation and then crossed it and
forced his way through some gorse and came upon a

sunken road, that crossed the hill in a gorse-lined cutting. He struggled down the steep bank. At its foot, regardless of him, unaware of him, a man sat beside a motor bicycle with his fists gripped tight and his head downcast, swearing. A county map was crumpled in his hand. " Damn !" he cried and flung the map to the ground and kicked it and put his foot on it.

Bealby slipped, came down the bank with a run and found himself in the road within a couple of yards of the blonde features and angry eyes of Captain Douglas. When he saw the Captain and perceived himself recognised, he flopped down—a done and finished Bealby. . . .

§ 7

He had arrived just in time to interrupt the Captain in a wild and reprehensible fit of passion.

The Captain imagined it was a secret fit of passion. He thought he was quite alone and that no one could hear him or see him. So he had let himself shout and stamp, to work off the nervous tensions that tormented him beyond endurance.

In the direct sense of the words the Captain was in love with Madeleine. He was in love quite beyond the bounds set by refined and decorous people to this dangerous passion. The primordial savage that lurks in so many of us was uppermost in him. He was not in love with her prettily or delicately, he was in love with her violently and vehemently. He wanted to be with her, he wanted to be close to her, he wanted to possess her and nobody else to approach her. He was so inflamed now that no other interest in life had any importance except as it aided or interfered with this desire. He had forced himself in spite of this fever in his blood to leave her in order to pursue Bealby, and now he was furiously regretting this firmness. He had expected to catch Bealby overnight and bring him back

27

to the hotel in triumph. But Bealby had been elusive. There she was, away there, hurt and indignant—neglected!

"A laggard in love," cried the Captain, "a dastard in war! God!—I run away from everything. First I leave the manœuvres, then her. Unstable as water thou shalt not prevail. Water! What does the confounded boy matter? What does he matter?

"And there she is. Alone! She'll flirt—naturally she'll flirt. Don't I deserve it? Haven't I asked for it? Just the one little time we might have had together! I fling it in her face. You fool, you laggard, you dastard! And here's this map!"

A breathing moment.

"How the *devil*," cried the Captain, "am I to find the little beast on this map?

"And twice he's been within reach of my hand!

"No decision!" cried the Captain. "No instant grip! What good is a soldier without it? What good is any man who will not leap at opportunity? I ought to have chased out last night after that fool and his oats. Then I might have had a chance!

"Chuck it! Chuck the whole thing! Go back to her. Kneel to her, kiss her, compel her!

"And what sort of reception am I likely to get?"

He crumpled the flapping map in his fist.

And then suddenly out of nowhere Bealby came rolling down to his feet, a dishevelled and earthly Bealby. But Bealby.

"Good Lord!" cried the Captain, starting to his feet and holding the map like a sword sheath. "What do you want?"

For a second Bealby was a silent spectacle of misery.

"Oooh! I want my *breckfuss*," he burst out at last, reduced to tears.

"Are you young Bealby?" asked the Captain, seizing him by the shoulder.

"They're after me," cried Bealby. "If they catch

me they'll put me in prison. Where they don't give
you anything. It wasn't me did it—and I 'aven't had
anything to eat—not since yesterday."

The Captain came rapidly to a decision. There
should be no more faltering. He saw his way clear
before him. He would act—like a whistling sword.
"Here! jump up behind," he said . . . "hold on
tight to me. . . ."

§ 8

For a time there was a more than Napoleonic swiftness in the Captain's movements. When Bealby's
pursuer came up to the hedge that looks down into
the sunken road, there was no Bealby, no Captain,
nothing but a torn and dishevelled county map, an
almost imperceptible odour of petrol and a faint sound
—like a distant mowing machine,—and the motor
bicycle was a mile away on the road to Beckinstone.
Eight miles, eight rather sickening miles, Bealby did to
Beckinstone in eleven minutes, and there in a little
coffee-house he was given breakfast with eggs and bacon
and marmalade (Prime!) and his spirit was restored to
him while the Captain raided a bicycle and repairing
shop and negotiated the hire of an experienced but
fairly comfortable wicker-work trailer. And so to
London through the morning sunshine, leaving tramps,
pursuers, policemen, handbills, bakers, market gardeners,
terrors of the darkness and everything upon the road
behind—and farther behind and remote and insignificant—and so to the vanishing point.

Some few words of explanation the Captain had
vouchsafed and that was all.

"Don't be afraid about it," he said. "Don't be in
the least bit afraid. You tell them about it, just simply
and truthfully, exactly what you did, exactly how you
got into it and out of it and all about it."

"You're going to take me up to a Magistrate, sir?"

"I'm going to take you up to the Lord Chancellor himself."

"And then they won't do anything?"

"Nothing at all, Bealby; you trust me. All you've got to do is to tell the simple truth. . . ."

It was pretty rough going in the trailer but very exciting. If you gripped the sides hard and sat quite tight nothing very much happened, and also there was a strap across your chest. And you went past everything. There wasn't a thing on the road the Captain didn't pass, lowing deeply with his great horn when they seemed likely to block his passage. And as for the burglary and everything, it would all be settled. . . .

The Captain also found that ride to London exhilarating. At least he was no longer hanging about; he was getting to something. He would be able to go back to her—and all his being now yearned to go back to her—with things achieved, with successes to show. He'd found the boy. He would go straight to dear old Uncle Chickney, and Uncle Chickney would put things right with Moggeridge, the boy would bear his testimony. Moggeridge would be convinced and all would be well again. He might be back with Madeleine that evening. He would go back to her, and she would see the wisdom and energy of all he had done, and she would lift that dear chin of hers and smile that dear smile of hers and hold out her hand to be kissed, and the lights and reflections would play on that strong soft neck of hers. . . .

They buzzed along stretches of common and stretches of straight-edged meadowland, by woods and orchards, by pleasant inns and slumbering villages and the gates and lodges of country houses.

These latter grew more numerous and presently they skirted a town, and then more road, more villages and at last signs of a nearness to London, more frequent houses, more frequent inns, hoardings and advertisements, an asphalted side-walk, lamps, a gasworks, laundries, a stretch of suburban villadom, a suburban railway station a suburbanised old town, an omnibus, the head of a tramline, a stretch of public common thick with notice-boards, a broad pavement, something-or-other parade, with a row of shops. . . .

London.

CHAPTER THE EIGHTH

How Bealby Explained

§ 1

LORD CHICKNEY was only slightly older than Lord Moggeridge, but he had not worn nearly so well. His hearing was not good, though he would never admit it, and the loss of several teeth greatly affected his articulation. One might generalise and say that neither physically nor mentally do soldiers wear so well as lawyers. The army ages men sooner than the law and philosophy; it exposes them more freely to germs, which undermine and destroy, and it shelters them more completely from thought, which stimulates and preserves. A lawyer must keep his law highly polished and up-to-date or he hears of it within a fortnight, a general never realises he is out of training and behind the times until disaster is accomplished. Since the magnificent retreat from Bondy-Satina in eighty-seven and his five weeks' defence of Barrowgast (with the subsequent operations) the abilities of Lord Chickney had never been exercised seriously at all. But there was a certain simplicity of manner and a very tall, very

836

drooping, grizzled old-veteran picturesqueness about him that kept him distinguished, he was easy to recognise on public occasions on account of his vast height and his vast blonde white moustaches, and so he got pointed out when greater men were ignored. The autograph collectors adored him. Every morning he would spend half an hour writing autographs and patriotic sentiments, and the habit was so strong in him that on Sundays, when there was no London post, and autograph writing would have been wrong anyhow, he filled the time in copying out the epistle and gospel for the day. And he liked to be well in the foreground of public affairs—if possible wearing his decorations. After the autographs he would work, sometimes for hours, for various patriotic and morally aggressive societies, and more particularly for those which opposed Socialism in every shape and form and those which sought to deprive working people, and particularly working girls, of the temptations that arise from unassigned leisure. He had a peculiar vague horror of Socialism, which he regarded as a compound of atheism, republicanism, blight, mildew, measles, and all the worst characteristics of a Continental sabbath. He wrote and toiled for these societies, but he could not speak for them on account of his teeth. For he had one peculiar weakness; he had faced death in many forms but he had never faced a dentist. The thought of dentists gave him just the same sick horror as the thought of Socialism. But it was a great grief to him that he could not speak his mind.

He was a man of blameless private life, a widower and childless. In later years he had come to believe that he had once been very deeply in love with his cousin Susan, who had married a rather careless husband named Douglas; both she and Douglas were dead now, but he maintained a touching affection for her two lively rather than satisfying sons. He called them his nephews, and by the continuous attrition of affection he had become their recognised uncle. He was glad when they came to him in their scrapes, and he liked to be seen about with them in public places. They regarded him with considerable confidence and respect, and an affection that they sometimes blamed themselves for as not quite warm enough for his merits. But there is a kind of injustice about affection.

He was really gratified when he got a wire from the less discreditable of these two bright young relations, saying, " Sorely in need of your advice. Hope to bring difficulties to you to-day at twelve."

He concluded very naturally that the boy had come to some crisis in his unfortunate entanglement with Madeleine Philips, and he was flattered by the trustfulness that brought the matter to him. He resolved to be delicate but wily, honourable, strictly honourable, but steadily, patiently separative. He paced his spacious study with his usual morning's work neglected, and rehearsed little sentences in his mind that might be effective in the approaching interview. There would probably be emotion. He would pat the lad on his shoulder and be himself a little emotional. " I understand, my boy," he would say, " I understand.

" Don't forget, my boy, that I've been a young man too."

He would be emotional, he would be sympathetic, but also he must be a man of the world. " Sort of thing that won't do, you know, my boy; sort of thing that people will *not* stand. . . . A soldier's wife has to be a soldier's wife and nothing else. . . . Your business is to serve the King, not—not some celebrity. Lovely, no doubt, I don't deny the charm of her—but on the hoardings, my boy. . . . Now don't you think—don't you *think?*—there's some nice pure girl somewhere, sweet as violets, new as the dawn, and ready to be *yours;* a girl I mean, a maiden fancy free, not—how shall I put it?—a woman of the world. Wonderful I admit—but seasoned. Public. My dear, dear boy,

I knew your mother when she was a girl, a sweet, pure girl—a thing of dewy freshness. Ah! Well I remember her! All these years, my boy— Nothing. It's difficult. . . ."

Tears stood in his brave old blue eyes as he elaborated such phrases. He went up and down mumbling them through the defective teeth and the long moustache and waving an eloquent hand.

§ 2

When Lord Chickney's thoughts had once started in any direction it was difficult to turn them aside. No doubt that concealed and repudiated deafness helped his natural perplexity of mind. Truth comes to some of us as a still small voice, but Lord Chickney needed shouting and prods. And Douglas did not get to him until he was finishing lunch. Moreover it was the weakness of Captain Douglas to talk in jerky fragments and undertones, rather than clearly and fully in the American fashion. "Tell me all about it, my boy," said Lord Chickney. "Tell me all about it. Don't apologise for your clothes. I understand. Motor bicycle and just come up. But have you had any lunch, Eric?"

"Alan, uncle,—not Eric. My brother is Eric."

"Well, I called him Alan. Tell me all about it. Tell me what has happened. What are you thinking of doing? Just put the position before me. To tell you the truth I've been worrying over this business for some time."

"Didn't know you'd heard of it, uncle. He can't have talked about it already. Anyhow,—you see all the awkwardness of the situation. They say the old chap's a thundering spiteful old devil when he's roused —and there's no doubt he was roused. . . . Tremendously. . . ."

Lord Chickney was not listening very attentively.

27*

Indeed he was also talking. "Not clear to me there was another man in it," he was saying. "That makes it more complicated, my boy, makes the row acuter. Old fellow, eh? Who?"

They came to a pause at the same moment.

"You speak so indistinctly," complained Lord Chickney. "*Who* did you say?"

"I thought you understood. Lord Moggeridge."

"Lord!— Lord Moggeridge! My dear Boy! But how?"

"I thought you understood, uncle."

"He doesn't want to marry her! Tut! Never! Why the man must be sixty if he's a day. . . ."

Captain Douglas regarded his distinguished uncle for a moment with distressed eyes. Then he came nearer, raised his voice and spoke more deliberately.

"I don't know whether you quite understand, uncle. I am talking about this affair at Shonts last week-end."

"My dear Boy, there's no need for you to shout. If only you don't mumble and clip your words—and turn head over heels with your ideas. Just tell me about it plainly. Who is Shonts? One of those Liberal peers? I seem to have heard the name. . . ."

"Shonts, uncle, is the house the Laxtons have; you know,—Lucy."

"Little Lucy! I remember her. Curls all down her back. Married the milkman. But how does *she* come in, Alan? The story's getting complicated. But that's the worst of these infernal affairs,—they always do get complicated. Tangled skeins—

> " ' *Oh what a tangled web we weave,*
> *When first we practise to deceive.*'

And now, like a sensible man, you want to get out of it."

Captain Douglas was bright pink with the effort to control himself and keep perfectly plain and straightforward. His hair had become like tow and little beads of perspiration stood upon his forehead.

"I spent last week-end at Shonts," he said. "Lord Moggeridge, also there, week-ending. Got it into his head that I was pulling his leg."

"Naturally, my boy, if he goes philandering. At his time of life. What else can he expect?"

"It wasn't philandering."

"Fine distinctions. Fine distinctions. Go on—anyhow."

"He got it into his head that I was playing practical jokes upon him. Confused me with Eric. It led to a rather first-class row. I had to get out of the house. Nothing else to do. He brought all sorts of accusations——"

Captain Douglas stopped short. His uncle was no longer attending to him. They had drifted to the window of the study and the General was staring with an excitement and intelligence that grew visibly at the spectacle of Bealby and the trailer outside. For Bealby had been left in the trailer and he was sitting as good as gold waiting for the next step in his vindication from the dark charge of burglary. He was very travel-worn and the trailer was time-worn as well as travel-worn, and both contrasted with the efficient neatness and newness of the motor bicycle in front. The contrast had attracted the attention of a tall policeman who was standing in a state of elucidatory meditation regarding Bealby. Bealby was not regarding the policeman. He had the utmost confidence in Captain Douglas, he felt sure that he would presently be purged of all the horror of that dead old man and of the brief unpremeditated plunge into crime, but still for the present at any rate he did not feel equal to staring a policeman out of countenance. . . .

From the window the policeman very largely obscured Bealby. . . .

Whenever hearts are simple there lurks romance.

Age cannot wither nor custom stale her infinite diversity. Suddenly out of your kindly diplomacies, your sane man-of-the-world intentions, leaps the imagination like a rocket, flying from such safe securities bang into the sky. So it happened to the old General. He became deaf to everything but the appearances before him. The world was jewelled with dazzling and delightful possibilities. His face was lit by a glow of genuine romantic excitement. He grasped his nephew's arm. He pointed. His grizzled cheeks flushed.

"That isn't," he asked with something verging upon admiration in his voice and manner, "a Certain Lady in disguise?"

§ 3

It became clear to Captain Douglas that if ever he was to get to Lord Moggeridge that day he must take his uncle firmly in hand. Without even attempting not to appear to shout he cried, "That is a little Boy. That is my Witness. It is Most Important that I should get him to Lord Moggeridge to tell his Story."

"What story?" cried the old commander pulling at his moustache and still eyeing Bealby suspiciously. . . .

It took exactly half an hour to get Lord Chickney from that inquiry to the telephone and even then he was still far from clear about the matter in hand. Captain Douglas got in most of the facts, but he could not eliminate an idea that it all had to do with Madeleine. Whenever he tried to say clearly that she was entirely outside the question, the General patted his shoulder and looked very wise and kind and said, "My dear Boy, I quite understand; I *quite* understand. Never mention a lady. *No.*"

So they started at last rather foggily—so far as things of the mind went, though the sun that day was brilliant —and because of engine trouble in Port Street the

General's hansom reached Little Tenby Street first and he got in a good five minutes preparing the Lord Chancellor tactfully and carefully before the bicycle and its trailer came upon the scene. . . .

§ 4

Candler had been packing that morning with un-usual solicitude for a week-end at Tulliver Abbey. His master had returned from the catastrophe of Shonts, fatigued, visibly aged and extraordinarily cross, and Candler looked to Tulliver Abbey to restore him to his former self. Nothing must be forgotten; there must be no little hitches, everything from first to last must go on oiled wheels, or it was clear his lordship might develop a desperate hostility to these excursions, excursions which Candler found singularly refreshing and entertaining during the stresses of the session. Tulliver Abbey was as good a house as Shonts was bad; Lady Checksammington ruled with the softness of velvet and the strength of steel over a household of admirably efficient domestics, and there would be the best of people there. Mr. Evesham perhaps, the Loopers, Lady Privet, Andreas Doria and Mr. Pernambuco, great silken mellow personages and diamond-like individuali-ties, amidst whom Lord Moggeridge's mind would be restfully active and his comfort quite secure. And as far as possible Candler wanted to get the books and papers his master needed into the trunk or the small valise. That habit of catching up everything at the last moment and putting it under his arm and the consequent need for alert picking up, meant friction and nervous wear and tear for both master and man.

Lord Moggeridge rose at half-past ten—he had been kept late overnight by a heated discussion at the Aristotelian—and breakfasted lightly upon a chop and coffee. Then something ruffled him; something that came with the letters. Candler could not quite make out what it was, but he suspected another pamphlet by Dr. Schiller. It could not be the chop because Lord Moggeridge was always wonderfully successful with chops. Candler looked through the envelopes and letters afterwards and found nothing diagnostic, and then he observed a copy of *Mind* torn across and lying in the waste-paper basket.

"When I went out of the room," said Candler discreetly examining this. "Very likely it's that there Schiller after all."

But in this Candler was mistaken. What had disturbed the Lord Chancellor was a coarsely disrespectful article on the Absolute by a Cambridge Rhodes scholar written in that flighty facetious strain that spreads now like a pestilence over modern philosophical discussion. "Does the Absolute, on Lord Moggeridge's own showing, mean anything more than an eloquent oiliness uniformly distributed through space?" and so on.

Pretty bad!

Lord Moggeridge early in life had deliberately acquired a quite exceptional power of mental self-control. He took his perturbed mind now and threw it forcibly into the consideration of a case upon which he had reserved judgment. He was to catch the 3.35 at Paddington, and at two he was smoking a cigar after a temperate lunch and reading over the notes of this judgment. It was then that the telephone bell became audible, and Candler came in to inform him that Lord Chickney was anxious to see him at once upon a matter of some slight importance.

"Slight importance?" asked Lord Moggeridge.

"Some slight importance, my lord."

"Some? Slight?"

"'Is lordship, my lord, mumbles rather now 'is back teeth 'ave gone," said Candler, "but so I understand 'im."

"These apologetic assertive phrases annoy me, Candler," said Lord Moggeridge over his shoulder.

" You see," he turned round and spoke very clearly, " either the matter is of importance or it is not of importance. A thing must either be or not be. I wish you would manage—when you get messages on the telephone—. . . . But I suppose that is asking too much. . . . Will you explain to him, Candler, when we start, and—ask him, Candler—ask him what sort of matter it is."

Candler returned after some parleying.

" So far as I can make 'is lordship out, my lord, 'e says 'e wants to set you right about something, my lord. He says something about a *little* misapprehension."

" These diminutives, Candler, kill sense. Does he say what sort—what sort—of *little* misapprehension?"

" He says something—I'm sorry, my lord, but it's about Shonts, my lord."

" Then I don't want to hear about it," said Lord Moggeridge.

There was a pause. The Lord Chancellor resumed his reading with a deliberate obviousness; the butler hovered.

" I'm sorry, my lord, but I can't think exactly what I ought to say to 'is lordship, my lord."

" Tell him—tell him that I do not wish to hear anything more about Shonts for ever. Simple."

Candler hesitated and went out, shutting the door carefully lest any fragment of his halting rendering of this message to Lord Chickney should reach his master's ears.

Lord Moggeridge's powers of mental control were, I say, very great. He could dismiss subjects from his mind absolutely. In a few instants he had completely forgotten Shonts and was making notes with a silver-cased pencil on the margins of his draft judgment.

§ 5

He became aware that Candler had returned.

" 'Is lordship, Lord Chickney, my lord, is very persistent, my lord. 'E's rung up twice. 'E says now that 'e makes a personal matter of it. Come what may, 'e says, 'e wishes to speak for two minutes to your lordship. Over the telephone, my lord, 'e vouchsafes no further information."

Lord Moggeridge meditated over the end of his third after-lunch cigar. His man watched the end of his left eyebrow as an engineer might watch a steam gauge. There were no signs of an explosion. "He must come, Candler," his lordship said at last. . . .

"Oh, Candler!"

"My lord?"

"Put the bags and things in a conspicuous position in the hall, Candler. Change yourself, and see that you look thoroughly like trains. And in fact have everything ready, *prominently* ready, Candler."

Then once more Lord Moggeridge concentrated his mind.

§ 6

To him there presently entered Lord Chickney.

Lord Chickney had been twice round the world and he had seen many strange and dusky peoples and many remarkable customs and peculiar prejudices, which he had never failed to depise, but he had never completely shaken off the county family ideas in which he had been brought up. He believed that there was an incurable difference in spirit between quite good people like himself and men from down below like Moggeridge, who was the son of an Exeter chorister. He believed that these men from nowhere always cherished the profoundest respect for the real thing like himself,

that they were greedy for association and gratified by
notice, and so for the life of him he could not approach
Lord Moggeridge without a faint sense of condescen-
sion. He saluted him as "my *dear* Lord Moggeridge,"
wrung his hand with effusion, and asked him kind,
almost district-visiting questions about his younger
brother and the aspect of his house. "And you are
just off, I see, for a week-end."

These amenities the Lord Chancellor acknowledged
by faint gruntings and an almost imperceptible movement of his eyebrows. "There was a matter," he said,
"some *little* matter, on which you want to consult
me?"

"Well," said Lord Chickney and rubbed his
chin. "*Yes*. Yes, there *was* a little matter, a little
trouble——"

"Of an urgent nature?"

"Yes. Yes. Exactly. Just a little complicated, you
know, not quite simple." The dear old soldier's manner
became almost seductive. "One of these difficult little
affairs, where one has to remember that one is a man of
the world, you know. A little complication about a
lady, known to you both. But one must make concessions, one must understand. The boy has a witness.
Things are not as you supposed them to be."

Lord Moggeridge had a clean conscience about ladies;
he drew out his watch and looked at it—aggressively.
He kept it in his hand during his subsequent remarks.

"I must confess," he declared, "I have not the
remotest idea. . . . If you will be so good as to be—
elementary. What *is* it all about?"

"You see I knew the lad's mother," said Lord
Chickney. "In fact——" He became insanely confidential—"Under happier circumstances—don't mis-
understand me, Moggeridge; I mean no evil—but
he might have been my son. I feel for him like a
son. . . ."

§ 7

When presently Captain Douglas, a little heated from his engine trouble, came into the room—he had left Bealby with Candler in the hall—it was instantly manifest to him that the work of preparation had been inadequately performed.

"One minute more, my dear Alan," cried Lord Chickney.

Lord Moggeridge with eyebrows waving and watch in hand was of a different opinion. He addressed himself to Captain Douglas.

"There *isn't* a minute more," he said. "What is all this—this philoprogenitive rigmarole about? Why have you come to me? My cab is outside *now*. All this about ladies and witnesses;—what *is* it?"

"Perfectly simple, my lord! You imagine that I played practical jokes upon you at Shonts. I didn't. I have a witness. The attack upon you downstairs, the noise in your room——"

"Have I any guarantee——?"

"It's the steward's boy from Shonts. Your man outside knows him. Saw him in the steward's room. He made the trouble for you—and me, and then he ran away. Just caught him. Not exchanged thirty words with him. Half a dozen questions. Settle Everything. Then you'll know—nothing for you but the utmost respect."

Lord Moggeridge pressed his lips together and resisted conviction.

"In consideration," interpolated Lord Chickney, "feelings of an old fellow. Old soldier. Boy means no harm."

With the rudeness of one sorely tried the Lord Chancellor thrust the General aside. "Oh!" he said, "Oh!" and then to Captain Douglas. "One minute. Where's your witness? . . ."

The Captain opened the door. Bealby found himself bundled into the presence of two celebrated men.

" Tell him," said Captain Douglas. " And look sharp about it."

" Tell me plainly," cried the Lord Chancellor. " And be—*quick*."

He put such a point on " quick " that it made Bealby jump.

" Tell him," said the General more gently. " Don't be afraid."

" Well," began Bealby after one accumulating pause, " it was 'im told me to do it. 'E said you go in there——"

The Captain would have interrupted but the Lord Chancellor restrained him by a magnificent gesture of the hand holding the watch.

" He told you to do it!" he said. " I knew he did. Now listen ! He told you practically to go in and do anything you could."

" Yessir." Woe took possession of Bealby. " I didn't do any 'arm to the ole gentleman."

" But *who* told you?" cried the Captain. " *Who* told you?"

Lord Moggeridge annihilated him with arm and eyebrows. He held Bealby fascinated by a pointing finger.

" Don't do more than answer the questions. I have thirty seconds more. He told you to go in. He *made* you go in. At the earliest possible opportunity you got away?"

" I jest nipped out——"

" Enough ! And now, sir, how dare you come here without even a plausible lie? How dare you after your intolerable tomfoolery at Shonts confront me again with fresh tomfoolery? How dare you drag in your gallant and venerable uncle in this last preposterous—I suppose you would call it—*lark?* I suppose you had prepared that little wretch with some fine

story. Little you know of False Witness! At the first
question, he breaks down! He does not even begin
his lie. He at least knows the difference between my
standards and yours. Candler! Candler!"

Candler appeared.

"These—these *gentlemen* are going. Is everything
ready?"

"The cab is at the door, m'lord. The usual cab."

Captain Douglas made one last desperate effort.
"Sir!" he said. "My lord——"

The Lord Chancellor turned upon him with a face
that he sought to keep calm, though the eyebrows
waved and streamed like black smoke in a gale.
"Captain Douglas," he said, "you are probably not
aware of the demands upon the time and patience of a
public servant in such a position as mine. You see the
world no doubt as a vastly entertaining fabric upon
which you can embroider your—your facetious arrangements. Well, it is not so. It is real. It is earnest.
You may sneer at the simplicity of an old man, but
what I tell you of life is true. Comic effect is not, believe me, its goal. And you, sir, you, sir, you impress
me as an intolerably foolish, flippant and unnecessary
young man. Flippant. Unnecessary. Foolish."

As he said these words Candler approached him
with a dust coat of a peculiar fineness and dignity, and
he uttered the last words over his protruded chest while
Candler assisted his arms into the sleeves.

"My lord," said Captain Douglas again, but his
resolution was deserting him.

"*No,*" said the Lord Chancellor, leaning forward in
a minatory manner while Candler pulled down the tail
of his jacket and adjusted the collar of his overcoat.

"Uncle," said Captain Douglas.

"*No,*" said the General, with the curt decision of a
soldier and turned exactly ninety degrees away from
him. "You little know how you have hurt me, Alan!
You little know. I couldn't have imagined it. The

Douglas strain!   False Witness—and insult.   I am
sorry, my dear Moggeridge, beyond measure."

"I quite understand—you are as much a victim as
myself.   Quite.   A more foolish attempt—   I am sorry
to be in this hurry——"

"Oh!   You damned little fool," said the Captain
and advanced a step towards the perplexed and shrinking
Bealby.   "You imbecile little trickster!   What do you
mean by it?"

"I didn't mean anything——!"

Then suddenly the thought of Madeleine, sweet and
overpowering, came into the head of this distraught
young man.   He had risked losing her, he had slighted
and insulted her and here he was—entangled.   Here
he was in a position of nearly inconceivable foolishness,
about to assault a dirty and silly little boy in the
presence of the Lord Chancellor and Uncle Chickney.
The world, he felt, was lost, and not well lost.   And
she was lost too.   Even now while he pursued these
follies she might be consoling her wounded pride. . . .

He perceived that love is the supreme thing in life.
He perceived that he who divides his purposes scatters
his life to the four winds of Heaven.   A vehement
resolve to cut the whole of this Bealby business pounced
upon him.   In that moment he ceased to care for
reputation, for appearances, for the resentment of Lord
Moggeridge or the good intentions of Uncle Chickney.

He turned, he rushed out of the room.   He escaped
by unparalleled gymnastics the worst consequences
of an encounter with the Lord Chancellor's bag which
the under-butler had placed rather tactlessly between
the doors, crossed the wide and dignified hall, and in
another moment had his engine going and was struggling
to mount his machine in the street without.   His face
expressed an almost apoplectic concentration.   He
narrowly missed the noses of a pair of horses in the
carriage of Lady Beach Mandarin, made an extraordinary curve to spare a fishmonger's tricycle, shaved

the front and completely destroyed the gesture of that eminent actor manager, Mr. Pomegranate, who was crossing the road in his usual inadvertent fashion, and then he was popping and throbbing and banging round the corner and on his way back to the lovely and irresistible woman who was exerting so disastrous an influence upon his career. . . .

§ 8

The Captain fled from London in the utmost fury and to the general danger of the public. His heart was full of wicked blasphemies, shoutings and self-reproaches, but outwardly he seemed only pinkly intent. And as he crossed an open breezy common and passed by a milestone bearing this inscription, "To London Thirteen Miles," his hind tyre burst conclusively with a massive report. . . .

§ 9

In every life there are crucial moments, turning points, and not infrequently it is just such a thing as this, a report, a sudden waking in the night, a flash upon the road to Damascus that marks and precipitates the accumulating new. Vehemence is not concentration. The headlong violence of the Captain had been no expression of a single-minded purpose, of a soul all gathered together to an end. Far less a pursuit had it been than a flight, a flight from his own dissensions. And now—now he was held.

After he had attempted a few plausible repairs and found the tyre obdurate, after he had addressed ill-chosen remonstrances to some unnamed hearer, after he had walked some way along the road and back in an indecision about repair shops in some neighbouring town, the last dregs of his resistance were spent. He perceived that he was in the presence of a Lesson. He sat down by the roadside some twenty feet from the disabled motor bicycle, and, impotent for further effort, frankly admitted himself overtaken.   He had not reckoned with punctures.

The pursuing questions came clambering upon him and would no longer be denied; who he was and what he was and how he was, and the meaning of this Rare Bate he had been in, and all those deep questions that are so systematically neglected in the haste and excitement of modern life.

In short, for the first time in many headlong days he asked himself simply and plainly what he thought he was up to?

Certain things became clear, and so minutely and exactly clear that it was incredible that they had ever for a moment been obscure.   Of course Bealby had been a perfectly honest little boy, under some sort of misconception, and of course he ought to have been carefully coached and prepared and rehearsed before he was put before the Lord Chancellor.   This was so manifest now that the Captain stared aghast at his own inconceivable negligence.   But the mischief was done.   Nothing now would ever propitiate Moggeridge, nothing now would ever reconcile Uncle Chickney. That was—settled.   But what was not settled was the amazing disorder of his own mind.   Why had he been so negligent, what had come over his mind in the last few weeks?

And this sudden strange illumination of the Captain's mind went so far as perceiving that the really important concern for him was not the accidents of Shonts but this epilepsy of his own will.   Why now was he rushing back to Madeleine?   Why?   He did not love her. He knew he did not love her.   On the whole, more than anything else he resented her.

But he was excited about her, he was so excited that these other muddles, fluctuations, follies, came as a natural consequence from that.   Out of this excitement came those wild floods of angry energy that made him career about——

"Like some damned Cracker," said the Captain.

"For instance," he asked himself, "*now?* what am I going for?"

"If I go back she'll probably behave like an offended Queen. Doesn't seem to understand anything that does not focus on herself. Wants a sort of Limelight Lover. . . .

"She *relies* upon exciting me!

"She relies upon exciting everyone!—she's just a woman specialised for excitement."

And after meditating through a profound minute upon this judgment, the Captain pronounced these two epoch-making words: "*I won't!*"

§ 10

The Captain's mind was now in a state of almost violent lucidity.

"This sex stuff," he said, "first I kept it under too tight and now I've let it rip too loose.

"I've been just a distracted fool, with my head swimming with meetings and embraces and—frills."

He produced some long impending generalisations.

"Not a man's work, this Lover business. Dancing about in a world of petticoats and powder puffs and attentions and jealousies. Rotten game. . . . Played off against some other man. . . .

"I'll be hanged if I am. . . .

"Have to put women in their places. . . .

"Make a hash of everything if we don't. . . ."

Then for a time the Captain meditated in silence and chewed his knuckle. His face darkened to a scowl. He swore as though some thought twisted and tormented him. "Let some other man get her! Think of her with some other man.

"I don't care," he said, when obviously he did.
"There's other women in the world.

"A man—a man mustn't care for *that*. . . .

"It's this or that," said the Captain, "anyhow. . . ."

§ 11

Suddenly the Captain's mind was made up and done.
He arose to his feet and his face was firm and tranquil
and now nearer pallor than pink. He left his bicycle
and trailer by the wayside even as Christian left his
burden. He asked a passing nurse-girl the way
to the nearest railway station and thither he went.
Incidentally and because the opportunity offered he
called in upon a cyclist's repair shop and committed his
abandoned machinery to its keeping. He went straight
to London, changed at his flat, dined at his club and
caught the night train for France—for France and whatever was left of the grand manœuvres.

He wrote a letter to Madeleine from the Est train
next day, using their customary endearments, avoiding
any discussion of their relations and describing the
scenery of the Seine valley and the characteristics of
Rouen in a few vivid and masterly phrases.

"If she's worth having she'll understand," said the
Captain, but he knew perfectly well she would not
understand.

Mrs. Geedge noted this letter among the others,
and afterwards she was much exercised by Madeleine's
behaviour. For suddenly that lady became extraordinarily gay and joyous in her bearing, singing
snatches of song and bubbling over with suggestions
for larks and picnics and wild excursions. She patted
Mr. Geedge on the shoulder and ran her arm through
the arm of Professor Bowles. Both gentlemen received
these familiarities with a gawky coyness that Mrs.
Geedge found contemptible. And moreover Madeleine

drew several shy strangers into their circle. She invited the management to a happy participation.

Her great idea was a moonlight picnic. "We'll have a great camp-fire and afterwards we'll dance—this very night."

"But wouldn't it be better to-morrow?"

"To-night!"

"To-morrow perhaps Captain Douglas may be back again. And he's so good at all these things."

Mrs. Geedge knew better because she had seen the French stamp on the letter, but she meant to get to the bottom of the business, and thus it was she said this.

"I've sent him back to his soldiering," said Madeleine serenely. "He has better things to do."

§ 12

For some moments after the unceremonious departure of Captain Douglas from the presence of Lord Moggeridge, it did not occur to anyone, it did not occur even to Bealby, that the Captain had left his witness behind him. The General and the Lord Chancellor moved into the hall, and Bealby, under the sway of a swift compelling gesture from Candler, followed modestly. The same current swept them all out into the portico, and while the under-butler whistled up a hansom for the General, the Lord Chancellor with a dignity that was at once polite and rapid, and with Candler gravely protective and a little reproving, departed. Bealby, slowly apprehending their desertion, regarded the world of London with perplexity and dismay. Candler had gone. The last of the gentlemen was going. The under-butler, Bealby felt, was no friend. Under-butlers never are.

Lord Chickney in the very act of entering his cab had his coat-tail tugged. He looked inquiringly.

"Please, sir, there's me," said Bealby.

Lord Chickney reflected. " Well ?" he said.

The spirit of Bealby was now greatly abased. His face and voice betrayed him on the verge of tears. " I want to go 'ome to Shonts, sir."

"Well, my boy, go 'ome—go home I mean to Shonts."

" 'E's gone, sir," said Bealby. . . .

Lord Chickney was a good-hearted man, and he knew that a certain public kindliness and disregard of appearances, looks far better and is infinitely more popular than a punctilious dignity. He took Bealby to Waterloo in his hansom, got him a third-class ticket to Chelsome, tipped a porter to see him safely into his train and dismissed him in the most fatherly manner.

§ 13

It was well after tea-time, Bealby felt, as he came once more within the boundaries of the Shonts estate.

It was a wiser and a graver Bealby who returned from this week of miscellaneous adventure. He did not clearly understand all that had happened to him; in particular he was puzzled by the extreme annoyance and sudden departure of Captain Douglas from the presence of Lord Moggeridge; but his general impression was that he had been in great peril of dire punishment and that he had been rather hastily and ignominiously reprieved. The nice old gentleman with the long grey moustaches had dismissed him to the train at last with a quality of benediction. But Bealby understood now better than he had done before that adventures do not always turn out well for the boy hero, and that the social system has a number of dangerous and disagreeable holes at the bottom. He had reached the beginnings of wisdom. He was glad he had got away from the tramp and still gladder that he had got away from Crayminster; he was sorry that he would never see the beautiful lady again, and perplexed and perplexed.

And also he was interested in the probability of his mother having toast for tea. . . .

It must, he felt, be a long time after tea-time,— quite late. . . .

He had weighed the advisability of returning quietly to his windowless bedroom under the stairs, putting on his little green apron and emerging with a dutiful sang-froid as if nothing had happened, on the one hand, or of going to the gardens on the other. But tea—with eatables—seemed more probable at the gardens. . . .

He was deflected from the direct route across the park by a long deep trench, that someone had made and abandoned since the previous Sunday morning. He wondered what it was for. It was certainly very ugly. And as he came out by the trees and got the full effect of the façade, he detected a strangely bandaged quality about Shonts. It was as if Shonts had recently been in a fight and got a black eye. Then he saw the reason for this; one tower was swathed in scaffolding. He wondered what could have happened to the tower. Then his own troubles resumed their sway.

He was so fortunate as not to meet his father in the gardens, and he entered the house so meekly that his mother did not look up from the cashmere she was sewing. She was sitting at the table sewing some newly dyed black cashmere.

He was astonished at her extreme pallor and the drooping resignation of her pose.

" Mother !" he said and she looked up convulsively and stared, stared with bright round astonished eyes.

" I'm sorry, mother, I 'aven't been quite a good steward's-room boy, mother. If I could 'ave another go, mother. . . ."

He halted for a moment, astonished that she said nothing, but only sat with that strange expression and opened and shut her mouth.

" Reely—I'd *try,* mother. . . ."

LOVE AND MR. LEWISHAM

" Great Spirits and Great Businesse doe keepe out this weak Passion . . . yet Love can finde Entrance not only into an open Heart but also into a Heart well fortified, if Watch be not well kept."— FRANCIS BACON.

CHAPTER THE FIRST

Introduces Mr. Lewisham

THE opening chapter does not concern itself with Love—indeed that antagonist does not certainly appear until the third—and Mr. Lewisham is seen at his studies. It was ten years ago; and in those days he was assistant master in the Whortley Proprietary School, Whortley, Sussex, and his wages were forty pounds a year, out of which he had to afford fifteen shillings a week during term time to lodge with Mrs. Munday, at the little shop in the West Street. He was called "Mr." to distinguish him from the bigger boys, whose duty it was to learn, and it was a matter of stringent regulation that he should be addressed as "Sir."

He wore ready-made clothes, his black jacket of rigid line was dusted about the front and sleeves with scholastic chalk, and his face was downy and his moustache incipient. He was a passable-looking youngster of eighteen, fair-haired, indifferently barbered and with a quite unnecessary pair of glasses on his fairly prominent nose—he wore these to make himself look older, that discipline might be maintained. At the particular moment when this story begins he was in his bedroom. An attic it was, with lead-framed dormer windows, a slanting ceiling and a bulging wall, covered, as a number of torn places witnessed, with innumerable strata of florid old-fashioned paper.

To judge by the room, Mr. Lewisham thought little of Love but much on Greatness. Over the head of the bed, for example, where good folks hang texts, these truths asserted themselves, written in a clear, bold, youthfully flourishing hand : " Knowledge is Power," and " What man has done man can do "—man in the second instance referring to Mr. Lewisham. Never for a moment were these things to be forgotten. Mr. Lewisham could see them afresh every morning as his head came through his shirt. And over the yellow-painted box upon which—for lack of shelves—Mr. Lewisham's library was arranged, was a " *Schema*." (Why he should not have headed it " Scheme," the editor of the *Church Times,* who calls his miscellaneous notes " Varia," is better able to say than I.) In this scheme, 1892 was indicated as the year in which Mr. Lewisham proposed to take his B.A. degree at the London University with " hons. in all subjects," and 1895 as the date of his " gold medal." Subsequently there were to be " pamphlets in the Liberal interest," and such like things duly dated. " Who would control others must first control himself," remarked the wall over the wash-hand stand, and behind the door against the Sunday trousers was a portrait of Carlyle.

These were no mere threats against the universe; operations had begun. Jostling Shakespeare, Emerson's Essays, and the penny Life of Confucius, there were battered and defaced school books, a number of the excellent manuals of the Universal Correspondence Association, exercise books, ink (red and black) in penny bottles, and an india-rubber stamp with Mr.

Lewisham's name. A trophy of bluish-green South Kensington certificates for geometrical drawing, astronomy, physiology, physiography, and inorganic chemistry, adorned his further wall. And against the Carlyle portrait was a manuscript list of French irregular verbs.

Attached by a drawing-pin to the roof over the wash-hand stand, which—the room being an attic—sloped almost dangerously, dangled a Time-Table. Mr. Lewisham was to rise at five, and that this was no vain boasting, a cheap American alarum clock by the books on the box witnessed. The lumps of mellow chocolate on the papered ledge by the bed-head, endorsed that evidence. "French until eight," said the time-table curtly. Breakfast was to be eaten in twenty minutes; then twenty-five minutes of "literature"—to be precise, learning extracts (preferably pompous) from the plays of William Shakespeare—and then to school and duty. The time-table further prescribed Latin Composition for the recess and the dinner hour ("literature," however, during the meal), and varied its injunctions for the rest of the twenty-four hours according to the day of the week. Not a moment for Satan and that "mischief still" of his. Only three-score and ten has the confidence, as well as the time, to be idle.

But just think of the admirable quality of such a scheme! Up and busy at five, with all the world about one horizontal, warm, dreamy-brained or stupidly hullish; if roused, roused only to grunt and sigh and roll over again into oblivion. By eight three hours' clear start, three hours' knowledge ahead of everyone. It takes, I have been told by an eminent scholar, about a thousand hours of sincere work to learn a language completely—after three or four languages much less—which gives you, even at the outset, one each a year before breakfast. The gift of tongues—picked up like mushrooms! Then that "literature"—an astonishing conception! In the afternoon mathematics and the sciences. Could anything be simpler or more magnificent? In six years Mr. Lewisham will have his five or six languages, a sound, all-round education, a habit of tremendous industry, and be still but four and twenty. He will already have honour in his university and ampler means. One realises that those pamphlets in the Liberal interest will be no obscure platitudes. Where Mr. Lewisham will be at thirty stirs the imagination. There will be modifications of the Schema, of course, as experience widens. But the spirit of it—the spirit of it is a devouring flame!

He was sitting facing the diamond-framed window, writing, writing fast, on a second yellow box that was turned on end and empty, and the lid was open, and his knees were conveniently stuck into the cavity. The bed was strewn with books and copygraphed sheets of instructions from his remote correspondence tutors. Pursuant to the dangling time-table he was, you would have noticed, translating Latin into English.

Imperceptibly the speed of his writing diminished. " *Urit me Glyceræ nitor* " lay ahead and troubled him. " Urit me," he murmured, and his eyes travelled from his book out of window to the vicar's roof opposite and its ivied chimneys. His brows were knit at first and then relaxed. " *Urit me !*" He had put his pen into his mouth and glanced about for his dictionary. *Urare ?*

Suddenly his expression changed. Movement dictionary-ward ceased. He was listening to a light tapping sound—it was a footfall—outside.

He stood up abruptly, and stretching his neck peered through his unnecessary glasses and the diamond panes down into the street. Looking acutely downward he could see a hat daintily trimmed with pinkish white blossom, the shoulder of a jacket, and just the tips of nose and chin. Certainly the stranger who sat under the gallery last Sunday next the Frobishers. Then, too, he had seen her only obliquely. . . .

He watched her until she passed beyond the window

frame. He strained to see impossibly round the corner. . . .

Then he started, frowned, took his pen from his mouth. "This wandering attention!" he said. "The slightest thing! Where was I? Tcha!" He made a noise with his teeth to express his irritation, sat down, and replaced his knees in the upturned box. "Urit me," he said, biting the end of his pen and looking for his dictionary.

It was a Wednesday half-holiday late in March, a spring day glorious in amber light, dazzling white clouds and the intensest blue, casting a powder of wonderful green hither and thither among the trees and rousing all the birds to tumultuous rejoicings; a rousing day, a clamatory insistent day, a veritable herald of summer. The stir of that anticipation was in the air, the warm earth was parting above the swelling seeds, and all the pine-woods were full of the minute crepitation of opening bud scales. And not only was the stir of Mother Nature's awakening in the earth and the air and the trees, but also in Mr. Lewisham's youthful blood, bidding him rouse himself to live—live in a sense quite other than that the Schema indicated.

He saw the dictionary peeping from under a paper, looked up "Urit me," appreciated the shining "nitor" of Glycera's shoulders, and so fell idle again to rouse himself abruptly.

"I *can't* fix my attention," said Mr. Lewisham. He took off the needless glasses, wiped them, and blinked his eyes. This confounded Horace and his stimulating epithets! A walk?

"I won't be beat," he said—incorrectly—replaced his glasses, brought his elbows down on either side of his box with resonant violence, and clutched the hair over his ears with both hands. . . .

In five minutes' time he found himself watching the swallows curving through the blue over the vicarage garden.

"Did ever man have such a bother with himself as me?" he asked vaguely but vehemently. "It's self-indulgence does it—sitting down's the beginning of laziness."

So he stood up to his work, and came into permanent view of the village street. "If she has gone round the corner by the post office, she will come in sight over the palings above the allotments," suggested the unexplored and undisciplined region of Mr. Lewisham's mind. . . .

She did not come into sight. Apparently she had not gone round by the post office after all. It made one wonder where she had gone. Did she go up through the town to the avenue on these occasions? . . . Then abruptly a cloud drove across the sunlight, the glowing street went cold and Mr. Lewisham's imagination submitted to control. So "*Mater sæva cupidinum,*" "The untameable mother of desires"—Horace (Book II. of the Odes) was the author appointed by the university for Mr. Lewisham's matriculation—was, after all, translated to its prophetic end.

Precisely as the church clock struck five Mr. Lewisham, with a punctuality that was indeed almost too prompt for a really earnest student, shut his Horace, took up his Shakespeare, and descended the narrow curved uncarpeted staircase that led from his garret to the living room in which he had his tea with his landlady, Mrs. Munday. That good lady was alone, and after a few civilities Mr. Lewisham opened his Shakespeare and read from a mark onward—that mark, by-the-by, was in the middle of a scene—while he consumed mechanically a number of slices of bread and whort jam.

Mrs. Munday watched him over her spectacles and thought how bad so much reading must be for the eyes, until the tinkling of her shop-bell called her away to a customer. At twenty-five minutes to six he put the book back in the window-sill, dashed a few crumbs from his jacket, assumed a mortar-board cap that was lying on the tea-caddy, and went forth to his evening "preparation duty."

The West Street was empty and shining golden with the sunset. Its beauty seized upon him, and he forgot to repeat the passage from Henry VIII. that should have occupied him down the street. Instead he was presently thinking of that insubordinate glance from his window and of little chins and nose-tips. His eyes became remote in their expression. . . .

The school door was opened by an obsequious little boy with "lines" to be examined.

Mr. Lewisham felt a curious change of atmosphere on his entry. The door slammed behind him. The hall with its insistent scholastic suggestions, its yellow marbled paper, its long rows of hat-pegs, its disreputable array of umbrellas, a broken mortar-board and a tattered and scattered *Principia*, seemed dim and dull in contrast with the luminous stir of the early March evening outside. An unusual sense of the greyness of a teacher's life, of the greyness indeed of the life of all studious souls, came and went in his mind. He took the "lines," written painfully over three pages of exercise book, and obliterated them with a huge G. E. L., scrawled monstrously across each page. He heard the familiar mingled noises of the playground drifting in to him through the open schoolroom door.

CHAPTER THE SECOND

"As the Wind Blows"

A FLAW in that pentagram of a time-table, that pentagram by which the demons of distraction were to be excluded from Mr. Lewisham's career to Greatness, was the absence of a clause forbidding study out of doors. It was the day after the trivial window peeping of the last chapter that this gap in the time-table became apparent, a day if possible more gracious and alluring than its predecessor, and at half-past twelve, instead of returning from the school directly to his lodging, Mr. Lewisham escaped through the omission and made his way—Horace in pocket—to the park gates and so to the avenue of ancient trees that encircles the broad Whortley domain. He dismissed a suspicion of his motive with perfect success. In the avenue—for the path is but little frequented—one might expect to read undisturbed. The open air, the erect attitude, are surely better than sitting in a stuffy, enervating bed-

870

room. The open air is distinctly healthy, hardy, simple. . . .

The day was breezy, and there was a perpetual rustling, a going and coming in the budding trees.

The network of the beeches was full of golden sunlight, and all the lower branches were shot with horizontal dashes of new-born green

> " *Tu, nisi ventis*
> *Debes ludibrium, cave.*"

was the appropriate matter of Mr. Lewisham's thoughts, and he was mechanically trying to keep the book open in three places at once, at the text, the notes and the literal translation, while he turned up the vocabulary for *ludibrium,* when his attention, wandering dangerously near the top of the page, fell over the edge and escaped with incredible swiftness down the avenue. . . .

A girl wearing a straw hat adorned with white blossom, was advancing towards him. Her occupation, too, was literary. Indeed, she was so busy writing that evidently she did not perceive him :

Unreasonable emotions descended upon Mr. Lewisham—emotions that are unaccountable on the mere hypothesis of a casual meeting. Something was whispered; it sounded suspiciously like "It's her!" He advanced with his fingers in his book, ready to retreat to its pages if she looked up, and watched her over it. *Ludibrium* passed out of his universe. She was clearly unaware of his nearness, he thought, intent upon her writing, whatever that might be. He wondered what it might be. Her face, foreshortened by her downward regard, seemed infantile. Her fluttering skirt was short, and showed her shoes and ankles. He noted her graceful, easy steps. A figure of health and lightness it was, sunlit, and advancing towards him, something, as he afterwards recalled, with a certain astonishment, quite outside the Schema.

Nearer she came and nearer, her eyes still downcast

28*

He was full of vague, stupid promptings towards an uncalled-for intercourse. It was curious she did not see him. He began to expect almost painfully the moment when she would look up, though what there was to expect—! He thought of what she would see when she discovered him, and wondered where the tassel of his cap might be hanging—it sometimes occluded one eye. It was of course quite impossible to put up a hand and investigate. He was near trembling with excitement. His paces, acts which are usually automatic, became uncertain and difficult. One might have thought he had never passed a human being before. Still nearer, ten yards now, nine, eight. Would she go past without looking up? . . .

Then their eyes met.

She had hazel eyes, but Mr. Lewisham being quite an amateur about eyes, could find no words for them. She looked demurely into his face. She seemed to find nothing there. She glanced away from him among the trees, and passed, and nothing remained in front of him but an empty avenue, a sunlit, green-shot void.

The incident was over.

From far away the soughing of the breeze swept towards him, and in a moment all the twigs about him were quivering and rustling and the boughs creaking with a gust of wind. It seemed to urge him away from her. The faded dead leaves that had once been green and young sprang up, raced one another, leapt, danced and pirouetted, and then something large struck him on the neck, stayed for a startling moment, and drove past him up the avenue.

Something vividly white! A sheet of paper—the sheet upon which she had been writing!

For what seemed a long time he did not grasp the situation. He glanced over his shoulder and understood suddenly. His awkwardness vanished. Horace in hand, he gave chase, and in ten paces had secured the fugitive document. He turned towards her, flushed with triumph, the quarry in his hand. He had as he picked it up seen what was written, but the situation dominated him for the instant. He made a stride towards her, and only then understood what he had seen. Lines of a measured length and capitals! Could it really be—? He stopped. He looked again, eyebrows rising. He held it before him, staring now quite frankly. It had been written with a stylographic pen. Thus it ran:

"*Come! Sharp's the word.*"

And then again,

"*Come! Sharp's the word.*"

And then,

"*Come! Sharp's the word.*"
"*Come! Sharp's the word.*"

And so on all down the page, in a boyish hand uncommonly like Frobisher ii.'s.

Surely! "I say!" said Mr. Lewisham, struggling with the new aspect and forgetting all his manners in his surprise. . . . He remembered giving the imposition quite well: Frobisher ii. had repeated the exhortation just a little too loudly—had brought the thing upon himself. To find her doing this jarred oddly upon certain vague preconceptions he had formed of her. Somehow it seemed as if she had betrayed him. That of course was only for the instant.

She had come up with him now. "May I have my sheet of paper, please?" she said with a catching of her breath. She was a couple of inches less in height than he. Do you observe her half-open lips, said Mother Nature in a noiseless aside to Mr. Lewisham—a thing he afterwards recalled. In her eyes was a touch of apprehension.

"I say," he said, with protest still uppermost. "You oughtn't to do this."

"Do what?"

"This. Impositions. For my boys."

She raised her eyebrows, then knitted them momentarily, and looked at him. "Are *you* Mr. Lewisham?"

she asked with an affectation of entire ignorance and discovery.

She knew him perfectly well, which was one reason why she was writing the imposition, but pretending not to know gave her something to say.

Mr. Lewisham nodded.

" Of all people ! Then "—frankly—" you have just found me out."

" I am afraid I have," said Lewisham. " I am afraid I *have* found you out."

They looked at one another for the next move. She decided to plead in extenuation.

" Teddy Frobisher is my cousin. I know it's very wrong, but he seemed to have such a lot to do and to be in *such* trouble. And I had nothing to do. In fact, it was *I* who offered. . . ."

She stopped and looked at him. She seemed to consider her remark complete.

That meeting of the eyes had an oddly disconcerting quality. He tried to keep to the business of the imposition. " You ought not to have done that," he said, encountering her steadfastly.

She looked down and then into his face again. " No," she said, " I suppose I ought not to. I'm very sorry."

Her looking down and up again produced another unreasonable effect. It seemed to Lewisham that they were discussing something quite other than the topic of their conversation; a persuasion patently absurd and only to be accounted for by the general disorder of his faculties. He made a serious attempt to keep his footing of reproof.

" I should have detected the writing, you know."

" Of course you would. It was very wrong of me to persuade him. But I did—I assure you. He seemed in such trouble. And I thought———"

She made another break, and there was a faint deepening of colour in her cheeks. Suddenly, stupidly, his own adolescent cheeks began to glow. It became necessary to banish that sense of a duplicate topic forthwith.

"I can assure you," he said, now very earnestly, "I never give a punishment, never, unless it is merited. I make that a rule. I—er—*always* make that a rule. I am very careful indeed."

"I am really sorry," she interrupted with frank contrition. "It *was* silly of me."

Lewisham felt unaccountably sorry she should have to apologise, and he spoke at once with the idea of checking the reddening of his face. "I don't think *that*," he said with a sort of belated alacrity. "Really, it was kind of you, you know—very kind of you indeed. And I know that—I can quite understand that—er—your kindness. . . ."

"Ran away with me. And now poor little Teddy will get into worse trouble for letting me. . . ."

"Oh no," said Mr. Lewisham, perceiving an opportunity and trying not to smile his appreciation of what he was saying. "I had no business to read it as I picked it up—absolutely no business. Consequently. . . ."

"You won't take any notice of it? Really!"

"Certainly not," said Mr. Lewisham.

Her face lit with a smile, and Mr. Lewisham's relaxed in sympathy. "It is nothing—it's the proper thing for me to do, you know."

"But so many people wouldn't do it. Schoolmasters are not usually so—chivalrous."

He was chivalrous! The phrase acted like a spur. He obeyed a foolish impulse.

"If you like——" he said.

"What?"

"He needn't do this. The Impot., I mean. I'll let him off."

"Really?"

"I can."

"It's awfully kind of you."

"I don't mind," he said. "It's nothing much. If you really think. . . ."

He was full of self-applause for this scandalous sacrifice of justice.

"It's awfully kind of you," she said.

"It's nothing, really," he explained, "nothing."

"Most people wouldn't——"

"I know."

Pause.

"It's all right," he said. "Really."

He would have given worlds for something more to say, something witty and original, but nothing came.

The pause lengthened. She glanced over her shoulder down the vacant avenue. This interview—this momentous series of things unsaid was coming to an end! She looked at him hesitatingly and smiled again. She held out her hand. No doubt that was the proper thing to do. He took it, searching a void, tumultuous mind in vain.

"It's awfully kind of you," she said again as she did so.

"It don't matter a bit," said Mr. Lewisham, and sought vainly for some other saying, some doorway remark into new topics. Her hand was cool and soft and firm, the most delightful thing to grasp, and this observation ousted all other things. He held it for a moment, but nothing would come.

They discovered themselves hand in hand. They both laughed and felt "silly." They shook hands in the manner of quite intimate friends, and snatched their hands away awkwardly. She turned, glanced timidly at him over her shoulder, and hesitated. "Good-bye," she said, and was suddenly walking from him.

He bowed to her receding back, made a seventeenth-century sweep with his college cap, and then some hitherto unexplored regions of his mind flashed into revolt.

Hardly had she gone six paces when he was at her side again.

"I say," he said with a fearful sense of his temerity and raising his mortar-board awkwardly as though he was passing a funeral. "But that sheet of paper. . . ."

"Yes," she said, surprised—quite naturally.

"May I have it?"

"Why?"

He felt a breathless pleasure, like that of sliding down a slope of snow. "I would like to have it."

She smiled and raised her eyebrows, but his excitement was now too great for smiling. "Look here!" she said, and displayed the sheet crumpled into a ball. She laughed—with a touch of effort.

"I don't mind that," said Mr. Lewisham laughing too. He captured the paper by an insistent gesture and smoothed it out with fingers that trembled.

"You don't mind?" he said.

"Mind what?"

"If I keep it?"

"Why should I?"

Pause. Their eyes met again. There was an odd constraint about both of them, a palpitating interval of silence.

"I really *must* be going," she said suddenly, breaking the spell by an effort. She turned about and left him with the crumpled piece of paper in the fist that held the book, the other hand once more lifting the mortar-board in a dignified salute.

He watched her receding figure. His heart was beating with remarkable rapidity. How light, how living she seemed! Little round flakes of sunlight raced down her as she went. She walked fast, then slowly, looking sideways once or twice but not back, until she reached the park gates. Then she looked towards him, a remote, friendly little figure, made a gesture of farewell, and disappeared.

His face was flushed and his eyes bright. Curiously

enough, he was out of breath. He stared for a long time at the vacant end of the avenue. Then he turned his eyes to his trophy gripped against the closed and forgotten Horace in his hand.

CHAPTER THE THIRD

The Wonderful Discovery

ON Sunday it was Lewisham's duty to accompany the boarders twice to church. The boys sat in the gallery above the choir, facing the organ loft and at right angles to the general congregation. It was a prominent position, and made him feel painfully conspicuous, except in moods of exceptional vanity when he used to imagine that all these people were thinking how his forehead and his certificates accorded. He thought a lot in those days of his certificates and forehead, but little of his honest, healthy face beneath it. (To tell the truth there was nothing very wonderful about his forehead.) He rarely looked down the church, as he fancied to do so would be to meet the collective eye of the congregation regarding him. So that in the morning he was not able to see that the Frobishers' pew was empty until the litany.

But in the evening, on the way to church, the Frobishers and their guest crossed the market-square as his string of boys marched along the west side. And the guest was arrayed in a gay new dress, as if it were already Easter, and her face set in its dark hair came with a strange effect of mingled freshness and familiarity. She looked at him calmly! He felt very awkward and was for cutting his new acquaintance. Then hesitated, and raised his hat with a jerk as if to Mrs. Frobisher. Neither lady acknowledged his salute, which may possibly have been a little unexpected. Then young Siddons dropped his hymn-book, stooped to pick it up, and Lewisham almost fell upon him. . . . He entered church in a mood of black despair.

But consolation of a sort came soon enough. As *she* took her seat she distinctly glanced up at the gallery, and afterwards as he knelt to pray, he peeped between his fingers and saw her looking up again. She was certainly not laughing at him.

In those days much of Lewisham's mind was still an unknown land to him. He believed among other things that he was always the same consistent intelligent human being, whereas under certain stimuli be became no longer reasonable and disciplined but a purely imaginative and emotional person. Music, for instance, carried him away, and particularly the effect of many voices in unison whirled him off from almost any state of mind to a fine massive emotionality. And the evening service at Whortley church—at the evening service surplices were worn—the chanting and singing, the vague brilliance of the numerous candle flames, the multitudinous unanimity of the congregation down there, kneeling, rising, thunderously responding, invariably inebriated him. Inspired him, if you will, and turned the prose of his life into poetry. And Chance, coming to the aid of Dame Nature, dropped just the apt suggestion into his now highly responsive ear.

The second hymn was a simple and popular one, dealing with the theme of Faith, Hope and Charity, and having each verse ending with the word "Love." Conceive it, long drawn out and disarticulate——

Faith will van . . . ish in . . . to sight,
Hope be emp . . . tied in deli . . . ight,
Love in Heaven will shine more bri . . . ight
There . . . fore gi . . . ve us . . . Love.

At the third repetition of the refrain, Lewisham looked down across the chancel and met her eyes for a brief instant. . . .

He stopped singing abruptly. Then the consciousness of the serried ranks of faces below there, came with almost overwhelming force upon him, and he dared not look at her again. He felt the blood rushing to his face.

Love! The greatest of these. The greatest of all things. Better than fame. Better than knowledge. So came the great discovery like a flood across his mind, pouring over it with the cadence of the hymn and sending a tide of pink in sympathy across his forehead. The rest of the service was phantasmagorial background to that great reality—a phantasmagorial background a little inclined to stare. He, Mr. Lewisham, was in Love.

"A . . . men." He was so preoccupied that he found the whole congregation subsiding into their seats, and himself still standing, rapt. He sat down spasmodically, with an impact that seemed to him to re-echo through the church.

As they came out of the porch into the thickening night he seemed to see her everywhere. He fancied she had gone on in front, and he hurried up the boys in the hope of overtaking her. They pushed through the throng of dim people going homeward. Should he raise his hat to her again? . . . But it was Susie Hopbrow in a light-coloured dress—a raven in dove's plumage. He felt a curious mixture of relief and disappointment. He would see her no more that night.

He hurried from the school to his lodging. He wanted very urgently to be alone. He went upstairs to his little room and sat before the upturned box on which his Butler's Analogy was spread open. He did not go to the formality of lighting the candle. He leant back and gazed blissfully at the solitary planet that hung over the vicarage garden.

He took out of his pocket a crumpled sheet of paper, smoothed and carefully refolded, covered with a writing not unlike that of Frobisher ii., and after some maidenly hesitation pressed this treasure to his lips. The Schema and the time-table hung in the darkness like the mere ghosts of themselves.

Mrs. Munday called him thrice to his supper.

He went out immediately after it was eaten and wandered under the stars until he came over the hill behind the town again, and clambered up the back to the stile in sight of the Frobishers' house. He selected the only lit window as hers. Behind the blind, Mrs. Frobisher, thirty-eight, was busy with her curl-papers— she used papers because they were better for the hair— and discussing certain neighbours in a fragmentary way with Mr. Frobisher, who was in bed. Presently she moved the candle to examine a faint discoloration of her complexion that rendered her uneasy.

Outside, Mr. Lewisham (eighteen) stood watching the orange oblong for the best part of half an hour, until it vanished and left the house black and blank. Then he sighed deeply and returned home in a very glorious mood indeed.

He awoke the next morning feeling extremely serious, but not clearly remembering the overnight occurrences. His eye fell on his clock. The time was six and he had not heard the alarum; as a matter of fact the alarum had not been wound up. He jumped out of bed at once and alighted upon his best trousers amorphously dropped on the floor instead of methodically cast over a chair. As he soaped his head he tried, according to his rules of revision, to remember the overnight reading. He could not for the life of him. The truth came to him as he was getting into his shirt. His head, struggling in its recesses, became motionless, the handless cuffs ceased to dangle for a minute. . . .

Then his head came through slowly with a surprised expression upon his face. He remembered. He remembered the thing as a bald discovery, and without a touch of emotion. With all the achromatic clearness, the unromantic colourlessness of the early morning. . . .

Yes. He had it now quite distinctly. There had been no overnight reading. He was in Love.

The proposition jarred with some vague thing in his mind. He stood staring for a space, and then began looking about absent-mindedly for his collar-stud. He paused in front of his Schema, regarding it.

CHAPTER THE FOURTH

Raised Eyebrows

"WORK must be done anyhow," said Mr. Lewisham. But never had the extraordinary advantages of openair study presented themselves so vividly. Before breakfast he took half an hour of open-air reading along the allotments land near the Frobishers' house; after breakfast and before school he went through the avenue with a book, and returned from school to his lodgings circuitously through the avenue, and so back to the avenue for thirty minutes or so before afternoon school. When during these periods of open-air study Mr. Lewisham was not looking over the top of his book, then commonly he was glancing over his shoulder. And at last whom should he see but——!

He saw her out of the corner of his eye, and he turned away at once, pretending not to have seen her. His whole being was suddenly irradiated with emotion. The hands holding his book gripped it very tightly. He did not glance back again, but walked slowly and steadfastly, reading an ode that he could not have translated to save his life, and listening acutely for her approach.

And after an interminable time, as it seemed, came a faint footfall and the swish of skirts behind him.

He felt as though his head was directed forward by a clutch of iron.

"Mr. Lewisham," she said close to him, and he turned with a quality of movement that was almost convulsive. He raised his cap clumsily.

He took her extended hand by an afterthought, and held it until she withdrew it. "I am so glad to have met you," she said.

"So am I," said Lewisham simply.

They stood facing one another for an expressive moment, and then by a movement she indicated her intention to walk along the avenue with him. "I wanted so much," she said looking down at her feet, "to thank you for letting Teddy off, you know. That is why I wanted to see you." Lewisham took his first step beside her. "And it's odd, isn't it," she said looking up into his face, "that I should meet you here in just the same place. I believe. . . . Yes. The very same place we met before."

Mr. Lewisham was tongue-tied.

"Do you often come here?" she said.

"Well," he considered—and his voice was most unreasonably hoarse when he spoke— "No. No. . . . That is— At least not often. Now and then. In fact I like it rather for reading and that sort of thing. It's so quiet."

"I suppose you read a great deal?"

"When one teaches one has to."

"But you. . . ."

"I'm rather fond of reading, certainly. Are you?"

"I *love* it."

Mr. Lewisham was glad she loved reading. He would have been disappointed had she answered differently. But she spoke with real fervour. She *loved* reading! It was pleasant. She would understand him a little perhaps. "Of course," she went on, "I'm not clever like some people are. And I have to read books as I get hold of them."

" So do I," said Mr. Lewisham, " for the matter of that. . . . Have you read . . . Carlyle?"

The conversation was now fairly under way. They were walking side by side beneath the swaying boughs. Mr. Lewisham's sensations were ecstatic, marred only by a dread of some casual boy coming upon them. She had not read *much* Carlyle. She had always wanted to, even from quite a little girl—she had heard so much about him. She knew he was a Really Great Writer, a *very* Great Writer indeed. All she *had* read of him she liked. She could say that. As much as she liked anything. And she had seen his house in Chelsea.

Lewisham, whose knowledge of London had been obtained by excursion trips on six or seven isolated days, was much impressed by this. It seemed to put her at once on a footing of intimacy with this imposing Personality. It had never occurred to him at all vividly that these Great Writers had real abiding places. She gave him a few descriptive touches that made the house suddenly real and distinctive to him. She lived quite near, she said, at least within walking distance, in Clapham. He instantly forgot the vague design of lending her his " *Sartor Resartus* " in his curiosity to learn more about her home. " Clapham—that's almost in London, isn't it ? " he said.

" Quite," she said, but she volunteered no further information about her domestic circumstances. " I like London," she generalised, " and especially in winter." And she proceeded to praise London, its public libraries, its shops, the multitudes of people, the facilities for " doing what you like," the concerts one could go to, the theatres. (It seemed she moved in fairly good society.) " There's always something to see even if you only go out for a walk," she said, " and down here there's nothing to read but idle novels. And those not new."

Mr. Lewisham had regretfully to admit the lack of such culture and mental activity in Whortley. It made him feel terribly her inferior. He had only his bookishness and his certificates to set against it all—and she had seen Carlyle's house! "Down here," she said, "there's nothing to talk about but scandal." It was too true.

At the corner by the stile, beyond which the willows were splendid against the blue with silvery aments and golden pollen, they turned by mutual impulse and retraced their steps. "I've simply had no one to talk to down here," she said. "Not what *I* call talking."

"I hope," said Lewisham, making a resolute plunge, "perhaps while you are staying at Whortley. . . ."

He paused perceptibly, and she, following his eyes, saw a voluminous black figure approaching. "We may," said Mr. Lewisham, resuming his remark, "chance to meet again, perhaps."

He had been about to challenge her to a deliberate meeting. A certain delightful tangle of paths that followed the bank of the river had been in his mind. But the apparition of Mr. George Bonover, headmaster of the Whortley Proprietary School, chilled him amazingly. Dame Nature no doubt had arranged the meeting of our young couple, but about Bonover she seems to have been culpably careless. She now receded illimitably, and Mr. Lewisham, with the most unpleasant feelings, found himself face to face with a typical representative of a social organisation which objects very strongly *inter alia* to promiscuous conversation on the part of the young unmarried junior master.

"—chance to meet again, perhaps," said Mr. Lewisham, with a sudden lack of spirit.

"I hope so too," she said.

Pause. Mr. Bonover's features, and particularly a bushy pair of black eyebrows, were now very near, those eyebrows already raised, apparently to express a refined astonishment.

" Is this Mr. Bonover coming?" she asked.

" Yes."

Prolonged pause.

Would he stop and accost them? At any rate this frightful silence must end. Mr. Lewisham sought in his mind for some remark wherewith to cover his employer's approach. He was surprised to find his mind a desert. He made a colossal effort. If they could only talk, if they could only seem at their ease! But this blank incapacity was eloquent of guilt. Ah!

" It's a lovely day, though," said Mr. Lewisham. " Isn't it?"

She agreed with him. " Isn't it?" she said.

And then Mr. Bonover passed, forehead tight reefed so to speak, and lips impressively compressed. Mr. Lewisham raised his mortar-board, and to his astonishment, Mr. Bonover responded with a markedly formal salute—mock clerical hat sweeping circuitously—and the regard of a searching, disapproving eye, and so passed. Lewisham was overcome with astonishment at this improvement on the nod of their ordinary commerce. And so this terrible incident terminated for the time.

He felt a momentary gust of indignation. After all, why should Bonover or anyone interfere with his talking to a girl if he chose? And for all he knew they might have been properly introduced. By young Frobisher, say. Nevertheless, Lewisham's spring-tide mood relapsed into winter. He was, he felt, singularly stupid for the rest of their conversation, and the delightful feeling of enterprise that had hitherto inspired and astonished him when talking to her had shrivelled beyond contempt. He was glad—positively glad—when things came to an end.

At the park gates she held out her hand. " I'm afraid I have interrupted your reading," she said.

" Not a bit," said Mr. Lewisham warming slightly. " I don't know when I've enjoyed a conversation. . . ."

"It was—a breach of etiquette, I am afraid my speaking to you, but I did so want to thank you. . . ."

"Don't mention it," said Mr. Lewisham, secretly impressed by the etiquette.

"Good-bye." He stood hesitating by the lodge, and then turned back up the avenue in order not to be seen to follow her too closely up the West Street.

And then, still walking away from her, he remembered that he had not lent her a book as he had planned, nor made any arrangement ever to meet her again. She might leave Whortley anywhen for the amenities of Clapham. He stopped and stood irresolute. Should he run after her? Then he recalled Bonover's enigmatical expression of face. He decided that to pursue her would be altogether too conspicuous. Yet. . . . So he stood in inglorious hesitation, while the seconds passed.

He reached his lodging at last to find Mrs. Munday halfway through dinner.

"You get them books of yours," said Mrs. Munday, who took a motherly interest in him, "and you read and you read, and you take no account of time. And now you'll have to eat your dinner half cold and no time for it to settle proper before you goes off to school. It's ruination to a stummik—such ways."

"Oh, never mind my stomach, Mrs. Munday," said Lewisham, roused from a tangled and apparently gloomy meditation; "that's *my* affair." Quite crossly he spoke for him.

"I'd rather have a good sensible actin' stummik than a full head," said Mrs. Munday, "any day."

"I'm different, you see," snapped Mr. Lewisham, and relapsed into silence and gloom.

("Hoity toity!" said Mrs. Munday under her breath.)

CHAPTER THE FIFTH

Hesitations

Mʀ. BONOVER, having fully matured a Hint suitable for the occasion, dropped it in the afternoon while Lewisham was superintending cricket practice. He made a few remarks about the prospects of the first eleven by way of introduction, and Lewisham agreed with him that Frobisher i. looked like shaping very well this season.

A pause followed and the headmaster hummed. "By-the-by," he said, as if making conversation and still watching the play; "I, ah—understood that you, ah—were a *stranger* to Whortley."

"Yes," said Lewisham, "that's so."

"You have made friends in the neighbourhood?"

Lewisham was troubled with a cough and his ears—those confounded ears—brightened. "Yes," he said, recovering. "Oh yes. Yes. I have."

"Local people, I presume."

"Well, no. Not exactly." The brightness spread from Lewisham's ears over his face.

890

"I saw you," said Bonover, "talking to a young lady in the avenue. Her face was somehow quite familiar to me. Who *was* she?"

Should he say she was a friend of the Frobishers? In that case Bonover, in his insidious amiable way, might talk to the Frobisher parents and make things disagreeable for her. "She was," said Lewisham, flushing deeply with the stress on his honesty and dropping his voice to a mumble, "a . . . a . . . an old friend of my mother's. In fact, I met her once at Salisbury."

"Where?"

"Salisbury."

"And her name?"

"Smith," said Lewisham, a little hastily and repenting the lie even as it left his lips.

"Well *hit*, Harris!" shouted Bonover, and began to clap his hands. "Well *hit*, sir."

"Harris shapes very well," said Mr. Lewisham.

"Very," said Mr. Bonover. "And—what was it? Ah! I was just remarking the odd resemblances there are in the world. There is a Miss Henderson—or Henson—stopping with the Frobishers—in the very same town, in fact, the very picture of your Miss . . ."

"Smith," said Lewisham, meeting his eye and recovering the full crimson note of his first blush.

"It's odd," said Bonover, regarding him pensively.

"Very odd," mumbled Lewisham, cursing his own stupidity and looking away.

"*Very*—very odd," said Bonover.

"In fact," said Bonover, turning towards the schoolhouse, "I hardly expected it of you, Mr. Lewisham."

"Expected what, sir?"

But Mr. Bonover feigned to be already out of earshot.

"Damn!" said Mr. Lewisham. "Oh!—*damn!*"— a most objectionable expression and rare with him in those days. He had half a mind to follow the headmaster and ask him if he doubted his word. It was only too evident what the answer would be.

He stood for a minute undecided, then turned on his heel and marched homeward with savage steps. His muscles quivered as he walked, and his face twitched. The tumult of his mind settled at last into angry indignation.

"Confound him!" said Mr. Lewisham, arguing the matter out with the bedroom furniture. "Why the *devil* can't he mind his own business?"

"Mind your own business, sir!" shouted Mr. Lewisham at the wash-hand stand. "Confound you, sir, mind you own business!"

The wash-hand stand did.

"You overrate your power, sir," said Mr. Lewisham a little mollified. "Understand me! I am my own master out of school."

Nevertheless, for four days and some hours after Mr. Bonover's Hint, Mr. Lewisham so far observed its implications as to abandon open-air study and struggle with diminished success to observe the spirit as well as the letter of his time-table prescriptions. For the most part he fretted at accumulating tasks, did them with slipshod energy or looking out of window. The Career constituent insisted that to meet and talk to this girl again meant reproof, worry, interference with his work for his matriculation, the destruction of all "Discipline," and he saw the entire justice of the insistence. It was nonsense this being in love; there wasn't such a thing as love outside trashy novelettes. And forthwith his mind went off at a tangent to her eyes under the shadow of her hat brim, and had to be lugged back by main force. On Thursday when he was returning from school he saw her far away down the street, and hurried in to avoid her, looking ostentatiously in the opposite direction. But that was the turning-point. Shame overtook him. On Friday his belief in love was warm and living again, and his heart full of remorse for laggard days.

On Saturday morning his preoccupation with her was so vivid that it distracted him even while he was teaching that most teachable subject, algebra; and by the end of the school hours the issue was decided and the Career in headlong rout. That afternoon he would go whatever happened, and see her and speak to her again. The thought of Bonover arose only to be dismissed. And besides——

Bonover took a siesta early in the afternoon.

Yes, he would go out and find her and speak to her. Nothing should stop him.

Once that decision was taken his imagination became riotous with things he might say, attitudes he might strike, and a multitude of vague fine dreams about her. He would say this, he would say that, his mind would do nothing but circle round this wonderful pose of lover. What a cur he had been to hide from her so long! What could he have been thinking about? How *could* he explain it to her, when the meeting really came? Suppose he was very frank——.

He considered the limits of frankness. Would she believe he had not seen her on Thursday?—if he assured her that it was so?

And, most horrible, in the midst of all this came Bonover with a request that he would take "duty" in the cricket field instead of Dunkerley that afternoon. Dunkerley was the senior assistant master, Lewisham's sole colleague. The last vestige of disapprobation had vanished from Bonover's manner; asking a favour was his autocratic way of proffering the olive branch. But it came to Lewisham as a cruel imposition. For a fateful moment he trembled on the brink of acquiescence. In a flash came a vision of the long duty of the afternoon —she possibly packing for Clapham all the while. He turned white. Mr. Bonover watched his face.

"*No*," said Lewisham bluntly, saying all he was sure of, and forthwith racking his unpractised mind for an excuse. "I'm sorry I can't oblige you, but . . . my arrangements . . . I've made arrangements, in fact, for the afternoon."

Mr. Bonover's eyebrows went up at this obvious lie, and the glow of his suavity faded. "You see," he said, "Mrs. Bonover expects a friend this afternoon, and we rather want Mr. Dunkerley to make four at croquet. . . ."

"I'm sorry," said Mr. Lewisham, still resolute, and making a mental note that Bonover would be playing croquet.

"You don't play croquet by any chance?" asked Bonover.

"No," said Lewisham, "I haven't an idea."

"If Mr. Dunkerley had asked you? . . ." persisted Bonover, knowing Lewisham's respect for etiquette.

"Oh! it wasn't on that account," said Lewisham, and Bonover with eyebrows still raised and a general air of outraged astonishment left him standing there, white and stiff, and wondering at his extraordinary temerity.

CHAPTER THE
SIXTH

The Scandalous Ramble

AS soon as school was dismissed Lewisham made a gaol-delivery of his outstanding impositions, and hurried back to his lodgings, to spend the time until his dinner was ready—Well? . . . It seems hardly fair, perhaps, to Lewisham to tell this; it is doubtful, indeed, whether a male novelist's duty to his sex should not restrain him, but, as the wall in the shadow by the diamond-framed window insisted, "*Magna est veritas et prævalebit.*" Mr. Lewisham brushed his hair with elaboration, and ruffled it picturesquely, tried the effect of all his ties and selected a white one, dusted his boots with an old pocket-handkerchief, changed his trousers because the week-day pair was minutely frayed at the heels, and inked the elbows of his coat where the stitches were a little white. And, to be still more intimate, he studied his callow appearance in the glass from various points of view, and decided that his nose might have been a little smaller with advantage. . . .

Directly after dinner he went out, and by the shortest path to the allotment lane, telling himself he did not care if he met Bonover forthwith in the street. He did not know precisely what he intended to do, but he was quite clear that he meant to see the girl he had met in the avenue. He knew he should see her. A sense of obstacles merely braced him and was pleasurable. He went up the stone steps out of the lane to the stile that overlooked the Frobishers', the stile from which he had watched the Frobisher bedroom. There he seated himself with his arms folded, in full view of the house.

That was at ten minutes to two. At twenty minutes to three he was still sitting there, but his hands were deep in his jacket pockets, and he was scowling and kicking his foot against the step with an impatient monotony. His needless glasses had been thrust into his waistcoat pocket—where they remained throughout the afternoon—and his cap was tilted a little back from his forehead and exposed a wisp of hair. One or two people had gone down the lane, and he had pretended not to see them, and a couple of hedge-sparrows chasing each other along the side of the sunlit, wind-rippled field had been his chief entertainment. It is unaccountable, no doubt, but he felt angry with her as the time crept on. His expression lowered.

He heard someone going by in the lane behind him. He would not look round—it annoyed him to think of people seeing him in this position. His once eminent discretion, though overthrown, still made muffled protests at the afternoon's enterprise. The feet down the lane stopped close at hand.

"Stare away," said Lewisham between his teeth. And then began mysterious noises, a violent rustle of hedge twigs, a something like a very light foot-tapping.

Curiosity boarded Lewisham and carried him after the briefest struggle. He looked round, and there she was, her back to him, reaching after the spiky blossoming blackthorn that crested the opposite hedge. Remarkable accident! She had not seen him!

In a moment Lewisham's legs were flying over the

stile. He went down the steps in the bank with such impetus that it carried him up into the prickly bushes beside her. "Allow me," he said, too excited to see she was not astonished.

"Mr. Lewisham!" she said in feigned surprise, and stood away to give him room at the blackthorn.

"Which spike will you have?" he cried overjoyed. "The whitest? The highest? Any!"

"That piece," she chose haphazard "with the black spike sticking out from it."

A mass of snowy blossom it was against the April sky, and Lewisham, struggling for it—it was by no means the most accessible—saw with fantastic satisfaction a lengthy scratch flash white on his hand, and turn to red.

"Higher up the lane," he said, descending triumphant and breathless, "there is blackthorn. . . . This cannot compare for a moment. . . ."

She laughed and looked at him as he stood there flushed, his eyes triumphant, with an unpremeditated approval. In church, in the gallery, with his face fore-shortened, he had been effective in a way, but this was different. "Show me," she said, though she knew this was the only place for blackthorn for a mile in either direction.

"I knew I should see you," he said by way of answer. "I felt sure I should see you to-day."

"It was our last chance almost," she answered with as frank a quality of avowal. "I'm going home to London on Monday."

"I knew," he cried in triumph. "To Clapham?" he asked.

"Yes. I have got a situation. You did not know that I was a shorthand clerk and typist, did you? I am. I have just left the school, the Grogram School. And now there is an old gentleman who wants an amanuensis."

"So you know shorthand?" said he. "That

accounts for the stylographic pen.   Those lines were written. . . .   I have them still."

She smiled and raised her eyebrows.   "Here," said Mr. Lewisham tapping his breast-pocket.

"This lane," he said—their talk was curiously inconsecutive—"some way along this lane, over the hill and down, there is a gate, and that goes—I mean, it opens into the path that runs along the river bank.   Have you been?"

"No," she said.

"It's the best walk about Whortley.   It brings you out upon Immering Common.   You *must*—before you go."

"*Now?*" she said with her eyes dancing.

"Why not?"

"I told Mrs. Frobisher I should be back by four," she said.

"It's a walk not to be lost."

"Very well," said she.

"The trees are all budding," said Mr. Lewisham, "the rushes are shooting, and all along the edge of the river there are millions of little white flowers floating on the water.   *I* don't know the names of them, but they're fine. . . .   May I carry that branch of blossom?"

As he took it their hands touched momentarily . . . and there came another of those significant gaps.

"Look at those clouds," said Lewisham abruptly remembering the remark he had been about to make and waving the white froth of blackthorn.   "And look at the blue between them."

"It's perfectly splendid.   Of all the fine weather the best has been kept for now.   My last day.   My very last day."

And off these two young people went together in a highly electrical state—to the infinite astonishment of Mrs. Frobisher, who was looking out of the attic window—stepping out manfully and finding the whole world lit and splendid for their entertainment. The things they discovered and told each other that afternoon down by the river!—that spring was wonderful, young leaves beautiful, bud scales astonishing things, and clouds dazzling and stately!—with an air of supreme originality! And their naïve astonishment to find one another in agreement upon these novel delights! It seemed to them quite outside the play of accident that they should have met each other.

They went by the path that runs among the trees along the river bank, and she must needs repent and wish to take the lower one, the towing path, before they had gone three hundred yards. So Lewisham had to find a place fit for her descent, where a friendly tree proffered its protruding roots as a convenient balustrade, and down she clambered with her hand in his.

Then a water-vole washing his whiskers gave occasion for a sudden touching of hands and the intimate confidence of whispers and silence together. After which Lewisham essayed to gather her a marsh mallow at the peril, as it was judged, of his life, and gained it together with a bootful of water. And at the gate by the black and shiny lock, where the path breaks away from the river, she overcame him by an unexpected feat, climbing gleefully to the top rail with the support of his hand, and leaping down, a figure of light and grace, to the ground.

They struck boldly across the meadows, which were gay with lady's smock, and he walked, by special request, between her and three matronly cows—feeling as Perseus might have done when he fended off the sea-monster. And so by the mill, and up a steep path to Immering Common. Across the meadows Lewisham had broached the subject of her occupation. "And are you really going away from here to be an amanuensis?" he said, and started her upon the theme of herself, a theme she treated with a specialist's enthusiasm. They dealt with it by the comparative

method, and neither noticed the light was out of the
sky until the soft feet of the advancing shower had
stolen right upon them.

"Look!" said he.   "Yonder!   A shed," and they
ran together.   She ran laughing, and yet swiftly and
lightly.   He pulled her through the hedge by both
hands, and released her skirt from an amorous bramble,
and so they came into a little black shed in which sheltered a rusty harrow of gigantic proportions.   He noted
how she still kept her breath after that run.

She sat down on the harrow and hesitated.   "I
must take off my hat," she said, "that rain will spot
it," and so he had a chance of admiring the sincerity
of her curls—not that he had ever doubted them.   She
stooped over her hat, pocket-handkerchief in hand,
daintily wiping off the silvery drops.   He stood up at
the opening of the shed and looked at the country outside through the veil of the soft vehemence of the
April shower.

"There's room for two on this harrow," she said.

He made inarticulate sounds of refusal, and then
came and sat down beside her, close beside her, so that
he was almost touching her.   He felt a fantastic desire
to take her in his arms and kiss her, and overcame the
madness by an effort.   "I don't even know your name,"
he said, taking refuge from his whirling thoughts in
conversation.

"Henderson," she said.

"*Miss* Henderson?"

She smiled in his face—hesitated.   "Yes—*Miss*
Henderson."

Her eyes, her atmosphere were wonderful.   He had
never felt quite the same sensation before, a strange
excitement, almost like a faint echo of tears.   He was
for demanding her Christian name.   For calling her
"dear" and seeing what she would say.   He plunged
headlong into a rambling description of Bonover and
how he had told a lie about her and called her Miss

Smith, and so escaped this unaccountable emotional crisis. . . .

The whispering of the rain about them sank and died, and the sunlight struck vividly across the distant woods beyond Immering. Just then they had fallen again into a silence that was full of daring thoughts for Mr. Lewisham. He moved his arm suddenly and placed it so that it was behind her on the frame of the harrow.

"Let us go on now," she said abruptly. "The rain has stopped."

"That little path goes straight to Immering," said Mr. Lewisham.

"But, four o'clock?"

He drew out his watch and his eyebrows went up. It was already nearly a quarter past four.

"Is it past four?" she asked, and abruptly they were face to face with parting. That Lewisham had to take "duty" at half-past five seemed a thing utterly trivial. "Surely," he said, only slowly realising what this parting meant. "But must you? I—I want to talk to you."

"Haven't you been talking to me?"

"It isn't that. Besides—no."

She stood looking at him. "I promised to be home by four," she said. "Mrs. Frobisher has tea. . . ."

"We may never have a chance to see one another again."

"Well?"

Lewisham suddenly turned very white.

"Don't leave me," he said, breaking a tense silence and with a sudden stress in his voice. "Don't leave me. Stop with me yet—for a little while. . . . You . . . You can lose your way."

"You seem to think," she said forcing a laugh, "that I live without eating and drinking."

"I have wanted to talk to you so much. The first time I saw you. . . . At first I dared not . . . I did not know you would let me talk. . . . And now, just as I am—happy, you are going."

He stopped abruptly. Her eyes were downcast. "No," she said, tracing a curve with the point of her shoe. "No. I am not going."

Lewisham restrained an impulse to shout. "You will come to Immering?" he cried, and as they went along the narrow path through the wet grass, he began to tell her with simple frankness how he cared for her company. "I would not change this," he said, casting about for an offer to reject, "for—anything in the world. . . . I shall not be back for duty. I don't care. I don't care what happens so long as we have this afternoon."

"Nor I," she said.

"Thank you for coming," he said in an outburst of gratitude. "Oh, thank you for coming," and held out his hand. She took it and pressed it, and so they went on hand in hand until the village street was reached. Their high resolve to play truant at all costs had begotten a wonderful sense of fellowship. "I can't call you Miss Henderson," he said. "You know I can't. You know . . . I must have your Christian name."

"Ethel," she told him.

"Ethel," he said and looked at her, gathering courage as he did so. "Ethel," he repeated. "It is a pretty name. But no name is quite pretty enough for you, Ethel . . . *dear*. . . ."

The small shop in Immering lay back behind a garden full of wallflowers, and was kept by a very fat and very cheerful little woman, who insisted on regarding them as brother and sister, and calling them both "dearie." These points conceded she gave them an admirable tea of astonishing cheapness. Lewisham did not like the second condition very much, because it seemed to touch on his latest enterprise. But the tea and the bread and butter and the whort jam were like no food on earth. There were wallflowers, heavy scented, in a jug upon the table, and Ethel admired them, and when they set out again the little old lady insisted on her taking a bunch with her.

It was after they left Immering that this ramble, properly speaking, became scandalous. The sun was already a golden ball above the blue hills in the west—it turned our two young people into figures of flame—and yet, instead of going homeward, they took the Wentworth road that plunges into the Forshaw woods. Behind them the moon, almost full, hung in the blue sky above the tree-tops, ghostly and indistinct, and slowly gathered to itself such light as the setting sun left for it in the sky.

Going out of Immering they began to talk of the future. And for the very young lover there is no future but the immediate future.

"You must write to me," he said, and she told him she wrote such *silly* letters. "But I shall have reams to write to you," he told her.

"How are you to write to me?" she asked, and they discussed a new obstacle between them. It would never do to write home—never. She was sure of that with an absolute assurance. "My mother—" she said and stopped.

That prohibition cut him, for at that time he had the makings of a voluminous letter-writer. Yet it was only what one might expect. The whole world was unpropitious—obdurate indeed. . . . A splendid isolation *à deux*.

Perhaps she might find some place where letters might be sent to her? Yet that seemed to her deceitful.

So these two young people wandered on, full of their discovery of love, and yet so full too of the shyness of adolescence that the word "Love" never passed their lips that day. Yet as they talked on, and the kindly dusk gathered about them, their speech and their hearts came very close together. But their speech

29*

would seem so threadbare, written down in cold blood, that I must not put it here. To them it was not threadbare.

When at last they came down the long road into Whortley, the silent trees were black as ink and the moonlight made her face pallid and wonderful, and her eyes shone like stars. She still carried the blackthorn from which most of the blossoms had fallen. The fragrant wallflowers were fragrant still. And far away, softened by the distance, the Whortley band, performing publicly outside the vicarage for the first time that year, was playing with unctuous slowness a sentimental air. I don't know if the reader remembers it, that favourite melody of the early eighties :

"*Sweet dreamland faces, passing to and fro (pum, pum)*
Bring back to Mem'ry days of long ago-o-o-oh."

was the essence of it, very slow and tender and with an accompaniment of pum, pum. Pathetically cheerful that pum, pum, hopelessly cheerful indeed against the dirge of the air, a dirge accentuated by sporadic vocalisation. But to young people things come differently.

"I *love* music," she said.

"So do I," said he.

They came on down the steepness of West Street. They walked athwart the metallic and leathery tumult of sound into the light cast by the little circle of yellow lamps. Several people saw them and wondered what the boys and girls were coming to nowadays, and one eye-witness even subsequently described their carriage as "brazen." Mr. Lewisham was wearing his mortar-board cap of office—there was no mistaking him. They passed the Proprietary School and saw a yellow picture framed and glazed, of Mr. Bonover taking duty for his aberrant assistant master. And outside the Frobisher house at last they parted perforce.

"Good-bye," he said for the third time. "Good-bye, Ethel."

She hesitated. Then suddenly she darted towards him. He felt her hands upon his shoulders, her lips soft and warm upon his cheek, and before he could take hold of her she had eluded him, and had flitted into the shadow of the house. "Good-bye," came her sweet, clear voice out of the shadow, and while he yet hesitated an answer, the door opened. He saw her, black in the doorway, heard some indistinct words, and then the door closed and he was alone in the moonlight, his cheek still glowing from her lips. . . .

So ended Mr. Lewisham's first day with Love.

CHAPTER THE SEVENTH

The Reckoning

A ND after the day of Love came the days of Reckoning. Mr. Lewisham was astonished—overwhelmed almost—by that Reckoning, as it slowly and steadily unfolded itself. The wonderful emotions of Saturday carried him through Sunday, and he made it up with the neglected Schema by assuring it that She was his Inspiration, and that he would work for Her a thousand times better than he could possibly work for himself. That was certainly not true, and indeed he found himself wondering whither the interest had vanished out of his theological examination of Butler's Analogy. The Frobishers were not at church for either service. He speculated rather anxiously why?

Monday dawned coldly and clearly—a Herbert Spencer of a day—and he went to school sedulously assuring himself there was nothing to apprehend. Day boys were whispering in the morning apparently about him, and Frobisher ii. was in great request. Lewisham overheard a fragment. "My mother *was* in a wax," said Frobisher ii.

At twelve came an interview with Bonover, and

906

voices presently rising in angry altercation and audible to Senior-assistant Dunkerley through the closed study door. Then Lewisham walked across the schoolroom, staring straight before him, his cheeks very bright.

Thereby Dunkerley's mind was prepared for the news that came the next morning over the exercise books. "When?" said Dunkerley.

"End of next term," said Lewisham.

"About the girl that's been staying at the Frobishers?"

"Yes."

"She's a pretty bit of goods. But it will mess up your matric next June," said Dunkerley.

"That's what I'm sorry for."

"It's scarcely to be expected he'll give you leave to attend the exam. . . ."

"He won't," said Lewisham shortly, and opened his first exercise book. He found it difficult to talk.

"He's a greaser," said Dunkerley. "But there!—what can you expect from Durham?" For Bonover had only a Durham degree and Dunkerley, having none, inclined to be particular. Therewith Dunkerley lapsed into a sympathetic and busy rustling over his own pile of exercises. It was not until the heap had been reduced to a book or so that he spoke again—an elaborate point.

"Male and female created He them," said Dunkerley ticking his way down the page. "Which (tick, tick) was damned hard (tick, tick) on assistant masters."

He closed the book with a snap and flung it on the floor behind him. "You're lucky," he said. "I *did* think I should be first to get out of this scandalising hole. You're lucky. It's always acting down here. Running on parents and guardians round every corner. That's what I object to in life in the country : it's so confoundedly artificial. *I* shall take jolly good care *I* get out of it just as soon as ever I can. You bet."

"And work those patents?"

"Rather, my boy. Yes. Work those patents. The Patent Square Top Bottle! Lord! Once let me get to London. . . ."

"I think _I_ shall have a shot at London," said Lewisham.

And then the experienced Dunkerley, being one of the kindest young men alive, forgot certain private ambitions of his own—he cherished dreams of amazing patents—and bethought him of agents. He proceeded to give a list of these necessary helpers of the assistant master at the gangway—Orellana, Gabbitas, The Lancaster Gate Agency, and the rest of them. He knew them all—intimately. He had been a "nix" eight years. "Of course that Kensington thing may come off," said Dunkerley, "but it's best not to wait. I tell you frankly—the chances are against you."

The "Kensington thing" was an application for admission to the Normal School of Science at South Kensington, which Lewisham had made in a sanguine moment. There being an inadequate supply of qualified science teachers in England, the Science and Art Department is wont to offer free instruction at its great central school, and a guinea a week, to select young pedagogues who will bind themselves to teach science after their training is over. Dunkerley had been in the habit of applying for several years, always in vain, and Lewisham had seen no harm in following his example. But then Dunkerley had no green-grey certificates.

So Lewisham spent all that "duty" left him of the next day composing a letter to copy out and send the several scholastic agencies. In this he gave a brief but appreciative sketch of his life, and enlarged upon his discipline and educational methods. At the end was a long and decorative schedule of his certificates and distinctions, beginning with a good-conduct prize at the age of eight. A considerable amount of time was required to recopy this document, but his modesty upheld him. After a careful consideration of the time-table, he set aside the midday hour for "Correspondence."

He found that his work in mathematics and classics was already some time in arrears, and a "test" he had sent to his correspondence tutor during those troublous days after the meeting with Bonover in the Avenue, came back blottesquely indorsed: "Below Pass Standard." This last experience was so unprecedented and annoyed him so much that for a space he contemplated retorting with a sarcastic letter to the tutor. And then came the Easter recess, and he had to go home and tell his mother, with a careful suppression of details, that he was leaving Whortley. "Where you have been getting on so well!" cried his mother.

But that dear old lady had one consolation. She observed he had given up his glasses—he had forgotten to bring them with him—and her secret fear of grave optical troubles that were being "kept" from her, was alleviated.

Sometimes he had moods of intense regret for the folly of that walk. One such came after the holidays, when the necessity of revising the dates of the Schema brought before his mind, for the first time quite clearly, the practical issue of this first struggle with those mysterious and powerful influences the spring-time sets a-stirring. His dream of success and fame had been very real and dear to him, and the realisation of the inevitable postponement of his long anticipated matriculation, the doorway to all the other great things, took him abruptly like an actual physical sensation in his chest.

He sprang up, pen in hand, in the midst of his corrections, and began pacing up and down the room. "What a fool I have been!" he cried. "What a fool I have been!"

He flung the pen on the floor and made a rush at an

ill-drawn attempt upon a girl's face that adorned the
end of his room, the visible witness of his slavery. He
tore this down and sent the fragments of it scattering. . . .

"Fool!"

It was a relief—a definite abandonment. He stared
for a moment at the destruction he had made, and then
went back to the revision of the time-table, with a
mutter about "silly spooning."

That was one mood. The rarer one. He watched
the posts with far more eagerness for the address to
which he might write to her than for any reply to
those reiterated letters of application, the writing of
which now ousted Horace and the higher mathematics
(Lewisham's term for conics) from his attention. Indeed
he spent more time meditating the letter to her than
even the schedule of his virtues had required.

Yet the letters of application were wonderful com-
positions; each had a new pen to itself and was for the
first page at least in a handwriting far above even his
usual high standard. And day after day passed and that
particular letter he hoped for still did not come.

His moods were complicated by the fact that, in
spite of his studied reticence on the subject, the reason
of his departure did in an amazingly short time get
"all over Whortley." It was understood that he had
been discovered to be "fast," and Ethel's behaviour
was animadverted upon with complacent indignation—
if the phrase may be allowed—by the ladies of the
place. Pretty looks were too often a snare. One boy
—his ear was warmed therefor—once called aloud
"Ethel," as Lewisham went by. The curate, a curate
of the pale-faced, large-knuckled, nervous sort, now
passed him without acknowledgment of his existence.
Mrs. Bonover took occasion to tell him that he was a
"mere boy," and once Mrs. Frobisher sniffed quite
threateningly at him when she passed him in the
street. She did it so suddenly she made him jump.

This general disapproval inclined him at times to depression, but in certain moods he found it exhilarating, and several times he professed himself to Dunkerley not a little of a blade. In others, he told himself he bore it for *her* sake. Anyhow he had to bear it.

He began to find out too, how little the world feels the need of a young man of nineteen—he called himself nineteen, though he had several months of eighteen still to run—even though he adds prizes for good conduct, general improvement, and arithmetic, and advanced certificates signed by a distinguished engineer and headed with the Royal Arms, guaranteeing his knowledge of geometrical drawing, nautical astronomy, animal physiology, physiography, inorganic chemistry and building construction, to his youth and strength and energy. At first he had imagined headmasters clutching at the chance of him, and presently he found himself clutching eagerly at them. He began to put a certain urgency into his applications for vacant posts, an urgency that helped him not at all. The applications grew longer and longer until they ran to four sheets of note-paper—a pennyworth in fact. "I can assure you," he would write, "that you will find me a loyal and devoted assistant." Much in that strain. Dunkerley pointed out that Bonover's testimonial ignored the question of moral character and discipline in a marked manner, and Bonover refused to alter it. He was willing to do what he could to help Lewisham, in spite of the way he had been treated, but unfortunately his conscience . . .

Once or twice Lewisham misquoted the testimonial—to no purpose. And May was halfway through, and South Kensington was silent. The future was grey.

And in the depths of his doubt and disappointment came her letter. It was typewritten on thin paper. "Dear," she wrote simply, and it seemed to him the most sweet and wonderful of all possible modes of address, though as a matter of fact it was because she had forgotten his Christian name and afterwards forgotten the blank she had left for it.

"Dear, I could not write before because I have no room at home now where I can write a letter, and Mrs. Frobisher told my mother falsehoods about you. My mother has surprised me dreadfully—I did not think it of her. She told me nothing. But of that I must tell you in another letter. I am too angry to write about it now. Even now you cannot write back, for *you must not send letters here.* It would *never* do. But I think of you, dear "—the "dear" had been erased and re-written—" and I must write and tell you so, and of that nice walk we had, if I never write again. I am very busy now. My work is rather difficult and I am afraid I am a little stupid. It is hard to be interested in anything just because that is how you have to live, is it not? I dare say you sometimes feel the same of school. But I suppose everybody is doing things they don't like. I don't know when I shall come to Whortley again, if ever, but very likely you will be coming to London. Mrs. Frobisher said the most horrid things. It would be nice if you could come to London, because then perhaps you might see me. There is a big boy's school at Chelsea, and when I go by it every morning I wish you were there. Then you would come out in your cap and gown as I went by. Suppose some day I was to see you there suddenly!"

So it ran, with singularly little information in it, and ended quite abruptly, "Good-bye, dear. Good-bye, dear," scribbled in pencil. And then, "Think of me sometimes."

Reading it, and especially that opening "dear," made Lewisham feel the strangest sensation in his throat and chest, almost as though he was going to cry. So he laughed instead and read it again, and went to and fro in his little room with his eyes bright and that precious writing held in his hand. That "dear" was just as if she had spoken—a voice suddenly heard. He thought of her farewell, clear and sweet, out of the shadow of the moonlit house.

But why that "If I never write again," and that abrupt ending? Of course he would think of her.

It was her only letter. In a little time its creases were worn through.

Early in June came a loneliness that suddenly changed into almost intolerable longing to see her. He had vague dreams of going to London, to Clapham, to find her. But you do not find people in Clapham as you do in Whortley. He spent an afternoon writing and re-writing a lengthy letter, against the day when her address should come. If it was to come. He prowled about the village disconsolately, and at last set off about seven and retraced by moonlight almost every step of that one memorable walk of theirs.

In the blackness of the shed he worked himself up to the pitch of talking as if she were present. And he said some fine brave things.

He found the little old lady of the wallflowers with a candle in her window, and drank a bottle of ginger beer with a sacramental air. The little old lady asked him, a trifle archly, after his sister, and he promised to bring her again some day. "I'll certainly bring her," he said. Talking to the little old lady somehow blunted his sense of desolation. And then home through the white indistinctness in a state of melancholy that became at last so fine as to be almost pleasurable.

The day after that mood a new "text" attracted and perplexed Mrs. Munday, an inscription at once mysterious and familiar, and this inscription was:

Mizpah.

It was in Old English lettering and evidently very carefully executed.

Where had she seen it before?

It dominated all the rest of the room at first, it flaunted like a flag of triumph over "discipline" and the time-table and the Schema. Once indeed it was taken down, but the day after it reappeared. Later a list of scholastic vacancies partially obscured it, and some pencil memoranda were written on the margin.

And when at last the time came for him to pack up and leave Whortley, he took it down and used it with several other suitable papers—the Schema and the time-table were its next-door neighbours—to line the bottom of the yellow box in which he packed his books : chiefly books for that matriculation that had now to be postponed.

CHAPTER THE EIGHTH

The Career Prevails

$\mathcal{T}$HERE is an interval of two years and a half and
the story resumes with a much maturer Mr. Lewisham,
indeed no longer a youth but a man, a legal man, at any
rate, of one and twenty years. Its scene is no longer
little Whortley embedded among its trees, ruddy banks,
parks and common land, but the grey spaciousness of
West London.

And it does not resume with Ethel at all. For that
promised second letter never reached him, and though
he spent many an afternoon during his first few months
in London, wandering about Clapham, that arid waste
of people, the meeting that he longed for never came.
Until at last after the manner of youth, so gloriously
recuperative in body, heart, and soul, he began to forget.

The quest of a " crib " had ended in the unexpected
fruition of Dunkerley's blue paper. The green-blue
certificates had, it seemed, a value beyond mural decoration, and when Lewisham was already despairing of any
employment for the rest of his life, came a marvellous
blue document from the Education Department promising inconceivable things. He was to go to London and

be paid a guinea a week for listening to lectures— lectures beyond his most ambitious dreams! Among the names that swam before his eyes was Huxley—Huxley and then Lockyer! What a chance to get! Is it any wonder that for three memorable years the Career prevailed with him?

You figure him on his way to the Normal School of Science at the opening of his third year of study there. (They call the place the Royal College of Science in these latter days.) He carried in his right hand a shiny black bag, well stuffed with textbooks, notes, and apparatus for the forthcoming session; and in his left was a book that the bag had no place for, a book with gilt edges, and its binding very carefully protected by a brown paper cover.

The lapse of time had asserted itself upon his upper lip in an inaggressive but indisputable moustache, in an added inch or so of stature, and in his less conscious carriage. For he no longer felt that universal attention he believed in at eighteen; it was beginning to dawn on him indeed that quite a number of people were entirely indifferent to the fact of his existence. But if less conscious, his carriage was decidedly more confident— as of one with whom the world goes well.

His costume was, with one exception, a tempered black—mourning put to hard uses, and "cutting up rusty." The mourning was for his mother, who had died more than a year before the date when this story resumes, and had left him property that capitalised at nearly a hundred pounds, a sum which Lewisham hoarded jealously in the Savings Bank, paying only for such essentials as university fees, and the books and instruments his brilliant career as a student demanded. For he was having a brilliant career after all, in spite of the Whortley check, licking up paper certificates indeed like a devouring flame.

(Surveying him, Madam, your eye would inevitably have fallen to his collar—curiously shiny, a surface like wet gum. Although it has practically nothing to do with this story, I must, I know, dispose of that before I go on, or you will be inattentive. London has its mysteries, but this strange gloss on his linen! "Cheap laundresses always make your things blue," protests the lady. "It ought to have been blue-stained, generously frayed, and loose about the button, fretting his neck. But this gloss . . ." You would have looked nearer, and finally you would have touched—a charnel-house surface, dank and cool! You see, Madam, the collar was a patent waterproof one. One of those you wash overnight with a tooth-brush, and hang on the back of your chair to dry, and there you have it next morning, rejuvenesced. It was the only collar he had in the world, it saved three pence a week at least, and that, to a South Kensington "science teacher in training," living on the guinea a week allowed by a parental but parsimonious government, is a sum to consider. It had come to Lewisham as a great discovery. He had seen it first in a shop window full of indiarubber goods, and it lay at the bottom of a glass bowl in which goldfish drifted discontentedly to and fro. And he told himself that he rather liked that gloss.)

But the wearing of a bright red tie would have been unexpected—a bright red tie after the fashion of a South-Western railway guard's! The rest of him by no means dandiacal, even the vanity of glasses long since abandoned. You would have reflected. . . . Where had you seen a crowd—red ties abundant and in some way significant? The truth has to be told. Mr. Lewisham had become a Socialist!

That red tie was indeed but one outward and visible sign of much inward and spiritual development. Lewisham, in spite of the demands of a studious career, had read his Butler's Analogy through by this time, and some other books; he had argued, had had doubts, and called upon God for "Faith" in the silence of the night—"Faith" to be delivered immediately if Mr.

Lewisham's patronage was valued, and which nevertheless was not so delivered. . . . And his conception of
his destiny in this world was no longer an avenue of
examinations to a remote Bar and political eminence
"in the Liberal interest (D.V.)." He had begun to
realise certain aspects of our social order that Whortley
did not demonstrate, begun to feel something of the
dull stress deepening to absolute wretchedness and pain,
which is the colour of so much human life in modern
London. One vivid contrast hung in his mind symbolical. On the one hand were the coalies of the
Westbourne Park yards, on strike and gaunt and hungry,
children begging in the black slush, and starving
loungers outside a soup kitchen; and on the other,
Westbourne Grove, two streets further, a blazing array
of crowded shops, a stirring traffic of cabs and carriages,
and such a spate of spending that a tired student in
leaky boots and graceless clothes hurrying home was continually impeded in the whirl of skirts and parcels and
sweetly pretty womanliness. No doubt the tired
student's own inglorious sensations pointed the moral.
But that was only one of a perpetually recurring series
of vivid approximations.

Lewisham had a strong persuasion, an instinct it may
be, that human beings should not be happy while others
near them were wretched, and this gay glitter of prosperity had touched him with a sense of crime. He still
believed people were responsible for their own lives; in
those days he had still to gauge the possibilities of moral
stupidity in himself and his fellow-men. He happened
upon "Progress and Poverty" just then, and some
casual numbers of the "Commonweal," and it was
only too easy to accept the theory of cunning, plotting capitalists and landowners, and faultless, righteous,
martyr workers. He became a Socialist forthwith. The
necessity to do something at once to manifest the new
faith that was in him was naturally urgent. So he went
out and (historical moment) bought that red tie!

" Blood colour, please," said Lewisham meekly to the young lady at the counter.

" *What* colour?" said the young lady at the counter, sharply.

" A bright scarlet, please," said Lewisham, blushing. And he spent the best part of the evening and much of his temper in finding out how to tie this into a neat bow. It was a plunge into novel handicraft—for previously he had been accustomed to made-up ties.

So it was that Lewisham proclaimed the Social Revolution. The first time that symbol went abroad a string of stalwart policemen were walking in single file along the Brompton Road. In the opposite direction marched Lewisham. He began to hum. He passed the policemen with a significant eye and humming the *Marseillaise*. . . .

But that was months ago, and by this time the red tie was a thing of use and wont.

He turned out of the Exhibition Road through a gateway of wrought iron, and entered the hall of the Normal School. The hall was crowded with students carrying books, bags, and boxes of instruments, students standing and chattering, students reading the framed and glazed notices of the Debating Society, students buying notebooks, pencils, rubber, or drawing pins from the privileged stationer. There was a strong representation of new hands, the paying students, youths and young men in black coats and silk hats or tweed suits, the scholar contingent, youngsters of Lewisham's class, raw, shabby, discordant, grotesquely ill-dressed and awe-stricken; one Lewisham noticed with a sailor's peaked cap gold-decorated, and one with mittens and very genteel grey kid gloves; and Grummett the perennial Official of the Books was busy among them.

" Der Zozalist!" said a wit.

Lewisham pretended not to hear and blushed vividly. He often wished he did not blush quite so much, seeing he was a man of one and twenty. He looked studiously away from the Debating Society notice board, whereon " G. E. Lewisham on Socialism " was announced for the next Friday, and struggled through the hall to where the Book awaited his signature. Presently he was hailed by name, and then again. He could not get to the Book for a minute or so, because of the hand-shaking and clumsy friendly jests of his fellow-" men."

He was pointed out to a raw hand, by the raw hand's experienced fellow-townsman, as " that beast Lewisham —awful swat. He was second last year on the year's work. Frightful mugger. But all these swats have a touch of the beastly prig. Exams—Debating Society— more Exams. Don't seem to have ever heard of being alive. Never goes near a Music Hall from one year's end to the other."

Lewisham heard a shrill whistle, made a run for the lift and caught it just on the point of departure. The lift was unlit and full of black shadows; only the sapper who conducted it was distinct. As Lewisham peered doubtfully at the dim faces near him, a girl's voice addressed him by name.

" Is that you, Miss Heydinger?" he answered. " I didn't see. I hope you have had a pleasant vacation."

CHAPTER THE NINTH

Alice Heydinger

*W*HEN he arrived at the top of the building he stood aside for the only remaining passenger to step out before him. It was the Miss Heydinger who had addressed him, the owner of that gilt-edged book in the cover of brown paper. No one else had come all the way up from the ground floor. The rest of the load in the lift had emerged at the "astronomical" and "chemical" floors, but these two had both chosen "zoology" for their third year of study, and zoology lived in the attics. She stepped into the light, with a rare touch of colour springing to her cheeks in spite of herself. Lewisham perceived an alteration in her dress. Perhaps she was looking for and noticed the transitory surprise in his face.

The previous session—their friendship was now nearly a year old—it had never once dawned upon him that she could possibly be pretty. The chief thing he had been able to recall with any definiteness during the vacation was that her hair was not always tidy and that even when it chanced to be so, she was nervous about it; she distrusted it. He remembered her gesture while she talked, a patting exploration that verged on the exasperating. From that he went on to remember that its colour was on the whole fair, a light brown. But he had forgotten her mouth, he had failed to name the colour of her eyes. She wore glasses, it is true. And her dress was indefinite in his memory—an amorphous dinginess.

And yet he had seen a good deal of her. They were not in the same course, but he had made her acquaintance on the committee of the school Debating Society. Lewisham was just then discovering Socialism. That had afforded a basis of conversation—an incentive to intercourse. She seemed to find something rarely interesting in his peculiar view of things, and, as chance would have it, he met her accidentally quite a number of times, in the corridors of the schools, in the big Education Library, and in the Art Museum. After a time those meetings appear to have been no longer accidental.

Lewisham for the first time in his life began to fancy he had conversational powers. She resolved to stir up his ambitions—an easy task. She thought he had exceptional gifts and that she might serve to direct them; she certainly developed his vanity. She had matriculated at London University and they took the Intermediate Examination in Science together in July—she a little unwisely—which served, as almost anything will serve in such cases, as a further link between them. She failed; but that in no way diminished Lewisham's regard for her. On the examination days they discoursed about Friendship in general, and things like that, down the Burlington Arcade during the lunch time—Burlington Arcade undisguisedly amused by her learned dinginess and his red tie—and among other things that were said she reproached him for not reading poetry. When they parted in Piccadilly after the examination, they agreed to write about poetry and themselves during the holidays, and then she lent him, with a touch of hesitation, Rossetti's poems. He began to forget what had at first been very evident to him, that she was two or three years older than he.

Lewisham spent the vacation with an unsympathetic but kindly uncle who was a plumber and builder. His uncle had a family of six, the eldest eleven, and Lewisham made himself agreeable and instructive. Moreover he worked hard for the culminating third year of his studies (in which he had decided to do great things) and he learnt to ride the Ordinary Bicycle. He also thought about Miss Heydinger, and she, it would seem, thought about him.

He argued on social questions with his uncle, who was a prominent local Conservative. His uncle's controversial methods were coarse in the extreme. Socialists, he said, were thieves. The object of Socialism was to take away what a man earned and give it to " a lot of lazy scoundrels." Also rich people were necessary. " If there weren't well-off people, how d'ye think I'd get a livin'? Hey? And where'd *you* be then?" Socialism, his uncle assured him, was " got up " by agitators. " They get money out of young Gabies like you, and they spend it on champagne." And thereafter he met Mr. Lewisham's arguments with the word " Champagne " uttered in an irritating voice, followed by a luscious pantomime of drinking.

Naturally Lewisham felt a little lonely, and perhaps he laid stress upon it in his letters to Miss Heydinger. It came to light that she felt rather lonely too. They discussed the question of True as distinguished from Ordinary Friendship, and from that they passed to Goethe and Elective Affinities. He told her how he looked for her letters, and they became more frequent. Her letters were indisputably well written. Had he been a journalist with a knowledge of "*per thou*." he would have known each for a day's work. After the practical plumber had been asking what he expected to make by this here science of his, re-reading her letters was balsamic. He liked Rossetti—the exquisite sense of separation in "The Blessed Damozel" touched him. But on the whole he was a little surprised at Miss Heydinger's taste in poetry. Rossetti was so sensuous . . . so florid. He had scarcely expected that sort of thing.

Altogether he had returned to the schools decidedly more interested in her than when they had parted. And the curious vague memories of her appearance as something a little frayed and careless, vanished at sight of her emerging from the darkness of the lift. Her hair was in order, as the light glanced through it it looked even pretty, and she wore a well-made dark-green and black dress, loose-gathered as was the fashion in those days, that somehow gave a needed touch of warmth to her face. Her hat too was a change from the careless lumpishness of last year, a hat that, to a feminine mind, would have indicated design. It suited her—these things are past a male novelist's explaining.

"I have this book of yours, Miss Heydinger," he said.

"I am glad you have written that paper on Socialism," she replied, taking the brown-covered volume.

They walked along the little passage towards the biological laboratory side by side, and she stopped at the hat pegs to remove her hat. For that was the shameless way of the place, a girl student had to take her hat off publicly, and publicly assume the holland apron that was to protect her in the laboratory. Not even a looking-glass!

"I shall come and hear your paper," she said.

"I hope you will like it," said Lewisham at the door of the laboratory.

"And in the vacation I have been collecting evidence about ghosts—you remember our arguments. Though I did not tell you in my letters."

" I'm sorry you're still obdurate," said Lewisham. " I thought that was over."

" And have you read ' Looking Backwards ' ? "

" I want to."

" I have it here with my other books, if you'd care for me to lend it to you. Wait till I reach my table. My hands are so full."

They entered the laboratory together, Lewisham holding the door open courtly-wise, Miss Heydinger taking a reassuring pat at her hair. Near the door was a group of four girls, which Miss Heydinger joined, holding the brown-covered book as inconspicuously as possible. Three of them had been through the previous two years with her, and they greeted her by her Christian name. They had previously exchanged glances at her appearance in Lewisham's company.

A morose elderly young demonstrator brightened momentarily at the sight of Lewisham. " Well, we've got one of the decent ones anyhow," said the morose elderly young demonstrator, who was apparently taking an inventory, and then brightening still more at a fresh entry. " Ah! and here's Smithers."

CHAPTER THE TENTH

In the Gallery of Old Iron

AS one goes into the South Kensington Art Museum from the Brompton Road, the Gallery of Old Iron is overhead to the right. But the way thither is exceedingly devious and not to be revealed to everybody, since the young people who pursue science and art thereabouts set a peculiar value on its seclusion. The gallery is long and narrow and dark, and set with iron gates, iron-bound chests, locks, bolts and bars, fantastic great keys, lamps, and the like, and over the balustrade one may lean and talk of one's finer feelings and regard Michael Angelo's horned Moses, or Trajan's Column (in plaster) rising gigantic out of the hall below and far above the level of the gallery. And here on a Wednesday afternoon were Lewisham and Miss Heydinger, the Wednesday afternoon immediately following that paper upon Socialism that you saw announced on the notice board in the hall.

The paper had been an immense success, closely

926

reasoned, delivered with a disciplined emotion, the redoubtable Smithers practically converted, the reply after the debate methodical and complete, and it may be there were symptoms of that febrile affection known to the vulgar as "swelled 'ed." Lewisham regarded Moses and spoke of his future, Miss Heydinger for the most part watched his face.

"And then?" said Miss Heydinger.

"One must bring these views prominently before people. I believe still in pamphlets. I have thought . . ." Lewisham paused, it is to be hoped through modesty.

"Yes?" said Miss Heydinger.

"Well—Luther, you know. There is room, I think, in Socialism, for a Luther."

"Yes," said Miss Heydinger, imagining it. "Yes—that would be a grand way."

So it seemed to many people in those days. But eminent reformers have been now for more than seven years going about the walls of the Social Jericho, blowing their own trumpets and shouting—with such small result beyond incidental displays of ill-temper within, that it is hard to recover the fine hopefulness of those departed days.

"Yes," said Miss Heydinger. "That would be a grand way."

Lewisham appreciated the quality of personal emotion in her voice. He turned his face towards her, and saw unstinted admiration in her eyes. "It would be a great thing to do," he said, and added, quite modestly, "if only one could do it."

"*You* could do it."

"You think I could?" Lewisham blushed vividly—with pleasure.

"I do. Certainly you could set out to do it. Even to fail hopelessly would be Great. Sometimes . . ."

She hesitated. He looked expectation. "I think sometimes it is greater even to fail than to succeed."

30

"I don't see that," said the proposed Luther, and his eyes went back to the Moses. She was about to speak and changed her mind.

Contemplative pause.

"And then, when a great number of people have heard of your views?" she said presently.

"Then I suppose we must form a party and . . . bring things about."

Another pause—full, no doubt, of elevated thoughts.

"I say," said Lewisham quite suddenly. "You do put—well—courage into a chap. I shouldn't have done that Socialism paper if it hadn't been for you." He turned round and stood leaning with his back to the Moses, and smiling at her. "You do help a fellow," he said.

That was one of the vivid moments of Miss Heydinger's life. She changed colour a little. "Do I?" she said, standing straight and awkward and looking into his face. "I'm . . . glad."

"I haven't thanked you for your letters," said Lewisham. "And I've been thinking . . ."

"Yes?"

"We're first-rate friends, aren't we? The best of friends."

She held out her hand and drew a breath. "Yes," she said as they gripped. He hesitated whether to hold her hand. He looked into her eyes, and at that moment she would have given three-quarters of the years she had still to live, to have had eyes and features that could have expressed her. Instead, she felt her face hard, the little muscles of her mouth twitching insubordinate, and fancied that her self-consciousness made her eyes dishonest.

"What I mean," said Lewisham, "is—that this will go on. We're always going to be friends, side by side."

"Always. Just as I am able to help you—I will help you. However, I can help you, I will."

"We two," said Lewisham gripping her hand.

Her face lit. Her eyes were for a moment touched with the beauty of simple emotion. "We two," she said, and her lips trembled and her throat seemed to swell. She snatched her hand back suddenly and turned her face away. Abruptly she walked towards the end of the gallery, and he saw her fumbling for her handkerchief in the folds of the green and black dress.

She was going to cry!

It set Lewisham marvelling—this totally inappropriate emotion.

He followed her and stood by her. Why cry? He hoped no one would come into the little gallery until her handkerchief was put away. Nevertheless he felt vaguely flattered. She controlled herself, dashed her tears away, and smiled bravely at him with reddened eyes. "I'm sorry," she said, gulping.

"I am so glad," she explained.

"But we will fight together. We two. I *can* help you. I know I can help you. And there is such Work to be done in the world!"

"You are very good to help me," said Lewisham, quoting a phrase from what he had intended to say before he found out that he had a hold upon her emotions.

"No!

"Has it ever occurred to you," she said abruptly, "how little a woman can do alone in the world?"

"Or a man," he answered after a momentary meditation.

So it was Lewisham enrolled his first ally in the cause of the red tie—of the red tie and of the Greatness that was presently to come. His first ally; for hitherto—save for the indiscretion of his mural inscriptions—he had made a secret of his private ambitions. In that now half-forgotten love affair at Whortley even, he had, in spite of the considerable degree of intimacy attained, said absolutely nothing about his Career.

CHAPTER THE ELEVENTH

Manifestations

MISS HEYDINGER declined to disbelieve in the spirits of the dead, and this led to controversy in the laboratory over Tea. For the girl students, being in a majority that year, had organised Tea between four o'clock and the advent of the extinguishing police-man at five. And the men students were occasionally invited to Tea. But not more than two of them at a time really participated, because there were only two spare cups after that confounded Simmons broke the third.

Smithers, the square-headed student with the hard grey eyes, argued against the spirits of the dead with positive animosity, while Bletherley, who displayed an orange tie and lank hair in unshorn abundance, was vaguely opened-minded. "What is love?" asked Bletherley, "surely that at any rate is immortal!" His remark was considered irrelevant and ignored.

Lewisham, as became the most promising student

930

of the year, weighed the evidence—comprehensively under headings. He dismissed the mediumistic *séances* as trickery.

"Rot and imposture," said Smithers loudly, and with an oblique glance to see if his challenge reached its mark. Its mark was a grizzled little old man with a very small face and very big grey eyes, who had been standing listlessly at one of the laboratory windows until the discussion caught him. He wore a brown velvet jacket and was reputed to be enormously rich. His name was Lagune. He was not a regular attendant, but one of those casual outsiders who are admitted to laboratories that are not completely full. He was known to be an ardent spiritualist—it was even said that he had challenged Huxley to a public discussion on materialism, and he came to the biological lectures and worked inter-mittently in order, he explained, to fight disbelief with its own weapons. He rose greedily to Smithers' controversial bait.

"I say *no!*" he said, calling down the narrow labora-tory and following his voice. He spoke with the ghost of a lisp. "Pardon my interrupting, sir. The question interests me profoundly. I hope I don't intrude. Excuse me, sir. Make it personal. Am I a—fool, or an impostor?"

"Well," parried Smithers with all a South Kensing-ton student's want of polish, "that's a bit personal."

"Assume, sir, that I am an honest observer."

"Well?"

"I have *seen* spirits, *heard* spirits, *felt* the touch of spirits." He opened his pale eyes very widely.

"Fool, then," said Smithers in an undertone which did not reach the ears of the spiritualist.

"You may have been deceived," paraphrased Lewisham.

"I can assure you . . . others can see, hear, feel. I have tested, sir. Tested! I have some scientific training and I have employed tests. Scientific and exhaustive tests! Every possible way. I ask you, sir —have you given the spirits a chance?"

"It is only paying guineas to humbugs," said Smithers.

"There you are! Prejudice! Here is a man denies the facts and consequently *won't* see them, won't go near them."

"But you wouldn't have every man in the three kingdoms who disbelieved in spirits, attend *séances* before he should be allowed to deny?"

"Most assuredly yes. Most assuredly yes! He knows nothing about till then."

The argument became heated. The little old gentleman was soon under way. He knew a person of the most extraordinary gifts, a medium . . .

"Paid?" asked Smithers.

"Would you muzzle the ox that treadeth out the corn?" said Lagune promptly.

Smithers's derision was manifest.

"Would you distrust a balance because you bought it? Come and see." Lagune was now very excited and inclined to gesticulate and raise his voice. He invited the whole class incontinently to a series of special *séances.* "Not all at once—the spirits—new influences." But in sections. "I warn you we may get nothing. But the chances are . . . I would rejoice infinitely. . . ."

So it came about that Lewisham consented to witness a spirit-raising. Miss Heydinger it was arranged should be there, and the sceptic Smithers, Lagune, his typist and the medium would complete the party. Afterwards there was to be another party for the others. Lewisham was glad he had the moral support of Smithers. "It's an evening wasted," said Smithers, who had gallantly resolved to make the running for Lewisham in the contest for the Forbes medal. "But I'll prove my case. You see if I don't." They were given an address in Chelsea.

The house, when Lewisham found it at last, proved a large one with such an air of mellowed dignity that he was abashed. He hung his hat up for himself beside a green-trimmed hat of straw in the wide, rich-toned hall. Through an open door he had a glimpse of a palatial study, book-shelves bearing white busts, a huge writing-table lit by a green-shaded electric lamp and covered thickly with papers. The housemaid looked, he thought, with infinite disdain at the rusty mourning and flamboyant tie, and flounced about and led him upstairs.

She rapped, and there was a discussion within. "They're at it already, I believe," she said to Lewisham confidentially. "Mr. Lagune's always at it."

There were sounds of chairs being moved, Smithers' extensive voice making a suggestion and laughing nervously. Lagune appeared opening the door. His grizzled face seemed smaller and his big grey eyes larger than usual.

"We were just going to begin without you," he whispered. "Come along."

The room was furnished even more splendidly than the drawing-room of the Whortley Grammar School, hitherto the finest room (except certain of the State Apartments at Windsor) known to Lewisham. The furniture struck him in a general way as akin to that in the South Kensington Museum. His first impression was an appreciation of the vast social superiority of the chairs; it seemed impertinent to think of sitting on anything quite so stately. He perceived Smithers standing with an air of bashful hostility against a bookcase. Then he was aware that Lagune was asking them all to sit down. Already seated at the table was the Medium, Chaffery, a benevolent-looking, faintly shabby gentleman with bushy iron-grey side-whiskers, a wide, thin-lipped mouth tucked in at the corners, and a chin like the toe of a boot. He regarded Lewisham critically and disconcertingly over gilt glasses. Miss Heydinger was quite at her ease and began talking at once. Lewisham's replies were less confident than they had been in the Gallery of Old Iron; indeed there was almost a reversal of their positions. She led and he was abashed. He felt obscurely that she had taken an advantage of him. He became aware of another girlish figure in a dark dress on his right.

Everyone moved towards the round table in the centre of the room, on which lay a tambourine and a little green box. Lagune developed unsuspected lengths of knobby wrist and finger directing his guests to their seats. Lewisham was to sit next to him, between him and the Medium; beyond the Medium sat Smithers with Miss Heydinger on the other side of him, linked to Lagune by the typist. So sceptics compassed the Medium about. The company was already seated before Lewisham looked across Lagune and met the eyes of the girl next that gentleman. It was Ethel! The close green dress, the absence of a hat, and a certain loss of colour made her seem less familiar, but did not prevent the instant recognition. And there was recognition in her eyes.

Immediately she looked away. At first his only emotion was surprise. He would have spoken, but a little thing robbed him of speech. For a moment he was unable to remember her surname. Moreover, the strangeness of his surroundings made him undecided. He did not know what was the proper way to address her—and he still held to the superstition of etiquette. Besides—to speak to her would involve a general explanation to all these people. . . .

" Just leave a pin-point of gas, Mr. Smithers, please," said Lagune, and suddenly the one surviving jet of the gas chandelier was turned down and they were in darkness. The moment for recognition had passed.

The joining of hands was punctiliously verified, the circle was linked little finger to little finger. Lewisham's abstraction received a rebuke from Smithers. The

Medium, speaking in an affable voice, premised that he could promise nothing, he had no "*directing*" power over manifestations. Thereafter ensued a silence. . . .

For a space Lewisham was inattentive to all that happened.

He sat in the breathing darkness, staring at the dim elusive shape that had presented that remembered face. His mind was astonishment mingled with annoyance. He had settled that this girl was lost to him for ever. The spell of the old days of longing, of the afternoons that he had spent after his arrival in London, wandering through Clapham with a fading hope of meeting her, had not returned to him. But he was ashamed of his stupid silence, and irritated by the awkwardness of the situation. At one moment he was on the very verge of breaking the compact and saying "Miss Henderson" across the table. . . .

How was it he had forgotten that "Henderson?" He was still young enough to be surprised at forgetfulness.

Smithers coughed, one might imagine with a warning intention.

Lewisham, recalling his detective responsibility with an effort, peered about him, but the room was very dark. The silence was broken ever and again by deep sighs and a restless stirring from the Medium. Out of this mental confusion Lewisham's personal vanity was first to emerge. What did she think of him? Was she peering at him through the darkness even as he peered at her? Should he pretend to see her for the first time when the lights were restored? As the minutes lengthened it seemed as though the silence grew deeper and deeper. There was no fire in the room, and it looked for lack of that glow chilly. A curious scepticism arose in his mind as to whether he had actually seen Ethel or only mistaken someone else for her. He wanted the *séance* over in order that he might look at her again. The old days at Whortley came out of his

30*

memory with astonishing detail and yet astonishingly free from emotion. . . .

He became aware of a peculiar sensation down his back, that he tried to account for as a draught. . . .

Suddenly a beam of cold air came like a touch against his face, and made him shudder convulsively. Then he hoped that she had not marked his shudder. He thought of laughing a low laugh to show he was not afraid. Someone else shuddered too, and he perceived an extraordinarily vivid odour of violets. Lagune's finger communicated a nervous quivering.

What was happening?

The musical box somewhere on the table began playing a rather trivial, rather plaintive air that was strange to him. It seemed to deepen the silence about him, an accent on the expectant stillness, a thread of tinkling melody spanning an abyss.

Lewisham took himself in hand at this stage. What *was* happening? He must attend. Was he really watching as he should do? He had been wool-gathering. There were no such things as spirits, mediums were humbugs, and he was here to prove that sole remaining Gospel. But he must keep up with things —he was missing points. What was that scent of violets? And who had set the musical box going. The Medium of course : but how? He tried to recall whether he had heard a rustling or detected any movement before the music began. He could not recollect. Come! he must be more on the alert than this!

He became acutely desirous of a successful exposure. He figured the dramatic moment he had prepared with Smithers—Ethel a spectator. He peered suspiciously into the darkness.

Somebody shuddered again, someone opposite him this time. He felt Lagune's finger quiver still more palpably, and then suddenly the raps began, abruptly, all about him. *Rap!*—making him start violently. A swift percussive sound, tap, rap, dap, under the table, under the chair, in the air, round the cornices. The Medium groaned again and shuddered, and his nervous agitation passed sympathetically round the circle. The music seemed to fade to the vanishing point and grew louder again.

How was it done?

He heard Lagune's voice next him speaking with a peculiar quality of breathless reverence. "The alphabet?" he asked, "shall we—shall we use the alphabet?"

A forcible rap under the table.

"No!" interpreted the voice of the Medium.

The raps were continued everywhere.

Of course it was trickery. Lewisham endeavoured to think what the mechanism was. He tried to determine whether he really had the Medium's little finger touching his. He peered at the dark shape next him. There was a violent rapping with an almost metallic resonance far away behind them. Then the raps ceased, and over the healing silence the little jet of melody from the musical box played alone. And after a moment that ceased also. . . .

The stillness was profound. Mr. Lewisham was now highly strung. Doubts assailed him suddenly, and an overwhelming apprehension, a sense of vast occurrences gathered above him. The darkness was a physical oppression. . . .

He started. Something had stirred on the table. There was the sharp ping of metal being struck. A number of little crepitating sounds like paper being smoothed. The sound of wind without the movement of air. A sense of a presence hovering over the table.

The excitement of Lagune communicated itself in convulsive tremblings; the Medium's hand quivered. In the darkness on the table something faintly luminous, a greenish-white patch, stirred and hopped slowly among the dim shapes.

The object, whatever it was, hopped higher, rose slowly in the air, expanded. Lewisham's attention followed this slavishly. It was ghostly—unaccountable —marvellous. For the moment he forgot even Ethel. Higher and higher this pallid luminosity rose overhead, and then he saw that it was a ghostly hand and arm, rising, rising. Slowly, deliberately, it crossed the table, seemed to touch Lagune, who shivered. It moved slowly round and touched Lewisham. He gritted his teeth.

There was no mistaking the touch, firm and yet soft, of finger-tips. Almost simultaneously, Miss Heydinger cried out that something was smoothing her hair, and suddenly the musical box set off again with a reel. The faint oval of the tambourine rose, jangled, and Lewisham heard it pat Smithers in the face. It seemed to pass overhead. Immediately a table somewhere beyond the Medium began moving audibly on its castors.

It seemed impossible that the Medium, sitting so still beside him, could be doing all these things— grotesquely unmeaning though they might be. After all. . . . .

The ghostly hand was hovering almost directly in front of Mr. Lewisham's eyes. It hung with a slight quivering. Ever and again its fingers flapped down and rose stiffly again.

Noise! A loud noise it seemed. Something moving? What was it he had to do!

Lewisham suddenly missed the Medium's little finger. He tried to recover it. He could not find it. He caught, held and lost an arm. There was an exclamation. A faint report. A curse close to him bitten in half by the quick effort to suppress it. Tzit! The little pin-point of light flew up with a hiss.

Lewisham, standing, saw a circle of blinking faces turned to the group of two this sizzling light revealed. Smithers was the chief figure of the group; he stood triumphant, one hand on the gas tap, the other gripping the Medium's wrist, and in the Medium's hand—the incriminatory tambourine.

" How's this, Lewisham," cried Smithers, with the shadows on his face jumping as the gas flared.

" *Caught!*" said Lewisham loudly, rising in his place and avoiding Ethel's eyes.

" What's this?" cried the Medium.

" Cheating," panted Smithers.

" Not so," cried the Medium. " When you turned up the light . . . put my hand up . . . caught tambourine . . . to save head."

" Mr. Smithers," cried Lagune. " Mr. Smithers, this is very wrong. This—shock——"

The tambourine fell noisily to the floor. The Medium's face changed, he groaned strangely and staggered back. Lagune cried out for a glass of water. Everyone looked at the man, expecting him to fall, save Lewisham. The thought of Ethel had flashed back into his mind. He turned to see how she took this exposure in which he was such a prominent actor. He saw her leaning over the table as if to pick up something that lay across it. She was not looking at him, she was looking at the Medium. Her face was set and white. Then, as if she felt his glance, her eyes met his.

She started back, stood erect, facing him with a strange hardness in her eyes.

At the moment Lewisham did not grasp the situation. He wanted to show that he was acting upon equal terms with Smithers in the exposure, and for the moment her action simply directed his attention to the object towards which she had been leaning, a thing of shrivelled membrane, a pneumatic glove, lying on the table. This was evidently part of the mediumistic apparatus. He pounced and seized it.

" Look!" he said holding it towards Smithers. " Here is more! What is this?"

He perceived that the girl started. He saw Chaffery, the Medium, look instantly over Smithers' shoulders, saw his swift glance of reproach at the girl. Abruptly the situation appeared to Lewisham; he perceived her complicity. And he stood, still in the attitude of triumph, with the evidence against her in his hand! But his triumph had vanished.

"Ah!" cried Smithers, leaning across the table to secure it. "*Good* old Lewisham! . . . Now we *have* it. This is better than the tambourine."

His eyes shone with triumph. "Do you see, Mr. Lagune?" said Smithers. "The Medium held this in his teeth and blew it out. There's no denying this. This wasn't falling on your head, Mr. Medium, was it? *This*—this was the luminous hand!"

CHAPTER THE TWELFTH

Lewisham is Unaccountable

THAT night, as she went with him to Chelsea station, Miss Heydinger discovered an extraordinary moodiness in Lewisham. She had been vividly impressed by the scene in which they had just participated. For a time she had believed in the manifestations, and the swift exposure had violently revolutionised her ideas. The details of the crisis were a little confused in her mind. She ranked Lewisham with Smithers in the scientific triumph of the evening. On the whole she felt elated. She had no objection to being confuted by Lewisham. But she was angry with the Medium. " It is dreadful," she said. " Living a lie! How can the world grow better, when sane, educated people use their sanity and enlightenment to darken others? It is dreadful!

" He was a horrible man—such an oily, dishonest voice. And the girl—I was sorry for her. She must have been oh!—bitterly ashamed or why should she have burst out crying? That did distress me. Fancy crying

941

like that! It was—yes—*abandon*. But what can one do?"

She paused. Lewisham was walking along, looking straight before him, lost in some grim argument with himself.

"It makes me think of 'Sludge, the Medium,'" she said.

He made no answer.

She glanced at him suddenly. "Have you read 'Sludge, the Medium?'"

"Eigh?" he said, coming back out of infinity. "What? I beg your pardon. Sludge, the Medium? I thought his name was—it *was*—Chaffery."

He looked at her, clearly very anxious upon this question of fact.

"But I mean Browning's 'Sludge.' You know—the poem."

"No—I'm afraid I don't," said Lewisham.

"I must lend it to you," she said. "It's splendid. It goes to the very bottom of this business."

"Does it?"

"It never occurred to me before. But I see the point clearly now. If people, poor people, are offered money if phenomena happen, it's too much. They are *bound* to cheat. It's bribery—immorality!"

She talked in panting little sentences, because Lewisham was walking in heedless big strides. "I wonder how much—such people—could earn honestly."

Lewisham slowly became aware of the question at his ear. He hurried back from infinity. "How much they could earn honestly? I haven't the slightest idea."

He paused. "The whole of this business puzzles me," he said. "I want to think."

"It's frightfully complex, isn't it?" she said—a little staggered.

But the rest of the way to the station was silence. They parted with the hand-clasp they took a pride in—a little perfunctory so far as Lewisham was concerned on this occasion. She scrutinised his face as the train moved out of the station, and tried to account for his mood. He was staring before him at unknown things— as if he had already forgotten her.

He wanted to think! But two heads, she thought, were better than one in a matter of opinion. It troubled her to be so ignorant of his mental states. "How we are wrapped and swathed about—soul from soul!" she thought, staring out of the window at the dim things flying by outside.

Suddenly a fit of depression came upon her. She felt alone—absolutely alone—in a void world.

Presently she returned to external things. She became aware of two people in the next compartment eyeing her critically. Her hand went patting at her hair.

CHAPTER THE THIRTEENTH

Lewisham Insists

ETHEL HENDERSON sat at her machine before the window of Mr. Lagune's study, and stared blankly at the greys and blues of the November twilight. Her face was white, her eyelids were red from recent weeping, and her hands lay motionless in her lap. The door had just slammed behind Lagune.

"Heigh-ho!" she said. "I wish I was dead. Oh! I wish I was out of it all."

She became passive again. "I wonder what I have *done*," she said, "that I should be punished like this."

She certainly looked anything but a Fate-haunted soul, being indeed visibly and immediately a very pretty girl. Her head was shapely and covered with curly dark hair, and the eyebrows above her hazel eyes were clear and dark. Her lips were finely shaped, her mouth was not too small to be expressive, her chin small, and her neck white and full and pretty. There is no need to lay stress upon her nose—it sufficed. She was of a mediocre height, sturdy rather than slender, and her dress was of a pleasant, golden-brown material with the easy sleeves and graceful line of those æsthetic days. And she sat at her typewriter and wished she was dead and wondered what she had *done*.

The room was lined with bookshelves and conspicuous therein was a long row of foolish pretentious volumes, the "works" of Lagune—the witless, meandering imitation of philosophy that occupied his life. Along the cornices were busts of Plato, Socrates and Newton. Behind Ethel was the great man's desk with its green-shaded electric light, and littered with proofs and copies of *Hesperus,* "A paper for Doubters," which with her assistance he edited, published, compiled, wrote, and (without her help) paid for and read. A pen, flung down forcibly, quivered erect with its one surviving nib in the blotting pad. Mr. Lagune had flung it down.

The collapse of the previous night had distressed him dreadfully, and ever and again before his retreat he had been breaking into passionate monologue. The ruin of a life-work it was, no less. Surely she had known that Chaffery was a cheat. Had she not known? Silence. "After so many kindnesses—— "

She had interrupted him with a wailing "Oh, I know —I know."

But Lagune had been remorseless and insisted she had betrayed him, worse—made him ridiculous! Look at the "work" he had undertaken at South Kensington— how could he go on with that now? How could he find the heart? When his own typist sacrificed him to her stepfather's trickery? "Trickery!"

The gesticulating hands became active, the grey eyes dilated with indignation, the piping voice eloquent.

"If he hadn't cheated you, someone else would," was Ethel's inadequate muttered retort, unheard by the seeker after phenomena.

It was perhaps not so bad as dismissal, but it certainly lasted longer. And at home was Chaffery, grimly malignant at her failure to secure that pneumatic glove. He had no right to blame her, he really had not; but a disturbed temper is apt to falsify the scales of justice. The tambourine, he insisted, he could have explained by saying he put up his hand to catch it and protect his head directly Smithers moved. But the pneumatic glove there was no explaining. He had made a chance for her to secure it when he had pretended to faint. It was rubbish to say anyone could have been looking on the table then—rubbish.

Beside that significant wreck of a pen stood a little carriage clock in a case, and this suddenly lifted a slender voice and announced *five*. She turned round on her stool and sat staring at the clock. She smiled with the corners of her mouth down. "Home," she said, "and begin again. It's like battledore and shuttlecock. . . .

"I *was* silly. . . .

"I suppose I've brought it on myself. I ought to have picked it up, I suppose. I had time. . . .

"Cheats . . . just cheats.

"I never thought I should see him again. . . .

"He was ashamed, of course. . . . He had his own friends."

For a space she sat still, staring blankly before her. She sighed, rubbed a knuckle in a reddened eye, rose.

She went into the hall where her hat, transfixed by a couple of hat pins, hung above her jacket, assumed these garments, and let herself out into the cold grey street.

She had hardly gone twenty yards from Lagune's door before she became aware of a man overtaking her and walking beside her. That kind of thing is a common enough experience to girls who go to and from work in London, and she had had perforce to learn many things since her adventurous Whortley days. She looked stiffly in front of her. The man deliberately got in her way so that she had to stop. She lifted eyes of indignant protest. It was Lewisham—and his face was white.

He hesitated awkwardly and then in silence held out his hand. She took it mechanically. He found his voice. "Miss Henderson," he said.

"What do you want?" she asked faintly.

"I don't know," he said. . . . "I want to talk to you."

"Yes?" Her heart was beating fast.

He found the thing unexpectedly difficult.

"May I——? Are you expecting——? Have you far to go? I would like to talk to you. There is a lot. . . ."

"I walk to Clapham," she said. "If you care . . . to come part of the way. . . ."

She moved awkwardly. Lewisham took his place at her side. They walked side by side for a moment, their manner constrained, having so much to say that they could not find a word to begin upon.

"Have you forgotten Whortley?" he asked abruptly.

"No."

He glanced at her; her face was downcast. "Why did you never write?" he asked bitterly.

"I wrote."

"Again, I mean."

"I did—in July."

"I never had it."

"It came back."

"But Mrs. Munday. . . ."

"I had forgotten her name. I sent it to the Grammar School."

Lewisham suppressed an exclamation.

"I am very sorry," she said.

They went on again in silence. "Last night," said Lewisham at length. "I have no business to ask. But——"

She took a long breath. "Mr. Lewisham," she said. "That man you saw—the Medium—was my stepfather."

"Well?"

"Isn't that enough?"

Lewisham paused. "No," he said.

There was another constrained silence. "No," he said less dubiously. "I don't care a rap what your stepfather is. Were *you* cheating?"

Her face turned white. Her mouth opened and closed. "Mr. Lewisham," she said deliberately, "you may not believe it, it may sound impossible, but on my honour . . . I did not know—I did not know for certain, that is—that my stepfather. . . ."

"Ah!" said Lewisham, leaping at conviction. "Then I was right. . . ."

For a moment she stared at him, and then, "I *did* know," she said, suddenly beginning to cry. "How can I tell you? It is a lie. I *did* know. I *did* know all the time."

He stared at her in white astonishment. He fell behind her one step, and then in a stride came level again. Then, a silence, a silence that it seemed would never end. She had stopped crying, she was one huge suspense, not daring even to look at his face. And at last he spoke.

"No," he said slowly. "I don't mind even that. I don't care—even if it was that."

Abruptly they turned into the King's Road, with its roar of wheeled traffic and hurrying foot-passengers, and forthwith a crowd of boys with a broken-spirited Guy involved and separated them. In a busy highway of a night one must needs talk disconnectedly in shouted snatches or else hold one's peace. He glanced at her face and saw that it was set again. Presently she turned southward out of the tumult into a street of darkness and warm blinds, and they could go on talking again.

"I understand what you mean," said Lewisham. "I know I do. You knew but you did not want to know. It was like that."

But her mind had been active. "At the end of this road," she said, gulping a sob, "you must go back. It was kind of you to come, Mr. Lewisham. But you were ashamed—you are sure to be ashamed. My employer is a spiritualist, and my stepfather is a professional Medium, and my mother is a spiritualist. You were quite right not to speak to me last night. Quite. It was kind of you to come, but you must go back. Life is hard enough as it is. . . . You must go back at the end of the road. Go back at the end of the road. . . ."

Lewisham made no reply for a hundred yards. "I'm coming on to Clapham," he said.

They came to the end of the road in silence. Then at the kerb corner she turned and faced him. "Go back," she whispered.

"No," he said obstinately, and they stood face to face at the cardinal point of their lives.

"Listen to me," said Lewisham. "It is hard to say what I feel. I don't know myself. . . . But I'm not going to lose you like this. I'm not going to let you slip a second time. I was awake about it all last night. I don't care where you are, what your people are, nor very much whether you've kept quite clear of this medium humbug. I don't. You will in future. Anyhow. I've had a day and night to think it over. I had to come and try to find you. It's you. I've never forgotten you. Never. I'm not going to be sent back like this."

"It can be no good for either of us," she said as resolute as he.

"I shan't leave you."

"But what is the good? . . ."

"I'm coming," said Lewisham, dogmatically.

And he came.

He asked her a question point blank and she would not answer him, and for some way they walked in grim silence. Presently she spoke with a twitching mouth. "I wish you would leave me," she said. "You are quite different from what I am. You felt that last night. You helped find us out. . . ."

"When first I came to London I used to wander

about Clapham looking for you," said Lewisham, "week after week."

They had crossed the bridge and were in a narrow little street of shabby shops near Clapham Junction before they talked again. She kept her face averted and expressionless.

"I'm sorry," said Lewisham, with a sort of stiff civility, "if I seem to be forcing myself upon you. I don't want to pry into your affairs—if you don't wish me to. The sight of you has somehow brought back a lot of things. . . . I can't explain it. Perhaps—I had to come to find you—I kept on thinking of your face, of how you used to smile, how you jumped from the gate by the lock, and how we had tea . . . a lot of things."

He stopped again.

"A lot of things."

"If I may come?" he said, and went unanswered. They crossed the wide streets by the Junction and went on towards the Common.

"I live down this road," she said, stopping abruptly at a corner. "I would rather . . ."

"But I have said nothing."

She looked at him with her face white, unable to speak for a space. "It can do no good," she said. "I am mixed up with this. . . ."

She stopped.

He spoke deliberately. "I shall come," he said, "to-morrow night."

"No," she said.

"But I shall come."

"No," she whispered.

"I shall come." She could hide the gladness of her heart from herself no longer. She was frightened that he had come, but she was glad and she knew he knew that she was glad. She made no further protest. She held out her hand dumbly. And on the morrow she found him awaiting her even as he had said.

CHAPTER THE
FOURTEENTH

Mr. Lagune's Point of View

FOR three days the Laboratory at South Kensington saw nothing of Lagune, and then he came back more invincibly voluble than ever. Everyone had expected him to return apostate, but he brought back an invigorated faith, a propaganda unashamed. From some source he had derived strength and conviction afresh. Even the rhetorical Smithers availed nothing. There was a joined battle over the insufficient tea-cups, and the elderly young assistant demonstrator hovered on the verge of the discussion, rejoicing, it is supposed, over the entanglements of Smithers. For at the outset Smithers displayed an overweening confidence and civility, and at the end his ears were red and his finer manners lost to him.

Lewisham, it was remarked by Miss Heydinger, made but a poor figure in this discussion. Once or twice he seemed about to address Lagune, and thought better of it with the words upon his lips.

Lagune's treatment of the exposure was light and vigorous. "The man Chaffery," he said, "has made a clean breast of it. His point of view——"

"Facts are facts," said Smithers.

"A fact is a synthesis of impressions," said Lagune; "but that you will learn when you are older. The thing is that we were at cross purposes. I told Chaffery you were beginners. He treated you as beginners—arranged a demonstration."

"It *was* a demonstration," said Smithers.

"Precisely. If it had not been for your interruptions. . . ."

"Ah!"

"He forged elementary effects. . . ."

"You can't but admit that."

"I don't attempt to deny it. But, as he explained—the thing is necessary—justifiable. Psychic phenomena are subtle, a certain training of the observation is necessary. A medium is a more subtle instrument than a balance or a borax bead, and see how long it is before you can get assured results with a borax bead! In the elementary class, in the introductory phase, conditions are too crude. . . ."

"For honesty."

"Wait a moment. *Is* it dishonest—rigging a demonstration?"

"Of course it is."

"Your professors do it."

"I deny that in toto," said Smithers, and repeated with satisfaction, "in toto."

"That's all right," said Lagune, "because I have the facts. Your chemical lecturers—you may go downstairs now and ask, if you disbelieve me—always cheat over the indestructibility of matter experiment—always. And then another—a physiography thing. You know the experiment I mean? To demonstrate the existence of the earth's rotation. They use—they use——"

"Foucault's pendulum," said Lewisham. "They use a rubber ball with a pin-hole hidden in the hand, and blow the pendulum round the way it ought to go."

"But that's different," said Smithers.

"Wait a moment," said Lagune, and produced a piece of folded printed paper from his pocket. "Here is a review from *Nature* of the work of no less a person than Professor Greenhill. And see—a convenient pin is introduced into the apparatus for the demonstration of virtual velocities! Read it—if you doubt me. I suppose you doubt me."

Smithers abruptly abandoned his position of denial "in toto." "This isn't my point, Mr. Lagune; this isn't my point," he said. "These things that are done in the lecture theatre are not to prove facts, but to give ideas."

"So was my demonstration," said Lagune.

"We didn't understand it in that light."

"Nor does the ordinary person who goes to Science lectures understand it in that light. He is comforted by the thought that he is seeing things with his own eyes."

"Well, I don't care," said Smithers; "two wrongs don't make a right. To rig demonstrations is wrong."

"There I agree with you. I have spoken plainly with this man Chaffery. He's not a full-blown professor, you know, a highly salaried ornament of the rock of truth like your demonstration-rigging professors here, and so I can speak plainly to him without offence. He takes quite the view they would take. But I am more rigorous. I insist that there shall be no more of this. . . ."

"Next time—" said Smithers with irony.

"There will be no next time. I have done with elementary exhibitions. You must take the word of the trained observer—just as you do in the matter of chemical analysis."

"Do you mean you are going on with that chap when he's been caught cheating under your very nose?"

"Certainly. Why not?"

Smithers set out to explain why not, and happened on confusion. "I still believe the man has powers," said Lagune.

"Of deception," said Smithers.

"Those I must eliminate," said Lagune. "You might as well refuse to study electricity because it escaped through your body. All new science is elusive. No investigator in his senses would refuse to investigate a compound because it did unexpected things. Either this dissolves in acid or I have nothing more to do with it—eh? That's fine research!"

Then it was the last vestiges of Smithers' manners vanished. "I don't care *what* you say," said Smithers. "It's all rot—it's all just rot. Argue if you like—but have you convinced anybody? Put it to the vote?"

"That's democracy with a vengeance," said Lagune. "A general election of the truth half-yearly, eh?"

"That's simply wriggling out of it," said Smithers. "That hasn't anything to do with it at all."

Lagune, flushed but cheerful, was on his way downstairs when Lewisham overtook him. He was pale and out of breath, but as the staircase invariably rendered Lagune breathless he did not remark the younger man's disturbance. "Interesting talk," panted Lewisham. "Very interesting talk, sir."

"I'm glad you found it so—very," said Lagune.

There was a pause, and then Lewisham plunged desperately. "There is a young lady—she is your typist. . . ."

He stopped from sheer loss of breath.

"Yes?" said Lagune.

"Is she a medium or anything of that sort?"

"Well," Lagune reflected. "She is not a medium, certainly. But—why do you ask?"

"Oh! . . . I wondered."

"You noticed her eyes, perhaps. She is the stepdaughter of that man Chaffery—a queer character but indisputably mediumistic. It's odd the thing should have struck you. Curiously enough I myself have fancied she might be something of a psychic—judging from her face."

"A what?"

"A psychic—undeveloped of course. I have thought once or twice. Only a little while ago I was speaking to that man Chaffery about her."

"Were you?"

"Yes. He of course would like to see any latent powers developed. But it's a little difficult to begin, you know."

"You mean—she won't?"

"Not at present. She is a good girl, but in this matter she is—timid. There is often a sort of disinclination—a queer sort of feeling—one might almost call it modesty."

"I see," said Lewisham.

"One can override it usually. I don't despair."

"No," said Lewisham shortly. They were at the foot of the staircase now. He hesitated. "You've given me a lot to think about," he said with an attempt at an offhand manner. "The way you talked upstairs"; and turned towards the book he had to sign.

"I'm glad you don't take up quite such an intolerant attitude as Mr. Smithers," said Lagune; "very glad. I must lend you a book or two. If your *cramming* here leaves you any time, that is."

"Thanks," said Lewisham shortly, and walked away from him. The studiously characteristic signature quivered and sprawled in an unfamiliar manner.

"I'm *damned* if he overrides it," said Lewisham, under his breath.

CHAPTER THE FIFTEENTH

Love in the Streets

LEWISHAM was not quite clear what course he meant to take in the high enterprise of foiling Lagune, and indeed he was anything but clear about the entire situation. His logical processes, his emotions and his imagination seemed playing some sort of snatching game with his will. Enormous things hung imminent, but it worked out to this, that he walked home with Ethel night after night for—to be exact—seven and sixty nights. Every week night through November and December, save once when he had to go into the far East to buy himself an overcoat, he was waiting to walk with her home. A curious, inconclusive affair, that walk, to which he came nightly full of vague longings and which ended invariably under an odd shadow of disappointment. It began outside Lagune's most punctually at five, and ended—mysteriously—at the corner of a side road in Clapham, a road of little yellow houses with sunk basements and tawdry decorations of stone. Up that road she vanished night after night, into a grey mist and the shadow beyond a feeble yellow gas-lamp, and he would watch her vanish, and then sigh and turn back towards his lodgings.

They talked of this and that, their little superficial

ideas about themselves and of their circumstances and tastes, and always there was something, something that was with them unspoken, unacknowledged, which made all these things unreal and insincere.

Yet out of their talk he began to form vague ideas of the home from which she came. There was, of course, no servant, and the mother was something meandering, furtive, tearful in the face of troubles. Sometimes of an afternoon or evening she grew garrulous. "Mother does talk so—sometimes." She rarely went out of doors. Chaffery always rose late, and would sometimes go away for days together. He was mean, he allowed only a weekly twenty-five shillings for housekeeping and sometimes things grew unsatisfactory at the week-end. There seemed to be little sympathy between mother and daughter; the widow had been flighty in a dingy fashion, and her marriage with her chief lodger Chaffery had led to unforgettable sayings. It was to facilitate this marriage that Ethel had been sent to Whortley, so that was counted a mitigated evil. But these were far-off things, remote and unreal down the long, ill-lit vista of the suburban street which swallowed up Ethel nightly. The walk, her warmth and light and motion close to him, her clear little voice and the touch of her hand; that was reality.

The shadow of Chaffery and his deceptions lay indeed across all these things, sometimes faint, sometimes dark and present. Then Lewisham became insistent, his sentimental memories ceased, and he asked questions that verged on gulfs of doubt. Had she ever " helped "? She had not, she declared. Then she added that twice at home she had " sat down " to complete the circle. She would never help again. That she promised—if it needed promising. There had already been dreadful trouble at home about the exposure at Lagune's. Her mother had sided with her stepfather and joined in blaming her. But was she to blame?

" Of *course* you were not to blame," said Lewisham.

Lagune, he learnt, had been unhappy and restless for the three days after the *séance*—indulging in wearisome monologue—with Ethel as sole auditor (at twenty-one shillings a week). Then he had decided to give Chaffery a sound lecture on his disastrous dishonesty. But it was Chaffery gave the lecture. Smithers, had he only known it, had been overthrown by a better brain than Lagune's, albeit it spoke through Lagune's treble.

Ethel did not like talking of Chaffery and these other things. "If you knew how sweet it was to forget it all," she would say; "to be just us two together for a little while." And, "What good *does* it do to keep on?" when Lewisham was pressing. Lewisham wanted very much to keep on at times, but the good of it was a little hard to demonstrate. So his knowledge of the situation remained imperfect and the weeks drifted by.

Wonderfully varied were those seven and sixty nights, as he came to remember in after life. There were nights of damp and drizzle, and then thick fogs, beautiful, isolating, grey-white veils, turning every yard of pavement into a private room. Grand indeed were these fogs, things to rejoice at mightily, since then it was no longer a thing for public scorn that two young people hurried along arm in arm, and one could do a thousand impudent, significant things with varying pressure and the fondling of a little hand (a hand in a greatly mended glove of cheap kid). Then indeed one seemed to be nearer that elusive something that threaded it together. And the dangers of the street corners, the horses looming up suddenly out of the dark, the carters with lanterns at their horses' heads, the street lamps, blurred smoky orange at one's nearest, and vanishing at twenty yards into dim haze, seemed to accentuate the infinite need of protection on the part of a delicate young lady who had already traversed three winters of fogs, thornily alone. Moreover, one could come right down the quiet street where she lived, half-way to the steps of her house, with a delightful sense of enterprise.

The fogs passed all too soon into a hard frost, into nights of starlight and presently moonlight, when the lamps looked hard, flashing like rows of yellow gems, and their reflections and the glare of the shop windows were sharp and frosty and even the stars hard and bright, snapping noiselessly (if one may say so) instead of twinkling. A jacket trimmed with imitation Astrakhan replaced Ethel's lighter coat, and a round cap of Astrakhan her hat, and her eyes shone hard and bright, and her forehead was broad and white beneath it. It was exhilarating, but one got home too soon and so the way from Chelsea to Clapham was lengthened, first into a loop of side streets, and then when the first pulverulent snows told that Christmas was at hand, into a new loop down King's Road, and once even through the Brompton Road and Sloane Street, where the shops were full of decorations and entertaining things.

And under circumstances of infinite gravity, Mr. Lewisham secretly spent three-and-twenty shillings out of the vestiges of that hundred pounds, and bought Ethel a little gold ring set with pearls. With that there must needs be a ceremonial, and on the verge of the snowy, foggy Common she took off her glove and the ring was placed on her finger. Whereupon he was moved to kiss her—on the frost-pink knuckle next to an inky nail.

"It's silly of us," she said. "What can we do?— ever?"

"You wait," he said, and his tone was full of vague promises.

Afterwards he thought over those promises, and another evening went into the matter more fully, telling her of all the brilliant things that he held it was possible for a South Kensington student to do and be—of headmasterships, northern science schools, inspectorships, demonstratorships, yea, even professorships. And then, and then— To all of which she lent a willing and incredulous ear, finding in that dreaming a quality of fear as well as delight.

31

The putting on of the pearl-set ring was mere ceremonial, of course; she could not wear it either at Lagune's or at home; so instead she threaded it on a little white satin ribbon and wore it round her neck— "next her heart." He thought of it there warm "next her heart."

When he had bought the ring he had meant to save it for Christmas before he gave it to her. But the desire to see her pleasure had been too strong for him.

Christmas Eve, I know not by what deceit on her part, these young people spent together all day. Lagune was down with a touch of bronchitis and had given his typist a holiday. Perhaps she forgot to mention it at home. The Royal College was in vacation and Lewisham was free. He declined the plumber's invitation; "work" kept him in London, he said, though it meant a pound or more of added expenditure. These absurd young people walked sixteen miles that Christmas Eve, and parted warm and glowing. There had been a hard frost and a little snow, the sky was a colourless grey, icicles hung from the arms of the street lamps, and the pavements were patterned out with frond-like forms that were trodden into slides as the day grew older. The Thames they knew was a wonderful sight, but that they kept until last. They went first along the Brompton Road. . . .

And it is well that you should have the picture of them right; Lewisham in the ready-made overcoat, blue cloth and velvet collar, dirty tan gloves, red tie, and bowler hat; Ethel in a two-year-old jacket, and hat of curly Astrakhan; both pink-cheeked from the keen air, shyly arm in arm occasionally, and very alert to miss no possible spectacle. The shops were varied and interesting along the Brompton Road, but nothing to compare with Piccadilly. There were windows in Piccadilly so full of costly little things it took fifteen minutes to get them done, card shops, drapers' shops full of foolish, entertaining attractions. Lewisham, in spite of his old

animosities, forgot to be severe on the Shopping Class,
Ethel was so vastly entertained by all these pretty follies.

Then up Regent Street by the place where the sham
diamonds are, and the place where the girls display
their long hair, and the place where the little chickens
run about in the window, and so into Oxford Street,
Holborn, through to Ludgate Hill, St. Paul's Churchyard, and on to Leadenhall and the markets where
turkeys, geese, ducklings and chickens—turkeys predominant, however—hang in rows by the thousand.

"I *must* buy you something," said Lewisham, resuming a topic.

"No, no," said Ethel with her eye down a vista of
innumerable birds.

"But I *must*," said Lewisham. "You had better
choose it, or I shall get something wrong." His mind
ran on brooches and clasps.

"You mustn't waste your money, and besides, I have
that ring."

But Lewisham insisted.

"Then—if you must—I am starving. Buy me something to eat."

An immense and memorable joke. Lewisham plunged
recklessly—orientally—into an awe-inspiring place with
mitred napkins. They lunched on cutlets—stripped the
cutlets to the bone—and little crisp brown potatoes, and
they drank between them a whole half bottle of—some
white wine or other, selected by Lewisham in an offhand
way from the list. Neither of them had ever taken wine
at a meal before. One-and-ninepence it cost him, Sir,
and the name of it was Capri! It was really very passable Capri—a manufactured product, no doubt, but
warming and aromatic. Ethel was aghast at his magnificence and drank a glass and a half.

Then, very warm and comfortable, they went down
by the Tower, and the Tower Bridge with its crest of
snow, huge pendant icicles, and the ice blocks choked in
its side arches, was seasonable seeing. And as they had

had enough of shops and crowds they set off resolutely along the desolate Embankment homeward.

But indeed the Thames was a wonderful sight that year! Ice-fringed along either shore, and with drift-ice in the middle reflecting a luminous scarlet from the broad red setting sun, and moving steadily, incessantly seaward. A swarm of mewing gulls went to and fro, and with them mingled pigeons and crows. The buildings on the Surrey side were dim and grey and very mysterious, the moored, ice-blocked barges silent and deserted, and here and there a lit window shone warm. The sun sank right out of sight into a bank of blue, and the Surrey side dissolved in mist save for a few insoluble spots of yellow light, that presently became many. And after our lovers had come under Charing Cross Bridge the Houses of Parliament rose before them at the end of a great crescent of golden lamps, blue and faint, halfway between the earth and sky. And the clock on the Tower was like a November sun.

It was a day without a flaw, or at most but the slightest speck. And that only came at the very end.

"Good-bye, dear," she said. "I have been very happy to-day."

His face came very close to hers. "Good-bye," he said, pressing her hand and looking into her eyes.

She glanced round, she drew nearer to him. "*Dearest* one," she whispered very softly, and then, "Good-bye."

Suddenly he became unaccountably petulant, he dropped her hand. "It's always like this. We are happy. *I* am happy. And then—then you are taken away. . . ."

There was a silence of mute interrogations.

"Dear," she whispered, "we must wait."

A moment's pause. "*Wait!*" he said, and broke off. He hesitated. "Good-bye," he said as though he was snapping a thread that held them together.

CHAPTER THE SIXTEENTH

Miss Heydinger's Private Thoughts

*T*HE way from Chelsea to Clapham and the way from South Kensington to Battersea, especially if the former is looped about a little to make it longer, come very near to each other. One night close upon Christmas two friends of Lewisham's passed him and Ethel. But Lewisham did not see them, because he was looking at Ethel's face.

"Did you see?" said the other girl, a little maliciously.

"Mr. Lewisham—wasn't it?" said Miss Heydinger in a perfectly indifferent tone.

Miss Heydinger sat in the room her younger sister called her "Sanctum." Her Sanctum was only too evidently an intellectualised bedroom, and a cheap wallpaper of silvery roses peeped coquettishly from between her draped furniture. Her particular glories were the writing-desk in the middle of the room and the microscope on the unsteady octagonal table under the window. There were bookshelves of workmanship patently feminine in their facile decoration and structural in-

963

stability, and on them an array of glittering poets, Shelley, Rossetti, Keats, Browning, and odd volumes of Ruskin, South Place Sermons, Socialistic publications in torn paper covers, and above, science textbooks and note-books in an oppressive abundance. The autotypes that hung about the room were eloquent of æsthetic ambi-tions and of a certain impermeability to implicit mean-ings. There was the Mirror of Venus by Burne-Jones, Rossetti's Annunciation, Lippi's Annunciation, and the Love and Life and Love and Death of Watts. And among other photographs was one of last year's Debat-ing Society Committee, Lewisham smiling a little weakly near the centre, and Miss Heydinger out of focus in the right wing. And Miss Heydinger sat with her back to all these things in her black horsehair armchair, staring into the fire, her eyes hot and her chin on her hand.

" I might have guessed—before," she said. " Ever since that *séance*. It has been different. . . ."

She smiled bitterly. " Some shop girl . . ."

She mused. " They are all alike, I suppose. They come back—a little damaged, as the woman says in ' Lady Windermere's Fan.' Perhaps he will. I wonder. . . .

" Why should he be so deceitful? Why should he act to me? . . .

" Pretty, pretty, pretty—that is our business. What man hesitates in the choice? He goes his own way, thinks his own thoughts, does his own work . . .

" His dissection is getting behind—one can see he takes scarcely any notes. . . ."

For a long time she was silent. Her face became more intent. She began to bite her thumb, at first slowly, then faster. She broke out at last into words again.

" The things he might do, the great things he might do. He is able, he is dogged, he is strong. And then comes a pretty face! Oh God! *Why* was I made with heart and brain?" She sprang to her feet, with her hands clenched and her face contorted. But she shed no tears.

Her attitude fell limp in a moment. One hand dropped by her side, the other rested on a fossil on the mantelshelf, and she stared down into the red fire.

"To think of all we might have done! It maddens me!

"To work, and think, and learn. To hope and wait. To despise the petty arts of womanliness, to trust to the sanity of man . . .

"To awake like the foolish virgins," she said, "and find the hour of life is past!"

Her face, her pose, softened into self-pity.

"Futility . . .

"It's no good. . . ." Her voice broke.

"I shall never be happy. . . ."

She saw the grandiose vision of the future she had cherished, suddenly rolled aside and vanishing, more and more splendid as it grew more and more remote—like a dream at the waking moment. The vision of her inevitable loneliness came to replace it, clear and acute. She saw herself alone and small in a huge desolation—infinitely pitiful, Lewisham callously receding. With "some shop girl." The tears came, came faster, until they were streaming down her face. She turned as if looking for something. She flung herself upon her knees before the little armchair, and began an incoherent sobbing prayer for the pity and comfort of God.

The next day one of the other girls in the biological course remarked to her friend that "Heydinger-dingery" had relapsed. Her friend glanced down the laboratory. "It's a bad relapse," she said. "Really . . . I couldn't . . . wear my hair like that."

She continued to regard Miss Heydinger with a critical eye. She was free to do this because Miss Heydinger was standing, lost in thought, staring at the December fog outside the laboratory windows. "She looks white," said the girl who had originally spoken. "I wonder if she works hard."

"It makes precious little difference if she does," said her friend. "I asked her yesterday what were the bones in the parietal segment, and she didn't know one. Not one."

The next day Miss Heydinger's place was vacant. She was ill—from overstudy—and her illness lasted to within three weeks of the terminal examination. Then she came back with a pallid face and a strenuous unavailing industry.

CHAPTER THE SEVENTEENTH

In the Raphael Gallery

IT was nearly three o'clock, and in the Biological Laboratory the lamps were all alight. The class was busy with razors cutting sections of the root of a fern to examine it microscopically. A certain silent frog-like boy, a private student who plays no further part in this story, was working intently, looking more like a frog than usual—his expression modest with a touch of effort. Behind Miss Heydinger, jaded and untidy in her early manner again, was a vacant seat, an abandoned microscope and scattered pencils and note-books.

On the door of the class-room was a list of those who had passed the Christmas examination. At the head of it was the name of the aforesaid frog-like boy; next to him came Smithers and one of the girls bracketed together. Lewisham ingloriously headed the second class, and Miss Heydinger's name did not appear—there was, the list asserted, "one failure." So the student pays for the finer emotions.

967   31*

And in the spacious solitude of the museum gallery devoted to the Raphael cartoons, sat Lewisham, plunged in gloomy meditation. A negligent hand pulled thoughtfully at the indisputable moustache, with particular attention to such portions as were long enough to gnaw.

He was trying to see the situation clearly. The shadow of that defeat lay across everything, blotted out the light of his pride, shaded his honour, threw everything into a new perspective. The rich prettiness of his love-making had fled to some remote quarter of his being. Against the frog-like youngster he felt a savage animosity. And Smithers had betrayed him. He was angry, bitterly angry with "swats" and "muggers" who spent their whole time grinding for these foolish chancy examinations. Nor had the practical examination been altogether fair, and one of the questions in the written portion was quite outside the lectures. Biver, Professor Biver, was an indiscriminating ass, he felt assured, and so too was Weeks, the demonstrator. But these obstacles could not blind his intelligence to the manifest cause of his overthrow, the waste of more than half his available evening, the best time for study in the twenty-four hours, day after day. And that was going on steadily, a perpetual leakage of time. To-night he would go to meet her again, and begin to accumulate to himself ignominy in the second part of the course, the botanical section, also. And so, reluctantly rejecting one cloudy excuse after another, he clearly focussed the antagonism between his relations to Ethel and his immediate ambitions.

Things had come so easily to him for the last two years that he had taken his steady upward progress in life as assured. It had never occurred to him, when he went to intercept Ethel after that *séance,* that he went into any peril of that sort. Now he had had a sharp reminder. He began to shape a picture of the frog-like boy at home—he was a private student of the upper middle class—sitting in a convenient study with a writing-table, book-shelves and a shaded lamp—Lewisham worked at his chest of drawers with his great coat on, and his feet in the lowest drawer wrapped in all his available linen—and in the midst of incredible conveniences the frog-like boy was working, working, working. Meanwhile Lewisham toiled through the foggy streets, Chelsea-ward, or, after he had left her, tramped homeward—full of foolish imaginings.

He began to think with bloodless lucidity of his entire relationship to Ethel. His softer emotions were in abeyance, but he told himself no lies. He cared for her, he loved to be with her and to talk to her and please her, but that was not all his desire. He thought of the bitter words of an orator at Hammersmith, who had complained that in our present civilisation even the elemental need of marriage was denied. Virtue had become a vice. "We marry in fear and trembling, sex for a home is the woman's traffic, and the man comes to his heart's desire when his heart's desire is dead." The thing which had seemed a mere flourish, came back now with a terrible air of truth. Lewisham saw that it was a case of divergent ways. On the one hand that shining staircase to fame and power that had been his dream from the very dawn of his adolescence, and on the other hand—Ethel.

And if he chose Ethel, even then would he have his choice? What would come of it? A few walks more or less! She was hopelessly poor, he was hopelessly poor, and this cheat of a Medium was her stepfather! After all she was not well-educated, she did not understand his work and his aims. . . .

He suddenly perceived with absolute conviction that after the *séance* he should have gone home and forgotten her. Why had he felt that irresistible impulse to seek her out? Why had his imagination spun such a strange web of possibilities about her? He was involved now, foolishly involved. . . . All his future was a sacrifice to this transitory ghost of love-making in the streets. He pulled spitefully at his moustache.

His picture began to shape itself into Ethel and her mysterious mother and the vague dexterous Chaffery holding him back, entangled in an impalpable net, from that bright and glorious ascent to performance and distinction. Leaky boots and the splashings of cabs as his portion for all his life. Already the Forbes Medal, the immediate step, was as good as lost. . . .

What on earth had he been thinking about? He fell foul of his upbringing. Men of the upper or middle classes were put up to these things by their parents; they were properly warned against involving themselves in this love nonsense before they were independent. It was much better. . . . .

Everything was going. Not only his work—his scientific career, but the Debating Society, the political movement, all his work for Humanity. . . . Why not be resolute—even now? . . . Why not put the thing clearly and plainly to her? Or write? If he wrote now he could get the advantage of the evening at the Library. He must ask her to forego these walks home— at least until the next examination. *She* would understand. He had a qualm of doubt whether she would understand. . . . He grew angry at this possibility. But it was no good mincing matters. If once he began to consider her— Why should he consider her in that way? Simply because she was unreasonable!

Lewisham had a transitory gust of anger.

Yet that abandonment of the walks insisted on looking mean to him. And she would think it mean. Which was very much worse, somehow. *Why* mean? Why should she think it mean? He grew angry again.

The portly museum policeman who had been watching him furtively, wondering why a student should sit in front of the "Sacrifice of Lystra" and gnaw lips and nails and moustache, and scowl and glare at that masterpiece, saw him rise suddenly to his feet with an air of resolution, spin on his heel, and set off with a quick step out of the gallery. He looked neither to the right nor the left. He passed out of sight down the staircase.

"Gone to get some more moustache to eat, I suppose," said the policeman reflectively. . . .

"One 'ud think something had bit him."

After some pensive moments the policeman strolled along down the gallery and came to a stop opposite the cartoon.

"Figgers is a bit big for the houses," said the policeman, anxious to do impartial justice. "But that's Art. I lay '*e* couldn't do anything . . . not arf so good."

CHAPTER THE EIGHTEENTH

The Friends of Progress Meet

THE night next but one after this meditation saw a new order in the world. A young lady dressed in an Astrakhan-edged jacket and with a face of diminished cheerfulness marched from Chelsea to Clapham alone, and Lewisham sat in the flickering electric light of the Education Library, staring blankly over a business-like pile of books at unseen things.

The arrangement had not been effected without friction, the explanation had proved difficult. Evidently she did not appreciate the full seriousness of Lewisham's mediocre position in the list. "But you have *passed* all right," she said. Neither could she grasp the importance of evening study. "Of course I don't know," she said judicially; "but I thought you were learning all day." She calculated the time consumed by their walk as half an hour, "just one half hour," she forgot that he had to get to Chelsea and then to return to his lodgings. Her customary tenderness was veiled by an only too apparent resentment. First at him, and then when he protested, at Fate. "I suppose it *has* to be," she said. "Of course it doesn't matter, I suppose, if we *don't* see each other quite so often," with a quiver of pale lips.

He had returned from the parting with an uneasy mind, and that evening had gone in the composition of a letter that was to make things clearer. But his scientific studies rendered his prose style hard, and things he could whisper he could not write. His justification indeed did him no sort of justice. But her reception of it made her seem a very unreasonable person. He had some violent fluctuations. At times he was bitterly angry with her for her failure to see things as he did. He would wander about the museum conducting imaginary discussions with her and even making scathing remarks. At other times he had to summon all his power of acrid discipline and all his memories of her resentful retorts, to keep himself from a headlong rush to Chelsea and unmanly capitulation.

And this new disposition of things endured for two weeks. It did not take Miss Heydinger all that time to discover that the disaster of the examination had wrought a change in Lewisham. She perceived those nightly walks were over. It was speedily evident to her that he was working with a kind of dogged fury; he came early, he went late. The wholesome freshness of his cheek paled. He was to be seen on each of the late nights amidst a pile of diagrams and textbooks in one of the less draughty corners of the Educational Library, accumulating piles of memoranda. And nightly in the Students' "club" he wrote a letter addressed to a stationer's shop in Clapham, but that she did not see. For the most part these letters were brief, for Lewisham, South Kensington fashion, prided himself upon not being "literary," and some of the more despatch-like wounded a heart perhaps too hungry for tender words.

He did not meet Miss Heydinger's renewed advances

with invariable kindness. Yet something of the old relations were presently restored. He would talk well to her for a time, and then snap like a dry twig. But the loaning of books was resumed, the subtle process of his æsthetic education that Miss Heydinger had devised. "Here is a book I promised you," she said one day, and he tried to remember the promise.

The book was a collection of Browning's Poems, and it contained "Sludge"; it also happened that it contained "The Statue and the Bust"—that stimulating lecture on half-hearted constraints. "Sludge" did not interest Lewisham, it was not at all his idea of a medium, but he read and re-read "The Statue and the Bust." It had the profoundest effect upon him. He went to sleep—he used to read his literature in bed because it was warmer there, and over literature nowadays it did not matter as it did with science if one dozed a little—with these lines stimulating his emotions :

> "*So weeks grew months, years; gleam by gleam*
> *The glory dropped from their youth and love,*
> *And both perceived they had dreamed a dream.*"

By way of fruit it may be to such seed, he dreamed a dream that night. It concerned Ethel, and at last they were a-marrying. He drew her to his arms. He bent to kiss her. And suddenly he saw her lips were shrivelled and her eyes were dull, saw the wrinkles seaming her face! She was old! She was intolerably old! He woke in a kind of horror and lay awake and very dismal until dawn, thinking of their separation and of her solitary walk through the muddy streets, thinking of his position, the leeway he had lost and the chances there were against him in the battle of the world. He perceived the colourless truth; the Career was improbable, and that Ethel should be added to it was almost hopeless. Clearly the question was between these two. Or should he vacillate and lose both? And then his wretchedness gave place to that anger that comes of perpetually thwarted desires. . . .

It was on the day after this dream that he insulted Parkson so grossly. He insulted Parkson after a meeting of the " Friends of Progress " at Parkson's rooms.

No type of English student nowadays quite realises the noble ideal of plain living and high thinking. Our admirable examination system admits of extremely little thinking at any level, high or low. But the Kensington student's living is at any rate insufficient, and he makes occasional signs of recognition towards the cosmic process.

One such sign was the periodic gathering of these " Friends of Progress," an association begotten of Lewisham's paper on Socialism. It was understood that strenuous things were to be done to make the world better, but so far no decisive action had been taken.

They met in Parkson's sitting-room, because Parkson, being a Whitworth Scholar and in receipt of one hundred pounds a year, was the only one of the Friends opulent enough to have a sitting-room. The Friends were of various ages, mostly very young. Several smoked and others held pipes which they had discontinued smoking—but there was nothing to drink except coffee, because that was the utmost they could afford. Dunkerley, an assistant master in a suburban school, and Lewisham's former colleague at Whortley, attended these assemblies through the introduction of Lewisham. All the Friends wore red ties except Bletherley, who wore an orange one to show that he was aware of Art, and Dunkerley wore a black one with blue specks because assistant masters in small private schools have to keep up appearances. And their simple procedure was that each talked as much as the others would suffer.

Usually the self-proposed " Luther of Socialism "—ridiculous Lewisham!—had a thesis or so to maintain, but this night he was depressed and inattentive. He sat with his legs over the arm of his chair by way of indicating the state of his mind. He had a packet of

Algerian cigarettes (twenty for fivepence) and appeared chiefly concerned to smoke them all before the evening was out. Bletherley was going to discourse of " Woman under Socialism," and he brought a big American edition of Shelley's works and a volume of Tennyson, including the " Princess," both bristling with paper tongues against his marked quotations. He was all for the abolition of " monopolies," and the crèche was to replace the family. He was unctuous when he was not pretty-pretty, and his views were evidently unpopular.

Parkson was a man from Lancashire, and a devout Quaker; his third and completing factor was Ruskin, with whose work and phraseology he was saturated. He listened to Bletherley with a marked disapproval, and opened a vigorous defence of that ancient tradition of loyalty that Bletherley had called the monopolist institution of marriage. " The pure and simple old theory—love and faithfulness," said Parkson, " suffices for me. If we are to smear our political movements with this sort of stuff . . ."

" Does it work?" interjected Lewisham, speaking for the first time.

" What work?"

" The pure and simple old theory. I know the theory. I believe in the theory. Bletherley's Shelley-witted. But it's theory. You meet the inevitable girl. The theory says you may meet her anywhen. You meet too young. You fall in love. You marry—in spite of obstacles. Love laughs at locksmiths. You have children. That's the theory. All very well for a man whose father can leave him five hundred a year. But how does it work for a shopman? . . . An assistant master like Dunkerley? Or . . . Me?"

" In these cases one must exercise restraint," said Parkson. " Have faith. A man that is worth having is worth waiting for."

" Worth growing old for?" said Lewisham.

" Chap ought to fight," said Dunkerley. " Don't

see your difficulty, Lewisham. Struggle for existence keen, no doubt, tremendous in fact—still. In it—may as well struggle. Two—join forces—pool the luck. If I saw a girl I fancied so that I wanted to, I'd marry her to-morrow. And my market value is seventy *non res.*"

Lewisham looked round at him eagerly, suddenly interested. "*Would* you?" he said. Dunkerley's face was slightly flushed.

"Like a shot. Why not?"

"But how are you to live?"

"That comes after. If . . ."

"I can't agree with you, Mr. Dunkerley," said Parkson. "I don't know if you have read 'Sesame and Lilies,' but there you have, set forth far more fairly than any words of mine could do, an ideal of a woman's place . . ."

"All rot—'Sesame and Lilies,'" interrupted Dunkerley. "Read bits. Couldn't stand it. Never *can* stand Ruskin. Too many prepositions. Tremendous English, no doubt, but not my style. Sort of thing a wholesale grocer's daughter might read to get refined. *We* can't afford to get refined."

"But would you really marry a girl . . .?" began Lewisham, with an unprecedented admiration for Dunkerley in his eyes.

"Why not?"

"On—?" Lewisham hesitated.

"Forty pounds a year *res.* Whack! Yes."

A silent youngster began to speak, cleared an accumulated huskiness from his throat and said, "Consider the girl."

"Why *marry?*" asked Bletherley, unregarded.

"You must admit you are asking a great thing when you want a girl . . ." began Parkson.

"Not so. When a girl's chosen a man, and he chooses her, her place is with him. What is the good of hankering? Mutual. Fight together."

"Good!" said Lewisham suddenly emotional. "You talk like a man, Dunkerley. I'm hanged if you don't."

"The place of Woman," insisted Parkson, "is the Home. And if there is no home——! I hold that, if need be, a man should toil seven years——as Jacob did for Rachel——ruling his passions, to make the home fitting and sweet for her . . ."

"Get the hutch for the pet animal," said Dunkerley. "No. I mean to marry a *woman*. Female sex always *has* been in the struggle for existence——no great damage so far——always will be. Tremendous idea——that struggle for existence. Only sensible theory you've got hold of, Lewisham. Woman who isn't fighting square side by side with a man——woman who's just kept and fed and petted is . . ." He hesitated.

A lad with a spotted face and a bulldog pipe between his teeth supplied a Biblical word.

"That's shag," said Dunkerley. "I was going to say 'a harem of one.'"

The youngster was puzzled for a moment. "I smoke Perique," he said.

"It will make you just as sick," said Dunkerley.

"Refinement's so beastly vulgar," was the belated answer of the smoker of Perique.

That was the interesting part of the evening to Lewisham. Parkson suddenly rose, got down "Sesame and Lilies," and insisted upon reading a lengthy mellifluous extract that went like a garden roller over the debate, and afterwards Bletherley became the centre of a wrangle that left him grossly insulted and in a minority of one. The institution of marriage, so far as the South Kensington student is concerned, is in no immediate danger.

Parkson turned out with the rest of them at half-past ten, for a walk. The night was warm for February and the waxing moon bright. Parkson fixed himself upon Lewisham and Dunkerley, to Lewisham's intense annoyance——for he had a few intimate things he could have said to the man of Ideas that night. Dunkerley lived north, so that the three went up Exhibition Road to High Street, Kensington. There they parted from Dunkerley, and Lewisham and Parkson turned southward again for Lewisham's new lodging in Chelsea.

Parkson was one of those exponents of virtue for whom the discussion of sexual matters has an irresistible attraction. The meeting had left him eloquent. He had argued with Dunkerley to the verge of indelicacy, and now he poured out a vast and increasingly confidential flow of talk upon Lewisham. Lewisham was distraught. He walked as fast as he could. His sole object was to get rid of Parkson. Parkson's sole object was to tell him interesting secrets about himself and a Certain Person with a mind of extraordinary Purity of whom Lewisham had heard before.

Ages passed.

Lewisham suddenly found himself being shown a photograph under a lamp. It represented an asymmetrical face singularly void of expression, the upper part of an " art " dress, and a fringe of curls. He perceived he was being given to understand that this was a Paragon of Purity, and that she was the particular property of Parkson. Parkson was regarding him proudly and apparently awaiting his verdict.

Lewisham struggled with the truth. " It's an interesting face," he said.

" It is a face essentially beautiful," said Parkson quietly but firmly. " Do you notice the eyes, Lewisham ?"

" Oh, yes," said Lewisham. " Yes. I see the eyes."

" They are . . . innocent. They are the eyes of a little child."

" Yes. They look that sort of eye. Very nice, old man. I congratulate you. Where does she live ?"

" You never saw a face like that in London," said Parkson

"*Never,*" said Lewisham decisively.

"I would not show that to everyone," said Parkson. "You can scarcely judge all that pure-hearted, wonderful girl is to me." He returned the photograph solemnly to its envelope, regarding Lewisham with an air of one who has performed the ceremony of blood-brotherhood. Then taking Lewisham's arm affectionately—a thing Lewisham detested—he went on to a copious outpouring on Love—with illustrative anecdotes of the Paragon. It was just sufficiently cognate to the matter of Lewisham's thoughts to demand attention. Every now and then he had to answer, and he felt an idiotic desire—albeit he clearly perceived its idiocy—to reciprocate confidences. The necessity of fleeing Parkson became urgent—Lewisham's temper under these multitudinous stresses was going.

"Every man needs a Lode Star," said Parkson—and Lewisham swore under his breath.

Parkson's lodgings were now near at hand to the left, and it occurred to him this boredom would be soonest ended if he took Parkson home. Parkson consented mechanically, still discoursing.

"I have often seen you talking to Miss Heydinger," he said. "If you will pardon my saying it . . ."

"We are excellent friends," admitted Lewisham. "But here we are at your diggings."

Parkson stared at his "diggings." "There's Heaps I want to talk about. I'll come part of the way at any rate to Battersea. Your Miss Heydinger, I was saying . . ."

From that point onwards he made casual appeals to a supposed confidence between Lewisham and Miss Heydinger, each of which increased Lewisham's exasperation. "It will not be long before you also, Lewisham, will begin to know the infinite purification of a Pure Love. . . ." Then suddenly, with a vague idea of suppressing Parkson's unendurable chatter, as one motive at least, Lewisham rushed into the confidential.

"I know," he said. "You talk to me as though . . . I've marked out my destiny these three years." His confidential impulse died as he relieved it.

"You don't mean to say Miss Heydinger—?' asked Parkson.

"Oh, *damn* Miss Heydinger!" said Lewisham, and suddenly, abruptly, uncivilly, he turned away from Parkson at the end of the street and began walking away southward, leaving Parkson in mid-sentence at the crossing.

Parkson stared in astonishment at his receding back and ran after him to ask for the grounds of this sudden offence. Lewisham walked on for a space with Parkson trotting by his side. Then suddenly he turned. His face was quite white and he spoke a tired voice.

"Parkson," he said, "you are a fool! . . . You have the face of a sheep, the manners of a buffalo, and the conversation of a bore. Pewrity indeed! . . . The girl whose photograph you showed me has eyes that don't match. She looks as loathsome as one would naturally expect. . . . I'm not joking now. . . . Go away!"

After that Lewisham went on his southward way alone. He did not go straight to his room in Chelsea, but spent some hours in a street in Battersea, pacing to and fro in front of a possible house. His passion changed from savagery to a tender longing. If only he could see her to-night! He knew his own mind now. To-morrow he was resolved he would fling work to the dogs and meet her. The things Dunkerley had said had filled his mind with wonderful novel thoughts. If only he could see her now!

His wish was granted. At the corner of the street two figures passed him: one of these, a tall man in glasses and a quasi-clerical hat, with coat collar turned up under his grey side-whiskers, he recognised as Chaffery; the other he knew only too well. The pair passed him without seeing him, but for an instant the lamplight fell upon her face and showed it white and tired.

Lewisham stopped dead at the corner, staring in blank astonishment after these two figures as they receded into the haze under the lights. He was dumbfounded. A clock struck slowly. It was midnight. Presently down the road came the slamming of their door.

Long after the echo died away he stood there. " She has been at a *séance;* she has broken her promise. She has been at a *séance,* she has broken her promise," sang in perpetual reiteration through his brain.

And then came the interpretation. " She has done it because I have left her. I might have told it from her letters. She has done it because she thinks I am not in earnest, that my love-making was just boyishness . . .

" I knew she would never understand."

CHAPTER THE NINETEENTH

Lewisham's Solution

THE next morning Lewisham learnt from Lagune that his intuition was correct, that Ethel had at last succumbed to pressure and consented to attempt thought-reading. "We made a good beginning," said Lagune rubbing his hands. "I am sure we shall do well with her. Certainly she has powers. I have always felt it in her face. She has powers."

"Was much . . . pressure necessary?" asked Lewisham by an effort.

"We had—considerable difficulty. Considerable. But of course—as I pointed out to her—it was scarcely possible for her to continue as my typist unless she was disposed to take an interest in my investigations——"

"You did that?"

"Had to. Fortunately Chaffery—it was his idea, I must admit——"

Lagune stopped astonished. Lewisham, after making an odd sort of movement with his hands, had turned round and was walking away down the laboratory.

983

Lagune stared, confronted by a psychic phenomenon beyond his circle of ideas. "Odd!" he said at last, and began to unpack his bag. Ever and again he stopped and stared at Lewisham, who was now sitting in his own place and drumming on the table with both hands.

Presently Miss Heydinger came out of the specimen room and addressed a remark to the young man. He appeared to answer with considerable brevity. He then stood up, hesitated for a moment between the three doors of the laboratory, and walked out by that opening on the back staircase. Lagune did not see him again until the afternoon.

That night Ethel had Lewisham's company again on her way home and their voices were earnest. She did not go straight home, but instead they went up under the gas lamps to the vague spaces of Clapham Common to talk there at length. And the talk that night was a momentous one. "Why have you broken your promise?" he said.

Her excuses were vague and weak. "I thought you did not care so much as you did," she said. "And when you stopped these walks—nothing seemed to matter. Besides—it is not like *séances* with spirits . . ."

At first Lewisham was passionate and forcible. His anger at Lagune and Chaffery blinded him to her turpitude. He talked her defences down. "It is cheating," he said. "Well—even if what *you* do is not cheating, it is delusion—unconscious cheating. Even if there is something in it, it is wrong. True or not, it is wrong. Why don't they thought-read each other? Why should they want you? Your mind is your own. It is sacred. To probe it!—I won't have it! I won't have it! At least you are mine to that extent. I can't think of you like that—bandaged. And that little fool pressing his hand on the back of your neck and asking questions. I won't have it! I would rather kill you than that."

" They don't do that!"

" I don't care! that is what it will come to. The bandage is the beginning. People must not get their living in that way anyhow. I've thought it out. Let them thought-read their daughters and hypnotise their aunts, and leave their typists alone."

" But what am I to do?"

" That's not it. There are things one must not suffer anyhow, whatever happens! Or else—one might be made to do anything. Honour! Just because we are poor— Let him dismiss you! *Let* him dismiss you. You can get another place——"

" Not at a guinea a week."

" Then take less."

" But I have to pay sixteen shillings every week."

" That doesn't matter."

She caught at a sob. " But to leave London—I can't do it. I can't."

" But how?— Leave London?" Lewisham's face changed.

" Oh! life is *hard*," she said. " I can't. They— they wouldn't let me stop in London."

" What do you mean?"

She explained if Lagune dismissed her she was to go into the country to an aunt, a sister of Chaffery's who needed a companion. Chaffery insisted upon that. " Companion they call it. I shall be just a servant— she has no servant. My mother cries when I talk to her. She tells me she doesn't want me to go away from her. But she's afraid of him. ' Why don't you do what he wants?' she says."

She sat staring in front of her at the gathering night. She spoke again in an even tone.

" I hate telling you these things. It is you . . . If you didn't mind . . . But you make it all different. I could do it—if it wasn't for you. I was . . . I *was* helping . . . I had gone meaning to help if anything went wrong at Mr. Lagune's. Yes—that night.

No . . . don't! It was too hard before to tell you
But I really did not feel it . . . until I saw you there.
Then all at once I felt shabby and mean."

"Well—" said Lewisham.

"That's all. I may have done thought-reading, but
I have never really cheated since—*never*. . . . If you
knew how hard it is . . ."

"I wish you had told me that before."

"I couldn't. Before you came it was different. He
used to make fun of the people—used to imitate
Lagune and make me laugh. It seemed a sort of joke."
She stopped abruptly. "Why did you ever come on
with me? I told you not to—you *know* I did."

She was near wailing. For a minute she was silent.

"I can't go to his sister's," she cried. "I may be a
coward—but I can't."

Pause. And then Lewisham saw his solution straight
and clear. Suddenly his secret desire had become his
manifest duty.

"Look here," he said, not looking at her and pulling
his moustache. "I won't have you doing any more of
that damned cheating. You shan't soil yourself any
more. And I won't have you leaving London."

"But what am I to do?" Her voice went up.

"Well—there is one thing you can do. If you
dare."

"What is it?"

He made no answer for some seconds. Then he
turned round and sat looking at her. Their eyes
met. . . .

The grey of his mind began to colour. Her face
was white and she was looking at him, in fear and
perplexity. A new tenderness for her sprang up in
him—a new feeling. Hitherto he had loved and
desired her sweetness and animation—but now she was
white and weary-eyed. He felt as though he had forgotten her and suddenly remembered. A great longing
came into his mind.

" But what is the other thing I can do?"

It was strangely hard to say. There came a peculiar sensation in his throat and facial muscles, a nervous stress between laughing and crying. All the world vanished before that great desire. And he was afraid she would not dare, that she would not take him seriously.

" What is it?" she said again.

" Don't you see that we can marry?" he said with the flood of his resolution suddenly strong and steady. " Don't you see that is the only thing for us? The dead lane we are in! You must come out of your cheating, and I must come out of my . . . cramming. And we—we must marry."

He paused and then became eloquent. " The world is against us, against—us. To you it offers money to cheat—to be ignoble. For it *is* ignoble! It offers you no honest way, only a miscrable drudgery. And it keeps you from me. And me too it bribes with the promise of success—if I will desert you . . . You don't know all . . . We may have to wait for years—we may have to wait for ever, if we wait until life is safe. We may be separated. . . . We may lose one another altogether. . . . Let us fight against it. Why should we separate? Unless True Love is like the other things —an empty cant. This is the only way. We two— who belong to one another."

She looked at him, her face perplexed with this new idea, her heart beating very fast. " We are so young," she said. " And how are we to live? You get a guinea."

" I can get more—I can earn more. I have thought it out. I have been thinking of it these two days. I have been thinking what we could do. I have money."

" You have money?"

" Nearly a hundred pounds."

" But we are so young— And my mother . . ."

" We won't ask her. We will ask no one. This is

our affair.   Ethel! this is *our* affair.   It is not a question of ways and means—even before this—— I have thought . . . Dear one!—*don't* you love me?"

She did not grasp his emotional quality.   She looked at him with puzzled eyes—still practical—making the suggestion arithmetical.

"I could typewrite if I had a machine.   I have heard——"

"It's not a question of ways and means.   Now. Ethel—I have longed——"

He stopped.   She looked at his face, at his eyes now eager and eloquent with the things that never shaped themselves into words.

"*Dare* you come with me?" he whispered.

Suddenly the world opened out in reality to her as sometimes it had opened out to her in wistful dreams. And she quailed before it.   She dropped her eyes from his.   She became a fellow-conspirator.   "But, how——?"

"I will think how.   Trust me!   Surely we know each other now— Think!   We two——"

"But I have never thought——"

"I could get apartments for us both.   It would be so easy.   And think of it—think—of what life would be!"

"How can I?"

"You will come?"

She looked at him, startled.   "You know," she said, "you must know I would like—I would love——"

"You will come."

"But dear—!   Dear, if you *make* me——"

"Yes!" cried Lewisham triumphantly.   "You will come."   He glanced round and his voice dropped. "Oh! my dearest! my dearest . . ."

His voice sank to an inaudible whisper.   But his face was eloquent.   Two garrulous, home-going clerks passed opportunely to remind him that his emotions were in a public place.

CHAPTER THE TWENTIETH

The Career is Suspended

ON the Wednesday afternoon following this — it was hard upon the botanical examination—Mr. Lewisham was observed by Smithers in the big Education Library reading in a volume of the British Encyclopædia. Beside him were the current Whitaker's Almanack, an open note-book, a book from the Contemporary Science Series, and the Science and Art Department's Directory. Smithers, who had a profound sense of Lewisham's superiority in the art of obtaining facts of value in examinations, wondered for some minutes what valuable tip for a student in botany might be hidden in Whitaker, and on reaching his lodgings spent some time over the landlady's copy. But really Lewisham was not studying botany, but the art of marriage according to the best authorities. (The book from the Contemporary Science Series was Professor Letourneau's " Evolution of Marriage." It was interesting certainly, but of little immediate use.)

From Whitaker Lewisham learnt that it would be

possible at a cost of £2 6s. 1d. or £2 7s. 1d. (one of the items was ambiguous) to get married within the week—that charge being exclusive of vails—at the district registry office. He did little addition sums in the note-book. The church fees he found were variable, but for more personal reasons he rejected a marriage at church. Marriage by certificate at a registrar's involved an inconvenient delay. It would have to be £2 7s. 1d. Vails—ten shillings, say.

Afterwards, without needless ostentation, he produced a cheque-book and a deposit-book, and proceeded to further arithmetic. He found that he was master of £61 4s. 7d. Not a hundred as he had said, but a fine big sum—men had started great businesses on less. It had been a hundred originally. Allowing five pounds for the marriage and moving, this would leave about £56. Plenty. No provision was made for flowers, carriages or the honeymoon. But there would be a typewriter to buy. Ethel was to do her share. . . .

"It will be a devilish close thing," said Lewisham with a quite unreasonable exultation. For, strangely enough, the affair was beginning to take on a flavour of adventure not at all unpleasant. He leant back in his chair with the note-book closed in his hand. . . .

But there was much to see to that afternoon. First of all he had to discover the district superintendent registrar, and then to find a lodging whither he should take Ethel—their lodging, where they were to live together.

At the thought of that new life together that was drawing so near, she came into his head, vivid and near and warm. . . .

He recovered himself from a day dream. He became aware of a library attendant down the room leaning forward over his desk, gnawing the tip of a paper knife after the fashion of South Kensington library attendants, and staring at him curiously. It occurred to Lewisham that thought reading was one of the most possible things in the world.   He blushed, rose clumsily and took the volume of the Encyclopædia back to its shelf.

He found the selection of lodgings a difficult business.   After his first essay he began to fancy himself a suspicious-looking character, and that perhaps hampered him.   He had chosen the district southward of the Brompton Road.   It had one disadvantage—he might blunder into a house with a fellow-student. . . . Not that it mattered vitally.   But the fact is, it is rather unusual for married couples to live permanently in furnished lodgings in London.   People who are too poor to take a house or a flat commonly find it best to take part of a house or unfurnished apartments. There are in London to every couple living in furnished apartments, a hundred in unfurnished rooms (" with the use of kitchen ").   To the discreet landlady the absence of furniture predicates a dangerous want of capital. The first landlady Lewisham interviewed didn't like ladies, they required such a lot of attendance, the second was of the same mind, the third told Mr. Lewisham he was " youngish to be married," the fourth said she only " did " for single " gents."   The fifth was a young person with an arch manner, who liked to know all about people she took in, and subjected Lewisham to a searching cross-examination.   When she had spitted him in a downright lie or so, she expressed an opinion that her rooms " would scarcely do," and bowed him amiably out.

He cooled his ears and cheeks by walking up and down the street for a space, and then tried again.   This landlady was a terrible and pitiful person, so grey and dusty she was, and her face deep lined with dust and trouble and labour.   She wore a dirty cap that was all askew.   She took Lewisham up into a threadbare room on the first floor.   " There's the use of a piano," she said, and indicated an instrument with a front of torn green silk.   Lewisham opened the keyboard and evoked a vibration of broken strings.   He took one further

32

survey of the dismal place. "Eighteen shillings," he said. "Thank you . . . I'll let you know." The woman smiled with the corners of her mouth down, and without a word moved wearily towards the door. Lewisham felt a transient wonder at her hopeless position, but he did not pursue the inquiry.

The next landlady sufficed. She was a clean-looking German woman, rather smartly dressed; she had a fringe of flaxen curls and a voluble flow of words, for the most part recognisably English. With this she sketched out remarks. Fifteen shillings was her demand for a minute bedroom and a small sitting-room, separated by folding doors on the ground floor, and her personal services. Coals were to be "sixpence a kettle," she said—a pretty substitute for scuttle. She had not understood Lewisham to say he was married. But she had no hesitation. "Aayteen shillin'," she said imperturbably. "Paid furs day ich wik. . . . See?" Mr. Lewisham surveyed the rooms again. They looked clean, and the bonus tea vases, the rancid, gilt-framed oleographs, two toilet tidies used as ornaments, and the fact that the chest of drawers had been crowded out of the bedroom into the sitting-room, simply appealed to his sense of humour. "I'll take 'em from Saturday next," he said.

She was sure she would like them and proposed to give him his book forthwith. She mentioned casually that the previous lodger had been a captain and had stayed three years. (One never hears by chance of lodgers stopping for a shorter period.) Something happened (German) and now he kept his carriage—apparently an outcome of his stay. She returned with a small penny account-book, a bottle of ink and an execrable pen, wrote Lewisham's name on the cover of this, and a receipt for eighteen shillings on the first page. She was evidently a person of considerable business aptitude. Lewisham paid, and the transaction terminated. "Szhure to be gomfortable," followed him comfortingly to the street.

Then he went on to Chelsea and interviewed a fatherly

gentleman at the Registrar's office. The fatherly gentleman was chubby-faced and spectacled, and his manner was sympathetic but business-like. He "called-back" each item of the interview. "And what can I do for you? You wish to be married! By licence?"

"By licence."

"By licence!"

And so forth. He opened a book and made neat entries of the particulars.

"The lady's age?"

"Twenty-one."

"A very suitable age . . . for a lady."

He advised Lewisham to get a ring and said he would need two witnesses.

"*Well*—" hesitated Lewisham.

"There is always someone about," said the superintendent registrar. "And they are quite used to it."

Thursday and Friday Lewisham passed in exceedingly high spirits. No consciousness of the practical destruction of the Career seems to have troubled him at this time. Doubt had vanished from his universe for a space. He wanted to dance along the corridors. He felt curiously irresponsible and threw up an unpleasant sort of humour that pleased nobody. He wished Miss Heydinger many happy returns of the day, *apropos* of nothing, and he threw a bun across the refreshment room at Smithers and hit one of the Art School officials. Both were extremely silly things to do. In the first instance he was penitent immediately after the outrage, but in the second he added insult to injury by going across the room and asking in an offensively suspicious manner if anyone had seen his bun. He crawled under a table and found it at last, rather dusty but quite eatable, under the chair of a lady art student. He sat down by Smithers to eat it, while he argued with the Art official. The Art official said the manners of the Science students were getting unbearable, and threatened to bring the matter before the refreshment-room Committee. Lewisham said it was a pity to make such a fuss about a trivial thing, and proposed that the Art official should throw his lunch—steak and kidney pudding—across the room at him, Lewisham, and so get immediate satisfaction. He then apologised to the official and pointed out in extenuation that it was a very long and difficult shot he had attempted. The official then drank a crumb, or breathed some beer, or something of that sort, and the discussion terminated. In the afternoon, however, Lewisham, to his undying honour, felt acutely ashamed of himself. Miss Heydinger would not speak to him.

On Saturday morning he absented himself from the schools, pleading by post a slight indisposition, and took all his earthly goods to the booking-office at Vauxhall Station. Chaffery's sister lived at Tongham, near Farnham, and Ethel, dismissed a week since by Lagune, had started that morning, under her mother's maudlin supervision, to begin her new slavery. She was to alight either at Farnham or Woking, as opportunity arose, and return to Vauxhall to meet him. So that Lewisham's vigil on the main platform was of indefinite duration.

At first he felt the exhilaration of a great adventure. Then, as he paced the long platform, came a philosophical mood, a sense of entire detachment from the world. He saw a bundle of uprooted plants beside the portmanteau of a fellow-passenger and it suggested a grotesque simile. His roots, his earthly possessions, were all downstairs in the booking-office. What a flimsy thing he was! A box of books and a trunk of clothes, some certificates and scraps of paper, an entry here and an entry there, a body not over strong—and the vast multitude of people about him—against him—the huge world in which he found himself! Did it matter anything to one human soul save her if he ceased to exist forthwith? And miles away perhaps she also was feeling little and lonely. . . .

Would she have trouble with her luggage? Suppose

her aunt were to come to Farnham Junction to meet her? Suppose someone stole her purse? Suppose she came too late! The marriage was to take place at two. . . . Suppose she never came at all! After three trains in succession had disappointed him his vague feelings of dread gave place to a profound depression. . . .

But she came at last, and it was twenty-three minutes to two. He hurried her luggage downstairs, booked it with his own, and in another minute they were in a hansom—their first experience of that species of conveyance—on the way to the Registrar's office. They had said scarcely anything to one another, save hasty directions from Lewisham, but their eyes were full of excitement, and under the apron of the cab their hands were gripped together.

The little old gentleman was business-like but kindly. They made their vows to him, to a lean black-bearded clerk and a lady who took off an apron in the nether part of the building to attend. The little old gentleman made no long speeches. "You are young people," he said slowly, "and life together is a difficult thing. . . . Be kind to each other." He smiled, and held out a friendly hand.

Ethel's eyes glistened and she found she could not speak.

CHAPTER THE TWENTY-FIRST

Home

*T*HEN a furtive payment of witnesses, and Lewisham was beside her. His face was radiant. A steady current of workers going home to their half-holiday rest poured along the street. On the steps before them lay a few grains of rice from some more public nuptials.

A critical little girl eyed our couple curiously and made some remark to her ragamuffin friend.

"Not them," said the ragamuffin friend. "They've only been askin' questions."

The ragamuffin friend was no judge of faces.

They walked back through the thronged streets to Vauxhall Station, saying little to one another, and there Lewisham, assuming as indifferent a manner as he could command, recovered their possessions from the booking-office by means of two separate tickets and put them aboard a four-wheeler. His luggage went outside, but the little brown portmanteau containing Ethel's trousseau was small enough to go on the seat in front of them. You must figure a rather broken-down four-wheeler

996

bearing the yellow-painted box and the experienced trunk and Mr. Lewisham and all his fortunes, a despondent fitful horse, and a threadbare venerable driver, blasphemous *sotto voce* and flagellant, and an ancient coat with capes. When our two young people found themselves in the cab again a certain stiffness of manner between them vanished and there was more squeezing of hands. " Ethel *Lewisham*," said Lewisham several times, and Ethel reciprocated with " Husbinder " and " Hubby dear," and took off her glove to look again in an ostentatious manner at a ring. And she kissed the ring.

They were resolved that their newly-married state should not appear, and with considerable ceremony it was arranged that he should treat her with off-hand brusqueness when they arrived at their lodging. The Teutonic landlady appeared in the passage with an amiable smile and the hope that they had had a pleasant journey, and became voluble with promises of comfort. Lewisham having assisted the slatternly general servant to carry in his boxes, paid the cabman a florin in a resolute manner and followed the ladies into the sitting-room.

Ethel answered Madam Gadow's inquiries with admirable self-possession, followed her through the folding-doors and displayed an intelligent interest in a new spring mattress. Presently the folding-doors were closed again. Lewisham hovered about the front room pulling his moustache and pretending to admire the oleographs, surprised to find himself trembling. . . .

The slatternly general servant reappeared with the chops and tinned salmon he had asked Madame Gadow to prepare for them. He went and stared out of the window, heard the door close behind the girl, and turned at a sound as Ethel appeared shyly through the folding-doors.

She was suddenly domestic. Hitherto he had seen her without a hat and jacket only on one indistinct dramatic occasion. Now she wore a little blouse of soft, dark red material, with a white froth about the wrists and that pretty neck of hers. And her hair was a new wonderland of curls and soft strands. How delicate she looked and sweet as she stood hesitating there. These gracious moments in life! He took two steps and held out his arms. She glanced at the closed door of the room and came flitting towards him. . . .

CHAPTER THE TWENTY-SECOND

Epithalamy

FOR three indelible days Lewisham's existence was a fabric of fine emotions, life was too wonderful and beautiful for any doubts or forethought. To be with Ethel was perpetual delight—she astonished this sister-less youngster with a thousand feminine niceties and refinements. She shamed him for his strength and clumsiness. And the light in her eyes and the warmth in her heart that lit them!

Even to be away from her was a wonder and in its way delightful. He was no common Student, he was a man with a Secret Life. To part from her on Monday near South Kensington station and go up Exhibition Road among all the fellows who lived in sordid, lonely lodgings and were boys to his day-old experience! To neglect one's work and sit back and dream of meeting again! To slip off to the shady churchyard behind the Oratory when, or even a little before, the midday bell woke the great staircase to activity, and to meet a smiling face and hear a soft voice saying sweet foolish things! And after four another meeting and the walk home— their own home.

No little form now went from him and flitted past

a gas lamp down a foggy vista, taking his desire with her. Never more was that to be. Lewisham's long hours in the laboratory were spent largely in a dreamy meditation, in—to tell the truth—the invention of foolish terms of endearment: "Dear Wife," "Dear Little Wife Thing," "Sweetest Dearest Little Wife," "Dillywings." A pretty employment! And these are quite a fair specimen of his originality during those wonderful days. A moment of heart-searching in that particular matter led to the discovery of hitherto un-dreamt-of kindred with Swift. For Lewisham, like Swift and most other people, had hit upon the Little Language. Indeed it was a very foolish time.

Such section cutting as he did that third day of his married life—and he did very little—was a thing to marvel at. Bindon, the botany professor, under the fresh shock of his performance, protested to a colleague in the grill-room that never had a student been so foolishly overrated.

And Ethel too had a fine emotional time. She was mistress of a home—*their* home together. She shopped and was called "Ma'am" by respectful good-looking shopmen; she designed meals and copied out papers of notes with a rich sense of helpfulness. And ever and again she would stop writing and sit dreaming. And for four bright weekdays she went to and fro to accompany and meet Lewisham and listen greedily to the latest fruits of his imagination.

The landlady was very polite and conversed enter-tainingly about the very extraordinary and dissolute servants that had fallen to her lot. And Ethel disguised her newly wedded state by a series of ingenious pre-varications. She wrote a letter that Saturday evening to her mother—Lewisham had helped her to write it—making a sort of proclamation of her heroic departure and promising a speedy visit. They posted the letter so that it might not be delivered until Monday.

She was quite sure with Lewisham that only the

possible dishonour of mediumship could have brought their marriage about—she sank the mutual attraction beyond even her own vision. There was more than a touch of magnificence, you perceive, about this affair.

It was Lewisham had persuaded her to delay that reassuring visit until Monday night. "One whole day of honeymoon," he insisted, was to be theirs. In his prenuptial meditations he had not clearly focussed the fact that even after marriage some sort of relations with Mr. and Mrs. Chaffery would still go on. Even now he was exceedingly disinclined to face that obvious necessity. He foresaw, in spite of a resolute attempt to ignore it, that there would be explanatory scenes of some little difficulty. But the prevailing magnificence carried him over this trouble.

"Let us at least have this little time for ourselves," he said, and that seemed to settle their position.

Save for its brevity and these intimations of future trouble it was a very fine time indeed. Their midday dinner together, for example—it was a little cold when at last they came to it on Saturday—was immense fun. There was no marked subsidence of appetite; they ate extremely well in spite of the meeting of their souls, and in spite of certain shiftings of chairs and hand claspings and similar delays. He really made the acquaintance of her hand then for the first time, plump white hands with short white fingers, and the engagement ring had come out of its tender hiding-place and acted as keeper to the wedding ring. Their eyes were perpetually flitting about the room and coming back to mutual smiles. All their movements were faintly tremulous.

She professed to be vastly interested and amused by the room and its furniture and her position, and he was delighted by her delight. She was particularly entertained by the chest of drawers in the living room, and by Lewisham's witticisms at the toilet tidies and the oleographs.

And after the chops and most of the tinned salmon and the very new loaf were gone they fell to with fine effect upon a tapioca pudding. Their talk was fragmentary. "Did you hear her call me *Madame?* *Mádáme*—so! And presently I must go out and do some shopping. There are all the things for Sunday and Monday morning to get. I must make a list. It will never do to let her know how little I know about things. . . . I wish I knew more."

At the time Lewisham regarded her confession of domestic ignorance as a fine basis for facetiousness. He developed a fresh line of thought, and condoled with her on the inglorious circumstances of their wedding. "No bridesmaids," he said; "no little children scattering flowers, no carriages, no policemen to guard the wedding presents, nothing proper—nothing right. Not even a white favour. Only you and I."

"Only you and I. *Oh!*"

"This is nonsense," said Lewisham, after an interval.

"And think what we lose in the way of speeches," he resumed. "Cannot you imagine the best man rising—'Ladies and gentlemen—the health of the bride.' That is what the best man has to do isn't it?"

By way of answer she extended her hand.

"And do you know," he said, after that had received due recognition, "we have never been introduced!"

"Neither have we!" said Ethel. "Neither have we! We have never been introduced!"

For some inscrutable reason it delighted them both enormously to think that they had never been introduced. . . .

In the later afternoon Lewisham, having unpacked his books to a certain extent and so forth, was visible to all men, visibly in the highest spirits, carrying home Ethel's shopping. There were parcels and cones in blue and parcels in rough grey paper and a bag of confectionery, and out of one of the side pockets of that East-end overcoat the tail of a haddock protruded from its paper. Under such magnificent sanctions and amid such ignoble circumstances did this honeymoon begin.

On Sunday evening they went for a long rambling walk through the quiet streets, coming out at last into Hyde Park. The early spring night was mild and clear and the kindly moonlight was about them. They went to the bridge and looked down the Serpentine, with the lights of Paddington yellow and remote. They stood there, dim little figures and very close together. They whispered and became silent.

Presently it seemed that something passed, and Lewisham began talking in his magnificent vein. He likened the Serpentine to Life, and found Meaning in the dark banks of Kensington Gardens and the remote bright lights. "The long struggle," he said, "and the lights at the end"—though he really did not know what he meant by the lights at the end. Neither did Ethel, though the emotion was indisputable. "We are Fighting the World," he said, finding great satisfaction in the thought. "All the world is against us—and we are fighting it all."

"We will not be beaten," said Ethel.

"How could we be beaten—together?" said Lewisham. "For you I would fight a dozen worlds."

It seemed a very sweet and noble thing to them under the sympathetic moonlight, almost indeed too easy for their courage, to be merely fighting the world.

"You 'aven't bin married ver' long," said Madam Gadow with an insinuating smile, when she readmitted Ethel on Monday morning after Lewisham had been swallowed up by the Schools.

"No, I haven't *very* long," admitted Ethel.

"You are ver' 'appy," said Madam Gadow, and sighed.

"I was ver' 'appy," said Madam Gadow.

CHAPTER THE TWENTY-THIRD

Mr. Chaffery at Home

THE golden mists of delight lifted a little on Monday, when Mr. and Mrs. G. E. Lewisham went to call on his mother-in-law and Mr. Chaffery. Mrs. Lewisham went in evident apprehension, but clouds of glory still hung about Lewisham's head, and his manner was heroic. He wore a cotton shirt and linen collar, and a very nice black satin tie that Mrs. Lewisham had bought on her own responsibility during the day. She naturally wanted him to look all right.

Mrs. Chaffery appeared in the half light of the passage as the top of a grimy cap over Ethel's shoulder and two black sleeves about her neck. She emerged as a small, middle-aged woman, with a thin little nose between silver-rimmed spectacles, a weak mouth and perplexed eyes, a queer little dust-lined woman with the oddest resemblance to Ethel in her face. She was trembling visibly with nervous agitation.

She hesitated, peering, and then kissed Mr. Lewisham effusively. "And this is Mr. Lewisham!" she said as she did so.

She was the third thing feminine to kiss Lewisham

since the promiscuous days of his babyhood. " I was
so afraid—There !" She laughed hysterically.

" You'll excuse my saying that it's comforting to see
you—honest like and young. Not but what Ethel . . .
He has been something dreadful," said Mrs. Chaffery.
" You didn't ought to have written about that mesmeris-
ing. And of all letters that which Jane wrote—there !
But he's waiting and listening——"

" Are we to go downstairs, Mums ?" asked Ethel.

" He's waiting for you there," said Mrs. Chaffery.
She held a dismal little oil lamp, and they descended a
tenebrous spiral structure into an underground breakfast-
room lit by gas that shone through a partially frosted
globe with cut-glass stars. That descent had a distinctly
depressing effect upon Lewisham. He went first. He
took a deep breath at the door. What on earth was
Chaffery going to say ? Not that he cared, of course.

Chaffery was standing with his back to the fire,
trimming his finger-nails with a pocket-knife. His gilt
glasses were tilted forward so as to make an inflamed
knob at the top of his long nose, and he regarded
Mr. and Mrs. Lewisham over them with—Lewisham
doubted his eyes for a moment—but it was positively a
smile, an essentially waggish smile.

" You've come back," he said quite cheerfully over
Lewisham to Ethel. There was a hint of falsetto in
his voice.

" She has called to see her mother," said Lewisham.
" You, I believe, are Mr. Chaffery ?"

" I would like to know who the Deuce *you* are ?"
said Chaffery, suddenly tilting his head back so as to
look through his glasses instead of over them, and
laughing genially. " For thorough-going Cheek I'm inclined to think you take the Cake. Are you the Mr.
Lewisham to whom this misguided girl refers in her
letter ?"

" I am."

" Maggie," said Mr. Chaffery to Mrs. Chaffery,

"there is a class of being upon whom delicacy is lost—
to whom delicacy is practically unknown. Has your
daughter got her marriage lines?"

"Mr. Chaffery!" said Lewisham, and Mrs. Chaffery
exclaimed, "James! How *can* you?"

Chaffery shut his penknife with a click and slipped it
into his vest-pocket. Then he looked up again, speaking in the same equal voice. "I presume we are civilised
persons prepared to manage our affairs in a civilised way.
My stepdaughter vanishes for two nights and returns
with an alleged husband. I at least am not disposed to
be careless about her legal position."

"You ought to know her better——" began Lewisham.

"Why argue about it?" said Chaffery gaily, pointing
a lean finger at Ethel's gesture, "when she has 'em in
her pocket? She may just as well show me now. I
thought so. Don't be alarmed at my handling them.
Fresh copies can always be got at the nominal price of
two-and-seven. Thank you. Lewisham, George Edgar.
One and twenty. And . . . You—one and twenty!
I never did know your age, my dear, exactly, and now
your mother won't say. Student! Thank you. I am
greatly obliged. Indeed I am greatly relieved. And
now, what have you got to say for yourselves in this
remarkable affair?"

"You had a letter," said Lewisham.

"I had a letter of excuses—the personalities I over-
look . . . Yes, sir—they were excuses. You young
people wanted to marry—and you seized an occasion.
You did not even refer to the fact that you wanted to
marry in your letter. Pure modesty! But now you
have come here married. It disorganises this household,
it inflicts endless bother on people, but never you mind
that! I'm not blaming *you*. Nature's to blame!
Neither of you know what you are in for yet. You
will. You're married and that is the great essential
thing. . . . (Ethel, my dear, just put your husband's
hat and stick behind the door.) And you, sir, are so

good as to disapprove of the way in which I earn my living?"

"Well," said Lewisham. "Yes—I'm bound to say I do."

"You are really *not* bound to say it. The modesty of inexperience would excuse you."

"Yes, but it isn't right—it isn't straight."

"Dogma," said Chaffery. "Dogma!"

"What do you mean by dogma?" asked Lewisham.

"I mean, dogma. But we must argue this out in comfort. It is our supper hour, and I'm not the man to fight against accomplished facts. We have inter-married. There it is. You must stop to supper—and you and I must thresh these things out. We've involved ourselves with each other and we've got to make the best of it. Your wife and mine will spread the board, and we will go on talking. Why not sit in that chair instead of leaning on the back? This is a home—*domus* —not a debating society—humble in spite of my mani-fest frauds. . . . That's better. And in the first place I hope—I do so hope "—Chaffery was suddenly very impressive—" that you're not a Dissenter."

"Eh!" said Lewisham, and then, "No! I am *not* a Dissenter."

"That's better," said Mr. Chaffery. "I'm glad of that. I was just a little afraid— Something in your manner. I can't stand Dissenters. I've a peculiar dis-like to Dissenters. To my mind it's the great drawback of this Clapham. You see . . . I have invariably found them deceitful—invariably."

He grimaced and dropped his glasses with a click against his waistcoat buttons. "I'm very glad of that," he said, replacing them. "The Dissenter, the Non-conformist Conscience, the Puritan, you know, the Vegetarian and Total Abstainer, and all that sort of thing, I cannot away with them. I have cleared my mind of cant and formulæ. I've a nature essentially Hellenic. Have you ever read Matthew Arnold?"

" Beyond my scientific reading——"

" Ah ! you *should* read Matthew Arnold—a mind of singular clarity. In him you would find a certain quality that is sometimes a little wanting in your scientific men. They are apt to be a little too phenomenal, you know, a little too objective. Now I seek after noumena. Noumena, Mr. Lewisham ! If you follow me——?"

He paused, and his eyes behind the glasses were mildly interrogative. Ethel re-entered without her hat and jacket, and with a noisy square black tray, a white cloth, some plates and knives and glasses, and began to lay the table.

" *I* follow you," said Lewisham, reddening. He had not the courage to admit ignorance of this remarkable word. " You state your case."

" I seek after *noumena*," repeated Chaffery with great satisfaction, and gesticulated with his hand, waving away everything but that. " I cannot do with surfaces and appearances. I am one of those nympholepts, you know, nympholepts. . . . Must pursue the truth of things ! the elusive fundamental. . . . I make a rule, I never tell myself lies—never. There are few who can say that. To my mind—truth begins at home. And for the most part—stops there. Safest and seemliest ! *you* know. With most men—with your typical Dissenter *par excellence*—it's always gadding abroad, calling on the neighbours. You see my point of view?"

He glanced at Lewisham, who was conscious of an unwonted opacity of mind. He became wary, as wary as he could manage to be on the spur of the moment.

" It's a little surprising, you know;" he said very carefully, " if I may say so—and considering what happened —to hear *you* . . ."

" Speaking of truth? Not when you understand my position. Not when you see where I stand. That is what I am getting at. That is what I am naturally anxious to make clear to you now that we have inter-married, now that you are my stepson-in-law. You're young, you know, you're young, and you're hard and fast. Only years can give a mind *tone*—mitigate the varnish of education. I gather from this letter—and your face—that you are one of the party that participated in that little affair at Lagune's."

He stuck out a finger at a point he had just seen. "By-the-by!—That accounts for Ethel," he said.

Ethel rapped down the mustard on the table. "It does," she said, but not very loudly.

"But you had met before?" said Chaffery.

"At Whortley," said Lewisham.

"I see," said Chaffery.

"I was in— I was one of those who arranged the exposure," said Lewisham. "And now you have raised the matter, I am bound to say ——"

"I knew," interrupted Chaffery. "But what a shock that was for Lagune!" He looked down at his toes for a moment with the corners of his mouth tucked in. "The hand dodge wasn't bad, you know," he said with a queer sidelong smile.

Lewisham was very busy for a moment trying to get this remark in focus. "I don't see it in the same light as you do," he explained at last.

"Can't get away from your moral bias, eh? Well, well. We'll go into all that. But apart from its moral merits—simply as an artistic trick—it was not bad."

"I don't know much about tricks ——"

"So few who undertake exposures do. You admit you never heard or thought of that before—the bladder, I mean. Yet it's as obvious as tintacks that a medium who's hampered at his hands will do all he can with his teeth, and what *could* be so self-evident as a bladder under one's lapel? What could be? Yet I know psychic literature pretty well and it's never been suggested even! Never. It's a perpetual surprise to me how many things are *not* thought of by investigators. For one thing, they never count the odds against them, and that puts them wrong at the start. Look at it! I am by nature tricky. I spend all my leisure standing or sitting about and thinking up or practising new little tricks, because it amuses me immensely to do so. The whole thing amuses me. Well—what is the result of these meditations? Take one thing : I know eight and forty ways of making raps—of which at least ten are original. Ten original ways of making raps." His manner was very impressive. "And, some of them simply tremendous raps. There !"

A confirmatory rap exploded—as it seemed between Lewisham and Chaffery.

" *Eh?*" said Chaffery.

The mantelpiece opened a dropping fire, and the table went off under Lewisham's nose like a cracker.

"You see?" said Chaffery, putting his hands under the tail of his coat. The whole room seemed snapping its fingers at Lewisham for a space.

"Very well, and now take the other side. Take the severest test I ever tried. Two respectable professors of physics—not Newtons, you understand, but good, worthy, self-important professors of physics—a lady anxious to prove there's a life beyond the grave, a journalist who wants stuff to write—a person, that is, who gets his living by these researches just as I do— undertook to test me. Test *me!* . . . Of course they had their other work to do, professing physics, professing religion, organising research, and so forth. At the outside they don't think an hour a day about it, and most of them had never cheated anybody in their existence, and couldn't, for example, travel without a ticket for a three-mile journey and not get caught, to save their lives. . . . Well—you see the odds?"

He paused. Lewisham appeared involved in some interior struggle.

"You know," explained Chaffery, "it was quite an accident you got me—quite. The thing slipped out of my mouth. Or your friend with the flat voice wouldn't have had a chance. Not a chance."

Lewisham spoke like a man who is lifting a weight. "All *this,* you know, is off the question. I'm not disputing your ability. But the thing is . . . it isn't right."

"We're coming to that," said Chaffery.

"It's evident we look at things in a different light."

"That's it. That's just what we've got to discuss. Exactly!"

"Cheating is cheating. You can't get away from that. That's simple enough."

"Wait till I've done with it," said Chaffery with a certain zest. "Of course it's imperative you should understand my position. It isn't as though I hadn't one. Ever since I read your letter I've been thinking over that. Really!—a justification! In a way you might almost say I had a mission. A sort of prophet. You really don't see the beginning of it yet."

"Oh, but hang it!" protested Lewisham.

"Ah! you're young, you're crude. My dear young man, you're only at the beginning of things. You really must concede a certain possibility of wider views to a man more than twice your age. But here's supper. For a little while at any rate we'll call a truce."

Ethel had come in again bearing an additional chair, and Mrs. Chaffery appeared behind her, crowning the preparations with a jug of small beer. The cloth, Lewisham observed, as he turned towards it, had several undarned holes and discoloured places, and in the centre stood a tarnished cruet which contained mustard, pepper, vinegar, and three ambiguous dried-up bottles. The bread was on an ample board with a pious rim, and an honest wedge of cheese loomed disproportionate on a little plate. Mr. and Mrs. Lewisham were seated facing one another, and Mrs. Chaffery sat in the broken chair because she understood its ways.

"This cheese is as nutritious and unattractive and indigestible as Science," remarked Chaffery, cutting and passing wedges. "But crush it—so—under your fork, add a little of this good Dorset butter, a dab of mustard, pepper—the pepper is very necessary—and some malt vinegar, and crush together. You get a compound called Crab and by no means disagreeable. So the wise deal with the facts of life, neither bolting nor rejecting, but adapting."

"As though pepper and mustard were not facts," said Lewisham, scoring his solitary point that evening.

Chaffery admitted the collapse of his image in very complimentary terms, and Lewisham could not avoid a glance across the table at Ethel. He remembered immediately afterwards that Chaffery was a slippery scoundrel whose blame was better than his praise.

For a time the Crab engaged Chaffery, and the conversation languished. Mrs. Chaffery asked Ethel formal questions about their lodgings, and Ethel's answers were buoyant. "You must come and have tea one day," said Ethel, not waiting for Lewisham's endorsement, "and see it all."

Chaffery astonished Lewisham by suddenly displaying a complete acquaintance with his status as a South Kensington teacher in training. "I suppose you have some money beyond that guinea," said Chaffery off-handedly.

"Enough to go on with," said Lewisham, reddening.

"And you look to them at South Kensington to do something for you—a hundred a year or so, when your scholarship is up?"

"Yes," said Lewisham a little reluctantly. "Yes. A hundred a year or so. That's the sort of idea. And there's lots of places beyond South Kensington, of course, even if they don't put me up there."

"I see," said Chaffery; "but it will be a pretty close shave for all that—one hundred a year. Well, well— there's many a deserving man has to do with less," and after a meditative pause he asked Lewisham to pass the beer.

"Hev you a mother living, Mr. Lewisham?" said

Mrs. Chaffery suddenly, and pursued him through the tale of his connections. When he came to the plumber, Mrs. Chaffery remarked with an unexpected air of consequence, that most families have their poor relations. Then the air of consequence vanished again into the past from which it had arisen.

Supper finished, Chaffery poured the residuum of the beer into his glass, produced a Broseley clay of the longest sort, and invited Lewisham to smoke. "Honest smoking," said Chaffery, tapping the bowl of his clay, and added : "In this country—cigars—sound cigars—and honesty rarely meet."

Lewisham fumbled in his pocket for his Algerian cigarettes, and Chaffery having regarded them unfavourably through his glasses, took up the thread of his promised apologia. The ladies retired to wash up the supper things.

"You see," said Chaffery, opening abruptly so soon as the clay was drawing, "about this cheating—I do not find life such a simple matter as you do."

"*I* don't find life simple," said Lewisham, "but I do think there's a Right and a Wrong in things. And I don't think you have said anything so far to show that spiritualistic cheating is Right."

"Let us thresh the matter out," said Chaffery, crossing his legs, "let us thresh the matter out. Now "—he drew at his pipe—"I don't think you fully appreciate the importance of Illusion in life, the Essential Nature of Lies and Deception of the body politic. You are inclined to discredit one particular form of Imposture, because it is not generally admitted—carries a certain discredit, and—witness the heel edges of my trouser legs, witness yonder viands—small rewards."

"It's not that," said Lewisham.

"Now I am prepared to maintain," said Chaffery, proceeding with his proposition, "that Honesty is essentially an anarchistic and disintegrating force in

society, that communities are held together and the
progress of civilisation made possible only by vigorous
and sometimes even violent Lying; that the Social Contract is nothing more nor less than a vast conspiracy of
human beings to lie to and humbug themselves and one
another for the general Good. Lies are the mortar that
bind the savage individual man into the social masonry.
There is the general thesis upon which I base my justification. My mediumship, I can assure you, is a particular instance of the general assertion. Were I not of
a profoundly indolent, restless, adventurous nature, and
horribly averse to writing, I would make a great book of
this and live honoured by every profound duffer in the
world."

" But how are you going to prove it ? "

" Prove it ! It simply needs pointing out. Even
now there are men—Bernard Shaw, Ibsen, and such like
—who have seen bits of it in a new-gospel-grubbing sort
of fashion. What is man ? Lust and greed tempered
by fear and an irrational vanity."

" I don't agree with that," said Mr. Lewisham.

" You will as you grow older," said Chaffery.
" There's truths you have to grow into. But about this
matter of Lies—let us look at the fabric of society, let
us compare the savage. You will discover the only
essential difference between savage and civilised is this :
The former hasn't learnt to shirk the truth of things,
and the latter has. Take the most obvious difference—
the clothing of the civilised man, his invention of
decency. What *is* clothing ? The concealment of
essential facts. What is decorum ? Suppression ! I
don't argue against decency and decorum, mind you, but
there they are—essentials to civilisation and essentially
' *suppressio veri*.' And in the pockets of his clothes our
citizen carries money. The pure savage has no money.
To him a lump of metal is a lump of metal—possibly
ornamental—no more. That's right. To any lucid-
minded man it's the same or different only through the

gross folly of his fellows. But to the common civilised man the universal exchangeability of this gold is a sacred and fundamental fact. Think of it! Why should it be? There isn't a why! I live in perpetual amazement at the gullibility of my fellow-creatures. Of a morning sometimes, I can assure you, I lie in bed fancying that people may have found out this swindle in the night, expect to hear a tumult downstairs and see your mother-in-law come rushing into the room with a rejected shilling from the milkman. 'What's this?' says he. 'This Muck for milk?' But it never happens. Never. If it did, if people suddenly cleared their minds of this cant of money, what would happen? The true nature of man would appear. I should whip out of bed, seize some weapon, and after the milkman forthwith. It's becoming to keep the peace, but it's necessary to have milk. The neighbours would come pouring out—also after milk. Milkman, suddenly enlightened, would start clattering up the street. After him! Clutch— tear! Got him! Over goes the cart— Fight if you like, but don't upset the can! . . . Don't you see it all—perfectly reasonable every bit of it. I should return, bruised and bloody, with the milk-can under my arm. Yes—*I* should have the milk-can—I should keep my eye on that. . . . But why go on? You of all men should know that life is a struggle for existence, a fight for food. Money is just the lie that mitigates our fury."

"No," said Lewisham; "no! I'm not prepared to admit that."

"What *is* money?"

Mr. Lewisham dodged. "You state your case first," he said. "I really don't see what all this has to do with cheating at a *séance*."

"I weave my defence from this loom, though. Take some aggressively respectable sort of man—a bishop, for example."

"Well," said Lewisham, "I don't much hold with bishops."

"It doesn't matter. Take a professor of science, walking the earth. Remark his clothing, making him a decent citizen, concealing the fact that physically he is a flabby, pot-bellied degenerate. That is the first Lie of his being. No fringes round *his* trousers, my boy. Notice his hair, groomed and clipped, the tacit lie that its average length is half an inch, whereas in nature he would wave a few score yard-long hairs of ginger grey to the winds of heaven. Notice the smug suppressions of his face. In his mouth are Lies in the shape of false teeth. Then on the earth somewhere poor devils are toiling to get him meat and corn and wine. He is clothed in the lives of bent and thwarted weavers, his way is lit by phossy jaw, he eats from lead-glazed crockery—all his ways are paved with the lives of men. . . . Think of the chubby, comfortable creature! And, as Swift has it—to think that such a thing should deal in pride! . . . He pretends that his blessed little researches are in some way a fair return to these remote beings for their toil, their suffering; pretends that he and his parasitic career are payment for their thwarted desires. Imagine him bullying his gardener over some transplanted geraniums, the thick mist of lies they stand in, so that the man does not immediately, with the edge of a spade, smite down his impertinence to the dust from which it rose. . . . And his case is the case of all comfortable lives. What a lie and sham all civility is, all good breeding, all culture and refinement, while one poor ragged wretch drags hungry on the earth!"

"But this is Socialism!" said Lewisham. "*I*——"

"No Ism," said Chaffery, raising his rich voice. "Only the ghastly truth of things—the truth that the warp and the woof of the world of men is Lying. Socialism is no remedy, no *ism* is a remedy; things are so."

"I don't agree——" began Lewisham.

"Not with the hopelessness, because you are young, but with the description you do."

" Well—within limits."

" You agree that most respectable positions in the world are tainted with the fraud of our social conditions. If they were not tainted with fraud they would not be respectable. Even your own position— Who gave you the right to marry and prosecute interesting scientific studies while other young men rot in mines?"

" I admit——"

" You can't help admitting. And here is my position Since all ways of life are tainted with fraud, since to live and speak the truth is beyond human strength and courage—as one finds it—is it not better for a man that he engage in some straightforward comparatively harmless cheating, than if he risk his mental integrity in some ambiguous position and fall at last into self-deception and self-righteousness? That is the essential danger. That is the thing I always guard against. Heed that! It is the master sin. Self-righteousness."

Mr. Lewisham pulled at his moustache.

" You begin to take me. And after all, these worthy people do not suffer so greatly. If I did not take their money some other impostor would. Their huge conceit of intelligence would breed perhaps some viler swindle than my facetious rappings. That's the line our doubting bishops take, and why shouldn't I? For example, these people might give it to Public Charities, minister to the fattened secretary, the prodigal younger son. After all, at worst, I am a sort of latter-day Robin Hood; I take from the rich according to their incomes. I don't give to the poor certainly, I don't get enough. But—there are other good works. Many a poor weakling have I comforted with Lies, great thumping, silly Lies, about the grave! Compare me with one of those rascals who disseminate phossy jaw and lead poisons, compare me with a millionaire who runs a music hall with an eye to feminine talent, or an underwriter, or the common stockbroker. Or any sort of lawyer. . . .

" There are bishops," said Chaffery, " who believe in

Darwin and doubt Moses. Now I hold myself better than they—analogous perhaps but better—for I do at least invent something of the tricks I play—I do do that."

"That's all very well," began Lewisham.

"I might forgive them their dishonesty," said Chaffery, "but the stupidity of it, the mental self-abnegation—Lord! If a solicitor doesn't swindle in the proper shabby-magnificent way, they chuck him for unprofessional conduct." He paused. He became meditative, and smiled faintly.

"Now some of *my* dodges," he said with a sudden change of voice, turning towards Lewisham, his eyes smiling over his glasses and an emphatic hand patting the table-cloth; "some of *my* dodges are *damned* ingenious, you know—*damned* ingenious—and well worth double the money they bring me—double."

He turned towards the fire again, pulling at his smouldering pipe and eyeing Lewisham over the corner of his glasses.

"One or two of my little things would make Maskelyne sit up," he said presently. "They would set that mechanical orchestra playing out of pure astonishment. I really must explain some of them to you—now we have intermarried."

It took Mr. Lewisham a minute or so to re-form the regiment of his mind, disordered by its headlong pursuit of Chaffery's flying arguments. "But on your principles you might do almost anything!" he said.

"Precisely!" said Chaffery.

"But——"

"It is rather a curious method," protested Chaffery; "to test one's principles of action by judging the resultant actions on some other principle, isn't it?"

Lewisham took a moment to think. "I suppose that is so," he said, in the manner of a man convinced against his will.

He perceived his logic insufficient. He suddenly

thrust the delicacies of argument aside. Certain sentences he had brought ready for use in his mind came up and he delivered them abruptly. "Anyhow," he said, "I don't agree with this cheating. In spite of what you say, I hold to what I said in my letter. Ethel's connection with all these things is at an end. I shan't go out of my way to expose you, of course, but if it comes in my way I shall speak my mind of all these spiritualistic phenomena. It's just as well that we should know about where we are."

"That is clearly understood, my dear stepson-in-law." said Chaffery. "Our present object is discussion."

"But Ethel——"

"Ethel is yours," said Chaffery. "Ethel is yours," he repeated after an interval, and added pensively— "to keep."

"But talking of Illusion," he resumed, dismissing the sordid with a sign of relief, "I sometimes think with Bishop Berkeley, that all experience is probably something quite different from reality. That consciousness is *essentially* hallucination. I here, and you, and our talk —it is all Illusion. Bring your Science to bear—what am I? A cloudy multitude of atoms, an infinite interplay of little cells. Is this hand that I hold out, me? This head? Is the surface of my skin any more than a rude average boundary? You say it is my mind that is me? But consider the war of motives. Suppose I have an impulse that I resist—it is *I* resist it—the impulse is outside me, eh? But suppose that impulse carries me and I do the thing— that impulse is part of me, is it not? Ah! My brain reels at these mysteries! Lord! what flimsy fluctuating things we are—first this, then that, a thought, an impulse, a deed and a forgetting, and all the time madly cocksure we are ourselves. And as for you—you who have hardly learned to think for more than five or six short years, there you sit, assured, coherent, there you sit in all your inherited original sin —Hallucinatory Windlestraw! — judging and condemning. *You* know Right from Wrong! My boy, so did Adam and Eve . . . *so soon as they'd had dealings with the father of lies!*

At the end of the evening whisky and hot water were produced, and Chaffery, now in a mood of great urbanity, said he had rarely enjoyed anyone's conversation so much as Lewisham's, and insisted upon everyone having whisky. Mrs. Chaffery and Ethel added sugar and lemon. Lewisham felt an instantaneous mild surprise at the sight of Ethel drinking grog.

At the door Mrs. Chaffery kissed Lewisham an effusive good-bye and told Ethel she really believed it was all for the best.

On the way home Lewisham was thoughtful and preoccupied. The problem of Chaffery assumed enormous proportions. At times indeed even that good man's own philosophical sketch of himself as a practical exponent of mental sincerity touched with humour and the artistic spirit, seemed plausible. Lagune was an undeniable ass, and conceivably psychic research was an incentive to trickery. Then he remembered the matter in his relation to Ethel. . . .

"Your stepfather is a little hard to follow," he said at last, sitting on the bed and taking off one boot. "He's dodgy—he's so confoundedly dodgy. One doesn't know where to take hold of him. He's got such a break he's clean bowled me again and again."

He thought for a space, and then removed his boot and sat with it on his knee. "Of course! . . . all that he said was wrong—quite wrong. Right is right and cheating is cheating, whatever you say about it."

"That's what I feel about him," said Ethel at the looking-glass. "That's exactly how it seems to me."

CHAPTER THE TWENTY-FOURTH

The Campaign Opens

ON Saturday Lewisham was first through the folding doors. In a moment he reappeared with a document extended. Mrs. Lewisham stood arrested with her dress skirt in her hand, astonished at the astonishment on his face. "*I* say!" said Lewisham; "just look here!"

She looked at the book that he held open before her, and perceived that its vertical ruling betokened a sordid import, that its list of items in an illegible mixture of English and German was lengthy. "1 kettle of coals 6d." occurred regularly down that portentous array and buttoned it all together. It was Madam Gadow's first bill. Ethel took it out of his hand and examined it closer. It looked no smaller closer. The overcharges were scandalous. It was curious how the humour of calling a scuttle "kettle" had evaporated.

That document, I take it, was the end of Mr. Lewisham's informal honeymoon. Its advent was the snap of that bright Prince Rupert's drop; and in a moment— Dust. For a glorious week he had lived in the persuasion that life was made of love and mystery, and now he was reminded with singular clearness that it was begotten of a struggle for existence and the Will to

Live. "Confounded imposition!" fumed Mr. Lewisham, and the breakfast table was novel and ominous, mutterings towards anger on the one hand and a certain consternation on the other. "I must give her a talking to this afternoon," said Lewisham at his watch, and after he had bundled his books into the shiny black bag, he gave the first of his kisses that was not a distinct and self-subsisting ceremony. It was usage and done in a hurry, and the door slammed as he went his way to the schools. Ethel was not coming that morning, because by special request and because she wanted to help him she was going to copy out some of his botanical notes which had fallen into arrears.

On his way to the schools Lewisham felt something suspiciously near a sinking of the heart. His preoccupation was essentially arithmetical. The thing that engaged his mind to the exclusion of all other matters is best expressed in the recognised business form.

Dr.		£	s.	d.	*Cr.*	£	s.	d.
Cash in hand					By bus fares to South Kensington (late)		2	
Mr. L.	..	13	10	4½	By 6 lunches at the Students' Club	5	2½	
Mrs. L.	..		12	7				
At Bank	..	45	0	0	By 2 packets of cigarettes (to smoke after dinner)		6	
To Scholarship		1	1	0	By marriage and elopement ..	4	18	10
					By necessary subsequent additions to bride's trousseau ..		16	1
					By housekeeping exs.	1	1	4½
					By "A ew little things" bought by housekeeper ..		15	3½
					By Madam Gadow for coal, lodging and attendance (as per account rendered) ..	1	15	0
					By missing			4
					By balance	50	11	2
		£60	3	11½		£60	3	11½

From this it will be manifest to the most unbusinesslike that, disregarding the extraordinary expenditure on the marriage, and the by no means final "few little things " Ethel had bought, outgoings exceeded income by two pounds and more, and a brief excursion into arithmetic will demonstrate that in five and twenty weeks the balance of the account would be nothing.

But that guinea a week was not to go on for five and twenty weeks, but simply for fifteen, and then the net outgoings will be well over three guineas, reducing the "law" accorded our young couple to two and twenty weeks. These details are tiresome and disagreeable, no doubt, to the refined reader, but just imagine how much more disagreeable they were to Mr. Lewisham, trudging meditative to the schools. You will understand his slipping out of the laboratory and betaking himself to the Educational Reading-room; and how it was that the observant Smithers, grinding his lecture notes against the now imminent second examination for the "Forbes," was presently perplexed to the centre of his being by the spectacle of Lewisham intent upon a pile of current periodicals, the *Educational Times,* the *Journal of Education,* the *Schoolmaster, Science and Art,* the *University Correspondent, Nature,* the *Athenæum,* the *Academy,* and the *Author.*

Smithers remarked the appearance of a notebook, the jotting down of memoranda. He edged into the bay nearest Lewisham's table and approached him suddenly from the flank. "What are *you* after?" said Smithers in a noisy whisper and with a detective eye on the papers. He perceived Lewisham was scrutinising the advertisement columns, and his perplexity increased.

"Oh—nothing," said Lewisham blandly, with his hand falling casually over his memoranda; "what's your particular little game?"

"Nothing much," said Smithers, "just mooching round. You weren't at the meeting last Friday?"

He turned a chair, knelt on it, and began whispering over the back about Debating Society politics. Lewisham was inattentive and brief. What had he to

33

do with these puerilities. At last Smithers went away foiled, and met Parkson by the entrance. Parkson, by-the-bye, had not spoken to Lewisham since their painful misunderstanding. He made a wide detour to his seat at the end table, and so, and by a singular rectitude of bearing and a dignified expression, showed himself aware of Lewisham's offensive presence.

Lewisham's investigations were twofold. He wanted to discover some way of adding materially to that weekly guinea by his own exertions, and he wanted to learn the conditions of the market for typewriting. For himself he had a vague idea, an idea subsequently abandoned, that it was possible to get teaching work in evening classes during the month of March. But except by reason of sudden death, no evening class in London changes its staff after September until July comes round again. Private tuition, moreover, offered many attractions to him, but no definite proposals. His ideas of his own possibilities were youthful, or he would not have spent time in noting the conditions of application for a vacant professorship in physics at the Melbourne University. He also made a note of the vacant editorship of a monthly magazine devoted to social questions. He would not have minded doing that sort of thing at all, though the proprietor might. There was also a vacant curatorship in the Museum of Eton College.

The typewriting business was less varied and more definite. Those were the days before the violent competition of the half-educated had brought things down to an impossible tenpence the thousand words, and the prevailing price was as high as one-and-six. Calculating that Ethel could do a thousand words in an hour and that she could work five or six hours in the day, it was evident that her contributions to the household expenses would be by no means despicable; thirty shillings a week perhaps. Lewisham was naturally elated at this discovery. He could find no advertisements of authors

or others seeking typewriting, but he saw that a great
number of typists advertised themselves in the literary
papers.   It was evident Ethel also must advertise.
"'Scientific phraseology a speciality' might be put,"
meditated Lewisham.   He returned to his lodgings in
a hopeful mood with quite a bundle of memoranda of
possible employment.   He spent five shillings upon
stamps on the way.

After lunch, Lewisham—a little short of breath—
asked to see Madam Gadow.   She came up in the most
affable frame of mind; nothing could be further from
the normal indignation of the British landlady.   She
was very voluble, gesticulatory and lucid, but unhappily bi-lingual, and at all the crucial points German.
Mr. Lewisham's natural politeness restrained him from
too close a pursuit across the boundary of the two imperial tongues.   Quite half an hour's amicable discussion led at last to a reduction of sixpence, and all parties
professed themselves satisfied with this result.

Madam Gadow was quite cool even at the end.   Mr.
Lewisham was flushed in the face, red-eared, and his
hair slightly disordered; but that sixpence was at any
rate an admission of the justice of his claim.   "She
was evidently trying it on," he said almost apologetically
to Ethel.   "It was absolutely necessary to present a
firm front to her.   I doubt if we shall have any trouble
again. . . .

"Of course what she says about kitchen coals is
perfectly just."

Then the young couple went for a walk in Kensington Gardens, and—the spring afternoon was so warm
and pleasant—sat on two attractive green chairs near
the band-stand, for which Lewisham had subsequently
to pay twopence.   They had what Ethel called a
"serious talk."   She was really wonderfully sensible
and discussed the situation exhaustively.   She was particularly insistent upon the importance of economy in
her domestic disbursements and deplored her general

ignorance very earnestly. It was decided that Lewisham should get a good elementary textbook of domestic economy for her private study. At home Mrs. Chaffery guided her house by the oracular items of "Enquire Within upon Everything," but Lewisham considered that work unscientific.

Ethel was also of opinion that much might be learnt from the sixpenny ladies' papers—the penny ones had hardly begun in those days. She had bought such publications during seasons of affluence, but chiefly, as she now deplored, with an eye to the trimming of hats and suchlike vanities. The sooner the typewriter came the better. It occurred to Lewisham with unpleasant suddenness that he had not allowed for the purchase of a typewriter in his estimate of their resources. It brought their "law" down to twelve or thirteen weeks.

They spent the evening in writing and copying a number of letters, addressing envelopes and enclosing stamps. There were optimistic moments.

"Melbourne's a fine city," said Lewisham, "and we should have a glorious voyage out." He read the application for the Melbourne professorship out loud to her, just to see how it read, and she was greatly impressed by the list of his accomplishments and successes. "I did not know you knew *half* those things," she said, and became depressed at her relative illiteracy. It was natural, after such encouragement, to write to the scholastic agents in a tone of assured consequence.

The advertisement for typewriting in the *Athenæum* troubled his conscience a little. After he had copied out his draft with its "Scientific phraseology a speciality," fine and large, he saw the notes she had written out for him. Her hand-writing was still round and boyish, even as it had appeared in the Whortley avenue, but her punctuation was confined to the erratic comma and the dash, and there was a disposition to spell the imperfectly legible along the line of least resistance. However, he dismissed that matter with a resolve to read over and correct anything in that way that she might have sent her to do. It would not be a bad idea, he thought parenthetically, if he himself read up some sound authority on the punctuation of sentences.

They sat at this business quite late, heedless of the examination in botany that came on the morrow. It was very bright and cosy in their little room with their fire burning, the gas lit and the curtains drawn, and the number of applications they had written made them hopeful. She was flushed and enthusiastic, now flitting about the room, now coming close to him and leaning over him to see what he had done. At Lewisham's request she got him the envelopes from the chest of drawers. "You *are* a help to a chap," said Lewisham, leaning back from the table. "I feel I could do anything for a girl like you—anything."

"*Really!*" she cried. "Really! Am I really a help?"

Lewisham's face and gesture were all assent. She gave a little cry of delight, stood for a moment, and then by way of practical demonstration of her unflinching helpfulness, hurried round the table towards him with arms extended. "You dear!" she cried.

Lewisham, partially embraced, pushed his chair back with his disengaged arm, so that she might sit on his knee. . . .

Who could doubt that she was a help?

CHAPTER THE TWENTY-FIFTH

The First Battle

LEWISHAM'S inquiries for evening teaching and private tuition were essentially provisional measures. His proposals for a more permanent establishment displayed a certain defect in his sense of proportion. That Melbourne professorship, for example, was beyond his merits, and there were aspects of things that would have affected the welcome of himself and his wife at Eton. At the outset he was inclined to regard the South Kensington scholar as the intellectual salt of the earth, to overrate the abundance of " decent things " yielding from one hundred and fifty to three hundred a year, and to disregard the competition of such inferior enterprises as the universities of Oxford, Cambridge, and the literate North. But the scholastic agents to whom he went on the following Saturday did much in a quiet way to disabuse his mind.

Mr. Blendershin's chief assistant in the grimy little office in Oxford Street cleared up the matter so vigorously that Lewisham was angered. "Head Master of an endowed school, perhaps!" said Mr. Blendershin's chief assistant. "Lord!—why not a bishopric? I say"—as Mr. Blendershin entered smoking an assertive cigar—"one and twenty, *no* degree, *no* games, two years' experience as junior—wants a headmastership of an endowed school!" He spoke so loudly that it was inevitable the selectors of clients in the waiting-room should hear, and he pointed with his pen.

"Look here!" said Lewisham hotly; "if I knew the ways of the market I shouldn't come to you."

Mr. Blendershin stared at Lewisham for a moment. "What's he done in the way of certificates?" asked Mr. Blendershin of the assistant.

The assistant read a list of 'ologies and 'ographies. "Fifty-resident," said Mr. Blendershin concisely— "that's your figure. Sixty, if you're lucky."

"*What?*" said Mr. Lewisham.

"Not enough for you?"

"Not nearly."

"You can get a Cambridge graduate for eighty resident—and grateful," said Mr. Blendershin.

"But I don't want a resident post," said Lewisham.

"Precious few non-resident shops," said Mr. Blendershin. "Precious few. They want you for dormitory supervision—and they're afraid of your taking pups outside."

"Not married by any chance?" said the assistant suddenly, after an attentive study of Lewisham's face.

"Well- -er." Lewisham met Mr. Blendershin's eye. "Yes," he said.

The assistant was briefly unprintable. "Lord! you'll have to keep that dark," said Mr. Blendershin. "But you have got a tough bit of hoeing before you. If I was you I'd go on and get my degree now you're so near it. You'll stand a better chance."

Pause.

"The fact is," said Lewisham slowly and looking

at his boot toes, " I must be doing *something* while I am getting my degree."

The assistant whistled softly.

" Might get you a visiting job, perhaps," said Mr. Blendershin speculatively. " Just read me those items again, Binks." He listened attentively. " Objects to religious teaching!—Eh?" He stopped the reading by a gesture. " That's nonsense. You can't have everything, you know. Scratch that out. You won't get a place in any middle-class school in England if you object to religious teaching. It's the mothers—bless 'em! Say nothing about it. Don't believe—who does? There's hundreds like you, you know—hundreds. Parsons—all sorts. Say nothing about it——"

" But if I'm asked?"

" Church of England. Every man in this country who has not dissented belongs to the Church of England. It'll be hard enough to get you anything without that."

" But——" said Mr. Lewisham. " It's lying."

" Legal fiction," said Mr. Blendershin. " Everyone understands. If you don't do that, my dear chap, we can't do anything for you. It's journalism, or London docks. Well, considering your experience—say docks."

Lewisham's face flushed irregularly. He did not answer. He scowled and tugged at the still by no means ample moustache.

" Compromise, you know," said Mr. Blendershin, watching him kindly. " Compromise."

For the first time in his life Lewisham faced the necessity of telling a lie in cold blood. He glissaded from the austere altitudes of his self-respect and his next words were already disingenuous.

" I won't promise to tell lies if I'm asked," he said aloud. " I can't do that."

" Scratch it out," said Blendershin to the clerk. " You needn't mention it. Then you don't say you can teach drawing."

"I can't," said Lewisham.

"You just give out the copies," said Blendershin, "and take care they don't see you draw, you know."

"But that's not teaching drawing——"

"It's what's understood by it in *this* country," said Blendershin. "Don't you go corrupting your mind with pedagogueries. They're the ruin of assistants. Put down drawing. Then there's shorthand——"

"Here, I say!" said Lewisham.

"There's shorthand, French, book-keeping, commercial geography, land measuring——"

"But I can't teach any of those things!"

"Look here," said Blendershin, and paused. "Has your wife or you a private income?"

"No," said Lewisham.

"Well?"

A pause of further moral descent, and a whack against an obstacle. "But they will find me out," said Lewisham.

Blendershin smiled. "It's not so much ability as willingness to teach, you know. And *they* won't find you out. The sort of schoolmaster we deal with can't find anything out. He can't teach any of these things himself—and consequently he doesn't believe they *can* be taught. Talk to him of pedagogics and he talks of practical experience. But he puts 'em on his prospectus, you know, and he wants 'em on his time-table. Some of these subjects—— There's commercial geography, for instance. What *is* commercial geography?"

"Barilla," said the assistant biting the end of his pen, and added pensively, "*and* blethers."

"Fad," said Blendershin. "Just fad. Newspapers talk rot about commercial education, Duke of Devonshire catches on and talks ditto—pretends he thought of it himself—much *he* cares—parents get hold of it —schoolmasters obliged to put something down, consequently assistants must. And that's the end of the matter!"

33*

"*All* right," said Lewisham catching his breath in a faint sob of shame. "Stick 'em down. But mind—a non-resident place."

"Well," said Blendershin, "your science may pull you through. But I tell you it's hard. Some grant-earning grammar school may want that. And that's about all, I think. Make a note of the address. . . ."

The assistant made a noise, something between a whistle and the word "Fee." Blendershin glanced at Lewisham and nodded doubtfully.

"Fee for booking," said the assistant; "half a crown. Postage—in advance—half a crown."

But Lewisham remembered certain advice Dunkerley had given him in the old Whortley days. He hesitated. "No," he said. "I don't pay that. If you get me anything there's the commission—if you don't——"

"We lose," supplied the assistant.

"And you ought to," said Lewisham. "It's a fair game."

"Living in London?" asked Blendershin.

"Yes," said the clerk.

"That's all right," said Mr. Blendershin. "We won't say anything about the postage in that case. Of course it's the off season, and you mustn't expect anything at present very much. Sometimes there's a shift or so at Easter. . . . There's nothing more. . . . Afternoon. Anyone else, Binks?"

Messrs. Maskelyne, Smith and Thrums did a higher class of work than Blendershin, whose specialities were lower class private establishments and the cheaper sort of endowed schools. Indeed, so superior were Maskelyne, Smith and Thrums that they enraged Lewisham by refusing at first to put him on their books. He was interviewed briefly by a young man dressed and speaking with offensive precision, whose eye adhered rigidly to the waterproof collar throughout the interview.

"Hardly our line," he said, and pushed Lewisham a

form to fill up. "Mostly upper class and good preparatory schools here, you know."

As Lewisham filled up the form with his multitudinous "'ologies" and "'ographies," a youth of ducal
appearance entered and greeted the precise young man
in a friendly way. Lewisham, bending down to write,
perceived that this professional rival wore a very long
frock coat, patent leather boots, and the most beautiful
grey trousers. His conceptions of competition enlarged.
The precise young man by a motion of his eyes directed
the newcomer's attention to Lewisham's waterproof
collar, and was answered by raised eyebrows and a faint
tightening of the mouth. "That bounder at Castleford has answered me," said the newcomer in a fine
rich voice. "Is he any bally good?"

When the bounder at Castleford had been discussed
Lewisham presented his paper, and the precise young
man with his eye still fixed on the waterproof collar
took the document in the manner of one who reaches
across a gulf. "I doubt if we shall be able to do anything for you," he said reassuringly. "But an English
mastership may chance to be vacant. Science doesn't
count for much in *our* sort of schools, you know.
Classics and good games—that's our sort of thing."

"I see," said Lewisham.

"Good games, good form, you know, and all that
sort of thing."

"I see," said Lewisham.

"You don't happen to be a public-school boy?" asked
the precise young man.

"No," said Lewisham.

"Where were you educated?"

Lewisham's face grew hot. "Does that matter?" he
asked with his eye on the exquisite grey trousering.

"In our sort of school—decidedly. It's a question of
tone, you know."

"I see," said Lewisham, beginning to realise new
limitations. His immediate impulse was to escape the

eye of the nicely dressed assistant master. "You'll
write, I suppose, if you have anything," he said, and
the precise young man responded with alacrity to his
doorward motion.

"Often get that kind of thing?" asked the nicely
dressed young man when Lewisham had departed.

"Rather. Not quite so bad as that, you know.
That waterproof collar—did you notice it? Ugh!
And—'I see.' And the scowl and the clumsiness of
it. Of course *he* hasn't any decent clothes—he'd go
to a new shop with one tin box! But that sort of thing
—and board school teachers—they're getting everywhere! Only the other day—Rowton was here."

"Not Rowton of Pinner?"

"Yes, Rowton of Pinner. And he asked right out
for a board school master. He said, 'I want someone
who can teach arithmetic.'"

He laughed. The nicely dressed young man meditated over the handle of his cane. "A bounder of that
kind can't have a particularly nice time," he said, "anyhow. If he does get into a decent school, he must get
tremendously cut by all the decent men."

"Too thick-skinned to mind that sort of thing, I
fancy," said the scholastic agent. "He's a new type.
This South Kensington place and the polytechnics are
turning him out by the hundred. . . ."

Lewisham forgot his resentment at having to profess a religion he did not believe, in this new discovery
of the scholastic importance of clothing. He went
along with an eye to all the shop windows that afforded
a view of his person. Indisputably his trousers *were*
ungainly, flapping abominably over his boots and
bagging terribly at the knees, and his boots were not
only worn and ugly but extremely ill blacked. His
wrists projected offensively from his coat sleeves, he
perceived a huge asymmetry in the collar of his jacket,
his red tie was askew and ill tied, and that waterproof
collar! It was shiny, slightly discoloured, suddenly

clammy to the neck. What if he did happen to be well equipped for science teaching? That was nothing. He speculated on the cost of a complete outfit. It would be difficult to get such grey trousers as those he had seen for less than sixteen shillings and he reckoned a frock coat at forty shillings at least—possibly even more. He knew good clothes were very expensive. He hesitated at Poole's door and turned away. The thing was out of the question. He crossed Leicester Square and went down Bedford Street disliking every well-dressed person he met.

Messrs. Danks and Wimborne inhabited a bank-like establishment near Chancery Lane, and without any conversation presented him with forms to fill up. Religion? asked the form. Lewisham paused and wrote "Church of England."

Thence he went to the College of Pedagogues in Holborn. The College of Pedagogues presented itself as a long-bearded, corpulent, comfortable person with a thin gold watch chain and fat hands. He wore gilt glasses and had a kindly confidential manner that did much to heal Lewisham's wounded feelings. The 'ologies and 'ographies were taken down with polite surprise at their number. "You ought to take one of our diplomas," said the stout man. "You would find no difficulty. No competition. And there are prizes—several prizes—in money."

Lewisham was not aware that the waterproof collar had found a sympathetic observer.

"We give courses of lectures, and have an examination in the theory and practice of education. It is the only examination in the theory and practice of education for men engaged in middle and upper class teaching in this country. Except the Teacher's Diploma. And so few come—not two hundred a year. Mostly governesses. The men prefer to teach by rule of thumb, you know. English characteristic—rule of thumb. It doesn't do to say anything of course

—but there's bound to be—something happen—something a little disagreeable—somewhen, if things go on as they do. American schools keep on getting better—German too. What used to do won't do now. I tell this to you, you know, but it doesn't do to tell everyone. It doesn't do. It doesn't do to do anything. So much has to be considered. However . . . But you'd do well to get a diploma and make yourself efficient. Though that's looking ahead."

He spoke of looking ahead with an apologetic laugh as though it was an amiable weakness of his. He turned from such abstruse matters and furnished Lewisham with the particulars of the college diplomas, and proceeded to other possibilities. "There's private tuition," he said. "Would you mind a backward boy? Then we are occasionally asked for visiting masters. Mostly by girls' schools. But that's for older men—married men, you know."

"I am married," said Lewisham.

"*Eh?*" said the College of Pedagogues, startled.

"I *am* married," said Lewisham.

"Dear me," said the College of Pedagogues gravely, and regarding Mr. Lewisham over gold-rimmed glasses. "Dear me! And I am more than twice your age, and I am not married at all. One and twenty! Have you—have you been married long?"

"A few weeks," said Lewisham.

"That's very remarkable," said the College of Pedagogues. "Very interesting. . . . *Really!* Your wife must be a very courageous young person. . . . Excuse me! You know—— You will really have a hard fight for a position. However—it certainly makes you eligible for girls' schools; it does do that. To a certain extent, that is."

The evidently enhanced respect of the College of Pedagogues pleased Lewisham extremely. But his encounter with the Medical, Scholastic and Clerical Agency that holds by Waterloo Bridge was depressing again, and after that he set out to walk home. Long before he reached home he was tired, and his simple pride in being married and in active grapple with an unsympathetic world had passed. His surrender on the religious question had left a rankling bitterness behind it; the problem of the clothes was acutely painful. He was still far from a firm grasp of the fact that his market price was under rather than over one hundred pounds a year, but that persuasion was gaining ground in his mind.

The day was a greyish one, with a dull cold wind, and a nail in one of his boots took upon itself to be objectionable. Certain wild shots and disastrous lapses in his recent botanical examination, that he had managed to keep out of his mind hitherto, forced their way on his attention. For the first time since his marriage he harboured premonitions of failure.

When he got in he wanted to sit down at once in the little creaky chair by the fire, but Ethel came flitting from the newly bought typewriter with arms extended and prevented him. "Oh!—it *has* been dull," she said.

He missed the compliment. "*I* haven't had such a giddy time that you should grumble," he said, in a tone that was novel to her. He disengaged himself from her arms and sat down. He noticed the expression of her face.

"I'm rather tired," he said by way of apology. "And there's a confounded nail I must hammer down in my boot. It's tiring work hunting up these agents, but of course it's better to go and see them. How have you been getting on?"

"All right," she said regarding him. And then, "You *are* tired. We'll have some tea. And—let me take off your boot for you, dear. Yes—I will."

She rang the bell, bustled out of the room, called for tea at the staircase, came back, pulled out Madam Gadow's ungainly hassock and began unlacing his boot.

Lewisham's mood changed. "You *are* a trump, Ethel," he said; "I'm hanged if you're not." As the laces flicked he bent forward and kissed her ear. The unlacing was suspended and there were reciprocal endearments. . . .

Presently he was sitting in his slippers, with a cup of tea in his hand, and Ethel, kneeling on the hearthrug with the firelight on her face, was telling him of an answer that had come that afternoon to her advertisement in the *Athenæum*.

"That's good," said Lewisham.

"It's a novelist," she said with a light of pride in her eyes, and handed him the letter. "Lucas Holderness, the author of 'The Furnace of Sin' and other stories."

"That's first rate, said Lewisham with just a touch of envy, and bent forward to read by the firelight.

The letter was from an address in Judd Street, Euston Road, written on good paper and in a fair round hand such as one might imagine a novelist using. "Dear Madam," said the letter; "I propose to send you, by registered letter, the MS. of a three-volume novel. It is about 90,000 words—but you must count the exact number."

"How I shall count I don't know," said Ethel.

"I'll show you a way," said Lewisham. "There's no difficulty in that. You count the words on three or four pages, strike an average, and multiply."

"But of course, before doing so I must have a satisfactory guarantee that my confidence in putting my work in your hands will not be misplaced and that your execution is of the necessary high quality."

"Oh!" said Lewisham; "that's a bother."

"Accordingly I must ask you for references."

"That's a downright nuisance," said Lewisham. "I suppose that ass Lagune . . . But what's this? 'Or, failing references, for a deposit . . .' That's reasonable, I suppose."

It was such a moderate deposit too—merely a guinea.
Even had the doubt been stronger, the aspect of helpful
hopeful little Ethel eager for work might well have
thrust it aside. "Sending him a cheque will show him
we have a banking account behind us," said Lewisham
—his banking was still sufficiently recent for pride.
"We will send him a cheque. That'll settle *him* all
right."

That evening after the guinea cheque had been
despatched, things were further brightened by the
arrival of a letter of atrociously jellygraphed advices from
Messrs. Danks and Wimborne. They all referred to
resident vacancies for which Lewisham was manifestly
unsuitable, nevertheless their arrival brought an encouraging assurance of things going on, of shifting and unstable places in the defences of the beleaguered world.
Afterwards, with occasional endearments for Ethel, he
set himself to a revision of his last year's notebooks, for
now the botany was finished, the advanced zoological
course—the last lap, as it were, for the Forbes medal—
was beginning. She got her best hat from the next
room to make certain changes in the arrangement of its
trimming. She sat in the little chair, while Lewisham,
with documents spread before him, sat at the table.

Presently she looked up from an experimental arrangement of her cornflowers, and discovered Lewisham
no longer reading, but staring blankly at the middle of
the table-cloth with an extraordinary misery in his eyes.
She forgot the cornflowers and stared at him.

"Penny," she said after an interval.

Lewisham started and looked up. "*Eh?*"

"Why were you looking so miserable?" she asked.

"*Was* I looking miserable?"

"Yes. And *cross!*"

"I was thinking just then that I would like to boil
a bishop or so in oil."

"My dear!"

"They know perfectly well the case against what they

teach, they know it's neither madness nor wickedness nor any great harm to others, not to believe, they know perfectly well that a man may be as honest as the day, and right—right and decent in every way—and not believe in what they teach. And they know that it only wants the edge off a man's honour, for him to profess anything in the way of belief. Just anything. And they won't say so. I suppose they want the edge off every man's honour. If a man is well off they will truckle to him no end, though he laughs at all their teaching. They'll take gold plate from company promoters and rent from insanitary houses. But if a man is poor and doesn't profess to believe in what some of them scarcely believe themselves, they wouldn't lift a finger to help him against the ignorance of their followers. Your stepfather was right enough there. They know what's going on. They know that it means lying and humbug for any number of people, and they don't care. Why should they? *They've* got it down all right. They're spoilt and why shouldn't we be?"

Lewisham having selected the bishops as scapegoats for his turpitude, was inclined to ascribe even the nail in his boot to their agency.

Mrs. Lewisham looked puzzled. She realised his drift.

"You're not," she said, and dropped her voice, "an *infidel?*"

Lewisham nodded gloomily. "Aren't you?" he said.

"Oh no," said Mrs. Lewisham.

"But you don't go to church, you don't——"

"No, I don't," said Mrs. Lewisham; and then with more assurance, "But I'm not an infidel."

"Christian?"

"I suppose so."

"But a Christian—— What do you believe?"

"Oh! to tell the truth, and do right, and not hurt or injure people and all that."

"That's not a Christian. A Christian is one who believes."

"It's what *I* mean by a Christian," said Mrs. Lewisham.

"Oh! at that rate anyone's a Christian," said Lewisham. "We all think it's right to do right and wrong to do wrong."

"But we don't all do it," said Mrs. Lewisham, taking up the cornflowers again.

"No," said Lewisham, a little taken aback by the feminine method of discussion. "We don't all do it— certainly." He stared at her for a moment—her head was a little on one side and her eyes on the corn-flowers—and his mind was full of a strange discovery. He seemed on the verge of speaking, and turned to his notebook again.

Very soon the centre of the table-cloth resumed its sway.

The following day Mr. Lucas Holderness received his cheque for a guinea. Unhappily it was crossed. He meditated for some time and then took pen and ink and improved Lewisham's careless " one " to " five " and touched up his unticked figure one to correspond.

You perceive him, a lank, cadaverous, good-looking man with long black hair and a semi-clerical costume of quite painful rustiness. He made the emendations with grave carefulness. He took the cheque round to his grocer. His grocer looked at it suspiciously.

"You pay it in," said Mr. Lucas Holderness, "if you've any doubts about it. Pay it in. *I* don't know the man or what he is. He may be a swindler for all I can tell. *I* can't answer for him. Pay it in and see. Leave the change till then. I can wait. I'll call round in a few days' time."

"All right, wasn't it?" said Mr. Lucas Holderness in a casual tone two days later.

"Quite, sir," said the grocer with enhanced respect,

and handed him his four pounds thirteen and sixpence change.

Mr. Lucas Holderness, who had been eyeing the grocer's stock with a curious intensity, immediately became animated and bought a tin of salmon. He went out of the shop with the rest of the money in his hand, for the pockets of his clothes were old and untrustworthy. At the baker's he bought a new roll.

He bit a huge piece of the roll directly he was out of the shop, and went on his way gnawing. It was so large a piece that his gnawing mouth was contorted into the ugliest shapes. He swallowed by an effort, stretching his neck each time. His eyes expressed an animal satisfaction. He turned the corner of Judd Street biting again at the roll, and the reader of this story, like the Lewishams, hears of him no more.

CHAPTER THE TWENTY-SIXTH

The Glamour Fades

AFTER all, the rosy love-making and marrying and Epithalamy are no more than the dawns of things, and to follow comes all the spacious interval of white laborious light. Try as we may to stay those delightful moments, they fade and pass remorselessly; there is no returning, no recovering, only—for the foolish—the vilest peep-shows and imitations in dens and darkened rooms. We go on—we grow. At least we age. Our young couple, emerging presently from an atmosphere of dusk and morning stars, found the sky gathering greyly overhead and saw one another for the first time clearly in the light of every day.

It might perhaps witness better to Lewisham's refinement if one could tell only of a moderated and dignified cooling, of pathetic little concealments of disappointment and a decent maintenance of the sentimental atmosphere. And so at last daylight. But our young couple were too crude for that. The first intimations of their lack of identity have already been described, but it would be tedious and pitiful to tell of all the little intensifications, shade by shade, of the conflict of their individualities. They fell out, dear lady! They came to conflict of words. The stress of perpetual worry was upon them, of dwindling funds and the anxious search for work that would not come. And on Ethel lay long, vacant, lonely hours in dull surroundings. Differences arose from the most indifferent things; one night Lewisham lay awake in unfathomable amazement because she had convinced him she did not care a rap for the Welfare of Humanity, and deemed his Socialism a fancy and an indiscretion. And one Sunday afternoon they started for a walk under the pleasantest auspices, and returned flushed and angry, satire and retort flying free—on the score of the social conventions in Ethel's novelettes. For some inexplicable reason Lewisham saw fit to hate her novelettes very bitterly. These encounters indeed were mere skirmishes for the most part, and the silences and embarrassments that followed ended sooner or later in a "making up," tacit or definite, though once or twice this making up only re-opened the healing wound. And always each skirmish left its scar, effaced from yet another line of their lives the lingering tints of romantic colour.

There came no work, no added income for either of them, saving two trifles, for five long months. Once Lewisham won twelve shillings in the prize competition of a penny weekly, and three times came infinitesimal portions of typewriting from a poet who had apparently seen the *Athenæum* advertisement. His name was Edwin Peak Baynes and his handwriting was sprawling and unformed. He sent her several short lyrics on scraps of paper with instructions that he desired "three copies of each written beautifully in different styles" and "*not* fastened with metal fasteners but with silk thread of an appropriate colour." Both of our young people were greatly exercised by these instructions. One fragment was called " Bird Song," one " Cloud Shadows," and one " Eryngium," but Lewisham thought they might be spoken of collectively as Bosh. By way of payment, this poet sent, in contravention of the postal regulations, half a sovereign stuck into a card, asking her to keep the balance against future occasions. In a little while, greatly altered copies of these lyrics were returned by the poet in person, with this enigmatical instruction written across the cover of each : " This style I like, only if possible more so."

Lewisham was out, but Ethel opened the door, so this endorsement was unnecessary. " He's really only a boy," said Ethel, describing the interview to Lewisham, who was curious. They both felt that the youthfulness of Edwin Peak Baynes detracted something from the reality of this employment.

From his marriage until the final examination in June, Lewisham's life had an odd amphibious quality. At home were Ethel and the perpetual aching pursuit of employment, the pelting irritations of Madam Gadow's persistent overcharges, and so forth, and amid such things he felt extraordinarily grown up; but inter-calated with these experiences were those intervals at Kensington, scraps of his adolescence, as it were, lying amidst the new matter of his manhood, intervals during which he was simply an insubordinate and disappoint-ing student with an increasing disposition to gossip. At South Kensington he dwelt with theories and ideals as a student should; at the little rooms in Chelsea—they grew very stuffy as the summer came on, and the accu-mulation of the penny novelettes Ethel favoured made a litter—there was his particular private concrete situa-tion, and ideals gave place to the real.

It was a strangely narrow world, he perceived dimly, in which his manhood opened. The only visitors were the Chafferys. Chaffery would come to share their supper, and won upon Lewisham in spite of his roguery by his incessantly entertaining monologue and by his expressed respect for and envy of Lewisham's scientific attainments. Moreover, as time went on Lewisham found himself more and more in sympathy with Chaffery's bitterness against those who order the world. It was good to hear him on bishops and that sort of people. He said what Lewisham wanted to say, beautifully. Mrs. Chaffery was perpetually flitting out of the house as Lewisham came home, a dim, black, nervous, untidy little figure. She came because Ethel, in spite of her expressed belief that love was "all in all," found married life a little dull and lonely while Lewisham was away. And she went hastily when he came, because of a certain irritability that the struggle against the world was developing. He told no one at Kensington about his marriage, at first because it was such a delicious secret and then for quite other reasons. So there was no overlapping. The two worlds began and ended sharply at the wrought-iron gates. But the day came when Lewisham passed those gates for the last time and his adolescence ended altogether.

In the final examination of the biological course, the examination that signalised the end of his income of a weekly guinea, he knew well enough that he had done badly. The evening of the last day's practical work found him belated, hot-headed, beaten, with ruffled hair and red ears. He sat to the last moment doggedly struggling to keep cool and to mount the ciliated funnel of an earthworm's nephridium. But ciliated funnels come not to those who have shirked the laboratory practice. He rose, surrendered his paper to the morose elderly young assistant demonstrator who had welcomed him so flatteringly eight months before, and walked down the laboratory to the door where the rest of his fellow-students clustered.

Smithers was talking loudly about the "twistiness" of the identification, and the youngster with the big ears was listening attentively.

" Here's Lewisham ! How did *you* get on, Lewisham ?" asked Smithers, not concealing his assurance.

" Horribly," said Lewisham shortly, and pushed past.

" Did you spot D ?" clamoured Smithers.

Lewisham pretended not to hear.

Miss Heydinger stood with her hat in her hand and looked at Lewisham's hot eyes. He was for walking past her, but something in her face penetrated even his disturbance. He stopped.

" Did you get out the nephridium ?" he said as graciously as he could.

She shook her head. " Are you going downstairs ?" she asked.

" Rather," said Lewisham with a vague intimation in his manner of the offence Smithers gave him.

He opened the glass door from the passage to the staircase. They went down one tier of that square spiral in silence.

" Are you coming up again next year ?" asked Miss Heydinger.

" No," said Lewisham. " No, I shall not come here again. Ever."

Pause. " What will you do ?" she asked.

" I don't know. I have to get a living somehow. It's been bothering me all the session."

" I thought—" She stopped. " Will you go down to your uncle's again ?" she said.

" No. I shall stop in London. It's no good going out of things into the country. And besides—I've quarrelled rather with my uncle."

" What do you think of doing?—teaching ?"

" I suppose it will be teaching. I'm not sure. Anything that turns up."

" I see," she said.

They went on down in silence for a time.

" I suppose you will come up again ?" he asked.

" I may try the botanical again—if they can find room. And, I was thinking—sometimes one hears of things. What is your address? So that if I heard of anything——"

Lewisham stopped on the staircase and thought. "Of course," he said. He made no effort to give her the address, and she demanded it again at the foot of the stairs.

"That confounded nephridium——!" he said. "It has put everything out of my head."

They exchanged addresses on leaflets torn from Miss Heydinger's little notebook.

She waited at the Book in the hall while he signed his name. At the iron gates of the Schools she said: "I am going through Kensington Gardens."

He was now feeling irritated about the addresses, and he would not see the implicit invitation. "I am going towards Chelsea."

She hesitated a moment, looking at him—puzzled. "Good-bye then," she said.

"Good-bye," he answered, lifting his hat.

He crossed the Exhibition Road slowly with his packed glazed bag, now seamed with cracks, in his hand. He went thoughtfully down to the corner of the Cromwell Road and turned along that to the right so that he could see the red pile of the Science Schools rising fair and tall across the gardens of the Natural History Museum. He looked back towards it regretfully.

He was quite sure that he had failed in this last examination. He knew that any career as a scientific man was now closed to him for ever. And he remembered now how he had come along this very road to that great building for the first time in his life, and all the hopes and resolves that had swelled within him as he had drawn near. That dream of incessant unswerving work! Where might he have reached if only he had had singleness of purpose to make it a reality? . . .

And in these gardens it was that he and Smithers and Parkson had sat on a seat hard by the fossil tree and discoursed of Socialism together before the great paper was read. . . .

"Yes," he said, speaking aloud to himself; "yes— *that's* all over too.   Everything's over."

Presently the corner of the Natural History Museum came between him and his receding Alma Mater.   He sighed and turned his face towards the stuffy little rooms at Chelsea, and the still unconquered world.

CHAPTER THE TWENTY-SEVENTH

Concerning a Quarrel

IT was late in September that this particular quarrel occurred. Almost all the roseate tints seemed gone by this time, for the Lewishams had been married six months. Their financial affairs had changed from the catastrophic to the sordid; Lewisham had found work. An army crammer named Captain Vigours wanted someone energetic for his mathematical duffers, and to teach geometrical drawing and what he was pleased to call "Sandhurst Science." He paid no less than two shillings an hour for his uncertain demands on Lewisham's time. Moreover, there was a class in lower mathematics beginning at Walham Green where Lewisham was to show his quality. Fifty shillings a week or more seemed credible—more might be hoped for. It was now merely a case of tiding over the interval until Vigours paid. And meanwhile the freshness of Ethel's blouses departed, and Lewisham refrained from the repair of his boot, which had cracked across the toe.

1050

The beginning of the quarrel was trivial enough. But by the end they got to generalities. Lewisham had begun the day in a bad temper and under the cloud of an overnight passage of arms—and a little incident that had nothing to do with their ostensible difference lent it a warmth of emotion quite beyond its merits. As he emerged through the folding door he saw a letter lying among the sketchily laid breakfast things, and Ethel's attitude suggested the recoil of a quick movement; the letter suddenly dropped. Her eyes met his and she flushed. He sat down and took the letter—a trifle awkwardly perhaps. It was from Miss Heydinger. He hesitated with it halfway to his pocket, then decided to open it. It displayed an ample amount of reading, and he read. On the whole he thought it rather a dull sort of letter, but he did not allow this to appear. When it was read he put it carefully in his pocket.

That formally had nothing to do with the quarrel. The breakfast was already over when the quarrel began. Lewisham's morning was vacant, and he proposed to occupy it in the revision of certain notes bearing upon " Sandhurst Science." Unhappily the search for his notebook brought him into collision with the accumulation of Ethel's novelettes.

" These things are everywhere," he said after a gust of vehement handling. " I *wish* you'd tidy them up sometimes."

" They were tidy enough till you began to throw them about," Ethel pointed out.

" Confounded muck! it's only fit to be burnt," Lewisham remarked to the universe, and pitched one viciously into the corner.

" Well you tried to write one, anyhow," said Ethel, recalling a certain " Mammoth " packet of note-paper that had come on an evil end before Lewisham found his industrial level. This reminiscence always irritated him exceedingly.

" Eh?" he said sharply

"You tried to write one," repeated Ethel—a little unwillingly.

"You don't mean me to forget that."

"It's you reminded me."

He stared hostility for a space.

"Well, the things make a beastly litter anyhow, there isn't a tidy corner anywhere in the room. There never is."

"That's just the sort of thing you always say."

"Well—*is* there?"

"Yes, there is."

"*Where?*"

Ethel professed not to hear. But a devil had possession of Lewisham for a time. "It isn't as though you had anything else to do," he remarked, wounding dishonourably.

Ethel turned. "If I *put* those things away," she said with tremendous emphasis on the "put," "you'd only say I'd hidden them. What *is* the good of trying to please you?"

The spirit of perversity suggested to Lewisham, "None apparently."

Ethel's cheeks glowed and her eyes were bright with unshed tears. Abruptly she abandoned the defensive and blurted out the thing that had been latent so long between them. Her voice took a note of passion. "Nothing I can do ever does please you, since that Miss Heydinger began to write to you."

There was a pause, a gap. Something like astonishment took them both. Hitherto it had been a convention that she knew nothing of the existence of Miss Heydinger. He saw a light. "How did you know?" he began, and perceived that line was impossible. He took the way of the natural man; he ejaculated an "Ugh!" of vast disgust, he raised his voice. "You *are* unreasonable!" he cried in angry remonstrance. "Fancy saying that! As though you ever tried to please me! Just as though it wasn't all the other way about!" He stopped—struck by a momentary perception of injustice. He plunged at the point he had shirked. " How did you know it *was* Miss Heydinger——?"

Ethel's voice took upon itself the quality of tears. " I wasn't *meant* to know, was I ?" she said.

" But how ?"

" I suppose you think it doesn't concern me ? I suppose you think I'm made of stone ?"

" You mean—you think——?"

" Yes—I *do*."

For a brief interval Lewisham stared at the issue she had laid bare. He sought some crushing proposition, some line of convincing reasoning, with which to overwhelm and hide this new aspect of things. It would not come. He found himself fenced in on every side. A surging, irrational rage seized upon him.

" Jealousy !" he cried. " Jealousy ! Just as though—Can't I have letters about things you don't understand —that you *won't* understand ? If I asked you to read them you wouldn't—— It's just because——"

" You never give me a *chance* to understand."

" Don't I ?"

" No !"

" Why !—at first I was always trying. Socialism, religion—all those things. But you don't care—you won't care. You won't have that I've thought over these things at all, that I care for these things ! It wasn't any *good* to argue. You just care for me in a way—and all the rest of me—doesn't matter ! And because I've got a friend . . ."

" Friend !"

" Yes—*friend !*"

" Why !—you hide her letters !"

" Because I tell you you wouldn't understand what they are about. But, pah ! I won't argue. I *won't !* You're jealous and there's the end of the matter !"

" Well, who *wouldn't* be jealous ?"

He stared at her as if he found the question hard to

see. The theme was difficult—invincibly difficult. He surveyed the room for a diversion. The notebook he had disinterred from her novelettes lay upon the table and reminded him of his grievance of ruined hours. His rage exploded. He struck out abruptly towards fundamental things. He gesticulated forcibly. "This can't go on!" he cried, "this can't go on! How can I work? How can I do anything?"

He made three steps and stood in a clear space.

"I won't *stand* it—I won't go on at this! Quarrels—bickerings—discomfort. Look there! I meant to work this morning. I meant to look up notes! Instead of which you start a quarrel——"

The gross injustice raised Ethel's voice to an outcry. "*I* didn't start the quarrel——"

The only response to this was to shout, and Lewisham shouted. "You start a quarrel!" he repeated. "You make a shindy! You spring a dispute—jealousy!—on me! How can I do anything? How can one stop in a house like this? I shall go out. Look here!—I shall go out. I shall go to Kensington and work there!"

He perceived himself wordless, and Ethel was about to speak. He glared about him, seeking a prompt climax. Instant action was necessary. He perceived Huxley's "Vertebrata" upon the side-table. He clutched it, swaying it through a momentous arc, and hurled it violently into the empty fireplace.

For a second he seemed to be seeking some other missile. He perceived his hat on the chest of drawers, seized it and strode tragically from the room.

He hesitated with the door half closed, then opened it wide and slammed it vehemently. Thereby the world was warned of the justice of his rage, and so he passed with credit into the street.

He went striding heedless of his direction through the streets dotted with intent people hurrying to work, and presently habit turned his feet towards the Brompton Road. The eastward trend of the morning traffic caught

him.   For a time, save for a rebellious ingredient of
wonder at the back of his mind, he kept his anger white
and pure.   Why had he married her?   was the text to
which he clung.   Why in the name of destiny had he
married her?   But anyhow he had said the decisive thing.
He would not stand it!   It must end.   Things were
intolerable and they must end.   He meditated devast-
ating things that he might presently say to her in pursu-
ance of this resolution.   He contemplated acts of cruelty.
In such ways he would demonstrate clearly that he would
not stand it.   He was very careful to avoid inquiring
what it was he would not stand.

How in the name of destiny had he come to marry
her?   The quality of his surroundings mingled in some
way with the quality of his thoughts.   The huge distended buildings of corrugated iron in which the Art
Museum (of all places!) culminates, the truncated
Oratory all askew to the street, seemed to have a similar
quarrel with fate.   How in the name of destiny?   After
such high prolusions!

He found that his thoughts had carried him past the
lodge of the museum.   He turned back irritably and
went through the turnstile.   He entered the museum
and passed beneath the gallery of Old Iron on his way
to the Education Library.   The vacant array of tables,
the bays of attendant books had a quality of refuge. . . .

So much for Lewisham in the morning.   Long before
midday all the vigour of his wrath was gone, all his
passionate conviction of Ethel's unworthiness.   Over a
pile of neglected geological works he presented a face of
gloom.   His memory presented a picture of himself as
noisy, overbearing, and unfair.   What on earth had it
all been about?

By two o'clock he was on his way to Vigours', and his
mood was acute remorse.   Of the transition there can
be no telling in words, for thoughts are more subtle
than words and emotions infinitely vaguer.   But one
thing at least is definite, that a memory returned.

34

It drifted in to him, through the glass roof of the Library far above. He did not perceive it as a memory at first, but as an irritating obstacle to attention. He struck the open pages of the book before him with his flat hand. " Damn that infernal hurdy-gurdy !" he whispered.

Presently he made a fretful movement and put his hands over his ears.

Then he thrust his books from him, got up, and wandered about the Library. The organ came to an abrupt end in the middle of a bar, and vanished in the circumambient silence of space.

Lewisham standing in a bay closed a book with a snap and returned to his seat.

Presently he found himself humming a languid tune, and thinking again of the quarrel that he had imagined banished from his mind. What in the name of destiny had it all been about? He had a curious sense that something had got loose, was sliding about in his mind. And as if by way of answer emerged a vision of Whortley —a singularly vivid vision. It was moonlight and a hillside, the little town lay lit and warm below, and the scene was set to music, a lugubriously sentimental air. For some reason this music had the quality of a barrel organ—though he knew that properly it came from a band—and it associated with itself a mystical formula of words, drawling words :

" *Sweet dreamland fa—ces passing to and fro,*
  Bring back to mem'ry, days of long ago—oh !"

This air not only reproduced the picture with graphic vividness, but it trailed after it an enormous cloud of irrational emotion, emotion that had but a moment before seemed gone for ever from his being.

He recalled it all ! He had come down that hillside and Ethel had been with him. . . .

Had he really felt like that about her?

" Pah !" he said suddenly and reverted to his books.

But the tune and the memory had won their footing, they were with him through his meagre lunch of milk and scones—he had resolved at the outset he would not go back to her for the midday meal—and on his way to Vigours' they insisted on attention. It may be that lunching on scone and milk does in itself make for milder ways of thinking. A sense of extraordinary contradiction, of infinite perplexity, came to him.

"But then," he asked, "how the devil did we get to *this?*"

Which is indeed one of the fundamental questions of matrimony.

The morning tumults had given place to an almost scientific calm. Very soon he was grappling manfully with the question. There was no disputing it, they had quarrelled. Not once but several times lately they had quarrelled. It was real quarrelling—they had stood up against one another, striking, watching to strike, seeking to wound. He tried to recall just how things had gone—what he had said and what she had replied. He could not do it. He had forgotten phrases and connections. It stood in his memory not as a sequence of events but as a collection of disconnected static sayings; each saying blunt, permanent, inconsecutive like a graven inscription. And of the scene there came only one picture—Ethel with a burning face and her eyes shining with tears.

The traffic of a cross street engaged him for a space. He emerged on the further side full of the vivid contrast of their changed relations. He made a last effort to indict her, to show that she was entirely to blame for the transition. She had quarrelled with him, she had quarrelled deliberately because she was jealous. She was jealous of Miss Heydinger because she was stupid. But now these accusations faded like smoke as he put them forth. But the picture of two little figures back there in the moonlit past did not fade. It was in the narrows of Kensington High Street that he abandoned her arraignment. It was beyond the Town Hall that he made the new step. Was it, after all, just possible that in some degree he himself rather was the chief person to blame?

It was instantly as if he had been aware of that all the time.

Once he had made that step, he moved swiftly. Not a hundred paces before the struggle was over, and he had plunged headlong into the blue abyss of remorse. And all these things that had been so dramatic and forcible, all the vivid brutal things he had said, stood no longer graven inscriptions but in letters of accusing flame. He tried to imagine he had not said them, that his memory played him a trick, tried to suppose he had said something similar perhaps but much less forcible. He attempted with almost equal futility to minimise his own wounds. His endeavour served only to measure the magnitude of his fall.

He had recovered everything now, he saw it all. He recalled Ethel sunlit in the avenue, Ethel white in the moonlight before they parted outside the Frobisher house, Ethel as she would come out of Lagune's house greeting him for their nightly walk, Ethel new wedded, as she came to him through the folding doors radiant in the splendour his emotions threw about her. And at last Ethel angry, dishevelled and tear-stained in that ill-lit, untidy little room. All to the cadence of a hurdy-gurdy tune! From that to this! How had it been possible to get from such an opalescent dawning to such a dismal day? What was it had gone? He and she were the same two persons who walked so brightly in awakened memory; he and she who had lived so bitterly through the last few weeks of misery!

His mood sank for a space to the quality of groaning. He implicated her now at most as his partner in their failure—"What a mess we have made of things!" was his new motif. "What a mess!"

He knew love now for what it was, knew it for something more ancient and more imperative than reason.

He knew now that he loved her, and his recent rage, his hostility, his condemnation of her seemed to him the reign of some exterior influence in his mind. He thought incredulously of the long decline in tenderness that had followed the first days of their delight in each other, the diminution of endearment, the first yielding to irritability, the evenings he had spent doggedly working, resisting all his sense of her presence. "One cannot always be love-making," he had said, and so—they were slipping apart. Then in countless little things he had not been patient, he had not been fair. He had wounded her by harshness, by unsympathetic criticism, above all by his absurd secrecy about Miss Heydinger's letters. Why on earth had he kept those letters from her? as though there was something to hide! What was there to hide? What possible antagonism could there be? Yet it was by such little things that their love was now like some once valued possession that had been in brutal hands, it was scratched and chipped and tarnished, it was on its way to being altogether destroyed. Her manner had changed towards him, a gulf was opening that he might never be able to close again.

"No, it *shall* not be!" he said, "it shall not be!"

But how to get back to the old footing? how to efface the things he had said, the things that had been done?

Could they get back?

For a moment he faced a new possibility. Suppose they could not get back! Suppose the mischief was done! Suppose that when he slammed the door behind him it locked, and was locked against him for ever!

"But we *must!*" said Lewisham, "we must!"

He perceived clearly that this was no business of reasoned apologies. He must begin again, he must get back to emotion, he must thrust back the overwhelming pressure of everyday stresses and necessities that was crushing all the warmth and colour from their lives. But how? How?

He must make love to her again. But how to begin—
how to mark the change? There had been making-up
before, sullen concessions and treaties. But this was
different. He tried to imagine something he might say,
some appeal that he might make. Everything he thought
of was cold and hard, or pitiful and undignified, or
theatrical and foolish. Suppose the door *was* closed!
If already it was too late! In every direction he was
confronted by the bristling memories of harsh things.
He had a glimpse of how he must have changed in her
eyes, and things became intolerable for him. For now
he was assured he loved her still with all his heart.

And suddenly came a florist's window, and in the
centre of it a glorious heap of roses.

They caught his eye before they caught his mind.
He saw white roses, virginal white, roses of cream and
pink and crimson, the tints of flesh and pearl, rich, a
mass of scented colour, visible odours, and in the midst
of them a note of sullen red. It was as it were the very
colour of his emotion. He stopped abruptly. He turned
back to the window and stared frankly. It was gorgeous,
he saw, but why so particularly did it appeal to him?

Then he perceived as though it was altogether self-
evident what he had to do. This was what he wanted.
This was the note he had to strike. Among other
things because it would repudiate the accursed worship
of pinching self-restraint that was one of the incessant
stresses between them. They would come to her with a
pure unexpectedness, they would flame upon her.

Then, after the roses, he would return.

Suddenly the grey trouble passed from his mind; he
saw the world full of colour again. He saw the scene
he desired bright and clear, saw Ethel no longer bitter
and weeping, but glad as once she had always seemed
glad. His heart-beats quickened. It was giving had
been needed, and he would give.

Some weak voice of indiscreet discretion squeaked and

vanished. He had, he knew, a sovereign in his pocket.
He went in.

He found himself in front of a formidable young lady
in black, and unprepared with any formula. He had
never bought flowers before. He looked about him for
an inspiration. He pointed at the roses. " I want those
roses," he said. . . .

He emerged again with only a few small silver coins
remaining out of the sovereign he had changed. The
roses were to go to Ethel, properly packed; they were
to be delivered according to his express direction at six
o'clock.

"Six o'clock," Lewisham had reiterated very earnestly.

" We quite understand," the young lady in black had
said, and had pretended to be unable to conceal a smile.
" We're *quite* accustomed to sending out flowers."

CHAPTER THE TWENTY-EIGHTH

The Coming of the Roses

AND the roses miscarried!

When Lewisham returned from Vigours' it was already nearly seven. He entered the house with a beating heart. He had expected to find Ethel excited, the roses displayed. But her face was white and jaded. He was so surprised by this that the greeting upon his lips died away. He was balked! He went into the sitting-room and there were no roses to be seen. Ethel came past him and stood with her back to him looking out of the window. The suspense was suddenly painful. . . .

He was obliged to ask, though he was certain of the answer, "Has nothing come?"

Ethel looked at him. "What did you think had come?"

"Oh! nothing."

She looked out of the window again. "No," she said slowly, "nothing has come."

He tried to think of something to say that might bridge the distance between them, but he could think

1062

of nothing. He must wait until the roses came. He took out his books and a gaunt hour passed to supper time. Supper was a chilly ceremonial set with necessary over-polite remarks. Disappointment and exasperation darkened Lewisham's soul. He began to feel angry with everything—even with her—he perceived she still judged him angry and that made him angry with her. He was resuming his books and she was helping Madam Gadow's servant to clear away, when they heard a rapping at the street door. "They have come at last," he said to himself brightening, and hesitated whether he should bolt or witness her reception of them. The servant was a nuisance. Then he heard Chaffery's voice, and whispered a soft "damn!" to himself.

The only thing to do now if the roses came was to slip out into the passage, intercept them and carry them into the bedroom by the door between that and the passage. It would be undesirable for Chaffery to witness that phase of sentiment. He might flash some dart of ridicule that would stick in their memory for ever.

Lewisham tried to show that he did not want a visitor. But Chaffery was in high spirits and could have warmed a dozen cold welcomes. He sat down without any express invitation in the chair that he preferred.

Before Mr. and Mrs. Chaffery the Lewishams veiled whatever trouble might be between them beneath an insincere cordiality, and Chaffery was soon talking freely, unsuspicious of their crisis. He produced two cigars. "I had a wild moment," he said. "'For once,' said I, 'the honest shall smoke the admirable—or the admirable shall smoke the honest,' whichever you like best. Try one? No? Those austere principles of yours! There will be more pleasure then. But really, I would as soon you smoked it as I. For to-night I radiate benevolence."

He cut the cigar with care, he lit it with ceremony, waiting until nothing but honest wood was burning on the match, and for fully a minute he was silent, evolving

34*

huge puffs of smoke. And then he spoke again, punctuating his words by varied and beautiful spirals. "So far," he said, "I have only trifled with knavery."

As Lewisham said nothing he resumed after a pause.

"There are three sorts of men in the world, my boy, three and no more—and of women only one. There are happy men and there are knaves and fools. Hybrids I don't count. And to my mind knaves and fools are very much alike."

He paused again.

"I suppose they are," said Lewisham flatly, and frowned at the fireplace.

Chaffery eyed him. "I am talking wisdom. To-night I am talking a particular brand of wisdom. I am broaching some of my oldest and finest, because—as you will find one day—this is a special occasion. And you are distrait!"

Lewisham looked up. "Birthday?" he said.

"You will see. But I was making golden observations about knaves and fools. I was early convinced of the absolute necessity of righteousness if a man is to be happy. I know it as surely as there is a sun in the heavens. Does that surprise you?"

"Well, it hardly squares——"

"No. I know. I will explain all that. But let me tell you the happy life. Let me give you that, as if I lay on my deathbed and this was a parting gift. In the first place, mental integrity. Prove all things, hold fast to that which is right. Let the world have no illusions for you, no surprises. Nature is full of cruel catastrophies, man is a physically degenerate ape, every appetite, every instinct, needs the curb; salvation is not in the nature of things but whatever salvation there may be is in the nature of man; face all these painful things. I hope you follow that?"

"Go on," said Lewisham, with the debating-society taste for a thesis prevailing for a minute over that matter of the roses.

"In youth, exercise and learning; in adolescence, ambition, and in early manhood, love—no footlight passion." Chaffery was very solemn and insistent, with a lean extended finger, upon this point.

"Then marriage, young and decent, and then children and stout honest work for them, work too for the State in which they live; a life of self-devotion, indeed, and for sunset a decent pride—that is the happy life. Rest assured that is the happy life; the life Natural Selection has been shaping for man since life began. So a man may go happy from the cradle to the grave—at least— passably happy. And to do this needs just three things —a sound body, a sound intelligence, and a sound will. . . . A sound will."

Chaffery paused on the repetition.

"No other happiness endures. And when all men are wise, all men will seek that life. Fame! Wealth! Art!—the Red Indians worship lunatics, and we are still by way of respecting the milder sorts. But I say that all men who do not lead that happy life are knaves and fools. The physical cripple, you know, poor devil, I count a sort of bodily fool."

"Yes," weighed Lewisham, "I suppose he is."

"Now a fool fails of happiness because of his insufficient mind, he miscalculates, he stumbles and hobbles, some cant or claptrap whirls him away; he gets passion out of a book and wife out of the stews, or he quarrels on a petty score; threats frighten him, vanity beguiles him, he fails by blindness. But the knave who is not a fool fails against the light. Many knaves are fools also—*most* are—but some are not. I know—I am a knave but no fool. The essence of your knave is that he lacks the will, the motive capacity to seek his own greater good. The knave abhors persistence. Strait is the way and narrow the gate; the knave cannot keep to it and the fool cannot find it."

Lewisham lost something of what Chaffery was saying by reason of a rap outside. He rose, but Ethel was before him. He concealed his anxiety as well as he could, and was relieved when he heard the front door close again and her footsteps pass into the bedroom by the passage door. He reverted to Chaffery.

"Has it ever occurred to you," asked Chaffery, apparently apropos of nothing, "that intellectual conviction is no motive at all? Any more than a railway map will run a train a mile."

"Eh?" said Lewisham. "Map—run a train a mile —of course, yes. No, it won't."

"That is precisely my case," said Chaffery. "That is the case of your pure knave everywhere. We are not fools—because we know. But yonder runs the highway, windy, hard and austere, a sort of dry happiness that will endure; and here is the pleasant by-way—lush, my boy, lush, as the poets have it, and with its certain man-trap among the flowers. . . ."

Ethel returned through the folding doors. She glanced at Lewisham, remained standing for awhile, sat down in the basket chair as if to resume some domestic needlework that lay upon the table, then rose and went back into the bedroom.

Chaffery proceeded to expatiate on the transitory nature of passion and all glorious and acute experiences. Whole passages of that discourse Lewisham did not hear, so intent was he upon those roses. Why had Ethel gone back into the bedroom? Was it possible—? Presently she returned, but she sat down so that he could not see her face.

"If there is one thing to set against the wholesome life it is adventure," Chaffery was saying. "But let every adventurer pray for an early death, for with adventures come wounds, and with wounds come sickness, and —except in romances—sickness effects the nervous system. Your nerve goes. Where are you then, my boy?"

"Sh! what's that?" said Lewisham.

It was a rap at the house door. Heedless of the flow of golden wisdom, he went out at once and admitted a gentleman friend of Madam Gadow, who passed along the passage and vanished down the staircase. When he returned Chaffery was standing to go.

" I could have talked with you longer," he said, " but you have something on your mind, I see. I will not worry you by guessing what. Some day you will remember. . . ." He said no more but laid his hand on Lewisham's shoulder.

One might almost fancy he was offended at something.

At any other time Lewisham might have been propitiatory, but now he offered no apology. Chaffery turned to Ethel and looked at her curiously for a moment. " Good-bye," he said, holding out his hand to her.

On the doorstep Chaffery regarded Lewisham with the same curious look, and seemed to weigh some remark. " Good-bye," he said at last with something in his manner that kept Lewisham at the door for a moment looking after his stepfather's receding figure. But immediately the roses were uppermost again.

When he re-entered the living room he found Ethel sitting idly at her typewriter, playing with the keys. She got up at his return and sat down in the armchair with a novelette that hid her face. He stared at her, full of questions. After all, then, they had not come. He was intensely disappointed now, he was intensely angry with the ineffable young shop-woman in black. He looked at his watch and then again, he took a book and pretended to read and found himself composing a scathing speech of remonstrance to be delivered on the morrow at the flower-shop. He put his book down, went to his black bag, opened and closed it aimlessly. He glanced covertly at Ethel and found her looking covertly at him. He could not quite understand her expression.

He fidgeted into the bedroom and stopped as dead as a pointer.

He felt an extraordinary persuasion of the scent of

roses. So strong did it seem that he glanced outside the room door, expecting to find a box there, mysteriously arrived. But there was no scent of roses in the passage.

Then he saw close by his foot an enigmatical pale object, and stooping, picked up the creamy petal of a rose. He stood with it in his hand, perplexed beyond measure. He perceived a slight disorder of the valence of the dressing-table and linked it with this petal by a swift intuition.

He made two steps, lifted the valence, and behold! there lay his roses crushed together!

He gasped like a man who plunges suddenly into cold water. He remained stooping with the valence raised.

Ethel appeared in the half doorway and her expression was unfamiliar. He stared at her white face.

"Why on earth did you put my roses here?" he asked.

She stared back at him. Her face reflected his astonishment.

"Why did you put my roses here?" he asked again.

"Your roses!" she cried. "What! Did *you* send those roses?"

CHAPTER THE TWENTY-NINTH

Thorns and Rose Petals

HE remained stooping and staring up at her, realising the implication of her words only very slowly.

Then it grew clear to him.

As she saw understanding dawning in his face, she uttered a cry of consternation. She came forward and sat down upon the little bedroom chair. She turned to him and began a sentence. "I," she said and stopped, with an impatient gesture of her hands. "*Oh!*"

He straightened himself and stood regarding her. The basket of roses lay overturned between them.

"You thought these came from someone else?" he said, trying to grasp this inversion of the universe.

She turned her eyes. "I did not know," she panted. "A trap. . . . Was it likely—they came from you?"

"You thought they came from someone else," he said.

"Yes," she said, "I did."

"Who?"

"Mr. Baynes."

"That boy!"

"Yes—that boy."

"Well!"

Lewisham looked about him—a man in the presence of the inconceivable.

"You mean to say you have been carrying on with that youngster behind my back?" he asked.

She opened her lips to speak and had no words to say.

His pallor increased until every tinge of colour had left his face. He laughed and then set his teeth. Husband and wife looked at one another.

"I never dreamt," he said in even tones.

He sat down on the bed, thrusting his feet among the scattered roses with a sort of grim satisfaction. "I never dreamt," he repeated, and the flimsy basket kicked by his swinging foot hopped indignantly through the folding doors into the living-room and left a trail of blood-red petals.

They sat for perhaps two minutes and when he spoke again his voice was hoarse. He reverted to former formula. "Look here," he said, and cleared his throat. "I don't know whether you think I'm going to stand this, but I'm not."

He looked at her. She sat staring in front of her, making no attempt to cope with disaster.

"When I say I'm not going to stand it," explained Lewisham, "I don't mean having a row or anything of that sort. One can quarrel and be disappointed over—other things—and still go on. But this is a different thing altogether.

"Of all dreams and illusions! . . . Think what I have lost in this accursed marriage. And *now* . . . You don't understand—you won't understand."

"Nor you," said Ethel, weeping but neither looking at him nor moving her hands from her lap where they lay helplessly. "*You* don't understand."

"I'm beginning to."

He sat in silence gathering force. "In one year," he said, "all my hopes, all my ambitions have gone. I know

I have been cross and irritable—I know that. I've been pulled two ways. But . . . I bought you these roses."

She looked at the roses, and then at his white face, made an imperceptible movement towards him, and became impassive again.

"I do think one thing. I have found out you are shallow, you don't think, you can't feel things that I think and feel. I have been getting over that. But I did think you were loyal——"

"I *am* loyal," she cried.

"And you think—Bah!—you poke my roses under the table!"

Another portentous silence. Ethel stirred and he turned his eyes to watch what she was about to do. She produced her handkerchief and began to wipe her dry eyes rapidly, first one and then the other. Then she began sobbing. "I'm . . . as loyal as you . . . anyhow," she said.

For a moment Lewisham was aghast. Then he perceived he must ignore that argument.

"I would have stood it—I would have stood anything if you had been loyal—if I could have been sure of you. I am a fool, I know, but I would have stood the interruption of my work, the loss of any hope of a Career, if I had been sure you were loyal. I . . . I cared for you a great deal."

He stopped. He had suddenly perceived the pathetic. He took refuge in anger.

"And you have deceived me! How long, how much, I don't care. You have deceived me. And I tell you "—he began to gesticulate—" I'm not so much your slave and fool as to stand that! No woman shall make me *that* sort of fool, whatever else— So far as I am concerned, this ends things. This ends things. We are married—but I don't care if we were married five hundred times. I won't stop with a woman who takes flowers from another man——"

"I *didn't,*" said Ethel.

Lewisham gave way to a transport of anger. He caught up a handful of roses and extended them, trembling. "What's *this?*" he asked. His finger bled from a thorn, as once it had bled from a blackthorn spray.

"I *didn't* take them," said Ethel. "I couldn't help it if they were sent."

"Ugh!" said Lewisham. "But what is the good of argument and denial? You took them in, you had them. You may have been cunning, but you have given yourself away. And our life and all this"—he waved an inclusive hand at Madam Gadow's furniture—"is at an end."

He looked at her and repeated with bitter satisfaction, "At an end."

She glanced at his face and his expression was remorseless. "I will not go on living with you," he said, lest there should be any mistake. "Our life is at an end."

Her eyes went from his face to the scattered roses. She remained staring at these. She was no longer weeping, and her face, save about the eyes, was white.

He presented it in another form. "I shall go away."

"We never ought to have married," he reflected. "But . . . I never expected *this!*"

"I didn't know," she cried out, lifting up her voice. "I *didn't* know. How could *I* help! *Oh!*"

She stopped and stared at him with hands clenched, her eyes haggard with despair.

Lewisham remained impenetrably malignant.

"I don't *want* to know," he said, answering her dumb appeal. "That settles everything. *That!*" He indicated the scattered flowers. "What does it matter to me what has happened or hasn't happened? Anyhow— oh! I don't mind. I'm glad. See? It settles things.

"The sooner we part the better. I shan't stop with you another night. I shall take my box and my portmanteau into that room and pack. I shall stop in there to-night, sleep in a chair or *think*. And to-morrow I shall settle up with Madam Gadow and go. You can go back . . . to your cheating."

He stopped for some seconds. She was deadly still. " You wanted to, and now you may. You wanted to, before I got work. You remember? You know your place is still open at Lagune's. I don't care. I tell you I don't care *that*. Not that! You may go your own way—and I shall go mine. See? And all this rot— this sham of living together when neither cares for the other—I don't care for you *now*, you know, so you needn't think it—will be over and done with. As for marriage—I don't care *that* for marriage—it can't make a sham and a blunder anything but a sham.

" It's a sham, and shams have to end, and that's the end of the matter."

He stood up resolutely. He kicked the scattered roses out of his way and dived beneath the bed for his port-manteau. Ethel neither spoke nor moved, but remained watching his movements. For a time the portmanteau refused to emerge, and he marred his stern resolution by a half audible " Come here—damn you !" He swung it into the living-room and returned for his box. He proposed to pack in that room.

When he had taken all his personal possessions out of the bedroom, he closed the folding doors with an air of finality. He knew from the sounds that followed that she flung herself upon the bed, and that filled him with grim satisfaction.

He stood listening for a space, then set about packing methodically. The first rage of discovery had abated, he knew quite clearly that he was inflicting grievous punishment and that gratified him. There was also indeed a curious pleasure in the determination of a long and painful period of vague misunderstanding by this unexpected crisis. He was acutely conscious of the silence on the other side of the folding doors, he kept up a succession of deliberate little noises, beat books together and brushed clothes, to intimate the resolute prosecution of his preparations.

That was about nine o'clock. At eleven he was still busy . . .

Darkness came suddenly upon him. It was Madam Gadow's economical habit to turn off all her gas at that hour unless she chanced to be entertaining friends.

He felt in his pocket for matches and he had none. He whispered curses. Against such emergencies he had bought a brass lamp and in the bedroom there were candles. Ethel had a candle alight, he could see the bright yellow line that appeared between the folding doors. He felt his way presently towards the mantel, receiving a blow in the ribs from a chair on the way, and went carefully amidst Madam Gadow's once amusing ornaments.

There were no matches on the mantel. Going to the chest of drawers he almost fell over his open portmanteau. He had a silent ecstasy of rage. Then he kicked against the basket in which the roses had come. He could find no matches on the chest of drawers.

Ethel must have the matches in the bedroom, but that was absolutely impossible. He might even have to ask her for them, for at times she pocketed matches. . . . There was nothing for it but to stop packing. Not a sound came from the other room.

He decided he would sit down in the armchair and go to sleep. He crept very carefully to the chair and sat down. Another interval of listening and he closed his eyes and composed himself for slumber.

He began to think over his plans for the morrow. He imagined the scene with Madam Gadow, and then his departure to find bachelor lodgings once more. He debated in what direction he should go to get suitable lodgings. Possible difficulties with his luggage, possible annoyances of the search loomed gigantic. He felt greatly irritated at these minor difficulties. He wondered if Ethel also was packing. What particularly would she do? He listened but he could hear nothing. She was very still. She was really very still! What could she be doing? He forgot the bothers of the morrow in his new interest. Presently he rose very softly and listened. Then he sat down again impatiently. He tried to dismiss his curiosity about the silence by recapitulating the story of his wrongs.

He had some difficulty in fixing his mind upon this theme, but presently his memories were flowing freely. Only it was not wrongs now that he could recall. He was pestered by an absurd idea that he had again behaved unjustly to Ethel, that he had been headlong and malignant. He made strenuous efforts to recover his first heat of jealousy—in vain. Her remark that she had been as loyal as he, became an obstinate ·headline in his mind. Something arose within him that insisted upon Ethel's possible fate if he should leave her. What particularly would she do? He knew how much her character leant upon his. Good Heavens! What might she not do?

By an effort he succeeded in fixing his mind on Baynes. That helped him back to the harsher footing. However hard things might be for her she deserved them. She deserved them!

Yet presently he slipped again, slipped back to the remorse and regrets of the morning time. He clutched at Baynes as a drowning man clutches at a rope, and recovered himself. For a time he meditated on Baynes. He had never seen the poet, so his imagination had scope. It appeared to him as an exasperating obstacle to a tragic avenging of his honour that Baynes was a mere boy—possibly even younger than himself.

The question, "What will become of Ethel?" rose to the surface again. He struggled against its possibilities. No! That was not it! That was her affair.

He felt inexorably kept to the path he had chosen, for all the waning of his rage. He had put his hand to the plough. "If you condone this," he told himself, "you might condone anything. There are things one *must* not stand." He tried to keep to that point of view—assuming for the most part out of his imagination what it was he was not standing. A dim sense came to him of how much he was assuming. At any rate she must have flirted! . . . He resisted this reviving perception of justice as though it was some unspeakably disgraceful craving. He tried to imagine her with Baynes.

He determined he would go to sleep.

But his was a waking weariness. He tried counting. He tried to distract his thoughts from her by going over the atomic weights of the elements. . . .

He shivered, and realised that he was cold and sitting cramped on an uncomfortable horsehair chair. He had dozed. He glanced for the yellow line between the folding doors. It was still there but it seemed to quiver. He judged the candle must be flaring. He wondered why everything was so still.

Now why should he suddenly feel afraid.

He sat for a long time trying to hear some movement, his head craning forward in the darkness. . . .

A grotesque idea came into his head that all that had happened a very long time ago. He dismissed that. He contested an unreasonable persuasion that some irrevocable thing had passed. But why was everything so still?

He was invaded by a prevision of unendurable calamity.

Presently he rose and crept very slowly and with infinite precautions against noise, towards the folding doors. He stood listening with his ear near the yellow chink.

He could hear nothing, not even the measured breathing of a sleeper.

He perceived that the doors were not shut but slightly ajar. He pushed against the inner one very gently and opened it silently. Still there was no sound of Ethel. He opened the door still wider and peered into the room. The candle had burnt down and was flaring in its socket. Ethel was lying half undressed upon the bed, and in her hand and close to her face was a rose.

He stood watching her, fearing to move. He listened hard and his face was very white. Even now he could not hear her breathing.

After all, it was probably all right. She was just asleep. He would slip back before she woke. If she found him——

He looked at her again. There was something in her face——

He came nearer, no longer heeding the sounds he made. He bent over her. Even now she did not seem to breathe.

He saw that her eyelashes were still wet, the pillow by her cheek was wet. Her white, tear-stained face hurt him. . . .

She was intolerably pitiful to him. He forgot everything but that and how he had wounded her that day. And then she stirred and murmured indistinctly a foolish name she had given him.

He forgot that they were going to part for ever. He felt nothing but a great joy that she could stir and speak. His jealousy flashed out of being. He dropped upon his knees.

"Dear," he whispered. "Is it all right? I . . . I could not hear you breathing. I could not hear you breathing."

She started and was awake.

"I was in the other room," said Lewisham in a voice full of emotion. "Everything was so quiet. I was afraid—I did not know what had happened. Dear—Ethel dear. Is it all right?"

She sat up quickly and scrutinised his face. "Oh! let me tell you," she wailed. "Do let me tell you. It's nothing. It's nothing. You wouldn't hear me. You wouldn't hear me. It wasn't fair—before you had heard me. . . ."

His arms tightened about her. "Dear," he said, "I knew it was nothing. I knew. I knew."

She spoke in sobbing sentences. "It was so simple. Mr. Baynes . . . something in his manner . . . I knew he might be silly . . . Only I did so want to help you." She paused. Just for one instant she saw one untellable indiscretion as it were in a lightning flash. A chance meeting it was, a "silly" thing or so said, a panic, retreat. She would have told it—had she known how. But she could not do it. She hesitated. She abolished it—untold. She went on : "and then, I thought he had sent the roses and I was frightened. . . . I was frightened."

"Dear one," said Lewisham. "Dear one.! I have been cruel to you. I have been unjust. I understand. I *do* understand. Forgive me. Dearest—forgive me."

"I did so want to do something for you. It was all I could do—that little money. And then you were angry. I thought you didn't love me any more because I did not understand your work. . . . And that Miss Heydinger—Oh! it was hard."

"Dear one," said Lewisham, "I do not care your little finger for Miss Heydinger."

"I know how I hamper you. But if you will help me. Oh! I would work, I would study. I would do all I could to understand."

"Dear," whispered Lewisham. "*Dear.*"

"And to have *her*——"

"Dear," he vowed, "I have been a brute. I will end all that. I will end all that."

He took her suddenly into his arms and kissed her.

"Oh, I *know* I'm stupid," she said.

"You're not. It's I have been stupid. I have been unkind, unreasonable. All to-day . . . I've been thinking about it. Dear! I don't care for anything— It's *you.* If I have you nothing else matters. . . . Only I get hurried and cross. It's the work and being poor.

Dear one, we *must* hold to each other. All to-day—
It's been dreadful. . . ."

He stopped. They sat clinging to one another.

"I do love you," she said presently with her arms
about him. "Oh! I do—*do*—love you."

He drew her closer to him.

He kissed her neck. She pressed him to her.

Their lips met.

The expiring candle streamed up into a tall flame,
flickered, and was suddenly extinguished. The air was
heavy with the scent of roses.

CHAPTER THE THIRTIETH

A Withdrawal

ON Tuesday Lewisham returned from Vigours' at five—at half-past six he would go on to his science class at Walham Green—and discovered Mrs. Chaffery and Ethel in tears. He was fagged and rather anxious for some tea, but the news they had for him drove tea out of his head altogether.

"He's gone," said Ethel.

"Who's gone? What! Not Chaffery?"

Mrs. Chaffery, with a keen eye to Lewisham's behaviour, nodded tearfully over an experienced handkerchief.

Lewisham grasped the essentials of the situation forthwith, and trembled on the brink of an expletive. Ethel handed him a letter.

For a moment Lewisham held this in his hand asking questions. Mrs. Chaffery had come upon it in the case of her eight-day clock when the time to wind it came round. Chaffery, it seemed, had not been home since Saturday night. The letter was an open one addressed to Lewisham, a long rambling would-be clever letter, oddly inferior in style to Chaffery's conversation.

It had been written some hours before Chaffery's last visit; his talk then had been perhaps a sort of codicil.

"The inordinate stupidity of that man Lagune is driving me out of the country," Lewisham saw. "It has been at last a definite stumbling block—even a legal stumbling block, I fear. I am off. I skedaddle. I, break ties. I shall miss our long refreshing chats—you had found me out and I could open my mind. I am sorry to part from Ethel also, but thank Heaven she has you to look to! And indeed they both have you to look to, though the 'both' may be a new light to you."

Lewisham growled, went from page 1 to page 3—conscious of their both looking to him now—even intensely —and discovered Chaffery in a practical vein.

"There is but little light and portable property in that house in Clapham that has escaped my lamentable improvidence, but there are one or two things; the iron-bound chest, the bureau with a broken hinge, and the large air pump, distinctly pawnable if only you can contrive to get them to a pawnshop. You have more Will power than I—I never could get the confounded things downstairs. That iron-bound box was originally mine, before I married your mother-in-law, so that I am not altogether regardless of your welfare and the necessity of giving some equivalent. Don't judge me too harshly."

Lewisham turned over sharply without finishing that page.

"My life at Clapham," continued the letter, "has irked me for some time, and to tell you the truth, the spectacle of your vigorous young happiness—you are having a very good time, you know, fighting the world— reminded me of the passing years. To be frank in self-criticism, there is more than a touch of the New Woman about me, and I feel I have still to live my own life. What a beautiful phrase that is—to live one's own life! —redolent of honest scorn for moral plagiarism. No *Imitatio Christi* in that. . . . I long to see more of men and cities. . . . I begin late, I know, to live my own life, bald as I am and grey-whiskered; but better late than never. Why should the educated girl have the monopoly of the game? And after all, the whiskers will dye. . . .

"There are things—I touch upon them lightly—that will presently astonish Lagune." Lewisham became more attentive. "I marvel at that man, grubbing hungry for marvels amidst the almost incredibly marvellous. What can be the nature of a man who gapes after Poltergeists with the miracle of his own silly existence (inconsequent, reasonless, unfathomably weird) nearer to him than breathing and closer than hands and feet. What is *he* for, that he should wonder at Poltergeists? I am astonished these by no means flimsy psychic phenomena do not turn upon their investigators, and that a Research Society of eminent illusions and hallucinations does not pursue Lagune with sceptical inquiries. Take his house —expose the alleged man of Chelsea! *A priori* they might argue that a thing so vain, so unmeaning, so strongly beset by cackle, could only be the diseased imagining of some hysterical phantom. Do *you* believe that such a thing as Lagune exists? I must own to the gravest doubts. But happily his banker is of a more credulous type than I. . . . Of all that Lagune will tell you soon enough."

Lewisham read no more. "I suppose he thought himself clever when he wrote that rot," said Lewisham bitterly, throwing the sheets forcibly athwart the table. "The simple fact is, he's stolen, or forged, or something—and bolted."

There was a pause. "What will become of Mother?" said Ethel.

Lewisham looked at Mother and thought for a moment. Then he glanced at Ethel.

"We're all in the same boat," said Lewisham.

"I don't want to give any trouble to a single human being," said Mrs. Chaffery.

"I think you might get a man his tea, Ethel," said

Lewisham sitting down suddenly; "anyhow." He drummed on the table with his fingers. "I have to get to Walham Green by a quarter to seven."

"We're all in the same boat," he repeated after an interval, and continued drumming. He was chiefly occupied by the curious fact that they were all in the same boat. What an extraordinary faculty he had for acquiring responsibility! He looked up suddenly and caught Mrs. Chaffery's tearful eye directed to Ethel and full of distressful interrogation, and his perplexity was suddenly changed to pity. "It's all right, Mother," he said. "I'm not going to be unreasonable. I'll stand by you."

"Ah!" said Mrs. Chaffery. "As if I didn't know!" and Ethel came and kissed him.

He seemed in imminent danger of universal embraces.

"I wish you'd let me have my tea," he said. And while he had his tea he asked Mrs. Chaffery questions and tried to get the new situation into focus.

But even at ten o'clock when he was returning hot and jaded from Walham Green he was still trying to get the situation into focus. There were vague ends and blank walls of interrogation in the matter, that perplexed him.

He knew that his supper would be only the prelude to an interminable " talking over," and indeed he did not get to bed until nearly two. By that time a course of action was already agreed upon. Mrs. Chaffery was tied to the house in Clapham by a long lease and thither they must go. The ground floor and first floor were let unfurnished, and the rent of these practically paid the rent of the house. The Chafferys occupied basement and second floor. There was a bedroom on the second floor formerly let to the first floor tenants, that he and Ethel could occupy, and in this an old toilet table could be put for such studies as were to be prosecuted at home. Ethel could have her typewriter in the subterranean breakfast-room. Mrs. Chaffery and Ethel must do the catering and the bulk of the housework, and as soon as possible, since letting lodgings would not square with Lewisham's professional pride, they must get rid of the lease that bound them and take some smaller and more suburban residence. If they did that without leaving any address it might save their feelings from any return of the prodigal Chaffery.

Mrs. Chaffery's frequent and pathetic acknowledgments of Lewisham's goodness only partly relieved his disposition to a philosophical bitterness. And the practical issues were complicated by excursions upon the subject of Chaffery, what he might have done, and where he might have gone, and whether by any chance he might not return.

When at last Mrs. Chaffery, after a violent and tearful kissing and blessing of them both—they were " good dear children," she said—had departed, Mr. and Mrs. Lewisham returned into their sitting-room. Mrs. Lewisham's little face was enthusiastic. " You're a Trump," she said, extending the willing arms that were his reward. " I know," she said, " I know, and all to-night I have been loving you. Dear! Dear! Dear. . . ."

The next day Lewisham was too full of engagements to communicate with Lagune, but the following morning he called and found the psychic investigator busy with the proofs of *Hesperus*. He welcomed the young man cordially nevertheless, conceiving him charged with the questions that had been promised long ago—it was evident he knew nothing of Lewisham's marriage. Lewisham stated his case with some bluntness.

" He was last here on Saturday," said Lagune. " You have always been inclined to suspicion about him. Have you any grounds ?"

" You'd better read this," said Lewisham, repressing a grim smile, and he handed Lagune Chaffery's letter.

He glanced at the little man ever and again to see if he had come to the personal portion, and for the rest of the time occupied himself with an envious inventory of the writing appointments about him. No doubt the boy with the big ears had had the same sort of thing . . .

When Lagune came to the question of his real identity he blew out his cheeks in the most astonishing way but made no other sign.

"Dear, dear!" he said at last. "My bankers!"

He looked at Lewisham with the exaggerated mildness of his spectacled eye. "What do you think it means?" he asked. "Has he gone mad? We have been conducting some experiments involving—considerable mental strain. He and I and a lady. Hypnotic——"

"I should look at my cheque-book if I were you."

Lagune produced some keys and got out his cheque-book. He turned over the counterfoils. "There's nothing wrong here," he said, and handed the book to Lewisham.

"Um," said Lewisham. "I suppose this— I say, *is this* right?"

He handed back the book to Lagune, open at the blank counterfoil of a cheque that had been removed. Lagune stared and passed his hand over his forehead in a confused way. "I can't see this," he said.

Lewisham had never heard of post hypnotic suggestion and he stood incredulous. "You can't see that?" he said. "What nonsense!"

"I can't see it," repeated Lagune.

For some seconds Lewisham could not get away from stupid repetitions of his inquiry. Then he hit upon a collateral proof. "But look here! Can you see *this* counterfoil?"

"Plainly," said Lagune.

"Can you read the number?"

"Five thousand two hundred and seventy-nine."

"Well, and this?"

"Five thousand two hundred and eight-one."

"Well—where's five thousand two hundred and eighty?"

Lagune began to look uncomfortable. "Surely,"

he said, "he has not— Will you read it out—the cheque, the counterfoil I mean, that I am unable to see."

"It's blank," said Lewisham with an irresistible grin.

"Surely," said Lagune, and the discomfort of his expression deepened. "Do you mind if I call in a servant to confirm——?"

Lewisham did not mind, and the same girl who had admitted him to the *séance* appeared. When she had given her evidence she went again. As she left the room by the door behind Lagune her eyes met Lewisham's, and she lifted her eyebrows, depressed her mouth and glanced at Lagune with a meaning expression.

"I'm afraid," said Lagune, "that I have been shabbily treated. Mr. Chaffery is a man of indisputable powers—indisputable powers; but I am afraid—I am very much afraid he has abused the conditions of the experiment. All this—and his insults—touch me rather nearly."

He paused. Lewisham rose. "Do you mind if you come again?" asked Lagune with gentle politeness.

Lewisham was surprised to find himself sorry.

"He was a man of extraordinary gifts," said Lagune. "I had come to rely upon him. . . . My cash balance has been rather heavy lately. How he came to know of that I am unable to say. Without supposing, that is, that he had very remarkable gifts."

When Lewisham saw Lagune again he learnt the particulars of Chaffery's misdeed and the additional fact that the "lady" had also disappeared. "That's a good job," he remarked selfishly. "There's no chance of *his* coming back." He spent a moment trying to imagine the "lady"; he realised more vividly than he had ever done before the narrow range of his experience, the bounds of his imagination. These people also— with grey hair and truncated honour—had their emotions! Even it may be glowing! He came back to facts. Chaffery had induced Lagune when hypnotised to sign a blank cheque as an "autograph." "The strange thing is," explained Lagune, "it's doubtful if he's legally accountable. The law is so peculiar about hypnotism, and I certainly signed the cheque, you know."

The little man, in spite of his losses, was now almost cheerful again on account of a curious side issue. "You may say it is coincidence," he said, "you may call it a fluke, but I prefer to look for some other interpretation. Consider this. The amount of my balance is a secret between me and my bankers. He never had it from *me,* for I did not know it—I hadn't looked at my pass-book for months. But he drew it all in one cheque, within seventeen and sixpence of the total. And the total was over five hundred pounds!"

He seemed quite bright again as he culminated.

"Within seventeen and sixpence," he said. "Now how do you account for that, eh? Give me a materialistic explanation that will explain away all that. You can't. Neither can I."

"I think I can," said Lewisham.

"Well—what is it?"

Lewisham nodded towards a little drawer of the bureau. "Don't you think—perhaps "—a little ripple of laughter passed across his mind—" he had a skeleton key?"

Lagune's face lingered amusingly in Lewisham's mind as he returned to Clapham. But after a time that amusement passed away. He declined upon the extraordinary fact that Chaffery was his father-in-law, Mrs. Chaffery his mother-in-law, that these two and Ethel constituted his family, his clan, and that grimy graceless house up the Clapham hillside was to be his home. Home! His connection with these things as a point of worldly departure was as inexorable now as though he had been born to it. And a year ago, except for a fading reminiscence of Ethel, none of these people had existed for him. The ways of Destiny! The happenings of the last few months, foreshortened in perspective, seemed to have almost a pantomimic rapidity. The thing took him suddenly as being laughable; and he laughed.

His laugh marked an epoch. Never before had Lewisham laughed at any fix in which he had found himself. The enormous seriousness of adolescence was coming to an end; the days of his growing were numbered. It was a laugh of infinite admissions.

CHAPTER THE THIRTY - FIRST

In Battersea Park

NOW although Lewisham had promised to bring things to a conclusion with Miss Heydinger, he did nothing in the matter for five weeks, he merely left that crucial letter of hers unanswered. In that time their removal from Madam Gadow's into the gaunt house at Clapham was accomplished—not without polyglot controversy—and the young couple settled themselves into the little room on the second floor even as they had arranged. And there it was that suddenly the world was changed—was astonishingly transfigured—by a whisper.

It was a whisper between sobs and tears, with Ethel's arms about him and Ethel's hair streaming down so that it hid her face from him. And he too had whispered, dismayed perhaps a little, and yet feeling a strange pride, a strange novel emotion, feeling altogether different from the things he had fancied he might feel when this thing that he had dreaded should come. Suddenly he perceived finality, the advent of the solution, the reconciliation of the conflict that had been waged so long. Hesitations were at an end—he took his line.

Next day he wrote a note and two mornings later he started for his mathematical duffers an hour before it was absolutely necessary, and instead of going directly to Vigours', went over the bridge to Battersea Park. There waiting for him by a seat where once they had met before, he found Miss Heydinger pacing. They walked up and down side by side, speaking for a little while about indifferent topics, and then they came upon a pause . . .

"You have something to tell me?" said Miss Heydinger abruptly.

Lewisham changed colour a little. "Oh yes," he said; "the fact is—" He affected ease. "Did I ever tell you I was married?"

"*Married?*"

"Yes."

"Married!"

"Yes," a little testily.

For a moment neither spoke. Lewisham stood without dignity staring at the dahlias of the London County Council, and Miss Heydinger stood regarding him.

"And that is what you have to tell me?"

Mr. Lewisham turned and met her eyes. "Yes!" he said. "That is what I have to tell you."

Pause. "Do you mind if I sit down," asked Miss Heydinger in an indifferent tone.

"There is a seat yonder," said Lewisham, "under the tree."

They walked to the seat in silence.

"Now," said Miss Heydinger, quietly. "Tell me whom you have married."

Lewisham answered sketchily. She asked him another question and another. He felt stupid and answered with a halting truthfulness.

"I might have known," she said, "I might have known. Only I would not know. Tell me some more. Tell me about her."

Lewisham did. The whole thing was abominably

disagreeable to him, but it had to be done, he had promised Ethel it should be done. Presently Miss Heydinger knew the main outline of his story, knew all his story except the emotion that made it credible. "And you were married—before the second examination?" she repeated.

"Yes," said Lewisham.

"But why did you not tell me of this before?" asked Miss Heydinger.

"I don't know," said Lewisham. "I wanted to— that day, in Kensington Gardens. But I didn't. I suppose I ought to have done so."

"I think you ought to have done so."

"Yes, I suppose I ought . . . But I didn't. Somehow—it has been hard. I didn't know what you would say. The thing seemed so rash, you know, and all that."

He paused blankly.

"I suppose you had to do it," said Miss Heydinger presently, with her eyes on his profile.

Lewisham began the second and more difficult part of his explanation. "There's been a difficulty," he said, "all the way along—I mean—about you, that is. It's a little difficult— The fact is, my wife, you know— She looks at things differently from what we do."

"We?"

"Yes—it's odd, of course. But she has seen your letters——"

"You didn't show her——?"

"No. But, I mean, she knows you write to me, and she knows you write about Socialism and Literature and—things we have in common—things she hasn't."

"You mean to say she doesn't understand these things?"

"She's not thought about them. I suppose there's a sort of difference in education——"

"And she objects——?"

"No," said Lewisham, lying promptly. "She doesn't *object* . . ."

"Well?" said Miss Heydinger, and her face was white.

"She feels that— She feels—she does not say, of course, but I know she feels that it is something she ought to share. I know—how she cares for me. And it shames her—it reminds her— Don't you see how it hurts her?"

"Yes. I see. So that even that little—" Miss Heydinger's breath seemed to catch and she was abruptly silent.

She spoke at last with an effort. "That it hurts *me*," she said, and grimaced and stopped again.

"No," said Lewisham, "that is not it." He hesitated.

"I *knew* this would hurt you."

"You love her. You can sacrifice——"

"No. It is not that. But there is a difference. Hurting *her*—she would not understand. But you— somehow it seems a natural thing for me to come to you. I seem to look to you— For her I am always making allowances——"

"You love her."

"I wonder if it *is* that makes the difference. Things are so complex. Love means anything—or nothing. I know you better than I do her, you know me better than she will ever do. I could tell you things I could not tell her. I could put all myself before you—almost—and know you would understand— Only——"

"You love her."

"Yes," said Lewisham lamely and pulling at his moustache. "I suppose . . . that must be it."

For a space neither spoke. Then Miss Heydinger said "*Oh!*" with extraordinary emphasis.

"To think of this end to it all! That all your

promise . . . What is it she gives that I could not
have given?

"Even now! Why should I give up that much of
you that is mine? If she could take it— But she
cannot take it. If I let you go—you will do nothing.
All this ambition, all these interests will dwindle and
die, and she will not mind. She will not understand.
She will think that she still has you. Why should she
covet what she cannot possess? Why should she be
given the thing that is mine—to throw aside?"

She did not look at Lewisham, but before her, her
face a white misery.

"In a way—I had come to think of you as something belonging to me . . . I shall—still."

"There is one thing," said Lewisham after a pause;
"it is a thing that has come to me once or twice
lately. Don't you think that perhaps you over-estimate
the things I might have done? I know we've talked of
great things to do. But I've been struggling for half a
year and more to get the sort of living almost anyone
seems able to get. It has taken me all my time. One
can't help thinking after that, perhaps the world is a
stiffer sort of affair . . ."

"No," she said decisively. "You could have done
great things.

"Even now," she said, "you may do great things—
If only I might see you sometimes, write to you sometimes— You are so capable and—weak. You must
have somebody— That is your weakness. You fail in
your belief. You must have support and belief—unstinted support and belief. Why could I not be that
to you? It is all I want to be. At least—all I want
to be now. Why need she know? It robs her of
nothing. I want nothing— she has. But I know of
my own strength too I can do nothing. I know that
with you . . . It is only knowing hurts her. Why
should she know?"

Mr. Lewisham looked at her doubtfully. That

phantom greatness of his, it was that lit her eyes. In that instant at least he had no doubts of the possibility of his Career. But he knew that in some way the secret of his greatness and this admiration went together. Conceivably they were one and indivisible. Why indeed need Ethel know? His imagination ran over the things that might be done, the things that might happen, and touched swiftly upon complication, confusion, discovery.

"The thing is, I must simplify my life. I shall do nothing unless I simplify my life. Only people who are well off can be—complex. It is one thing or the other——"

He hesitated and suddenly had a vision of Ethel weeping as once he had seen her weep with the light on the tears in her eyes.

"No," he said almost brutally. "No. It's like this— I can't do anything underhand. I mean—I'm not so amazingly honest—now. But I've not that sort of mind. She would find me out. It would do no good and she would find me out. My life's too complex. I can't manage it and go straight. I—you've overrated me. And besides— Things have happened. Something—" He hesitated and then snatched at his resolve. "I've got to simplify—and that's the plain fact of the case. I'm sorry, but it is so."

Miss Heydinger made no answer. Her silence astonished him. For nearly twenty seconds perhaps they sat without speaking. With a quick motion she stood up and at once he stood up before her. Her face was flushed, her eyes downcast.

"Good-bye," she said suddenly in a low tone and held out her hand.

"But," said Lewisham and stopped. Miss Heydinger's colour left her.

"Good-bye," she said, looking him suddenly in the eyes and smiling awry. "There is no more to say, is there? Good-bye."

He took her hand. "I hope I didn't——"

"Good-bye," she said impatiently, and suddenly disengaged her hand and turned away from him. He made a step after her.

"Miss Heydinger," he said, but she did not stop. "Miss Heydinger." He realised that she did not want to answer him again. . . .

He remained motionless, watching her retreating figure. An extraordinary sense of loss came into his mind, a vague impulse to pursue her and pour out vague passionate protestations. . . .

Not once did she look back. She was already remote when he began hurrying after her. Once he was in motion he quickened his pace and gained upon her. He was within thirty yards of her as she drew near the gates.

His pace slackened. Suddenly he was afraid she might look back. She passed out of the gates, out of his sight. He stopped, looking where she had disappeared. He sighed and took the pathway to his left that led back to the bridge and Vigours.

Halfway across this bridge came another crisis of indecision. He stopped, hesitating. An impertinent thought obtruded. He looked at his watch and saw that he must hurry if he would catch the train for Earl's Court and Vigours. He said Vigours might go to the devil.

But in the end he caught his train.

CHAPTER THE THIRTY-SECOND

The Crowning Victory

*T*HAT night about seven Ethel came into their room
with a waste-paper basket she had bought for him,
and found him sitting at the little toilet table at which
he was to "write." The outlook was, for a London
outlook, spacious, down a long slope of roofs towards
the Junction, a huge sky of blue passing upward to the
darkling zenith and downward into a hazy bristling
mystery of roofs and chimneys, from which emerged
signal lights and steam puffs, gliding chains of lit window carriages and the vague vistas of streets. She
showed him the basket and put it beside him, and then
her eye caught the yellow document in his hand.
"What is that you have there?"

He held it out to her, "I found it—lining my yellow
box. I had it at Whortley."

She took it and perceived a chronological scheme. It
was headed "Schema," there were memoranda in the
margin, and all the dates had been altered by a hasty
hand.

"Hasn't it got yellow?" she said.

That seemed to him the wrong thing for her to say.
He stared at the document with a sudden accession of

sympathy. There was an interval. He became aware
of her hand upon his shoulder, that she was bending
over him. "Dear," she whispered, with a strange
change in the quality of her voice. He knew she was
seeking to say something that was difficult to say.

"Yes?" he said presently.

"You are not grieving?"

"What about?"

"*This*."

"No!"

"You are not—you are not even sorry?" she said.

"No—not even sorry."

"I can't understand that. It's so much——"

"I'm glad," he proclaimed. "*Glad*."

"But—the trouble—the expense—everything—and
your work?"

"Yes," he said, "that's just it."

She looked at him doubtfully. He glanced up at
her, and she questioned his eyes. He put his arm
about her, and presently and almost absent-mindedly she
obeyed his pressure and bent down and kissed him.

"It settles things," he said holding her. "It joins us.
Don't you see? Before . . . But now it's different.
It's something we have between us. It's something
that . . . It's the link we needed. It will hold us
together, cement us together. It will be our life. This
will be my work now. The other . . ."

He faced a truth. "It was just . . . vanity!"

There was still a shade of doubt in her face, a wist-
fulness.

Presently she spoke.

"Dear," she said.

"Yes?"

She knitted her brows. "No!" she said. "I can't
say it."

In the interval she came into a sitting position on
his knees.

He kissed her hand, but her face remained grave,

and she looked out upon the twilight. "I know I'm stupid," she said. "The things I say . . . aren't the things I feel."

He waited for her to say more.

"It's no good," she said.

He felt the onus of expression lay on him. He too found it a little difficult to put into words. "I think I understand," he said, and wrestled with the impalpable. The pause seemed long and yet not altogether vacant. She lapsed abruptly into the prosaic. She started from him.

"If I don't go down, Mother will get supper . . ."

At the door she stopped and turned a twilight face to him. For a moment they scrutinised one another. To her he was no more than a dim outline. Impulsively he held out his arms. . . .

Then at the sound of a movement downstairs she freed herself and hurried out. He heard her call "Mother! You're not to lay supper. You're to rest."

He listened to her footsteps until the kitchen had swallowed them up. Then he turned his eyes to the Schema again and for a moment it seemed but a little thing.

He picked it up in both hands and looked at it as if it was the writing of another man, and indeed it was the writing of another man. "Pamphlets in the Liberal Interest," he read, and smiled.

Presently a train of thought carried him off. His attitude relaxed a little, the Schema became for a time a mere symbol, a point of departure, and he stared out of the window at the darkling night. For a long time he sat pursuing thoughts that were half emotions, emotions that took upon themselves the shape and substance of ideas. The deepening current stirred at last among the roots of speech.

"Yes, it was vanity," he said. "A boy's vanity. For me—anyhow. I'm too two-sided . . . Two-sided? . . . Commonplace!"

"Dreams like mine—abilities like mine. Yes—any man! And yet . . . The things I meant to do!"

His thoughts went to his Socialism, to his red-hot ambition of world mending. He marvelled at the vistas he had discovered since those days.

"Not for us— Not for us.

"We must perish in the wilderness—Some day. Somewhen. But not for us. . . .

"Come to think, it is all the Child. The future is the Child. The Future. What are we—any of us—but servants or traitors to that? . . .

"Natural Selection—it follows . . . this way is happiness . . . must be. There can be no other."

He sighed. "To last a lifetime, that is.

"And yet—it is almost as if Life had played me a trick—promised so much—given so little! . . .

"No! One must not look at it in that way? That will not do! That will *not* do.

"Career! In itself it is a career—the most important career in the world. Father! Why should I want more?

"And . . . Ethel! No wonder she seemed shallow . . . She has been shallow. No wonder she was restless. Unfulfilled . . . What had she to do? She was drudge, she was toy . . .

"Yes. This is life. This alone is life! For this we were made and born. All these other things—all other things—they are only a sort of play . . .

"Play!"

His eyes came back to the Schema. His hands shifted to the opposite corner and he hesitated. The vision of that arranged Career, that ordered sequence of work and successes, distinction and yet further distinctions, rose brightly from the symbol. Then he compressed his lips and tore the yellow sheet in half, tearing very deliberately. He doubled the halves and tore again, doubled again very carefully and neatly until the Schema was torn into numberless little pieces. With it he seemed to be tearing his past self.

"Play," he whispered after a long silence.

"It is the end of adolescence," he said; "the end of empty dreams. . . ."

He became very still, his hands resting on the table, his eyes staring out of the blue oblong of the window. The dwindling light gathered itself together and became a star.

He found he was still holding the torn fragments. He stretched out his hand and dropped them into that new waste-paper basket Ethel had bought for him.

Two pieces fell outside the basket. He stooped, picked them up and put them carefully with their fellows.